THE EMERALD VALLEY

The Miners' Federation of Great Britain is engaged in a struggle to preserve your wages, working hours and general conditions. Every man in Warwickshire is expected to be loyal to the Federation and cease work after 30th April unless otherwise instructed by us.

'Llew – you don't mean you're going to *blackleg*?' Amy said, shocked.

His head came up. 'Have you got any better suggestions?'

'But it's our *own* people this strike is about!' Amy turned on the stool, her eyes blazing blue fire. 'My Dad, my brothers – *they're* the ones who've been exploited all these years. And now at last everybody's pulling together to try to get something done about it. You can't undermine that, Llew! You can't make money at their expense! I won't forgive you if you turn blackleg while my family and the friends and neighbours I grew up with are struggling for just a decent living wage – not half nor a quarter of what we take for granted. I mean it, Llew; I won't forgive you!'

Also in Arrow by Janet Tanner
THE BLACK MOUNTAINS

THE EMERALD VALLEY

Janet Tanner

ARROW

Published in the United Kingdom in 1987
by Arrow Books

1 3 5 7 9 0 8 6 4 2

Copyright © Janet Tanner 1985

The right of Janet Tanner to be identified as the author
of this work has been asserted by her in accordance
with the Copyright, Designs and Patents Act, 1988

First published in the United Kingdom in 1985 by Century

Arrow Books
The Random House Group Limited
20 Vauxhall Bridge Road, London, SW1V 2SA

Random House Australia (Pty) Limited
20 Alfred Street, Milsons Point, Sydney,
New South Wales 2061, Australia

Random House New Zealand Limited
18 Poland Road, Glenfield
Auckland 10, New Zealand

Random House (Pty) Limited
Endulini, 5a Jubilee Road, Parktown 2193, South Africa

The Random House Group Limited Reg. No. 954009

www.randomhouse.co.uk

A CIP catalogue record for this book is available from the British Library

Papers used by Random House are natural, recyclable products made from
wood grown in sustainable forests. The manufacturing processes conform to
the environmental regulations of the country of origin

Printed and bound in Great Britain by
Bookmarque Ltd, Croydon, Surrey

ISBN 0 09 950340 9

To my mother

Chapter One

The Ford motor lorry stood in the centre of the depot yard, square, squat and spanking brand-new. Its cab was painted green – a darker green than the grassy hillside that provided a backdrop to the yard on its south side – and the strong spring sunlight drove a straight shaft in through the windscreen and out through the small oval of glass at the rear of the driver's cab. It caught the yellow legend on the door also, making it stand out with a sharpness that was almost hurtful to the eye:

'L. ROBERTS. HAULAGE CONTRACTOR. HILLSBRIDGE.'

A few yards away a young woman stood looking thoughtfully at the lorry, one hand resting lightly against her narrow pleated skirt, the other playing restlessly with her honey-coloured curls, square-cut to a bouncing 'bingle' – the style that bridged the gap between the flattering bob and the fashionable but more severe shingle. Cornflower-blue eyes were narrowed behind long fair lashes and there was a determined set to the delicate, heart-shaped chin and the clearly defined mouth.

Amy Roberts knew what she wanted all right – just as she had always known. And what was more she was determined to get it – just as she usually did. The only thing that surprised her was that on this occasion getting her way had taken so long, and the person who had stood stubbornly in her way was the one she could usually get round the most easily – her husband, Llew. Generally, Llew would refuse her nothing. When those lips and eyes smiled together and the dimples played in her cheeks he was ready to weaken; when she put her arms around his neck and pressed her body against his – rounded and feminine beneath the boyish line of the clothes – he was lost.

1

But on this particular issue Llew Roberts had not weakened; this one thing he had continued to refuse. For after all, what man in his right mind would allow his wife to drive a lorry?

'Don't be so silly, Amy – of course you can't! You wouldn't be strong enough, for one thing.'

'I'm sure I would be,' she had argued. 'I cut my muscles helping my mother put the Monday washing through the mangle when I was still at school. And I still do it – every week – shirts and sheets *you've* made dirty, Llew Roberts.'

He had ignored the jibe. He disliked seeing his wife mangling washing – and the sooner he could afford to pay someone to do it for her, the better. But he did not want to see her driving a lorry either – the whole idea was preposterous.

'I'm sorry, Amy, I haven't got time to teach you.'

'It wouldn't take any time at all!' she had insisted. 'You've told me plenty of times about when you went up to Birmingham to collect your first lorry. You said you'd never even driven a car and they showed you where the gears were, three forward and one back, told you which way to turn the wheel to go left and right and left you to it. You drove all the way back to Hillsbridge on your own – eighty-odd miles. So how you can say *I* couldn't do it, I don't know!'

'But that was in 1922, Amy. This is 1926 and there's a lot more traffic on the roads now than there was then. Besides, I'm a man...'

'Hmm!' she had snorted. 'What difference does that make, I should like to know? I'm as clever as most of the men I know – and cleverer than quite a lot of them. I could have got a scholarship and stayed on at school if I'd wanted, like you did, only I didn't want to. But when I see some of the fatheads I was at school with driving and you say they can do it just because they're men – well, it's quite ridiculous.'

But Llew had refused to be moved, by threat or entreaty, by bribery or blackmail.

'No, Amy, you're not driving my lorry,' was all he would say, and so far Amy had had no chance to disobey. She had watched, waited and plotted for a chance to get her way, all without success – until today, when Llew had gone off on a long trip that would keep him away until late. And Amy had come to the depot yard with one purpose in mind – to drive the lorry as she had wanted to do for so long.

It had been a shock to discover that Llew had taken his old

lorry for the trip – the lorry that he had described in his story of 'three gears forward and one back, turn the wheel this way for left, this way for right.' She had heard it so often she felt sure she could have emulated Llew's success almost without trying. But for some reason it was the new lorry, collected only a fortnight ago, that now stood in the depot yard, gleaming and winking in the spring sunshine. For a moment Amy had hesitated. The new lorry was Llew's pride and joy. But she had had to wait so long for this chance to try to drive... and what he didn't know wouldn't hurt him.

As she stood looking at the lorry a lanky man in overalls crossed the yard towards her – Herbie Button, Llew's right-hand-man. Herbie's brother, Cliff, ran a taxi service in Hillsbridge and sometimes when he was fully booked for weddings and funerals Herbie helped him out. But there wasn't enough work to keep the two brothers fully occupied and two years ago Herbie had thrown in his lot with Llew Roberts.

'Afternoon, Mrs Roberts,' he greeted her, and even now, after two years, the name stuck like black treacle in his mouth. He had known her when she was a little girl, pretty, mischievous Amy Hall, and 'Mrs Roberts' did not come quite naturally. But it was what Llew insisted on, and Llew was the boss.

She tilted her head to look at him and he knew at once from her expression that she was up to something.

'Hello, Herbie.'

Oh yes, her 'butter wouldn't melt' expression was hiding something, he was sure of it. But he warmed towards her all the same. That was one thing about Amy Hall – Mrs Roberts. You could know she was after something, cooking up some scheme, using that charm of hers to get her own way, but it made no difference. You still couldn't help but like her.

'Didn't expect to see you today, Mrs Roberts,' he said conversationally. 'Little 'uns all right, are they?'

'Yes. Fine.' She dismissed the 'little 'uns' – her children – with a quick, impatient smile. Barbara, at three, was a charmer, with her mother's golden curls and blue eyes, and Maureen, though not quite a year, was already displaying a personality of her own. But they took up so much of her time that sometimes Amy almost resented them – though she always had the grace to feel guilty about it later. They were healthy and beautiful and she loved them – it was just that

3

there were now so many other things she wanted to do besides feeding and looking after them, washing and ironing and tidying up the muddles they made. Thank heavens there was no need to have a string of children any more, as women had had to in her mother's day, was all she could say ...

Herbie Button pushed his cap to the back of his head with a grimy hand.

'Well, we're not expecting Mr Roberts back until late. He and Ivor Burge have gone off down to ...'

'I know,' she cut in. 'And I want to be able to give him a surprise when he gets back, Herbie.'

The grimy fingers scratched in the hair that had previously been covered by his cap.

'Surprise? What sort of surprise, Mrs Roberts?'

Her lower lip tightened; small tucks appeared in her cheeks instead of dimples.

'I want to be able to drive the lorry.'

'What?' If she had said she wanted to take off for the moon he couldn't have been more surprised. There she stood, a slip of a girl in a pleated dress up to her knees and a pair of those shoes with the silly little heels that got thin in the middle and a gold gypsy bracelet just above her left elbow biting into the plump flesh without a hint of muscle in it, and told him she wanted to drive the lorry. 'Oh, you're joking, of course, Mrs Roberts,' he added in relief.

'No, I'm not joking.' Her chin came up and the expression in her eyes made the shock hit him all over again. She wasn't joking. He could see that now.

'Please, Herbie, don't tell me I can't,' she said, a slightly threatening note creeping into her voice. 'I've heard that quite often enough. I just want you to show me how. And there's no need to look so worried, either. I'll make sure Llew doesn't take it out on you; I shall tell him I made you.'

Herbie scratched his head again and settled his cap back squarely over it.

'Well, if you'm sure you know what you'm doing ...'

'I'm sure.' She reached up to open the cab and climbed up onto the running board, showing enough leg to make Herbie glance sideways in embarrassment – what were girls coming to! Then she was easing herself into the plump curve of the leather seat, as yet unsoiled by the daily round of grubby trousers, holding the wheel between her hands and stretching her feet out towards the pedals that were the

4

touchstone of the mystery of driving.

'Now just tell me, Herbie – this one's for when I want to go faster, is that right? And this one for when I want to stop?'

'You can't reach them, can you?' he accused.

'Of course I can!' It was an effort, but she could do it, just, by really stretching. If only I were a bit taller, Amy thought, as she did so often. Five feet two was something and nothing – she would have loved to be tall and willowy. But none of her family were big people and she just had to accept it. 'Now what?' she asked.

'Start the darned thing, I s'pose,' Herbie muttered.

'Will you do it for me, then?'

Shaking his head to emphasise that this whole episode was against his better judgement, Herbie cranked the handle and the engine spluttered into life. As the cab began to vibrate about her Amy felt a moment's panic, but this gave way quickly to exhilaration.

'Can I try the gears?' she shouted above the racket.

'Yes... but put your clutch in first. Thick pedal there!' Herbie cried, pointing.

She did as he said with a great deal of crashing at first, but gradually she got the feel of it.

'And where's reverse? How do I go backwards?' she asked, remembering Llew's first lesson.

'Back'ards? I shoulds't think 'ee wanna go for'ards first!' Agitation was thickening Herbie's Somerset dialect from his first careful, 'talking to the boss's wife' mode of conversation. Then, catching the flash of impatience in her eyes, he added hastily, ''Tis 'ere, look. You d' do it like this...'

'Can I try now? Can I go round the yard?'

Herbie cast around a quick, concerned eye. With Llew away with the other lorry there was not much she could hit, he supposed. Only the pile of chippings they had managed to save off the half-dozen loads they had run for the council, because Llew had thought they would fill up the worst of the potholes in the yard, and the latest load of pit-props waiting to be delivered to Midlington Pit. Midlington Pit was only half a mile back up the lane and as always the nearest was the one that got left until last...

'Go on then if you d' want to,' he said with a sigh.

That was enough for Amy. With legs and toes stretched almost into cramp she manipulated the pedals and the lorry jerked forward so suddenly that it made her almost cry out.

'Oh – I did it!' she wanted to say, but of course there was no time. The fence post was rushing up at her and, knuckles white with tension, she yanked on the steering wheel.

'Ease up! Ease her up now!' Herbie shouted, running after her. As she did as he said and the lorry straightened out, running along parallel with the river that bounded the yard on the south side, she felt the sense of exhilaration returning along with the quickening adrenalin.

This was fun – and it was easy! Press this pedal and the lorry surged forward, press that one and it slowed down. Pull the wheel – yes, and round it went – easy as riding a bicycle, easier really for Amy had never felt very safe wobbling along on two wheels. But here, high in the lorry cab, lip held tight between her teeth in a paroxysm of concentration, nerves and muscles strained to singing life, she was enjoying herself – just as she had known she would.

At the bottom of the yard were some outbuildings and a tarpaulin-covered shed with a wood-plank step that Llew used as an office. As she neared them she swung the wheel again so that she travelled in a loose arc to face the way she had started. Then she stopped for a moment to savour her success.

'There you be then, missus. Done now, 'ave you?' Herbie came panting over, a look of relief lightening his permanently anxious expression.

She tilted her head, looking at him directly out of the side window of the cab, her eyes sparkling.

'No, I haven't done, Herbie! I've only just started!'

He swore under his breath and though she did not hear what he said she sensed that he might be about to put his foot down. A new wave of determination surged through her; if he thought she was going to get this far and give up, he was very much mistaken!

With a quick, decisive movement she banged the lorry into gear again and juggled the pedals. As it jerked forward Herbie shouted, 'Hoi!' and ran after it while Amy, afraid he might jump onto the running board and forcibly stop her, pressed her foot down harder on what she thought of as the 'Go' pedal. With Herbie still running after it, the lorry careered across the yard, out through the gate and, slowing slightly, across the river bridge. Then, with a yank of the wheel Amy turned right, driving for the first time in her life on the highway.

6

Llew Roberts' Transport Depot was situated in a finger of valley that followed the river out of Hillsbridge. It was bounded on one side by steep green fields that fell away from the road to Frome and Warminster, and on the other by the railway embankment and, beyond that, ridges of 'batch' as colliery waste tips were known in this part of the world. Twenty-five pits the faulted Somerset seams had thrown up, and the narrow ridges of waste that ran along above the railway lines and in the shadow of the larger, mountainous mounds had come from only two or three of them. There was no tipping now on the section that overlooked the depot – the trucks carried the waste further along to a new incline – and in an effort to hide the ugly black ridges fir trees had been planted in neat rows. At this time of year – late April – they looked attractive, fresh and green but in summer it would be a different story. The sparks from passing trains would set the trees ... or the coal-dust ... or both alight, and the fires would burn for days, running along in the combustible ground to emerge in a new spot, spreading devastation and leaving behind charred brown skeletons.

Sometimes the fires had to be tackled from above, but mostly the fire-engine approached them across the very bridge where Amy was now driving, taking water from the river to try to douse the flames.

Today, however, there was no fire and the bridge and the road were mercifully clear. Amy swung the lorry out into the road, jogging steadily along the flat valley floor with the fields becoming steep, well-kept allotments to her left and the impressive wooden mill buildings rising on her right. The river shelved here into a small weir and the mill made use of the water power as it had done for generations to grind wheat to flour and process animal feedstuffs. As always the mill was hard at work; a sack of grain was on the pulley half-way up the tall mill-tower as Amy chugged by and the man manipulating it stopped for a moment to turn and watch the lorry pass.

A few yards and the lane became a slope, curving up towards the main Frome Road. Briefly Amy felt a qualm of fear as she faced the decision: which way to turn? Undoubtedly it would be easier to swing round to the right and go down the hill past Starvault Pit. But that way would lead her inevitably into the centre of Hillsbridge, and for all her natural bubbling confidence Amy did not think she was quite ready for that. Besides, the two colliery horses were pulling a load of trucks on the lines that ran across the road from the pit to the sidings – more waste to be taken to the black 'batches' and tipped – and she was not quite sure she would be able to stop.

'It would be awful if I were to run into them,' she thought, and choosing the lesser of the two evils she put her foot hard down on the 'go' pedal and pulled the wheel round to make the sharp left turn that would take her on up the hill.

For a few moments the lorry juddered and protested and Amy thought it was going to stop altogether. Then somehow it pulled itself together. Going uphill might be slow, noisy and bone-shaking, she thought, but at least there was less chance of hitting something at this speed. Up, up, she crept – the hill seemed to go on for ever. Up, up... with houses on one side of the road and allotments and fields falling away on the other – those same fields that bounded the valley where she had been just a few moments ago. With the road clear and empty ahead of her, Amy risked a quick peep. Yes, there was the depot yard – and that minuscule man-figure in cap and blue overalls would be Herbie, still there, still pacing, probably wondering what on earth to do next. Amy giggled. It was easy to imagine the kind of things he would be muttering through the Woodbine he would have lit the moment he had failed to catch her going through the gates. Llew thought she was ignorant of the language the men used when they were out of hearing of ladies, and she let him go on thinking it. But she knew, all right, and it amused her now to think of Herbie swearing away with colourful adjectives peppering his every remark.

From the centre of Hillsbridge to the point where it first began to flatten out, Frome Hill was a good mile long; three-quarters of the way up, Amy decided that maybe she had gone far enough for her first trip out. She was approaching the yard and squat grey-stone buildings of the Iron Foundry – just beyond it was a lane that led back down into the valley, and Amy swung left into it.

At its neck the lane was cobbled, but as it dropped away from the main road it became steadily more uneven. Potholes broke the surface and as the front wheels of the lorry dropped into them the shock ran up the steering column and into Amy's hands. She hung on tightly, keeping as straight a course as she could between the grassy banks and the hedges, heavy with spring growth. This was not as easy as going uphill, especially as she had to stretch all the time now in order to keep her foot on the brake. Half-way down she felt her toes going into cramp. She eased off a little and the lorry surged forward. There was a bend coming up – past that she would have to be careful because she knew it was the steepest and narrowest part, around a triangle of grass where the moon-daisies grew thickly during the summer months, then a sharp turn to take her back onto the lower road – unless she wanted to run away and crash into the river! Gritting her teeth in extreme concentration, she pressed her foot down onto the brake again. Hold it – hold it . . .

As she came around the bend she saw it – a red Morgan three-wheeler sports car coming up fast and right in the middle of the lane. There was time for just a moment's cold panic as she stepped on the brake and pulled the wheel hard into the left. But her aching foot slid, not getting the pressure she needed, and the lorry jerked forward. Again she stabbed for the brake, but it was too late. The sports car had taken avoiding action too, but as she lurched to a stop she caught the mudguard a glancing blow, spinning the Morgan away from her. Her own wheel turned and, unable to hold it, she ran into the bank, jolting up briefly so that for a moment she was afraid the lorry was going to overturn. Then it subsided again, coming to rest in the lane some yards below the sports car she had hit.

'Oh, my Lord!' said Amy, pulling on the hand-brake with trembling hands and closing her eyes against acceptance of what had happened.

The hiatus was short-lived. Moments later the door of the lorry cab was wrenched open and she found herself looking down at one of the angriest men she had ever had to face in her life.

It seemed to Amy in that frightened moment that everything about him was dark. Dark hair, springing thickly, dark eyes blazing with fury, dark lines contorting his face around a dark moustache. And he was tall enough not to be dwarfed even though he was standing in the road while she was perched high in the cab. In his leather jacket and flying boots he cut a figure that was both awesome and unavoidable.

Amy knew who he was. She had recognised him the moment she saw him, had recognised the car too, though she had never before come into such close or uncomfortable contact with him. Everyone in Hillsbridge knew Ralph Porter. His timber merchants' business was the biggest in the district, with a virtual monopoly for the supply of pit-props to the collieries, and many said he was the richest man in Hillsbridge next to the colliery owners themselves. More than once as he had struggled for a share of business Amy had heard Llew, her husband, curse Ralph Porter, saying he was 'in with the nobs' and had it 'all sewn up'.

But it was not only his money and his thriving business which made Ralph Porter stand out from the crowd. There was the fact that although he was in his early thirties and a most eligible man, he had never married, but lived all alone with his housekeeper and an invalid sister for whom he provided a home in his rambling house at the bottom of the lane down which Amy had been driving – Porter's Hill. There were also the motors he drove – the sporty three-wheeled Morgans that were winning all the races in their class at Montlhery Track in France, but which were seldom seen in the quiet roads around Hillsbridge – and there was the list of decorations he was reputed to have gained during the Great War. Put all together, Ralph Porter was a colourful character admired, even if in secret, by the young men, dreamed about as a romantic figure by the young women and the children, and described as 'a card' by those old enough to feel indulgent towards him.

Facing him now, however, after being the cause of damage to his precious Morgan motor car, Amy felt none of these things. She experienced only an odd blend of acute embarrassment and pure terror – both unusual emotions for her.

'What the hell do you think you're up to? Look what you've done to my car!'

The moment's silence when they had glared at one another was shattered by his voice. It was as dark as the rest of him – a bark, almost – and it made Amy tremble all the more.

'I'm sorry,' she said weakly. 'I couldn't stop.'

'That's bally obvious!' he bellowed. 'You came down there like a steam engine – and right in the middle of the road, too. This hill's not suitable for lorries; you ought to know that.'

'I thought it would be all right,' Amy said helplessly. She wished her teeth would stop chattering.

'You've no business here anyway. Don't you know it's private?'

'I didn't think...'

'I don't suppose you *did*. And now...' He broke off, his eyes narrowing as if he was only just seeing her clearly enough to register her sex. 'What's a woman doing driving a lorry anyway?' he demanded. 'You ought to stay where you belong – in the kitchen!'

The remark struck at a raw chord in Amy's make-up and the first tongue of annoyance rippled razor-sharp through the minefield of embarrassment and shock.

'Why should I?'

'Why should you? I would have thought it was damned clear enough why you should. You're not capable of handling a motor vehicle, are you?'

His tone combined with the scorn and derision in his face to twist Amy's own anger a notch tighter. Why was she taking all the blame just because she was a woman?

'It was your fault as well, you know!' she flared. 'I couldn't help being in the middle of the road with a lorry. You weren't exactly in the side yourself!'

She saw a muscle work furiously at the side of his mouth and in spite of her anger felt another moment of sharp fear.

'Dammit, woman, it's my hill! I shall drive up it any way I like!'

'Then you must expect somebody to run into you,' Amy went on, determined not to be bullied. 'I know you say it's private and if you own it I suppose you must be right. But people *do* use it, and if you don't want them to you ought to put up a notice saying so!'

'Now there's so much traffic on the roads I probably will,' he snarled. 'In the meantime, what do you intend to do about this?'

Amy's anger died as quickly as it had risen and she began to tremble again. 'What do you mean?'

'I mean my car. You caused this accident and you're going to have to pay for it. Who are you insured with?'

Through the rising tide of panic Amy tried desperately to think, but her thoughts were curdled like thick stale cream.

'I don't know.'

'You'll have to find out then, won't you? Who owns it?'

Her jaw felt unsteady now, as wobbly as her hands and

legs. Almost inaudibly she whispered, 'My husband.'

'He's Llew Roberts, the haulier, is he?'

He made it sound menial, but Amy was too upset now to notice.

'Yes.'

'Now we're getting somewhere. Though what he's thinking of letting you loose on the roads, I can't imagine.' He opened his jacket, feeling in one of the inside pockets and drawing out a card, gold-embossed on glossy white. 'This is where he can find me. And I shall be expecting to hear from him very shortly – this evening, perhaps!'

'Not this evening. He's away and won't be back until late.'

One eyebrow registered disbelief and Amy went on quickly, 'It's true!'

'All right. Tomorrow, then. Otherwise he'll be hearing from my solicitor.'

Without waiting for her agreement he turned and strode back up the hill, leaving the door of the lorry cab swinging open. In the mirror on its long-angled arm she saw him go to his car and inspect the newly buckled mudguard, anger still showing in every taut line of his shoulders and back. Then, not wanting to see any more, she turned away. Tears were singing inside her head now and burning her throat and although ahead of her the lane still ran its sunlit course between the burgeoning hedges, it seemed she was seeing it through a haze.

'Damn, damn, damn!' said Amy, spreading out her hands across the steering wheel and pounding in an effort to ease the tension bottled up inside her without giving way to her tears. *'Damn!'*

But it didn't help much. Even a word like 'damn' which would certainly cause her mother if not her husband to raise a disapproving eyebrow if she was heard to use it, did nothing to numb the sense of shock or smooth the path back to the depot. Herbie would be the first person she would have to explain to and she was not looking forward to it.

He's an employee, I don't have to answer to him! she told herself, but that didn't help any more than saying 'damn'. Perhaps she did not have to answer to Herbie, but that wouldn't stop him from making a few pretty caustic remarks or alter the way he would look at her . . . and it was all so embarrassing. Wilful she might be – and determined to get her own way – but Amy still liked people to approve of her.

Their good opinion mattered a great deal to her, though she would have died rather than admit it. And as for looking a fool, that was a prospect she could not abide.

I shan't admit to anyone that it might have been my fault! she decided. I shall tell them he came up the hill in that racing car of his so fast I had no chance to avoid him.

Already she found herself almost believing it.

There was still a more immediate problem, though. The lorry engine had cut out when she hit the bank and Amy was not at all sure how to start it again.

Well, there was only one answer – walk back to the depot. It wouldn't look good, but short of asking Ralph Porter for assistance it was the only way.

Gathering all the shreds of her tattered self-esteem, Amy pushed open the cab door and climbed down onto the running-board. The cotton-reel shape of her heels almost unbalanced her as she landed in the road, but mercifully she managed to remain on her feet. She did not dare to look at the damage to Llew's new lorry. For the moment, she decided she would rather not know.

For just a second she stood holding on to the door handle, steadying herself, then she smoothed down the pleated skirt over her hips and without a backward glance at either lorry, car or Ralph Porter, she set out down over the hill.

*

Greenslade Terrace – 'the Rank', as everyone who lived there knew it – basked sleepily in the warmth of the late April sunshine. Perched as it was across the south-facing side of the valley bowl, high above Hillsbridge, it was ideally placed to make the most of the warm weather that was so welcome after the long hard winter – the fronts of the houses saw little sunshine, it was true, but no one in Greenslade Terrace lived in the front of their houses. Front rooms were reserved for special occasions, for weddings, christenings and funerals – and for laying out the dead. The backs of the houses were where the living was done – the cooking and washing and ironing, the eating and gossiping and playing. And when the sun shone the doors and windows all along the Rank would open like the buds on the horse chestnut trees in the centre of Hillsbridge and stay open, letting fresh air into cramped sculleries and kitchens where coal fires burned winter and summer alike for cooking as well as heat.

This afternoon, the first really warm day of the year, the doors had opened and one by one inhabitants had emerged on one pretext or another to enjoy the sunshine.

At No. 19, Colwyn Yelling, wounded and shell-shocked in the Great War and now carrying on his new trade as a bootmaker in what had once been his mother's washhouse, sat on the back step to cut a piece of leather to shape. At No. 10, Charlie Durrant, henpecked husband of the temperate chapel-bumper Martha, scourge of the rank, made the excuse that he had to see to his seed potatoes in order to escape into the sunshine for a quiet half-hour away from his wife's constant nagging. And next door but one at No. 12, Molly Clements hung out yet another line of washing to billow in the breeze above the gardens which sloped away into the valley beyond the blocks of privies and washhouses.

The woman who stood in the doorway of No. 11, however, needed no excuse for being there. Her grandchildren were with her for the afternoon – two of them, at any rate – and when they were there it was reason enough to stop work for a few hours, sun or no sun.

Charlotte Hall hitched eleven-month-old Maureen higher on her hip and pointed across the yard to where a golden-haired, blue-eyed toddler was busily arranging a doll in a doll's pram, home-made from an orange box and a set of wheels.

'Look, my love, what's Barbara doing? She's going to take her baby for a walk, is she? Going to shop for a pound of bacon and a ha'porth of suet.'

'Da,' said Maureen loudly, pulling a strand of her grandmother's hair loose from her bun. 'Da-da-da!'

Charlotte Hall let her do it and smiled. Why was it, she wondered, that it was so much easier to have patience with your grandchildren than with your own children? Because you knew at the end of the day you could hand them back, perhaps; because in the end all the problems of bringing them up, the discipline and the decisions, were someone else's responsibility.

Seven children of her own she had raised and she never remembered feeling about any of them in quite the way she felt about her grandchildren – except perhaps little Florrie who had caught the whooping-cough and died when she was not much older than Maureen was now. Death had

14

enshrined her in a special place in Charlotte's heart, preserved her for ever as a sweet-natured toddler who had not lived long enough to display human failings. Yes, if anything, Florrie was the only one she could equate with her grandchildren. And occasionally in the dead of night when James, her husband, was snoring chestily beside her, Charlotte would lie awake and pray that none of them would be taken as Florrie had been.

This afternoon, however, with the sun warming the grey stones of the houses and splintering into myriads of the spectrum wherever it collided with wide-open bedroom windows, death and its attendant griefs seemed very far away. Instead there was an expectancy in the air, the expectancy given off by the whole of nature as it bursts into new life. And Charlotte, with Maureen's plump little body warm in her arms, thought not of the past but relished the present.

Footsteps on the cobbled path that served the Rank made her look up and she saw a plump, faired-haired woman approaching with a shopping basket over her arm. It was Peggy Yelling, mother of Colwyn and Charlotte's best friend, who had brought almost every baby in the Rank into the world and laid out 'the old ones' when they passed away.

'Hello, Peg,' Charlotte greeted her. 'Going off down to shop, are you?'

'Yes, there's one or two things I want. And I hear they've got some more of that nice tasty cheese in down at the Co-op. Trouble is,' Peggy pulled a face, 'it doesn't last five minutes in our house.'

'No, I don't suppose it does. You've still got your boys to feed,' Charlotte said ruefully. She could remember the time when a pound of cheese hadn't lasted any time in her larder, either, when all the family were at home. But now it was only herself, James and Harry, the youngest boy – except of course when Ted, scallywag of the family, took it into his head to come home for a bit and settle down from his wanderings . . .

'You've got Amy's two girls again, I see,' Peggy went on, smiling indulgently at Barbara and poking Maureen's plump cheek with a teasing finger. 'Where's their Mam today?'

In spite of her friendship with Peggy, Charlotte sensed the unspoken criticism of Amy and bristled slightly. It was not for Peggy to judge and find wanting.

'She had to go to Llew's yard. He's away on a long trip,' she said shortly.

Peggy nodded, taking no umbrage.

'I see. Well, good luck to her. But she's fortunate to have you to have them, I must say. There's plenty that wouldn't.'

'I'm always glad to see my grandchildren,' Charlotte returned. 'I only wish the others were near enough to have so often. Well I do have Dolly's, of course, but...'

'But your Dolly's more of a one for her home, isn't she?' Peggy said, referring to the elder of Charlotte's daughters, plump, pretty, imperturbable Dolly who to everyone's surprise had played the field so widely before she settled down that even Charlotte had begun to think she would finish up an old maid. 'Proper little mother she is now, isn't she? And she keeps those boys of hers a treat.'

'Yes, she does,' Charlotte agreed without rancour. She knew what a job Dolly had making ends meet. Her husband, Victor Coleman, was a gardener and handyman at Captain Fish's, the big house at the top of the hill, but like Colwyn Yelling he had been shell-shocked in the war and sometimes had to take time off work, unpaid of course. But as Peggy said, Dolly was a good manager and always seemed satisfied with her lot – unlike Amy, who was forever trying to improve hers.

How could two sisters have the same mother and father and be so different? Charlotte wondered, as she had so often over the years.

'Well, I'd better be getting on down or they'll be shut before I get there,' Peggy said amicably, burying her finger once again in Maureen's plump chins. 'Bye-bye, my love. Bye-bye, Barbara.'

'Bye-bye, Auntie Peggy,' Barbara replied without looking up from her doll.

'Barbara, I expect your Mammy'll be here soon,' Charlotte said as Peggy turned the corner of the Rank and disappeared from view. 'We'd better go in and get you cleaned up ready for her.'

Barbara looked up, a small, mulish pout pursing her lips. How like Amy at her age! Charlotte thought. Looking at Barbara it was almost impossible to believe the passage of the years. Why, it seemed like only yesterday when it had been Amy who was playing along the Rank – though Amy had

preferred riding in her brothers' trucks to playing with dolls
– and if you let yourself dream for a moment you could
almost think it *was* Amy. Those golden curls with the white
ribbon tied in them, plump little legs bare above white socks
– no, Amy had worn long stockings and petticoats and
pinafores. Perhaps it was longer ago than it seemed. I'm
getting old without realising it, Charlotte thought.

'Mammy! Mammy!' Barbara's excited voice attracted
Charlotte's attention and she looked up to see Barbara drop
the blanket with which she had been covering her doll and
start to run along the Rank. Following the child with her
eyes, Charlotte saw a boyish-looking silhouette emerge from
the path that led down between the gardens, a short cut from
the valley below, 'bingled' curls turned golden by the sun, a
dress with a square-cut sailor collar and narrow pleated skirt
– much too short to be decent, Charlotte thought, but she
knew better than to say so. Amy, her younger daughter, had a
tongue as sharp as a whiplash if you upset her and Charlotte
had no desire to get on the wrong side of her this afternoon.

'Look, Maureen, it's your Mammy!' she said, pointing
while Maureen wriggled, stretching out chubby hands.

'Da-da-da!'

'No, not Da-da – Ma-ma!' Charlotte corrected.

Barbara had reached Amy now and was throwing herself
at her mother's legs, but Charlotte saw Amy steer her skirt
clear of the grubby hands. If Dolly had left one of her boys for
the afternoon, she would have had him up in her arms by
now, Charlotte thought, treating him to a real bear-hug. But
Amy was a good mother in her own way, even if it was not
Dolly's, and deep down Charlotte had some sympathy with
her. Like Amy she had sometimes felt resentful that there
should be nothing more to a woman's life than running a
home and all its comforts for the benefit of a mostly
ungrateful family.

'Let's go and meet Mammy then, shall we?' Charlotte
suggested and as they drew closer she called out, 'There you
are, then! They've been good girls, the two of them . . .'

Her voice trailed away. She could tell at a glance
something was wrong with Amy.

'What is it? What's the matter?' she asked sharply.

Amy looked down at Barbara, avoiding her eyes.

'Oh . . . nothing.'

'Something is,' Charlotte pressed her. 'Come on – come in

17

and have a cup of tea and tell me what it is.'

'Nothing!' Amy repeated, the impatience in her tone giving the lie to the word as surely as the closed-in expression on her face.

'All right, have it your way,' Charlotte sighed. 'We'll have a cup of tea anyway.'

She turned and led the way back to No. 11, pushing open the door with a hand slightly puffed by the rheumatism that plagued her, worse some times than others. In the scullery the saucepans from dinner still stood draining beside the sink, washed but not dried – another concession to the grandchildren being here. However busy she had been when her own children were small, she would never have left the washing-up about until half-way through the afternoon. Then she had always wanted to be abreast if not ahead of herself. Now, it was different. Life was rushing past – she was fifty-one years old – and she wanted to take time to enjoy things while she could.

The kitchen led directly off the scullery, a crowded homely room furnished with a settle, straight-backed serviceable chairs and a square table covered by a red chenille cloth. Photographs hung on the walls now, more recent than those which decorated the piano in the front room, and photos that Charlotte liked to have around – Fred, the son who had been killed in the Great War, smiling gravely, head erect above the scratchy collar of his army uniform; Dolly and Amy in the figured silk bridesmaids' dresses they had worn for the rather grand wedding of their brother Jack, the schoolteacher who had married 'up the scale'; and Jack himself – pictured with Stella, his bride and daughter of the manager of South Hill Pit – getting into the motor which had carried them from church to reception after the ceremony. Even now, five years later, Charlotte could still feel a thrill of pride remembering her Jack had been one of the first in Hillsbridge to have motors for his wedding instead of horses and traps, though at the time the glory had been slightly marred by the fear that she and James might let Jack down in front of his grand new relations.

This afternoon, however, Charlotte was not concerned with her gallery of photographs, however precious. She crossed the room to the fireplace, setting Maureen down on the bright rag rug, then stirring the coals and settling the kettle on the hob.

'It won't take a tick to boil,' she said. 'Is everything all right at the yard?'

'Yes,' Amy said, but again she spoke too quickly and Charlotte knew she was hiding something. Oh well, give her time...

They chatted while they waited for the kettle to boil and Charlotte, who was a keen royalist and had kept a scrapbook on the royal family from the time she was a little girl, got out her latest cuttings to show Amy – the reports of the birth at 17 Bruton Street of a new princess, daughter of the Duke and Duchess of York.

'They're calling her Elizabeth,' Charlotte said. 'Isn't that a lovely name? Though it's after her mother, of course.'

Amy smiled inattentively and Charlotte tried another tack.

'I don't like the sound of what's going on at the pits,' she said conversationally as she poured boiling water into her brown earthenware pot. 'From what our Harry was saying, it wouldn't surprise me if there was another strike.'

'Oh, Harry – what does he know about it?' Amy asked, dismissing her younger brother. 'I should think that after what happened in 1921, anyone with any sense would have realised strikes do more harm than good. Look at all the men who have never been able to get work since – our dad for one. Though of course it did make some pull themselves up by their boot-strings – Llew for one...'

Her voice wobbled suddenly and looking at her Charlotte saw that her eyes were shining with what looked suspiciously like tears.

'Amy, for goodness' sake, what's the matter?' she asked impatiently.

For a moment longer Amy looked at her blankly, but Charlotte was certain there was something bottled up behind those defences. And sure enough a second later her lips began to tremble.

'Oh, Mam... it's the lorry... Llew...'

Charlotte went cold. 'Do you mean there's been an accident?'

'Yes, but...' She broke off, seeing her mother's expression. 'Oh, not that sort of accident. Not Llew. Me.'

'*You?*'

'Yes.'

And then it was tumbling out and Charlotte stood with thumbs in the tie of her floral print cross-over apron,

19

listening in sheer disbelief.

'Whatever is Llew going to say?' she asked when Amy had finished.

'I don't know!' Amy wept. 'What am I going to do, Mam? He'll be furious!'

'And rightly so,' Charlotte chided her. 'You could have killed somebody. Or been killed yourself. I thought you had more sense, Amy. And as for running into Ralph Porter... well, that just puts the tin lid on it.'

'I know.' Amy pressed her knuckles into her mouth. 'I've never seen anybody so cross. Why of all the people in Hillsbridge did it have to be him?'

'Well, there's nothing for it, you'll just have to own up to Llew about what's happened,' Charlotte advised. 'Where's the lorry now – still in Porter's Hill?'

'No. Herbie Button fetched it back for me. But it's got an awful dent, Mam...'

'Oh, my Lord!' Charlotte said, suppressing a vision of Amy being thrown out into the street. Oh well, she and the children could always come home here if the worst came to the worst...

'Amy...' she began, but a creaking sound made them both stop short, looking anxiously towards the door that, cupboard-like, concealed the stairs.

'Dad's coming down!' Amy said in a panicky voice. 'Oh Mam, I don't want him to know!'

'All right,' Charlotte said softly, then, louder, 'Well, that's about the size of it, Amy. She's due in the summer and they reckon it could be twins!'

The door opened and James appeared. A small-built man who had been a collier all his working life, he now looked older than his fifty-eight years. His hair, once fair, was now white and sparse, his body, arms and hands blue-veined with the coal-dust, and his shoulders rounded protectively around the chest that was so often racked with that rasping, phlegmy cough that came in time to anyone who worked long enough in narrow seams breathing in black air.

But in spite of losing his health, a mate or two and finally his livelihood in the coalfield, James had retained that easygoing acceptance of his lot that seemed a characteristic of many of the men who worked the Somerset seams.

'Worse things happen at sea,' was his favourite saying whenever trouble struck. 'Worse things happen at sea,

Lotty,' he would say, his mild blue eyes staring into space as if gazing as an impassive observer on those things which were so much worse than anything he was called upon to face.

Sometimes his calm acceptance had comforted Charlotte, sometimes baffled and often irritated her. But let James once lose his temper and you knew about it. Just a handful of times in her married life she had seen him aroused and it was not an experience she wished to repeat.

Now, realising that Amy was anxious her father should not get to hear of her folly, Charlotte took over with an ease born of long habit.

'Well, well, you're awake then. You smelt the teapot, I reckon.' She winked at Amy. 'Your Dad's been having his afternoon "snooge".'

'Hello, Dad,' Amy said without surprise. 'Afternoon snooges' had been the order of the day for as long as she could remember. Once they had been confined to Sunday afternoons – a special weekend treat when James retreated to bed for a couple of hours with a cup of tea and the *News of the World*. Now that he no longer worked, the 'snooge' had encroached onto the week as well.

'Hello, Amy.' He fastened the neck of his vest and straightened his braces. 'Everything all right?'

Charlotte saw her swallow her tears.

'Yes, Dad, fine. I've just come for the children...'

Charlotte poured the tea and fetched a biscuit each for Barbara and Maureen. They chatted on for a while, discussing everything from the strike threat that was hanging over the coalfield to the latest gossip, but Charlotte could see that Amy was still very worried in spite of the brave face she was putting on, so she collected the children's things together earlier than usual and settled Barbara in the wedge seat on Maureen's pram.

'I think I'll be going, Mam. By the time I get home...'

'Yes, all right.' Charlotte kissed the children and managed to whisper in Amy's ear: 'Just own up, Amy, it's the best way.'

But the smile Amy gave her in return was wan, and as she watched her push the pram along the Rank Charlotte shook her head sadly.

Amy had wanted to tell her, just as she had always wanted to tell her mother of her troubles ever since she was a little girl. But in those days they had been mostly molehills masquerading as mountains and Charlotte had more often than not been able to suggest a way of putting things right.

Now it was not that easy any more. They really were mountains and Charlotte had no ready answers to the problems her children brought her.

'They've grown up now and will just have to sort it out for themselves,' she told herself as Amy reached the corner of the Rank and turned to wave. 'There's nothing I can do now.'

And with a sigh that summed up the helpless frustration of a woman used to making things happen she turned and went back into the house to pour another cup of tea for James and herself.

*

When at last the children were tucked up in bed and asleep, Amy Roberts lit a cigarette and took it through into the front room of her home.

Llew disliked her smoking – not only did he think it was a most unladylike habit, he didn't care for the smell of tobacco either, so she tried to keep it out of his way as far as possible. Not that she smoked a great deal anyway, just at times of stress or if she wanted something to help her to relax, and tonight without a doubt she needed a prop to help her get up the courage to face him with the news of what she had done to his lorry when he returned home. And there were two advantages to having that much-needed cigarette in the front room – firstly the smell of smoke would be less noticeable when he came in and would not put him off the cold meat and baked potato supper she had ready for him, and secondly if she stood by the window that overlooked the road, she would get early warning of his arrival.

Amy took an ashtray over and set it in the cream-painted wooden window sill, then leaned over to open the window and let some fresh air into the room. Strange how quickly it could begin to get musty at this time of year. She used the front room a good deal more than her mother had ever used the one at Greenslade Terrace, lighting a fire at least once or twice a week in winter and opening it up every day in summer, for she had always hated the feeling of any room in a house being a mausoleum. Nevertheless the stiff, rather formal furniture which she and Llew had bought second-hand because it was all they could afford, gave a 'best room' impression and there was a darkening of the wall around the window that looked and smelled suspiciously like damp.

'It's that paeony bush doing it,' Charlotte had told her when she had mentioned the damp patch. 'It's right against the wall and that's something that's often a nuisance. You want to get Llew to dig it out.'

'I suppose so,' Amy had replied doubtfully, but she hadn't mentioned it to Llew. She loved the paeony bush with its luxuriant leaves and huge pink flowers – it had been one of the first things to attract her when Llew had taken her to look at the house. Standing on the pavement outside, holding tightly to his hand and trying not to display too much of the excitement that was bubbling inside her in case any of the neighbours might be peeping out from behind their curtains, she had gazed in wonder at the square grey house, made angular by the jutting porch on one corner, with the fancy-patterned, green-painted gables and the oblong-shaped front room window with the paeony-bush beneath.

Hope Terrace, Llew had told her it was called when he had first suggested they should look at the house, and she had expected it to be almost identical to Greenslade Terrace. But it was much grander. Set on the main Frome road where the hill levelled out to run almost flat, a mile out of the centre of Hillsbridge, it gave the impression of being 'open', with a garden back and front, and the houses were clearly much larger than those in Greenslade Terrace. Best of all, the house they were looking at was an end one, so that the nearest neighbour on one side was the width of a drive away, and to Amy that lent it a very special air of distinction.

'Oh Llew, do you really think we could afford a house like this?' she had asked, eyes shining, and Llew, pleased by her response, had replied, 'Well, it might be a bit of a struggle, Amy, but if I'm going to be taken seriously as a haulage contractor, I think we ought to have a place of our own.'

She had nodded and again the pride had swelled in her. It was hard sometimes to believe her luck – that in that bleak year of 1922, with a generation of girls resigning themselves to being on the shelf because so many young men had been killed in the Great War, she should have caught a man like Llew who was not only good-looking and treated her well, but was also quite determined to get on and make his mark on the world, even if jobs were scarce and money hard to come by.

That was what had brought him to Somerset, he had told her – he and his family could see no prospect of getting work in their native South Wales, so they had sold up and moved, lock, stock and barrel, mother, father, three sons and two daughters. Unfortunately things were no better in Hillsbridge and when he discovered that, Llew had set about planning his own enterprise – his own haulage business.

Amy had known nothing of that, of course, when she first met him, it was something he had confided to her over the months as his dream grew. But all her life she was to tell people that she had known the very first time she saw him that he was different – and not just because he was a stranger in Hillsbridge.

'He had a sort of presence – you couldn't help but notice him,' Amy described it, her eyes going misty blue as she remembered the night when he had first walked into the weekly dance run by Madame Roland in the room beneath the Picture Palace.

From the time the dances had begun a year earlier, Amy had been an eager patron. After the strictures of war, a new mood had taken the country by storm and the young people were enjoying themselves with a more determined gaiety than ever before. The stars of the silent screen – Charlie Chaplin, Douglas Fairbanks and Mary Pickford – were their idols; the new music craze from America, known as jazz, was sweeping across the Atlantic and everyone everywhere wanted to learn to dance – and not only the old-fashioned waltz either. Classes mushroomed in every available hall, with teachers varying from the enthusiastic amateur to the bored professional anxious to turn a quick pound. In Hillsbridge the best of these without doubt was Madame Roland.

Twice a week she swept into town by train, disembarking onto the platform of the S. & D. Railway Station in a cloud of camphor and cheap French perfume that Reuben Tapper, the porter, reckoned 'could knock you sideways'; the older residents looked askance at her scarlet-painted lips and nails, the length of her skirts beneath her lush fur coat and the height of the Cuban heels on her shoes. The fashion of the day might be to look flat chested and boyish, but Madame Roland certainly did not believe in adhering to that; while most young women flattened their figures by every conceivable means, she accentuated her already voluptuous curves; and while the bob was all the rage as a hairstyle, Madame Roland continued to make the most of her thick black, waist-length tresses.

Because she was such a colourful figure, however, Madame Roland had no difficulty whatever in attracting a clientele for her dancing classes and dances. They came at first out of curiosity, to giggle and be scandalised, but having come they stayed. Madame Roland's were the best dances in Hillsbridge or for miles around and before long they became *the* place to be on a Saturday night.

To Amy – pretty, popular and light on her feet – the dances were the highlight of the week. After a brief romance with Winston Walker, the young solicitor who had defended her brother Ted when he had been charged with manslaughter a year earlier, she was fancy-free again – and playing the field for all it was worth. Long ago she had discovered the power of a demure smile accompanied by a sidelong glance, and though she was not as pretty as her older sister Dolly, Amy had the personality to make men swear she was. They buzzed around her like wasps round a jam-pot – the reason why her romance with Winston Walker had been so short-lived. Amy had liked Winston – he was pleasant, well-set-up and knew how to treat a lady – but the strain of having to continue to behave like one soon took its toll on her affection. Besides, Winston was rather serious for her and much too well-read. 'We'd bore one another to tears in no time,' Amy had explained to Charlotte, who was very disappointed when the match fell through. 'There are plenty of nice boys about who like the same things as I do.'

Sighing at the disappearance of her dream for Amy, Charlotte had been forced to agree. In spite of the war there were still plenty of lads in Hillsbridge with the same carefree attitude to life as Amy ... and most of them seemed to attend Madame Roland's dances!

On the Saturday night when Amy met Llew, she had gone to the dance with Edie Presley who lived at No. 15 Greenslade Terrace, and the minute they went in the boys started flocking around, asking them to dance and even trying to stake a claim to walk them home.

'I don't know what I'm doing yet – ask me later,' Amy replied to all these invitations, and it was a measure of her popularity that she was fairly confident that several of them at least would do so.

It had been past ten and the dance in full swing when the unexpected happened. Amy, dancing with Arthur Packer, the bookmaker's clerk, had her back to the door, but she was alerted by Arthur's, 'Hello, who's that, then?' and turned her head to see two strangers walking down the side of the hall.

At virtually first glance it was clear they were brothers – both had the same fresh boyish faces and brown hair springing from a deep 'widow's peak', both were neatly dressed in light blue suits. They were of similar build, tall and whippy, but they carried it well, making no attempt to slouch or blend into the background.

Arthur's query, it seemed, had been taken up by the rest of the dancers. Feet slowed, heads turned and the buzz of comment was almost loud enough to be heard over the swelling strains of 'Chick-chick-chick-chick-chicken, Lay a little egg for me'.

'Who are they?'

'Look as if they think they own the place...'

'Never seen them around here before...'

'Perhaps they're something to do with Madame Roland...'

The two young men crossed to a corner beside the stage and all eyes followed them. 'Looking as if they owned the place' was a harsh judgement, but there was some truth in it.

When the music stopped and Arthur escorted Amy back to her seat beside Edie Presley, the two girls added their whispers to the others watching the strangers surreptitiously.

'They're nice, aren't they, Amy? Do you think they might ask us to dance? Amy – *they're coming over!*'

Two pairs of eyes were hastily averted. They did not want to be caught looking. They lifted their noses in the air, chattering together with just the right degree of assumed animation and pretending not to notice until two blue suits drew level with their line of vision.

'Would you care to dance?'

'May I have the pleasure?'

The accents were faintly but unmistakably Welsh. The girls hesitated, wondering how the local lads would receive it if they danced so readily with these rather forward strangers, but as Edie put it later, 'We didn't want to make them feel awkward, did we?'

'All right, if you like,' she said, getting up and Amy followed suit, treating 'hers' to a long and searching look before allowing him to lead her on to the floor.

In spite of his height he was a good dancer. Amy, used to the local lads who were on the whole much shorter, was surprised by the easy gliding way he moved and liked the firm cool way his hand held hers. He was older, too, she judged, than the majority of the patrons – in his middle twenties, if her guess was anything to go by. They introduced themselves and conversed a little, but the talk was more about Madame Roland and the dance than any personal subjects and when she returned to her chair, Amy was not much the wiser about her partner apart from his name.

'Mine was called Llew Roberts,' she confided, trying not to let the lads see she was talking about them. 'What was yours?'

'Mine was Edwin. They're brothers.'

'I thought so. Did you find out what they're doing here?'

'They're moving to Hillsbridge. Renting a house up at South Hill. And there's another brother and two sisters.' Edie was justly proud of the information she had managed to glean in five minutes of twirling.

'But what do they do?'

'I don't know, I couldn't find out,' Edie grinned mischievously. 'But I will if they ask us to dance again.'

'Probably they won't. They'll want to get to know as many as possible,' Amy said. But she was wrong. A few minutes later and the two Roberts boys were back, snapping them up and almost monopolising them to the annoyance of the local lads. And later the two girls were able to compare notes to the effect that the newcomers had each asked to walk them home.

'Do you think we should?' Edie wondered anxiously.

Amy, who had liked Llew more each time she danced with him, tossed her head. 'I don't see why not.'

'Our boys won't like it. I could see Arthur Packer looking at you ever so black just now ...'

'Won't do him any harm,' Amy said airily. 'It'll keep him on his toes.'

And so it was arranged. The Roberts boys, carrying their dancing shoes under their arms, walked Amy and Edie through the centre of Hillsbridge where the lights were turned out at last in the Market Yard and the two pubs, the George and the Miners' Arms, faced one another across the main road, past the livery stables and forge and up the steep and winding Conygre Hill to Greenslade Terrace.

'You've got a long walk back up to South Hill,' Amy said.

'You're right the other side of the valley.'

Not that they seemed to mind. Like perfect gentlemen they left the two girls at their doors and to their disappointment made no mention of seeing them again. But the following week they were at Madame Roland's again and once more, to the fury of Arthur Packer and the other local lads, they monopolised the two girls who were undoubtedly the prettiest and liveliest unattached females in the place.

That night Llew asked Amy out and she was far more surprised than he was to find herself accepting.

I don't usually give in that easily; I like to lead them along a bit, she thought.

But Llew had a way with him – and for almost the first time in her life Amy was afraid that if she refused she might not be given a second chance.

After walking out with Llew for a few weeks, Amy began to be aware that she felt quite differently about him from the way she had felt about any of her other so-called 'young men'. Usually after a few meetings she would grow restless and impatient, longing to try the greener pasture on the other side of the fence. But the more she saw of Llew, the more she wanted to see, and try as she might she could not explain it even to herself.

He was such a contradiction in terms, she thought, and always unexpected. As she had observed the first time she met him, he had a self-confidence and a sense of purpose that seemed to add to his stature, a determination to make things happen – and happen the way he wanted them to. Yet he was also a dreamer. And when he shared them with her, Amy was surprised at the depth and intensity of his dreams.

'What are you going to do about a job?' she had asked him one evening.

It was a Sunday. Amy had been invited to the Roberts' rented home in South Hill Gardens, and when they had disposed of the ham sandwiches, seed cake and drop scones that Mrs Roberts had put in front of them, Llew had suggested a walk – in the hope, Amy guessed, of being out when the party for evening service at chapel was mustered. It was a pleasant evening and they skirted South Hill Pit and climbed through a V-gate into the fields that sloped steeply – as did most of the green areas around Hillsbridge – down to the valley beneath. The main bowl of the town was away to their right – dust-blackened buildings clustered around the railway sidings and pits, a horseshoe-shaped loop of shops, a church with a tower, and several chapels, and beneath them the valley that linked Hillsbridge with South Compton, the next town, looked peaceful and serene. There were no trains on the two railway lines that ran arrow-straight through the valley, and the overhanging branches hid even the gentle movement of the river. Only a few hens, strutting and clucking in a pen at the bottom of one of the gardens, seemed to be awake.

Sitting there in the shade of the thick hedge, staring into the valley across his drawn-up knees, Llew seemed to be in a trance and Amy, who had faced a barrage of queries from Charlotte about her latest young man and his prospects, repeated her question.

'What are you going to do about a job, Llew? There's not much work here just now – no more than in Glamorgan, I wouldn't have thought. Since the strike everything seems to be dead.'

'You're right,' Llew agreed. 'And if there is a job, I'm not likely to get it with the local lads wanting work as well. Employers are bound to be prejudiced.'

Amy's heart sank. Not only did she not relish the prospect of confessing to Charlotte that Llew was still unemployed, but if he was talking like this there was always the possibility that he might decide to move on.

'You don't hold out much hope, then?'

'Not really. But that doesn't bother me,' he replied.

Amy looked round sharply. 'Not bother you? Whatever do you mean?'

'I don't want to work for anybody else.' He wasn't looking at her. His eyes were narrowed so that his lashes, thick as a girl's, formed a screen for his thoughts. 'It's a mug's game, breaking your back to make someone else rich, and at the end of the day you've got nothing to show for it. I can't see the sense in that.'

Amy said nothing. True enough, it did not seem fair. She had watched her father and her eldest brother Jim working away their lives in the pit and she knew that during the winter months they had sometimes not seen daylight from one week's end to the next. Yet they still lived in miners' cottages while it was the owner, Sir Richard Spindler, who lived in style at Hillsbridge Down House. But right or wrong, it was the way of things. There were bosses and there were workers; it was a question of knowing your place.

'No, I'm going to be my own boss, Amy,' Llew went on, breaking into her thoughts. 'I made up my mind about that a long time ago.'

'But what could you do?' Amy asked.

'I'm going to get myself a lorry and go into the haulage business.'

'A *lorry*?'

'That's right. Horses and carts are going to be finished with soon. Motor transport is the thing of the future.'

'But what would you carry in it?' Amy was totally nonplussed. 'Nobody round here would want anything carried in *lorries*.'

'Well, that's where you're wrong,' Llew told her. 'This is a very good place to start. You see this valley?' He pointed down across the green slopes. 'They're going to put a road through here, joining Hillsbridge up with South Compton, to save having to go up South Hill and down past the cottages where your Jim lives. A straight road, straight up the valley, the same as the railway lines.'

'Yes, I know that,' Amy said with some impatience. She had read in the *Mercury*, the local paper, about the proposed new road – a scheme to give extra jobs for the unemployed in the district, it was said. 'But I don't see . . .'

'If they're building a road, they'll need to bring in the stuff to make it.' There was enthusiasm in Llew's voice now. 'Oh, I know they're going to use slag from the colliery waste-tips to fill in the foundations and that, they say, is going to go straight down over from South Hill Pit in trucks on an incline. But they're bound to need gravel and stone and stuff from the quarries. That's where I come in.'

'I see,' Amy said, still only half-believing. 'But you haven't got a lorry, Llew.'

His lips curved and for the first time he turned to look at her.

'No, but I'm getting one next week. I'm going up to Birmingham to get it.'

'Birmingham? Why Birmingham?'

'Because I'm buying it from a dealer there.'

'But you can't drive a motor, can you?'

'No, but I can learn. What do you think of that then, Amy?'

'I think it's lovely!' she said.

That had been the start of 'Llew Roberts, Haulage

Contractors'. Much to the amazement of Amy – and Charlotte – the lorry had materialised just as Llew had promised, and he was able to fix himself up with contracts to haul for the council, who were responsible for building the new road. For a time Llew's brother Eddie had come in on the venture. Amy had regretted that. For some reason she did not altogether trust Eddie, who had a plausible, rather sly manner, and she was glad when after some disagreement or other Llew had re-invested some of the money the council paid him to buy Eddie's lorry. That made it a two-vehicle concern, and when he managed to get a contract to haul some wood for pit-props he had to take on a driver to help him out.

'It's a risky business,' Charlotte said, shaking her head. But Amy was absolutely delighted. On the strength of the new contracts, Llew had asked her to marry him and she had accepted. Her early doubts had all melted now – she was head over heels in love with Llew and quite convinced he was going to make a success of the enterprise. What was more, she was determined to enjoy the status that would come from being the wife of a man who owned two lorries and employed a driver and a mate. Who cared if half Hillsbridge called him 'jumped-up' and secretly hoped to see him take a tumble? He would show them, she was certain of it – and so would she.

Not that things had worked out quite as she'd hoped of course, Amy thought, as she stood and smoked at the window of their house in Hope Terrace that evening four years later. Nothing had come easily. There had been days when Llew had worked until he was worn to a frazzle, only to have his bill defaulted on at the end of it, and nights when she had heard him pace the floor as he worried about meeting some expense or other or delivering a contract on time. There had been occasions when he had taken a gamble that had scared her out of her wits – such as when he had arranged to buy out his first copse and cut it without being sure he had a buyer. Everyone knew most of the contracts for the supply of wood for pit-props were sewn up – Ralph Porter, the timber merchant, had most of the owners and managers in his pocket – and Amy had been terrified Llew would find himself with a lot of wood on his hands and no outlet for it. But Edgar Tudgay at Lower Midlington had taken pity on him and bought the lot. Amy had had a new dress out of that – badly needed since Barbara and Maureen had come along, leaving her plumper than she had been before.

But on the whole she knew Llew was pleased.

'It might be hard work, but it's worth it if I know it's for our benefit,' was his motto, and Amy admired him for it while trying to involve herself in the business as much as he would let her.

'I could help with the booking, I'm sure I could!' she had suggested. 'I always liked figures at school.' And so, more to humour her than anything, Amy felt, Llew sometimes allowed her to go to the yard and make out the delivery tickets, filling in details like 'tare weights' and discolouring her fingers – and sometimes her face – with the 'blue-paper' that produced the magical second and third copies.

She was never allowed to touch the accounts, however, and bills and letters concerning the business she never saw. The postman usually delivered the letters before Llew left for the yard in the mornings and he took them with him, sorting them in his little office and bringing home any private correspondence that evening. Local letters sometimes arrived by the second post, but these Llew seemed less concerned about, a fact that puzzled Amy since most of his business was conducted locally. As for important items such as insurance on the motor lorries, she had not the faintest idea as to whom they were with or what they were about even; so on that April day after colliding so disastrously with Ralph Porter's Morgan, there was nothing Amy could do but wait for Llew's return . . . and confess what she had done.

The cigarette burned down and she stubbed it out, her hand shaking slightly, and got up. Stupid to sit here, watching for him and getting more and more nervous. It might be hours yet before he came home and there were a hundred and one things she could be doing.

With a decisive movement Amy leaned over, pushed open the window and tipped the contents of the ashtray into the paeony bush. Then, leaving the window slightly open to let out the last of the smoke, she went back to the living-room.

*

It was past 10 o'clock when Amy heard the front door open. Adrenalin began pumping through her veins again as she stood up on legs suddenly trembling and switched off the crystal set she had been listening to in order to occupy her mind.

Llew must be tired. He only came in by the front door when he was past walking round to the back. And she had to tell him ... oh Lord, thought Amy as she hurried through to the kitchen to return the kettle to the hob. She was just rearranging the table setting, the new loaf and the plate of cold meat, when she saw his shadow in the doorway and looked up, forcing a bright smile.

'Hello, you're home ...'

Then, as she saw the expression on his face, her voice died away. Llew only looked that way when he was very angry or very upset, and instinctively – without a word passing between them – Amy knew that somehow he had already heard what had happened to his lorry.

'Llew – I'm sorry, truly I am ...' she began, but he seemed not to hear her.

'That stupid fool Button!' he exploded, hurling his cap at the kitchen chair. 'What do you think he's done?'

'It wasn't his fault ...' Amy protested weakly, but Llew in full flow heard nothing.

'Hare-brained idiot! I thought he was supposed to be a responsible man and used to motors. But I leave him in charge for one day – one day! – and when I get back, what do I find? My new lorry with the front wing buckled – and when it's only been on the road less than a week! And there's worse, it seems. It was Ralph Porter he ran into, of all people! Ralph Porter in that three-wheeler Morgan of his. It couldn't be worse. Not if he'd run into the King of England, it couldn't be!'

'Llew ...' Amy was confused. Surprising enough that Llew should have known about the accident so soon – but why should he think it was Herbie who was responsible? 'How did you ...?'

'Well, I saw it, didn't I, when I took my lorry back to the yard. Funny – I nearly drove it home with me, but I didn't have too much petrol. And there in the yard is my new lorry, large as life, with the fender bent and the number-plate twisted.'

'But what makes you think it was Herbie?' Amy didn't know why she had said that, unless it was a case of anything to put off the evil moment when they would get to the crux of the conversation and she would have to confess...

'It couldn't have been anybody else. Ivor Burge was with me,' Llew said, referring to the young 'mate' he had taken on and was teaching to drive. 'I tell you, Amy, I was so mad I went to see Herbie straight away. And he had the cheek to try and make light of it!'

'Well, it was an accident ...' Amy interposed.

'I can't afford accidents like that.' Llew was loosening his collar and putting one foot on the chair to undo his boot. 'Especially not with Ralph Porter. I'd been hoping to sub-contract for him; he's bought up an entire wood out on Withydown Lane and I thought I might get in there and make enough to pay off the lorry. Fat chance I've got to do that now! His car was badly dented, according to Herbie; he had to help him push it out of the hedge – you know there's no reverse gear on those Morgans. I couldn't be bothered with it myself, but it's like a baby to him, they say. Well, I told Herbie straight – if that's the way you drive, you're no good to me.'

'Llew!' Amy was round-eyed now. 'You don't mean you've...?'

'Sacked him? Of course I have.' Llew sighed deeply and gesticulated towards the kettle which was singing on the hob. 'For goodness' sake, Amy, stop gawping and make me a cup of tea.'

'Oh!' said Amy, not so much trembling now as tingling all over with shock and surprise and guilt. This whole thing was much worse than she had thought: the lorry damaged before it was even paid for; Ralph Porter's pride, as well as his Morgan, dented; and a contract on which Llew had obviously been pinning a great deal lost and gone beyond recall. But all this paled before the fact that Herbie had been willing to take the blame for her – allowed Llew to sack him and still not said – though once it had got that far she supposed it had really snowballed out of his control. Funny, she had never thought he liked her much, for there was always an edge beneath the respect which made her feel he resented her. And now...

'Llew, you can't sack Herbie,' she stated.

'I've done it. Come on, Amy, make that pot of tea for goodness' sake.'

'You can't sack him because it wasn't his fault.'

'Try telling that to Ralph Porter.'

'Llew, will you listen to me!' she cried in exasperation. 'It wasn't Herbie driving the lorry. It was me!'

Llew sighed. 'Amy, I'm tired. I've had a long day. Let's just forget it now, eh?'

'I'm not making it up, Llew, just to save Herbie his job. I'm telling you the truth! Ask Ralph Porter if you don't believe me. It was me driving the lorry.'

'But you can't!'

'I know that now. That's why I ran into Ralph Porter, I suppose. But I thought I could. Herbie tried to stop me but I wouldn't listen . . .'

'Amy, I can't believe what I'm hearing! You mean you took the lorry out on the road?'

'Yes.'

'After I expressly forbade you to try?'

'Yes. I did so want to and you . . .'

'I was conveniently out of the way, breaking my back to make money for you to throw away . . . Amy, you haven't got a driving licence!'

'I didn't think anyone would be any the wiser . . .'

'You stupid woman! Don't you realise it's against the law to drive on the road without a licence? Oh my Lord, suppose the insurance won't stand it . . . That's why Herbie tried to cover up for you, I suppose.'

His hands made fists, the knuckles white, his lips drawn back from his teeth in a snarl of rage. In the four years she had known him, Amy had never seen him so angry and she cowered away as his fist came up, convinced he was going to strike her.

'Oh, Llew . . .' she sobbed.

His hands fastened on the curved back of the cane chair she had set at the table ready for him to have his supper and he lifted it effortlessly, swinging it behind him. The edge of the tablecloth went with it, a plate skidded off the edge of the table and smashed on the flagstone floor and a jug of milk overturned, swamping the loaf of bread on the china bread-plate.

'Llew, please!' Amy screamed, believing for a moment that he was going to lay about her with the chair. 'I'm sorry! *I'm sorry!*'

As she said it he brought the chair sharply round, throwing it as hard as he could across the kitchen. Amy stepped smartly aside and it smashed into the stone sink, splintering a leg and falling drunkenly to the floor. There was a moment's complete silence and then Llew turned, beating helplessly at the door-frame with his fist.

The moment of danger passed, Amy looked wildly round at the scene of destruction for which she knew she was to blame.

'And what good do you think that did?' she demanded boldly.

There was no reply. His anger spent now, Llew laid his forehead against the doorpost, looking such a picture of dejection that for the first time Amy thought of him rather than of herself, briefly seeing the events of the day through his eyes. He did work hard, too hard, driving himself to build up the business against a certain amount of opposition from the locals, and today had clearly been long and tiring for him. It wasn't much fun for him to come home to this.

She crossed the kitchen to Llew, winding her arms around him and laying her head against his back.

'I'm really sorry. And I'll try to put things right with Ralph Porter. Just tell me what to say and I'll go and see him and . . .'

Llew turned so violently that she was pushed aside and for once he made no attempt to pull her into his arms, as he usually did after a disagreement.

'No! I'll deal with this now and you will stay at home where you belong. And Amy, if you ever attempt to drive that lorry again, I promise you I'll put you across my knee and spank you!'

Amy said nothing. Llew was not a violent man and he had never laid a finger on her, but she felt this was no idle threat. And with a twinge of shame that was almost foreign to her nature, she knew that she had earned every bit of his anger.

I wish I could have the afternoon over again so that I could do it differently, Amy thought. I would never have gone down Porter's Hill if I had known what was going to happen.

But in spite of everything there was one thing she had no desire to change.

Give her the chance again, and she would still drive the lorry!

Chapter Two

In a shed at the end of the garden at No. 11 Greenslade Terrace, Harry Hall was watching his pigeons.

The shed was made of orange boxes and only just high enough for Harry to stand upright, but he didn't mind that. It was his own special place – his world which he had built with his own hands – and he enjoyed the feeling of privacy it gave him. Much to his mother's bewilderment he would stay here for hours, constructing new nesting boxes where the hen birds could sit on their eggs and then watching as they reared their young ... the tiny, almost bald chicks which they fed with their own regurgitated food until they were big enough to take seed. Sometimes when there were too many chicks, he had to shake the eggs to addle them so that the birds sat in vain. When this happened he went to the pigeon loft less often, for it made him feel sad to think that their efforts would be to no avail, but he did it all the same. Restricting the number of young was a necessary part of keeping pigeons and Harry accepted it as a fact of life, even though at the same time it stirred in him a feeling of injustice. Some things had to be done. Addling eggs was one of them.

That evening in late April, however, the young pigeons had all hatched out healthy and well; there would be some fine flying birds amongst them and Harry hoped that he would soon be able to enter one or two for a race. The Flying Club was big in Hillsbridge – pigeon fancying was a popular hobby amongst the miners, for you didn't need to be a millionaire to take part in it – and several of the members were well-known for their success. Deep down, Harry cherished a dream that maybe one day he too would have a pigeon so fast and with a homing instinct so strong that wherever it was released it would return to the loft more quickly than any of its fellow competitors. That would show the old-timers, he thought, and the idea of shining at something – even pigeon fancying – was an attractive one.

At sixteen, Harry was something of an enigma to all who knew him. The youngest of the Halls, he had the same fair hair and skin as his brothers, the same blue eyes and stubby fair lashes, the same compact build. With the exception of Jack, they had all gone to work in the pits as soon as they were old enough – though Ted, always known as 'a scallywag', had left now to wander round the country doing a variety of jobs and Fred, killed in France, would never set foot in the dark seams again. Harry had followed their lead without really knowing why. He had had the opportunity to stay on at school, for Mr Davies, the headmaster, had said he was sure Harry had the capability to gain a scholarship to the Higher Elementary at South Compton and Charlotte had encouraged – even begged – him to try. But Harry had not wanted to. With the same mulish stubbornness he had displayed ever since he was a small child, he had blankly refused and no amount of persuasion could make him change his mind.

'I'm going to leave and go down the pit,' he had told his mother when she had come home after being summoned to the school for an interview with William Davies. 'I told Mr Davies that when he had a go at me this afternoon.'

'I know you did. That's why he sent for me – to try to get some sense into your head,' Charlotte had said impatiently. 'He says it's a crime, Harry, to waste a brain like you've got. And he reckons that if you put your mind to it you could do every bit as well as our Jack.'

'Be a schoolmaster?' Harry asked incredulously. 'No, thanks!'

'What's wrong with being a schoolmaster, I'd like to know?' Charlotte demanded. She was very proud of Jack who, now that he was properly qualified, had got himself a post in a very nice village down the county where open rolling countryside met sea. When Harry only shrugged, she went on, 'You don't want to be a carting boy all your life, that I do know!'

'I won't be, don't worry about that,' Harry had replied.

Charlotte had snorted. Carting boys were the very lowest in the hierarchy of the men who worked in the narrow, dark seams beneath the green Somerset fields, and quite often they were still chained to their backbreaking work long after they could be termed 'boys'. Their job was to shift the coal hewn at the face by the 'breakers', dragging it by means of the infamous guss and crook through seams so narrow that they could only crawl on hands and knees.

When she had first come to the Somerset coalfield as a young bride, Charlotte had not known of the existence of the guss and crook, and at first when James had explained it to her she had laughed, certain he was 'pulling her leg'. After all, she had thought, who in their right minds would believe that anyone could expect a lad to pull a sleigh full of coal by means of a circle of tarred rope around his waist and passed between his legs? It was too monstrous to be true! Then, when James had finally called in a young lad from further down the Rank who had recently started work as a carting boy, and pulled up his shirt to reveal a raw and bleeding band of flesh around his waist where the rope had cut into it, her amusement had turned to horror.

'It's terrible!' she had cried in outrage. 'It shouldn't be allowed! If the roadways aren't big enough for tubs and ponies, they should *make* them big enough!'

But James had merely shrugged. 'It's the best way. And the lads soon get used to it. You don't know what you'm talking about, Lotty,' and she had been shocked by his easy acceptance, just as the politicians who fought in vain to get the contraption banned were shocked when their efforts were sneered at as 'interference' by the very men forced to use it.

How could a man ever accept it? she wondered. The pain of the raw rub marks might ease as use – and the urine they rubbed in – hardened the skin, but the ignominy of being regarded as a human donkey remained. Now, faced with yet another of her children subjecting himself to it, she felt bitter and impotent.

'Stop worrying, Mam,' Harry had advised her.

But of course she could not, and she had no intention of keeping her anxiety to herself either.

'It's easy to get into, but not so easy to get out, Harry,' she had said tartly, her mind returning to the events of a few years previously when another of her carting-boy sons had tried to exchange his way of life. 'Look at our Ted – when he tried to leave, the under-manager made all sorts of threats . . . told him that if he left he'd have to take his father with him.

'Of course I didn't know about it at the time – Ted saw to that, kept it to himself for the sake of his father's pride. And a good thing I didn't know, too – I'd have been down there quick-sharp and given them a piece of my mind.'

'But Ted's not carting now,' Harry had said reasonably.

'No, but if it hadn't been for the war he might be,' she responded. 'They've got you where they want you once you go into the pits, Harry. Try to get away and they kick up hell's delight.'

'They won't keep me if I don't want to stay,' Harry had replied. 'You ought to know me better than that, Mam.'

That had silenced Charlotte. She did know him, of course, and knew that once he had made up his mind about something it would take heaven and earth to move him. Yes, come to think of it, she pitied the under-manager or manager even who tried to blackmail Harry into doing something he did not want to do. And she could not see concern for anyone else stopping him as it had stopped Ted. In Harry's world, what he wanted was the prime consideration. It was not that he was selfish, just that he took no account of anyone else.

So in this as in most things Harry had got his own way. Shortly after his fourteenth birthday he left William Davies and the Board School and secured himself a job at Middle Pit in the centre of Hillsbridge where his father and his brothers Jim, Fred and Ted had worked before him.

Unlike them, however, he had felt no thrill of pride at entry into the world of men as he walked down the hill on that first morning with his bottle of cold tea, a cognocker of bread and cheese in his bait tin and a couple of tallow candles to light his way underground. He had no illusions about the life he was going to lead, for a while at least. He knew – without even having set foot in the open-sided cage that would carry him below – of the narrow, faulted seams where ceiling was floor and floor ceiling, the heat that made men work as near naked as they could and the stale dust-filled air, freshened in some places only by a hand-driven fan known as a 'Blow Georgie'. He knew about the diseases of the chest, the asthma and bronchitis that affected the older miners, for he had grown up with his father's rattling cough and seen him spit evil-looking phlegm into the fire from the time he could crawl. And he was aware too that the weekly wage, though riches to him, was barely enough to live on for a man struggling to keep a wife and family. But in his dogged way, Harry refused to allow himself to be put off by any of these things. Any work experience was better than none in these days of high unemployment, he reckoned. And it wasn't going to be for ever. As he had told his mother so forcibly, he had no more intention of remaining a carting boy than he had of becoming a schoolmaster. It was a stepping-stone, he felt, though at the moment a stepping-stone to what he was not quite sure.

Sometimes he thought about it as he lovingly tended his pigeons in their loft made of orange boxes, trying to identify the restlessness within him. What *was* it he wanted to do? There was an urge deep inside him so sharp that he sometimes felt he was hovering right on the brink of knowing, a sort of breathless anticipation and a stirring of excitement. He could remember feeling a little this way when he had been a child, rushing into the garden on a spring morning, smelling the freshness of the dew-wet garden, seeing a cabbage-white butterfly dance by, hearing the hens clucking contentedly in their coop at the end of the Clements' garden. The world had been there, new and full of limitless promise, and without being quite sure what he wanted from it, he had revelled in the feeling that whatever it was, he had only to decide and it would be his.

The same held true now. Harry got up with the dawn and spent most of the daylight hours far beneath the earth. He found himself accepted into the mining fraternity as his brothers had been before him, hearing for the first time in his life the conversation of men used to the company of other men, joining in the card schools and sending betting slips to the bookie, collecting his meagre wage at the end of the week and spending some of it on 'scrumpy', the rough cider they sold straight from the barrels in the Miners' Arms. And all the time he was conscious of waiting... waiting for something to show him the way ...

'Harry! Harry – are you in there?' His mother's voice, loud as the pit hooter when she wanted it to be, carried up the garden and Harry pushed open the door of the pigeon loft. He did not want Charlotte to come barging in and disturbing the birds.

After the dim light in the shed the evening sunshine made him blink and he stood for a moment shading his eyes, a compactly built young man in an open-necked shirt and a pair of rushy-duck trousers, his bright fair hair covered by a smart blue cap.

'What's up, Mam?'

Charlotte came near enough to speak without shouting. 'It's your Dad, Harry. He's not at all well.'

'I could see that at teatime.' Harry said. It was true – he had noticed the way James was hunching and wheezing, eating next to nothing – 'not enough to keep a bird alive' as Charlotte described it – and leaving the table long before the others had finished to sink exhausted into his chair by the fire.

'You could see how poorly he was, couldn't you?' Charlotte said anxiously. 'And now, if you like, he's talking about going down to the Miners' Arms. I've told him there's no sense in it, but he reckons he's got some runner beans he promised our Jim and they ought to be put in this weekend. South Compton Fair Day,' she added by way of explanation, referring to the local street fair that had been held every year since being granted a Royal Charter centuries ago, and which was used by many local people as a gardening almanac.

Harry said nothing. He knew what was coming.

'I told him if he'd forget about being so silly, you'd run down for him,' Charlotte went on. 'You needn't stay if you don't want to – I'd rather you weren't going in pubs at your age – but I don't want your father struggling up and down that hill and that's the truth.'

Harry sighed and nodded.

'All right. Tell him I'll go for him. Just let me shut up here.'

'No rush.' The evening breeze stirred a stray lock of Charlotte's hair and she raised a slightly puffy hand to tuck it back into her bun. 'Our Jim won't be there much before half-past eight, your Dad said.'

'All right.'

A faint smile lightened Charlotte's worried expression. Stubborn and opinionated as he could be at times, he was still her baby, youngest of the brood and the last she would have now. 'You're a good boy, Harry,' she said.

When she had gone back up the path Harry checked on his pigeons once more and locked up the house before following her. In the scullery he washed his hands at the stone sink and took off his cap to comb his hair. Then he went through into the kitchen.

'Mam says you've got some beans for me to take down for our Jim.'

James was sitting in his favourite chair beside the hob and as he turned his head with an effort Harry could see he had deteriorated quite a lot even since teatime, shrinking and slumping as he did when his chest was bad. The heavy rasp of his breathing filled the room.

'Ah – I wish you would, Harry.' The effort of speaking exhausted him for a moment. 'There's a few geranium plants too, though tell him not to put them in till May,' he went on when he could manage it. 'I'd come and get them for you, Harry, but I think I'd better stay where I be ...'

'I'll get them for him, don't you worry,' Charlotte said, adding with a snort, 'And you thought you were going to go down to the pub yourself! I said you were born silly!'

James opened his mouth to answer, but a fit of coughing took him and though he managed to bring up several sizable globules of phlegm, when the fit had subsided his breathing was worse than ever and he slumped back into his chair. Harry viewed him with alarm. He looked like a wizened old man and there was something very disturbing about the way his eyes, pale and watery, gazed fixedly into space as he fought for breath.

Harry had grown up with his father's 'turns', but this was as bad as he had ever seen him.

'I'll go and take the plants off Mam,' he said, grateful for an excuse to escape from the familiar room that seemed suddenly oppressive.

The plants were tied neatly in bundles with newspaper round them. James had clearly put in some time on them before the 'turn' came on. Charlotte gave Harry the beans in a tobacco tin to put into his pocket and stacked the plants together in a seed-box.

'Can you manage them like that, or shall I put them in my string bag?' she asked.

'I can manage them like that!' Harry said hastily. He had no intention of being seen in Hillsbridge carrying a string shopping bag, no matter what it contained!

'Here you are, then.' Charlotte handed it to him. 'Don't be late, now. And I wish you'd tell our Jim how bad his Dad is this time,' she added.

Harry nodded. 'I will. Don't worry.'

But as he walked along the Rank the sense of foreboding he had felt so strongly in the house melted away. Out of earshot of that awful rattling breathing and with the fresh air in his nostrils instead of the faint sickly-sweet smell that seemed to emanate from James when he was unwell, it was easy to tell himself it was just another of his father's 'turns'.

Harry settled the plants more comfortably in his arms and whistling a fairly tuneless version of 'The Sheik of Araby' he turned the corner and started down the hill.

*

The Miners' Arms was and always had been the 'local' for the men who worked the black seams at Middle Pit, South Hill, Starvault and the other collieries within the Hillsbridge bowl. It stood in the centre of the town, facing a rival hostelry, the George, across the width of the main Bath Road. But the George was the pub used by 'the nobs' – colliery managers and business men, the secretary of the Co-operative Society, the mill owner and Ralph Porter the timber merchant, known as the richest man in Hillsbridge. None of them would have been seen dead in the Miners' Arms, while the miners similarly avoided the George.

For them, the Miners' Arms had everything they could wish for – a skittle alley for noisy matches with other pubs in the district, a quoits bed where the men of Hillsbridge excelled themselves against all-comers, and a yard where homing pigeon crates could be stacked before being taken over to the railway station for despatch to various distant parts. In addition it had two good-sized rooms: a lounge, or 'best room' as it was known, and a public bar with sawdust on the floor and spittoons placed in strategic positions. Sometimes, for a change, the patrons visited the Working Men's Club, which boasted the attraction of a piano for live music and sing-songs, and if one miner wanted to see another he could be sure that if he didn't find him in the Miners' Arms he would be in the Club.

Tonight however, Harry went straight to the public bar at the Miners' Arms, climbing the three stone steps where the bookie's runner sometimes stood to collect his betting slips and pushing open the door to his left. The fuggy air came out to meet him. Anyone would think, mused Harry, that

44

after a day in the stale dusty air underground, the miners would want to breathe something purer in the evenings. But it didn't seem to occur to them. Almost every man in the bar, regardless of the state of his chest, had a cigarette either between his fingers or stuck to his lower lip, and the resulting smoke hung in a thick blanket below the yellowing ceiling and around the lamps.

A few men were ranged along the bar, but by far the biggest group were seated around two tables which they had pushed together.

One of the group, Ewart Brixey, a swarthy man in his early thirties, looked around as Harry came in, balancing his chair on its two back legs.

'Hey, Jim. Here's your young'un.'

Jim Hall put down his glass, looking up in surprise.

'Well, so it is! What are you doing here then, Harry?'

Jim was clearly a Hall. Even through the thicker cigarette fug that hung around the tables the family likeness was evident.

'I've come down for our Dad. He wasn't well and he had some beans and these geranium plants to give you.' Harry put them down on the table among the glasses. 'He says keep the geraniums out of the frost until May, but the beans ought to go in now if they're to be ready early summer.'

'Better get 'em in then, Jim,' Ewart said and Harry looked at him sharply. Ewart was such a strident character and he was never sure whether he was joking. This time, from the look of his face, Harry didn't think he *was* joking.

'You'll be wanting them. We shall all want plenty of stuff in our gardens if this strike comes off,' he went on.

The strike had been talked about since the threatened lock-out last summer, when the owners had wanted to make a sharp reduction in wages which were already only just above the breadline. It had been averted then because the Government had set up a National Commission, but that had issued its report last month and things were boiling up again now.

'You reckon it will come off, do you, Ewart?' Reuben Tapper, porter on the S. & D. Railway line, pressed him.

'I do!' Ewart maintained. 'Well, look at it like this, Reuben. How would you like to have to do longer hours for less pay? It's scandalous!'

'But I thought they was offering you better conditions,'

Reuben said in his slow way.

Ewart and a couple of others snorted loudly.

'That's a good 'un! Going to join up some of the smaller pits and call that progress! Well, it's no progress as far as I can see.'

'But baths. I heard they was going to put in baths at the pithead so you can have a wash before you go on home,' Reuben said mildly.

'So they say. But when? Half of us'll be coming up to retiring before they get round to doing that. And anyway, I'd sooner have my proper pay and wash in front of the fire, same as I've always done,' Ewart added triumphantly.

'So you reckon it's going to happen?' Reuben persisted.

'Unless the Government steps in, yes,' said Jim Hall. 'They did before and I'm in hopes they will again. There's still a couple of days to go to the end of April.'

'There's one thing about it,' put in Walter Clements, the quietly-spoken next-door neighbour of the Halls. 'At least this time the mining man won't be on his own. The trade unions are solid behind us.'

Ewart snorted again, hawked and aimed a globule of phlegm at the spittoon. At thirty-two he could already cough with the best of them.

'I'll believe that when I see it. Look at the strike back in '21. The railwaymen and the steel workers were supposed to back us up – and what happened? When the time came they saved their own skins and we were left to carry the can. This place has never been the same since. There were too bloody many who never got work again. Your father for one!' he said to Harry, who was listening with rapt attention.

'Our Dad? But I thought it was because of his chest he couldn't work...' Harry said, puzzled. The politics of the coalfield were never discussed at No.11 Greenslade Terrace.

'That's partly it, of course,' Ewart conceded. 'But 1921 was a sell-out. We went back – those of us who were lucky enough to get back – for less than we were getting before. And now they want us to take another cut. It's bloody scandalous, that's what it is!'

The men murmured agreement and Reuben Tapper muttered, 'A land fit for heroes, that's what it was s'posed to be. A land fit for heroes!'

'And heroes is what we be!' Ewart declared, warming to his subject. 'Look at the conditions we put up with! Working

46

down in that filthy hole, breathing muck into our lungs for years and then, when we'm fit for nothing because of it, thrown on the scrap-heap to cough and wheeze till we can't cough and wheeze no more. Look at your Dad, Harry, and the state he's in. It's all through the years he's spent underground. But does anybody give a bugger? Not likely!'

'Here, Harry, here's a drink for you.' Jim Hall, who had visited the bar during the conversation, put a half pint of cider down at Harry's elbow, but Harry hardly noticed. He had never really heard anyone talking like this before – or perhaps it was just that he had not listened. Underground, when he and the rest of his team stopped work to sit down and eat their cognocker, he chatted mostly to the other carting boys, swapping jokes and betting on who could be the first to entice a mouse out of the dark ground with a few crumbs of cheese. If the older men's talk was too serious, the lads merely ignored it. Even the threat of strike had gone largely over his head. Men often muttered about strikes – they had done so almost all the time since he started work in the pit. But nothing had come of it and Harry, who could remember very little about the 1921 confrontation, viewed it very much as people had viewed the boy who cried 'Wolf!'

No, he went to work, he did enough to bring home his money at the end of the week and if he behaved himself, his mother would give him back enough to have a night out. Every week she made some comment about wishing she did not have to take it from him, but he had always accepted it as a fact of life. Now, he thought of his father wheezing in his chair and the pieces clicked into place. His own meagre wage was going to help support the household because James could no longer work. Yet it wasn't James's fault; he was being penalised because of what the pits had done to him.

'Oh, yes, this strike's going to come all right, and the sooner we all stick together and show the bosses they can't treat us like slaves, the better it'll be for all of us!' Ewart finished. Then, grinning, he turned and held out his glass to Jim. 'Get us another pint, Jim, will 'ee – and another half for young Harry here while you're about it.'

'No, I don't want any more – I'd better be going on home,' Harry said, wishing all the same that he need not do so. He didn't want to leave the cheerful company in the bar – go home to hear his father's wheezing and see the anxious sidelong glances his mother kept giving her ailing husband.

Here in the smoky, hop-heavy atmosphere, he felt oddly free. But he knew his mother would not expect him to be away too long. It would worry her – and she had enough to worry about without him adding to it.

He pulled his cap onto his bright fair hair.

'Be seeing you, Jim,' he said. And set out to walk back up the hill that led to home.

*

At first Harry did not know what had woken him. He lay with the sheets pulled up to his chin listening to the tiny sounds of the night – the beams settling, the boards giving an occasional soft creak, an owl hooting as it winged its way across the valley. Then, louder than all these and much closer, he heard that awful breathless gasping which he had grown to know over the years... and to dread.

James was having another 'turn'.

Resisting the temptation to bury himself under the clothes and go back to sleep, Harry sat up to listen. James had been so much worse this time, worse even than during the really cold spell in the winter, and there was something so desperate in that noisy struggle for oxygen that it struck terror even to Harry's sixteen-year-old heart. But there was something not quite right, somehow, for the sounds seemed to come not from the bedroom next door but from downstairs. And as Harry strained his ears to listen, he heard the thud of something being knocked over.

For a second he froze, sitting bolt upright, eyes wide, fingers clawed around the hem of the blanket. He half-expected to hear the soft buzz of his mother's voice, low and anxious, but there was nothing except the terrible gasping, faster and harsher even than before and accompanied by a high-pitched moan.

Harry felt his blood begin to tingle oddly in his veins and fear seemed almost to stop his own breath. He ought to do something, he thought, and he ought to do it right away. Go and see if Mam was awake, perhaps? Or find out first just what was going on downstairs?

He pushed aside the covers. The moonlit linoleum was cold to his bare feet, but he hardly noticed as he padded across the floor and went down the steep, scrubbed wood stairs. The door at the foot was open a crack and Harry could see light from the kitchen slanting through. He put out a hand to push it open, but nothing happened; he pushed harder... still the door refused to budge. But the harsh breathing and the moaning was so close now that it might almost have been in his ear and it dawned on Harry that there could be only one reason for the door refusing to open, only one thing jamming it closed.

'Dad!' he said in an urgent whisper. 'Dad – are you all right?'

There was no reply, but the moaning grew louder.

'Oh dear. Oh dear... dear... dear...'

'Dad! You're there, aren't you? Dad, let me open the door...'

'James! Are you down there?'

Harry turned, his hand still on the door, to see Charlotte at the top of the stairs. 'Harry, what's happening?' she asked, her voice rising in panic as she made out the figure of her son.

'It's Dad,' Harry said urgently. 'He's been taken worse and I think he's fallen down right in the doorway. I can't get in to find out.'

Charlotte ran down the stairs and added her weight to Harry's.

'James!' she called. 'James – move, can't you! Just a bit? We can't get in to you.'

Still there was no response, only a period of quiet before the gasping and its accompanying moans began again.

'Oh my Lord, whatever shall we do?' Charlotte, who had woken from a deep, exhausted sleep to find the bed empty beside her, was more flustered than Harry could ever remember seeing her. 'If we can't open the door, we can't get to him.'

'But he's not that big,' Harry protested wonderingly.

'No, but he's a dead weight.' Her voice cracked as if she realised what she had said. 'James, listen, can't you help yourself? Roll – or wriggle? Just enough to let our Harry through.'

Sounds of effort came from the other side of the door, but it remained almost closed. Harry, hating the inaction, turned away.

'I'll go and see if I can get down out of the window. Then I could go round the outside.'

'You'd fall,' Charlotte predicted. 'And anyway, that

wouldn't do any good. You'd still have to break a window to get back in. It's all locked up and the key's in the back door.'

Harry swore, using one of the words he had picked up working underground, but in the tension of the moment Charlotte barely noticed.

'James, can you hear me!' she tried again.

'Y-ye-yes...' It was jerky, in time with the laboured gasps, but it was the first actual response they had had from him.

'Listen, you must move a bit,' she went on, speaking clearly as if to a child. 'We can't get out.'

The muted dragging sound was almost drowned by the heavy breathing, but Charlotte heard it.

'Push, Harry!' she entreated.

They pushed together and the door opened a little further, though it was still only a crack.

'Could you get through now, Harry?' she asked.

'I could try.' He turned sideways on, inching his shoulders through the space and trying to follow with his head. It was tight, very tight and Harry felt glad he was no bigger. A broader man would never make it, but he just might...

For the moment the effort of concentration made him forget his apprehension over what he might find on the other side of the door. But as he squeezed through the full horror hit him again.

James was slumped on the floor, half-sitting, half-lying against the door. His face was ashen, reflecting the look of a man who had found even the smallest movement beyond him. Every ounce of his strength was needed purely for the effort of breathing. And even that appeared to be a losing battle.

'Dad!' He dropped to his knees beside his father, but the liquid blue eyes seemed not to see him. They gazed into space somewhere over Harry's shoulder.

'Come on, Dad, we've got to move you,' he said. 'You can't stay there and Mam can't get out.'

He bent, lifting James's arms and winding them round his neck. Then he tried to straighten, using leverage and the strength that came from dragging putts of coal in narrow seams. It was far from easy, for as Charlotte had said James was a dead weight, but at last he managed to move him far enough for her to push open the door and get into the room. Then she and Harry together were able to get James to his feet and over to the sofa where she propped him up with all the cushions she could find at his back, supporting him against them as he threatened to fall forward.

'Harry – you'd better go for the doctor,' Charlotte said. She was slowly regaining her ability to take charge of a situation.

'But Mam...' he hesitated, unwilling to leave them.

'Don't argue, just do as I say.'

He ran up the stairs to his room, pulling on his clothes with the kind of haste usually reserved for mornings when he had overslept. But his fingers were trembling, so it took a long while to fasten the buttons and he was still fiddling with them as he clattered back down the stairs.

'Make haste, now,' Charlotte instructed as he took one last fearful look at James and let himself out. As he ran along the Rank, his hobnailed boots echoed on the stones. The doctor lived in one of the big houses in South Hill on the other side of the valley; it was quite a step, and Harry thought it would take him at least a quarter of an hour to get there, even if he ran all the way. Then he still had to persuade the doctor to come – and Harry had the uncomfortable feeling that there was not a great deal he could do, anyway. When James had a really bad turn, Charlotte invariably called the doctor, but from a conversation he had once overheard between his mother and Peggy Yelling, he suspected this had more to do with simplifying the formalities if this 'turn' should prove to be fatal than with expecting the doctor to be able to provide a miracle cure. For the miner who had spent his life at the face, breathing in the thickly-polluted air, there was no cure.

'And does anybody give a bugger?' Harry asked himself, unconsciously echoing what Ewart Brixey had said earlier in the Miners' Arms. 'Not likely!'

On the sofa in Greenslade Terrace his father could be gasping his last but no one cared – certainly not the nobs who owned the mines. They had grown rich on the efforts of men like James – the life-blood of the miners in their employ paid for the upkeep of their grand houses and bought the fine feather pillows and beds upon which right now they would be taking their rest. If their breathing was rough it would probably be from the effects of too many cigars – not too much coal-dust – and any aches and pains they might experience would be more likely the result of overeating and a drop too much to drink, Harry thought. It wasn't fair. It just wasn't fair.

His own legs were aching now, but it was nothing to the

fierce tightness in his chest that jarred with every jolting step he took. His father could be dying – might be dead, before he got back – and there was nothing he could do about it. Even when he had been there at his side, he had been powerless to help. Hating the way that made him feel, the anger drove him on through the empty streets of the sleeping town and up South Hill, where the miners had marched in force during the 1921 strike with the intention of tarring and feathering the general manager of the time. Climbing the hill took the last of his remaining breath and he was forced to a walk that seemed like a crawl as he turned into one of the steep drives leading to a house built in the side of the hill. Then, with no regard for the rest of the doctor's household, he began pulling on the doorbell with all the urgency the situation demanded.

Through years of practice, the doctor was a light sleeper. Within minutes he was opening his window to call out.

'It's all right, you can stop ringing now. I'm coming down.'

Harry waited, stamping with impatience, until the doctor appeared – a big, bluff man with a grey flannel dressing-gown straining across his rugby-player's chest.

'All right, lad, what the devil is it?'

'It's my Dad.' A small core of Harry's anger directed itself at the doctor, but he knew better than to show it. 'He's really bad – he can't breathe – he fell down and we couldn't get him up again . . .'

Dr Vezey snorted. 'Couldn't it have waited until morning?'

'I don't know . . . Mam said to get you . . .'

'Well, there's precious little I can do about it,' the doctor said testily. He had already had two broken nights this week – and with private patients too, not the sort who could be put off. 'Short of giving him a new pair of lungs, there's precious little *anyone* can do.'

Harry, terrified by a sudden vision of having run all the way home again to report that the doctor refused to attend, dug in his heels.

'But he's really bad – you must come!' He searched around for the worst thing he could think of. 'If he dies and you don't come, it'll be your fault!'

The strike went home. Dr Vezey drew himself up; he was not used to being spoken to in that tone by a patient. Most of them were so in awe of 'the doctor' that the women put on their best apron and the men doffed their caps before addressing him in reverential tones. As for the 'private patients' – the ones who would consider themselves his social equal – they had such preferential treatment they had no cause for complaint. They were always seen first and their medicines dispensed to them in neatly-wrapped packages. Most of them did not even come to the surgery, but were attended by him in their own homes, where he quite often took a glass of sherry with them after his diagnosis was completed. It was all very civilised, so that although he had been well-known as a terror on the rugby field in his younger days, Dr Frank Vezey was totally unused to confrontation off the field and in daily life. And now here was this young whipper-snapper, not even a 'panel patient' but one of those who belonged to 'the club', actually daring to threaten him!

'All right, lad, if he's as bad as you say, I'd better come,' he said, his tone implying that if Harry had been exaggerating he had better look out. 'How did you get here?'

'On shanks's pony,' Harry said. He was offended and angered by the doctor's attitude and it showed in his tone. 'I ran.'

'Hmm.' Dr Vezey considered. 'Well, if you'd like to wait, you can ride back with me in my motor.'

Harry was tempted to tell him what he could do with his motor, that he would run all the way back again before letting this conceited nob do him any favours. But before he could say anything, the doctor went on, 'Yes, you can show me which house it is – save me disturbing the rest of Hillsbridge. It is the middle of the night, you know.'

At last the doctor was ready and Harry felt a choking nervousness returning as he rattled through the sleeping town in the front passenger seat of Dr Vezey's Model T Ford. Suppose they were too late? Suppose his father had been unable to last out?

The light burning in the downstairs window of No.11, Greenslade Terrace shone out like a beacon in the night and Harry experienced a sudden fierce longing for the days when he had been a little boy and his brothers and sisters had lived at home. He remembered how his mother had once taken him on a day trip to Cheddar and an engine problem with the charabanc had meant it was dark before they got home again. There had been a magic in being out later than he had ever been out before, but the sight of that window pouring out brightness into the night had made a warm place inside him, and when his mother had opened the door and pushed him, yawning and blinking, inside, the welcoming safety that came from being part of a family had enveloped him. His three brothers had been there, Ted, Jack – and Fred, who had been killed in the war – and Dad too, all sitting up to the table for a bread and cheese supper. And Amy had been there, already undressed for bed, curled up on the sofa with her legs drawn up inside her nightdress and her hair in curling rags – she had persuaded James to let her stay up until Mam and Harry got home.

The memory was a fleeting one only and what had happened next he did not recall. It was the warmth and the safety that he remembered and craved. For the others had all left home now and he was the only one remaining. And in times of crisis such as this, the burden of being the man of the house fell onto his shoulders alone.

The doctor stopped the car and turned off the engine. Harry jumped out and as he opened the back door the loud rasp of his father's breathing came out to meet him. For once it was a welcome sound. Silence would have been ominous.

'In here, doctor,' he said, and had a quick glimpse of his father's rheumy blue eyes and ashen face, flushed now by the high spots of feverish colour, before being banished to the scullery while the examination took place.

From the other side of the door the murmur of voices – too low to understand – seemed to go on forever. Then, after what seemed a lifetime, the door opened again and Dr Vezey came out, Charlotte following.

'Good night then, doctor, and thank you. I'm sorry to have called you out . . .'

The doctor snorted and left without bidding good night to either mother or son. As the door closed after him, Harry turned to Charlotte anxiously.

'Well?'

Charlotte's face was drawn, the soft lamplight etching deep lines between nose and mouth.

'He didn't like the look of your father, I could tell. He's given me a prescription for cough mixture we can get in the morning and we're to try a steam kettle or two to get it loose. He's to be kept warm, but moved about frequently. I'll have to make up a bed for him here, of course. It won't be the first

54

time, but . . .' She broke off, bending her head and covering her face with her hands.

Harry hovered awkwardly. It wasn't like her to show emotion.

'Mam?'

She jerked upright again impatiently, swallowing hard and sniffing.

'It's all right, Harry. It's just that the doctor thinks his bed will have to stay down here this time. All this trouble with his breathing is playing his heart up – Vezey says he's shouldn't be doing the stairs.' She swallowed again. 'He says he mustn't do the hill either.'

'You mean . . .?'

Charlotte faced him squarely. The tears had gone now, all of them, but her eyes were black.

'If your Dad gets over this, he will have to take life very easy from now on. He won't be able to do any of the things he's used to doing, like his garden, or going down for a pint of an evening. He's going to be an invalid, you might say.'

'But that will be awful for him!' Harry protested.

'Yes, it will be, won't it?' Charlotte said. 'And he's not an old man, Harry – he won't be sixty for another couple of years. And do you know what the doctor said? That he's *lucky* – lucky to be alive. Lucky to be in a state like he's in!'

'Well, I suppose he is,' Harry said, thinking of men he knew who had succumbed to the chest disease before they were fifty even.

'*Lucky!*' Charlotte yelled. 'How can you stand there and say it? You don't know how short life is, my lad! It seems like only yesterday your Dad was young and healthy like you are – there's nothing in a year, nor ten years, as you get older. It just goes – gone! – before you can look round. And you'll be the next – especially if you stay in that filthy hole, carting coal. Oh Harry, can't you see that?'

Harry was staring into space and for him it seemed everything was coming together. The bosses who allowed terrible conditions underground to reduce a man to a pitiful heap of dust-clogged flesh and then discarded him when he was of no further use; the system that offered no real way out of the accompanying poverty; the attitude of the doctor and others like him to human beings they considered less worthy of decent treatment because of their station in life. Harry had known it already – known, as he had said, men who were thrown on the scrap-heap before they were forty – but because it had been other men and other families it had never seemed quite real before. Now it was James, his own father, who had lived through an agonising night to face a few more trying and pain-wracked years as an invalid, and suddenly the whole pattern was immediate and threatening. If it could happen to his father, then it could also happen to Jim, his brother. It could even happen to him. For a brief moment in time it seemed to Harry that he saw himself propped against the pillows in the steam-filled kitchen, struggling for breath, himself grown prematurely old in the dark, dust-filled seams.

His father had always accepted it as the way of things and Harry, trying to be a man like him, had adopted his views. Now, for the first time, he felt the injustice of it so sharply it was a physical pain, gnawing at him from within.

'Something ought to be done,' he muttered.

Charlotte snorted.

'All these years I've been saying that. Nobody ever seems to listen.'

'I'm listening,' said Harry and as the pain seared upwards through his veins it seemed to mutate, spreading and taking into itself that strange, unidentified sense of purpose that had been sleeping for so long on the borders of his conscious mind.

He had always known there was something he wanted to do that was more than carting coal for a weekly wage; more than breeding fine, swift homing pigeons; more even than marrying and raising a family. And he had been confident that one day the ambition would crystalise so that he was able to recognise it.

Now, at the age of sixteen, Harry stood in the lamplit kitchen and knew the moment had come. Something had to be done to improve the lot of men like his father. Someone had to speak for them – fight for them. Suddenly the sense of purpose was burning in him more brightly than the anger or the pain.

He would do it. As yet he didn't know how, but he would do it. Harry clenched his jaw and narrowed his blue eyes. And when he spoke, there was a firmness in his voice that, for all his youth, carried conviction.

'I'm listening, Mam! And I'll tell you something else. I'm going to make sure that people listen to me!'

*   *   *

For two days and two nights James fought for his life, breath by rasping breath. For two days and nights neighbours in the Rank watched the comings and goings of the family and the doctor, passing on the latest news of his condition together with the information that even if he got better, James Hall was likely to be bedridden from now on.

Then on the third day, the fever began to pass, the tortured breathing eased a little and the globules of phlegm began coming up once more to hiss and crackle in the fire.

But before the news that James was improving could be passed into the grapevine of gossip, Hillsbridge folk had something else to talk about – something which affected each and every one of them – the growing threat of an all-out strike in the pits, perhaps supported by every working man in England.

'Trades Unions Solid Behind Miners' ran a headline in the *Mercury* on the last Friday in April, beneath it the prophecy that the events of the day would be 'of exceptionally grave importance to the coal industry'. There was also a reprint of a notice which had been circulated by the Warwickshire Miners' Association.

'The Miners' Federation of Great Britain is engaged in a struggle to preserve your wages, working hours and general conditions. Every man in Warwickshire is expected to be loyal to the Federation and cease work after 30th April unless otherwise instructed by us.'

It spoke for all of them and summed up the crisis. Talks in London between unions and management, on which everyone had pinned their hopes, had ended in deadlock. Not even the Government had been able to do anything to help.

And the mining community in Hillsbridge sadly acknowledged that the struggle which could prove both long and bitter had begun.

Chapter Three

The strike which ordinary people had believed deep down could never happen took hold with a sudden ferocity that startled, frightened... and inspired.

'It's just like 1914 all over again,' said Charlotte – and so it was.

Then, thousands upon thousands of working men had rallied round to drive Kaiser Bill out of Belgium; now they downed tools without a word of protest to try to win a living wage for the miners. Trains and buses ground to a halt, newspapers ceased to appear, building sites took on the appearance of ghost towns.

'We'm bound to win now!' was the optimistic feeling in the bar at the Miners' Arms, and it was left to cynics like Stanley Bristow to wonder aloud how long it would last and what it would achieve.

'Stands to reason, they'll have to give in and play fair with us,' Ewart Brixey said triumphantly. 'We've brought the country to a halt.'

'But for how long?' Stanley Bristow asked. 'Oh, they've all come out on strike now because their unions have told them to. But I don't see it lasting. The unions can't afford to feed all of them and their families for more than a couple of weeks. And when they've got no money coming in and the larder's bare, they'll all be back at work before you can look round – see if I'm not right.'

'Get on with you!' Ewart scoffed. 'The working men of this country are sticking together this time.'

Stanley shook his head sadly. 'But it b'ain't their fight, Ewart. No man's going to see his own family go short when he's got nothing to gain from it. That's human nature. And 't won't last, I'm telling 'ee.'

'You'm bitter and twisted, Stanley, and you have been ever since the war when they had your horses,' Ewart said nastily. Until 1914 Stanley had been the proud owner of the livery stables, but the Government had requisitioned the horses he had treated like babies for service in France and Stanley had never got over it. Now, he planted his beer firmly on the table.

'You'm right there, Ewart. Beautiful creatures, they were, and I'd trust them before I'd trust any man. My horses wouldn't have let you down. The unions will.'

'Well, we shall have to wait and see about that, shan't we?' Ewart grinned round at the assembled company, wiping the beer foam off his chin with the back of his hand. 'But I'll promise you this, Stanley. This time we b'ain't going to give in. That's right, lads, isn't it?'

The chorus of agreement filled the bar. The miners were determined this time.

'Not a penny off the pay – Not a minute on the day' was their rallying call and they meant to stick to it.

At the moment they could feel only jubilation that most of the working men in the country were solidly behind them.

*

However, others in Hillsbridge were less pleased by the prospect of a General Strike.

Business men in the town knew that their profit margins, meagre as they already were, would be hit hard by a shortage of money amongst their customers; farmers worried over the spectre of thousands of gallons of milk having to be poured down the drain if there was no transport to take it away; and those who had need of buses or trains to take them to the city nine miles distant wondered if they could beat their leg-muscles into submission if they could beg, borrow or steal a bicycle. They felt sorry for the miners – who would not, especially when they lived in the same community and saw how badly they were paid for their back-breaking and dangerous work – but life for them had to go on. Many had clawed themselves a foothold on the ladder of survival by enterprise and sheer hard work; some were in debt for their trouble and faced ruin if the stoppage was prolonged.

One of these was Llew Roberts, but for him the problem was even more complex, for he found himself torn between loyalty to his wife's family and his own strong instinct for self-preservation. With everything in and around Hillsbridge at a standstill, Llew knew he could not rely on his usual customers to keep his two lorries busy. If the pits closed there would be no need for new pit-props, and when the strike became general he assumed the quarries would shut down too, so that the stock of stone or gravel to haul would soon be exhausted.

But that would not stop the bills coming in. The rent on the yard still had to be paid and the instalments on the new lorry, not to mention the cost of the damage Amy had caused by her attempt at driving. Llew seemed to have forgiven her for that now, but she felt guilty that she had added to his problems – running a business meant that money had to come from somewhere or all too soon the creditors would move in – and then the years of dedication and sheer hard work would count for nothing.

'I can't afford to have the lorries standing idle for long,' he said to Amy as they prepared for bed on the night the announcement of the General Strike was broadcast.

They had listened to it on the crystal set in the diningroom, their anxiety heightened by the deliberate calm of the announcer whose words had come, by virtue of the wonder of radio waves, direct into their home:

'The miners are on strike. The TUC has ordered other vital industries to join them from Tuesday...'

And then, no less awesome, the broadcast message from the Prime Minister himself: 'Keep steady. Remember peace on earth comes to men of good will.'

'Keep steady!' Llew said now, echoing the words. 'It's all very well for him; he doesn't stand to lose everything he's worked for.'

'You don't know that. He might – if they bring the Government down,' Amy said.

She was sitting on the stool in front of the dressing-table to brush her honey-coloured hair as she did every night. In the mirror she could see Llew perched on the edge of the bed, frozen in the attitude of unknotting his tie. From his inactivity she knew he was worried. Usually Llew was so tired he dropped his clothes where he stood and fell into bed in a matter of seconds.

'Well, I'm sorry, Amy. I can't concern myself about the Prime Minister,' he said vehemently. 'It's *me* I'm worried about. I've got to keep those lorries busy or we'll be in a real hole.'

'But how can you if nobody's working? The pits – the quarries...' She waved the brush at his reflected image. 'There won't be anything to carry.'

'You're wrong there,' Llew said. 'There's bound to be things to be carried. More than usual. It's just finding out what and where.'

Her nose wrinkled. 'More than usual? What do you mean?'

'People must eat. Supplies will have to be moved about. And with the railways on strike and the big transport companies...'

'Llew – you don't mean you're going to *blackleg*?' Amy said, shocked.

His head came up. 'Have you got any better suggestions?'

'But you *can't*!' Amy protested. 'It wouldn't be right! The whole point of sticking together is that if things get desperate enough the Government will force the owners to give in.'

'I can't help it, Amy. If I don't have my usual work, I must take what I can get. I can't afford *not* to. Others will, you'll see. There'll be those that come out of this richer than they were before; there always are.'

'But it's our *own* people this strike is about!' Amy turned on the stool, her eyes blazing blue fire. 'My Dad, my brothers – *they're* the ones who've been exploited all these years. And now at last everybody's pulling together to try to get something done about it. You can't undermine that, Llew!'

'I need the money. The business needs the money. I can't see it go to pot, Amy. Not now!'

He stood up to unbutton his shirt and she flew at him.

'You can't make money at their expense!'

His face darkened as it always did when his temper was barely under control, eyes narrowing, nostrils flaring. 'I don't want to have to remind you of this, Amy, but we would owe less money if you hadn't run the new lorry into Ralph Porter's car. I'm going to have to foot that bill myself – and I don't have a money-making bush at the end of the garden!'

'Oh, I see! It's my fault now!' Guilt made her tone sharp. 'You'll take the bread out of my family's mouths and it's all my doing!'

'Yes.' He took off his shirt, tossing it over the back of a small cane chair. 'Yes, if you want to see it like that. It's certainly your fault that we have to find a great deal more ready cash than we would otherwise.'

'Well, well!' Amy stood up and the stool rocked on its three legs. 'It's a good thing you've got someone to blame for turning blackleg, if you ask me.'

'Be as nasty as you like, Amy. It doesn't alter facts.'

'And the fact is you haven't forgiven me for driving your lorry.' She flounced to the bed, pulled back the bedspread and sat down. 'Well, let me tell *you* something. *I* won't forgive *you* if you turn blackleg while my family and the friends and neighbours I grew up with are struggling for just a decent living wage – not half nor a quarter of what we take for granted. I mean it, Llew; I won't forgive you!'

Llew shrugged, sitting down on his side of the bed.

'That's up to you. You've got two choices. Either you stick with me and let me do things my way – or you sink back to their level. It's up to you.'

'Their level!' Amy was bolt upright again, furious now. 'What do you mean, *their level*?'

'I mean doing without the things you've come to take for granted – like nice clothes for yourself and the children, a bit of beef on the table instead of scrag-ends, this house even. You send the washing out to be done, and you look forward to the day when you can have somebody in to help clean the house, though it's not so long since you were in service yourself. You like those things and I don't see why you shouldn't have them. But don't be a hypocrite, Amy. Don't pretend you're taking them under protest!'

'Oh!' She slid down, humping the clothes over her and turning her back on him. 'Sometimes I hate you, Llew Roberts!'

'I see,' he said, furious but controlled. They lay in silence for a moment, the air between them so cold it could have grown icicles. Then as the heat of her body next to his began to melt the ice a little the first teasing hint of desire crept in and he went on more softly, 'I see – hate me do you?'

'Yes.' She lay rigid. His hand slid over the curve of her arm, but she pretended not to notice.

'Amy, you're the limit.' He was cajoling now – her aggression had fuelled his desire and turned his anger into indulgent amusement. 'But I promise you something – you'll go far.'

'Not at the expense of my family, I won't!'

'We're your family now – Maureen and Barbara and me.'

She didn't answer, but neither did she move away as his hand moved round to cup her breast and his long body curled round the angry curve of her back.

'You don't hate me, Amy.' He nibbled her ear. 'You know I've done well. They could have done the same if they'd had the guts.'

She puckered her mouth. He was right, really. He had started with nothing, which just went to show what imagination and courage could achieve when they were coupled with sheer hard work. But imagination and self-belief were not gifts which were handed out to everybody. Good men, solid men like her father and brother Jim, would never have thought for a moment of stepping off the tramlines on which their lives ran.

'What me? No – I'm a miner!' would be their reaction if someone suggested they branch out. What had her mother said when Llew had gone in for his second lorry? 'It's a bit risky, isn't it?' They were trapped by the belief that the tried and trusted was safest and best, even if it was riddled with drawbacks. Risk and change were to be avoided at all costs. But all the same...

If everybody in Hillsbridge had started up a haulage business there would be no living in it for anybody, thought Amy. And why should Dad and Jim and all the others be penalised just because they were good, honest, hard-working men who asked for nothing more than enough money to make life a bit more pleasurable, and a little extra time to spend with their families?

'Amy...' As Llew eased her over to face him, covering her lips with his, she softened momentarily. Then as his hands moved the length of her back, moulding her to him, she was aware of a flash of impatience. Men! Why did they think this could solve everything?

'Llew...' she murmured.

'Mm?' His lips were in her hair.

'Promise me...'

'Promise... promise what?'

'That you won't blackleg...'

His reaction was immediate, pulling away from her and swearing.

'Llew!' She followed him. 'What did you do that for?'

He was as rigid now as she had been a few minutes earlier. 'Why couldn't you leave it?'

'Because I don't want you to do it, Llew.'

'What you want doesn't come into it, Amy. I'll do what I have to.'

'Llew...'

'I mean it, Amy. I'll do what I must – for all of us, whether you like it or not. I have too much at stake to do otherwise.'

'Llew...' She put her arms around him now, frightened suddenly by the turn this quarrel was taking. Rights and wrongs, what did it matter as long as she and Llew could be together and the children got a good start in life? She laid her face against his shoulder, but he made no move. 'Llew – please...'

She was begging him now to forget their differences and make love to her as he had wanted a few moments ago. But he misunderstood her.

'For goodness' sake, shut up about it, Amy. I've told you what I intend to do and I'm not going over it any more. I'm tired. So just let me go to sleep, will you?'

His tone was so hard, so cold that it distanced her all over again. She removed her face from his shoulder as if it was burning her, a sense of rejection and injustice lending venom to her tongue.

'All right, go to sleep if you can – though I couldn't with a thing like that on my conscience. Not that you've got one, have you? You're too selfish and greedy. And don't kid yourself you're doing it for us, either. It's for you and you'd do it anyway, so don't tar *us* with your dirt!'

He did not move, just asked coldly, 'Are you going to keep this up, Amy? Because if so...'

'Yes – what?'

'If so, I'm going downstairs to sleep on the sofa. I told you, I'm tired...'

'Oh, stay where you are. I shan't say another word,' she flung at him, adding under her breath, 'Perhaps not ever.'

But he did not reply and to her fury she heard his breathing become deeper and more rhythmic a few minutes later. He had gone to sleep and it was the first time since they had been married that he had done so without kissing her good night.

'Never let the sun go down on your anger,' Charlotte had

always said and Amy had tried to live by that. If they had an argument – and heaven only knew there were plenty of those – Amy always tried to see that it was made up before going to sleep. Realising that this time she had failed brought a knot of tears to her throat and at the same time reinforced her sense of anger and injustice.

'I'm certainly not going to cry over the likes of him!' she told herself severely. And although it was a long while before she too was able to fall asleep, Amy – always as stubborn as she was mercurial – kept to her word.

*

'Harry, Harry – are you awake?'

Charlotte put her head around the bedroom door and Harry gave up his half-hearted attempts at pretence and pushed back the covers from his face.

Strange – he would have thought after all the mornings when he had had to drag himself out of bed at the crack of dawn to stumble down the hill to Middle Pit, the lie-ins that this enforced break permitted might have seemed something of a luxury. But no, he hadn't really enjoyed them. The last two mornings since the start of the strike he had woken just as early as usual, lain for a while tossing and turning bad-temperedly because he felt cheated at not making the most of the rare opportunity to sleep late, eventually dozing off again for a while and finally waking with a thick head. And this morning had been as bad in its way. He had managed to sleep a little later, it was true, but then had been woken by somebody knocking at the back door and the bellowing voice of Dolly's husband, Victor, in the kitchen below.

Harry had huffed with irritation and pulled the clothes up over his head. Why the heck did Victor have to have such a loud voice? He was the gentlest of men, kind to Dolly, patient with the children and totally at home among the green, growing things in Captain's Fish's garden where he planted and transplanted, dug, hoed and pruned with all the quiet love of a real countryman. But his voice was like a foghorn. The shells that had shocked and damaged his nervous system in the trenches of France had also impaired his hearing, Dolly explained, but even understanding, Harry found it hard to be tolerant. He longed to tell Victor to keep his voice down, but Charlotte had forbidden him to mention the subject, saying that if anyone told him about it, it would have to be Dolly.

'Harry!' Charlotte said again and the undertone of anxiety in her voice made him raise himself on one elbow. He had not been worried by the sound of Victor's voice – pushing his bicycle up the hill on his way to work at Captain Fish's, Victor had to pass by the entrance to the Rank, so it was not unusual for him to call in with a message from Dolly, or to pick up or deliver some parcel which was being passed between mother and daughter. Now, however, the alarm system that had been working a little too efficiently for comfort since James's 'bad turn' began sending sharp shocks through Harry's veins and brought him wide-awake.

'What's up, Mam?' he asked.

'It's our Dolly. She's not well,' Charlotte said.

'Our Dolly?' Harry repeated, surprised. Dolly was as strong as a little horse – he could hardly remember her having a day's illness in her life.

'She's sick and bad, Victor says, been up half the night with it. He didn't like leaving her with the babies, only he had to go to work.'

'I don't see why,' Harry muttered.

'Well, because she's not fit to cope, of course!' Charlotte said impatiently.

'I didn't meant that,' Harry wriggled the pillow into a more comfortable position. 'I mean I don't see why he has to go to work with a General Strike on.'

'It doesn't affect him, that's why.' Charlotte, who never had much patience with industrial action – or rather, as she saw it, *in*-action – spoke sharply. 'No, I thought you could pop up there, Harry, and see if there's anything you can do to help.'

Harry's heart sank. He had planned a quiet morning with his pigeons and the prospect of entertaining and possibly even looking after two rumbustious toddlers did not appeal to him in the least.

'But there's nothing I could do...' he began.

'Rubbish!' Charlotte said shortly. 'You've had it too easy, my lad, being the youngest in the family. Everybody's always waited on you, that's the trouble.' She crossed to the window, pulling the curtains so that the early May sunshine came streaming in. 'I think I've got a bottle of medicine in the cupboard that might do her good – the stuff the doctor gave me when I had the gastric 'flu last year. You know I'm not a one for taking medicines, but I thought it might come in useful. And I'd like you to take it up to her.'

'All right... all right...' Harry said hastily.

'Get up then and I'll make you a cup of tea.'

'All right,' he said again.

When she had gone he got up, pulled on a shirt and his second-best trousers and padded down the stairs in his stockinged feet.

James was lying in his made-up bed on the sofa, still wheezing when he moved, and Harry muttered a greeting as he hurried through.

'What about your tea?' Charlotte called after him.

'Can't I have it out in the yard? It's a lovely morning.'

'You cannot! I never heard of such a thing. You come back in here and have it – and a bit of toast too, or you'll be feeling faint.'

He did as he was told, gobbled the toast and gulped the tea quickly in order to escape the claustrophobic atmosphere in the kitchen. Perhaps going up to Dolly's would have its advantages after all, he thought. He need not stay long and afterwards he could have a bit of time to himself.

Almost as he thought it, the mantelpiece clock began to chime and he glanced up at it. Eight o'clock.

'That clock's five minutes slow,' said Charlotte. 'I think you ought to be getting on, Harry.'

He took his jacket from behind the door and she stood waiting, the medicine bottle wrapped in a paper bag in her hand.

'Tell our Dolly I'm sorry I haven't got anything nice to send her. But I don't suppose she'd be feeling up to it anyway. And Harry... do see what you can do to help her, there's a good boy.'

Thankfully Harry escaped from the house, feeling guilty at the sense of relief that enveloped him. But at least he was glad to be able to help Dolly. She was a good sort with her easygoing way and ready smile, and the fact that she had already grown up and left home to go into service before he was born lent her an added glamour in his eyes.

Whistling, he turned the corner of the Rank and started down the hill. There was a girl in front of him – a girl carrying a satchel and a tennis racket and wearing the uniform of the Higher Elementary School at High Compton, but he scarcely noticed. He was still too deep in thought about Mam and Dad and Dolly. Down the hill he went, past the cottages where the gardens were already beginning to blaze with early summer colour, past the place where the spring water ran in a steady inviting stream from the wall that shored up the gardens of the big houses on the other side of the road. By the time he reached the foot of the hill where Stanley Bristow had had his livery stables and where the forge still shod horses, he had almost caught up with the girl, but he still spared her scarcely a glance. Then, as she drew level with the side door of the George and stepped off the pavement to cross the forecourt, he suddenly saw her trip and go sprawling. Books spilled from her open satchel, the tennis racket flew from her hand. For a moment she lay in an inelegant heap, then struggled quickly to her feet, looking around in embarrassment and trying to recover the scattered books.

'Hey – are you all right?' Harry asked.

'Yes...' She looked up at him, cheeks flushed, eyes suspiciously bright. Her uniform hat had fallen off, revealing a tangle of dark curls that framed a pretty, oval face, and though he did not know her name he recognised her as a girl who lived in Tower View, a terrace of houses higher up the hill than Greenslade Terrace.

'Let me help...' He bent down, retrieving the tennis racket and the furthest-flung of her books, and as she straightened up he saw the holes in the knees of her stockings revealing large bleeding grazes. 'You're not all right! You've skinned your knees!' he said.

She glanced down, surprised almost, then the dark eyes suddenly welled tears. 'Oh – my stockings!' And then, as the numbness receded and the sharp pain began: 'Ouch! They hurt!'

'I'll bet they do! You took a real tumble!' He picked up another book and handed it to her. 'Have you got a handkerchief?'

'Somewhere...' She fumbled in her pockets, fighting back the tears as she pulled out a small white square of fabric. Then she bent to dab ineffectively at the flow of blood.

He watched helplessly, trying to remember if his own handkerchief was clean enough to offer as a substitute bandage and deciding it was not a risk he could take. After a minute she straightened up, flexing her leg.

'Oh, I'm in such a mess! But if I go home I'll be late for school.'

'How are you getting there?' he asked.

'I've got to walk. The buses and trains aren't running. I started out nice and early and now . . .' Her lip wobbled.

'I should go home if I were you,' he suggested.

'No.' She hoisted her satchel on to her shoulder, took a step and winced. 'No – I've got to get to school.'

'Walk? Like that? All the way to South Compton?'

'Yes. Oh, what a fool I am!'

'Which way are you going?' He was walking along beside her. 'Up South Hill?'

She nodded, holding her lip tightly between her teeth.

'I'm going that way,' he said. 'Give me your satchel and I'll carry it for you.'

She shot him a nervous look.

'It's all right – I really am,' he said. 'My sister lives up that way and I'm going to see her.'

'Oh, yes.' He saw her relax slightly. 'You're Harry Hall, aren't you?'

It was his turn to look surprised. 'How did you know that?'

'Oh, I just know. You've got a brother Jack who's a teacher.'

'That's right. Come on, give me your satchel.'

This time she did as he said. She was limping badly, he noticed, though she was trying not to show it, and when they passed a group of people walking in the opposite direction who stared at her tattered stockings and bleeding knees, he glanced sideways at her and saw the hot colour come up in her cheeks.

'I must have twisted my ankle on the edge of the pavement,' she said with a rueful smile and it suddenly struck him how attractive she was, blushing and smiling like that. This was not something he'd noticed before, he'd dismissed her as a schoolgirl – and one of the nobs from the Higher Elementary, at that. Now he realised she could only be a year or so younger than he was and out of school uniform would probably look a very pretty young lady. The knowledge flustered him and he said quickly, 'You ought to be more careful.'

'I know. I'm always doing things like that,' she said and he got the feeling she was poking fun at herself and liked her for it.

They walked in silence for a few minutes, then she asked, 'You don't go to school, I suppose?'

'No. I work at Middle Pit, but we're on strike.'

As he said this, he found himself wishing for the first time that he had taken the scholarship as Mr Davies had urged. But at the same time he felt she was impressed by the fact that he was a working man.

'I just hope you win this strike,' she said. 'I think it's terrible what you have to put up with.'

'We'll win.' He said it with more confidence than he felt because he thought it sounded good, and was rewarded by a gleam of admiration in her eyes.

They were at the top of the hill now and up ahead of them, along the straight, he could see the rank of houses where Dolly lived.

Walking in silence, he considered. Should he go on a bit further with the girl? She was still less than half-way to school, and the company was probably helping her to forget the stinging of her knees. Besides, he was enjoying himself. Harry had never been a great one for running after girls. For the sake of his work mates he pretended he was, of course, but in fact he had never met one who really interested him before as this one did.

But the bottle of medicine Charlotte had given him for Dolly was bouncing against his side, reminding him that his sister needed him too. It would take him at least an extra forty minutes to walk all the way to South Compton even if he ran all the way back, and if Charlotte got to hear of it he would certainly get the length of her tongue. Regretfully Harry decided that Dolly was where his duty lay.

'I'd walk all the way with you, but my sister's not very well and she's on her own with the nippers,' he said apologetically.

'Oh, that's all right – I didn't expect you to do that,' she said.

But he saw her lip wobble again and he said impulsively, 'Well, I can't come all the way, but I will walk as far as the Chapel with you.'

'That's a long way! If your sister's waiting...'

'She doesn't know I'm coming and it will only take me a few minutes,' he assured her.

'No, you mustn't.' She stopped, catching at the strap of her satchel. 'If this is as far as you go, I'll be all right now.'

He let her take the satchel and as she hoisted it onto her shoulder she managed a wry smile.

'Bye-bye, then. And thanks!'

'It's OK,' he said, awkward suddenly, and he stood for a few moments in the entrance to Dolly's rank watching the girl walk on up the straight, slightly-sloping road, limping still but pushing on with determination. Then, with a sigh, he turned and walked down the path between the houses.

Although built on quite the other side of the valley, Dolly's rank was not unlike Greenslade Terrace, with a cobbled way running past the back doors wide enough for the delivery-men to drive their horses and carts, and blocks of privies and washhouses and sheds on the opposite side. The houses were similar in design, too. - downstairs a scullery, a front room and a living-room - known as the kitchen - and upstairs three bedrooms.

Even before he opened the back door Harry could hear the loud crying and his heart sank. Then, as he went in, he saw that Fred - the elder boy, and a rascal at 2½ - was climbing on top of the table in an effort to reach the cupboard, while Bob, a year younger, sat in a wailing heap in the middle of the floor. Of Dolly there was no sign.

'What do you think you're doing?' he asked Fred.

The boy glared at him. 'Fred hungry.'

'And Fred'll hurt, too, if he falls off that table.' Harry scooped him up, and Fred yelled angrily.

'No - no! Fred hungry!'

'Where's your Mam?' Harry asked.

Fred continued to shriek and Bob's wailing increased in volume to match it. Desperate to quieten them, Harry opened the cupboard and found a box of rusks, giving them one each.

'Here you are. Now shut up, for Pete's sake!'

At that moment the back door opened and Dolly appeared. A plump, pretty girl with rosy cheeks and her father's mild blue eyes, Dolly was normally the picture of health. Not so today; Harry was shocked by her ill appearance - as white as a ghost, with huge circles under her eyes - and she stood for a

71

moment gripping the door-post as if she might fall down.

'Oh, Harry – what are you doing here?' she asked weakly.

'Mam sent me. Victor said you were bilious and Mam looked out this bottle of stuff...' He pulled it out of his pocket, holding it out to her, but Dolly only laughed harshly.

'Ha! Much good that'll do me!'

'You can at least try it after I've brought it for you,' he said.

Dolly picked her way over the rusk-eating children on the floor and sank down in a chair.

'There's no point,' she said wearily.

Harry felt a chill of fear. 'What d'you mean, Doll?'

She shook her head, not answering, and the chill deepened.

'Dolly – what is it?' he pressed her.

'Oh, nothing, Harry,' she said a little impatiently. 'I haven't told anybody yet.'

'You haven't...' He was shaking now, as he had shaken when he found his father so ill. It was strange, but sickness had not been real to him before that, and now it was much *too* real – as real as Dolly's white face and dark hollow eyes. His glance moved to the children on the floor, stuffing the last of the rusks into their mouths and looking around for more like hungry birds. What would they do if anything happened to Dolly?

'Dolly, for goodness' sake – you're not really ill, are you?' he asked, and the terror in his voice must have pierced the fog of her sickness, because she laughed suddenly.

'Oh, don't worry, Harry. It's nothing nine months won't cure!'

'Nine... oh!' His voice trailed away as he realised what she meant. 'You're going to...?'

She mopped at her face with a handkerchief.

'Yes, that's right. I'm going to have another baby. And if you tell a soul, I'll never speak to you again. Nobody knows yet, not even Victor. I wanted to be sure before I said anything to anyone.'

'Oh,' Harry said again. And then, 'But were you ill like this before?'

She shook her head. 'No, not as bad as this. I was a bit queasy, it's true. But this time I've felt really terrible. Right from the start, you might say – the very first day. This is the worst, but I feel sick all the time, Harry, from morning to night.'

'Isn't there anything you can do?' Harry asked helplessly.

'It'll pass. It's passing now and I'll be better presently. Only I don't think I can face giving the boys their breakfast, I really don't. D'you think you could...?'

'Yes, what do they have?'

Following her instructions, he prepared bowls of rusks and hot milk, with a cup of weak tea for Fred and a bottle of sugar water for Bob. Now that their mother was in view once more and their tummies were full they had both stopped crying, but for all that they were still a noisy pair, with loud voices and so much surplus energy it was exhausting merely to watch them.

Harry wondered how Dolly would cope if she was ill again. 'Do you want me to come tomorrow morning?' he asked, when he had eventually done all the jobs he could to help her out.

'Oh, you don't want to bother like that,' she replied, but remembering the chaotic situation he had walked in on, he insisted.

'It's all right. With the strike on, I've nothing better to do.'

'You are a good boy,' Dolly said, hugging him, and Harry had the grace to feel slightly ashamed.

Yes, he did want to help his sister out, of course. But that was not the whole story. Already, at the back of his mind, he was busy working it out – if he left at the same time as he had done today, he might see the girl again. Yes, if he was honest, that was more than half the reason. He wanted to see her again... and he didn't even know her name! Stupid – he should have asked her. Well, if he saw her again tomorrow he would.

It never occurred to Harry when he got home to ask Charlotte if she knew who the girl was, any more than it occurred to him to break Dolly's confidence and explain her sickness. Harry could be a silent soul when he wanted to be. So when Charlotte asked after Dolly he simply said she was feeling a bit better now, but that he had offered to go back and help her out with the boys tomorrow anyway. He did not mention the girl at all, but he thought of her all right as he fiddled about in his pigeon loft, seeing her oval face with the dark eyes threatening to spill tears, and the determined mouth holding them back. Yes, he decided, tomorrow he would not only find out her name, he would walk a bit further with her.

It was at supper that he heard about the 'blackleg train' and when he did, his heart sank.

'There'll be some trains tomorrow,' Charlotte said, dishing up potatoes with the spoon clattering so loudly on the plate it could be heard all along the Rank. 'Molly Clements told me about it just now, when we were getting in the washing.'

'What do you mean – trains?' Harry asked. He had heard Molly Clements calling across the gardens to his mother while he was in with the pigeons, but had kept his head low. Molly Clements was known for a chatterer and he had not wanted to get caught up in a long conversation. Now, however, he pricked up his ears.

'Trains – there're going to be trains. The first one's due out from Bath at half-past eight,' Charlotte said patiently, adding a spoonful of leeks to the potatoes.

'How can there be trains? Everybody's on strike.' That was James, speaking from his corner of the sofa.

'Don't ask me how. Somebody's volunteered to drive them, I suppose.' Charlotte said a little shortly.

'Well, that's disgusting!' James pulled himself slightly more upright. 'How can we ever hope to win a strike when people are willing to cut our throats like that? Blackleg labour, that's what it'll be. College lads, no doubt, and toffs who don't know or care a bugger for the likes of us.'

He began to wheeze again, made short of breath by the effort of losing his temper, and Charlotte threw him a warning look.

'Don't upset yourself now, Dad. It's not worth it.'

'No, you're right, it's not worth it, but it's disgusting all the same,' James said sadly. 'A blackleg train! Well, now I've heard it all.'

Harry said nothing, but something inside him had gone very still, very quiet. If there was going to be a train at half-past eight, the strike would not be the only thing to suffer. His chance of seeing the girl again would be gone, too. She wouldn't walk all the way to South Compton if she could ride. Nobody would.

'Can you eat a bit more bacon?' Charlotte asked, her fork

hovering over his plate, and he shook his head.

Suddenly he did not have a great deal of appetite left. Disappointment was fermenting inside him like yeast, filling his stomach, bubbling and swelling . . . and his anger against the blackleg train and the men who would drive it grew too.

A General Strike ought to *be* general if it was to do any good – nothing moving anywhere. That way, the bosses would be forced to climb down the sooner and give the miners a decent living wage.

I wish I could do something about it, thought Harry. I wish there was some way I could stop it running.

The other night he had vowed to make someone hear him, but as yet his voice was not loud enough and he had no idea what to say. Now there might be an opportunity to hinder the strike-breakers and he could not think how to do that either.

But there must be a way, he decided. And if only he could find it, nobody would stop him carrying out his plan.

*

The idea came to him that evening as he was attending to his pigeons, delighting him so much that he laughed out loud, frightening the birds. It was simple – so simple he could not understand why he hadn't thought of it before – but it would be wonderfully effective in stopping the train.

Along the Rank he could hear the two youngest Clements boys, Tommy and Reg, playing a half-hearted game of football, and he decided to let them in on his plan. Reg, who was the same age as Harry, was always game for a bit of fun and Tommy, two years older, was one of the keenest young members of the Federation at Middle Pit.

Harry settled the birds and locked up the shed for the night. Then he went up the garden to Tommy and Reg. Although there were two years between them, the boys were as like as peas in a pod; people often mistook them for twins and sometimes confused them altogether. Harry, however, had lived next door to them all his life, and had no difficulty in knowing it was Reg who slammed the ball towards him as he rounded the corner of the washhouse. He fielded it with his chest, got a foot to it and kicked it back with such enthusiasm that it hit the wall, skidded past the two boys and sent Peggy Yelling's cat bounding for the safety of the gardens.

'Hey – watch it, you three – you'll be breaking a window in a minute!' Molly, the Clements boys' stepmother, yelled from her window and they grinned at one another. They might be past their middle teens now and working men all three of them, but they had been yelled at from kitchen windows since they were toddlers and the feeling of fellowship it aroused in them was as comfortable and familiar as the boots on their feet.

It was also just the right atmosphere for persuading the Clements boys to join him in his plan, thought Harry.

'Listen, lads, come here a minute,' he began. 'No – let's go round the corner. I want to talk to you.'

They rescued the ball and followed him, bouncing it idly on the stones. Then, once they were out of earshot of the houses and leaning against the wall of the sheds, Harry told them about the blackleg train and outlined his ideas for stopping it.

His suggestion was greeted by hoots of laughter and unstinted enthusiasm.

'Oh, that's brilliant!'

'You're a dark horse, Harry. Fancy thinking of something like that! Count us in!'

They talked for a while longer, working out a plan of attack, decided where to get the things they would need and speculating about what would happen if they were able to do as they planned.

'There'll be some red faces and no mistake!' Tommy chortled. 'That early train is always chock-a-block with people going from Bath to Wells or Shepton – and most of them toffs, too. If it can't get any further than Hillsbridge, they'll either have to walk or stay on it and go back again.'

'We'd better meet early then,' Harry said. 'It's easy enough for me, as I promised to go up and give our Dolly a hand. But what about you – will you be up?'

'I shall,' Tommy said. 'Our Reg would sleep till the cows come home, but I'll make sure he gets up tomorrow!'

Reg laughed aloud. 'Don't worry about me – wouldn't miss this for worlds!' he said.

It was a sentiment they all shared.

*

Harry was awake much earlier than he needed to be next morning. He got up, dressed and went downstairs, taking Charlotte and James completely by surprise.

'Whatever has got into you?' Charlotte asked, pouring him a cup of tea. 'I've never known you get up this early when you didn't have to.'

Harry shrugged evasively, glad he had arranged to meet the Clements boys along at the corner instead of outside the door. If Charlotte had seen them all together she would have smelled a rat.

'I thought I'd get up to our Dolly's nice and early,' he said and had the grace to blush when Charlotte praised him for his thoughtfulness.

At about a quarter to eight he escaped. Tommy and Reg were already waiting at the end of the Rank, sharing a Woodbine as they leaned against the wall of the end house.

'Ready, then?' he greeted them.

'Yes! We thought you weren't coming.'

'Let's get going then.'

They started off down the hill with jaunty step.

'Have you got what we need?' Tommy asked.

Harry's hands closed over a heavy metal padlock which was concealed in his pocket. Last night he had found it at the bottom of his father's toolbox after half an hour's frenzied searching when he had almost given up, thinking someone must have moved it and that the plan would have to be abandoned.

'I've got it,' he told them and they chortled in anticipation.

They were still laughing as they turned the corner at the bottom of the hill and their objective came in sight.

Here in the centre of the town two sets of railway lines bisected the main street, protected by level-crossing gates. Closest to Conygre Hill was the Somerset and Dorset – the line that ran from Bath to Shepton Mallet and beyond, passing on its way through South Compton where, in about half-an-hour's time, the blackleg train would run. At present the crossing gates were open, sealing off the line until such time as they were swung by means of a lever in the signal box to stop any traffic and allow the train a passage across the road.

But this was what Harry was determined should not happen. If the gates failed to open, the train would be unable to leave the station – and then it would have no option but to

77

turn around and go back to Bath, he reasoned.

And with a padlock as strong as the one in his pocket to fasten them together, those gates would take some opening!

As they neared the railway line, however, Harry swore. 'Sod it! There's somebody up in the signal box already!'

The others looked... and groaned with him. They had made their plans on the assumption that with the railways on strike and the blackleg train the only one due on the line this morning, some volunteer or other would go up to the signal box at the last moment to open the gates and go through the formality of lowering the signals. Finding someone already there was a blow. The signal box provided a wonderful vantage point and it would be virtually impossible to tamper with the gates without being seen from there.

'We should have done it last night, while it was dark,' Tommy grumbled.

'I know what we *should* have done – but it's a bit late now to worry about that.' Harry caught hold of Reg's sleeve, giving it a jerk. 'Let's go back round the corner and have a think.'

They retreated out of sight of the signal box and Tommy got out his Woodbines and passed them round. Then they squatted down on their haunches against the wall in the time-honoured fashion of miners.

'There's only one way to do it,' Harry said after a moment. 'And that's to wait until the train's due.'

'We shall be seen,' Tommy objected.

'Of course we shall. But at least that way they won't have time to do anything about it. We're going to be seen whenever we do it – are you worried?'

'No!' they said together.

'Right, we'll wait here then.'

The strike had cast an unnatural hush over the town. There were no hooters to blare their clarion call into the fresh morning air, no rattle of pit-boots on the pavements, no distant thundery rumble from the stone quarries away over the hills as there was so often on clear mornings. Instead there was only bird-song, the soft rush of the river that ran through the centre of Hillsbridge between the two sets of railway lines and the occasional clip-clop of a horse and cart to break the stillness.

After they had been there a few minutes, however, the lads

heard footsteps and voices and turned to see a group of older miners coming down the hill.

'Morning, boys – you coming to join the protest, be you?' they greeted Harry and the Clements brothers.

'Protest? What protest's that?' Tommy asked.

'You've heard about the train, haven't you? Well, we be going to stand on the platform and boo when it comes through,' one of the men replied.

Harry viewed them scornfully. How weak! he thought. A fat lot of good booing would do. But it was typical of the peaceable approach of Hillsbridge miners – they might have a reputation for rowdiness on a Saturday night, but when it came to standing up for their rights they were a law-abiding lot.

'We b'ain't the only ones,' one of the men said, seeing his look. 'There's more lads coming from the other way. You want to come over and make your voices heard wi' the rest of us.'

'All right, we'll be over later,' Harry agreed and when the older miners had gone, the lads had another laugh over their plan and settled back to wait again.

From where they were squatting, Harry had only to peep around the corner to be able to see the town clock in its tower above the market building, but the hands seemed to move with painful slowness.

'How are we going?' Tommy asked every so often.

'Another ten minutes.'

'S'pose the train's early?'

They looked at one another.

'Would we hear the bell from here?' Harry asked, referring to the bell that rang on the platform as the train passed through the next station up the line, to warn of its approach.

'I could get a bit closer,' Reg offered. 'If it was just me nobody would take any notice. Then I could tip you the wink.'

'All right – but walk naturally and don't make it look as if you've got anything to hide,' Harry instructed.

'If I'm caught I shall pretend to be our Tommy,' Reg said with a grin, tossing his Woodbine into the gutter.

'Thanks very much!' his brother called after him. However, a moment later as Reg came hurrying back, his face a picture, the amusement disappeared from his tone: 'What's the matter?'

'There's a policeman over by the station,' Reg informed

them. 'It looks like Sergeant Eyles.'

They all looked at one another. This was something else they had not bargained for.

'They must have thought there might be trouble,' Harry said. 'Damn all those men and their silly booing! Well, we'll just have to do our best, won't we?'

Reg was looking worried. 'You mean we're still going to do it?'

''Course we are.'

'But we'm bound to get caught.'

Harry's jaw was set in a stubborn line. Anyone who knew him would have been able to tell in a moment that it would take a whole army of police officers to stop him carrying out his plan.

'Well, I'm doing it. Whether you join in is up to you.'

There was a brief silence and then Tommy said evasively, 'It wouldn't be so noticeable, would it – only one?'

The sense of that was undeniable, but Harry felt a sharp sense of let-down all the same.

'How about attracting old Eyles' attention, so he's less likely to notice me?'

'Well – yes . . .' But the Clements boys didn't sound too keen. They had attracted the policeman's attention a great deal too much in their time – and usually without meaning to.

'What could we do?'

'Oh, I don't know. Go down under the subway and make a noise. Make it sound as if *you're* the ones doing something . . .'

Clearly they didn't like it, but there was little alternative. After a few moment's consultation they set off, crossing the forecourts of the George Hotel where the stalls spilled out from the Market Hall on market days and going – with as much obvious stealth as they could muster – down the steps and into the subway that ran under the railway line. From around the corner Harry watched. Knowing their reputation, as soon as he heard and saw them the chances were that Sergeant Eyles would go to investigate what they were up to, but he was out of Harry's sight so the timing would have to be more a matter of luck than judgement.

Harry waited a few moments, then ducked out from cover. There were a few people on the platform waiting for the blackleg train, he noticed, keeping well away from the line of angry miners, but of the policeman there was no sign.

Harry's fingers closed over the padlock in his pocket, easing it open and ready. There was no hope of any cover for him; he would just have to walk across the road, wind the chain around the gate-posts and hope that it worked.

Trying to look nonchalant, he approached the crossing. Then, as he reached the gates he pulled out the padlock and threaded the chain through the struts. His trembling hands made him awkward and slow and before he could loop the padlock onto the chain a shout went up.

'Hoi! You! What do you think you're doing?'

He looked up to see a gentleman clad in pinstripe trousers and bowler hat angrily waving an umbrella at him. Harry fought down a sudden urge to laugh. He had not known there was anyone in Hillsbridge who went to work dressed like that. It just went to show, there were two quite separate worlds in this little mining town. But this was not the time for social speculation. Panic was making Harry's adrenalin flow freely, for he knew the shout would attract the attention of Sergeant Eyles. With a quick movement, he snapped the padlock shut and jerked out the key.

'Hey – you!' the man shouted again. 'Yes – you, boy!'

As Harry turned to run he heard the heavy thud of police boots on the subway steps and hesitated as he realised whichever way he went he would have to pass one of them: the cane-waving pin-stripe gentleman or the sergeant. The choice was not a difficult one. Sergeant Eyles might not be as young as he used to be, but he had been a rugby player in his time and Harry felt instinctively that a flying tackle would not yet be beyond him. But the traveller looked about as athletic as Queen Victoria. As he shouted again Harry dived towards him, then cut a circular detour into the road and headed towards the second level crossing. Once over it, there were any number of places he could escape to and hide until they got tired of looking for him. He didn't think the police sergeant had seen who he was – all pit lads looked much the same in their rushy-duck trousers and caps and the Clements boys would certainly deny all knowledge of 'goings-on' at the gates. Behind him he heard Sergeant Eyles' whistle blown sharply and imperatively and he laughed, risking a look over his shoulder.

Then, as he turned back to look where he was going, the laughter died. Coming down South Hill were not one but half-a-dozen burly policemen, looking to Harry's horrified eyes as if every one was as good a rugby player as Sergeant Eyles – and about half his age into the bargain. They were the reinforcements, drafted to the area in case of trouble in this centre of the Somerset coalfield during the strike, and billeted in the big house at the top of South Hill. Harry had forgotten all about them – but clearly they had not forgotten the blackleg train and had been on their way to see it safely through Hillsbridge when they heard the local man's whistle.

Instinctively Harry swerved into Frome Road. In his hand was the key and his first thought was that if they caught him all his efforts would be wasted – they would simply unlock the padlock and that would be that. Here at the entrance to Frome Road the bank shelved steeply away from the road into the river – so steeply and so suddenly that the sweets and newspaper shop on the corner had its back supported by stilts that were built right into the river – and Harry ran to the low stone wall, leaned over and threw the key towards the water as hard as he could. It landed with a small, satisfying splash and Harry knew a moment's triumph. But the delay had cost him his advantage in the chase and as he turned to run again, the two fastest policemen were almost on top of him – a short, hard-fought chase and they had him.

His arms held behind his back, Harry did not even bother to struggle. He was caught and he knew it. But at least the train would not go through! By the time the two policemen had frogmarched him back to the bridge where Sergeant Eyles was waiting, the damage had been discovered and a great deal of huffing and puffing was going on.

'All right then, lad – where's the key?' the sergeant greeted him.

To his annoyance, Harry was unable to suppress a grin of triumph.

'You think you've been very clever, I suppose,' the policeman said shortly. 'Well, it's up to you. Tell me where it is here and now, or you cool off in a cell.'

This time Harry laughed aloud. 'I'll tell you, for all the good it'll do. I threw it in the river!'

Sergeant Eyles lifted his chin and shook his head slowly from side to side in an expression of utter disgust.

'Well, it's round to the station for you then, my lad, isn't it? And what your mother's going to say I don't know. Get him out of my sight!'

One of the constables jerked Harry's arms, turning him back towards the centre of town. But Harry had seen a figure coming past the George from the direction of Conygre Hill – a girl in the uniform of the Higher Elementary at South Compton – and he hung back against the rough grip.

It was her – the girl he had walked with yesterday and hoped to see again – still limping, but neat, tidy and purposeful . . . and carrying less than she had done yesterday. She had intended to catch the blackleg train, he supposed. But to his surprise, though she looked at him and at the policeman with a puzzled and concerned expression as she went by, she made no attempt to go into the station. Instead she marched on across the second set of railway lines and towards South Hill, only pausing occasionally to look back over her shoulder at the spectacle of her erstwhile companion being frogmarched in the direction of the police station by a squad of burly policemen.

In spite of his triumph, Harry felt a moment's regret that he could not explain to her what he had done and why. Perhaps she now thought he was a mischief-making lout – or even a criminal! But there it was, he could not explain, any more than he could ask her why she was walking when to all intents and purposes the town had believed there was a train running. As she passed the station and headed up the hill towards South Compton, she could not have known that the train would be very lucky to get any further than Hillsbridge before half the morning was past at the earliest.

'Come on there, look where you're going!' One of the constables admonished him, pushing him so roughly that Harry almost fell. But he resisted, standing still for a moment and listening while a grin spread once more across his face. That distant sound coming closer and louder all the while was the unmistakable chug of the blackleg train as it steamed down the valley.

Irrepressibly he turned to the constable holding on to his arm. 'Here it comes, then – but I'd like to see it get any further!' he said cheerfully.

And although the constable only glared and hastened him on, the smile stayed on his face. He had done what he intended. By the time they had found somebody to saw through the chain and release the gates there would be a few frayed tempers to say the least – and a point would have been made.

Yes, whatever he had coming to him it would be worth it, Harry decided. And for a very long time he would be proud to tell the story of how he had stopped the blackleg train single-handed.

*

Harry was at the police station for the best part of two hours, locked in a cell until Sergeant Eyles eventually returned from the scene of his triumph; then he was treated to the kind of roasting for which the bluff sergeant was noted.

'Aren't you going to have me up, then?' Harry asked when the policeman at last opened the door and told him to, 'Get on home, then!'

'Not this time, lad,' Sergeant Eyles said shortly. 'Try some damnfool trick like that again, though, and you won't be so lucky. Now clear off before I change my mind. And I should steer clear of those Clements boys if you know what's good for you,' he added as an afterthought. 'You can say what you like -- they put you up to it and if I had a scrap of evidence they'd be here along with you. They're trouble, those two.'

Harry knew better than to argue, but all the same he felt hurt that the Clements boys should be credited with his idea.

They were waiting for him, squatting with half-a-dozen other striking miners against the low wall that edged the road between the two sets of railway lines. When they saw Harry, they gave him a hero's welcome.

'They let you go, then?' Tommy asked when the hubbub had died down a bit.

'Yes, but not before they had me locked up in a cell.' Harry was enjoying himself now. 'And what about the train? It's gone, I see!'

They laughed. 'Only just. They had to get a hacksaw to cut through the chain. Oh, you missed it, Harry! It was a picture. And you haven't heard the best bit. There was this one bloke – stuck-up sort of toff, kept marching up and down looking at his pocket watch and saying it was only what you'd expect in a place like Hillsbridge. Well, Reg and me went round the Co-op and got a couple of eggs, then we hid behind the water tower and took aim next time he came strutting down the platform. And we got him lovely! One egg all down his suit and the other on the back of his neck. And we got away with it, too, though we was laughing so much we could hardly stand up.'

Harry laughed with them, but the mention of passengers on the blackleg train had reminded him of the girl.

'Did you see her?' he asked Tommy, describing her as best he could. 'She came down over our hill and then went on, walking. It didn't look as if she was going to catch the train.'

'Well, she wouldn't, would she?' Tommy replied. 'Don't you know who that was?'

'Wouldn't ask if I knew, would I?'

'That's George Young's daughter. You know George Young – he's a big noise in the Labour Party. You can bet he'd never let his daughter ride on a blackleg train.'

'Oh, is that who it is?' Harry said, pleased. He had really liked the girl and it was nice to think that she too had been opposed to the blackleg train – so opposed that she was prepared to walk the best part of three miles rather than ride on it.

Then suddenly he remembered that he was supposed to have been walking that way himself... to see Dolly! She would be wondering what had happened to him. Though since he was supposed to be there, at least his mother would not yet have begun to ask questions about where he was!

He grinned ruefully. There was going to be hell to pay when Charlotte found out what had happened. The wigging Sergeant Eyles had given him would be nothing with the one that his mother would hand out when she got to hear what he had done.

But it was worth it, all the same. The most worthwhile thing he had ever done in his life. And then and there Harry came to a decision.

It might have been his first act to further his new-found cause. But certainly it would not be his last.

Chapter Four

The atmosphere was strained in the Roberts household and had been since the night the General Strike was announced. Too many things had been said that night which would have been better left unsaid, and the quarrel had been slept on - something Amy had known instinctively was a dangerous state of affairs. The next morning they had maintained an icy politeness and although when Llew had left for the yard Amy had cooled down and made up her mind to put their differences behind her, as soon as she saw him again all her anger had boiled up once more.

No further mention was made of the work Llew intended to try to get while the strike held, but Amy knew he was looking for it all the same and the knowledge festered inside her. She could understand it in a way, knew that if he was to stay solvent he could not afford to have the lorries idle for long, but it made no difference. It was like turning against her own to be a party to it, and she felt strongly that the more solid the backing for the miners the shorter the struggle would be.

Listening to her crystal set, Amy followed the progress of the strike. With no national newspapers, the BBC was almost the only means of learning what was happening in the outside world - apart, of course, from the news sheet known as the *British Gazette* which was being put out by the Government - and which Amy felt was hopelessly biased - and the equally slanted view of *The British Worker*, printed and distributed by the trade union leaders. But the BBC seemed reasonably impartial, and Amy listened avidly to reports of marches and rallies, arrangements for the distribution of food in the cities - such as the closure of Hyde Park in London for use as a centre for the capital's milk supplies – and news of transport at a standstill, miles of docks silent and abandoned and lights switched off to conserve electricity.

But she was incensed by the reports of strike-breaking and each and every one refuelled her resentment against Llew. In London and the big cities, she heard, students were manning the buses – and some had been the subject of demonstrations, with gangs of strikers surrounding them, breaking the windows and even setting them on fire in a couple of cases. This pleased her, just as she was secretly pleased and proud when she heard of Harry's escapade concerning the blackleg train, though she knew Charlotte would be furious with him for involving himself in what she would term horseplay. Amy could still remember all too clearly her mother's distress when Ted had been arrested some years previously and charged with the manslaughter of Rupert Thorne, the solicitor responsible for the pregnancy and death of Ted's sweetheart Becky Church; she knew that Harry being hauled off to the police station would have been enough to stir up all the old feelings of horror at finding herself and her own on the wrong side of the law and shame for anything which caused the family to be 'talked about'.

How long the strike could last, however, Amy did not know. As the days dragged by with no sign of the government weakening, her confidence in its chances of success began to wane, though she would have died rather than admit this to Llew.

It was just too much, she thought, to expect others to put up with the hardship of a prolonged strike when it was not their battle. There were rumours, too, of riots in Birmingham, Manchester and Glasgow, with shooting in the streets, and although the BBC dismissed the stories as utter rubbish it was admitted that troops could be seen marching up and down Whitehall and tanks had been moved to strategic places in London, for all the world as if the country was at war.

No, it couldn't go on and in spite of her loyalty to the miners, her own folk, she found herself beginning to hope it would not continue. It was no fun to be worried sick about unpaid bills. It was no fun to go into Hillsbridge and see great gaggles of idle men and know that your own husband was betraying them. And it was no fun being at loggerheads with him, either.

If only the strike would end and we could get back to normal instead of forever being at one another's throats! Amy thought, and found herself remembering the argument they had had that morning. While making the bed she had noticed an envelope which had fallen on to the floor on Llew's side and was half covered by the drop of the bedspread. It had fallen out of his pocket when he was undressing, she supposed as she picked it up, glancing without a great deal of interest at the handwritten address and the postmark – which looked like Glamorgan. However Llew, who was combing his hair at the dressing-table mirror ready to go to work, noticed it in her hand and immediately swooped on it.

'That's mine!'

'I know it is,' she said, irritated by his tone. 'It was on the floor, that's all.'

'And how did it get there?'

'How should I know?' she returned, equalling his sharpness.

'You know I don't like you looking at my letters.'

'I wasn't going to look. I'm not the least bit interested in your letters,' she snapped back and all the antagonism was there again, just as it had been for almost a week now.

He is utterly unreasonable sometimes, thought Amy; though in her heart she knew his bad temper was the result of worry over the strike, it made no difference.

When he had left for the yard, the matter still rankled. It was true what she had said – she was not interested in his post. Most of it was connected with the business and she had no desire to see it. But there was no need for him to be so horrid and secretive; after all, she was his wife and this was 1926.

It was probably connected with some blackleg job he was taking on, she decided, and he knew that if she found out about it there would be more rows, more arguments.

'Oh, blast the strike!' said Amy aloud. 'The sooner it's over, the better I shall be pleased.'

And with a sigh she went on preparing breakfast for Maureen and Barbara.

*

As Llew unlocked the gates of the compound, he too was

thinking about the strike and the effects it was having on their lives.

The letter which had caused the upheaval this morning had nothing to do with blackleg work, but he was doing it all the same and he did not much like it. Knowing how thoroughly Amy disapproved was bad enough; in addition Llew himself came from another mining area – the South Wales coalfield – and he could understand her feelings perfectly. Deep down he felt a heel himself, but he had no option. Sorry as he was for the miners, just though he felt their grievances to be, he simply could not afford to support them.

Who would it help, he asked himself, if he went bankrupt and had to lose his lorries? He had worked hard to build up the business, damned hard, and he could not stand by and see it all disintegrate, whatever the rights and wrongs of the miners' quarrel with the coal-owners.

And there was no doubt that working while others were on strike was paying off. You could argue the morals and ethics of it to your heart's content – the fact was that there was money to be made if you were prepared to work for it and it was against Llew's nature not to be so prepared. Long ago he had decided that he would be one of life's survivors. Not for him the endless round of back-breaking work to line someone else's pocket. Llew wanted more than that, for himself and for his family. He wanted money to buy them – and himself – a few luxuries and set them up in life. He wanted to be looked up to as being a little above the ordinary run-of-the-mill worker. And most of all he wanted to feel he had achieved something, built it up himself from nothing by his ingenuity, perseverance and sheer hard work. Geared up as he was to striving for that aim, it was more than he could bear to lose opportunities and let work pass him by.

In the yard the lorries stood silently waiting for him. Although not members of any union, Herbie Button and Ivor Burge were of mining stock and they felt as Amy did about strike-breaking. When he had first mentioned to them the loads he intended to carry for the Government they had reacted much as she had done, and he had not pressed them. He valued Herbie in particular as an employee, and he wanted relations between them to return to normal as soon as possible after the strike was over. Carrying loads of food and provisions and even animal feedstuffs as he was, there

were usually plenty of willing hands to help him unload –
troops, students and special constables. It was here in the
yard that he missed Herbie most, for the older man had taken
on responsibility for maintaining the lorries – something
about which Llew had never been that knowledgeable – and
running the long journeys they were undertaking now, it
was imperative the vehicles were kept in good order. Besides
that, he was experiencing problems with the new lorry, the
one which Amy had driven into Ralph Porter's car; there was
something underneath the front axle that was rubbing and
he suspected it was plied out of true.

Today he had no loads to carry and Llew had decided he
ought to do what he could to locate the trouble with the lorry
and put it right. He crossed to the shed, pulled on a pair of
overalls to protect his clothes from the worst of the grease
and looked out the jack, blocks and a carry-all of tools. The
sun was warm as he took them out into the yard, and it
crossed his mind that if the weather held it would be that
much harder for the strike to bite. A cold spell or even a few
hard showers of rain and people would be crying out for coal
to make up a nice blaze. But with the sun shining like this a
fire could be banked in with small coals and kept low for
days, needed only for cooking and boiling a kettle.

In spite of Amy's accident the lorry still looked good, the
paintwork gleaming like new in the sunshine, and Llew felt
the same thrill of pride as he always experienced when
looking at it. If I never own another thing, I shall always feel
proud that I was able to get myself a brand-new lorry, he
thought. But perfect as it looked, there was damage
somewhere and it had to be put right.

He dropped to his hand and knees, trying to peer up
underneath the front offside of the lorry, but he was unable
to get close enough or at the right angle to really see
anything. Better have the wheel off, he decided, loosening
the nuts and positioning the jack beneath it. As he settled the
chocks beneath the axle he noticed the ground was not quite
level – the dry weather seemed to have accentuated the
uneven surface of the yard. But Llew decided it was safe
enough. To move it now would mean putting the wheel
back on again and re-positioning everything... and
wherever he moved to would probably be just as bad. He
adjusted the chocks and the jack, put his tools within easy

reach and slid carefully under the lorry. In the complete shadow it was dark and chill, the ground strikingly cold to his back through shirt and overalls.

I ought to get something to lie on, Llew thought.

He moved sideways to wriggle out again and as he did so he was suddenly horrifying aware of the lorry moving above him. He froze, sweat breaking out all over his body. My God – wasn't it safe? He had never thought...

Let me get out of here! Llew thought in panic. Let me get out! He moved again, lengthways, inching his legs out into the warm sunshine, fear trapping the breath in his lungs and making the blood sing in his ears. A little more... a little more... careful now... careful...!

He heard the creak, loud as thunder, not only in his ears but all around him. He heard it with every sweating pore and froze again, knowing somehow even as he did so that it was no good. In a split second's sheer terror his dilated eyes saw too clearly exactly what was going to happen and Llew knew with absolute certainty that he was going to die.

'Amy! My God!' he cried, but it was a scream of silence. And then, next moment, the world caved in around him.

*

It was mid-morning and Amy was getting the girls ready to go shopping. They sat side by side on the kitchen table, protesting mildly while Amy scrubbed their faces, hands and knees with a wet flannel and combed the tangles out of their curls.

'Mammy, can we go for a walk up the New Road to the echo?' Barbara asked.

The flat valley road to South Compton provided a pleasant riverside walk in summer and some way along it there was a wooden bridge over a spring crevice in the hillside from which a shouted 'Hello!' carried across the meadows, bounced off the five stone arches that carried the railway embankment and echoed satisfyingly round the valley. The girls loved to be taken up the New Road, which they had been told their father had had a hand in building, and particularly they loved the echo. Even Maureen, though she could not yet really talk, could usually be persuaded to shout 'Da!' loudly enough to set the air singing in response.

But this morning Amy did not feel like walking along to the echo. She was too preoccupied with the state of affairs between herself and Llew.

It could not go on, she thought. This morning's fresh flurry of bad-tempered words had made her realise that. The strike could drag out for weeks yet and she had no wish to go on living in this minefield of resentment and anger. She was not used to it – she and Llew had always been happy until now, with quarrels quickly forgotten. Besides, it was a most uncomfortable state of affairs and if there was one thing Amy hated it was discomfort. But this morning it was more than that. This morning she had the distinctly panicky feeling that if they did not bring an end to their differences, something really dreadful was going to happen. Why she felt this she had no idea. There was no rhyme or reason in it. But she felt it so strongly that it frightened her.

'Can we go to the echo, Mammy?' Barbara pressed her and Amy made up her mind.

'Not this morning. I want to call in at the yard and see Daddy. And by the time we've done that and the shopping, it will be time to come home and get your dinner.'

Barbara whined a bit and Amy decided a spot of bribery would not come amiss.

'If you're good, you shall have some chocolate drops.'

Barbara's eyes widened. Chocolate drops only came from the pocket of Uncle Ted when he visited them, or on very special occasions. They would be worth missing the echo for!

Amy finished dressing Maureen and put her in her pram so that she could not crawl about and get herself dirty again. Then she tidied her own hair at the mirror and touched her lips with colour, thankful that nature had given her the kind of looks that stayed good without much effort.

So many girls she had known who had been pretty, or presentable at the very least, had slipped into being downright plain since they had married and had children and Amy thought a good deal of this had to do with the fact that they no longer had time to spend on themselves. Well, she did not intend to let that happen to her – neither was she going to get fat as some of them did, from eating all the wrong things that were cheap as well as filling. How could you expect your husband to stay interested if you were a pasty, shapeless lump? You couldn't. At least Llew was still interested, still teased and flattered her and made love to her as if he fancied her, not just as though she was a convenient body to fumble with in the dark. Though it was more than a week since he had made love to her now, she remembered, and the thought was a sudden ache of longing inside her. She could not remember their being this way before, not ever, with this distance between them, preventing them from touching even; realising this frightened her again and confirmed her in the decision to go to the yard and try to put things tight.

Gathering her things together, she eased the pram out of the door and closed it behind her. Barbara, always a chatterbox, kept up an incessant stream of questions and comments as they started down the hill and Amy answered her in slightly preoccupied fashion.

There was a strange atmosphere hanging over the streets – a little like a bank holiday, but without the effervescent fizz of joy and fun. A group of miners were squatting together under the chestnut tree that overhung the pavement at the cross-roads, caps pushed to the backs of their heads, Woodbines or home-rolled cigarettes sticking to their lower lips, but their faces wore resigned expressions and their eyes stared into space. 'We've seen it all before,' those expressions seemed to say and they lowered Amy's spirits by another notch. At the doors of one or two houses, other men were squatting on the front steps or lounging against the door-posts with the same air of aimlessness, and Amy wondered how they would survive a long strike. They simply were not used to so much leisure. For them the unwritten law of life was work and more work and it took an earthquake, in the form of this forced hiatus, to stop them. But they would not enjoy the respite; they might join the football matches or billiards contests – their opponents the police drafted in to keep the peace – but only the very youngest of them would revel in the situation. The rest would be painfully aware of the consequences of a long stoppage and the hardship it would bring. For they knew that all the fervour in the world would not tip the scales in their balance – no, not even with right on their side. The balances were too heavily weighted for the employers, the coal-owners, the 'haves' of this world.

I'm almost one of those now, thought Amy. Is that why I've been taking it out so on Llew – because I realise I'm half-way to being on the other side of the fence now and I feel guilty about it? But would I honestly change back? Would I have my husband squatting at the door watching the world go by and only hoping vainly for a better future? Would I change places with the women going to shop this morning with almost-empty purses to look for something cheap and cheerful to fill their family's hungry bellies?

With her handbag bumping comfortably on the handles of the pram to remind her she had enough to spend, if not a fortune, Amy knew she would not and knowing this made her a little ashamed. It was easy to get on her high horse when it was not up to her to decide to keep the lorry wheels turning. In a brief, enlightening moment Amy realised that she wanted to 'have her cake and eat it too', as Mam would have put it – to reap the financial benefits of working while others were on strike, yet salve her social conscience at the same time by objecting to it.

Yes, if she was honest with herself, she had been rather unfair to Llew and now she was tingling with a sense of urgent need to put things right.

As they neared the opening to Porter's Hill Barbara ran on and turned into it, but Amy called her back.

'Not that way, Babs.'

'But we're going to see Daddy.'

'Yes, but we'll go the road way,' Amy told her, privately cursing herself for a coward. It would be quicker to go down Porter's Hill – but she didn't want to risk seeing Ralph Porter. The very thought of it made her quake inwardly. He's probably working somewhere, she told herself, but that was not enough to convince her. After all, he had been driving up the hill on that fateful day when she had taken the lorry down and besides, his house overlooked the road. He might be in his study and look out and see her. Perhaps he might call out and inform her again that it was a private road. She wouldn't put it past him...

Further down the hill, the valley opened up beneath them and Amy could see the yard with the lorries standing there. So Llew had not gone out, then; he'd been telling the truth when he said he had no job today. But from the stillness you would never know there was anyone there working, especially anyone as vitally energetic as Llew. At full stretch he moved the very air around him, Amy thought.

Just before the turning that led down to the yard was a

little shanty shop that sold sweets, biscuits, fruit and some provisions.

'Can I have my sweeties now?' Barbara asked, holding on to the handles of the pram and hopping up and down.

'You know you always have them when I've finished my shopping and not before,' Amy told her.

Barbara's face fell. 'Me want them now!' she pouted and Amy, visualising how the child would keep on and on while she was trying to talk to Llew, almost gave in. Only the fact that the sweets were always an end-of-shopping treat stopped her; break the habit and she could never enforce it again. But there was an alternative.

'Tell you what. We'll go shopping *before* we go to see Daddy,' she decided. 'No, it's no use throwing a tantrum, Babs, you can easily wait a little while for your sweeties.'

This same air of unreality which had been apparent in her road hung over the entire town of Hillsbridge. Today there were no ponies drawing the wagons of waste on the tramlines across the road outside Starvault Pit, and the great wheels that worked the cage were still. Just a few days before the strike, a firm of local steeplejacks had begun work erecting a new chimney to rid the town of the clouds of choking smoke and fumes that the old one had dispensed into the atmosphere of the valley bowl – now that too stood abandoned, a monument to the strike. Under the wall at the pavement's edge some Starvault miners squatted in a row, looking for all the world as if they were waiting for time to begin their shift at the colliery, except that they had no bait tins containing the customary cognocker of bread and cheese, no tallow candles, no jar of cold tea. Amy recognised a couple of them as men she had known since she was a child, but they did not speak and she had the uncomfortable feeling that there was hostility in their eyes as they watched her pass.

'That's her husband who's blacklegging,' she could imagine them saying, but for the first time she felt no real shame, only a sense of injustice that they did not understand. Walking down the road she found herself formulating all the arguments in her mind and wishing she could find the courage to say them aloud to the men with the accusing eyes.

As she had expected, the shops were less busy than usual. Only one week into the dispute they might be, but that had already meant one pay-day missed and Federation funds were not sufficient to bring strike pay up to wage levels, low as they were. In the Co-op where she bought tea, biscuits and sugar, she heard women swapping their tales of woe and in the confectionery shop she felt quite guilty buying jam tarts for tea when the talk over the counter was how soon cheap loaves of bread would be introduced to help feed the hungry strikers' families.

'Come on then, girls, we'll go and see Daddy now,' she said, giving Barbara her twist of chocolate buttons.

As they emerged from the confectionery shop a distinctive sound attracted her attention and she turned to see the town ambulance bowling along the road towards them.

There was no mistaking the ambulance. It had begun life in shell-shattered France during the Great War, ferrying the wounded and sometimes the dead to and from the field hospitals, and when the last reveille sounded and it was no longer needed it had come home to civilian duty. Now its main purpose seemed to be rescuing the victims of the numerous accidents that were happening as a result of so many inexperienced drivers and motor cyclists taking to the roads, and the moment she saw it Amy's first thought was that something of the kind had happened again.

'Look, girls, it's coming this way!' she said, and although she told herself it was nothing to do with her a small chill ran through her all the same, as it always did at sight of the vehicle.

'The ambulance! The ambulance!' Barbara cried excitedly and Maureen managed her customary, 'Da! Da!'

The ambulance passed them, turning the sharp corner into Frome Hill, and by the time they rounded it themselves had disappeared from sight.

Amy pushed the pram in silence, wondering what to say to Llew to explain her unexpected visit; then she realised what a perfectly idiotic thought that was. He was her husband and they had been married for four years. She didn't have to say anything by way of explanation; he would know, just by her being there, that she wanted to make amends. And his eyes would meet hers and he would smile at her the way he had smiled that first night at the dance under the Palace . . . the way that could still make her melt inside. And he would probably whisper in her ear: 'I'll see you tonight, Mrs Roberts!'

The corner of her mouth twisted upwards and she looked

at Maureen, who had fallen asleep against her pillow, and Barbara wedged in the little dickey seat, her mouth full of chocolate drops that had trickled a brown stream down her chin.

I couldn't be luckier, thought Amy. I have a loving husband, two lovely children and a house better than my mother would ever have dared dream of living in. Sometimes, just once in a while, I ought to stop and count my blessings instead of behaving like a spoilt child when things don't go my way. Sometimes I ought to go down on my knees and thank God for all I have in case he thinks I'm ungrateful and snatches it away...

She reached the turning to Mill Road and turned into it. The hill sloped away steeply for the first hundred yards and she had to hang on tightly to the handles of the pram to ensure it did not run away with the two children in it. As they went down the slope at a bit of a run Barbara chuckled with delight, but Maureen still slept.

'Try not to wake your sister,' said Amy.

Then the sound of a car engine behind her made her pull the pram into the side of the way and as it passed she noticed that the driver was Dr Vezey.

Funny, thought Amy, a little alarmed. First the ambulance and now the doctor, both going this way. Though she didn't *know* the ambulance had gone this way; it could have carried on straight up the main road and the doctor might be going to one of the miners' cottages in the Rank built underneath Midlington Batch. But she found herself hurrying a little more anyway, her heart beating just too fast for comfort, her knees trembling ever so slightly. As she came around the bend in the road by the mill and saw the doctor's car pulled up outside the gates to the depot yard, she went cold inside.

What was he doing there?

For a fraction of a moment her feet ceased moving; then, quite suddenly, she began to run.

'Mammy!' Barbara cried in alarm, but Amy took no notice of her.

A step or two more and she saw the ambulance too. Panic flooded through her.

'Mammy!' Barbara wailed.

'Be quiet!' she snapped.

There was a blue-overalled figure coming out of the depot gates. It was Herbie.

'Herbie!' she cried, running towards him. 'What is it? What's going on?'

Herbie was white. His gaunt face seemed to have aged ten years since last she had seen him. '*Herbie!*' she half-screamed.

He stood blocking her path as if, should she try to pass him, he would spread out his arms and stop her bodily. 'Don't go down there, Mrs Roberts,' he said.

'But why? What's happened?' she sobbed.

Herbie's eyes were great haunted pools. 'There's been an accident.'

'An accident? What do you mean, an accident? Llew? Where's Llew?'

'Mrs Roberts – don't!' Herbie caught at the pram handles. 'Come in the Mill a minute.'

'I don't want to go in the Mill! What's going on? For pity's sake, Herbie...' She was in utter panic now and the blue, sun-lit sky seemed to have gone dark. Her voice rose hysterically; Barbara, frightened, began to cry and the noise woke Maureen who screamed in unison.

'*Tell me!*' Amy demanded.

'Oh, Mrs Roberts, I don't know how – I told you – there's been an accident, a terrible accident. Mr Roberts...' He broke off, unable to form the words, but somehow there was no need. Amy only looked at him and knew.

'Oh, my God!' she whispered.

Every vestige of the shock she had already felt gathered together now into a icy torrent that rushed through her veins, blinding her, deafening her, sweeping away common sense and coherent thought. An accident. Llew. The ambulance. The doctor. Herbie looking like a ghost. An accident. Llew. Llew!

She looked around wildly.

'Take the pram, Herbie.'

'Mrs Roberts...'

'Do as I say!'

Too shaken to argue, he did so. In his oily blue overalls he made an incongruous picture holding the pram, with two screaming children in it.

Amy began to run down the road. The ambulance was moving towards the yard gates and she ran towards it, scrabbling at the firmly closed doors with her hands.

'Hey – wait a minute now!' There was a hand on her arm,

restraining her, and she turned to see Dr Vezey.

'Leave me!' She tried to shake herself free. 'My husband...'

'No,' Dr Vezey said simply.

'No? You mean it's not him...?' Her eyes were wild, puzzled.

'Mrs Roberts, I think you should come and sit in my car.'

'I don't want to! I want Llew!'

'Come on, now...' He urged her towards the Ford. 'Come with me, there's a good girl.'

In a dream she let him ease her into the front seat.

'I don't understand... I don't...'

'Now get a grip on yourself,' Dr Vezey said and suddenly there was a pool of ice within her so deep, so dark that she was drowning in it without a struggle or a whimper because every bit of her was frozen rigid.

'You mean...?'

'I'm sorry,' he said. 'There was nothing to be done. By the time he was found it was too late – not that it would have made any difference if anyone *had* been here...'

'He's dead,' she said softly and choked on the words. 'But how?'

'The lorry fell on him. He must have been underneath it. I'm so very sorry.'

'Oh no!' she said. The pool of ice was spreading, trickling through her veins, freezing wherever it touched and she couldn't believe this was really happening to her. It was like a bad dream, or a play where she was taking the leading role. But it wasn't true – it couldn't be! In a moment the office door would open and Llew would come out, stepping carefully down on to the wood plank step and coming across the yard towards her...

'What are you doing sitting in the doctor's car?' he would say. 'And where are the children?'

The children... She half turned to look for them. As she did so she saw the ambulance moving away through the gate and it brought the truth home to her as nothing the doctor could say had done. It was a brief and agonising glimpse through a peephole into another world and it took her breath.

Llew was in that ambulance and he was dead. He was dead – they were taking him away. As the realisation cut through to her Amy began to scream.

'No – no! I won't let them! Doctor – stop them! Stop them!'

'Amy!' Dr Vezey's voice sounded far away, coming from a plane of normality that was lost for ever. 'Are you going to stop that screaming, or am I going to slap your face?'

Her eyes widened as she stared at him and she stopped screaming. But the ice was still there, paralysing her, and the feeling of living a nightmare had descended all around her like a suffocating blanket, shutting off light and air, alienating her, making her whole body into a shaking, trembling jelly.

Dr Vezey's hands covered hers and his eyes, kind and concerned, peered at her from that other plane.

'All right now?'

She nodded because there was nothing else to do. But the nightmare fog was thickening, cloying around her face, seeping into her pores, ballooning inside her head and in a moment's overwhelming despair Amy felt she would never be all right again.

*

Throughout the next few days the heavy impenetrable sense of nightmare persisted, pierced only by moments of sharp, almost unbearable grief and made more uncomfortable by the feverish burning of her cheeks and eyes, the heaviness of her head and the ache in her chest and throat.

People came and went, moving like shadows through the grey world ... a policeman, an undertaker, the doctor ... all firm enough to draw the required response from her – and neighbours and family whose shocked faces were no comfort to her because they reflected her own emotions and reminded her too sharply that this unbelievable fiction was true. There were arrangements to make and she made them, letters to write, condolences to accept and she did it all within the world of that clammy suffocating fog. The children had to be seen to as well – and the mundane tasks of washing grubby faces, spooning soft-boiled egg into unwilling mouths and providing clean socks and knickers were the hardest of all, because they belonged to the old life and now they were distorted, like reflections in a seaside 'Hall of Mirrors'.

Charlotte had offered to have the children, but Amy had refused. With Llew snatched away from her so suddenly and cruelly she wanted the comfort of their nearness, even if that comfort was no more than a myth and the responsibility of caring for them a trial. At least it made her stay sane. At least it forced her to continue with a life of sorts and for that Amy thought she should be grateful.

The nights were the worst, when she lay awake in the big empty bed with nothing to cushion her from her emotions or separate her from her thoughts ... the torture of wondering exactly what had happened, exactly how he had died.

It had been Herbie who had found him – Herbie who, although nominally on strike, was much too loyal to stay away from the yard for long. He had gone in to find Llew crushed beneath the lorry. Each time she thought of it Amy shuddered and a part of her mind clicked off, shutting down on the full horror. What she could not ignore, however, was the realisation that when she had looked down across the valley to the yard on her way to the shops, Llew was already dead. No wonder the yard had looked so still! The lorry, parked so innocently in the centre of the compound, had been hiding a terrible secret. The thought almost made Amy cry out aloud and she pressed her hands to her mouth, forcing it back inside her so that the pain made her writhe.

But at least she had not been the one to find him. Cowardly though she felt herself to be, she was glad about that. It was Barbara, whimpering for sweets, who had saved her from that. Instead Herbie had found him and the shock seemed to have turned him into an old man overnight.

'Whatever will you do, Mrs Roberts?' he asked when she next saw him, but his broken voice made her feel that he was the one who needed comforting.

'I don't know yet, Herbie. I haven't been able to think straight,' she replied simply.

The funeral was arranged for the Wednesday. Amy had been terrified that with the strike going on there would be nobody to bury him, but the minister assured her there would be.

'We wouldn't put you through that, Amy,' he promised, laying a hand on her shoulder. 'If I had to dig the grave myself, I'd see that the dead were decently buried.'

The dead. The words tore another hole in the defensive fog that surrounded her. The dead. That meant Llew, just as Sergeant Eyles had meant Llew when he had talked about 'the body' whilst making arrangements for the post mortem.

'Don't call him "the body"!' she had wanted to cry. 'He's not "the body". He's my husband!' But the fog had sealed her lips and she had said nothing.

The body. The dead. And to the frock-coated undertaker, 'the deceased'.

'You'll be wanting one of my very best oak coffins, I'm sure,' he said in his sonorous voice. 'There are sure to be a lot of people wanting to pay their last respects to the deceased.'

'Are there?' Amy had said, sounding small and lost.

She had hoped for a quiet funeral, where her grief would be private and she would be supported only by those closest to her. But Llew's family was almost as big and sprawling as her own and he had become quite a public figure in the short time since he had come to Hillsbridge. There would be a great many people anxious to attend his funeral.

On the Wednesday morning Dolly arrived to help Amy with the preparations for entertaining the mourners afterwards. She looked peaky, but Amy was too wrapped up in herself to notice. Together they made sandwiches, cut up slab cake and set out cups and saucers, with the big brown earthenware teapot that Charlotte had loaned her and which was always used for family occasions.

About midday the flowers started to arrive, daffodils and narcissi fresh-picked from the neighbours' gardens, and the family cross which Amy had ordered and a big, impressive wreath from Llew's family, both delivered by the local florist. Their perfume soon permeated the house, though it was not a pleasant scent, thought Amy, but the oppressive smell of funerals. Then, soon after the flowers, the relatives began arriving – Jack, her teacher brother who had driven up from Devon with Stella, his wife; Ted, scallywag and drifter, who still managed to be her favourite and who had come so as to ride with her in the front car; and Llew's parents and brothers and sisters.

'If they're going to go from the house, I reckon our Mam should too,' Dolly whispered to Amy as she sliced cold ham, so Jack was despatched to fetch Charlotte and Harry.

Llew's mother, always an emotional woman, was in floods of tears and soon she started everyone else off. Only Amy remained aloof in her tight little world.

'What are you going to do?' She was asked again and again and she could only shake her head.

'I don't know. I haven't had time to think. I don't know...'

The cars arrived, impressive black. Amy had been offered

the ornate, horse-drawn hearse, but had refused it in favour of the stark modern motorised one. Illogically, perhaps, she had always had a fear of horses and her vision of them bolting with the hearse behind them fitted too easily into her present nightmare world.

Then she was sitting in the front car with hands locked together, eyes misted, head bursting with unshed tears. Ted squeezed her arm, saying nothing, but remembering perhaps the girl he had loved and lost – sweet, innocent, tyrannised Becky Church – and the sense of sharing communicated itself to her for a moment before the fog closed in again... that fog which made her feel quite alone, no matter who else was suffering or had suffered as she was.

The road blurred by... people stopping to look, the men removing their hats as a mark of respect, the women lowering their eyes. Amy saw them but was apart from them. Just so had she ridden with Llew on their wedding day, she thought, her hand in his, heart bursting with pride because the people who watched her pass by knew she was now Mrs Llew Roberts.

But what a short time ago that seemed – like only yesterday! The knot of tears expanded in her throat, threatening to spill over into her eyes and she swallowed hard. Her pride would not allow her to let those people see her cry.

For the next half hour Amy was called upon to do a great deal of swallowing. She held her chin high as she followed the coffin into the handsome grey stone chapel, holding tightly to Ted's arm. She bit her lip until the blood came as the voices swelled in 'Abide with Me' and the minister extolled Llew's virtues and lamented his death. Then she was following the coffin again along the main street to the churchyard. There were people standing in groups under the swelling trees but she did not notice their faces, or see whether they were strangers or friends. She saw only dark, silent forms and averted her eyes, holding on tight to the tears.

Up the steep grey path between the green grass and the gravestones, the angels with outspread wings, the marble book pages. Some graves were overgrown, almost hidden by the new spring grass, others were neat and bright with splashes of colour from daffodils and tulips, grape hyacinths and narcissi. It was when she saw the freshly dug grave that she almost choked on her tears and her fingers gripped convulsively at Ted's arm.

I can't bear it, she thought. I can't watch them lower him into that... that hole!

Her eyes swivelled around in panic and she fought against the urge to turn and run, away from the staring people, the sympathetic and the merely curious, away from the flower-decked coffin, away most of all from that sickeningly deep hole in the ground. She fought and won and felt the fog close in once more, claustrophobic and yet oddly comforting, for there was no way her legs could carry her anywhere except slowly straight ahead whilst it weighted her down. And through it she heard the words of the burial service, too familiar to the older people present, sharply new yet an unintelligible jumble to Amy.

The coffin was lowered, the handful of earth scattered onto it.

'Ashes to ashes, dust to dust...'

And then it was over, the minister was saying something comforting to her and Llew's mother weeping again – everyone, it seemed, was weeping except her.

Perhaps they think I don't care, thought Amy, bewildered by her own composure that masked such a sea of bleak grief. Perhaps they think that...

But it didn't matter. Nothing mattered except getting home again to privacy and normality. No, not normality. Private it might be, but it would never be normal again. Home was a house which had gown to deserve that name because of shared plans and dreams, shared love. Home was a shoulder to lay her head on, arms to hold her and ease the tension out of her body. Home was someone to warm her, baby her, depend on her, yell at her sometimes, but most of all to *be* there. Home was where Llew was – but Llew would never be there again. He was in a box in a hole in the ground with a scattering of earth upon it. All that was left to see of him was a brass plate bearing his name. And soon even that would be hidden from view by six feet of dark, cloying earth...

Oh Llew, oh Llew, she thought, you've gone for ever and I never even kissed you goodbye. I was so mean to you and you walked out in anger. And now I can never put it right, never...

The tears erupted in her throat and she could contain them

no longer. As they gurgled into her mouth, eyes and nose she stood motionless with hands clenched, body heaving.

'Amy!' It was Ted, but she could hardly hear him above the roaring in her ears. 'Come on, Amy, it's all right.'

Her cheeks were drenched, her lips parted to let the sobs escape, but still she did not move.

'Amy,' Charlotte was beside her, her arms circled her daughter and for a moment, as if she were a child again, Amy laid her head against her mother's chest. But there was no comfort there now. Once Mam had turned mountains into molehills, but that was no longer possible. Now the mountains were real and Mam, like the rest of mankind, was only human.

Sobs tore at her throat and her whole body shuddered with pain. Like a swimmer with stomach cramp she wanted to fold up and in on herself but even in her grief something stopped her, some small, civilised safety-curtain that dropped over the screaming portion of her mind and urged restraint. Mam was on one side of her, Ted on the other, steering her away towards the path, making her turn her back on Llew's grave. She went with them obediently for a few steps; then halted, looking over her shoulder.

The coffin was out of sight now, but the mound of earth surrounded by flowers was still visible and for a moment it seemed to her as if Llew himself was there, standing beside the grave and looking after her with something like pleading in his eyes.

Pleading? For what? Amy didn't know. Grief was blinding her, making her deaf, muzzing her mind.

Sometime, she thought, I shall know what to do. And when I know I'll come back and tell you, Llew. I promise.

Then she gave in to the urgings of Ted and Mam and let them walk her away down the grey stone path.

*

For the Hall and Roberts families, May the twelfth was a day so steeped in sadness that it would be forever remembered as the day of Llew's funeral. But that was not the reason for it passing into the annals of history.

Nor was Llew's funeral the main talking point in the bar at the Miners' Arms that evening. And it was not the reason behind the long faces and subdued manner of the regulars.

'We've been sold out again,' Ewart Brixey commented and he spoke for them all.

At lunchtime that day, while the Hall and Roberts families were gathering to lay Llew to rest, the news had been given in a BBC broadcast: the TUC General Council had decided to terminate the General Strike that night.

'I told 'ee there was no dependence in 'em!' Stanley Bristow commented with gloomy glee. 'I told 'ee 'twas no good expecting 'em to stick with 'ee when the going got rough.'

For a moment there was silence in the bar, then Ewart put down his glass on the table with a crash.

'Well, one thing's for very sure. They won't break us that easy. They'll find the mining man is sticking out for his principles. And whether they support us or not, they'll learn there's a hell of a lot of fight left in us yet!'

Chapter Five

For as long as Harry Hall could remember, Whit Tuesday had been the day of the Labour Party Fete.

It was not the only fete in Hillsbridge – there was the Foresters' Fete, held in the Glebe Field each August, not to mention the numerous garden parties and 'treats' organised by the church and the various chapels. But for most people in Hillsbridge the only one that really counted was the Labour Party Fete.

'Are you going, Harry?' Tommy Clements asked him as they idly kicked a football along the Rank.

'Too true I am! The General Secretary of the Federation is coming here, isn't he? I should like to hear what he's got to say. And Owen Wynn-Jones is speaking too.' Harry was enthusiastic. Platform speakers were always a feature of the Labour Party Fete and although in the past Harry had thought them a rather boring necessity to be lived through before the fun could begin, this year it was different. With the strike going on, everyone was more than ready to listen to words of encouragement, a clarion call to further efforts and the hope of victory in the not-too-distant future, and to have the General Secretary of the Federation actually here in Hillsbridge was more than anyone would have dared hope for. And besides him, Owen Wynn-Jones was a name to be reckoned with, an influential and well-respected man in the Labour movement who had been adopted as the party's candidate for the next General Election in a constituency adjoining Hillsbridge.

'Hmm. It'll be a lot of hot air, I expect.' Tommy aimed a vicious kick at the football, sending it bouncing into the wall. 'But there should be a bit of fun afterwards. There's going to be a six-a-side football match played on motor bikes, I heard – a local team against six lads who work for the motor cycle factory in Bristol. And at least this year we'm getting in the recreation ground for free.'

'If we'd had to pay, there'd be a lot who couldn't make it,' Harry observed.

It was true. The first strike pay had been doled out that week, but it was little enough. As half-members Harry, Tommy and Reg were entitled to only 4s each a week and no one knew how long even that could go on. Funds were still very low from the last stoppage and it was rumoured they would only last another two or three weeks at most.

As the day of the fete approached, excitement mounted as it always did in the town.

'Labour Party Fete next week,' they said to one another in pub bars, shops and billiard halls. 'Let's hope the weather keeps fine.'

The murmurings stirred nostalgic chords in Harry, and casting his mind back he found himself recalling the anticipation of a small boy thrusting his fist deep into the sawdust of a bran tub in search of small, mysterious parcels wrapped in crinkly paper, the tooth-breaking crunch of toffee apples and the contentment of being carried home shoulder-high through the dusk, sleepy and happy. He even remembered – or *thought* he remembered, for the tale had been told so many times – the occasion when Charlotte had entered him in the Fancy Dress Competition dressed as a diminutive John Bull. He had hated every moment, refused to join in the procession and screamed so loudly he had had to be taken home early in disgrace.

But that was only one year out of many. Mostly the Labour Party Fete was something to look forward to – and Harry was certainly looking forward to it this year, and not only because of the celebrities who would be attending.

It had occurred to him that there was a chance Margaret Young, the girl he had met walking to school during the strike, would be there. More than a chance, if it came to that. With her father, George Young, being the secretary of the local Labour Party, it was almost a certainty.

The day of the fete dawned dull and heavy, but at least it was fine. The procession which was due to leave the Market Place at one o'clock began forming up soon after noon, and when Harry and the two Clements boys came sauntering down the hill to join in they found the Town Silver Band already playing, the banners hoisted into position and legion upon legion of working men – all attired for the occasion in the 'uniform' of their best caps and jackets – lined up behind them.

'Is Mr Cook here?' Harry asked one of those closest to him. During the week there had been some doubts raised as to whether the Federation Secretary would after all be able to come, as he had been taken ill at a rally in South Wales and was reported to be still unfit.

'Oh ah, he's here,' the older miner confirmed. 'Said he'd have to be on his last legs before he'd let us down. He's up the front of the band with t'other big-wigs!'

Harry did his best to spot Mr Cook and Owen Wynn-Jones, but with a thousand or more men assembled it just wasn't possible. They were hidden behind the banners and a sea of caps. And he could see no sign of Margaret either, but she was probably already at the field and awaiting the arrival of the procession.

At last they were off and Harry felt as if he would burst with pride as the massed miners followed the stirring notes of the cornets and trombones of the Silver Band across the railway bridge and into the long winding Frome Hill. Behind the men came a hundred and more children, all in fancy dress and riding – for the sake of the little ones – in decorated wagons. Harry had spotted Fred and Bob, Dolly's two little boys, amongst them – Fred resplendent in a pair of dyed bloomers and knee socks, masquerading as Sir Walter Raleigh; Bob, his brother, his chubby face surrounded by a rim of shaped yellow crepe paper, his body clad in green pullover and leggings, purporting to be a sunflower. Today they and all the other children were to be given a free tea by courtesy of the Labour Party, and Harry felt a new thrust of pride and warmth as he savoured the wonderful heady sense of unity.

With a crowd as big as this one, two platforms had been erected in the field and Mr Cook, the main attraction, was to speak on both of them in turn. Having been at the back of the procession, Harry and the two Clements boys found themselves facing the platform where Mr Cook was going to do his 'second house', but impatient though he was to hear him, Harry was secretly pleased to notice that while the other platform was being chaired by Tom Heron – the worthy, but rather dull miners' agent – 'his' platform included both George Young and Owen Wynn-Jones.

Digging his hands into his pockets and settling himself comfortably, feet apart, Harry looked at them both with interest. Two men could hardly have been more different. Owen Wynn-Jones was a short, squat man who made up for his lack of height by a head of luxuriant silver-grey hair, an impressive gold watch-chain strung across his ample waistcoated chest, and an undeniable 'presence', while George Young, father of Margaret, was a gaunt giant, a foot taller than the would-be MP though his shoulders were bent into a permanent stoop. Yet both exuded the same sense of purpose – that dynamic determination that was uplifting every man, woman and child in the field today.

'Comrades and brothers.' George Young, acting as chairman, had begun to speak and his voice, slow and vibrant, carried clearly through the hush that had fallen over the crowd. 'I can't tell you how delighted I am to see such a large crowd here today to meet Mr Cook, our General Secretary, and also Owen Wynn-Jones, a man who one day without a doubt will sit at Westminster and help to govern our country with far more wisdom and compassion than is being shown at present.'

'Hooray!' shouted someone away to Harry's left and when the general murmur of agreement had died down, George Young continued.

'This is a great day for Somerset. We are one of the oldest coalfields in the country and during our history we have seen many stirring times and fought on more than one occasion for better conditions for miners. As far back as 1756 the Somerset men rebelled against their intolerable conditions and from then on, from time to time, we have had to take action in order to improve our position. But throughout our history, I do not believe we have ever encountered such problems as we now face. Yet I am not downhearted. Everywhere people are expressing sympathy with our cause and expressing it in tangible ways. Just today we have heard of a cheque for £270,000 being received from Russia, so Somerset miners will again get some pay this week.'

His last words were lost in loud cheers and he raised his hand to silence them.

'We mustn't drown old Tom Heron. He's doing his best down the other end,' Harry whispered to Tommy.

'Now, brothers, I shall not go on any longer,' George was saying. 'I'm a man of few words, as you well know, but I'm going to introduce you to someone I know will move you greatly by his words. He's a courageous man, a determined man, with a strong sense of right and justice, and he is here to back us in our struggle. Brothers, I have the honour to welcome here a man who embodies all our hopes and the hopes of the Labour Party: Mr Owen Wynn-Jones!'

Once again the applause rang out, echoing like a thunder roll above the heads of the assembled men, interspersed with appreciative whistles.

A large, solid chunk of a man edged in directly in front of Harry, and as he shifted slightly to restore his view of the platform he felt a touch on his arm. Turning quickly, he was surprised to find himself looking into the smiling face of Margaret Young.

How she had got there he had no idea and didn't stop to wonder either. Quick colour was rushing into his cheeks. He had wanted to see her . . . now suddenly, all he could think of was that the last time she had seen him he was being frogmarched away between two burly policemen after the episode of the level-crossing gates.

'Oh, hello,' he said, trying to sound a good deal more nonchalant than he was feeling.

'Hello.' She had such a sweet smile, wide and natural, with hardly a hint of shyness. It lit up her small, even features, making her look even prettier than he remembered her, Harry thought. And today, of course, he was seeing her for the first time out of school uniform. The square-cut neck of her dress revealed a slender, creamy throat and a crop of tantalising freckles along the line of her collar bone; the apple-green georgette skimming down to a dropped waist accentuated curves the gymslip had hidden.

'That's my Dad,' she said proudly, nodding towards the platform.

'Yes, I know. He spoke very well,' Harry said.

'He was up half the night practising,' Margaret confessed. 'Mum says he's not what you would call a natural speaker. It doesn't come easily to him. But I suppose when you really believe in something...'

She broke off, putting a quick finger to her own lips. Owen Wynn-Jones had stepped to the front of the platform and a reverential hush had fallen over the crowd. Even before the first rolling Welsh exhortation he had them spellbound, the magic that emanated from his rotund person silencing even the most irrepressible amongst them. They had heard it all before, of course; there was nothing new in being told that their lot was a hard one, that they were owed more consideration, better money and better conditions by the coal-owners, and that the fight to get these – long and bloody though it might be – must and would result in victory. The sentiments had been expressed in every corner of the coalfield, in pubs and clubs, at rallies, on street corners and at tea-tables over the modest strike-fare of bread and dripping. But oh, to hear it expressed like this in the ringing tones of the born orator!

The hush was complete. Every man, woman and child was silent and listening, holding their collective breath. Not a chesty old miner coughed, not a baby cried, not a dog barked. Even the cow somewhere out in the Co-op fields – who had been lowing all day for her calf – was silent and the cuckoo which flew a ceaseless path of song in the valley through the months of early summer seemed to have taken himself elsewhere.

To Harry, standing there in front of the makeshift platform, it was the most uplifting experience of his life. Thinking back on it in later years he was able to take it apart, separating each facet, each tiny, sensuous part – the sun breaking through the clouds to warm his face, the fresh sweet smell of grass newly trampled underfoot, the ranker odour of body sweat, the occasional tingling heat spreading across his bare arms when Margaret brushed against him, the sound of

111

that deep resonant voice filling each dancing atom of sunlit air making it sing with the music of the valleys. But on that May afternoon he experienced it only as one intoxicating whole, one heady draught that permeated all his senses at the same time so that he felt totally at one with the universe, encompassed as it was here in the football field, and utterly certain that with unity such as this, and right and justice on their side, there was no way they could fail.

Too soon – far, far too soon – Owen Wynn-Jones wound up his speech, finishing on a glorious crescendo that seemed for a moment to take Harry's breath away. Then, as the applause began, he felt the sense of loss seeping in – a trickle that soon became a torrent. While the spell lasted anything was possible. He had even been a part of the group on the platform – one of the leaders, active for the strike, not just a part of the herd waiting patiently to be shown the way. Imagination? Maybe. Or maybe it was premonition, thought Harry as a small flame of excitement flickered within him, fanned to life by the cheering unity of the crowd around him. Maybe one day it would be him up there on the platform urging on the men, fighting for what was right. Owen Wynn-Jones and the others were special, of course – it seemed to him that if it were dark fiery halos might be seen glowing around their heads. He could never hope to be like them; even the thought would be pure sacrilege. But there were ordinary working men like himself who played an active part in the union or the Labour Party or both.

Strange how little he knew about either organisation, he thought. The union was something he had joined when he had been handed his first wages, the Labour Party was the organisation working people voted for in Hillsbridge and had done since the first candidate was fielded. But since he was not yet old enough to vote, that had not made any great impression on him.

Now the fervour that had been smouldering in him since the night of his father's illness flared again and the determination to do something concrete to assist the cause of the working man grew.

'Do you have anything to do with the Labour Party?' he whispered to Margaret.

She laughed softly and he felt the quick colour rushing to his cheeks again. What was funny – that he would be interested in politics? But a moment later he was reassured.

'Living in my house, it would be difficult to avoid it,' she explained.

'Yes, I suppose it would...' He tried to visualise what it would be like to have George Young for a father and failed. 'Your father talks a lot about politics, I suppose,' he said lamely.

'Oh, I wouldn't say that. Well, he does, but not all the time,' she defended. 'He likes lots of other things as well. Music, books...'

'Oh!' Harry was speechless. Music to him was a good old sing-song composed of music hall favourites, Sankey's sacred songs and modern ditties such as 'Chick-Chick-Chick-Chicken' with Charlotte at the piano. And books had come into the house with Jack and gone out with him. That anybody should list either as a favourite pastime was beyond him.

'We do get roped in though,' Margaret went on. 'We have people to stay sometimes. Owen Wynn-Jones came to dinner and I expect he'll come back for some supper too.'

'Will he?' The awe that Harry was feeling was reflected in his eyes and she giggled again, causing the large miner in front of them to turn, glare and 'Shush!' loudly.

It was Margaret's turn to colour, her face going very serious. Harry realised they had committed the heinous crime of talking and laughing while the Labour Party treasurer was following up Owen Wynn-Jones' rousing speech with a mind-bogglingly dull rundown on the facts and figures of the Distress Fund balance sheet – a definite anti-climax!

'Do you fancy going up in the swing-boats when this part's over?' Harry whispered.

Margaret hesitated. 'Oh, I'd love to, only... I'm supposed to be helping out on the pound stall. We've got to raise as much money as we can today...'

Harry shrugged. He didn't want to push himself.

'All right. Maybe I'll see you later.'

'Yes, maybe.' He did not recognise the tiny edge of disappointment in her voice. Already his mind was returning to the speeches, to the feeling of unity and the spirit of determination.

I want to be a part of it, thought Harry. I want it more than I wanted a winning homing pigeon, more than I have ever wanted anything. I don't want to experience this comradeship just once or twice in a lifetime – I want to live and breathe it – *be* it. And I want to do my bit, however small, to help the cause.

*

What breeze there was on that Whit Tuesday afternoon was easterly, and from time to time it wafted the sound of the cornets and trombones of the Town Silver Band towards Hope Terrace, where Amy Roberts was attempting to do some ironing in the kitchen of her home.

Each time she heard it, sharp shafts of pain penetrated the thick fog of her grief and she wished she could slam the windows and doors and shut it out. Like the rest of her family she had always gone to the Labour Fete and it held for her, as it did for Harry, memories of carefree days that now seemed to her to have gone for ever. But the thought of the stifling heat which would result if she did shut up the house around her was almost as unbearable as the nostalgic sound of the band, so she told herself: You have to put up with it. You have to get used to life going on without Llew.

The flat-iron she was using had gone cold and was no longer removing the creases from the pile of handkerchiefs and petticoats and pillow-cases stacked beside her on the kitchen table. With an effort she plonked it down on the grid of the gas stove, wrapped her iron-holder around the flat that was heating over the flame and changed them over. As she replaced the fresh iron on the table the holder slipped slightly so that her finger touched the hot surface and she gasped, setting it down and sticking her finger in her mouth to remove the sting. But the pain was enough to bring the quick tears to her eyes – tears that had seemed to be so close to the surface this last week that they flowed over at every opportunity.

Stop it! Stop it! she ordered herself, but it was too late and she crumpled over the ironing board, her hand stuffed into her mouth.

Dear God, it was like living a nightmare. At times it seemed to her that she would wake from it and see Llew coming in through the door, smiling at her, taking her in his arms, saying, 'You silly girl, Amy – you didn't really think I'd gone for good, did you?'

But almost at once the knowledge would come rushing in

114

again, sharply fresh because of the respite. Llew would *not* come through the door. Llew was dead. She had seen him buried. And as the pain spread and grew, it merged once more into the all-consuming black hopelessness. She was alone for all time. Somehow she had to keep things going for the sake of the children when all she wanted to do was to bury herself deep as Llew was buried, away from the sympathy and the curiosity and the well-meaning offers of help. Somehow she had to go on living.

Naturally, there had been many offers of help – so many she had felt swamped by them. The neighbours had all been more than kind, but they were also embarrassed and their embarrassment created an awkwardness from which Amy could not wait to escape. Eddie, Llew's brother who had once owned part-shares in the business, had called on a number of occasions, but because of remembered differences between the brothers Amy felt less than comfortable with him too – she felt, stupidly perhaps, that he was constantly critical of everything with Llew's mark on it, and consequently she resented him. Then there was always Mam. She had taken the children for a day or two and had asked Amy for meals, but Amy did not want to eat any more than most of the time she wanted to talk. Sometimes she felt like pouring her heart out, it was true – going on and on about Llew and that last day and how she wished she could have it again, just once, so that she could tell him how sorry she was for being spoilt and pettish ... put things right. But talking did no good. Maybe it eased the blackness inside her for just a little while, but it was still there – a thick impenetrable cloud waiting to stifle her again, so that after a while the words died in her throat and she would break off to stare, unseeing, into space.

To the best of her ability Amy had tried to hide these moods for the sake of the children, just as she tried to hide the shivering fits that overtook her from time to time ... and the tears.

It was the shock, Mam said, and Amy was lucky not to have gone down with 'flu. But like everything else, the explanation fell into the pool of blackness and sank like a stone. Words were just that – empty, meaningless, tiny rafts to cling to for a moment in the sea of grief but gone too soon, leaving her storm-tossed and rudderless.

Which were the worst? she wondered – the days, or the

nights? During the days she wanted most of all to be left alone, but when night fell and she got her wish she found that unbearable too. Oh, the emptiness of the bed she had shared with Llew! How could she ever have luxuriated in being able to stretch out in it when he came late to bed? Now the expanse of it swamped her and she felt like drowning in it. And the quiet when the children were asleep was like the quiet of the grave.

This afternoon too, the house was quiet. Ruby Clark from next door had taken Maureen and Barbara down to the fete where Mam was going to look after them for the afternoon and when it was time for tea, Ruby would bring them back again. Left alone, Amy had decided to attack the pile of ironing which had collected in her laundry basket. But 'attack' was the wrong word. She had no heart for it. Lifting the iron was an effort, laying a petticoat out on the table a chore that required more energy than she possessed.

I should be able to forget myself for a little while in sheer hard work, she thought, remembering how Mam at times of stress had been prone to taking down every curtain in the house and washing them with almost frightening thoroughness. But grief had not taken her that way. Instead she felt weak and useless and everything she did, she did in a dream.

Now, before the iron could go cold on her, she laid a pillow-case out on the ironing blanket and flicked cold water onto it from the bowl that stood at her elbow. This hot weather was all very well, but it did make the washing dry so rock-hard if you forgot to bring it in from the line in time. And this week, remembering washing was right at the end of Amy's list of priorities.

She had just finished the pillow-case when the front door-bell rang, making her sigh wearily. Who could it be this time? Someone who had noticed she was missing from the fete and had come to see if she was all right? Oh, why couldn't they understand she just wanted to be left alone!

She went along the cool dim hall, kicking the carpet 'runner' into place as she went, and drew the bolts on the front door. Then her lips parted in a small 'Oh!' of surprise.

Standing on the doorstep, his tall frame almost blotting out the sun, was Ralph Porter. As a concession to the warm afternoon, he had exchanged his leather jacket for an open-necked shirt with the sleeves rolled back half-way to the elbows, but he was still wearing the flying boots and glancing past him Amy saw the bright red of the Morgan drawn up at the gate.

For a moment, grief forgotten, Amy felt nothing but the same acute embarrassment she had experienced on the afternoon she had run into him with the lorry. It might have happened across the great divide, in another lifetime, but the emotion she felt now was just the same, pure and unadulterated – the shame of a wilful child who has caused some catastrophe through disobedience.

Then the memory of their sharp disagreement joined the others and she drew herself up.

'Yes?' she said shortly.

'Mrs Roberts.' Those dark eyes were disconcerting in their directness. He was not angry now, yet he still conveyed the impression of power – and something else. Yes. Arrogance. That was it. He stood there on her doorstep and somehow managed to look as if he and not she were the owner.

'Yes,' she said again. 'What can I do for you?'

One eyebrow lifted in an expression of sardonic surprise.

'I would hardly have thought you needed to ask that. I've been expecting to hear from you.'

'You've been expecting...' She had begun to tremble, but she stared at him in disbelief. Surely he could not be referring to the accident? Surely not even *he* would come here knocking on her door to ask about repairs to a motor car with her husband not buried a week?

'That's right. You caused considerable damage, which is going to cost in the region of £20 to repair. Your husband contacted me shortly after the incident and promised to put things right, but that's several weeks ago now and nothing has been done.' His tone was hard, totally emotionless and she gasped.

'Well, of course it hasn't!'

The eyebrow lifted a fraction once again.

'Really? Then it's as well I'm here, isn't it? I ought to warn you, Mrs Roberts, I could very well have put the matter in the hands of my solicitor, but initially I thought I would deal with it myself and save us both legal costs. Of course, if you're going to prove difficult...'

'How could you?' she cried. 'How can you be so callous?'

117

A muscle moved fractionally in his cheek above the dark moustache.

'I'm sorry you see it that way, Mrs Roberts. I hardly see how you can expect to go haring around causing damage to other people's vehicles and not paying for it, no matter what your financial position. And I'm afraid that, insured or not, I intend to have you reimburse me. I would have preferred to discuss the matter with your husband, but...'

'Oh, would you indeed?' she flared. 'I doubt that. You think you can bully me, I dare say. Well, it's no more than I would have expected. Llew always said what you were. It's just that I would never have believed that *anyone*...'

'I'm a businessman, Mrs Roberts. Sympathy is not an emotion in which I can afford to indulge. If you want to make a success of *your* business, you would do well to remember that and do the same.'

Her knuckles were white as she gripped the door frame for support, but for the moment her anger and sense of outrage were stifling all other emotions.

'I will probably do that, Mr Porter. But I sincerely hope I never stoop to hounding the bereaved. My God, if Llew knew...' She broke off, fighting back the sudden rush of threatening tears and as her eyes swam she saw his face change.

'What did you say?'

'You'll get your money, Mr Porter,' she rushed on. 'But if you need it so badly that you have to behave in this way, all I can say is I'm sorry for you. Llew might not have been as good a businessman as you. He didn't make provision for something like this - he didn't even leave a will. But he worked hard and he had standards. At least he could hold his head up without fear of being accused of grave-robbing.'

'My God!' His voice was low, shocked. 'You don't mean he's dead?'

In her throat hysterical laughter bubbled wildly and was suppressed. Ralph Porter, uncrowned king of Hillsbridge, pretending ignorance. Ludicrous - utterly ludicrous!

'You must have known, Mr Porter,' she threw at him. 'You were afraid, I suppose, that with Llew gone you wouldn't be paid. Well, you need not worry. You'll get your twenty pounds, I'll see to that. Now get off my doorstep. Go on! *Get out!*'

Then, as the tears welled up once more, she caught at the

118

door, slamming it shut. But as she leaned against it, his arrogant face seemed to mock her still and she crumpled, her fingers drawing long, painful streaks down the wood panels.

'Beast! Beast!' she sobbed – hatred, humiliation and grief all merging, blurring and then exploding so that she seemed on fire with them.

And then, as grief predominated and the tears drenched her cheeks: 'Oh, Llew – Llew! Why did you have to die! Oh, Llew . . .'

On the pavement outside, Ralph Porter stood for a moment looking back at the house.

Dead – Llew Roberts? He had been a healthy young man when he had come to see Ralph a few weeks ago. A little too plausible for Ralph Porter's taste, perhaps, but no one ever died of being too plausible. What had happened? Something, obviously, during the time that he, Ralph, had been in Sweden arranging new timber contracts. But what?

As always when faced with an awkward situation, Ralph Porter took refuge in the aggression that was barely hidden beneath the shallow layer of seeming indifference.

How the hell was I supposed to know anyway? he asked himself.

And turning, he climbed into the driver's seat of the red three-wheeled Morgan.

＊

At the football field the spirit of the Labour Party Fête was being revived for many by a quick half-pint of best bitter in the small marquee known on site as 'the beer tent'. During the afternoon the ladies had refreshed themselves with cups of hot weak tea, scones and fairy cakes, and the children had all been given a free 'treat'. Now it was the turn of the men to absent themselves in shifts from the proceedings. The fun of the motor-cycle six-a-side football match was over and dancing had begun, but few of them liked dancing – not until it was dark enough to waltz their partners under the trees for a quick kiss and cuddle, anyway.

Just inside the flap of the tent, Harry Hall was downing his beer with one eye trained to look out for his mother. She would be going soon, he guessed – Ruby Clark had taken Barbara and Maureen home and with nothing now to keep

119

her Charlotte's thoughts would be turning to James, left at home on the sofa that comprised his world these days. He could have waited until he had seen her disappear out of the gate before he began drinking in earnest, Harry supposed, for though she knew he did it Charlotte did not really approve.

But Harry had been unable to stifle the fear that his mother might ask him to accompany either her or the children – or even walk up to Dolly's to see how she was feeling. Charlotte knew now that Dolly was expecting again and privately was not too pleased about it.

'You'd think they'd have had more sense – at least until the boys are a bit less of a handful,' Harry had overheard her say to James. 'There's no need for it now, like there was in our day.'

But Harry knew her irritability stemmed from concern – Dolly looked so pale and puffy even *he* was anxious about her – and he was becoming used to Charlotte's exhortations to 'take this up to our Dolly, there's a good boy'. Usually he did not mind. The long days of the strike were dragging by and it sometimes seemed to him that life would be composed for evermore of days spent chewing the penny gobstoppers on sticks that were having to take the place of the cigarettes they could no longer afford, and nights of dodging the law to pick coal on the slag-heaps, or batches as they were known locally.

Today however he did not want to be despatched to check on either Amy or Dolly. He was far too keen to have his half-pint of beer in the small marquee within earshot of the men who were trying to set the world – and the mining industry – to rights. From his vantage point just inside the flap he listened, and tried to see if the dignitaries were imbibing in the beer tent too. Tom Heron was here, certainly, his slightly tremulous Somerset-cultivated tones carrying above the buzz of genuine dialect. Tom was a 'townie' who had made the coalfield his career, and he had had the good sense to adapt the way he spoke in order to gain the confidence of Hillsbridge working folk. In the early years he had lived in terror of being found out and the habit of taking out every word and looking at it was responsible for the slight hesitancy that was apparent now, even though his mode of speech was now second nature. Yes, Tom was there right enough, his glass being topped up again and again as he held forth on the rights of the miners' case; and so was Eddie Roberts, Amy's brother-in-law and another mustard-keen member of the local Labour Party. But of Owen Wynn-Jones and George Young, there was no sign.

Harry sighed, his ambitions temporarily frustrated. Eddie Roberts might be related to him by marriage, but Harry did not care for him. In Mam's words, Eddie was 'a bit too big for his boots'. As for approaching Tom Heron with his ideas about joining the Labour Party, Harry would as soon have entered a lion's den. Tom knew he was only a relatively new member of the Federation – as likely as not he would pat him on the head and tell him to come back when he had grown up a bit.

But if George Young or Owen Wynn-Jones had been there, Harry felt he might very well have taken his courage in both hands and spoken to one of them. Great men they might be, but their greatness somehow made them more approachable than someone who knew him more intimately.

Or perhaps they just seem more approachable because they're not here, Harry thought with a flash of insight. I just think I could speak to them because I don't have to put it to the test.

'Hey – Harry – we thought we'd find you here.'

Harry turned to see Tommy and Reg Clements slipping in under the awning.

'Yes, we saw your Mam just now and she said to tell you she's gone on home.'

'On the loose, Harry, on the loose! Have another half of bitter.'

Harry dug his hand into his pocket and pulled out his loose change. The beer in the tent was being sold at a special cheap rate, but even so he did not think he could afford it. Besides, now he knew the Labour Party officials were not here, the appeal of the hop-heavy, smoky air had lessened.

'Have you seen Owen Wynn-Jones on your travels?' he enquired.

The two Clements boys looked at him as if he had taken leave of his senses.

'Who?'

'Owen Wynn-Jones – who made the speech?'

'Oh, him.' The Clements' interest in politics was predictably negligible. 'What do you want him for?'

Harry coloured. 'Oh, I don't know, I just wanted to see

him again,' he said and their ribald laughter made him think; coming out into the political arena was not going to be as easy as he had imagined. They were all on the same side, yes, but at his age and with no background for it, no one was going to take him seriously – or if they did, they would probably think him, like Eddie Roberts, 'too big for his boots'.

'I think I'll have a walk round outside, anyway,' Harry said. 'Get some fresh air.'

They shrugged. 'Suit yourself. You'll know where to find us.'

'Too true I will,' Harry joked.

Outside the beer tent it was soft dusk. The band was playing for the dancing: 'Ramona . . . I hear the mission bells above$ Ramona . . . they're ringing out their songs of love . . .' and on the square of field lit by the carbide lamps couples were waltzing. Harry stopped for a minute to watch them and saw, out of the corner of his eye, a figure he recognised standing alone under the trees.

Margaret!

Dare he go and speak to her again, Harry wondered, remembering she had turned down his invitation to go in the swinging-boats? But then – nothing venture nothing gain, and he could not imagine her actually snubbing him.

Trying to appear nonchalant, he sidled up to her. 'Hello. Finished on your stall, then?'

She half-turned, smiling. 'Oh yes. We sold out a long time ago; we did really well.'

'Good. Money for the kitty.'

Her face went serious. 'How can you joke about it? My Dad says . . .'

'Where is your Dad?' he asked.

'He's gone home. And Mum. They had to give Owen Wynn-Jones supper and then he has to get back to Wales. He's got another rally there tomorrow.'

'Oh, I see.' Harry tried to think of something clever or appreciative to say, but words failed him.

Just think of it! Owen Wynn-Jones having supper at her house – sitting at the table where she sat! He looked at her with respectful eyes and it seemed to him she had taken on some of the glamour of the great man.

'Would you like to dance?' he said.

'Oh – I'm not very good. We have lessons at school, but . . .'

122

'I'm not very good either,' he admitted. 'And I can't see how you can dance properly on grass either. When we go to Madame Roland's classes, the floor is polished up with French chalk or something and the really serious ones wear special shoes.'

'Special *shoes*?' She sounded fascinated.

'Yes. They take them in a bag so as not to wear them out of doors.'

'Oh!' Her eyes narrowed dreamily. 'I wish I could go to Madame Roland's.'

Harry seized his opportunity. 'I'll take you if you like.'

'*Would* you?' She broke off, biting her lip. 'Oh, it's no good, I'd never be allowed.'

'Why not?'

'Well, for one thing I'm supposed to be concentrating on my exams so that I can matriculate. It costs quite a lot for me to go to the Higher Elementary.'

'He pays for you?' Harry asked, surprised.

'Yes. £4 7s 6d a term.'

'But I thought if you got a scholarship...'

'That it's free? Yes, it is. But I didn't! For one thing we missed the time for applying and for another, I'm not really that clever. But I do want to do well. I don't want to let Dad down. I mean – paying for a *girl*. So many parents say they'd do it for a boy, but girls only get married anyway.'

'That's true enough, I suppose,' Harry said, thinking of Dolly and Amy. Matriculation was all very well, but not really necessary in order to run a home and have babies. 'You can't study all the time though,' he pressed her. 'And Madame Roland's is on a Saturday night. You could always have a lie-in on Sunday morning.'

'Oh no, I have to go to chapel.' She spoke fiercely, with none of the resentment Harry himself displayed on the occasions when Mam put her foot down and said it was about time *he* put in an appearance in the family pew.

'I've never seen you in chapel,' he said, trying to impress her with his doubtful piety.

'That's because you're Methodists. We're Baptists,' she said and he was startled to realise how much she knew about him. 'Anyway, I don't think Dad really approves of dancing. It's supposed to be one of the devices of the devil.'

'Your Dad thinks that?' Harry was amazed.

'He's not really one to lay down the law, but I have heard it said. And I'll tell you something he definitely *doesn't* approve of,' she added with a sly twinkle, 'and that's strong drink. You smell of it!'

Harry's face was a picture. 'Oh, I didn't know – I only had a half...'

'You should sign the pledge,' she said. 'Turn teetotal. It does you no good, you know. It's a waste of money and people do really awful things when they've had too much to drink.'

'Well, I haven't!' Harry said indignantly, feeling he had somehow been put to the test and failed miserably. 'I can't see that just a drop does any harm.'

'Maybe not.' She tilted her head to one side like a bird and red-gold bobbed hair fell tantalisingly over the square of freckled chest. 'You asked me to dance just now.'

'Well – yes...'

'Then let's – or have you changed your mind?'

'No, of course I haven't!'

Feeling a little nonplussed now that the invitation had caught up with him, Harry led her across the rough grass to the square where the dancing was in progress.

Dusk was falling rapidly now; in the beams of light from the carbide lamps moths pirouetted and swirled in their own waltzes and tarantellas and the crushed-grass smell overpowered the last remaining scent of hops in his nostrils.

With slight awkwardness he took hold of her, one hand tentatively resting on her waist, the other holding her hand. Her touch in contrast to his own moist palm was cool, but he could feel the warmth of her body through the thin georgette of her dress. He took a step and trod on her toe.

'Sorry...'

'It's all right. As long as you don't scratch my shoes; they're new...'

'Oh – sorry... sorry...'

Never, he thought, had he apologized so often in the course of just a few minutes. And he was the one who was supposed to go to Madame Roland's dancing classes! But everywhere he moved his feet, hers seemed to be there first. And when he was not stepping on her toes, they were colliding with other couples. He couldn't enjoy the dance, couldn't even enjoy the contact with her. All he could think of was that she would consider him a clumsy, drunken oaf.

But rescue was at hand in the bulky, sweating shape of the

MC. The dance became an 'elimination waltz' and to Harry's enormous relief the first quarter of dancers to be instructed to leave the floor included them.

'That's the end of our chances for a prize, then,' he said, trying to sound regretful.

'Yes, and I think it's time I went home anyway,' Margaret replied.

Harry tried to marshal his thoughts quickly. Did she really have to go home or was she just trying to get away from him? Should he risk suggesting he walked her home – or was that asking for a put-down? He tossed it over quickly in his mind, embarrassment and fear of humiliation warring with the desire to stay with her and the attraction of retaining a link, however tenuous, with the politician who was having supper at her home. There was no contest; the combination of two kinds of romance was irresistible.

'I'll come with you if you like,' Harry said graciously. 'We don't live far away from you, after all.'

'But don't you want to stay and have another drink?' she asked.

'No, I told you I've had enough,' Harry said. 'But there will be men about who have had a drop too much. It's not out of my way. And I'd like to see you home – if you'll let me,' he added.

She smiled, the generous smile that lit up her face, making it especially pretty.

'All right. I can't argue with that, can I?'

'And I promise not to tread on your toes,' Harry said drily.

Away from the field there seemed little to talk about. Harry's mind was suddenly occupied by such burning questions as whether he should hold her hand. He decided against it. He did not want to scare her off and after all she might not really have wanted him to see her home at all – just been unable to think of a way to refuse the offer.

Tired as they were and not hurrying, the walk took them a quarter of an hour or so. As they passed the end of the Rank Harry looked along with some apprehension – he did not want to be seen by any of the neighbours. But those who were not still at the fete were safely inside their houses and there were no calls of 'Evening, Harry!' heavy with innuendo.

Past the end of the Rank they continued to climb. The road twisted with the curve of the hill, forking towards the front entrance of Captain Fish's house where Dolly had been in service and Victor was still employed as gardener, but they by-passed that turning and instead took the next, parallel to it and even higher up the hill.

The houses that followed the road here were terraced, but superior to the Rank. Many boasted porches, some had their own front gates too. But a cobbled right-of-way ran along the back of them just the same and Margaret led the way between the houses to reach it.

Half-way along she stopped. 'This is it, then. Thanks for seeing me home.'

There was a light in her kitchen window, but the curtains were drawn. Was Owen Wynn-Jones still here, Harry wondered, sitting at the table in that lighted kitchen, eating cold meat and cheese and pickle?

'What time will he be going?' he asked, before he could stop himself.

'Who?' she asked.

'Owen Wynn-Jones.'

'Oh, I don't know.' Her tone was cool suddenly. How could she be that disinterested? Harry wondered. If he had her opportunity, he would not miss a minute with the great man.

But the subject was closed and there was nothing else to be said about it.

She turned towards the door. The light caught her hair, making it molten gold and throwing shadows on the tip-tilted nose and wide mouth, and suddenly he forget all about Owen Wynn-Jones.

'Can I see you again?' he asked.

For a brief moment he caught her hesitation and his heart sank. She didn't want to! Then she nodded. 'Yes, all right.'

'When? Tomorrow? It's Whit week – you're not at school ... and I'm not at work ...'

'You mean go somewhere in the day?'

'Yes – why not?'

'Like a picnic?'

'Well, yes.' The thought hadn't crossed his mind, but it sounded inviting.

'All right. Three o'clock. I'll bring some food – you need not worry about that ...'

'We're not actually starving yet,' he said with grim humour.

'Oh – I didn't mean ...'

'No, it's all right...' It was like the dancing – they were treading on one another's toes, trying hard not to trip.

From inside the house a woman's voice called: 'Margaret? Is that you?'

She unlatched the door. 'I'd better go.'

'All right – goodbye, then.'

Briefly she was framed in the brightly-lit doorway, then she was gone. Harry stood motionless for a moment. What a day! This was a Whit Tuesday he would not forget in a hurry.

Chapter Six

May became June and dreamed towards July. No spirals or clouds of black smoke belched from pit chimneys to mar the clarity of the sky, and the wheels that raised and lowered the cages stood motionless, like matchbox models against the tranquil blue.

In the mornings and late afternoons the sunshine bathed the town in golden light, casting shadows first one way and then the other across the hoop of the main street and transforming the uniform greyness of grimy stone to a hypnotic cocktail of light and shade. It shone, too, through the leaves of the horse chestnut trees at the mouth of the New Road, freckling the pavement and the wooden seats where shoppers could sit and rest and watch the world go by; and it sharpened the paint-box colours of the flowers that bloomed in the neatly kept beds just clear of the shadow of the trees – geraniums, vermilion red; delphiniums, brightest blue; marigolds, burnt orange.

The grassed areas were still fresh and green, too. Not yet sullied by the black dust that blew from passing coal-carts, they still matched the steeply rising fields which provided a backdrop to the town.

But if the clear, hot weather was fulfilling the early

promise of a good summer, the promises that had been made in rhetoric from the platform at the Whit Tuesday Labour Fete showed no sign of being honoured.

'The Lord only knows where it will end,' Charlotte said as she settled James in a chair in the scullery doorway. 'I'm sure I don't.'

James grunted, but could not summon up enough breath to reply. Even with Charlotte half-carrying him, it was as much as he could do to totter to the back door from his permanent bed on the sofa in the living-room, but it was so stiflingly hot there, even with the windows thrown open and the fire banked in as much as possible in order to conserve what coal they had left.

'Another couple of bucketfuls and it'll be gone,' Charlotte said, checking the coal-house with a practised eye. 'Then I shall have to send our Harry up to the wood to see what stick he can find.'

'Well, at least we b'ain't in the cold o' winter,' James managed chestily. All his life he had looked for the best in a situation and he had not changed now, in spite of his infirmity. 'Worse things happen at sea,' was still the motto he lived by.

It was a maxim that irritated Charlotte at times, though she grudgingly admired him for it and had often relied on it for comfort during the thirty-four years of their marriage. Now she said shortly, 'If it was winter, maybe the strike would be over sooner. Weather like this, folk can do without coal.'

James wheezed again, unbuttoning the neck of his vest and laying his chest bare to the sunshine.

'I suppose we do have something to be thankful for,' Charlotte continued, sitting herself down on the wooden form outside the door and spreading her skirts to catch what breeze there was going. 'We have got a bit put by. But it's not so much people of our age I worry about. It's the young ones with families. Like our Jim. However he's going to manage if it goes on much longer, I don't know.'

'Like you said though, Lotty, we have a lot to be thankful for,' James maintained. 'At least he's the only one of ours in that position. We can do what we can to help him out a bit.'

Charlotte clucked impatiently.

'There's a limit to what we can do though. We could send him some nice fresh stuff out of the garden if we had it, but with you laid up I don't know what it will be like this year. Our Harry's got no interest in the garden at all, and I can't manage it on top of everything else.'

James' rheumy eyes went far away and Charlotte could have bitten her tongue. James had always loved his garden – it was breaking his heart now to see it 'going to rack and ruin', as he put it.

'Of course, there's talk of sending the children away while the strike's on,' she said, changing the subject. 'I told you about that before, didn't I? I saw Jim's Sarah down the street and she mentioned it. Our Alex and May would be eligible to go. But Sarah's not keen. Naturally she doesn't want them to.'

'Go where?' James had the sneaking suspicion he might have been 'snooging' when Charlotte had imparted that particular piece of news.

'Oh I don't know where – away,' Charlotte said vaguely. 'To stay with people who can afford to look after them, feed them properly and all that. Sarah says it's supposed to be marvellous for them – like a holiday really and with all expenses found. A fund has been set up to pay their train fares and everything – the Lady Something-or-Other Fund – but Sarah doesn't think it would be all it's cracked up to be and I must say I agree with her. I mean, what if they weren't well? The first person they'd want would be their Mam and how could she get to them? She couldn't. Besides, I wouldn't much like the idea of somebody else paying to bring up my child and I know that's how Sarah feels.'

'So they won't be going, then?' James asked.

'Well, I couldn't say. Alex is a big boy for twelve and he eats as much as a man. And our May's almost as bad. I don't know if Sarah will be able to afford any say in it. She's not very keen, though, I can tell you, and the children say they're not going anywhere at least until after the bun-fight.'

'A bun-fight, eh?' James put in. 'I hadn't heard about that.'

'Well, a tea anyway, in the recreation field, with sports and that afterwards.'

James shifted slightly in his chair. The effort made him wheeze again and when he recovered he asked, 'Our Harry will be mixed up in that, I suppose?'

'More than likely.' Charlotte stretched and got up. 'If you ask me anything, our Harry is one of the few you could say is enjoying this strike! He's out morning, noon and night with that girl, doing this and that for the Relief Fund. He's even been neglecting his pigeons. Well, not *neglecting* them, but not paying them the attention he used to. I tell you this, James, I'd like to know just what the attraction is!'

James nodded, but as usual refused to be stirred.

'Oh well, Lotty, just as long as he's happy...'

'Yes, I suppose so,' Charlotte agreed.

To be happy was after all the very best a mother could wish for her children, even if the path to happiness was totally beyond her understanding. And if Harry was happy, she only wished she could say the same about Amy.

Charlotte sighed. When you had children, you always had something to worry about. What was the old saying? When they're babies they're a weight on your arm, but when they're grown they're a weight on your heart. How true it was! You wanted to do your best for them and yet there were times when you couldn't reach them, when you just had to stay back and let them find their own way. This was one of those times for Amy. She had offered support, done all she could and been painfully aware it was nowhere near enough.

But she'll get through, Charlotte comforted herself. She's tough, is Amy, and maybe in the end she will be the better for it. But oh, the fire was painful, she knew, and it was agony for her too to watch Amy burn.

'Sometimes I feel so darned tired,' she said now, but James only shook his head thoughtfully.

'Worse things happen at sea, m'dear. Worse things happen at sea.'

*

Towards the end of June Ted Hall came home for a few days, breezing in almost unannounced and causing Charlotte to put on her thinking cap as to how to feed and sleep him.

'If only you'd let me know you were coming!' she chided him.

'Well, I can always go again,' Ted teased.

'Nothing you do would surprise me,' Charlotte returned and it was true.

Even as a boy Ted had been the scallywag of the family, always into some mischief or other. When he was twelve he had passed the labour exam and gone to work on the screens in Middle Pit, but it was not long before he was in trouble with the gaffer and he had been transferred to carting underground so that James could keep an eye on him. Then, when war had broken out, he had been quick to join the Somersets, fought in France and been taken prisoner. It was typical that he should have survived almost unscathed while his mates were falling all around him, Charlotte had always thought. The same guardian angel had saved him in a terrible accident underground and taken him out of a pub on the Strand minutes before it received a direct hit from a German bomb. But though he had come through the war with barely a mark on him, his good fortune had not extended to his personal life. On his release, he had come home from the prison camp to find the girl he had loved and left behind dead while he was still alive, and his revenge on the man he held responsible for her death had landed him in court on a murder charge.

Even now Charlotte shuddered as she thought of it. Ted was not the kind who gave his heart easily. He was too fond of the good times, of a drink and a cigarette, a day at the races or a night entertaining with the concert party in which he had been one of the leading lights. But he had idolised Becky Church and sometimes Charlotte felt sure he would never get over her.

True, he had for a while courted Rosa Clements from next door. Rosa, the illegitimate daughter of Walter Clements' first wife Ada and a travelling fair man, was a bewitching if – to Charlotte's mind – strange young woman, and though Charlotte did not personally like her she had almost hoped that Ted would settle down with Rosa.

Rosa loved him, it was plain to see, and always had done from the days when, as a scraggly child in torn petticoats and stockings stuck with burrs from the fields and woods where she spent so many hours, she had followed him everywhere. And in many ways they were two of a kind – both a little wild and unconventional. Yes, little though Charlotte cared for the idea of her son marrying the daughter of a gypsy – and horrified though she had been when for a while Rosa had turned her attentions to Jack, Ted's studious and quiet-natured younger brother – she had resigned herself to Ted and Rosa making a match of it.

But it had not worked out. Ted had drifted off, doing a dozen different jobs in a dozen different places – labouring on a building site in Cardiff, cleaning the windows at Bush House in London, working on a cockle stall at Weymouth – and Rosa had gone to the nearby village of Withydown where she worked (and lived in) at the little Post Office Stores. She and Ted were still in touch, Charlotte knew, and he went to see her whenever he was at home. But Charlotte despaired of him ever settling down. The wanderlust was in his blood now, and she could not imagine it ever leaving him.

Had Charlotte but known it, her doubts were all shared by Rosa herself.

You must be crazy, Rosa would tell herself as she sold stamps and envelopes, postal orders and glue. Crazy to go on hoping for him to change, crazy to be here, ready and waiting, whenever he takes it into his head to come and look you up.

But all the while she knew she *would* go on waiting for him, until the ends of the earth if needs be. She had loved him for too long – there could never be anyone else for her now.

Not that it's for lack of chances, Rosa consoled herself.

Even in this day and age, with too many of the young men dead in the war and too many women left hopeless old maids, Rosa had not lacked suitors. Her looks – dark sloe eyes in a narrow face which maturity had turned beautiful, and a body lissom yet curved in all the right places – made sure of that.

But Rosa did not give a fig for any of them. She had fallen in love with Ted when she was no more than a scruffy urchin and her feelings had never wavered. Even now she could picture herself as a child of twelve, watching from the window on the day Jim had married Sarah – her round-eyed wonder at the loveliness of the bride in her cream silk dress with orange blossom in her hair, and her swelling love for Ted, so fair and handsome as he rode in the horse-drawn wagonette with the rest of the Hall family. She had dreamed even then that one day it might be her turn to ride in the wagonette with orange blossom in her hair and Ted, scrubbed and handsome, at her side, and nothing had ever come along to match that dream.

In those days she had made spells to try to bring him to her, just as she had later made spells to keep him safe during the war and, to her undying shame, to send Becky Church away. She had been convinced in those long-ago days that she was a witch; knowing she was different from the rest of her family, it had been an explanation which had pleased and excited her, giving her a mystery that was all her own and raising her above the shame she might otherwise have felt. 'I'm a witch-child,' she used to say, as she went to the woods to pick onion flowers and mutter over knotted ropes. But that was one more illusion she had lost along the way. Charlotte Hall had told her the truth about herself – and her father – in a moment of anger. From that day on Rosa had never 'made a spell', though sometimes she thought with awe of the outcome of some of her efforts and wondered if it was possible that, witch-child or not, there might have been something in it.

And sometimes too she was prone to flashes of premonition. These came at the most unexpected of moments and usually concerned Ted. For instance, Rosa knew almost without exception when he was going to make one of his visits – an unscheduled entry into her world for a few crazy, wonderful days. There was no pattern to her 'feelings' as she called them; she just *knew* with a knowledge that went deeper than hoping and she would think: 'Ted's coming today,' or 'When I get home, there'll be a letter from Ted,' and the joy would sing in her veins like a bubbling, cascading mountain stream. And it did not matter that in a few days he would be gone again – for the time being this did not even enter her head. Rosa knew how to live for the moment, not spoiling it with anxieties about the future.

And at least he did keep in touch. Ever since she had gone to court and given evidence for him when he had been up on that dreadful murder charge – perjured herself, in fact – there had been a bond between them which surpassed mere physical attraction. She had known all the time that he was innocent, of course, but because of his loyalty to Becky he had refused to give the evidence which would clear him; with that same unfailing intuition, she had also known that he would be found guilty unless someone did something to save him. She had been that someone and had gladly traded her reputation for his freedom. She had done it without hope of gain, simply because she loved him, and the relationship that had grown between them had been a bonus. She had even allowed herself to hope it might deepen and develop. But Ted had still been too unsettled by Becky's death, too restless. The grief had driven him away and now, five years later, he seemed no nearer settling down than ever he had.

But at least, Rosa consoled herself, he had not settled down with anyone else either. Whether there were girls in the towns where he worked she neither knew nor wanted to know. Her only concern was that when he came home it was to her, and the meetings were explosive and rewarding, enough to satisfy her until the next time – and the next. Between whiles she went on with her own life, as she was doing that June afternoon when she had the sudden joyous feeling that Ted was near again.

Was she right? The singing in her veins told her she was and as she served and counted returns she felt alert and alive, looking up quickly and eagerly each time the doorbell jangled.

It was almost closing time when he came. She glanced out of the window and saw him standing on the road outside, lighting a Woodbine. The sun was catching his fair hair and turning it to molten gold and her heart turned over, setting her whole body a-tingle. It was all she could do not to run to the door and call his name, but somehow she controlled herself, waiting as she always did for him to make the move and come to her.

When at last he came in she looked up with a smile, feigning surprise.

'Ted!'

'Rosa! How are you doing?'

'Fine. What are you doing home?'

'You sound like my mother! She almost showed me the door.'

'I'm not surprised. You love to give people shocks, don't you?'

'Only nice ones, I hope. Busy?'

'So-so. Nobody seems to have any money to spend these days. We shall be closing soon.'

'Good, I hope you haven't any plans for afterwards.'

'None that can't be scrapped. What did you have in mind?'

'You want me to tell you now?'

'Perhaps you'd better not,' she laughed.

'We'll go for a walk and I'll tell you then.'

'Sounds good.' Her heart was singing so that she could hardly speak. He waited while she packed up, leaning against the counter, and she could feel him watching her. He was as pleased to see her as she was to see him, she knew.

Perhaps this time, she thought. Perhaps this time it will be different.

In the fields above the village the grass was long, but not yet overgrown, filling the air with the sweet, fresh smell of summer. Because of the strike it was not tainted by pit smoke, but as Ted and Rosa climbed they saw white puffs of steam rising from a train on the railway embankment to merge with the fluffy clouds in the blue sky above.

The feel of the country she loved so much fused with the happiness of having Ted home once more, and there on the sloping field Rosa pirouetted.

'Careful, you'll fall!' Ted warned with a laugh, but she was sure-footed as a mountain goat. He reached for her; she twisted out of his reach. The early summer sun had already darkened her olive skin to a rich, blackish brown and the tanning enhanced the slimness of her legs and arms and made her eyes shine black as bits of newly-hewn coal; she looked to him like a bewitching stranger.

'Come here, Rosa,' he said, his voice thickening though he was still laughing.

'Why?' She twirled away again but this time he shot out a hand as she passed, grabbing her slender wrist.

'Got you!'

She laughed again, delight gurgling in her throat, but as he pulled her close the laughter died and the quick, flaming magic lit her body to trembling awareness.

'Rosa Clements, has anyone ever told you you're beautiful?' His mouth was close, his eyes smiling into her.

She tossed her head, her lips curving, teasing him. 'What do you think?'

'*I* think you're beautiful.'

He kissed her and they stood for a moment pressed close so that the shadow they threw on the sunlit field was of one, not two. Then slowly they sank until they were kneeling, then lying in the fragrant, scratchy grass.

Beneath his touch her body was soft and yielding, her breasts thrust with a sigh into the cup of his hand, her legs parting at the caress of his fingers. Her thighs were as smooth as her breasts, giving pleasure that drove out pain and her lips clung to his with the desperation born of weeks, months of waiting and longing. As he took her she moaned, deep in her throat, but it was as soft as the wind in the grass and as her body rose to meet the thrust of his the tide ebbed and flowed between them, waves breaking gently on a beach at the start, then building to the cacophony of the deepest, most tumultuous ocean.

She sobbed at the end, unwilling to let him go, wanting to hold him within and around her, but after a few moments he rolled away to lie beside her, and though the sun was warm on her face and on her bare arms and legs it did nothing to diminish the chill of loss.

He had gone from her already. She knew it even before they began to talk quietly, conversationally, like two friends rather than lovers. And she felt the sorrowful shaft of parting even before he confirmed he was leaving again the next day to look for seasonal work in one of the South Coast resorts.

But Rosa knew better than to let her feelings show. Frighten Ted off and she might lose him forever. What they shared was too precious for her to risk destroying it.

For the present, it had to be enough.

*

In years to come when she looked back on the summer of 1926, Amy Roberts was able to see it not only as a time of grief in her life and things coming to an end, but also as a time of new beginnings.

'I expect you were under the planet Uranus,' Dolly – who had become interested in 'the stars' when she and Cook worked together for Captain Fish – told Amy one day when they were reminiscing. But at the time, such frivolity was far from Amy's thoughts. There was simply no room for it, even if it had been in her nature to interest herself in what she privately dismissed as nonsense.

As the first numbing grief and disbelief began to disperse a little, allowing periods of coherent thought, Amy realised that there was far more to Llew's death than simply a personal tragedy.

There was the legal side to be sorted out, for foolishly Llew had never got around to making a will, and there was the business to plan a future for.

It was Eddie Roberts, Llew's brother, who first raised the subject of the business with Amy.

'Have you thought what you're going to do with it?' he asked her.

She looked at him blankly.

'The haulage business,' he said, speaking slowly as if to a child. 'Llew rented the yard, there are two lorries and a couple of employees who have to be paid. Something will have to be done about it.'

Get rid of it? Was that what he was saying? A muscle tightened in Amy's stomach. Oh, she never wanted to see the yard or the lorry again, it was true. For the rest of her life, she felt, she would continue to relive the nightmare of that morning whenever she looked down across the valley to the quiet spot where Llew had died. But get rid of it? It was Llew's creation. He had lived and breathed it, built it up from nothing by his own endeavours, died for it in the end.

'Amy?' Eddie was looking at her with those eyes that were exactly the same colour as Llew's, yet somehow managed to have a slightly cunning glint to them.

'I don't know,' she said impatiently. 'I can't think yet. Give me a chance, for goodness' sake, Eddie.'

'All right, all right!' he soothed her. 'We'll say no more about it for the moment. But the best thing you can do is to go and see the solicitor as soon as possible – put everything in his hands.'

Amy nodded dumbly. That was the only thing she could do, she supposed.

'Shall I make an appointment for you with Mr Clarence?' Eddie pressed her.

Amy hesitated. She was not fond of Arthur Clarence. He was fussy and frowsty and his office intimidated her. For a moment she thought wistfully of Winston Walker, who had helped Ted when he had been charged with murder. But Winston was a barrister, not a solicitor, and anyway she had not seen him for years. No, if she needed a solicitor it would have to be Arthur Clarence.

'I'll make the appointment. and I'll pick you up and run you down to his office in the car,' Eddie went on.

'Thank you,' Amy said flatly, wishing that Eddie would leave her alone. She disliked him calling on her and poking his nose into her affairs, but it seemed ungrateful to say so, especially when he was offering not only his support but also the services of his smart new Model T Ford which was grand enough to be confused with the doctor's.

'I'll be in touch then, Amy,' Eddie promised and when she had seen him to the door, her thoughts returned briefly to what he had said about the business.

137

She would have to come to some decision, she supposed, if only for the sake of Herbie and young Ivor Burge. They had not been paid since Llew's death and they wouldn't go on working for nothing for ever. But she couldn't think about it now, she *couldn't*.

Next day Eddie Roberts was back, tapping on the back door and letting himself in. Amy was upstairs making the beds and when she heard someone in the kitchen and came hurrying down, she stopped dead for a moment to see him there, for in the light blue suit that was identical to Llew's he looked so like him it might have been his ghost there in the kitchen.

Then, as the first shock subsided, Amy felt a stab of annoyance. What right did he have to come barging into her kitchen? She could have been undressed and washing at the sink for all he knew.

'Oh, Eddie – I thought you were a burglar,' she said coolly. 'What are you doing here?'

The irony was lost on Eddie as he leaned his tall frame comfortably against the stone sink.

'You'd better get changed. You're going to see Mr Clarence in half an hour.'

'I am?'

'There was a free appointment and so I grabbed it. The sooner you get things moving the better.'

'Yes, I suppose so. It's just that...' She floundered and hated herself for it. She was not usually like this – so weak and indecisive. But Llew's death seemed to have knocked all the stuffing out of her.

'What about the children?' she asked. 'Can we take them with us in the car?'

Eddie's face fell. 'Couldn't they go with one of your neighbours? If you have to wait a bit they'll get bored and get sticky fingers and dribble all over my seats...'

'All right, I'll see,' Amy agreed meekly.

It took the best part of twenty minutes to change her dress and tidy her hair, make arrangements for Barbara and Maureen to go next door with Ruby for an hour and lock up the house. As she pulled the front door shut behind her and walked down the path, Eddie looked impatiently at his watch.

'I'm sorry, Eddie, but I couldn't come any faster,' she apologised.

'It's all right. Just as long as we don't keep Mr Clarence waiting. And I don't want to have to push the engine too hard,' Eddie said, omitting to mention that from Amy's house to Arthur Clarence's office was all downhill.

The solicitor's office was on the first floor above one of the shops in Hillsbridge's main street and as she climbed the steep flight of stairs Amy was feeling unaccountably nervous. It did not help when, perched on a hard chair in the glorified cupboard that served as a waiting-room, she heard him muttering to his aged clerk about the problems of intestacy. And when at last she was facing him across the large, leather-topped desk with its litter of musty, pink-tape-tied files, his unsmiling expression – 'fit to turn the milk sour' as Mam would describe it – did little to restore her flagging confidence.

'It's a great pity Mr Roberts did not make a will,' he said accusingly. 'Things are so much easier with a will.'

'I don't suppose he expected to die yet awhile,' Amy apologised, her voice made tart by nervousness. 'You don't, do you, at twenty-six?'

Arthur Clarence fixed her with a disapproving stare.

'We none of us know when our time is going to come, Mrs Roberts. That's the point. And if we are only *prepared* . . .' He broke off, nodding and sighing both at the same time. 'Ah well, it's no use crying over spilt milk. What is done is done – or rather *not* done. Now you wish to apply, I understand, for Letters of Administration.'

'Do I?' Amy said helplessly.

'That's the procedure when there is no will. The estate will have to be divided up according to the intestacy rules. In order to set all this in motion I shall need all the relevant documents – deeds of the house, insurance policies, investments of any kind, accounts . . . Have them delivered to me and I can get things moving. There is really no need for you to bother your pretty head about any of it. In fact, I'm sure if you allow him, Mr Edwin Roberts will go through everything with you.'

Amy bristled, not liking the thought of anyone poking through Llew's ledgers and correspondence – certainly not Eddie. 'That won't be necessary,' she said coolly. 'I'm sure I can manage.'

'Well, yes. I simply thought that as he will be taking over the business . . .'

Amy's eyes widened. 'I beg your pardon?'

'The business. Mr Edwin Roberts will be running it once everything's settled...'

'Whatever gave you that idea?' Amy demanded.

'Well, I naturally assumed... a thriving business... you would want to keep it in the family...'

'Yes, that's true enough...'

'And Mr Edwin Roberts does some experience with haulage. Weren't he and your late husband partners at the outset? I should have thought he would be the ideal person...'

Amy's surprise was turning to anger. She thought of Eddie bamboozling her to see Arthur Clarence, making the appointment, barging uninvited into her kitchen and now sitting smugly outside in his precious Model T Ford while the solicitor outlined the best course of action to her – that her brother-in-law should take over the business Llew had worked so hard to build – Eddie, whom Llew had bought out because they could not agree on how things should be run. He had put Mr Clarence up to this, not a doubt of it. No wonder he had been so keen to get her here!

'No, Mr Clarence, I don't want Eddie involved,' Amy said. 'And he certainly won't be running the business.'

Her tone held echoes of her old, firm manner and Arthur Clarence pressed his fingertips together disapprovingly.

'Well, Mrs Roberts, you will need someone.' His lips curled slightly. 'You surely don't propose running the business yourself?'

It was an attempt at dusty-dry humour, but Amy was fired up now by outrage. Oh, it hadn't taken long, had it, for the vultures to move in? First Ralph Porter, then Eddie – even Arthur Clarence in a way, hoping to profit from the fact that she was a woman alone. Well, if they thought they were going to walk roughshod over her, they were very much mistaken.

Amy stood up.

'Run the business myself? Do you know, Mr Clarence, I might do that. Yes – I think I just might!'

When she emerged from the glass-panelled door at the foot of the stairs and saw Eddie smirking at her from the driver's seat of the Model T Ford, Amy experienced an urge to kick both him and the car. How dare he try to worm his way in like this?

She marched around and got into the passenger seat.

'Don't start the engine for a moment, Eddie,' she ordered.

'Why? What's wrong?' He was still smirking.

'Mr Clarence had the idea that you would be taking over the business. I don't know where he got it from, but I assured him he is quite mistaken.'

As she spoke she saw Eddie's face change. Guilt was written all over it and a dark flush was spreading upwards from his neck.

'I'm sure I don't know what you're getting at, Amy,' he protested.

'Don't you? I think you do,' Amy said. 'And I want to put you straight about my intentions. The business was Llew's baby, Eddie. You know what he put into it as well as I do – and in the end it cost him his life. Well, it's mine now – or it will be when all the legal stuff has been attended to. And I intend to do my best to keep it running – my way – the way Llew would have wanted. Is that clear?'

The dark flush had receded in Eddie's face now and he had turned very pale. For a moment he sat very still, saying nothing. Then his mouth hardened.

'Supposing it isn't all yours?'

'What do you mean?'

'All the business really consists of is a rented yard, a certain amount of goodwill and two lorries. Now if one of those lorries or even part of it was mine...'

'Don't be absurd!' Amy snapped.

'Llew died without leaving a will,' Eddie said. 'His estate will have to be divided up amongst his family.'

Amy was going cold with horror. 'I don't believe you! I'm his wife!'

'And I'm his brother.' The smirk was back on Eddie's face. 'Parents, brothers, sisters, they all get a mention. It's the law.'

'I don't believe you!' Amy said again. 'I'm going back to see Mr Clarence!'

Eddie looked at his watch. 'I can't wait, Amy. If you want a lift home...'

'I don't, thank you! I wouldn't ride in your car now if it meant I had to walk to Bath and back!' She opened the door, flouncing herself out. 'I'll fight it, Eddie. Don't worry about that!'

But as she flew up the stairs again she was almost weeping with anxiety. Supposing it was true and all Llew's family were entitled to a share? There were so many of them – brothers and sisters, mother, father...

Dear God in Heaven, there'll be nothing left for me and the children! Amy thought in panic.

At the top of the stairs she was intercepted by Josiah Horler, the aged clerk.

'Can I see Mr Clarence again, please?' she asked.

'I'm sorry. Mr Clarence has another client with him.'

'When they've finished, then?'

'Mr Clarence has a lunch appointment...'

'But I wouldn't keep him a moment!' Amy pleaded.

Josiah Horler regarded her disapprovingly. Flighty young girls in the office – what were things coming to?

'You can wait if you wish, but I can make no promises.'

'Oh, I'll wait!' Amy assured him. 'I'll wait if it takes all day!'

The next hour, it seemed to her, was the longest of her life. One client left, another was ushered in and still Amy sat on the hardbacked chair, shaking with horror as the enormity of the situation if there was anything in what Eddie said came home to her.

What will I do? Whatever will I do? Oh, they wouldn't take it, surely – not from his children even, if they'd take it from me? But Eddie would, he's just out for his own ends. And the others? I don't know. They're a funny lot... Oh, whatever would I *do*?

At last she could bear it no longer. Mr Clarence's door was still firmly closed, but she could see Josiah Horler bent over his ledgers and she went up to him.

'Mr Horler, do you know anything about the rules for when someone dies without making a will?'

He sighed at the interruption, but she saw him swell a little with pride all the same.

'Well, of course I do. I've been here, for the past forty years, Mrs Roberts. What is it you want to know?'

'How is the estate' – the word stuck in her throat – 'how is the estate divided up when there's no will? Amongst the family, I mean?'

Josiah's thin lips curved with a smile.

'The surviving spouse is entitled to the first thousand pounds free of duty, and to a life interest in one half of the remainder. The second half of the remainder is shared by the issue – the children of the deceased – immediately, and the

142

first half of the remainder on the death of their mother. If one of the children pre-deceases the parent...'

'No – no. I don't want to know about that,' Amy said impatiently. 'What about the rest of the family? Are they entitled to a share?'

It seemed to her another hour before he answered, but there had never been a more welcome sound than the precise crackling of his voice.

'Oh no. Not where there is issue...'

She could have kissed him.

'Oh thank you, Mr Horler – thank you!'

She ran down the stairs and into the sunlight. But as the relief faded into the commonplace, Amy realised just how angry she still was that Eddie should put her through this on top of everything else.

I never liked him, she thought, though I couldn't really be sure why. Now I know. Because beneath that plausible, hail-fellow-well-met is a selfish schemer. He doesn't care who he treads on to get his own way. Well, if he thinks he's going to get the better of me, he's got another think coming!

Before going home, Amy went to the little flower shop in South Hill and bought a bunch of flowers. Then she walked along the street to the churchyard.

Amongst the others, Llew's grave still looked fresh and new. Amy took the dead flowers out of the small pot she had placed there and refilled it with clean water and the fresh flowers. Then she sat back on her heels.

'Your Eddie's a rare one,' she said silently, as if holding an unspoken conversation with Llew. 'But don't worry, he won't get a penny of your money. And he's certainly not going to poke his nose into the business. I won't let him.'

And the voice came back, loud and clear as if he was standing right behind her: 'That's right. Mind you don't.'

A smile curved Amy's lips and she closed her eyes, feeling for a moment his presence all around her.

When she opened them again she remembered how she had looked back at the grave the day they had buried him. He had seemed to be standing there that day watching her go and pleading with her to do something – at the time she had not known what it was.

Now, suddenly, she was totally sure.

When she had told Arthur Clarence she would run the business herself it had been an automatic angry reaction – a way of hitting out. But it should have been more than that. Keeping on his business was what Llew wanted her to do. How she would do it, heaven alone knew. But at least she was going to try. And doing so would help to fill the empty place that he had left in her life.

Straightening up she blew a kiss at the grave, turned her back and set out for home.

During the next weeks Amy found herself almost too busy to grieve. She had fewer offers of help now – the novelty was beginning to wear off a little – and she found herself rushing madly to look after the children and get all the household chores done each day so that she could return to the task of sorting Llew's papers for anything that had to go to Arthur Clarence. At home, at the bottom of his shirt drawer, she found the papers relating to the house, together with the details of an insurance policy he had taken out on his life; in the shed at the yard that served as an office were copies of contracts, bills, invoices and all the documents relating to the lorries.

'Everything all right, Mrs Roberts?' Herbie asked when he looked in to see her absolutely swimming in it and she had sighed, running fingers stained with blue paper through her hair.

'Oh, I don't know, Herbie – it's all double-dutch to me.'

'Well, ah – I'm sure it would be to me too,' Herbie agreed blandly.

'If only he had let me help more, I'd understand it better,' she complained.

But Llew hadn't. He had wanted to do it all himself.

As Amy worked, Herbie hung around dutifully until eventually, in exasperation, she told him to go. He was a nice old stick, totally reliable, but she just couldn't work with him looking over her shoulder. Since she had told him she intended keeping the business on and asked him if he would continue to work for her, he seemed to think that part of his duty included mounting a permanent guard at her elbow. She would have to discuss it all with him in time, of course – how they were going to manage, whether they needed to take on another driver or mate, all the questions that Herbie, who had worked with Llew, would be much better qualified to answer than she was. But for the moment the most important thing was getting everything up together so that the grant of administration could be applied for.

The annoying thing was that every time she thought she was getting through it, another batch would arrive. Bills fell merrily through the letter box to lie on the mat alongside letters of condolence. And one day there was a letter addressed to Llew amongst them that struck her as being vaguely familiar. She stared at it for a moment, wondering why it was striking chords in her memory. The pale, creamy-yellow envelope addressed in a rounded, childish hand; the postmark, thick black and smudged but decipherable as Glamorgan... yes, of course, that was it! This was identical to the letter she had picked up from the bedroom floor on the morning of the accident – the letter he had snapped at her over: 'That's mine!'

She sighed. It was a bill, she supposed – someone else to whom Llew had owed money. That was why he had been so anxious to take the other letter away from her no doubt – he had not wanted her to know just how much money he owed.

But somehow the writing did not look very businesslike – and neither did the envelope, if it came to that...

'Mammy! Mammy! Maureen's spilled her milk!' The cry from the kitchen was loud and urgent and Amy ran to answer it.

Maureen certainly had spilled her milk – it was everywhere... in the butter, swimming on the bread plate, soaking her dress, her high-chair and the mat. So it was going to be one of those days!

Amy put the letter down on the window sill above the sink and set about clearing up the mess. The washing-up water had gone cold and she boiled the kettle to warm it up again. Then, when she had mopped up the worst of the milk she took Maureen upstairs to change her. When she came back to put the dress to soak before the milk turned sour and began to smell, she found that the letter had blown out of the window sill into the bowl of washing-up water below. Cursing, she pulled it out, but it was completely waterlogged and the ink had blurred into one massive smudge. Whatever it had said was no longer readable. Oh well, if it was a bill, whoever had sent it would just have to do so again, thought Amy. And if it wasn't a bill well, that was too bad. She had no time to worry about it. This morning she had another appointment with Arthur Clarence and if she didn't get a move on she would be late.

Somehow, however – mostly by managing to do two

things at the same time – she got there on time, running up the steep stairs to the solicitor's office just as the town clock was striking the hour.

'Ah – Mrs Roberts!' Josiah Horler had been noticeably nicer to her since she had asked his advice about the intestacy rules. 'Mr Clarence is expecting you, isn't he?'

'Yes,' said Amy, a little out of breath, and a few minutes later she was installed in the client's chair facing Arthur Clarence across the big, untidy desk.

'I think we can safely say everything's tied up now,' he told her with a satisfied smile. 'And you will be glad to hear that things have balanced out relatively well. If you would care to have a look at this statement . . .'

He pushed a sheet of paper towards her across the desk and Amy looked at it attentively while he explained in great detail every item listed on it.

The gist of it, she thought, was fairly straightforward, if Arthur Clarence had been able to make anything straightforward instead of wrapping it up in legal jargon.

The mortgage on the house had been paid off automatically on Llew's death and an insurance he had taken out on his life had covered the cost of the funeral and the outstanding payments on the lorry with a little to spare. By the time all the bills and expenses had been paid, the accounts more or less balanced. But to expect there to be a cash residue was over-optimistic.

'I hope there are no more bills outstanding,' Arthur Clarence said gravely. 'The margin is very narrow. Though of course there are assets that could be sold should the need arise.'

He meant the lorries, Amy assumed with a falling of her spirits. And there could be other bills to meet – the letter that had fallen into the washing-up water being one example. And there was still Ralph Porter to pay; she hadn't mentioned him to Arthur Clarence. Pride had prevented her, besides which she didn't consider that debt to be Llew's. It was hers, incurred by her own foolishness, and she had made up her mind she would pay him herself out of whatever money came to her.

Now, with a sinking heart, she realised there would be very little of that. And quite honestly she did not want to keep him waiting any longer.

She pondered the problem as she walked back up the

hill. Since she did not have the wherewithal to pay him, she would have to find it from somewhere. Was there something she could sell? Not the business assets – to get rid of them would make it that much more difficult to keep things going, as she was now determined she should. No, something private – something she could manage without...

Mentally she began an inventory of her possessions and realised just how little any of them were worth. To her, invaluable – but on the market, just so much second-hand junk. The only thing of value she owned was her engagement ring.

As it first flashed into her mind she dismissed the very thought. She could not possibly sell her engagement ring; it meant far too much to her. But as she considered and rejected every other possibility, it came back to nag her again and again.

The ring was worth money. It was antique – Llew had told her it had been left to him by an old lady for whom he used to run errands.

'She was a funny old soul,' he had explained. 'She always promised she would let me have it for the girl I'd one day marry. I thought at the time she was off her rocker, but I suppose she had this romantic streak – and no one else to leave it to.'

Amy had always thought it a lovely story and had enjoyed picturing the old lady and the notions she'd had to do her best for the bright and willing lad who had brought pleasure and company into her last lonely years. And the ring was certainly something to treasure – a ruby set with diamonds that seemed to hold in its warm red depths a reflection of every one of her happiest and most precious memories.

Before collecting the children from Ruby next door, Amy went upstairs and opened her jewellery box. Amongst the other worthless trinkets the ring glowed warm, bright and comforting. She took it out, remembering the day Llew had placed it on her finger. The future had stretched before them then, full of promise and pride and happiness had sung in her veins until she had felt she could burst with them. But how short that future had been!

The sharp ready tears thickened Amy's throat and she swallowed at them angrily. Crying would do no good; she had done enough of that during these last weeks to last a lifetime. What she had to do now was weigh things up, look at them dispassionately. Llew had given her the ring but he had also given her other things – a family, a home, a business. The ring was the symbol of it all, true, but it was only cold metal and cold stones. The children were living, breathing human beings and the business was a living memorial to Llew's enterprise and initiative. If it came to a choice and one or the other had to go, it was obvious which it should be. You couldn't sacrifice the future to a piece of sentimentality.

And yet . . .

Oh Llew, Llew – you gave it to me! I can't sell it! I can't!

She closed her fist around the ring, feeling it bite into her palm and wishing the pain would be enough to eclipse the pain inside her. What a choice! How can I do it? How can I bear to put this ring – my engagement ring – down on a counter and leave it there? Oh I can't – I can't!

But you must. The small calm voice of reason sounded to her very like Llew's and through the raging emotion and deep despair it spoke from a still, calm place inside her that was the eye of the storm.

You mustn't be sentimental. Whether or not you have the ring, nothing can take away the memories you hold in your heart. Pay off Ralph Porter and anyone else you owe money, so you can hold your head up high. And start again. Build something Llew would be proud of. That's what he would want you to do.

'Yes,' she said, speaking aloud. 'It is, isn't it?'

She opened her palm and glanced down at the ring one last time. Then quickly, before she could change her mind, she took a small cardboard box that had contained a gift of earrings out of a drawer and laid the ring inside on the soft blue jeweller's cotton wool. As she slipped the lid into place, hiding the ring from her view, she felt as if she was shutting up a part of herself. But resolutely she cut off the thoughts that would start uncontrollable emotions.

Don't think. Just do it! For Llew and for Barbara and Maureen. And to settle that despicable Ralph Porter and get him off your back.

Once the box was hidden in the depths of her bag it was almost as if the irreversible had been attained and the ring had already gone for ever. But even so there were many moments when she held firm and reminded herself: Don't think. Just do it!

Perhaps the worst moment came as she entered the jeweller's shop – immediately below the solicitor's office in the High Street.

Amy had hardly ever been in the shop before, unless it was to get a clock repaired, and she found the dim, cloistered atmosphere unnerving. Around the walls a dozen different clocks ticked a dozen different times; in the corner a walnut-cased grandfather with an intricately decorated face surveyed the shop as his own; and in a glass dome on a prominent shelf a stuffed owl fixed Amy with unwinking eye.

From a door at the back of the counter the jeweller emerged – Mr Cornick. She knew him by sight, a slightly-built man with thick lensed spectacles covering the eyes strained by concentrating on minute workings for three-quarters of his life.

'Good morning, Mrs Roberts,' he greeted her. 'Can I help you?'

Slightly surprised that he knew who she was, Amy took out the box and opened it onto the glass-topped counter that covered precious items, each marked with a tiny, coded tag.

Why did jewellers always mark their goods with letters instead of prices that everyone could understand? It added to the mystery.

'I wanted to sell this. Would you be interested?' she asked.

He picked it up, handling it carefully, took off his spectacles and inspected it through an eyeglass.

'I think it's worth quite a lot,' Amy ventured.

Mr Cornick pondered a few more moments, 'hemming' softly to himself, then disappeared through the door into the shop. Anxiously Amy waited. The dozen clocks ticked the minutes away. Then, just when she had begun to think he would never reappear, there he was, replacing the ring in its box and looking at her steadily with eyes made huge by the thick-lensed spectacles.

'If you want to sell, I could offer you twenty pounds.'

Twenty pounds! It was less than she had hoped for – barely enough to cover her debt to Ralph Porter.

'Thirty?' she ventured.

But he shook his head.

'I'm sorry, Mrs Roberts. It may be a long while before I can sell it again. As you say, it's a fine piece, but in a place like Hillsbridge there's not a great deal of call for expensive jewellery.'

She hesitated, then made up her mind. Really, if she wanted the money, she had very little choice.

'All right.'

'I'll tell you what I'll do.' Mr Cornick folded his hands on the counter. 'I want to be fair with you, Mrs Roberts. Say twenty pounds now and if I can sell the ring quickly – within a month, say – and for a good sum, I'll forward you an extra ten pounds. How would that be?'

'Oh, that would be very nice,' Amy said gratefully.

A few moments later, the bank-notes safely tucked away in her bag, Amy left the shop. It was done, then. The ring was gone, but at least she had the money to pay Ralph Porter. And she intended to see the debt settled that very evening.

*

Ralph Porter's house, Valley View, stood at the bottom of Porter's Hill – big, rambling and built of natural stone. It could have been very impressive indeed, thought Amy, but there was a slightly unkempt air about it that was surprising, considering it was owned by the man who was supposed to be one of the richest in Hillsbridge.

In the gardens that flowed away from the rear and side, and through which led the gate from the path, roses ran riot and an enormous fish-pond was almost hidden from the sun by water-lily leaves the size of meat-platters. The trees and bushes near the house seemed to be jostling for light and air too, some tall and strong, others stunted. But the lawns had been cut, though not manicured, and the honeysuckle and morning glory around the door gave off a hauntingly sweet perfume in the warm evening air.

As she hauled on the bell-pull and heard it jangle inside the house, Amy realised she was nervous.

Don't be! she told herself. Why should you have a single qualm about him? He's only a man. And once you've paid him he will have no hold over you at all.

After a few moments she heard the key clank in the lock and the door opened. It was not Ralph Porter but his housekeeper – a plump jelly of a woman with three chins, apple cheeks and small darting eyes.

'Is Mr Porter at home?' Amy enquired.

'Who wants him?'

'Amy Roberts. I won't keep him a moment.'

'I'll tell him.'

The housekeeper waddled off while Amy waited, drumming her fingers on her bag. Then, almost at once, the housekeeper was back.

'Mr Porter says to ask you in.'

Amy followed the rolling figure through the hall with its mosaic tiled floor and into a large, dim drawing-room. It was obviously a man's room, she thought. The furniture was heavy and comfortable looking rather than elegant and the prints on the walls were old maps of the locality and a set of cartoon drawings. There was not the least touch of femininity, not even a vase of flowers to brighten a dim corner, and it crossed Amy's mind to wonder why Ralph's invalid sister, who shared the house with him, it was said – though she was hardly ever seen – had had so little influence on it. Perhaps it was because he would not let her. It would be very like him to want to have things his way, even if it was her home too.

Amy crossed to look at one of the cartoons, then a sound behind her made her spin round and she saw Ralph Porter come into the room.

In the confines of the house his presence was more vital than ever, dominating the room by far more than merely his size. Instinctively Amy drew herself up.

'I won't keep you, Mr Porter. I just wanted to settle my debt with you.'

He stood with hands in pockets, surveying her with disconcerting squareness.

'How are you going to manage to do that?'

She bristled. 'I don't think that's any of your business.'

He laughed. 'You're quite right. It isn't any of my business. All right, settle your debt, Mrs Roberts, if it makes you happy.'

Angry words rose to her lips. If it made *her* happy indeed! Selling her precious ring and having nothing to show for it . . . But she bit her tongue. Say as little as possible. Pay him the money and leave with as much dignity as you can.

She pulled out the wad of notes and held them out to him. He took them, pushing them carelessly into his pocket.

'Aren't you going to count it?' she asked, surprised.

He shrugged. 'I trust you. One very important lesson you will learn in business is who you can and cannot trust. And in any case, if the full amount isn't there, I know where to find you.'

She was trembling with hostility. Why did he *do* this to her?

'It's all there, I assure you. And I would prefer you to count it while I'm here so that there can be no dispute about it afterwards.'

One corner of his mouth quirked.

'All right, if you insist. And aren't you going to ask me for a receipt while you're about it?'

She lifted her chin. 'That's up to you. But you won't get the money twice in any case.'

'Then I suggest we forget the matter.' He moved to the door, holding it open for her. 'How did you get here, Mrs Roberts? Walking? Or did you drive?'

She caught her lip between her teeth. He was laughing at her. She had sold her ring to repay him, but he took the money almost nonchalantly, as if it meant nothing whatever to him – which, with all he had, it probably didn't – and now he was laughing at her. The perfect beast.

'I'm afraid not all of us can afford the luxury of a car, Mr Porter,' she said stiffly, passing him and going back into the hall.

He opened the heavy door for her and the scent of the honeysuckle wafted in, encompassing them.

'Thank you, Mrs Roberts,' he said in the same condescending tone.

'I told you, Mr Porter, that I pay my debts. Good night.'

'Good night.'

She walked away down the path and as she turned to close the gate after her he was still there, watching her from the doorway.

Well, that's that, Amy said to herself. That's done. And let's hope it's the last I see of Mr Ralph Porter.

*

Two days later an envelope dropped through Amy's door containing ten crisp pound notes. The accompanying letter, written on a billhead for Mr Cornick the jeweller, was brief and to the point.

He had been able to sell her ring quickly and for more than he had expected. As promised, he was enclosing...

Amy stood for a moment, her stomach falling away. It was gone, then. Someone else would be putting it on their finger, admiring the winking ruby, putting it at night into their own jewellery box. Until now she had nursed the vague hope that somehow, miraculously, she might get the money to buy it back before Mr Cornick could sell it. But now that was not to be.

But oh, the extra ten pounds would be useful! It was like untold riches in her hand.

She called the children. 'Come on, Barbara, let's put Maureen in her pram. We'll go up to the little shop on the corner and buy you some sweeties. Would you like that?'

The children squealed in delight. There had been precious few treats this summer; Amy had been too worried about making ends meet. Now, squandering the few pence she had been keeping in her purse for emergencies, Amy felt like a millionairess – headily generous and wildly extravagant.

It was, she thought, a good feeling.

Chapter Seven

In the front room of George Young's house in Tower View, Harry Hall and Margaret Young sat on their heels on the floor in the midst of piles of clothes sufficient in Harry's opinion to fill the stalls for an entire jumble sale. The furniture – the fat, serviceable sofa and two matching easy-chairs – had been pushed back to accommodate them and more sacks, waiting to be emptied, leaned against the walls, the writing bureau and the small occasional table.

With the miners' strike now in its twelfth week, hardship was rife in Hillsbridge and the committee of the Distress Fund had put out a plea for clothing for the needy. It had been answered enthusiastically, with the better-off inhabitants donating good, unwanted cast-offs to swell the sackloads donated by 'the gentry', people from the big houses outside the district where the daughters of mining families were in service. Since George Young was the secretary of the local Labour Party and Gussie, his wife, was one of the leading lights on the committee of the Distress Fund, most of it was delivered direct to their home and parties of willing helpers sorted it for distribution to hard-pressed families.

Today Harry and Margaret were taking their turn in this hub of activity and though Harry would have been the first to admit his qualifications for the job were less than adequate, he was doing his best – instructed by an enthusiastic Margaret, who generously pointed out his mistakes in between working tirelessly herself.

'I should throw that away, Harry. Who on earth would be seen dead in that?' And: 'Harry – that blue piqué is a hat-and-coat set for a baby boy, not a girl. See – look at the way it buttons. So it goes on this pile here.'

Obediently Harry compiled with her instructions. Sorting good used clothes was not one of his favourite jobs. There were things he would rather do than check on whether a pram coat buttoned to the right or the left, and he could not see that it made much difference anyway. A pram coat was a pram coat and that was all there was to it.

But boring as sorting old clothes might be, at least it was working for the cause. Everyone had to start somewhere, Harry supposed, and if his starting point was a bit like preparing for a glorified jumble sale, well, he would just have to accept it and be grateful that he had the opportunity actually to be here, in George Young's house, with George Young's blessing.

Since the day of the Labour Fete, it seemed to Harry that his life had changed completely. Whereas before he had been aware first of a restlessness he could not understand, and then of a desire to do something for the miners' cause without having a single idea on how to begin, now suddenly he found himself in the thick of things – and it was all because of Margaret.

She was, Harry thought, different from any girl he had ever known. Not that he had known many this well – there had been girls in his class at school, of course, but mostly they had stayed together in giggling groups. And certainly she was nothing like either Dolly or Amy. Just why she was so different he was not sure – unless perhaps it was that she saw things on a much larger canvas while they judged the world solely on how it would affect them. Never in a million years, he thought, could he imagine either of them working in a kind of soup kitchen, doling out plates of food to the neediest members of the community. Dolly would do anything for her own family but tended to believe, like Charlotte, that charity began and ended at home, and Amy he didn't think would be seen dead in public in a pinafore no matter what the circumstances.

Margaret, however, took charity work of all kinds very seriously.

'It's only right to do what we can,' she said, but the sentiments deeply drilled into her since childhood somehow did not make her appear pious as they might have done. Perhaps this was because she genuinely wanted to help, not just to look good in the eyes of the community, Harry thought. And because, of course, she had the best sense of humour of anyone he knew – his brother Ted excepted.

Harry had discovered how real was her sense of humour on that first picnic they had taken together. Typically, Margaret had packed a basket not only with sandwiches, fruit cake and a jug of home-made lemonade, but also a bright checked tablecloth, plates, cups, knives and forks.

Harry had carried this without complaining down the hill, through the town, past the church and along the valley bottom where the river ran cool and clear beneath the overhanging trees. They had stopped for a while by the spot where the naturally-broadening river had been turned into a swimming pool and where galas and water polo matches took place, and Harry had wanted to roll up his trousers and dabble his feet – but Margaret would not let him.

'My Dad says the pool will have to be closed down,' she informed him. 'He thinks it's being polluted.'

'Pollu-what?' Harry asked, one trouser leg already rolled up to the knee.

'Polluted. It means that not very nice things are going into it.'

'You mean the cows walking in the river upstream? They've always been there,' Harry said reasonably.

'No, I don't mean the cows, though I don't fancy them either,' she said seriously. 'My Dad says that there's sewage

155

coming down under the Tump from the houses up at Eastover. And even worse... you know what's on the other side?'

He looked, but was able to see nothing but green fields and the tower of the church.

'Nope.'

'The churchyard,' she said. 'Dad says all kinds of nasty things could be draining into the water – out of the graves.'

'Oh, crikey!' Harry, who had just begun to dabble one toe, withdrew it hastily. 'You mean... ?'

'Yes, I do. Not very nice, is it? You could get an infection if you had a cut, my Dad says.'

Harry, trying not to look too anxious, examined his foot for signs of a cut or graze but found none. Perhaps being on strike had its advantages! Usually he was covered in scrapes and grazes.

'That is horrible,' he said again, wondering if being in local politics was like this all the time – carrying the cares of the world and knowing things it was more pleasant not to know.

They strolled on for a bit until they found a shady spot, dappled with sunlight. Because Margaret had brought up her father's name, Harry felt himself justified in asking a few pertinent questions; he found her so knowledgeable in the workings of local politics that he began to wonder how he had remained ignorant for so long. The smallest details of organisation were new to him, the subject was endless and fascinating – he could have gone on about it for ever. But after a while Margaret protested.

'Do we have to talk about the Labour Party all the time? I get enough of it at home.'

Harry coloured. The last thing he wanted was to bore her, but he couldn't think of another single topic of conversation and to his own annoyance, fell silent.

'Shall we eat, then?' she suggested.

He helped her lay out the tablecloth and set the places. The sandwiches were neat triangles, totally unlike the doorstep wedges that Charlotte called sandwiches, the cake was cut into even-sized squares. From the bottom of the hamper she produced a little cruet set and small matching jars for milk and sugar – a slight mystery, since there was only lemonade to drink. But Harry was fascinated by the gentle orderliness of the whole exercise.

'This is the life!' he said.

'You like it?' There was an eagerness in her face that twisted something deep within him. Suddenly he wanted to touch her and the desire was stronger than embarrassment. He reached out so that his fingers brushed hers and the warmth sent tremors through his veins.

For a moment he held his breath, half expecting her to pull away, but she sat motionless as if she too was holding her breath, and gaining courage he locked his fingers around hers, then slid them slowly up her wrist and forearm. Her skin felt soft and warm to his touch and the desire twisted within him again, sharper and more urgent. Slowly, slowly he moved towards her and she did not draw away ... closer, closer, until her face blurred out of focus and he thought he could feel her breath on his cheek. As their lips touched the world seemed to stand still – it was as if even his heart had stopped beating and time was suspended by the sweetness of her mouth. There was no contact between their bodies yet she drew him, every pore, every nerve ending, to an awareness centred in the gentle pressure of their lips and the delicate perfume of her skin. For timeless moments it lasted, precious, lingering, never-to-be-forgotten moments.

And then the idyll was shattered by a crashing in the bushes behind them and they sprang apart to see first one, then two or three, then a whole herd of heifers lumbering towards them.

Margaret screamed and leapt to her feet, the bottle of lemonade went over, swimming into the neat triangle sandwiches. Harry, too, had jumped violently; now, he waved his arms wildly at the cows.

'Get out of it!'

They stopped, regarding him with patient, curious eyes. Then the first, clearly the leader, moved slowly on, lumbering uncertainly towards the river and passing so close that the black coat brushed his bare arm. As before, the others followed. One hoof trod on a corner of the outspread tablecloth, leaving a muddy footprint, then one after the other they pushed, jostled and splashed their way into the river shallows.

Harry swore, then turned to Margaret. She was standing, hands pressed to her mouth, eyes wide above them.

'Are you all right?' he asked.

'Yes, I ...'

And then she began to laugh. It bubbled out of her, peal after peal of mirth. 'Oh Harry, I'm sorry, but it's just too funny! Those stupid cows...'

She dropped to her knees, righting the lemonade bottle and rescuing sandwiches, still laughing. 'They startled me so! I'm not *really* frightened of them. I'm not keen, mind you, but they're only heifers, aren't they? They're just curious...'

'Well, they managed to ruin our picnic,' Harry said.

'Oh, go on, they didn't! Though I think perhaps I *would* rather move from here. I don't much fancy being in the way when they all plough back again. And they leave smelly pats, too,' she added, wrinkling her nose.

So much for our first kiss, thought Harry as he helped her pack the basket again and move back to a piece of open field. But the warm feeling he had for her grew and her laughter was like music in his ears.

That evening when he took her home, Harry had no doubts about asking to see her again and on the second evening she asked him in for a cup of tea. Then Harry had been introduced to her father and to her sweet-faced, soft-voiced mother, an older replica of Margaret; when the conversation had turned inevitably to the strike, Harry had been impressed by their obvious sincerity.

George Young might have left the pits to work for the Co-operative Society, collecting orders, but his heart was clearly still very much with his former colleagues.

'It's a sad business,' he said now, solemnly swirling the tea in the cup held between two huge hands, 'that men should be treated no better than slaves... and the hardship doesn't bear thinking about. We do what we can, of course, helping out wherever we can and raising money for the Relief Fund. But it's little enough.'

'Dad contributes something to the fund every week out of his wages, don't you, Dad?' Margaret said proudly.

'Margaret!' George treated her to a reproving stare over the rim of his cup. 'You know I told you we don't talk about that.'

'But you do!' she protested. 'Ten shillings a week.'

George ignored her, but Gussie made small shushing movements at her.

'The trouble is that the employers seem determined to grind the men into the ground,' George went on, 'and the

158

government seem more than happy to stand by and let them do it. To ask a man to work longer hours for less pay, when he's already on the breadline – it's madness. They've no alternative but to strike. But it's going to be a hard struggle, make no mistake about that. And it's up to those of us who are able to shoulder some of the burden to raise funds, organise trips for the children, anything to make the load lighter.'

'If there's anything I can do...' Harry said, eager to impress as well as truly anxious to be involved.

George beamed approvingly.

'That's the spirit, my boy. There will be something, you may be sure of it,' he said and Harry glowed with pride.

George's approval had sustained Harry through the various tasks he had been set. With Margaret's mother Gussie heading the Relief Committee, the house in Tower View was the centre of operations and Harry found himself press-ganged into the most menial of tasks – peeling potatoes for the emergency canteen that operated twice a week in the Victoria Hall; picking dry sticks in the wood to deliver to the old folk who, with only a retired miner's allowance to rely on, had quickly run out; sweeping up, and even helping to wash the floor, following one fund-raising event after another. The jobs were ones he would never have done at home in a month of Sundays – things which, apart from picking up sticks, Charlotte would never have dreamed of asking him to do – but when Gussie or George asked he did it with pleasure.

For one thing Margaret was there, and any excuse to see Margaret was a good one.

For another, Harry felt that he was working his ticket towards becoming a member of the Labour Party.

He had not dared raise the subject with George yet, though it hovered on his lips whenever politics was discussed. But Harry told himself he must be patient. First let him show George Young he had a serious interest in helping others. Then, when the opportunity arose, he would be able to put himself forward and know he had earned the right to be taken seriously.

There were times, though, when the fervour of wanting to help palled a little – and sorting through piles of good used clothes on a summer afternoon was one of them.

A little impatiently, Harry thrust his hand into the sack

159

and drew out a concoction of white webbing, bones and elastic.

'What the dickens is this?'

It was not a serious question – he already had a pretty good idea what it was – but Margaret went into peals of laughter.

'You're not supposed to know.' She went to snatch it from him playfully. 'Give it to me, Harry. That definitely goes on the ladies' pile.'

Harry swung the garment out of her reach, jumping up to caper with it held around his own chest.

'Hey, what do you think? Does it suit me? I'm having this!'

The door clicked open and Harry froze as Gussie came into the room. She looked at him unsmiling for a moment, standing there with the corselette held around him, and he wished the floor would open up and swallow him.

'Oh, Mrs Young – I . . .'

She ignored him.

'Margaret, I wondered if you'd run down to Market Cottages for me when you've finished that. There's a young woman down there who's just had a baby and I've found a couple of really good nightshirts in the last lot of stuff – and some nappies, too. She might as well have them right away and get some use out of them.'

'All right – we've nearly finished here,' Margaret replied.

'Good girl.' Gussie stopped in the doorway to look back at Harry with a twinkle. 'But if Harry's going with you, I really don't think he ought to wear his corselette!'

As they walked down the hill to the town centre, Harry was still smarting with embarrassment at having been caught out playing the fool with the corselette. He felt this was not quite the image he wanted to present to the Youngs, either as a suitor for their daughter or as a serious young prospective member of the Labour Party. In fact, when he came to think of it, he seemed to be making a fool of himself with Margaret on all sides. Why couldn't things go right for him the way they did for other young men – his brothers, for instance? Jim, of course, was too old to compare himself with, but Jack was a war hero and a pillar of the community in the small seaside town where he was a schoolmaster, while Ted had always been able to charm the birds off the trees.

Margaret, however, seemed not to be worried by his lack of *savoir faire* – she walked alongside him with a perky step, laughing and chatting and so totally at ease that he found it difficult to believe he was her senior.

As they reached the foot of the hill he noticed a young woman with a child standing outside the George and looking around somewhat uncertainly. He glanced curiously in her direction. It was unusual in Hillsbridge to see a woman waiting outside a pub – even though it would not be open for several hours yet, it was somehow deemed not to be quite nice, the mark of a woman who was no better than she should be. And this one certainly looked poor, Harry thought – painfully thin, her dark hair screwed tightly into a knot at the nape of her neck and her cotton dress well-worn and washed-out. The child, a boy of seven or eight, was as thin as his mother, with a pert urchin face and a shock of brown hair cut with the aid of a pudding basin. Like her, his clothes looked well-worn and the darns in the elbows of his jersey were apparent even at a casual glance.

The young woman looked towards them and Harry hastily averted his eyes. Then, as he and Margaret drew level, she took a nervous step away from the doorway of the George, planting herself almost in their path.

'Excuse me!' There was a lilt to her voice that was unmistakably Welsh. Harry had thought she was a stranger in Hillsbridge and her accent confirmed it. 'Excuse me ... I wonder, could you tell me if there's anywhere here where I could put up for the night?'

Besides the lilt there was strain in her voice. She looked and sounded weary – ill, even. Harry and Margaret exchanged glances.

'You mean you're looking for somewhere to stay?'

'Just for tonight. I thought the pub ... but I didn't like to go in ...'

'Well there's Manor House along the street – they take paying guests,' Harry suggested.

'And Mrs Moon in Glebe Bottoms takes lodgers,' Margaret added.

The woman bit her lip. She looked, Harry thought, as if she had all the cares of the world on her frail shoulders.

'Which would be cheapest? I haven't got much money ...'

'Mrs Moon, I should think,' Harry said and gave her directions.

The woman thanked them and hoisted a carpet bag up on to her shoulder with an effort. Then, with a sharp, 'Come on then!' to the boy, she started off and Harry and Margaret went on their way. But neither could resist glancing at her over their shoulders and Margaret's sunny mood seemed to have been overtaken by anxiety.

'Poor thing, she looked awful! Do you think I should have taken her up home and asked Mum if she had room to sleep her? We could have managed it. There's the little spare room off the landing...'

'She'll be all right with Mrs Moon,' Harry assured her.

'I suppose so.' Margaret looked far from convinced. 'I wonder who she is and what she's doing here?'

'I don't know, but we'd better get on and deliver this stuff for your Mum,' Harry said, changing the subject. 'Whoever she is, she's got nothing to do with us.'

'I suppose not,' Margaret agreed, trying to put the woman and her child out of her mind. A mystery they might be, but as Harry had said, they had nothing to do with her.

Chapter Eight

Amy had spent most of that day at the yard, checking through ledgers and work-sheets and trying to sort out with Herbie some kind of blueprint for the future of Roberts Haulage.

Not that Herbie was much help. He tried to be, granted, but Amy could tell he had no confidence whatever in her as his new employer, and his slow, painstaking way of talking to her about the business was almost as off-putting as the out-and-out opposition her plans had received from others – notably her own family.

'I don't think you should attempt it, Amy. It'll be too much for you and you'll only make yourself bad,' Charlotte had said. 'Besides, what are you going to do about the children? You can't have them running about with lorries loading and unloading. It wouldn't be safe.'

Amy had turned on her most pleading expression.

'I was hoping you might help me out there, Mam. I know you love having them...'

'Yes, I do, sometimes. But every day... And it might be too much for your father.'

'Don't bring me into it, Lottie,' James had wheezed from his bed in the corner of the living-room. 'They cheer me up. I'm cut off enough as it is, cooped up here. And Barbara likes giving her grampie his medicine, don't you, my duck?'

Barbara climbed up on to the bed to prove her agreement and Charlotte, deserted by her ally, had been forced into retreat.

'Well, if it's helping you out, Amy, I suppose I could. But what people will say – you down at the yard and doing a man's work – I don't know!'

'I don't care what they say!' Amy declared.

It was not quite true, for she did care. But it made no difference anyway. She had made up her mind that the business should survive and she had no intention of giving up just because people might talk.

Predictably, some of the strongest opposition had come from Eddie Roberts.

Denied his chance of taking over his brother's business, he too was determined to 'have his say' on the subject of Amy's venture.

'It's downright ridiculous,' he told her. 'You don't know the first thing about it.'

'Nor did Llew when he started.' Amy's chin was high, her mouth a tight determined line. 'Nor do you, if it comes to that.'

'But we're men.'

Amy tossed her head. 'And what has that to do with anything?'

'A great deal, I should say.'

'I can't see why. As regards the paper-work, I'm as able as any man once I find my way around it. And anything I don't understand, I shall change and do it my way. As for the manual work, I shall take on an extra hand as soon as I can afford it.'

'You won't be *able* to afford it,' Eddie said nastily.

'Oh, and why not?'

'Because you're forgetting something. To get work you'll have to deal with men. And men won't deal with a woman.'

'We shall see about that,' Amy said, wishing she felt as confident as she sounded.

'You won't be able to go into the places where they do business. A lot of deals are talked over and made in the pub. And that will be out so far as you're concerned.'

'When they see what a good business I run, they'll come to me,' she declared.

Eddie laughed scornfully and she turned on him.

'Leave me alone, Eddie. I've got enough to do without quarrelling with you.'

'I'm not quarrelling. I'm only trying to help.'

'Well, I can do without your help. I haven't forgotten how you were hoping for a share of Llew's estate. Thank goodness the law is fairer than you, that's all I can say.'

Eddie reddened. 'I wouldn't have taken your money, Amy. Surely you don't think ...'

'I don't know what I think. But if *you* think you're going to talk me out of doing this, I can tell you you're wasting your breath.'

Eddie had given up then, though Amy felt uncomfortably sure it was only a temporary respite. When he wanted something Eddie was like a terrier with a bone – and he wanted Llew's business.

I'll show him, Amy thought. I'll show them all!

But saying was a great deal easier than doing, as she soon discovered. Herbie could drive one lorry for the time being, with young Ivor Burge as mate, and eventually she hoped to take on another driver. But at present there was next-to-nothing to do. The contracts with the colliery companies on which Llew had relied were worthless as long as the miners' strike lasted, and she had little idea as to how to go about obtaining new business. But at least the grant of administration had been received, so she was free to do things her own way and the first step, she decided, was to go through the books and discover who Llew had dealt with in the past so that she could contact them and seek out new jobs.

That was what she had been doing that afternoon, making a list of likely customers; tomorrow she would make a start on trying to persuade them to do business with Roberts Haulage.

For the moment, however, she had reverted to her other role as mother to Barbara and Maureen. From the yard, she had walked up to Greenslade Terrace and, at Charlotte's insistence, stopped for a welcome cup of tea before starting out on the long trek home.

It was a warm, almost muggy afternoon and the sky was overcast for the first time for weeks, so that Amy thought there might be thunder in the air. As she pushed the pram, with Barbara dragging alongside, she realised she had a headache coming on and she sighed with impatience. She hated it when she had a headache; not only was it unpleasant, it also meant she didn't have the energy or concentration for all the things she had to do. Sickness was a luxury she could not afford.

Ahead of her on the hill she saw the figure of another woman with a child, dragging up the long climb. She looks about the way I feel, thought Amy – worse if anything, for even with the pram Amy was making ground on her. As the hill flattened out, however, she was still too far ahead for Amy to be able to see who she was. Then she turned into one of the gateways of the houses on the road.

It almost looked as if she went into my gate! thought Amy idly. She couldn't have, of course. It must have been next door. I wonder who she is?

Barbara was pulling on the pram, slowing Amy down, so she lifted her up into the little dickey seat and they covered the last few hundred yards at a much faster pace.

Then, as her house came into view, Amy almost stopped short in surprise. She had been right in thinking the woman with the child had turned into her gateway – they were standing at her front door and knocking on the knocker!

After the initial shock Amy began to hurry again, almost as if she thought the pair might disappear into thin air if she didn't catch them quickly. Her first thought as she went up the path towards them was how ill the woman looked; her second was to wonder if they had not made a mistake and gone to the wrong house. But as she approached the woman turned towards her, a look of what appeared to be guilt making her thin features even more pinched.

'Did you want me?' Amy asked.

'Well, not exactly...' The accent was Welsh, the tone almost apologetic. 'I was looking for Mr Roberts. Mr Llew Roberts?'

'Mr Roberts.' Inexplicably Amy felt weak inside. 'What do

you want him for?'

The woman hesitated. 'Does it matter? I just want to see him.'

'I'm sorry.' Amy's voice was hard.

The woman pulled her cardigan defensively around her thin body. 'You're Mrs Roberts, I suppose? I heard he was married. I won't keep him long, I promise, but I must see him.'

'It's not possible,' Amy said, warding off the woman's protest. 'He's not with us any more.'

'You mean he's left you?' A curious, unreadable expression pinched the woman's careworn features.

'No.' Amy took a deep breath – it still hurt to say it out loud. 'He's dead.'

The woman blanched; all the colour drained from her already-pale cheeks and she seemed to sway on her feet. '*What?* What did you say?'

The look of her disconcerted Amy and when she spoke her voice was correspondingly sharp.

'He was killed. There was an accident. So I'm sorry – your journey has been wasted.'

'Dead!' The woman was trembling visibly, shock written all over her. 'So that's why I haven't heard from him! Dead! Oh *duw* – I didn't know...'

It was Amy's turn to blanch. There was something she did not understand here... something she didn't like...

'Who are you?' she demanded.

The woman made an effort to control herself.

'I'm sorry... I'm Sibyl James. I knew Llew in Glamorgan, before he moved here...' She broke off, pressing a shaking hand to her face. 'I'm sorry... it's such a shock...'

A curtain at the next-door window moved and Amy got out her front-door key.

'You'd better come inside.'

'Oh – I don't know... I don't know what to do now...'

The curtain moved again. Amy opened the door, lifted Barbara down and pushed her inside. Then she turned to scoop up Maureen.

'Come on. We'll have a cup of tea.'

She led the way in and uncertainly the woman and child followed. In the kitchen the woman stood with the carpet-bag still over her shoulder, arms wrapped around her skinny frame.

166

'Sit down,' Amy said.

As if her legs would no longer support her the woman did as she was bid.

'Oh, I'm sorry...' she said again. 'I shouldn't have come, I suppose. But I was desperate, see? I didn't know what else to do. When... when did he die?'

'At the beginning of May. He had an accident at the yard.' Amy was filling the kettle, lighting the gas.

'So that's why I haven't heard. I wrote to him, see? Twice. But he didn't answer. It was so unlike him.'

At the mention of letters Amy jumped and then stood motionless remembering the cream envelopes with the Glamorgan postmarks. Had this woman sent them? It certainly sounded like it. But why – why? And why hadn't Llew told her about the woman? They had always told one another everything...

The woman was rocking back and forth on her chair, moaning softly, and at first Amy was too preoccupied with her own shocked thoughts to notice what she was saying. Then half a dozen words detached themselves from the rest.

'He always sent so regular, see...'

'Sent regular?' Amy repeated sharply. 'What are you talking about – sent regular?'

The woman moaned again, nodding towards the child.

'For Huw. He always sent money for Huw. After my Idris died, anyway.'

Amy caught her breath. Her fingers were too numb suddenly to hold the matchbox and it dropped to the floor unnoticed.

'Idris?'

'My husband. He got killed underground. A stone fell on him. And now you tell me Llew's gone too. Oh *duw, duw* ...'

Amy leaned forward, her knuckles white on the scrubbed wood table top.

'Wait a minute. I'm not following you. Are you trying to tell me that Llew supported your child? And I knew nothing about it? Why should he do that?'

The woman was crying now, her mouth slack, her chin wobbling. She brushed at the deep dark circles beneath her eyes with the back of her fingers and fumbled in the pocket of her cardigan for a handkerchief.

'You didn't know then? He never told you.'

'Told me what?' Amy almost shouted at her.

167

'About Huw.' She indicated the child who stood scowling beside her. 'Huw. His boy.'

'His *what*?'

'His boy – Llew was his father, see?' The words were tumbling out now, fast as a mountain stream. 'He and I ... well, we acted silly. I was a married woman and I should have know better, but you know how it is...'

'No,' Amy said, 'I *don't* know how it is.' Her voice was tight and hard and her headache was worse suddenly, compressing her brain so that she could not think straight.

The woman shook her head impatiently.

'Llew ... Llew and me ... don't you see? We ... well, they call it improper conduct in court, don't they? Though I've never seen where 'improper' comes in. Daft, more like. All this trouble for a few minutes' pleasure. But the fact is, foolishness or not, Huw is Llew's boy. My Idris never got to hear of it, God be praised, and he brought Huw up as his own. But now he's gone and I've had to ask Llew to do right by his own flesh and blood...'

As she spoke Amy stood, stunned into silence, unable to believe what she was hearing. It couldn't be happening.

'I wouldn't ask, only he promised,' the woman whined and something in Amy snapped.

'I think you'd better leave,' she said, drawing herself up very straight.

The effect on the woman was immediate and shocking. She half-rose, leaning forward onto the table, her eyes wide and imploring, her mouth working.

'Oh no ... please – you must help me! I don't know what to do. I've no money – nothing. I wouldn't ask for myself, but Huw...'

'I'm sorry,' Amy cut her off. 'I have no money either and I can't help you. And if you think you can come here making ridiculous claims about my husband, you are very much mistaken. Now get out before I call the police.'

'Oh! Oh!' the woman sobbed and the boy stepped forward, putting a protective arm around her. Amy, her head throbbing unbearably, glanced down at him and met his eyes, glaring defiant blue fire at her. Immediately she went cold. Blue eyes with that dark hair? Unusual. And Llew's eyes had been blue.

No! Stop it! she screamed silently to herself. Don't think it for a moment – it's not true!

Venting her feelings, Amy marched to the back door and threw it open. 'Go on, get out of my house!' she ordered. 'Take your sob stories elsewhere. I've got troubles enough of my own.'

The woman's eyes implored her for a moment. Her face was still ravaged by tears, but she made no effort to wipe them away. Then she straightened, hoisting the pathetic carpet-bag onto her shoulder and pulling the darned cardigan tightly around her as if it was the only protection left to her.

'All right, I know I'm not welcome here and I shouldn't blame you really, only I do. Because if Llew was here, he wouldn't let Huw suffer. He always promised that if anything happened between me and Idris he would see Huw was all right. And he did. Sent regular. He was one up in the world on us, see? But now . . . well, I can see you don't want to know. So we'll just leave you to your nice house and your fine clothes and all the things you've got because it was legal-like with you and Llew. And I hope God forgives you for what you're doing to us!'

Amy could no longer control the trembling. It was so violent even her teeth were chattering with it and her head seemed to throb in time. 'And I hope He forgives you for what you've done to me. Now get out – and don't come back.'

They went, the woman without a backward glance, holding on to the shattered remnants of her pride as she hung on to her threadbare jacket; the boy, his face contracted into a tight scowl beneath his pudding-basin haircut, glaring at her over his shoulder and managing to collide with his mother's heels as he did so.

Amy slammed the door after them, pressing her full weight against it as if she was afraid that anything less would allow the door to open again and re-admit them.

'Oh, my God, oh, my God!' she whispered over and over again as the waves of shock and distress washed over her.

'Mammy? Mammy? What is it?' Barbara, who had been hiding like a mouse in the larder, came running out crying and even Maureen, sitting in the middle of the rag rug, began to wail.

'Nothing. It's all right, children. Everything's all right.'

Amy scooped them both close to her, trying to eclipse the image of that ghastly woman and her child by the warmth and wholesomeness of their plump little bodies.

But she could not. That Welsh voice was still there in her ears, and the look of the two of them seemed imprinted indelibly on her vision. And the things the woman had said! Terrible things – ridiculous things! It couldn't be true that Llew had had an affair with a woman like that! She was a scarecrow – thin and scraggy as last week's neck of mutton – and she must be able to give him getting on for ten years. As for claiming that Llew had supported the child . . . well, that was even less believable. He couldn't have done it without Amy knowing . . . could he? And if he could, he wouldn't . . . would he? But she couldn't forget those letters with the Glamorgan postmark, one which had fallen into the washing-up water and the other which she had picked up from the bedroom floor and Llew had snatched away from her. All too clearly now she seemed to hear his voice, impatient, panicky, perhaps: 'Give it to me! That's mine!'

No, he certainly hadn't wanted her to see it.

'Twice I've written and not heard anything,' the woman – Sibyl, was that her name? – had said. Twice. Two letters addressed in a childish, unbusinesslike hand. One a few weeks ago and one on the day Llew had died.

But what had happened to that first letter? Amy wondered suddenly. Llew had taken it from her that morning, yet it had not been returned with his clothes and it was not amongst the papers in his office. Could it be that someone who was in the know had deliberately removed it to stop her from finding it? Or had Llew himself destroyed it so that there was no danger of Amy learning the truth?

'No!' Amy sobbed, twisting her head against the panels of the door, her arms encompassing Barbara and Maureen. 'No – I won't believe it. It's lies – all lies! And you can make anything seem the way you want it to. Anything! Llew wouldn't . . . he couldn't!'

Behind her the kettle began to whistle imperatively and trying to get a grip on herself, she put the children away from her.

'There now – go and find something to do, Barbara. Mammy's going to make your tea. Everything's all right now.'

A little tremulously Barbara went, and Amy set Maureen down on the rag rug once more. Automatically she fetched the teapot, warmed it and poured boiling water onto the tea leaves. The aroma was familiar and steadying, even lifting her headache momentarily, but inwardly she was still a jelly of churning thoughts and emotions.

Everything was all right, she had told the children. But dear God, was it never going to be all right again! She couldn't stand it any more – just one thing on top of the other, endless shocks and turmoil. What next? What next?

As she poured the tea the kitchen was illuminated suddenly, startling her, then as thunder rolled overhead she identified the source of the illumination – lightning. The sky outside the kitchen window darkened without her noticing and now a flurry of rain began, splattering forcefully against the panes. A thunderstorm. She had never cared much for thunderstorms. As a child Mam had comforted her by saying it was the people in the sky moving their furniture about and even when she had become a grown woman, she had been glad of Llew's arms around her through the worst of the storm. But now she had neither Mam nor Llew and the thunder seemed as nothing compared with the storms she had been through in the last months.

'Raining! Raining! Pram getting wet!' cried Barbara, running back into the kitchen and Amy, remembering the pram left outside the front door, was jerked away from her emotional ponderings to more mundane matters.

As she ran to get it in, she spared one brief thought for the woman and her child. They would be caught in the storm, no doubt.

Too bad, thought Amy. They're not my responsibility and that woman has no one to blame but herself. Coming here and making trouble. I hope she gets pneumonia!

Then, with an attempt to return to normality, she went back to the kitchen to make the children's tea.

*

Hillsbridge was buzzing and for once, in that summer of 1926, the talk was not of the strike.

'Have you heard the latest?' Peggy Yelling asked Charlotte, popping her head around the kitchen door. 'Some woman lodging with Mrs Moon down in Glebe Bottoms has been and died!'

'Is that right?' Charlotte, never a great one for gossip, had little interest in Mrs Moon or her lodgers, dead or alive.

'Yes. She came the day before yesterday with a little boy,

171

knocking on the door and looking for somewhere to stay. Mrs Moon let her have a room; then that same night she was took bad. She didn't get out of bed yesterday, it seems, and Mrs Moon knew she wasn't well, but never realised just how bad she was. Well, she never did have much sense, did she? Anyway, last night she heard the boy screaming and went in to see what was wrong and there she was – breathing her last! Mrs Moon got the doctor to her then, but it was too late. She was gone. It just goes to show, doesn't it – if you take in strangers you never know what you're letting yourself in for. I mean, it's no joke, is it?'

'No joke at all,' Charlotte agreed. 'What's going to happen to the boy, Peg?'

Peggy shrugged her plump shoulders.

'They'll take him to the Union, I suppose.'

'Hazebury?'

'I suppose so. Until they can find out if there are any relations that can take care of him. It's no place for a lad though, is it, down there with all the funny folk?'

Charlotte glanced at Barbara and Maureen, playing at dolls' tea-parties in the scullery, and shuddered.

'No, you're right there. It's awful to think of it. Where are they from, Peggy? Does anybody know?'

'I couldn't say – though they reckon she was a Welshie.'

'A Welshie, was she?' Charlotte stopped, remembering how Harry had come home a couple of afternoons ago and said that he and Margaret had met a woman and child in town looking for lodgings; she repeated the story now to Peggy.

'That must have been her, I'll bet you a shilling!' said Peggy triumphantly, glad to have another smidgin of information about the mystery woman. Not that Peggy was really a gossip, more that as midwife and ministrant to the dead in her own small area at least, she did like to know all the 'ins and outs', as she put it. 'Well, all I can say is, I hope somebody to do with them turns up, for the sake of the poor little lamb.'

'Yes, we must hope so,' Charlotte agreed.

*

A couple of hours later, when Amy came for the children and Charlotte made their customary pot of tea, she was concerned by how pale and drawn her daughter looked.

'Have you been doing too much, Amy?' she asked.

'No more than usual,' Amy said, a little snappily.

Charlotte looked at her closely.

'Well, you don't look too good to me. You can overdo it, you know, then you'll be no use to anybody. You'll end up like that poor woman who was lodging at Mrs Moon's.'

'What woman?' Amy asked idly, her mind obviously elsewhere.

'Some poor soul with a little boy. Put up with Mrs Moon for the night, got took bad and now she's dead.' She set down the tea and stopped short. 'Whatever is the matter, Amy?'

Amy did not answer; she had turned chalk-white and looked, thought Charlotte, as if she had seen a ghost.

'Amy!' she said again, more sharply. 'Are you all right?'

'Oh, my God!' said Amy. 'Who was it, did you say?'

'Nothing to do with us,' Charlotte reassured her. 'She was Welsh, I heard. Only came for the one night. I don't know what was wrong with her, Peggy didn't say. But our Harry saw a woman with a little boy down by the George the day before, looking for somewhere to put up for the night, and he did say how poorly she looked. So you see, you can't be too careful. You don't want our Barbara and Maureen to end up like that poor little boy, now do you? He'll have to go to Hazebury Union unless they can find somebody to take him, Peggy reckoned.'

Still Amy said nothing, but the look of her was alarming Charlotte.

'Look, Amy, why don't you stay and have a bit of tea with us?' she suggested. 'I've got some cold pork that ought to be eaten before it goes bad.'

'No, it's all right, thank you,' Amy said in a strained voice.

'It wouldn't be any trouble, and if it would save you having to go home and cook...'

'No – I'm not hungry, thank you,' Amy said in the same strained tone. 'Don't fuss, Mam, I'm all right, really.'

'Well, you don't look all right to me!' Charlotte pronounced.

But there was nothing she could do about it. If Amy wouldn't stay, she wouldn't. She had always been too wilful for her own good, thought Charlotte anxiously.

All the same, she couldn't understand why the story about the woman at Mrs Moon's had upset her so – unless of course she was worried, as Charlotte had suggested, that if she was not careful she might end up the same way.

I don't know, I'm sure, Charlotte said to herself. And long after Amy had left, anxiety about the way things were going for her daughter niggled at her.

*

In the middle of the night Amy sat bolt upright in bed and knew that at last she had made up her mind what she was going to do.

Ever since Mam had told her about the woman dying, she had been unable to think of anything else – not even the minor triumph she had scored that afternoon by securing a job hauling a load of gravel for one of the local quarries. She had worked hard persuading the quarry owner to give Roberts Haulage a chance and if the job was well done she hoped there would be more – maybe even a short-term contract of sorts.

The thought of the woman had been haunting her all the time, of course. Even when she was talking to the quarry owner it had been there, not in her mind exactly but in her emotions, so that every time she mentioned Llew's name there was a sinking feeling deep inside her and a bitter taste in her mouth. But she had pressed on, determined not to be distracted by the wicked mischief-making of some unknown woman.

And then, this afternoon, Mam had told her the woman was dead. Dead! Of course, she *had* looked terrible now that Amy came to think about it, consumptive almost, but at the time she had been too outraged by her revelations to feel any concern for her at all. Now she was overwhelmed by shock and guilt, and also concerned for the child who might have to be taken to Hazebury Union. Mam had said they were in hopes that some other relative would turn up to prevent that happening, but Amy realised that if the woman had been telling the truth there was no one *to* turn up. She had said she had no one and that Idris, her husband, had been killed in an accident underground.

She must have been in the same boat as me, Amy thought. Only I've got Mam and the rest of the family as well as the house and the business, and it sounded as though she had nothing and no one. And that poor little boy will have to go to Hazebury or somewhere very like it...

174

Every time she thought of it she shuddered, remembering the skinny frame, the thin urchin face and the blue eyes. Blue eyes – Llew's eyes? Oh no, surely even if the rest of the story was true – and as yet Amy was still desperately trying not to believe it – even given that, he couldn't be Llew's son. Llew's son would be big and strong, like his father. Wouldn't he? Unless of course he had been so starved of good food he had never grown properly. Not having the right things to eat could do awful things to you. Amy had seen what happened to the children of the poor families in Hillsbridge – those whose mothers cut their hair with the aid of a pudding-basin and let them go to school with their feet hanging out of their shoes. Some of them grew strong and wiry, it was true, but the others had one thing after another wrong with them: persistent hacking coughs, scarlet fever, diptheria, rickets which made their legs go bandy. And even the wiry ones tended to go down with such illnesses as pneumonia as they got older – more than one who had been at school with Amy was now dead and gone – and the others had lost all their looks very early on in life.

Perhaps that was what happened to the woman ... Amy found it hard to think of her as Sibyl. Perhaps she had been a good-looking girl before deprivation caught up with her. In her mind's eye Amy tried to picture the thin face and screwed-back hair. That made her look worse, of course; put a little more flesh on her and a bit of colour in her cheeks, let the hair down and she might look very different indeed. Attractive, even.

The thought made Amy feel sick, but for the first time she tried to face it squarely. Was there any truth in what she had said? Had Llew found her attractive? He must have known her, that much was certain. She would never have come otherwise. And – another sick realisation which had come to Amy during the endless pondering – she must have had some contact with him since he had come to Hillsbridge – since their marriage, even – or the woman could not have known where to find him.

No, there had to be some basis of truth in the story somewhere.

But the child ... Llew's? That she had not been able to stomach, had not wanted to think about until now, when she discovered that one way or another he was orphaned.

That night, after the children were in bed, Amy had

175

prowled the house, unable to settle in one place for two minutes at a stretch. Before coming to bed she had looked in on them, both fast asleep, and her heart had turned over. They had lost their father, yes, but their lives were still almost as before, their futures secure. But this other child, this boy – Huw was his name? How frightened and lost he must be tonight, with perhaps nothing but an orphanage to look forward to.

In bed she had tossed and turned, unable to sleep. And one thought kept coming to her again and again. She must find out – she must know the truth. But how? There really was only one way, though she shrank from it. She would have to go and see her mother-in-law. Perhaps Mrs Roberts would be able to tell her.

Next morning after she had left Barbara and Maureen with Charlotte, Amy caught a bus from Hillsbridge to High Compton, where the Roberts family now lived in a neat, square end-of-terrace. Since coming to Hillsbridge the entire family seemed to have thrived, with Mr Roberts senior and Eddie both going into the insurance business; Ivor, the next brother, apprenticed as a carpenter; and Megan and Gwyneth, the two daughters, both trained in shorthand and typewriting, with positions in offices in High Compton.

This elevated social standing suited Llew's mother, Annie Roberts, very well. She was, in her way, a snob – labelled privately by Charlotte as the sort she would like to 'take down a peg or two' – and Amy had never felt totally comfortable with her. 'She's so correct it hurts,' Amy once told Dolly after an exhausting meal at Llew's home, with serviettes in silver serviette rings and a bewildering array of cutlery including a fish service such as Amy had never set eyes on before – let alone used. 'I couldn't enjoy what I was eating; I was too afraid of doing something wrong.'

Those days had long since passed, but there was still no warmth in Amy's relationship with her mother-in-law. Despite being Llew's wife and the mother of his two daughters, she still felt Annie would exclude her from the family circle if she could – a girl who had been in service would never quite match up to what she would have liked for her eldest son – and Amy disliked the way she constantly boasted about the achievements of her own family.

As for calling her 'Mother' or 'Mam', Amy had never been able to bring herself to do it. 'Gran' when the children were

176

present, she could just about manage – at all other times Llew's mother remained 'Mrs Roberts'.

Mrs Roberts' propriety extended also to the way she dressed – a hat and gloves for chapel; shoes and stockings whatever the weather, whenever she left the house; and house-shoes placed just inside the door for changing into as soon as she came in again. She also changed her attire at least three times a day, wearing a wrap-around pinafore for mornings, a neat apron for afternoons and a smart dress or skirt and blouse in the evenings. Her daily and weekly routine was so strictly adhered to that Amy had no doubt that on a Thursday morning, as this was, she would find Mrs Roberts engaged in 'doing the bedrooms', and sure enough, when she knocked at the door there was a short wait before she heard footsteps coming down the stairs.

'Amy – good gracious, what a surprise!' Predictably, Mrs Roberts' smile was less than welcoming, for she disliked her routine being interrupted, but she had no option but to add, 'You'd better come in.'

Amy followed her into the prim living-room where the china figurines were set exactly equidistant along the mantelpiece and family portraits hung symmetrically around the walls. Instead of the usual chenille cloth, a cut-glass vase in its own bowl graced the table, but it was empty. Mrs Roberts did not care for flowers in the house – they made too much mess.

'Well, Amy, to what do we owe this visit?' Mrs Roberts asked, motioning for Amy to sit down in one of the over-stuffed arm-chairs with the lace-edged antimacassars.

'I want to talk to you . . . about Llew,' Amy said, obediently perching herself on the edge of the seat.

Instant tears filled Mrs Roberts' blue eyes.

'Oh, I don't know that I can. It upsets me so,' she demurred.

'I'm sorry, but it's important,' Amy persisted. 'I want to go back to when you lived in Wales. Did you ever know a woman called Sibyl James?'

She knew at once that she had touched on a sore point. The tears vanished and Mrs Roberts' face hardened.

'I couldn't say, I'm sure.'

'Please think, Mrs Roberts. A woman in her thirties – thin, dark. And she had a husband who was a miner – an Idris James.'

177

'A miner!' Mrs Roberts' lips tightened. 'We never had more to do with the miners than we could help.'

Amy ignored the implied insult. 'But did you know anyone of that name?'

Mrs Roberts brushed an imaginary speck of dust from the arm of her chair. 'I might have done, I suppose.'

Amy felt the skin on the back of her neck begin to prick. There was something; Mrs Roberts did not want to talk about it and her silence was as telling as any words. But with so much at stake, Amy had to press her for more.

'Did Llew know her?'

For a moment there was no sound in the room but the ticking of the mantel clock. Then Mrs Roberts gesticulated impatiently.

'Oh, all right, if you really want to know I should think everyone in the Rhondda Valley knew Sibyl James. She got a real name for herself – and not one any decent woman would want, I can tell you. Why her husband put up with it, I can't imagine. A quiet sort he was, not in our class mind you, but never one to get himself in trouble. But for some reason he saw fit to go and join the Army when the war started and she was left to her own devices. Of course, that was just what she wanted.'

The palms of Amy's hands were damp and she rubbed them against her skirt.

'And what about Llew?' she asked quietly.

Mrs Roberts clicked her teeth, distressed.

'Llew was just a boy at the time. He had a delivery round for the grocer's – used to be out there on his bike with the orders. Well ... it started. Llew should have known better, of course, but a woman like that knows how to get round any man, let alone a young impressionable lad. And of course, he was so good-looking ...' Her eyes filled with tears again and she blinked them away. 'As soon as I found out what was going on I put a stop to it, naturally. That was the end of his delivery round, as you can imagine.'

Amy was aware of a glimmer of hope. 'And that was all there was to it?'

Mrs Robert's face hardened. 'No, it wasn't. He must have gone on seeing her on the QT. A couple of years later it was – nearly the end of the war – and I found out he'd been with her again. Well, I was beside myself. I went straight out to see her and I told her straight that if she didn't leave him alone, I'd have the law on her. And that's when she had the brass-faced neck to say what she did.'

Amy felt weak. All this in Llew's past and she knew nothing of it.

'What did she say?' she asked.

Mrs Roberts moved impatiently.

'What do you want to bring all this up for? It's over and done with, years ago. Why don't you just leave it alone?'

Amy swallowed. 'Because it may not be over and done with,' she said. 'She told you she was going to have a child. Is that what you don't want to tell me, Mrs Roberts?'

'Well, I never heard such nonsense!' Annie Roberts was bristling, her hands now constantly brushing at the arm of the chair. 'To say a thing like that about our Llew! I told her there and then, it cut no ice with me. It was just wickedness on more wickedness. A lot of evil lies. There she stood, as brazen as you like, accusing my boy of being the father of the baby she was expecting. I told her she'd have to prove it in a court of law and I'd like to see her do *that*, and she said so long as her husband accepted the child as his she wouldn't bother to prove anything. I couldn't believe it, that any woman could be so downright wicked. And I told her so, straight.'

'So what happened?' Amy asked through dry lips.

'Well, I suppose she must have palmed off the baby on her husband,' Annie Roberts said. 'It could have been his all along, for all I know. Whichever, we didn't hear any more from her. She knew she had her master in me, and if she'd taken Llew to court we would have wiped the floor with her. So that's it. Now you know the story – and much good may it do you. As for her, I don't ever want to see her or hear her name again.'

Amy's nails were digging deep crescents in the damp palms of her hands.

'You won't be seeing her again.'

Annie Roberts' eyes narrowed. 'I beg you pardon?'

'She's dead,' Amy said.

Annie's mouth opened in an expression of surprise, then she shrugged.

'Oh well, I'd be a hypocrite if I said I was sorry.' Then, as the thought struck her, she sat forward, looking closely at Amy. 'How do you know she's dead? Why are you here, Amy, asking all these questions?'

Amy swallowed at the lump of nerves that was pulsing in her throat.

'Because she came to see me the day before she died,' she replied.

In that first startled moment Annie Roberts' face was a picture of disbelief. Then a murderous expression darkened her features.

'The mischief-maker! That's her all over! Oh – I wish she'd come to see *me*! What did she say?'

'That she was in need of financial help. That Llew had been sending her money since her husband had been killed underground. And she couldn't understand why it had stopped.'

'The minx! Llew ... sending her money! As if he would – and without you knowing!'

'I think he must have been sending it,' Amy said. Admitting it aloud was one of the hardest things she had ever done in her life. 'It all fits together too well and what you have told me simply confirms it.'

'But don't you see – the father of her child could have been any one of half-a-dozen. She's no proof, she never did have.'

'Llew must have thought it was his,' Amy said softly.

'What?' Annie Roberts was speechless.

'Llew must have thought it was his,' Amy repeated, as if she was trying to explain to herself. 'And if it's true – if that little boy is his son – then we must do something about it.'

'Like what, may I ask?'

'I don't know. But we can't let him go into the Union or an orphanage.'

'Why can't we? It's no business of ours.'

'How can you say that?' Amy demanded. 'If he is Llew's son, it means he's your grandchild. Doesn't that count for anything with you?'

Mrs Roberts drew herself up. 'Don't try to make me feel guilty, Amy. I don't believe Llew had a son and that's an end to it.'

'Then you won't help me?' Amy asked in a small voice.

'Help you? What do you mean – help you?'

Amy stood up, pacing the cold blue carpet square.

'Last night I lay awake for hours, thinking. And I made up my mind. If there is a chance that that boy is Llew's son, no matter who his mother was I'm going to see he's looked after. It's what Llew would have wanted.'

'Amy – have you taken leave of your senses?' Annie
Roberts got to her feet also. 'You don't want to broadcast the
past now; it's over and done with. And think how people
would talk! They'd love to have something to say about us.
You can't drag Llew's name through the mud – not now,
when he's not here to defend himself. You can't *do* it!'

'And I can't stand by and see his son go into an
orphanage,' retorted Amy.

'So what do you think you can do?' Annie Roberts asked
unpleasantly.

'I don't know. Offer him a home, I suppose, if it comes to
that.' Amy was amazed to hear herself saying aloud the half-
formed thought which had bombarded her during the night.

'A home... Amy, now I know you're not feeling well. Sit
down, put your feet up, let me make you a cup of tea...'

'There's nothing wrong with me,' Amy said deliberately.
'And I'm sorry if you don't like the idea, Mrs Roberts, but I
couldn't live with myself if I didn't do what's right. There's a
little boy, about seven years old, left all alone in the world
and he might be as much your grandchild as Barbara or
Maureen.'

'Oh, what rubbish!' Annie Roberts had always made a
great show of her affection for the girls and resented the fact
that Charlotte saw a great more of them than she did –
though whenever she was asked to help out with baby-sitting
or something similar she was invariably too busy with the
pattern of chores which must be adhered to or die! 'Amy, for
goodness' sake, you mustn't go saying such things outside
these four walls. Think of the poppy-show you'll make of
yourself! Think of *us* if you can't think of Llew – his father,
for instance, with the insurance rounds... and Eddie too.
Men would be cashing in their policies rather than have
them knocking at the door and seeing their wives when they
were out of the way at work.'

'Oh, how stupid!' Amy retorted.

'It's not stupid. "You can't trust those Roberts men where
there's a woman concerned" – I can just hear them and what
they'd say now. That sort of thing spreads like wildfire. And
then what about Eddie's ambitions for the council? Who
would vote for him if it was known that his brother –'

'Eddie's quite capable of looking after himself, I'm sure,'
Amy cut in.

Annie Roberts was almost wringing her hands.

'Then if you can't think of them, Amy, at least think of *me*. Oh, *duw*, the shame of it! I could never hold my head up again. We'd have to move away, somewhere we're not known, start all over again – and I'm not sure I could stand it at my age. Oh *duw, duw* ...'

Amy moved impatiently. 'Don't make it any harder for me, Mrs Roberts, please.'

'And what's *your* mother going to say about all this, I'd like to know? For the Lord's sake, Amy ...'

Amy felt sick as a glimpse of what lay in store for her – the arguments, the difficulties, the opposition, the gossip – flickered in front of her eyes. But resolutely she pushed it all away.

'I'd better be going.'

'Amy – don't go! Please, talk it over first ...'

Amy opened the door. 'I don't want to talk.'

'Amy – please ... oh, you don't know how this is upsetting me ...'

'I wonder, Mrs Roberts, if you have any idea how *I* feel about it?' Amy said wearily. 'It's all been a complete shock. But at least I'm glad to say that I still know right from wrong.'

'Amy ...'

Tears were stinging her eyes, but she was determined not to let the older woman see them. She marched out of the house with head high, ears deliberately deaf to the frenzied pleadings of her mother-in-law who followed her, flapping and distraught.

'Amy – I can't bear it! Amy, for the Lord's sake ...'

The smells of the morning hit her – the garden fresh after the recent rain, hot tar from the tar-spraying machine that was being pulled slowly up the main road by a plodding council horse. Smells from another, far-off life when everything had been simple and sweet ... and she ached suddenly with the overwhelming desire to return to it. But it was no good. There could be no going back; she could only go on.

Amy brushed her eyes with the back of her hand. Could she shoulder this new burden? As she had said to Llew's mother, if she did not, she would be unable to live with herself. But could she live *with* it?

Into her mind's eye came a sudden vision of Charlotte, her mother. When she had been young it had always seemed to her that Charlotte was a tower of strength. Of late Amy had forgotten that earlier, childhood vision, for it was blurred now with the passage of years and with Charlotte as she now was – middle-aged, a little tired, no longer a fighter because she had no need to be. But life had not treated her gently, she had had troubles and to spare – two children buried in infancy, a son lost in France, another standing in court on a murder charge, a husband whose health she had seen slowly but surely destroyed.

All those things and more, countless trials, countless griefs, yet somehow she had remained a rock in the eyes of all her children.

If only I can be like her! Amy thought. If only to my own family I can be the rock that she has been to us. Can I do it? I don't know! I'm *me*, not her – Amy, not Charlotte. I'm the little girl with ribbons in my hair, spoiled youngest daughter, petted, loved... how can I be like that?

You can be because you have to be.

It was like a voice inside her, firm, cold almost. It brought no comfort, only a sense of bleak despair. She didn't *want* to be the rock Charlotte had been. She didn't *want* the family to lay their troubles on her. She wanted to be free, careless, happy Amy. But what she wanted had very little to do with it, for she couldn't choose. Well... she could. She could choose to get on a train and go as far as possible from Hillsbridge and from those who would depend on her. But she *wouldn't* do it. So, when there was nothing left but to do what you had to do – well, then, you did it.

Amy caught her lip between her teeth, mentally squaring her shoulders to accept the burdens that were being placed there.

'I won't opt out. I won't take the coward's way, like Mrs Roberts, saying 'I can't stand it' and 'I can't bear it' and 'it upsets me'.

I'll be strong if it kills me. I'll do what's right even if I'm crucified for it. And God grant that the tears I shed in the process, I am able to shed alone.

Chapter Nine

If Amy had encountered opposition to her plan to carry on Llew's haulage business, it was nothing to the opposition she met when she attempted to 'do right by' Llew's illegitimate son.

There were so many people to face – so many explanations to make – and all the while trying to be discreet.

Mrs Moon, at least, was one busybody Amy was able to avoid. She had got shot of the Welsh boy who had been orphaned under her roof at the very first opportunity, and by the time Amy had made up her mind to take responsibility for him, he had been removed from the lodging house to the Manse; there the minister and his wife were looking after Huw while enquiries were made as to any relatives the boy might have in Wales. But it seemed there were none and the minister, in consultation with the other leading figures in the parish, had agreed that there was little alternative but to send Huw to an Industrial School. It was far from being an ideal solution – Industrial School was the new name for Reformatory School and for a boy to be sent there along with hardened young trouble-makers and criminals for no better reason than that he had been orphaned, seemed rough justice indeed. But what alternative was there?

And then Amy Roberts had arrived, knocking at the Manse door with a story that was almost unbelievable. The shocked minister and his wife listened to what she had to say, agreed to keep the details of Huw's parentage confidential and considered the offer she had to make – that she was willing to take in the boy and give him a home and perhaps later, when the Bill now going through Parliament was made law, to adopt him formally.

'Without going into it all thoroughly, I don't know

whether *that* would be possible,' the minister said anxiously. 'What I do know is that it's a magnificent offer and legal adoption or not, as the boy has no relatives, I can see no reason why he should not come to you and be grateful for it.'

Amy nodded. 'I would give him a good home, I promise. I shall need a day or two to make the necessary arrangements, of course, but after that...'

'It's not going to be easy for you, Amy.' The minister thrust his hands deep into his pockets, regarding her seriously. 'You must remember that as a woman alone...'

'I've already given it a great deal of thought,' Amy said, anxious to avoid a lecture, 'and I'm sure it's what Llew would have wanted.'

'If you say so.' The minister rocked on his heels. 'And if it's God's will, I'm certain He will give you the strength to carry it through.'

Amy's face momentarily betrayed her scepticism. Privately she could not help feeling that the events of the last months indicated that she had somehow fallen out of favour with God.

The minister smiled, briefly and sadly.

'On a more practical level, I hope you will feel able to turn to me, as His representative, if you need to do so. Now, perhaps it would be a good idea for me to have the boy down and tell him what you propose to do for him.'

Amy felt a quick flicker of apprehension. She was more nervous of facing the boy with his sharp urchin face and those disconcerting blue eyes than she had been of confronting any of the figures of authority.

'You won't tell him...?'

'I see no need for that. We don't want to make things any worse for the poor boy than they must be, do we?' Alice...' He turned to his gentle but colourless wife, hovering in the background. 'Fetch Huw down, will you?'

The moment the boy came into the room, Amy sensed his antagonism. Cleaner and tidier Huw might be, but he was also somehow wilder, a young cub facing a hostile world alone. In vain Amy tried to tell herself that after all he had been through his defences were bound to be up – that did not help. Faced with his mutinous, resentful expression she felt it was she who was on the defensive, she who was the vulnerable one.

The minister made the introductions, explaining the

situation in simple language he might have used to a Sunday School pupil.

'This is Mrs Roberts, my boy. She has offered to look after you and give you a home.'

The boy stood there, lower lip jutting, eyes narrowed with a hatred that turned Amy cold inside.

'I'd like you to come home with me, Huw,' she said.

There was silence in the room, which the minister eventually broke:

'Well, my boy, and what do you say to that?'

The boy shrugged, his shoulders tightening so that he looked like a taut trip-wire. 'I want to go home.'

'But there's no one there to look after you,' the minister said gently.

Another shrug. 'Don't need anyone. I want to go home!'

Cautiously Amy went towards him. 'Huw . . .'

He took a step back, glaring at her.

'Huw,' the minister intervened. 'Don't be a silly boy, now. Mrs Roberts is being very kind. You don't know how lucky you are to have someone willing to take responsibility for you. Come now!'

But still there was no response.

'Leave me to talk to him, Amy,' the minister said quietly. 'I'm sure that in a day or two he'll come round and have the good sense to be grateful. You go ahead and make the necessary arrangements at your end and leave the rest to me.'

Amy nodded, glad that the interview was at an end.

But as she left the Manse she remembered that what could be the most awkward confrontation was still to come. She had yet to tell Charlotte – and she simply had no idea how to begin.

Climbing the hill to Greenslade Terrace, she tried to compose different openings in her imagination, but none sounded convincing. And she didn't know whether to be relieved or sorry when a somewhat disgruntled Charlotte raised the subject herself almost as soon as she got inside the door.

'Amy – Peggy's just come back from Hillsbridge with the most ridiculous story. How it got started, I don't know, but Peggy heard a tale that you had been to see Mrs Moon and offered to take that Welsh boy off her hands.'

Amy flushed. 'Yes. Mam – I want to talk to you.'

186

'Talk to me? What about? Amy – you're not saying there's any truth in it, surely?'

'Yes, Mam, there is...'

'Amy, for the Lord's sake! What could you do?'

'Mam, listen! He wasn't at Mrs Moon's any more; she couldn't keep him there – or wouldn't. The minister's wife was looking after him for the time being, while they tried to find out whether he had any family back in Wales. But it seems there is no one, and they had decided to send him to one of these so-called Industrial Schools, where they send bad boys to be taught a lesson.'

'You mean like a prison?' Charlotte said. 'Well, it's awful, I grant you that, but it's nothing to do with you, Amy. You've got enough on your plate.'

'It is to do with me, Mam,' Amy said and Charlotte moved impatiently.

'Whatever are you talking about, Amy? What could it have to do with you?'

Amy looked around the familiar room. On his sofa, James was 'snooging' the afternoon away, Harry was nowhere in evidence – Amy guessed he was out with Margaret Young again, doing something for the Labour Party – and the children were outside playing in the Rank, their eager shouts confirming that they were well and truly occupied.

There would never be a better opportunity than now.

Charlotte was pulling an aggressive face and Amy sighed.

'Mam, put the kettle on, will you? There's a lot to tell, and it will go down a darn sight better with a cup of tea.'

Her tone told Charlotte she was serious and with a narrow look at her daughter, she did as she was bid. Then, over a cup of her strongest, sweetest brew, Amy brought her up to date on the story, sparing no details. When she had finished she looked up warily, longing for – and half-expecting – Charlotte's support. But there she was to be disappointed.

'Well, Amy, I don't know what to say, I'm sure,' her mother said at last. 'It's a pretty kettle of fish and no mistake!'

'But you do see, don't you, that I've got to do something?' Amy pressed her. 'I can't let that poor little boy be taken into a reform school. I feel guilty enough as it is.'

'Guilty? Why should *you* feel guilty?' Charlotte demanded.

'Packing her off like I did. I wouldn't even listen.'

'Well, of course you wouldn't. I wouldn't have, I know!'

187

'But she was ill. I could see she was ill and I didn't even give her a cup of tea. And then the storm came and I suppose getting soaked through was like the last straw. If it hadn't been for that, she might be alive today; that's what I can't forget.'

'Don't talk silly, Amy,' Charlotte reprimanded. 'You weren't to know. And you can't go taking on somebody else's child just because of that.'

'Not someone else's child. Llew's.'

'You don't know that, you've only got her word for it. Mrs Roberts said she was a real flibbertijibbet. Now, put it out of your mind, do!'

'I can't,' Amy said, and recognising her stubborn expression, Charlotte's heart sank.

'Be sensible!' she tried again. 'You couldn't cope with him on your own, Amy. A boy needs a man around the place. It's not just now that you've got to think of. It's when he gets older; he might be ever such a naughty boy . . . with a mother like that . . .'

'I could make him know,' said Amy. 'And if he got really out of hand I could get our Jim to have a go at him – or even Harry. Harry's growing up now.'

Charlotte pulled a face.

'And what about the money side of it? Boys are expensive – I should know! They eat you out of house and home and their clothes don't last five minutes. I shall never forget our Ted – wore his best Sunday-going suit across the field once when he was supposed to be at chapel, got it muddy and washed it out in the river! That's the sort of thing you have to expect with boys.'

Amy said nothing and Charlotte pressed on:

'Money doesn't grow on trees, Amy, and you want to be able to keep a good table and keep the girls looking nice. And you don't know yet whether you're going to be able to make the business pay.'

'I shall have to sell the house,' Amy said.

'What?' Charlotte banged down her cup. 'Sell the house? Amy – you can't do that!'

'I shall have to,' Amy said in the same calm, stubborn voice. 'Oh, not just because of the boy. I've been thinking about it anyway. If I could get a smaller place, it would give me a bit of capital to play with while I'm trying to get the business sorted out.'

'But Amy, it's such a nice place – and you've got it lovely! Oh, you don't want to sell the house!' Charlotte sounded really distressed.

'No, I don't want to, but I haven't much choice,' Amy said. 'Don't go on about it, Mam – you only make it worse.'

'Well, where would you go? I couldn't have you here – not with your Dad...'

'I wouldn't think of it; you do enough. And you needn't think that if they let me have the boy that would mean extra work for you, either. I've already thought of that. When he's not at school, he can come to the yard with me; he'll be useful as he gets older.'

'Well, Amy, it sounds to me as if you've made up your mind. I don't know why you came here asking me...' Charlotte sounded faintly huffy.

'I didn't ask you, Mam,' Amy said quietly. 'I just wanted to let you know what I'm going to do. And I hoped you might approve.'

'Well, I shan't, Amy. I can't approve of something like this. You're worrying me to death, I don't mind telling you.'

Amy stood up. 'I'm sorry you see it like that, Mam. You always brought us up to do what we think is right, even if it isn't the easy way, and that's what I'm doing.'

'Amy...' Charlotte rose too, distressed. 'I'm only thinking of your good.'

'Look, Mam.' There was a slight tremble in Amy's voice. 'I don't honestly think you've got any idea how I feel. You've been lucky; you've had Dad thirty years. I only had Llew for five and it wasn't enough. I loved him and now he's gone. I've got to hang on to him any way I can. That's why I must keep the business going, whatever it costs me. It's like keeping part of Llew alive. And I've got to do what he would have wanted me to do.'

'But he wouldn't have expected this! He wouldn't have wanted you to take on...'

'Mam!' Amy said warningly.

Charlotte shook her head, tired suddenly.

'Well, I don't know what your Dad's going to say, I'm sure. It'll finish him, this will. He'll never stand it...'

The back door slammed. Harry!

'It's time we were going,' Amy said hastily, suddenly unable to face any more.

She collected the girls' things together, made them kiss

their Granny and Grampie and when Uncle Harry swung them high in the air as they always begged him to, she laughed at their squeals of delight. But out in the Rank the depression weighed down on her so that she felt like crying.

If only Mam had given her one word of encouragement! If only she had said, 'Yes, Amy, you are doing the right thing.' But she hadn't, and Amy knew she would not. Oh, she might come around sufficiently to offer some concrete help, but it was moral support Amy wanted just now more than anything else – someone to talk things over with and help her think of solutions, not place obstacles in her path.

That evening, when she had put the children to bed, the worries which had beset her ever since she reached her decision were still swimming round and round inside her head.

What effect was it going to have on Barbara and Maureen to have the boy in the house? she wondered anxiously. She would have less time for them by the time she had cared for the boy too, and money would be even more scarce for she couldn't see that she could expect financial help from any outside source, especially if eventually she was able to adopt Huw legally.

The only solution would be the one she had mentioned to Charlotte – sell the house and find somewhere cheaper. But another house would still have to have three bedrooms; Huw couldn't share a room with the girls.

I hope he won't be a bad influence on them, she worried. It was all very well to dismiss it blithely when Charlotte suggested he might be a bad boy, but quite another to still the doubts in her own heart. Huw had a look about him that was both wild and stubborn, the look of a boy who was worldly wise and, judging by what she could remember of his mother, Amy doubted he had ever been disciplined in his life.

Supposing he turned out to be a liar, a cheat, a thief? How would she handle him – and what sort of redress would she have if she failed?

And leaving aside the big issues – the things so overwhelming that it was almost pointless to spend time and energy worrying about them – what about the small day-to-day problems such as his schooling, his clothes, what time she should make him go to bed, even?

Bringing up your own children was one thing. You

learned as you went along. But a boy of seven or eight ... the list of problems both moral and practical was endless ... and daunting.

Preferring action to worrying, once the children were settled Amy decided to prepare the spare room in readiness for Huw.

It was the small front room next to her own, and since they had occupied the house it had become a kind of glory-hole. It was furnished, yes, but anything for which there was no obvious home found its way into the spare room. Her own out-of-season clothes filled the small wardrobe, the drawers of the small dressing-table provided storage space for keepsakes, articles of bed-linen which had been wedding presents and never yet used, some rag dolls she had bought at a bazaar for the children's Christmas presents and a host of other odds and ends. Amy sorted them, trying to be methodical, but it was difficult to keep her mind on the job. Huw had nothing to put into the empty drawers – nothing – and the emptiness was frightening. But she couldn't expect him to occupy a room full of other people's possessions.

And what to do with it all?

It will have to go into the attic for the time being, Amy decided. Until we move. Then there will have to be an almighty turnout and a lot of it will have to go.

Somehow the thought was the trigger for her pent-up emotions. It was weeks now since Amy had cried – there simply hadn't been time. Now, sitting in the jumble of possessions she and Llew had accumulated, despair overcame her once more and so suddenly she was powerless to combat it.

What will I do? How can I do it alone? I don't know. I don't know ...

She sobbed, her hand stuffed into her mouth so as not to disturb the children. Then after a while she regained control of herself and began sorting again, though the tears still streamed down her cheeks.

And then, at the back of the wardrobe, she found it.

My teddy bear! she thought, pulling out the battered toy. One ear was almost gone – Barbara had found the teddy once when she was a baby and chewed it before Amy could take it away from her and hide it again, but it was still unmistakably the bear of her own childhood and as she looked at it the years seemed to roll away.

Just nine years old she had been, not much older than Huw was now, when she had been given the bear. She had had a terrible accident – fallen backwards into a tub of boiling water which had been drawn to bath the baby in the Clements' house next door to her old home in Greenslade Terrace. The scalding had been dreadful – parboiled more than scalded, the doctor had said – and even now the memory of the screaming pain made her wince. As if in a dream, she could remember the things they had said about it when they thought she could not hear: that she might not survive because of the danger of infection, and that if she did she might not walk again.

At the time she hadn't cared. She had been unable to think beyond pain, which had reached unbearable proportions when her dressings were changed daily – clean washed sheeting to cover the raw patches, carron oil to help it heal. The one thing which had made it all bearable had been the doctor, Oliver Scott. He was young, much younger than any other doctor she had ever known, and so kind. She had fallen in love with him, heart and soul. Each day she had waited for his visit, thinking not of the painful dressing change to come but of his pale, good-looking face, his freckled forearms and the way his eyes seemed to disappear into creases when he smiled. He had sat with her much longer than he should – 'neglecting my other patients, but who cares?' he had said to her once – so in her nine-year-old heart she had been sure he loved her too.

She remembered thinking that she must get well for him. With Oliver to live for, she must not die! She remembered planning, too. One day they would be married and she would go to chapel riding in the ribbon-decked pony and trap as brides did. And then they would live together and he would be able to tell her stories and sit by her bed and hold her hand all the time, not just when she was ill and not really able to appreciate it.

And the panacea had worked. Miraculously Amy had begun to get well. For thirteen weeks she lay on her stomach on the kitchen sofa, then she had to be pushed out in her old push-chair until they taught her, with great patience, to walk again. Almost a year out of her life, a year of pleasure and pain, small triumphs and crushing setbacks, a year she would never forget.

But as her body healed, Amy's heart began to break. Oliver

Scott came less often now and she felt more bereft and lonely than she had ever felt in her life. Depression began to set in, depression fuelled by boredom and the taut feel of healing skin, broken only by such moments of wonderful joy as when, on a visit to his parents, he remembered to send her a postcard – a jolly, bright picture of a plump, bare-bottomed child sitting on a drum, with the caption: 'I'm sitting on it so's you can't beat it.' 'Well, I don't know, the doctor sending that!' Charlotte had said. But Amy had kept it beside her bed, insurance against the growing feeling that Oliver no longer cared.

He's forgotten me, Amy had thought. He's forgotten all about me. She lost interest in everything, lying listlessly while the blackness inside her head made her wish she had died after all.

And then one day Mam had brought her the brown paper parcel.

'Dr Scott left this for you. It's for Christmas really. But I don't suppose he'd mind if I let you open it now.'

Her heart had swelled. Oliver had not forgotten. With eager fingers she tore at the paper and extracted the contents. A card, inscribed: 'To the bravest little girl I ever met.' A whole pound of butterscotch when butterscotch usually came in ounces, not pounds. And the teddy!

She had never seen a teddy before. Teddies were brand-new toys, fresh from America and named for some politician or other: Amy thought it was the most wonderful thing she had ever been given.

Satisfied, she had tucked it under her arm, holding it close. In the months that followed, it went everywhere with her, brightening the dark moments and giving her a feeling of warmth and comfort.

Even when Oliver Scott married Grace O'Halloran, Hal's eldest daughter, and left Hillsbridge, the bear had not been put aside. Amy had been sad for a little while, yes, wishing he could have waited for her, but she was getting better all the time and life was beginning to open out again for her. She was out of the tunnel into daylight, and the bear was with her.

Now, all those years on, she sat in the small front bedroom of her home looking at the bear and feeling once more the warmth and comfort she had felt then.

That crisis in her life had come and gone and she had

survived. Others who had had similar accidents had not been so lucky, she knew. The severity of a scalding in uncooled bath water had claimed their lives, but not hers. And if she could survive that, she could survive anything else life might throw at her. She was a fighter. She had fought then, and she would fight now.

With a small, determined smile, Amy took the bear and hid it in her jumper drawer. She would have liked to put it on her bed, but if Barbara or Maureen found it they would want to play with it and she didn't want it damaged. Better to keep it and bring it out sometimes to remind herself that however dark life sometimes seemed, there was always a way of fighting through. Better to preserve it as a memento of what she had been through – and what she could go through again, if necessary.

Heartened and refreshed, Amy returned to the task of clearing the guest room for the new small visitor who had added yet another dimension to her already topsy-turvy life.

Chapter Ten

'Harry – hey, Harry, what d'you think?' Reg Clements turned the corner of the Rank just as Harry emerged from his pigeon loft, and half-running along the cobbled path, his pale freckled face showing two red highspots of anger. 'What d' you think – there's a man gone in to work this morning at Middle Pit!'

'Who's that, then?'

'"Nosey" Parker, from down Market Cottages. He went in when the safety men did and stayed about three-quarters of an hour. He was seen, of course, and all the men who were down on the Bridge got round the gates to give him a cheer when he came out.'

'A cheer?'

'Well, you know, kick up a din and let him know how we

feel about blacklegs. Cor – I wouldn't be in his shoes now, darned if I would!'

'Well, the dirty creep!' Harry said.

It was the last week of August and the strike showed no signs of ending. There were rumours from time to time, it was true, raising the hopes of men who had tightened their belts week after week as the Relief Fund dwindled and their weekly payments fell far below the breadline. From five shillings for full members and two-and-sixpence for boys such as Harry and Reg, the payments had been halved, and this week there was to be no handout at all. But the majority of the men were as determined as ever. This time there could be no surrender; they could not afford to give in and go back to work for less money than they had been earning when they came out – not after all they'd been through. So they let their children go away to stay with people who could afford to keep them, accepted what charity there was with as much dignity as they could muster, and met each new day of inactivity with faces grown gaunt and grim, but eyes that burned with the fervent belief that in the end justice would surely prevail.

Some, it was true, behaved in a way that Charlotte described as 'letting themselves down'. After one rally in Bath, Ewart Brixley – still a hothead though he was now old enough to know better – had been amongst a gang of a dozen or fifteen men who had tried to scramble into one taxi-cab. In the ensuing struggle the taxi driver had been assaulted and a policeman who came to take things in hand had his helmet knocked off. The man responsible for that had been given three months' hard labour and Ewart had been lucky not to be amongst the gaggle who got a month for being drunk and disorderly.

'There's no sense in it – that sort of thing does no good at all,' Charlotte said when she heard. 'I hope you've got more gump than to get yourself mixed up in anything like that, Harry!'

Harry had not bothered to reply. Privately he agreed with his mother, but it would have sounded a bit stick-in-the-mud coming from a boy of his age if he had said so. And in any case, if she didn't know him better than that by now, she should do.

He was working as hard and as tirelessly as ever – harder, perhaps, for as money grew shorter the dances and concerts

195

raised less and the Relief Fund began to be dependent on the regular contributions of sympathisers – not only big concerns such as the Co-op, but individuals like George Young, who somehow managed to make sufficient sacrifices themselves so as to contribute ten shillings a week out of their own meagre pay-packets.

The strike had brought fun, of course, as well as despair. The young people made the most of their freedom and thoroughly enjoyed the nightly dances that were held in the various recreation grounds around the outskirts of Hillsbridge. And it had also brought tragedy. One little boy who had left Hillsbridge Station with a group of colliers' children for a fortnight under canvas paid for by the Lady Slessor Fund, was back less than a week later in a pitifully small oak coffin with silver-plated fittings. Riding on a load of hay he had slipped off, rolled down the bank and under the rear wheels of the wagon.

'It's terrible!' said Charlotte, who was in town when the hearse bringing him back passed slowly through. 'Just think if it was our Alex or May!'

'Where is it they've gone?' asked Peggy, who was with her.

'Down to Eastleigh, in Hampshire. The two of them are together with some well-to-do businessman. They'll be coming back full of grand ideas, if I know anything about it. Our Sarah didn't want them to go, that I do know, but what can you do?'

That was just it. What could anyone do but tighten their belts, look for ways to survive and hope and pray it would all be over soon. Which was why there was so much anger at the thought of one man strike-breaking.

'Reckon he'll go in again tomorrow?' Harry asked Reg.

'Dunno. Shall we walk down and see?'

'Yes. Can do.'

The next day was fine, bright and warm. Altogether it had been a brilliant summer, apart from a few violent thunderstorms such as the one which had killed five cows, a bull and a horse in a field out beyond Withydown with one huge flash, and thrown six hikers to the ground on the road to Bath. But today the skies were clear and blue as Harry, Tommy and Reg walked down the hill.

Though they were early themselves, there was already quite a crowd gathered in the Market Yard and outside the Miners' Arms. 'Nosey' Parker would have to pass that way in order to get home to Market Cottages from Middle Pit and the men were determined he should not slip past without their making him aware of their disapproval.

'Blackleg!' one man muttered and another added: 'If this was still the war, they'd be handing him a white feather.'

'Good idea. That'd show 'un!'

Someone was despatched to raid the hen-pens down in Glebe Bottom in search of a white feather.

'Bring enough and get some tar from thick tar-spraying machine they'm doing the roads with and we could tar and feather 'un!' someone else added.

Harry began to feel uneasy. He hoped this was not going to get out of hand. But the feather-seeker was soon back empty-handed, complaining of being chased out of the hen-pens by an irate cottager wielding her sweeping brush, and almost at the same time Sergeant Eyles came marching around the corner with a force of the extra police strength which had been drafted into Hillsbridge in case of trouble.

That would put paid to any really crazy schemes, Harry thought with a sense of relief. He had no wish to see any of his mates sent off for three months' hard labour.

The crowd settled down to waiting once more. Harry was surprised at the number of women there – it was almost as if they were angrier on behalf of their menfolk than the men were themselves. One group, a noisy cluster from 'Batch Row' – one of the poorest areas in Hillsbridge – were in a huddle under the wall of the Miners' Arms, and from the amount of gesticulating and head-wagging and the occasional loud shriek of laughter, Harry suspected they were up to something. This was no laughing matter, and a few minutes ago the women had been anything but amused.

'What do you reckon that lot think is so funny?' he asked Tommy, who only shrugged.

'Dunno. Oh, I don't half wish I had a fag!'

The others agreed. They had not experienced real hardship as some families had done. Molly Clements, the boys' stepmother, was a good manager like Charlotte, and at this time of year the gardens were mercifully full of vegetables. But oh, it seemed so long since they had been able to enjoy the luxury of a few shillings to jingle in their pockets, a packet of Woodbines and a pint of beer!

'Look out – isn't that "Nosey" coming now?' Reg said.

Sure enough, a small bent figure in working togs had

emerged from the colliery gates. 'Nosey' Parker was older than many of them – forty if he was a day – and the best part of thirty years spent underground had given him the unmistakable gait of a miner. As he walked towards them, head bent against the expected jeers and catcalls, Harry saw the police begin to move in. There might be abuse for the blackleg miner, but there would be no violence ... or so it seemed.

But Harry – and the police – had reckoned without the women. As 'Nosey' approached, they watched closely in a silence that contrasted sharply with the noisy barracking of the men. Then, as if at a given signal, they swooped, surrounding him.

'Stinking rat!'

'Want a bath before you go home, Nosey? You don't want to go home dirty, do you?'

The police began to run towards the heaving group. They had anticipated any trouble would come from the men, not the women, and before they could get within striking distance a dozen eager hands had overcome Nosey's flapping struggles. Three of the women held his arms pinioned, two more held down his feet while the others tore at his clothing. Then, just as the first policeman reached the perimeter of the group, another woman came running out of the Miners' Arms carrying a pail. The policeman made to stop her, but she dodged him nimbly and as the others parted to let her through she hurled the water. Some splashed the policeman, quite a lot drenched the attacking women. But most went exactly where it had been intended to go – over 'Nosey' Parker. After the first shrieks the laughter began, unquenched by the angry shouts of the police, and as the women scattered 'Nosey' was exposed to Harry's view – a sad, scrawny figure in dripping, dirty-white underpants.

He hasn't been underground at all! Harry thought indignantly. No miner would think of wearing long underpants under his rushyduck trousers – it was much too hot!

But it was a passing thought only.

Harry's brother Ted would probably have laughed as loudly as anyone at the sight of 'Nosey'; Fred, who had been killed in the war, or Jim, might have stared unmoved; Jack might have been faintly disgusted by the vulgarity. But Harry felt none of these things.

With a wisdom beyond his years Harry found himself looking beyond the stark fact that 'Nosey' had betrayed his comrades and seeing what lay behind it – the despair, the heart-searching, the hunger and desperation. And the same sense of helpless anger that had filled him when he looked at his bedridden father rose in his craw again – anger that an honest, sober, hard-working man should be subjected to such indignity through the need to keep his family.

With the police after them the Batch Row women had scattered, and it looked as if several arrests had been made. 'Nosey', trying to look as if he didn't care a hang, pulled up his soaking trousers, buttoned them and continued his walk between the jeering men to the irreverent piping notes of a penny whistle. Sickened, Harry turned away.

'They say his son's coming with the trucks later on to get his coal allowance,' said Tommy, who had slipped off to be in the thick of the excitement. 'Shall we hang around and wait for un?'

Harry shook his head. 'I think I'm going home, Tom.'

'Why? What's the matter?'

Harry hesitated, wishing he had the courage to say out loud that he had no stomach for any more tormenting of one of their own, but the words refused to come.

'Oh nothing – I just want my dinner,' he muttered.

'I s'pose we might as well come too,' Tommy agreed and Reg added, 'It was a good laugh, though, wasn't it? Served old "Nosey" right!'

'I felt sorry for him,' Harry ventured.

'Sorry for him? Sorry for a *blackleg!*' the Clements boys chorused and Harry retreated.

'Well, he must have felt a real fool . . .'

'And so he should!' Tommy stated. 'I would have done far worse if I'd had half a chance.'

Harry said nothing. One day, he thought; one day I'll stand up and say that it's all wrong for miner to be set against miner . . . and this is what poverty does for you. But for the moment, no one would listen or take the slightest notice.

'Come on then, lads, last one up the hill is a lazy scoundrel!' he joked.

. . . And tried not to feel a Judas as he turned his back on the despair and frustration of those still in the thick of the protest.

Chapter Eleven

In the back bedroom of the house in Hope Terrace, a small boy stood kicking disconsolately at the skirting board with the rounded toe of brand-new brown leather sandals, while in the pockets of his equally new grey flannel shorts, his hands made small tight fists.

'I hate her!' he muttered, thrusting his full lower lip forward with each word. 'I hate her!'

But though the pain inside him was worse even than when he had scrumped a bellyful of half-ripe apples, he did not cry. At eight years old Huw James was not only tough, he was also bright as a button. Tears did no good. He had learned that a long time ago, playing in the back streets of Pontypridd. Tears were for sissies. If you got hurt, you hit out. It was the only way.

But until now, however much hitting out he had done, there had always been home to go back to – a small, dark, safe cottage in the shadow of the slag-heaps – and Mam, who had laughed a lot even when things went wrong, and who hugged him close with arms so thin he could almost circle them with his eight-year-old hands, and who washed the mud and blood and jam off his face and hands every night before he went to bed.

Until a year ago, there had been the man he called 'Dad' too, but only ever on the sidelines. Dad was of medium height and beefy-broad, a taciturn man who had spent little time in the cottage and less with Huw. The boy had thought nothing of this; in his experience, mothers stayed at home and fathers went out to work and to the pub. Some fathers, it was true, also sang in the male voice choir once a week. Occasionally Huw and his friends had stopped outside the practice hall to listen to the soaring resonance that filled the whole air like thunder, making every particle sing with it; it had taken his breath away to think that glorious noise was made by a lot of men you wouldn't look at twice if you saw them walking down the street alone ... men like Jones the butcher and Williams the milk, and the family of six brothers who lived at the top end of his Rank and went everywhere together.

But Dad was not in the choir and Huw had accepted this as a fact of life just as he accepted that Dad never went to chapel on Sundays, and was more likely to give him a cuff round the ear than a word of praise.

Sometimes, just sometimes, Dad would come out of that self-imposed silence to tell Huw stories about the war; in years to come these sessions, all too brief and all too seldom, were the only thing about Dad that Huw remembered with pleasure.

Dad had been in the war almost from the beginning, he had told Huw, rushing off to a recruiting station the moment hostilities commenced and before the Government put a ban on the enlistment of miners. He had fought on the Western Front and seen mates fall all around him, but miraculously the wounds he had suffered had not been serious enough to keep him out of the lines for long and the tales he had to tell of coal-box shells and machine guns, of muddy war – devastated countryside and rotting corpses, of heroics and comradeship, suffering and glory, had fascinated Huw. Even when he was too young to understand, the feeling of it all had drawn him, and from the time he could crawl he had played at soldiers, worming on his stomach between the legs of the kitchen table and attacking – with Dad's bicycle pump for a gun – from behind the sofa and chairs that crammed the dark little living-room.

The trouble was, as Huw discovered as he grew older, that all too often Dad's reminiscences of the war ended in one of his morose moods. All too often the feeling of warm companionship and latent excitement that Huw experienced during the telling would begin to fade as he saw the dark look begin to descend on Dad's blunt features. Always he tried to hang on to it.

'What then? What else?' he would press Idris, but the more he pressed, the blacker his father's mood would become.

'That's it. There's nothing more. It's all over and done with a long time ago,' Idris would growl, and bewildered though he was by the change in mood, Huw would know it was time to clear out and leave Dad in peace – or risk a clout.

Apart from the war games, Dad never played with Huw. It would never have occurred to either of them. As soon as he was old enough, Huw was out with the other boys in the Rank, trailing behind them at first and then becoming accepted as one of the pack. With them he played the usual games – wrapping a brick in brown paper and placing it in the centre of the footpath, only to jerk it away when some busybody or other tried to pick it up; or teasing elderly householders by means of a length of cotton attached to their door-knocker and a vantage point behind the walls of bushes so as to give it a quick jerk each time the unfortunate victim had gone back to the kitchen once more. In more law-abiding moments they played 'tag' and 'off-ground touch', cricket and football; when there was extra steam to let off they fought, either as individuals or in a gang, rolling on the ground with the ferocity of street fighters twice and three times their age – rolling, gouging, grabbing and kicking. Nobody, with the exception of his dictatorial schoolmaster, ever told Huw he should not fight. Mam sometimes shook her head at the state of him, but there was always an amused look somewhere at the back of her eyes and Dad would only say:

'Scrapping again? Ah well, you've got to learn, Huw.'

Huw learned. First how to defend himself; then how to attack; then, to his pleased amazement, that attack was the best form of defence anyway. He was not a big boy but scrawny really, like his mother, yet he was strong and fearless and soon had his place in the pecking order of the back streets of Pontypridd, respected and challenged by boys who were bigger, and older, than he.

Altogether, life had been a pretty satisfactory affair for Huw. He played hookey whenever he could both from school and chapel, and he learned different ways of dodging Dad's clips and cuffs. The poor meals served up were no different from what they had ever been – he knew nothing else – but by the age of seven he was wise enough to know how to supplement his diet by pinching a handful of gobstoppers from the counter in 'Jones the Sweets' shop; and sometimes, if he could distract old Jones for long enough, some mint shrimps or bullseyes too. He was out from morning till night, winter and summer alike, and if Mam wondered where he went when it rained, she never actually got around to asking – and certainly Huw would never have told her. Even Mam, who accepted most things with that half-smile of reproof, might have forbidden Huw to sneak into the pit offices by courtesy of a faulty window-catch. Huw had discovered it one night when they had been caught in a sudden storm, and he and the other boys classed the occupation as their greatest feat, savouring it whenever they could, growing more and more daring, but always being careful to leave no trace of their presence – and to return the window, by means of bent wire and string, to the position in which they had found it.

Yes, life was one long adventure, always different yet always the same, until tragedy impinged and cracks began to appear in the smooth surface of Huw's world.

It was late summer and Huw and the boys had been on the slag-heap behind the pit. Tipping had long since ceased there and the lads liked to climb to the top and slide down – sometimes on sacks; sometimes, if they were lucky, on an old tin tray. Officials would yell at them if they saw them, but that failed to stop them and dodging officialdom only added to the spice. And that morning they were at the very summit, the supreme vantage point, when they saw the activity in the valley below.

The appearance of the ambulance always caused a stir. Like the Hillsbridge vehicle, it had once been a field ambulance in France and after the war had been detailed for civilian duty. When they saw it in the road below the boys had all stopped what they were doing in order to look. Clearly somebody had been hurt underground. But they were too far away to make out the small, scurrying figures, or to get any clue as to the identity of the man on the stretcher – still . . . very still . . . covered by the dark grey blanket.

Strangely they said nothing, not even to each other, and when the ambulance had gone and the scene returned to normal, they took their tin trays and slid merrily down the slag-heap, shrieking and whooping and completely careless that someone had been seriously injured – killed even. But when he went home and turned the corner of his street, Huw found that for some reason his feet were dragging and there was a hollowness inside him which, had he known the word for it, he might have called apprehension or even dread. But he did not understand it, so he went on along the street with a jaunty step and burst in on a scene that would be imprinted on his mind for ever afterwards.

Mam was there, standing in the centre of the room with her hands pressed to her face, weeping. Two of the neighbours were there too, and a black-grimed man Huw recognised as one of the deputies from the pit. But after the first surprised glance his eyes were drawn irresistibly to the still figure laid out on the sofa. Dad . . . but a Dad who lay motionless, a Dad from whose face every trace of coal-dust had been washed so that he looked waxy-pale in the light creeping in through the closed curtains.

Huw stopped in his tracks, his blue eyes going wide.

'Dad?' he said, going towards the sofa.

But one of the neighbours moved quickly to intercept him, restraining him with a warning touch. And then Mam was there too, in front of him, blotting out his view of that strange greyish thing that looked like Dad and yet was . . .

'Oh, Huw – Huw . . . !' Mam's arms were around him, the thinness of them digging into his back and crushing him so that he fought her in panic. 'He's gone . . . gone. You're all I've got now. Oh, Huw . . .'

'Come on now, don't upset yourself, Sibyl love . . . And don't frighten the child . . .' The neighbours took charge, calming the distraught woman, easing Huw away, putting a mug of strong brewed tea into his hands; somehow he found himself acting almost normally, trying to impress them by his calmness, though he hardly knew what to make of what was going on.

Later, when the neighbours had gone and he was upstairs in the tiny room that led off his parents' bedroom, Mam had talked to him. She told him that there had been an accident underground and a large stone had fallen on Dad.

'He didn't have a chance,' she said sadly. 'All through the war he went, with hardly a scratch, and then to be killed here in Ponty! It's a funny old life; you'll learn that, Huw.'

Huw had listened quietly, wishing Mam would stop going on about it. He was embarrassed by her talking, just as he was embarrassed when she put her arms around him. He wished he could get out with the boys again, have a bit of fun and forget that all this was happening. He felt no grief, just puzzlement and a little resentment. And he hoped that never again, as long as he lived, would he have to see anyone else looking as Dad had looked.

For a while after the funeral – when Dad was actually taken into chapel for the first time Huw could ever remember – life reverted to normal. Huw hardly missed him – their paths had crossed too seldom in his lifetime to have formed anything of a pattern – and it was more comfortable by far to get out with the boys and stay out as if nothing had changed.

But it had ... and before long there was no escaping the repercussions. Whereas before Mam had seemed to let troubles roll off her like water off a duck's back, now she cried often and after a while even Huw could scarcely fail to notice the way she looked. More than once during the year that followed, she was ill, and each time it took her longer than before to get up and about again. She coughed long and often, bouts that racked her thin body and kept Huw awake at night – Huw, who always fell into bed so tired that Mam had said many a time you could drive a coach and horses through the room and he would never hear them. And without admitting it, Huw had begun to be frightened.

He had tried not to show it, of course, even when Mam packed their things into a carpet bag and took him on the train to a place called Hillsbridge.

'Why can't I stay at home?' he had asked her.

And Mam had snapped the way she snapped so often these days: 'You just *can't*. You have to come with me, see?'

Looking back afterwards, Huw was never quite sure when the visit stopped being boring and began to be a nightmare.

Was it when Mam took him to see that awful woman, who shouted and made her cry? Or was it when he was woken in the night by the shaking of the bed they were sharing and the sound of the hard, racking cough he had come to fear. He had turned over, humping the clothes over his head, but though that muffled the sound a little it could not prevent him from feeling the continued restless movement of the bed.

Next morning Mam had tried to get up, but she was too ill. Huw had stayed with her, partly because she kept hanging on to him and begging him not to leave her, partly because for the first time in his life he had met someone who frightened him – the dragon of a woman whose house they were staying in, Mrs Moon. She didn't look like a monster, Huw thought in puzzlement. She was small – almost as small as he was – with soft white hair and a flowered pinafore. But oh! the venomous expression that innocuous little face was capable of conjuring up! And how shrill was her voice with its unfamiliar accent, harsh-sounding to Huw's ears after the lilt of the valleys. Huw had escaped from colliery managers, policemen and threatening neighbours, wriggling out of a dozen and more tweaking ear-holds. He had been up before the headmaster more often, he maintained, than any other boy in the school and always emerged laughing – even if it was a laugh that held back tears of pain. But none of them had frightened him as Mrs Moon did. Afterwards, in his mind she was also woven in as an integral part of the nightmare.

It was on the second night that it happened.

All day as Mam coughed – trying to keep it quiet so as not to call down the wrath of Mrs Moon for disturbing her – she had tossed and turned as though she could not bear the bedclothes over her and he had been aware of a sense of impending doom. It seemed to fill the room with the ominous heaviness that precedes a thunderstorm. That evening, unable to bear it any longer, he pushed up the sash window and escaped for a while to wander and explore in this strange and hostile town. When he returned he was more afraid of being caught by Mrs Moon than of what he would find in Mam's room, and when he went in head-first over the sill and caught sight of her, his heart seemed to stop beating.

She looked just as Dad had looked – waxy-white, skin shiny and drawn tight over the bones of her face. For a moment he thought she was already dead. Cautiously, heavy with dread, he crept towards her and bent over the still, white form. And when her hand moved suddenly, fastening around his arm, he screamed and screamed, shocked beyond caring about anything. Then, as the door opened, his scream became sobs of fear. He had done it now – Mrs Moon was coming. And Mam was not dead at all ... she was alive. He could see the faint flutter of her eyelashes and hear the soft mew of her breathing.

'What's going on here? What ...?' Mrs Moon broke off, as shocked as Huw had been as her searching gaze settled on the unnaturally pale woman in the bed. 'Oh my Lord, whatever is the matter with your mother? We shall have to get the doctor to her. Why didn't you tell me, you stupid boy?'

She grabbed his arm to put him aside but Huw, veteran of dozens of encounters with angry adults, assumed she was about to mete out punishment so he twisted violently and kicked out. Mrs Moon screamed in pain and anger as the toe of his heavy boot connected with her bony leg, but Huw did not wait for anything. Seizing his advantage he sped through the door and away, running, running, until his breath came in short, painful bursts and his legs shook beneath him.

He stopped, doubling up while he caught his breath, then straightened and looked around. He had run along a road that was parallel with the railway line and beyond it an embankment rose, coal-dust black and covered with trees. There was something familiar and welcoming about the embankment – the first place since he had come to Hillsbridge that did not make him feel totally alien – and it drew Huw. Nimbly he climbed through the strand-wire fence and scooted across the railway line. To his relief no one saw him – you got yelled at for wandering about on railway lines, too. Then he was at the foot of the embankment, scrambling up the first steep part and sending small avalanches of dust and dirt down behind him.

It was cool amongst the trees, cool and somehow safe. Huw climbed until he found a really thick trunk and wedged himself behind it. He knew he ought to go back and face Mrs Moon's wrath, but he didn't want to. And he didn't want to see Mam looking like that again, either. He wanted her to have some of her old colour back in her cheeks; to look the way she used to before Dad died.

How long Huw stayed on the embankment he never knew, though afterwards there were certain sounds that always conjured it up for him once more – the whistle of trains on the line below as they approached the station; their even puffing, so close at hand; the distant clanging of church bells, for it was practice night at the Tower. There were smells, too – the pine needles and the damp, dusty earth all around him, and in the air the teasing whiff of a couch fire. Each time a train went by clouds of smoke rose, fogging the spaces between the trees. But still Huw sat there, wedged against the solid trunk.

It was only when darkness began to fall that he realised he could not stay here all night. Reluctantly, aware he would be in for trouble when he returned to 'the digs', he slid back down the embankment and picked his way across the railway lines. The light was failing fast and for a panicky moment he wondered if he would be able to find his way back. But landmarks presented themselves along the way and sooner than he expected he found himself nearing the house of torment. Lights were blazing out of every window. *I've done it now*, thought Huw.

There was nothing for it but to go in, but he hoped that he might be able to slip by the dragon unnoticed and into the room he was sharing with Mam. He tried the door and the handle turned; stealthily he pushed at it, then froze. Through the widening crack he could see the unmistakable dark blue of a policeman's uniform.

She went for the law! thought Huw in panic. She sent for the law because I kicked her!

His first instinct was to run again, but his path was blocked by someone coming in at the gate – a very large lady with a bag. He hesitated and was lost. Strong fingers gripped his shoulder and a booming voice with that strange, ugly accent announced:

'So there you are! Where have you been, eh, lad?'

Realising there was no escape, Huw tried a different approach. 'Mam? Where's my Mam?'

For a moment there was silence in the small, overcrowded hallway, and the quality of it panicked Huw. He looked around from one to the other – Mrs Moon, pinched-looking; the policeman, stern yet somehow sad; the newcomer – the large lady with the bag – her face set in a curious expression that somehow looked like pretend-solemnity. As he looked, fear seemed to explode in him like a roman candle on fireworks night, sending showers of small burning sparks through all his veins.

'Mam! Mam!' he cried, struggling against the grip on his shoulder.

'Now you wait a minute.' Huw did not perceive the note of kindness in the policeman's voice; he only felt the restraining hand and as before he kicked out wildly. The policeman momentarily slackened his grip just as Mrs Moon had done and Huw, the practised escaper, took advantage of it. Before any of them could stop him, he was across the hall and in the doorway of their room where he stopped again, his knees turning to jelly.

Mam was lying where he had left her, looking whiter and more waxy than ever, if such a thing were possible. Only now there was no flutter of her eyelashes, no gently rasping breath.

'Mam – Mam!' He threw himself towards her, willing it not to be true. 'Mam – wake up! Wake up!'

But already in his eight-year-old heart he knew. Mam was dead, just as Dad had been. No shouting, no crying, no shaking would wake her. And as he felt the policeman's hand on his shoulder once again, Huw began to cry for the first time since he could remember.

The days that followed would always be a merciful blur in his memory. There were questions – so many questions! – who was he, where did he come from, had he any relations? After the first instinctive reaction to lie, he told them the truth, but the answer to the last question was a definite negative. There was no one. As long as Huw could remember, it had been just Mam and Dad and himself.

After the questions there were discussions – always conducted just out of his hearing, though certain words and phrases were audible: 'Orphan', 'local guardians', 'burial on the parish'. There were rooms, mostly lighter and brighter than the cottage he had called home, but with walls that seemed to press in on him until he wanted to scream to escape. Most of all there were people, hemming him in even more closely than the walls: Mrs Moon, a bristling hedgehog of indignation that Mam should be so inconsiderate as to die in her house; the large lady with her too-solemn-to-be-true expression; the policeman, kind enough, but Huw had an innate distrust of the law. Then there was the minister's wife, putting her arms around him and calling him 'my poor lamb'. She meant well, but he hated her solicitous fussing even more than he hated Mrs Moon's hostility. And lastly there was 'the woman'.

'The woman' was named Mrs Roberts though some people, the minister's wife included, called her 'Amy'. But Huw could not think of her as anything but 'the woman' and he hated her with a venom that was stronger than his hatred for all the others put together.

'The woman' had made Mam cry. She had turned them out of her house when Mam could hardly stand up because she was so tired and ill, and in his own mind Huw held her entirely responsible for his mother's death. But because of some arrangement he did not understand, he had been taken to her home – the very house out of which she had turned him and his mother so unceremoniously – and given a room of his own. 'The small bedroom' the woman had called it, but Huw thought it was huge... huge – and horrible. It was so *tidy*, with a washstand with a special well for the jug and basin, a small wardrobe and something she called a 'dressing-table' beside the bed. The rug on the linoleum-covered floor was wool, not the rag rugs he was used to, and there was a cottony bedspread as well as blankets on the bed.

And it was not only the room that was tidy – *he* was expected to be tidy to match it! The day after he arrived there, 'the woman' had taken him to an outfitter's shop and bought him shorts and some shirts, short grey socks and sandals. Then she had taken away his own clothes, washed them and hung them out on the line and taken his boots to the menders. Huw could not remember the last time his boots had been mended; they were back now, standing in the corner of the kitchen, but not looking like *his* boots any more. There were new thick soles on them and brand-new laces.

The tidiness had not stopped with his clothes, either. 'The woman' made him wash twice a day, once in the morning and again before he went to bed at night – and he was expected to wash his hands before meals too. She would have him looking like those two prissy little girls of hers if she had her way, he thought, with another gush of hatred reserved especially for Barbara and Maureen in their frilly frocks and white ankle socks, with ribbons in their freshly-washed hair. But she would not get her way, for he did not intend to stay long enough for that. He was going to run away – back to Wales.

What he would do when he got there, Huw was not at all clear. But for the moment that didn't matter. Just let him get away from here, back amongst his friends, amongst people who talked the way he talked, in streets he knew. He had already worked out how to get out of the house; there was a drainpipe conveniently close by his window and a big, soft paeony bush underneath. He could shin down without any trouble; then he would make for the railway. He and Mam had come on a train and he would go on a train. He had no money, but he had seen plenty of trains with trucks and wagons on the back and was sure he would be able to slip into one unnoticed. After that ... well, he'd work it out as he went along. The important thing was to get away without the woman noticing.

Somewhere in the house, downstairs, a door slammed and then he heard footsteps on the stairs. There was a tap at his door and it opened.

'All right, Huw?'

It was her – 'the woman'! He couldn't look at her, he hated her too much. He aimed another kick at the skirting board.

'It's bedtime,' she said.

Bedtime. At home he never went to bed until it was dark – not even then if he didn't feel like it. There was so much fun to be had when it was dark.

'Would you like a biscuit and a glass of milk?'

He started to shake his head, then reconsidered. Her biscuits at least were nice – ginger nuts – and if he was going a long way on the train he might be hungry. He risked a cautious look and saw her offering him the tin and a glass of milk.

'Look, I'll put it down here for you.' She came into the room and put down the small tray on the dressing-table. 'Then you can have one if you feel like it. All right?'

With the biscuits safely deposited there was no need to look any more; he knew she would not take them away. He gazed unseeingly out of the window.

'Don't forget to have a wash before you go to bed, will you?'

Still he said nothing and he heard her sigh.

'Good night, Huw.'

He grunted. At least she didn't kiss him good night as the minister's wife had done when he had been staying there. That at least was something to be grateful for!

The door closed again and he heard her go into the girls' room, and then her own. He crossed to the tray, stuffed a ginger nut into his mouth and washed it down with milk. Then he filled his pockets with as many biscuits as he could cram in and lay down on the bed, covering himself with the cotton bedspread just in case she looked in again. He didn't think she would, but could not be sure.

After what seemed a lifetime the house became completely quiet. No more bumps and creaks from the room next door, no sounds of life at all. It was pitch dark outside now – not even the gas-lamp on the pavement outside was alight. Huw felt his eyes growing heavy and jerked himself upright. He mustn't go to sleep, for if he did he would have to spend another day in this awful place. Gingerly he slipped out of bed. He wished he knew where his own clothes were, but he had no idea where she had put them. But his boots – he couldn't go without them; if his friends saw him in these sissy sandals when he got home, he would be a laughing-stock.

Holding his breath, he began to turn the handle of the bedroom door ... slowly, slowly, just a little at a time; then in the same stealthy manner he opened the door. At one point it squeaked, a tiny, wailing noise – and he froze, ready to rush back to bed and pull the clothes over himself again. But there was no sound from the room opposite.

He took a careful step and a board creaked. Again he froze, looking down at his feet, still encased in the hated sandals. Why hadn't he taken them off? Well, it was too late now. If he tried to take them off in the dark, he might topple over and make a real row.

Carefully he crept on, along the narrow landing and down the stairs. It was a slow, tortuous exercise. Too many of the stairs creaked, even if he kept to the very edges, and each time he froze, listening for some sign from 'the woman's' bedroom that she had heard him.

If she comes out I shall pretend I was sleep-walking, he decided. But the house was as silent as before.

At the foot of the stairs the narrow hall led back towards the kitchen. Once that was negotiated the rest would be easy. The kitchen door was ajar and it was well away from 'the woman's' bedroom.

Sometime during his journey down the stairs the moon must have come out from behind the clouds, for it was illuminating the kitchen with a cold whiteness. By its light Huw was able to locate his boots, standing in the corner. He unbuckled the hated sandals and thrust his feet into the boots, but they felt so stiff and restrictive that he decided for the sake of easy, quiet movement it would be best to stick to the sandals. He put them back on and strung the boots around his neck by means of a knot in the brand-new laces.

Then he looked around and the light of the moon showed him something which cheered him – the key in the back door. If he could get out this way there would be no need for a stealthy climb back up the stairs and an uncertain descent via the drainpipe.

Eagerly he tried the key and it turned, but still the door would not open. Then he noticed the heavy bolt at the top; he could not reach it unaided, but had to get a chair to stand on. And oh! the noise the bolt made as he drew it! Loud enough to waken the whole house. Huw clambered down off the chair, poised for flight, but to his surprise there was no sound to indicate 'the woman' had heard. Perhaps she was dead like Mam, he thought, and though this sent a shiver through him, the idea pleased him. Now when he turned the handle and pulled on the door once more it opened, and as the cool night air rushed in to meet him he forgot everything else in the sweet heady draught of freedom.

He had to be very careful for just a little longer, going down the drive at the side of the house which ran almost under 'the woman's' bedroom window. Keeping close by the hedge he crept along and then, as the road opened up before him, he could no restrain himself no longer. There was a strip of grass along the edge of the pavement and the moment his feet encountered this he began to run.

A little way down the hill he saw two figures in the distance coming towards him and dodged into a gateway to hide until they had gone by. They were rolling and singing and a little the worse for drink and had not the slightest idea that he was there, crouched behind the hedge, but it made Huw nervous and he decided to get off the main road as soon as he could.

The very next turning was Porter's Hill. Huw had never been down the hill, but he knew where it ended – in the valley just the other side of the river from the railway lines. 'The woman' had taken him to the yard where her lorries were kept and on the way back Barbara had wanted to walk up the hill, but for some reason 'the woman' had refused. 'No, we're not going that way. It's a private road, Babs.' 'Me go! Me go!' Barbara had piped, and 'the woman's' voice had gone sharp as it had when she had spoken to his mother. 'If you do, Mr Porter will see you and come after you. Now do as I tell you, Babs!'

She had made Mr Porter sound a little like 'the bogey man' but Huw was not going to let that stop him. He hardly supposed Mr Porter would be able to see him in the dark and even if he did, Huw was very experienced at running away from miserable old men.

As he turned into the hill, the high hedges on each side shut out the moon and the gravel crunched underneath his feet. At first he tried to run again, but the ground was too uneven when you couldn't see where you were going and he had to settle for a hurried, loping walk.

When the dark bulk of the house came into view over a

slightly less unkempt section of hedge, he looked towards it warily. There were lights still burning at several of the windows, but otherwise no signs of life. Huw kept close in the shadow of the hedge and hurried on.

At the bottom of the hill he hesitated. Which way now? Hillsbridge Station was away down the valley to his left, but he was unsure whether to go there would be the best plan. It only increased his chances of getting caught before he had had the chance to get very far. But the other way to his right led eventually to Lower Midlington Pit; he had seen the chimney and the headgear towering above the trees and hedgerows, and the batch too – a long low mound of dust and waste that ran out from the hillside like a spur. With the railway so close to the pit, there were bound to be sidings – and sidings meant trucks waiting to be shunted out on to the main line. Huw knew all about trucks and sidings, for he had watched them work long enough to know the routine. His heart thumped with excitement as he ran nimbly along the lane which was fast becoming little more than a track. Once into a truck he could be away, far away from this awful place by first light. Then he could go anywhere he chose.

Or so he thought for a few blissful moments, before he remembered! The trucks would not be carrying coal or anything else from the pit at the moment. The pits were on strike!

Huw stopped, his breath coming unevenly. How could he have been so stupid as to forget something like that! Oh well, there was nothing for it, he would have to go into Hillsbridge and risk the main sidings after all.

He turned and began to trot back along the track. But this time his mind was busy with how he could find a train and stow away on it without being caught, and he forgot the potholes and large stray stones that were strewn along the way. Unexpectedly he stumbled on one of them, his foot turned and before he could save himself he had gone sprawling in the track.

At Huw's age a fall was nothing – an everyday occurrence almost – and as soon as he hit the ground he began to bounce up again, waiting for the expected stinging to begin in his hands and knees, the first sharp warning of gravel rash. Instead, as he tried to stand he was aware of a flash of red-hot pain in his ankle and with a cry he collapsed back onto the ground. Oh, but it hurt! After a moment the worst of the pain subsided and he tried again, but the instant his weight went on the foot, it was as bad as ever and he almost fell for the second time, hopping wildly on his good foot until he collided with the thorn hedge. Grasping it to save himself, the prickles went deep into his already skinned palms and at the same moment, or so it seemed, his knees began to sting so that he was a ball of pain.

Slowly he subsided, sitting on the grass beneath the hedge and gritting his teeth to keep from crying. Then, rather gingerly, he began to probe his ankle; he could tell it was swelling already, for it was bulging over the strap of his sandal. This would never have happened if he had had his boots on, Huw thought. Perhaps even now if he put them on he could walk.

He unbuckled his sandal and took the boots from around his neck. But try as he might there was no way he could force his foot into the boot, not even when he yanked the lace out right down to the toe, and the effort brought tears to his eyes again.

I've broken it, he thought. I've broken my bleeding ankle!

For a few moments he sat there in the hedge, trying to decide what to do next. He couldn't walk – but he couldn't stay here either. The night had turned chill and the cold was beginning to get to him, seeping up through the seat of his pants from the dampish grass and whispering over his bare arms. He shivered violently and the shiver seemed to throb in his ankle and set up a new and sharper burning in his gravel rash. Misery overcame Huw and for the first time for as long as he could remember, he was unable to hold back the tears. Suppressed so long, they ran in rivers down his screwed-up face while he mewed with soft sobs, as much because he was ashamed of his own babyish reaction as because of the pain. Then, after a few minutes, he snivelled convulsively and wiped his face on the back of his hand.

He was trembling with the cold now and the moment he tried to move again he noticed it. As he pulled himself to his feet, carefully refraining from putting any weight on the injured ankle, his whole body contracted... shoulders rounding in, chin drooping. With an effort he managed to keep his balance and bend to pick up his boots, stringing them round his neck again, but the sandal he left where it lay. He would not be able to get it on again either, but he was not going to be fussed carrying it.

Bracing himself, he took one short quick step on his injured foot and then a slower step with the weight on the other. He was doing it, but he would never get anywhere at this rate!

For long painful minutes he limped on, but with every step the pain became more excruciating and Huw knew he was going to have to sit down and rest. He knew the ankle could not be broken, otherwise he would have been unable to put any weight on it at all. He remembered one of his friends in Ponty breaking a leg once and the bone had stuck out through the skin.

It isn't broken, it's just sore, Huw told himself, deciding that if he could rest for a bit, then it would probably be well enough to go on again. But where to rest? The bank had proved much too cold and damp and there was nowhere – no houses, except...

He paused for a moment, collecting his breath, as the large squat outline of Valley View appeared over the hedges. A house that size was bound to have outbuildings – a coal-house, a garden shed or *something*.

With renewed effort he hopped on, around the garden perimeter to the gate. The lights seemed to have been extinguished now, all but one at an upstairs window. Taking his courage in both hands, Huw opened the gate. The slight creak sounded loud in the quiet of the night, but he was now almost past caring. Keeping as far as possible into the shadow of the trees, he hopped through the lower part of the garden. It was rather overgrown and he thanked his stars for that, but when he got to what looked like a potting-shed, he was disappointed. It was a stone lean-to only, completely open to the cold night air.

Well, there was nothing for it – he would have to get closer to the house and hope he was not seen. Huw resumed his slow, painful progress. As he neared the house he noticed a small casement at the top of the kitchen window was open and wished he could take advantage of it.

Had it not been for his foot, he could have gone in and found enough food to last him for days – and perhaps money too. But since he could barely walk, climbing was out of the question. Resigned, he hobbled on, his feet making no sound in the soft grass except for the occasional snapping of a dead twig.

The outbuildings were at the far end of the garden, a

cluster of low, brick-built sheds. The first one he came to was the coal-house and not caring how dirty he would get, Huw crawled inside and pulled the door shut after him. On one side the coal was stacked high behind pieces of wooden board; as the fuel was used up, so the pieces of board would be removed one by one to lower the barrier, then with a fresh delivery they would be slotted in again to contain it. Huw never stopped to wonder at the amount of coal still being stored here even in the middle of a pit strike. He was too busy moving the buckets and shovels from the far corner and arranging a pile of sacks into a bed where he could flop down.

Even lowering himself was painful, but at least the sacks protected him from the cold stone. Now that he had stopped again, he realised just how cold he was – 'shrammed', Mam would say. And he was tired too, his eyes beginning to drop with weariness in spite of the pain and the cold.

They would probably find him here in the morning, frozen to death, he thought sleepily, recalling a song Mam used to sing him about a boy who had died in the snow in Switzerland . . . he thought it was Switzerland. A snatch of it came back to him.

> Next morning by the faithful hound
> Half-buried in the snow was found,
> Still bearing in his hand of ice,
> A banner with the strange device – Exelsior!

The song always had a haunting feel to it and if the young Huw had ever experienced romance, this was it. Briefly he felt it again, as if he were the boy hero. But it was a fleeting impression only; there was nothing really very romantic about being cold and in pain. It was just horrid!

With an awkward movement Huw drew his knees up to his chin, clasping his shivering arms round them. Just a little sleep. Just for a little while. Then he would go on again . . .

'What the hell are you doing here?'

Hard, powerful voice, shattering sleep; heavy hand on his shoulder.

Huw's eyes snapped open. It was daylight, sunless grey brightness angling in through the open door and cutting a flat plane across the stacked coal. But there was a figure between him and the light . . . tall, bulky and – to Huw – threatening.

217

Was this the Mr Porter the woman had warned about? Huw had no intention of waiting to find out. Like a panther he gathered himself and sprang. Nine times out of ten the suddenness of his move would have guaranteed success, but not this time. The moment he moved the pain was back, taking him by surprise; the grasp on his shoulder slackened for a moment only, then tightened, hauling him to his feet yelping like a hurt puppy.

'Come out of there and let's have a look at you!'

Huw had never been one to give in gracefully and in the coal-house doorway he made one more attempt to escape, balancing on his good foot and lashing out with the other. But he had forgotten it was bare; his soft toes connected uselessly with the trousered leg and a shock-wave of pain reverberated to the swollen tendons. However, his yelp evoked no sympathy and the man continued to half-drag, half-carry him across the path to where a jelly of a woman stood with arms akimbo, quivering with indignation.

'This is your intruder, Mrs Milsom. Not much of a specimen, is he?'

The fat woman snorted, her sharp little eyes running curiously over Huw as he wriggled uncomfortably beneath her scrutiny.

'I don't know you, do I?' she said accusingly after a moment.

Huw made no reply; on these occasions it was safer to remain silent and wait for an opportunity to escape.

'You ought to be ashamed of yourself!' she went on. 'This is private property, did you know that? A terrible fright you gave me.' Her lips tightened to give extra venom to her glare and then she turned to her employer. 'I thought he was dead, Mr Porter, honest I did. I thought somebody had murdered him and put him in our coal-house!'

So this *was* Mr Porter, thought Huw. Why, oh why, had he stopped here last night? But really, there had been no choice. Everything had gone wrong . . .

'Right, lad, you've got some questions to answer. Inside!' Mr Porter pushed him towards the kitchen door, but the fat woman stood her ground.

'He can't come in here, Mr Porter, not like that. He's as black as a pot!'

'That's what spending the night in a coal-house does for you.' Ralph Porter eyed the black face, hands and knees; then, as his glance reached the bare foot, he asked, 'Where's your shoe, lad?'

Huw's eyes narrowed, lips tightened above his jutting chin, but he did not answer.

'Hurt your foot, have you?' the man went on. 'Well, at least I suppose that means you won't run away if I let go of you.' He released his hold on Huw's collar and Huw thought of making a dash for it, but realised the impossibility of such a course of action and stayed where he was.

'All right, that's enough messing about. I want to know who you are.' The tone was so hard, so pitiless that Huw felt like crying again. No wonder 'the woman' had made him sound like a bogey man; to those prissy girls he would probably be just that. But being yelled at and hauled about by angry adults was nothing new to Huw and he had no intention of giving in and telling where he had come from. If Mr Porter didn't know that, he couldn't send him back – could he? Huw sealed his lips.

At his continued silence a look of anger darkened Ralph Porter's face.

'Come on – who?' he demanded again, and this time he caught the lobe of Huw's ear, twisting it between finger and thumb so that the boy squealed and twisted with it. But still he did not answer.

'All right, if you won't tell me, then I shall take you to the police station,' Ralph Porter threatened.

Beneath the powdering of black coal-dust Huw turned pale. If there was one thing he hated, it was the law.

'Are you going to tell me or do I get out my car and take you to the police station?' Mr Porter repeated.

Huw's mind ran in desperate circles and then, suddenly, he was inspired.

'I'm Billy Williams,' he supplied.

It was a song back home – 'My name is Billy Williams and I come from Pontypridd' – but Ralph Porter wouldn't know that.

'And what are you doing here, Billy Williams?'

Again inspiration struck. 'I ran away from home.'

'I see. And where's home?'

'Ponty – Pontypridd,' said Huw, praying silently: 'Let him say he'll send me back there!'

But there was no lightening of that thunderous expression.

'Well, in that case it's the police station anyway, isn't it?'

Huw bit his lip. 'Couldn't you just put me on the train?' he ventured.

Ralph Porter's eyes narrowed. 'Now why should I do that? Why should you want me to?'

'No reason,' Huw shrugged miserably. 'Except I want to go home.'

'And so you shall, but not at my expense. You haven't any money, I suppose?'

'No.'

'Did you rick your ankle trying to get into my house to steal some?'

'No, *sir*.' Huw stared at him mutinously and Ralph Porter swivelled impatiently. 'Come on then, let's get going. I've a day's work ahead of me and I won't have time for breakfast – thanks to you.'

Movement at the gate attracted their attention; it was the postman.

'Morning, Mr Porter, sir. Morning, Mrs Milsom.' Then, as he noticed Huw, 'Hey, what are you doing here, young feller-me-lad?'

Ralph Porter's brows beetled. 'You know this boy?'

'Know him? Oh ah, I know him. He's the lad what's staying with Amy Roberts up at Hope Terrace...'

'Is he indeed!' Ralph Porter swung round angrily. 'Is this true?'

Huw's eyes fell away and the finger and thumb grabbed his ear lobe again, twisting it to make Huw look up at him.

'Is this true, I said?'

'Yes,' Huw whispered.

'Why did you lie to me, then?' Voice, louder than ever, tweak sharper. '*Why?*'

And Huw cracked.

'Because I *have* run away. Because I want to go home. I don't want to live with her! I want to go back to Ponty – back to my mates. But I hurt my foot and I couldn't walk.'

'He's the lad whose mother died,' the postman supplied, glad to be able to show his superior knowledge. 'Amy Roberts has given him a home. You should be ashamed of yourself, my lad, running off and causing all this trouble after all she's been an' gone an' done for you!' he said to Huw.

Ralph Porter muttered what sounded to Huw a little like: 'Amy Roberts! I might have known!' Then he caught Huw's shoulder roughly and began bundling him across the path to where a red three-wheeler car stood in the drive.

'Right, lad, in! And if Mrs Roberts has any sense, when I get you home she'll give me leave to tan your hide more soundly than it's been tanned for years!'

*

Amy discovered Huw was missing when she went to wake him. At first she had stood in the doorway, staring in disbelief at the neatly-made bed with only the top cover rumpled down. Huw making his bed like that? Unheard of! Since he had come here she had insisted he did it himself, but unless she ran behind him it was always a higgledy-piggledy mess.

Then it occurred to her to wonder where Huw was. Not downstairs, certainly, since she had just come up from having her own breakfast. A small alarm bell sounded in her head and she checked her own bedroom and the girls' room.

'Have you seen Huw this morning?' she asked Barbara, who was sitting up in bed dressing Greta, her doll. Barbara shook her head and Amy hurried downstairs again. The toilet door was wide open – clearly he was not there. With growing alarm she looked into the front room which was also empty.

'Huw!' she called 'Huw – where are you?'

But the house was quiet. And then she noticed that the back door had been unlocked.

At once she became very worried indeed. For some reason it never occurred to her that Huw might have gone out for an early morning walk; she knew with a certainty that defied explanation that he had run away.

The certainty did not stop her checking the outhouses, though. She sped around them and then looked up and down the road, fighting a rising sense of panic. What next? She *had* to find him. She couldn't go to the minister's wife and admit that after all the fuss she had made to get him, she had just lost him. But where would he go, a boy of eight? He didn't know Hillsbridge well – only the main ways where she had taken him. What would he be looking for? Freedom? Or something more...?

She stood in the midst of the morning clutter in the kitchen chewing her lips. Silly boy! Why had he done it? She had known he was unhappy, but that was only to be expected and she had tried so hard to make him feel at home. Not that that would be enough, of course. For a child who had lost his mother, how could it be? But she had made up her mind to do her best, first by gaining his confidence while she provided for his everyday needs, and later perhaps being able to give him the love and care he would have missed if he had had to go into a home.

As she stood undecided about the best course of action, Amy heard a car in the road outside – unusual at this time of the morning – and a few moments later there came a knocking at the front door.

Amy went cold. Too many shocks in too short a space of time had sapped her natural resilience. What had happened now? Please God Huw was all right! If he wasn't she would never forgive herself.

She hurried to open the door. The first thing she saw was Ralph Porter's bulk and she took an involuntary step backwards. Then she noticed the small figure at his side – shrinking back, looking as if he wished he could become invisible.

'Oh Huw, thank goodness!' she burst out.

'He does belong here, then?' Ralph Porter's tone was heavy with irony.

'Yes – yes, but how... ?'

'He spent the night in my coal-house. Apparently he was trying to get back to Pontypridd, but he damaged his ankle.'

'Oh yes – oh Huw! Your poor ankle! How did it happen? What did you do?'

'If you're going to conduct an inquest I shall leave you to it,' Ralph Porter said sarcastically. 'Some of us have work to do. But I suggest a good hiding might be in order.'

Amy got hold of Huw and pulled him in through the doorway, planting herself between man and boy as if she expected a physical attack at any moment.

'I don't think that will be necessary,' she said stiffly.

One eyebrow lifted. 'Really? A boy who causes this much trouble should be made to understand that it doesn't pay. If I had charge of him, I think I could guarantee he wouldn't try it again.'

Amy made no answer. She was thinking she could well understand any boy running away repeatedly if he was in the charge of Ralph Porter.

'Well, thank you for bringing him home, anyway,' she said stiffly, and Huw could sense the antagonism between them. 'I'm very grateful.'

'Not at all,' he said with an ironic smile.

When he had gone, Amy turned to Huw. 'Oh Huw, why did you do it? I was so worried about you! Aren't you happy here?' Her voice was anxious, tearful almost and it took Huw by surprise; he had expected her to be mad.

'I wanted to go home,' he said.

'Oh, Huw!' Her face crumpled softly. 'Huw, dear, you can't. There's nobody there any more.'

'My friends.'

'But they wouldn't be able to look after you, and if there's nobody to look after you it would mean being taken into some kind of institution. Don't you understand?'

'I wouldn't care,' he said stubbornly, 'as long as I was home.'

'Oh Huw, you would! You wouldn't have a room of your own and you'd have to share everything with the other boys, even those you disliked. You wouldn't be able to come and go as you pleased and the food wouldn't be very nice. And there would be nobody to care for you specially. No one. That's what would be worst of all.'

He said nothing and she smiled sadly.

'And if you were to run away they would probably beat you when they got you back, like Mr Porter wanted to.'

His head drooped. He ached all over, his foot throbbed and he was very hungry.

'Come on inside, Huw.' She put an arm around his shoulders in spite of the coal-dust, helping him into the kitchen. 'You'd better have a wash.'

Hated words ... but somehow this morning they sounded less threatening – there was a comfortable, familiar ring to them. She drew water in a bowl at the sink and sat him down on the edge of the table as she did the girls, washing his face, hands and legs with soap and flannel.

'You'll have to go into the tub after breakfast, but for now we'll make it a lick and a promise. Oh Huw, your hands and knees! They're covered in gravel rash! And your ankle ... !'

She bathed the grazes in disinfectant water. In some places the dirt had got in and Huw winced as she sponged it out. Then she covered the raw places with lint and sticky tape and put a bandage around his ankle.

'Where's your sandal?' she asked.

'I don't know. Somewhere down in the lane. I lost it.'

'Well, I certainly hope it turns up. New sandals are an expensive item. We shall have to go that way and look for it.' But there was only anxiety in her tone, not reproach, and he felt the first stab of guilt.

'I'll go and look for it,' he offered.

'Not on that ankle, you won't.' But she didn't say she would be afraid to let him out of her sight again and for that he was grateful.

Should he say he was sorry? But in his short life Huw had never apologised to anyone and he couldn't begin now. Only as he looked at her, he felt the beginnings of something like warmth instead of the usual rush of hatred.

'Sit up then, Huw, and I'll make you some breakfast. I expect you're hungry, aren't you?' she said now. As the smell of bacon filled the kitchen a few moments later, Huw laid his head on his arms on the table and fell fast asleep.

Chapter Twelve

Relentlessly the days marched on through autumn towards winter and still the strike dragged on. Rumours of this settlement and that were rife, but the blue and silver days of September became the glorious red-browns of October and nothing had changed, except that belts were tighter and hearts heavier.

As if it believed that such a summer as this had been would never come again, the whole of nature strained back to hold onto it. The trees in the rectory garden clung desperately to their leaves instead of shedding them early to form a russet carpet on the pavement they overhung. Along the ridge of batches above the railway line, the firs and pines stood green and bushy against the deep blue of the sky; a haze of flies still hung over the steeply sloping fields made marshy by springs that burst from the depths of the hillsides and trickled over the stones and mud patches towards the much depleted river.

But when at last the first nip in the air hardened to a bite, folk who had been hungry all summer found that they were now cold as well. In the mornings and evenings the smell of woodsmoke mingled with the seasonal aroma of bonfires as fires were kindled and stoked on what sticks the lads had been able to bring in from the woods; and men began sneaking to the batches after dark to pick coal and bring it home in sacks and home-made trucks.

It was against the law of course and if they were caught they could go to prison, but it was happening everywhere.

'Did you read about those miners in Abertillery who were going to a colliery in the mountain after dark and working it?' Charlotte asked Amy when she came to get the children one night. 'It sounds as if half the pit was there!'

'How do they know that?' Amy asked shortly.

'Because the police caught them. Well, at least, they caught eight, but it said in the paper that many more made their escape and sixty-two bags of coal were recovered.'

Charlotte glanced at Amy, half-expecting another sharp retort. She was so bad-tempered these days, not at all interested in the sort of pleasant chat in which she and her mother had indulged in the old days, and Charlotte knew it was because she was tired and overwrought.

On this occasion, however, Amy said nothing. It was Harry who spoke, coming indoors with Huw after letting him help feed the pigeons.

'You can't blame them though, can you?'

'Blame them?' Charlotte turned on him. 'What do you mean – can't blame them?'

'Well, when they see their families cold and hungry and the coal's there for the taking...'

'That doesn't make it right,' Charlotte said stubbornly. 'It's still stealing.'

'You don't say "no" to a sackful of the batch.'

'That's different,' Charlotte maintained. 'A bit like that doesn't make any difference to anybody – and it's stuff that's been thrown out as waste. These men were mining new coal and stealing it, I don't care what you say.'

Amy and Harry exchanged amused glances. Strict honesty was and always had been one of Mam's hobby-horses – and if something that it suited her to be party to was perhaps less worthy than the standards she proclaimed, then you could be sure there would be some circumstance that made it totally 'different'.

'I don't know what things are coming to, I'm sure,' she went on now, mixing batter in a bowl for the 'Johnny-cakes' she was making for tea. 'You never know what you're going to hear next these days. And what these silly men don't realise is that when they do something dishonest like that, they have to live with it for the rest of their lives.'

'I don't suppose conscience will keep them awake so much as cold or an empty belly,' said Harry.

'Harry, I wish you wouldn't use that word!' Charlotte reproved him. 'You know I don't like to hear it. Can't you say "stomach" like I always brought you up to?'

Another amused glance passed between brother and sister. For all her seeming propriety, Mam was not above using a choice word or two when the fancy took her!

'Anyway, it wasn't their consciences I was talking about,' Charlotte continued, returning to her theme. 'The bosses will have it in for them, you can bet a shilling. When they start taking men on again, those that stole or made trouble will be the last in line. Naturally. They won't trust them.'

'The Federation will see to it that they're not victimised,' Harry said, helping himself to a currant intended for the Johnny-cakes.

'Oh yes, and how are they going to do that?' Charlotte scoffed. 'Don't talk rot, Harry! No – they'll be marked men, I'm telling you, in the mines and out of them. Because it will be a fat lot of good them trying to get a job elsewhere with a police record!'

She swung round to get the heavy frying-pan out of the cupboard beneath the range and saw the look on Harry's face – thoughtful, anxious, guilty almost.

'What are you looking like that for?' she demanded.

Harry shook his head, saying nothing.

'*You* haven't been up to something you shouldn't, have you?'

'No, of course not. Chance would be a fine thing,' Harry replied, but the wariness was still there about his eyes.

'Well, I hope not,' Charlotte said. 'You have a good future ahead of you if you don't let yourself down.'

Amy laughed out loud – a small, scornful snort – and Harry snapped, 'Oh, for goodness' sake, Mam!' in much the same short tone that Charlotte was becoming used to hearing from her youngest daughter.

Charlotte pursed her lips.

It had come to something when her children talked to her in this way. There were times when she wished they were small again – young enough to make them know, and small enough to gain pleasure from the little things of life instead of always trying to appear too big for their boots.

'It's time we were going, Mam,' Amy said suddenly and Charlotte extracted her revenge.

'Would you like one of your Grandma's Johnny-cakes, Barbara?' she asked the little girl, who was curled up in her laundry basket playing 'boats'. 'I expect Mammy will wait while you have one.'

'But you haven't even started cooking them yet,' Amy protested above Barbara's excited affirmatives and Maureen's piping echo.

'It won't take me long. You know how *you* loved Johnny-cakes when you were little, Amy. I'll do one for Barbara and Maureen first.' She looked up to enjoy Amy's impotent annoyance and instead found herself looking at Huw. He was standing by the table saying nothing, but his eyes, huge and round as he regarded the Johnny-cakes, spoke volumes.

Charlotte had been totally against Amy taking him in – still was, if it came to that. They had managed to keep the truth of it quiet, thank goodness, but still it had caused talk in Hillsbridge and Charlotte had had her work cut out explaining to people why Amy had done such a thing. More often than not she had resorted to blaming Amy's grief at Llew's death: 'There are times when I don't think she knows what she's doing – or cares. All she could think of was that there was this little boy homeless and he was Welsh, like Llew. So she took him in. I tried to talk her out of it, but you know our Amy. And all credit to her, I say . . .'

Privately though, she had the strongest misgivings about the wisdom of Amy's action and in the dark of the night shuddered not only about what Hillsbridge would say if the truth were learned, but also what the future held for the newest member of her daughter's family – a boy born to and raised by a woman who was not only a foreigner, but also 'no better than she should be'. 'Bad blood will out,' Charlotte would think to herself. 'He'll be nothing but trouble for our Amy and she'll live to regret the day she made such a rash decision.'

But just now the young devil she conjured up in her worst nightmares seemed little in evidence, and Charlotte saw instead a little boy overwhelmed by passionate longing.

'Would *you* like a Johnny-cake, Huw?' she asked.

He almost jumped. It was the first time she had ever spoken to him civilly – if at all! Instead of defiance there was disbelief and the clearly-etched fear that this mirage had been offered him only to be snatched away.

He nodded. 'Yes.'

'Yes, *please*. Here you are, then, I'll put one in for you too,' Charlotte said; and tossing her head with satisfaction at this minor victory over her two children who seemed these days to delight in putting her in her place, Charlotte thought:

'And you two can put *that* in your pipe and smoke it!'

*

Tea over, Harry pushed back his chair and got up.

'Going out, then?' Charlotte asked unnecessarily.

'To Margaret's, yes.'

'I might have known – you're never anywhere else these days,' said Charlotte, whose bad temper had still not quite evaporated.

Harry did not reply and as he walked up the hill his feet seemed to drag. It was not that he didn't want to see Margaret; he did. But he also had things on his mind – things he could only think over alone. For that day he had come to hear about the latest piece of mischief planned by the striking miners of Hillsbridge, only this particular idea went far beyond a joke.

Plans were under way to wreck the winding gear at Middle Pit – a move designed not only to prevent any 'blackleg labour' from going underground, but also to show the bosses that the men were reaching the end of their tether.

Naturally enough, the hot-headed Ewart Brixey was the instigator.

'It's about time we showed 'em!' he had announced to the gathering of men, disgruntled at finding no pay-out for the third week running. 'We've got to show the bosses they can't go on treating us like this.'

'But Ewart, they can!' Walter Clements, father of the brood next door, was one of the old school, mild in speech, moderate in outlook. 'They've been treating us like this since last May, remember.'

'Only because we've let them! Well, we'll just have to show 'em we can get tough if we have to. Do some damage to their property so that they feel it where it hurts – in their pockets.'

There was a murmur of dissent amongst the men and Harry was secretly relieved. He had only been eleven years old during the last strike in 1921, but he could recall the mob that had marched up South Hill to manager O'Halloran's house with murder in their hearts and their minds set on doing as much damage as they could. Nothing had come of it, mainly thanks to the courage of Harry's brother Jack and the esteem in which he was held in the community, but Harry could well remember the charged atmosphere and now, with the wisdom of his sixteen years, he realised it was generated and sustained when ordinary angry men joined together in a mob.

When the majority of the men had moved off, Ewart came across to Harry and the Clements boys.

'They'm yellow-bellied, all of 'em,' he grumbled. 'We won't get nowhere if we don't do something to really show the bosses.'

'What did you have in mind, then, Ewart?' Tommy asked.

'You really want to know?'

''Course – I wouldn't ask otherwise, would I?'

'If I tell you, you'll only go and let on to somebody.'

'No, I won't!'

'All right.' Ewart lowered his voice conspiratorially. 'I reckon we ought to blow up the winding gear down at Middle Pit.'

'Blow up the winding gear? But what with?'

'Their own bloody explosives. There's enough in the powder store up the yard. Pity we can't get a shot-firer in on it.'

'You'd never get a shot-firer to mess about with his own explosives,' Reg Clements said.

Ewart shrugged. 'Well, I reckon I could do it myself anyway.'

'It's gelly.'

'Aw – kids' play. I've seen it done often enough.'

'Oh, you want to be careful, Ewart. You could blow your hand off easy as look at 'un . . .'

'If all you'm going to do is put the damper on it, you know what you can do.' He turned and stalked off, leaving the boys staring after him in awe.

'Do you reckon he's serious?'

'I do – you know Ewart.'

'Maybe he's right,' said Tommy. 'Maybe it is time we did something to show them.'

'Maybe.'

But Harry was still uneasy. He tried to forget what he had heard, but Charlotte's words about the long-term effects of 'foolishness' only served to worry him more.

It was not only the danger to Ewart himself if he started meddling with explosives. There was far more to it than that. Real damage could affect all their future. The bosses could be ruthless; blow up the head-gear at Middle Pit and it would cost thousands to get it in working order again. Suppose the bosses decided to have the last laugh and refused to shell out for repairs? Middle Pit would be closed permanently then and with the pit lost, all their jobs would be lost too.

But there's nothing I can do about it, Harry thought wretchedly. I'm in the know, but what use is that? Ewart would never listen to me.

That evening, sorting yet more used clothes for the Relief Fund, he was silent and morose.

'What's wrong then, Harry?' Margaret asked, sitting back on her heels to study his closed-in face.

Harry only shook his head. It would be a relief to share it with her, but if he did she would probably insist he told her father – or else she would tell him herself. And what could George Young do? He would probably go to the police – he was that kind of law-abiding person. And if the police were brought in, Ewart would very likely go to jail.

I can't do that to him, Harry thought in anguish. He's got a wife and youngsters and the bosses would make certain he never worked again.

'Harry...' Margaret wriggled closer to him, tucking her arm through his and tilting her head to look up at him with her most pleading expression. 'Don't be a misery. I hate it when you're a misery.'

Impatiently he shook himself free. 'Oh, leave me alone, can't you?'

She withdrew as if she had been shot, looking as if she might be going to cry, and he got up, aiming a kick at the pile of used clothing.

'I'm sick of all this. I'm sick of the whole bloody strike. I'm going home.'

'Harry!'

'Good night, Margaret.' He marched through into the kitchen where Gussie was busy letter-writing. 'Good night, Mrs Young. I'm going to get an early night,' he said, summoning civility.

'Oh, good night, Harry. Will we see you tomorrow?'

'I don't know.'

The night air cooled his flushed face, but did nothing to improve his humour or help him solve his dilemma.

He was in a cleft stick and he knew it. Nobody wanted to further the cause more than he did – sometimes he burned with the desire to help set the injustices to rights. But this was not the way to do it, he knew that instinctively – saw too clearly for comfort the possible consequences – yet was quite unable to think of a way to stop it. Whichever way he turned, he would be betraying someone.

If only I could be like the Clements boys! he thought enviously. They know about Ewart's plan too, but I don't suppose they'll lose any sleep over it. The Clements boys never lost sleep over anything. Forget it as they will, he told himself. But it did no good. The knowledge, the indecision and the fear of the consequences went on eating into him.

It was the same over the next few days, a constant nagging worry at the back of his mind. Every morning he woke fearful of what news he would hear, yet still unable to bring himself to do the unforgivable and 'split' on Ewart.

He was ashamed too of his outburst at Margaret, but although he duly presented himself at her home and made a token apology, he was still preoccupied and moody and when she tried to tease him out of it, it was all he could do to keep from snapping at her again. What did the strike mean to her really? She was cushioned against it, still going to school as if nothing was happening, still living the same charmed life with her concerned yet uninvolved parents. Working for the Labour Party was all very well, but what did they know about it? Torn apart by his divided loyalties, Harry felt he hated the whole world.

And then one morning came the news he had dreaded. Charlotte brought it back from Hillsbridge along with the day's shopping of meagre striker's family fare – broken biscuits, subsidised bread and a neck of mutton that would have to do three meals at the least.

'What do you think? Last night somebody tried to blow up the pit!'

Harry went cold.

'Blow up the pit? Whatever do you mean?' James enquired.

'Middle Pit!' Charlotte said. 'They were down at Middle Pit last night with explosives. Luckily the bosses had put in a night-watchman to try and catch the men who've been going in and nicking coal and he saw the shadow of a man, crouching about where he shouldn't have been.'

Harry tried to open his mouth to say something, but no words would come.

'Who was it then?' With an effort, James pulled himself bolt upright.

'I couldn't say.' Charlotte unbuttoned her coat and spread her hands out to the warmth of the fire. 'When he realised he'd been spotted, he made a run for it and got clean away. But they say the explosives he had there would have done so much damage the pit could have been shut down for good.'

'Well, well, damned fools, what be they going to do next?' James wheezed.

'What do you think about it, Harry?' Charlotte turned to him and Harry managed a noncommittal shrug.

'Don't *you* think it's stupid?' she pressed him and when he still said nothing, she clucked and tossed her head impatiently. 'I don't know, I'm sure, what the younger generation are coming to. You try to teach them right from wrong and still ... It'll be a tidy state of affairs when things are left to them if you ask me!'

'I'm going down to take a look at my pigeons,' Harry said, not wanting to argue. He was too shaky with relief that things had turned out this way. Not only had the attempt been thwarted and the explosives were now back in safe hands, but Ewart had escaped being caught and taken to court. It was the best possible result, but it was no thanks to him. He had known all about it, had been worried about it, but he'd done absolutely nothing.

For the first time it came to Harry that wanting to further the cause was not nearly as easy as he had once expected it to be. Things were not clear-cut black and white, with good on one side and bad on the other, and becoming involved had many facets he had not anticipated.

It meant making decisions and judgements, sometimes leading, sometimes making yourself unpopular, weighing up rights and wrongs and searching your conscience for the right action or inaction. Fervour was all very well, but it had to be tempered by many other qualities too.

Will I ever be able to do it? Harry wondered.

But for the moment at least the crisis had passed. The only explosions this November would come from the 'bangers' on Bonfire Night. And for the moment Harry could only be grateful.

Chapter Thirteen

Although it was still only November, the post office at Withydown was already getting busy for Christmas. But as she worked, Rosa Clements found her mind wandering time and again to Ted.

Perhaps, she thought, it's time to force a showdown. Perhaps, if Ted comes home for Christmas, I ought to say something about the way I feel, even if I *do* frighten him off. Because we can't go on this way for ever.

She had seen him twice since the June day when he had turned up unannounced, but nothing had changed and the optimism that had sustained her through the past years of waiting was beginning to wear a little thin.

The spark was still there between them when they were together, it was true, the wonderful soaring happiness that was enough to make her forget the lonely times both behind and ahead of her. But now it died too quickly, leaving her hollow and aching, and the memories were tarnished by doubt that Ted really cared for her at all. How could he, if he could leave her so easily and for so long? Was the truth of the matter that he still cared only for Becky and she, Rosa, was still a stop-gap?

Other memories came to haunt her now, sharp reminders of the hurt she had felt when the truth had become too obvious to allow excuses and explanations, and Rosa thought: I have to know. I have to have something to hold on to. If he does care, I can wait for him for ever. But if not...

'Will you be going home to Hillsbridge for Christmas this year, Rosa?' asked Mrs Cray, the elderly widowed owner of the post office.

And Rosa, her heart thumping with the momentousness of her decision, her small, darkly-beautiful face serious, replied without hesitation: 'Yes, Mrs Cray. I'll be going home.'

*

In the small makeshift office at the yard, Amy was poring over the books, her fingers stained from the blue-paper, her eyes aching from squinting at the figures and trying to make them tally to produce a more acceptable result. Things were not good, she thought. Ticking over, but not good. By the time she had paid Herbie and Ivor Burge and settled the account for rent due, there would not be much left over again. It was no use pretending; unless things soon took a turn for the better, she would have to do what she had been trying so hard to avoid and sell the house.

Although she had known from the beginning that this was probably inevitable and had tried to reconcile herself to it, still she had viewed the sale of the house as a last resort. It was not only the emotional upheaval of getting rid of the place she and Llew had chosen and lived in together, but also the practical difficulties of looking for something else suitable and then actually finding the time to move. Her days were already fully occupied from dawn to dusk and beyond.

But yesterday, quite by chance, she had heard of a cottage for sale in Batch Row which, although it was much smaller than her own house, at least had three bedrooms. When she had heard about it her stomach had seemed to fall away. It was all very well to talk blithely about selling up while she had nowhere to move to – a different thing altogether when it became a real possibility.

But there was no doubt about it, a smaller house would mean money in the bank and that in its turn would represent welcome security.

Amy glanced up, looking out across the yard to where one of the lorries stood idle, shrouded in November greyness. That was the trouble, of course, trying to run the business at half strength. Since Llew had bought the second lorry everything was geared to full employment for the two, or something approaching that, with Llew himself driving one and Herbie, when it was required, the other. But now to use both Amy would have to take on another man – and to be able to pay out extra wages, she must be assured of enough work to cover them. At the moment, that seemed like crying for the moon.

Biting her lip, Amy pored over the figures once more. In spite of the continuing strike she had managed to keep one lorry fairly well occupied. The hauling of gravel for the quarry company had now become a fairly regular thing; from that first uncertain job had come another... and another. But it was on a day-to-day basis with no contract involved, and already she waited with heart in mouth for Herbie to return each afternoon, anxious to know whether he had been asked to report back next morning.

'I reckon there's a couple more months in it at least,' he had told her. 'It will take them that long to finish the new road this lot's for.' But still she was afraid to depend on the work continuing. It only needed the quarry company to decide it was worth their while to purchase another lorry of their own – and that would be the end of it. Meanwhile, she was having to turn down the occasional casual job for the mill or a local farmer, because there was no one to drive the second lorry.

If only I could drive it myself! Amy thought, but she knew that would not solve her problem. Driving for fun was one thing, hauling was quite another. A man's strength was needed for loading and unloading and tough as she liked to think herself, Amy knew she couldn't do it.

No, if ever she was to expand enough to make the business secure, she needed another hand – two ideally. Young, untrained lads would suffice. Herbie had indicated that Ivor Burge had served his apprenticeship as a mate and was now competent to drive himself – but even young lads needed to be paid and the money she would get for the house would ensure there was enough in the bank to pay them, even if the lorry was sometimes standing idle. It was no use putting it off any longer. The house would have to go. And she really ought to go and look at the cottage in Batch Row right away before anyone else snapped it up. Not that that was very likely with money so short in Hillsbridge, but you never could tell.

Her mind made up, Amy snapped shut the ledger and scraped back her chair. As she emerged from the office a chill wind whistled across the yard, making her shiver, and she thought of the new winter coat Barbara needed. She had seen one in the Co-op, a pretty blue wool with a Peter Pan collar, but so far had been unable to afford it. Well, sell the house and she could.

And Barbara was not the only one who needed a winter coat, Amy remembered as a guilty afterthought. Huw would need one too and a boy's coat was likely to cost twice as much, unless she could persuade someone who did dressmaking to run one up for him...

Deep in thought, she left the yard and crossed the river bridge. Then, after listening carefully to make sure no trains were coming, she ducked under the wire and picked her way across the railway line to the lane that led to Batch Cottages. It was not well made-up. Dust kicked beneath her feet and as she drew level with the first of the cottages her heart sank. They looked so poky compared with her house – compared with Mam's even – the windows small and dark, the doors warped, the paintwork peeling. Three bedrooms? I can't imagine any of them being big enough to swing a cat in! Amy thought.

Nearer still and her depression deepened. The washing, strung up on lengths of line rope, looked grey and ragged and the children playing outside were grubby and be-draggled looking. Only determination kept her going until she reached the one cottage she had heard was for sale – the middle one of seven, even more dilapidated than the others if such a thing were possible.

The door was closed – no children were playing outside here. But as soon as she stopped and knocked they appeared from nowhere, a straggle of grimy boys and a little girl, standing in a silent circle to look at her. She knocked again and the door was opened by a tired elderly woman in a faded grubby overall.

'Yes?'

Amy opened her mouth to speak and breathed in the overpowering smell of cooked cabbage that had emanated with the woman from the cottage. She almost gagged, then recovered herself.

'I understand you want to sell your house?'

The woman looked her up and down, squinting.

'I don't want to, I've *got* to! My hubby bought it when the owners put the Rank up for sale and now he's gone I can't keep it up on my own. Why?'

'I'm interested in it.'

'Oh well, in that case . . .' The woman stood aside and Amy went into the cottage. No hall but straight into the living-room, and the smell of cooking cabbage so strong it almost took her breath.

She was amazed that anyone should own their own house here, but of course, most of them did not. When the Rank went up for sale they generally passed from one landlord to another and continued to live their drab, hand-to-mouth lives – kept poor by low wages, endless strings of children and menfolk who preferred to spend their meagre earnings in the pub and at the bookie's office rather than on their families. Mam would have a fit, she thought, remembering her mother's admonitions when she had been at school to 'keep away from the children from Batch Row'. 'You could catch all sorts,' she used to say, and remembering how often they had come to school with their heads shaved after a visit from the 'flea lady', Amy had known her mother was not referring only to germs. Now, she shuddered at the thought of her own children being associated with Batch Row.

She wouldn't let them play outside with the others, of course, but still the stigma would be there . . .

With the door shut the room was as dark as Amy had thought it would be – dark, stale and airless. There was a fire burning under the hob, the cabbage water spitting steadily into it, and Amy looked around trying to imagine her own furniture packed in. There would only be room for half of it – just the table and enough chairs for them to sit on, and perhaps at a push the sideboard. But that would be all. The china cabinet would have to go . . . and Llew's wing chair. Amy had heard of families eating in relays because they could not all sit down at once – here, it was easy to see why.

'This is it, then,' the woman said.

'Can I see the scullery?' Amy tried to keep her voice bright, but she felt it was coming from her boots.

The woman let her go ahead into the narrow passage that served as a scullery. A working surface formed by a board laid down on wooden cupboards ran the length of it, dominated by a bowl of potato pickings. Clearly there was no running water, but Amy had not expected there to be. The water would come from a communal tap across the yard, alongside the shared washhouse; and she knew the toilets were even further away – shared, free-standing wooden sheds half-way down the gardens.

237

'Thank you. And upstairs?'

She followed the woman back into the living-room and through a latched door. The stairs rose steep and bare, leading directly into the first of the bedrooms. Then one went through connecting doors into the second and third, all opening out one from the other and divided by only the flimsiest of partitions. Again they were so small that Amy knew most of her carefully acquired furniture would have to go. And there would be no privacy; the thinly screened walls would see to that.

She went to the window and looked out. From here the November day appeared even greyer. How could the view be more dismal than a bare depot yard? she wondered – but somehow it was. You did not expect a fine view from industrial premises, but when the only thing you could see from your bedroom window was the railway line and the cutting beyond, black with coal-dust and the soot from passing trains, it made the heart sink. She turned and almost fell over a china chamber pot, jutting out from beneath the bed.

'Well?' The woman was standing in the doorway, arms folded around her sagging bosom. She was almost bald, Amy noticed with surprise, with scraggly hair combed across her flaking pink scalp. Was that what living at Batch Row did for you?

'I shall have to think about it,' Amy said, her voice coming as before from some hollow deep inside her. 'I have a house to sell.'

'Yes, I know. You're Amy Roberts, aren't you? Amy Hall that was?'

Amy looked at her. 'Yes.'

'You don't know me, I don't expect, but you were at school with my George. Georgie Baker.'

'Oh, yes.' Amy remembered Georgie Baker – a thin, weasel-faced boy with a runny nose, one of a brood of Bakers. She had always thought him quite repulsive and had given him the widest possible berth. Could she possibly be considering living in the house where he had lived? What had she come down to?

'I'll let you know,' Amy said again. Claustrophobia was overcoming her – she had to get out of this place!

As the woman opened the door for her the cluster of children appeared again from nowhere, eyes rounded in pinched faces; when she began walking away they followed at a distance, one daring to call out a name that made her tighten in disgust.

Words like that from a child! How different from her own upbringing, with Mam getting worked up if they so much as dared to refer to their stomach as 'belly'.

I can't live there, she thought. I can't possibly raise my children in a place like that – no, not even to have the money to sink into the business. Something else will come up – it's bound to! Even if it means renting a place. I know that's not the same as owning a home and I would have to find rent every week, but at least I would have the capital behind me. And anything would be better than that dreadful house... anything!

But right now it did not solve her problem of the lorry standing idle, the books that only just balanced and the winter coats that would be needed before many more weeks had passed.

As she crossed the railway line once more the rain started, thick and fine, blowing with the wind, the heavy sky making it ominously clear that there was plenty up there to come down.

Another worry – when there was prolonged rain the river flooded and in especially bad times it would come right up into the yard. After the dry summer the river was still pretty low, but it was something to bear in mind. Flash floods could be more devastating than those which rose slowly and gave you time to prepare.

I must make sure all my paperwork is packed away on a top shelf before I go home at night, Amy thought – and perhaps it would be a good idea to move the lorry to the highest part of the yard. Remember to tell Herbie...

No! she thought suddenly. Why leave it to Herbie? I'll move it myself.

As she approached the lorry she felt a flutter of nervousness. It was the first time she had attempted to drive since that dreadful day when she had hit Ralph Porter's motor car. But she thought she had learned quite a lot since then – how to start the lorry, for one thing – from watching Herbie and Ivor day after day. And she suddenly felt about a thousand years older.

But when she attempted to crank the starting handle she realised that knowing how to do it was not quite the same as actually accomplishing the feat. The handle was stiff and heavy and no matter how hard Amy swung it she was unable to turn over the engine.

Drat! she thought, getting a fresh wind and trying again. But it was useless; she couldn't get it going.

'Having trouble, Mrs Roberts?'

The voice, right behind her, made her jump so that she let go of the handle, twisting round to see Ralph Porter standing there watching her with an amused expression on his darkly arrogant face.

'Mr Porter!' she said, thinking: What in the world does he want? 'I didn't hear you coming.'

Beneath the dark moustache one corner of his mouth twisted upwards.

'I should have thought after your last attempt, you would have given up trying to drive lorries.'

She made no reply. The nerve of the man, bringing that up again!

'What can I do for you?' she asked stiffly.

He raised an eyebrow. 'I came to talk business.'

'Oh!' Her surprise showed in her face and he said a little sarcastically. 'You are still in business, I take it?'

'Yes, of course.' The rain was coming down more heavily now and she raised a hand to brush a strand of wet, honey-coloured hair off her face. 'We'd better go inside.'

'That seems a good idea.'

She led the way across the yard to the office, opening the door and wishing he did not disconcert her in this way. How could any man make her feel such a fool just by a lift of the eyebrow, a twist of the mouth? Or was it the size of him? Without saying a word he seemed to dominate the small office, standing there in his leather flying-jacket and boots, particles of rain shimmering in the dark hair and moustache.

A pulse jumped suddenly in her throat and she moved to put the desk between them. 'What can I do for you then, Mr Porter?'

For a moment he didn't answer, though his eyes narrowed and he looked at her speculatively. Then he drew a silver cigarette case out of his pocket, flicking it open.

'Do you mind if I smoke?'

'No. Go ahead.'

He lit a cigarette, but did not offer her one. Typical, he's probably another of those who doesn't approve of women smoking, she thought. She unbuttoned her coat and sat down, then immediately wished she had not done so. It gave him such an advantage, towering over her.

'There's a chair behind you, Mr Porter,' she said tersely.

'Thanks.' He reached for it but instead of sitting, he turned it round and stood leaning his tall frame casually against the back. Determined not to be kept at this disadvantage she rose too, perching herself on the corner of the desk.

'Perhaps you should tell me why you're here, Mr Porter. If you've come to tell me you want more money for the repair of your car, I'm afraid you've wasted your journey. I believe I have already settled that debt in full.'

He drew smoke; behind it his eyes looked amused.

'It's not about the car. I told you, it's a matter of business.'

'Oh – what sort of business?'

'Your lorries are for hire, are they not?'

'Yes, but...'

'What are your terms?'

'Terms?'

'For the hire of your lorries. Really, Mrs Roberts, am I expressing myself that badly?'

Amy tried to shake herself out of the stupor of surprise. 'You mean you wish to contract the use of one of my lorries?'

'That's why I'm here, yes.'

'For what purpose?'

'I have a large amount of timber I want hauled. It's a sizable job, six weeks' work probably, and my own lorries are all fully occupied at the moment. The obvious answer is to sub-contract and as I have noticed one of your lorries lying idle...'

Illogically she felt her cheeks flame. He had noticed! Typical of him not to miss a thing like that. Of course his house was not far from the yard, but still...

'It's idle because I don't have another driver at the moment.'

'But you could get one?'

'Yes, of course, I have people I can call on,' she lied.

'Good. Then shall we say you could have a lorry at my timber yard on Monday morning at what... say, five?'

Amy swallowed; she could hardly believe this was happening. But say yes, a voice inside urged her. Don't worry about the hows, whys and wherefores at the moment. Just snap up this job like the manna from heaven that it is!

'Of course, if that's what you want,' she said, attempting to sound businesslike.

For a few minutes they discussed business details, hire charges and schedules, and Amy was surprised when he accepted her quotation without argument. Knowing Ralph Porter and his methods, she would have expected him to take advantage of her position. He knew she was desperate for business and it would have been so easy for him to try to squeeze the margins to their limits. But he did not. Oh yes, there was a raised eyebrow here and a biting remark there, but none of the really hard bargaining Amy would have expected.

What's he up to? she wondered.

At last, when the details had been agreed upon, Ralph Porter levered himself away from the chair. This gave Amy the excuse to rise too. though the difference in their height meant he still had the advantage.

'Well, if there's nothing more, Mr Porter...'

The corners of his mouth twitched. 'Not at the moment.'

'... I'm sure you'll find we can give you complete satisfaction.'

'I certainly hope so.'

There was a faintly mocking note in his voice and as she looked up his eyes – also faintly mocking – met and held hers and the pulse jumped in her throat again. Awkward, she looked away, but there was no escaping the power of his presence. She left the sanctuary of her desk in order to cross to the office door and open it, conscious of his eyes following her. Why was he looking at her like that? Why didn't he just go? But she could not be rude – not after he had given her the business she needed so badly. And besides, it wasn't actually unpleasant. Disconcerting – but not unpleasant...

She drew a deep breath. 'Thank you for trusting me with your business. I won't let you down.'

She held out her hand – it seemed the businesslike way to seal the agreement – but for what seemed an age he made no similar move. He looked almost amused by her gesture and she was about to withdraw her hand, feeling annoyed and confused, when he took it and his cool, strong fingers pressed hers for a moment.

'I'm sure you won't. But there's just one thing worrying me.'

'What's that?'

'It won't be *you*, will it, driving the lorry?'

The momentary bridge between them shattered and Amy withdrew her hand as suddenly as if she was being burned by his touch, but before she could think of a suitable reply he went on so smoothly that she knew he was laughing at her: 'It's all right, you don't have to answer that.'

'Good. Because if we are to work together successfully, I should appreciate it if you would let the past lie,' Amy said tartly.

'Very well, I shall do my best to respect your wishes.' But she still had the feeling that he was laughing at her and when he had gone, striding away across the wet yard to where his Morgan was parked in the lane outside, she could not believe the confused welter of her emotions.

How could he make her feel that way, she wondered – angry, awkward, yet also strangely aware of herself . . . and of him. He had come here and tossed a job into her lap almost casually – a job that might mean she could put off selling her house for a few weeks at least and still have some stability and growth for the business. She should be planning already how she was going to make it work. And yet, for the moment, she could think of nothing but the way he had looked at her.

She half-closed her eyes as she pictured it again; as she relived the confused moment when his eyes had met hers, something darted deep within her . . . sharp, piercing, sweet – a half-forgotten reaction to the nearness of a man. Fleetingly she was lifted, borne up on a wave of inexplicable excitement and unthinking breathless anticipation. Then, as suddenly, the wave broke, letting her come crashing down while the swirling yellow aftermath drove relentless ripples across the sandy expanse of her conscience and seeped guiltily into her heart.

The sound of a motor engine coming closer made her look up. It was Herbie, back from his day's gravel haulage. She went to the door of the office, watching him park the lorry. Thank heaven for Herbie, loyal, trusted and true. She could talk it all over with him – ask his advice about getting the extra men, decide which lorry should go to Ralph Porter and which continue with the gravel haulage - and know he would back her up.

Amy raised her chin and felt again a faint echo of the excitement and anticipation which had lifted her just now. Perhaps things were coming together after all. Perhaps there

243

was a future out there somewhere, if she could struggle on for a while longer over the stony ground.

'Can you come into the office for a minute, Herbie?' she called. 'I want to talk to you.' And as he came towards her across the wet yard with his unhurried, loping gait, hope grew in her. A new contract . . . extra staff to be taken on . . . even the rain appeared to be easing off . . . there wouldn't be a flash flood today, at any rate. All it needed now was for the strike to be settled and then things could be set fair.

'What is it, Mrs Roberts? What's wrong?' Herbie asked pessimistically and her lips curved upwards into something approaching her old, bright self.

'Nothing, Herbie. For once it's good news,' she told him. 'I think things are beginning to swing our way!'

*

But if things were looking brighter for Amy and the future of Roberts Haulage, for the mining families of Hillsbridge the outlook was still very black indeed.

The strike was close to being settled, it was true. Headlines in the *Hillsbridge Mercury* announced 'The End Really is in Sight' and few townsfolk disbelieved it. Everywhere the drift back to work had begun – 357,000 men in all, if the *Mercury* had it right – and letters from colliery workers appealing for peace were appearing in the correspondence columns.

But at what a cost! By the middle of November the Miners' Delegate Conference had decided to give their executive power to resume negotiations with the Government.

'That means they've already given in over the question of hours,' Walter Clements explained to the rest of his cronies in the now near-dry bar of the Miners' Arms, but really no explanation was needed. They knew only too well that things were not going their way, but they were too weary, too hungry and too heart-sore to fight any more. Strike pay was down to a meagre 3s a week and had been for three weeks now; not even food coupons distributed by the Miners' Relief Committee could do much to ease the distress now that winter was settling in.

Only stalwarts like Ewart Brixey remained solid for the strike, arguing with the wavering souls that, 'We can't give in now! What's it all been for, lads? Go back now and they'll have us over a barrel – we'll be even worse off than we was before!'

But the militants were now lone voices crying in the wilderness. The majority wanted only to return to some semblance of normality before Christmas. And on the last Thursday in November, they got their way.

At meetings all over the coalfields the vote was near unanimous. Back to work. Never mind the conditions. Just let's get back to work!

In their droves they headed for the colliery office to sign on – many, many more than there were jobs to fill after the long, damaging stoppage. And for the moment they could feel nothing but relief.

The strike was over. Soon the wheels would be turning again, bringing the rich black mineral up from the bowels of the earth.

The strike was over. There would be food on the tables and boots on cold, blistered feet. And soon it would be Christmas.

For a little while, at least, it was all the people of Hillsbridge knew or cared about.

Chapter Fourteen

During the month before Christmas Amy worked as she had never worked before. In the early days after Llew's death she had struggled on out of desperation, fighting wearily for survival. Now, with both lorries working again, four men on the payroll and a number of occasional jobs coming in besides the now-regular assignments of the quarry company and Ralph Porter's timber firm, Amy found she was throwing herself into each new day with fervour. There were still problems to be faced and plenty of them, but somehow the emphasis was shifted from holding a defensive position to one of attack, and the energy and enthusiasm ran through her veins with her blood, so that the early mornings and late nights no longer took their toll on her. She woke now not heavy from restless, worry-laden sleep, but tingling with the urgency of all there was to do; she marshalled the children with good-humoured efficiency; she took work home from the yard, poring over it when the household tasks were done, and she fell into bed tired but satisfied instead of weak and exhausted.

On the home front things were running a good deal more smoothly than she had dared hope – or perhaps it was just that she had no time to notice otherwise.

Huw had started school and though in the first few weeks he came home more than once with a bloodied nose, a black eye or a tear in the seat of his pants, Amy was relieved that he had settled in without any further attempts to run away. He still had a mutinous look about him, he still resisted any overtures of warmth, yet somehow she felt that she had made progress with him, despite the small amount of time she was able to spend with him.

Or, perhaps, because of it. A boy like Huw could not be rushed, she decided – fuss over him and he would feel stifled. As for the girls, they idolised Huw, trotting round behind him whatever he was doing until Amy had to tell them to leave him alone. Sometimes he came to the yard with her, playing a kind of hide-and-seek in the timber stacks and poking about with anything mechanical while she worked. Herbie treated him with the deepest suspicion, as likely as not to yell at him to 'Get out of it!' But Ivor Burge took a liking to Huw, finding jobs for him and even allowing him to ride in the lorry cab when there was room.

As a driver, Ivor had come on in leaps and bounds. He was young, strong and keen, with all Herbie's loyalty yet without the irritating knack Herbie had of making Amy feel he was indulging her, holding on to the strings while she played at transport management.

I'm being unfair, she told herself. Herbie is one in a million.

But the fact remained that she felt more comfortable telling Ivor what to do. And she had encountered a little resistance from Herbie when she announced the work schedules: Herbie to continue with the gravel haulage along with his new mate, Arty Dando, with Ivor carrying the timber for Ralph Porter.

'Leave Ivor doing something he knows about,' Herbie advised and Amy felt ridiculously guilty when she over-ruled him.

'No, I'd like him to take on the timber,' she said,

mollifying Herbie slightly by adding, 'It's very heavy work, Herbie, and I can't afford to risk you doing something to your back. I couldn't manage without you.'

So Ivor took on the timber . . . and a very good job he was making of it.

'He's a good worker, that lad of yours,' Ralph Porter said the first time he came to the yard to pay Amy for the hire of the lorry, and she glowed with pleasure. Ivor was 'home-grown' and it was almost as good to hear Ralph Porter praising him as it would have been to be complimented on one of the children.

Aloud, however, she merely said, 'I'm glad you're satisfied.'

'Very.' He was leaning his tall frame against the desk, looking at her with eyes narrowed in his dark face. 'I think we might be able to do quite a bit of business together. In fact, I was going to suggest that perhaps we could have dinner together one night in order to discuss it.'

Amy's flush of pleasure deepened to the scarlet of confusion.

'Oh – I don't really think that's necessary, is it?' she blurted, then wished she could have bitten off her tongue as he raised an eyebrow to give his face the familiar mocking expression.

'Perhaps not, but I always think it's very civilised to do business over a pleasant meal.'

'Yes, maybe,' she faltered. 'It's just that I have very little time for that kind of thing.'

His mouth quirked. 'Maybe you should make time? Think about it, anyway, and I shall ask you again. You wouldn't be committing yourself to anything. A lot of business might be conducted this way, but it's still quite within your power to say no to anything that doesn't appeal to you.'

'Yes – of course . . .'

'I'll see you in two weeks' time.' He left the office then and from the window she watched him cross the yard and climb into his distinctive motor car. Her pulses were beating a little too fast and her cheeks still burned with the confusion he seemed to start in her so easily.

Fool! she thought. What must he think of you? He probably meant nothing at all by asking you to have dinner with him – it's the kind of thing business people do. But could you take it like that? No – you had to jump to the wrong conclusion and make a fool of yourself.

But that was the way he affected her. He was so damned sure of himself it was disconcerting. So purposeful it made her weak by comparison, his dynamism and strength overshadowing any resolution she might make to be as cool and businesslike as he was. How did he manage it? He was a man of few words, he wasn't even flamboyant, but certainly there was no ignoring him.

It's probably his conceit, she decided. He expects everyone to kow-tow to him and so they do. But I have no intention of kow-towing to him – or to anyone.

By the time Ivor returned with the lorry, she had recovered herself sufficiently to check out the books and make up the wage-packets, although she still cringed inwardly every time she thought of the interview and the stupidity of her reaction to Ralph Porter's suggestion.

'Mr Porter is very pleased with you, Ivor,' she said, determined to mention his name normally. 'He says you're a good worker.'

Ivor's thin face lit up. 'I do my best, Mrs Roberts,' he mumbled.

She questioned him about the day's work and paid him his wages. Then, as he was about to leave, he turned back in the doorway.

'Oh, by the way, there was a bloke who works at Mr Porter's yard asking about you.'

'Asking about me?'

'One of the labourers. His name's Griffin – Ollie Griffin.'

'Griffin.' Amy racked her brains. 'One of the Griffins from Purldown?'

Ivor shrugged. 'I don't know. Reckon he must be.'

'What was he asking?'

'Oh, all sorts really. How you were getting on – how the business was going – all that kind of thing.'

'I hope you told him it's thriving,' Amy remarked sharply. She was very aware that half Hillsbridge was waiting for her to fail.

'Yes, I did, and he seemed very interested,' Ivor replied. 'The way he was talking, I wouldn't be surprised if he doesn't come to you for a job.'

'Oh, I shouldn't think so,' Amy said, but she couldn't help being pleased all the same. She had nothing to offer a prospective employee, but it was pleasant to think that someone might actually want to work for her – particularly a man who at present worked for Ralph Porter.

Perhaps I'm not the only person he causes to feel inadequate, she thought triumphantly. Perhaps his men feel the same way too.

As she continued with her work she forgot about Ollie Griffin. The next morning, however, a Saturday, she was somewhat surprised to see a young man wandering about outside the office and peering in through the windows when she called at the yard with the girls on the way to market. Thick-set, with slicked-back hair and dressed in a jacket and overalls, he was an unfamiliar figure to her, but as she crossed the yard to ask him what he thought he was doing she turned, noticed her and came towards her, beaming.

'Ah! Just the person I wanted to see!'

'Me?' Amy asked in surprise.

'That's right, you, love.' The familiarity in his attitude annoyed her slightly, but she could see he meant no harm.

The wind was whistling coldly around the yard, cutting through her coat and stinging her cheeks, and she got out her key and unlocked the office door.

'You'd better come in.'

He followed her, blowing on his hands.

'This is a cold one! Going to be a white Christmas, is it?'

She didn't answer but turned to face him. 'You wanted to see me, you said.'

'That's right. I'm Mr Griffin, Ollie Griffin. I was talking to one of your lads yesterday – Ivor, I think his name is. He said you might have a job for me, so I thought – strike while the iron's hot!'

Amy felt another stab of annoyance. 'I'm sorry, Mr Griffin, but I'm afraid you've had a wasted journey. I'm fully staffed at present.'

'Oh.' He looked put out but not deflated. 'Well, if you ever do want to take on anybody, bear me in mind, will you? I'm a good all-rounder, if I do say so myself. There's not much I can't turn my hand to – driving, labouring – and I know a fair bit about engines, too, if it comes to that.'

Amy looked at him closely. 'You work for Ralph Porter, don't you?'

'Worse luck.' Ollie Griffin drew a grubby handkerchief

out of his pocket and blew his nose noisily. 'He's a bugger to work for, though, and if I can fit myself up elsewhere I shall be glad.'

'You're not happy there, then?' Amy asked, unable to resist the opportunity for a little insight into Ralph Porter, employer.

Ollie stuffed his handkerchief back into his pocket.

'You said it! He'll keep a man down, given half a chance. When I went there I was supposed to be a driver. Promised me the earth, he did – reckoned he'd make me a foreman before the year was out. But it was just a lot of empty promises. Of course, he's a bully and like all bullies he doesn't like it if you stand up for yourself. He got his knife into me and put me back on labouring. No, I should be glad to see the back of that place, I can tell you.'

'I see,' Amy said. 'Well, as I say, Mr Griffin, I have nothing to offer you at the moment. But if the occasion should arise ...'

'Right. Thanks, love. I won't detain you any longer.'

After he had gone Amy felt ridiculously pleased with herself. It did wonders for the morale to have men actually coming to you for work – especially preferring you to someone like Ralph Porter as an employer. But of course at present it was hypothetical only. Two drivers and two mates for the two lorries was all she could possibly take on at the moment. Though if business continued to thrive, who knew ...?

'Mammy, I thought we were going to shop! Can't we go?' Barbara agitated and Amy got together the papers she had come to collect.

'Right, girls, we're on our way,' she said, stuffing them into her bag in rather unbusinesslike fashion. 'Market – here we come! And if you both behave yourselves, you shall have a quarter of mint shrimps to suck!'

*

Saturday morning was and always had been Amy's regular time for shopping. The market, of course, was open all day, becoming busier and more social as the hours passed. By the time the lamps were finally extinguished at past 9 o'clock, the atmosphere was almost like an extension of the fun-fair that wintered in the adjoining yard, with the Salvation Army

Band grouped in a circle playing rousing hymn tunes while people shopped for last-minute bargains. At this time of day, too, there was always plenty to see although, Amy thought with regret, a good deal less than when she was a child. Then there had been 'Smasher the Chinaware Man', throwing samples of his wares into the air and letting them crash to the ground to attract a crowd; Dr Quilley, the Indian quack, selling pills, potions and cure-alls in a jar; and Dr Rainbow, his partner, pulling teeth on an open wagon in full view of the interested onlookers. Those colourful characters had disappeared now. But there were still stalls of every description from cockles to cottons, cheap watches to cheese, and the cries of the vendors vied with the loud modern music continually played by the holder of the stall that sold the most up-to-date wind-up gramophones.

Most people in Hillsbridge visited the market at some time or another on a Saturday and so the following week Amy was not really surprised when she caught sight of Ollie Griffin sitting on one of the forms that surrounded the tea stall under the market clock, his hands clasped around a warming 'cuppa'. She was surprised, however, when he got up, left his tea and made a beeline for her.

'Morning, love.'

'Oh, good morning, Mr Griffin,' she said, a little coolly.

'Glad I saw you. Thought I'd tell you I've finished with Porter.'

'Oh, have you?' she said vaguely, busying herself with rearranging the shopping in her bag so as to keep the beef she had just bought in the meat market from dripping blood onto the rest of her purchases.

'That's right. Said I would, didn't I? I couldn't put up with him any longer. So if you've got a job going, don't forget me, will you?'

'I won't, but as I told you, I really don't need any more men at the moment.'

'Oh well, you never know what's round the next corner . . .'

Barbara was tugging impatiently at Amy's coat and she said, 'I must go.'

As she went on with her shopping, it crossed her mind to wonder if he had come to the market specially to see her. Possible. He seemed very keen to work for her. But then no one could be very enthralled with the idea of being out of work, especially with Christmas just around the corner.

Ralph Porter must indeed be a bad employer if a man chose to be unemployed rather than work for him, and again she felt a stab of satisfaction that she should be singled out as a better prospect. But she had nothing to offer Ollie Griffin at the moment and no likelihood of it either. Things were just ticking over nicely and she was delighted with the way the books had balanced this week. With luck she should be able to afford some little Christmas treats for the girls and Huw, without feeling too guilty about the extra expense. Not that she would be *extravagant*, of course, but as Llew had always said – what was Christmas if you couldn't do something a bit special . . .?

Llew. Amy's heart seemed to sink to a well somewhere deep inside her. This would be the first Christmas without Llew and she was dreading it. He had always made so much of the festivities, especially since they had had the children, bringing home bits and pieces to fill their stockings, springing small surprises and insisting, 'It's Christmas – enjoy yourself!'

But this year, Amy would have abolished Christmas altogether if she could. When families were all gathered together under their own roofs she knew the gap he had left would be excruciatingly apparent, and dreaded having to try to fill it for the sake of the children. One good thing was having Huw – at least that would make it a bit different. But she would be without the prop of the business for a few days at any rate, with too many things to remind her of the past.

Well, worry about that when the time comes, Amy told herself. Just be grateful for the way things are turning out.

A few days later, however, something happened to upset the equilibrium and make Amy rethink her plans for the business, when she arrived at the yard to find Arty Dando hanging about with a doleful expression on his face.

'What are you doing here, Arty?' she asked. 'Shouldn't you be picking up a load of gravel with Herbie?'

Arty's face brightened at the prospect of being the one to impart the news. 'Herbie's gone off to do the timber run this morning. Ivor Burge has been and gone and broke his leg.'

'Oh, no! But when? How?' Amy asked in horror.

'Last night, playing football. It snapped like a twig. Everybody in the field heard it,' Arty said with satisfaction. 'He won't be able to drive for a couple of months. So Herbie thought he'd better do Mr Porter's run first.'

'Oh, Lord!' The full implications of this development began to filter through to Amy and she felt herself going cold with horror. *Ivor* breaking his leg – it couldn't be worse. If it had been one of the mates, she could have managed, but a driver...

'Whatever am I going to do?' she wondered aloud.

And then it came to her: Ollie Griffin. It must have been fate which had sent him to her. He had said he could drive, so she'd better get in touch with him – and quickly.

'Do you know the Griffins?' she asked Arty. 'They live at Purldown, I think. You'd better get up there, find out where their house is and ask Ollie to come and see me. Straight away!'

Arty moved reluctantly. He had foreseen a pleasant lazy day messing about at the yard.

'How am I going to get there?'

'You'll have to walk, I suppose,' Amy said tartly. 'It won't hurt you; it's a nice dry day.'

Arty went and she was left to worry. Supposing Ollie Griffin had found other employment in the meantime? Well, it was useless to cross that bridge until she came to it. But she found it difficult to concentrate on anything for the good two hours it took before she saw Arty come back into the yard in the company of the broad, overalled figure of Ollie Griffin.

She sent up a silent prayer of thanks and set aside the pile of books on which she had been trying to work.

'Mr Griffin, I'm glad you could come. I'm in a bit of a spot.'

'Yes, Arty's been telling me.' Ollie Griffin was rubbing his hands together and beaming. It wasn't a very nice smile, she thought – but what had that got to do with it? The job demanded driving ability, not charm, and if Ollie was a good worker she could count herself lucky.

'You never know when you're going to need a good man, do you?' he went on with a leer.

Amy ignored the implication. 'You can drive, can't you?'

'Too true I can. You won't find a better driver in Hillsbridge.'

'And you could start right away?'

'Today if you like.'

'I should warn you that it's a temporary position only for the present,' Amy said. 'Just until Ivor's fit again. He's a good boy and I must keep the job open for him. But there's always the possibility that if business builds up I shall be able to run another lorry and put on another permanent crew. So the better you work now, promoting Roberts Haulage, the greater the chance of my being able to keep you on.'

'Fair enough,' Ollie agreed, adding, 'Of course, the old boy must be getting on a bit too, mustn't he?'

'Do you mean Herbie?' Amy asked, annoyed.

'Yes. A young man like me could give you a far better day's work . . .'

'Herbie is a valued employee and a friend,' Amy said stiffly. 'Please don't talk about him like that again.'

Ollie pulled a face. 'Oh, sorry!' But he didn't look it, as he stood grinning and rubbing his hands together.

Amy swallowed her dislike of him. 'You could start right away, you say?'

'Can do.'

'Then perhaps you and Arty could go and shift a few loads of gravel. They must be wondering why we haven't turned up this morning – I'm surprised they haven't been down here chasing us up.' If it had been Ralph Porter's work which had been left, *he* would have been down here riding his high horse by now, she thought. The quarry company people were more amenable – and further away. But she didn't want to risk upsetting them.

'Arty can show you where to go and from then on, just let them tell you what they want you to do,' she instructed.

'By the way, what about money?'

'Oh yes – money. I'll pay you the same as I pay Ivor.'

'I'm older and more experienced than him.'

'You'll be doing the same work. And anyway I can't afford to pay you more,' Amy said flatly.

Ollie looked at her for a moment, then his thick lips curled into a grin and one eye winked at her slowly and deliberately.

'I get it. I'm on probation. But if I can come up with the goods, it'll be a different story.'

'Maybe. We shall have to wait and see.' Amy's tone was crisp and businesslike. 'The lorry is over there and the sooner you get started, the better.'

When they had gone, trundling out of the yard, Amy sat in the office biting at the end of her pencil and thinking. Having a driver to call on in an emergency such as this had been a stroke of luck and it had taught her a lesson. She must never let herself be caught in such a position again. The mates must be taught to drive as soon as possible. In the meantime...

Perhaps the most sensible thing would be for Ollie to drive the lorry to Porter's timber yard tomorrow. After working for Ralph Porter, he must know the business inside and out and besides, as he had said, he was a good deal younger than Herbie when it came to dealing with an awkward commodity like timber. Herbie would probably object but she would have to be firm with him.

As she expected, when Herbie returned to the yard and she brought him up to date on developments, he was less than enthusiastic.

'Ollie Griffin? Oh, I don't know about that. I've never had a lot of time for those Griffins. They'm a funny lot...'

'Well, if he's no good he'll have to go,' Amy said. 'But he seems a willing worker.'

'Oh, they seem willing enough all right,' Herbie said enigmatically. 'It don't seem a very good idea to me to send him up to the timber yard though. If he used to work there...'

'Whyever not? He's the obvious one. Hauling timber will be second nature to him.'

'Yes, but you don't know what sort of feeling there'd be between him and Ralph Porter, do you?'

'Why should that make any difference?' Amy asked.

'I dunno,' Herbie shrugged. 'What's *he* got to say about it – Ollie Griffin?'

'I haven't told him yet.'

'Well, don't burn your boats until you have,' Herbie said darkly.

But when Ollie and Arty returned, Ollie was in high spirits.

'How did it go?' Amy enquired.

'Easy as pie!'

'Good. But tomorrow I should like you to take over the timber run.'

At once a smirk curled Ollie's mouth. 'To Ralph Porter's, you mean?'

'Yes. Have you any objection?'

'Objection my foot! I'll show the bugger...'

On the point of asking what he meant by that, Amy bit her

tongue. Now that Ollie Griffin was working for her she had no desire to be drawn into any gossip about business associates.

'I shall expect you to do it properly – not take the chance to settle old scores,' she said sternly.

'Now, would I do a thing like that? Not on your nellie . . .'

'That's all right, then,' said Amy. 'And I must say you've done well today. Carry on this way and you and I will get along famously.'

'I second that!' Ollie said heartily.

Next morning both lorries had gone out by the time Amy got to the yard and, feeling pleased with the way things were progressing, she went on with her work. But towards lunchtime she heard the sound of a motor car being raced into the yard and looked up to see Ralph Porter's red Morgan screaming to a stop outside the office.

Amy glanced at the calendar. It was not the day for settling his account, so what was he doing here? And why, for heaven's sake, was she turning into a jelly at the sight of him? Today, as proof against the elements in open-car motoring, he was wearing a leather flying helmet; as he climbed out of the car, he loosened the chin-strap and strode purposefully towards the office.

Supposing he has come to repeat his invitation to take me out to dinner! Amy thought in sudden panic. What shall I say this time?

As he opened the office door she got up to meet him.

'This is a surprise. I wasn't expecting . . .'

Her voice trailed away for his expression, cold and hard, was putting an end to social niceties.

'Mrs Roberts – you sent a different driver to my yard this morning,' he began without preamble. 'A man by the name of Ollie Griffin. I should be obliged if you would see to it that he's not sent again.'

'Really . . .?' He had knocked the wind right out of her sails.

'I thought that after I had expressed to you my satisfaction with young Burge, I could expect him to continue with the contract.'

'And he certainly would have done, except that he's at home with a broken leg,' Amy snapped. 'I had to find a replacement driver at short notice and I happened to know

256

Mr Griffin was looking for work. I consider I was lucky to get him.'

'Hmm!' Ralph Porter's mouth twisted. 'Well, that's a matter for conjecture, I assure you, Mrs Roberts. In fact, if you want my advice, you'll tell him where to get off and fast. That man's trouble!'

Amy lifted her chin. So that was it! There was ill-feeling between the two men and Ralph Porter, annoyed that Ollie had taken it upon himself to leave and worried no doubt about the stories he might spread concerning his former employer, intended using his influence to take his revenge . . . and possibly prevent Ollie from ever working again.

'He's only been with me a day, it's true,' Amy said. 'But from what I've seen of him, I'm perfectly satisfied . . .'

'You'll regret it,' he stated.

Amy felt her hackles rising. 'Ollie used to work for you, didn't he?' she asked.

'He did. I must confess that I was taken in by his apparent dedication in the beginning, though I comfort myself that I was very busy at the time – and it didn't take me very long to see through him. But you're a woman . . .'

'What has that got to do with it?' Amy asked, annoyed to think her sex was being dragged into this.

'Everything, I'm afraid. Griffin rather fancies himself with women. Perhaps you haven't noticed yet, but you'll need to watch him.'

'Watch him . . .?' Amy was growing crosser and crosser by the second. 'I really don't think I need a lecture from you on my employees. Just because he chose to leave you . . .'

'Oh, but he didn't. I sacked him!'

'Oh, but . . .' Amy was at a loss again. Typical, of course, that the two protagonists should differ in their accounts of what had happened. But hadn't Ollie Griffin told her a whole week earlier that he intended leaving Ralph Porter's employ at the first opportunity?

'I sacked him,' Ralph Porter went on, 'for a number of reasons. He is unreliable, he is not as honest as he might be, he has a loud mouth and he is overweeningly vain. Little things taken on their own, maybe, but add them all together and the man becomes a total liability, not worth the cost of the packet you put his wages in. Besides all that, he's a womaniser and I don't think you should trust him.'

'You don't? Well, I'm touched by your concern,' Amy said haughtily.

Ralph Porter swore. 'Dammit, woman, I'm trying to warn you for your own good.'

Now the devil was up in Amy.

'Are you sure you're not simply put out because Ollie Griffin prefers to work for me instead of you? Isn't this all sour grapes?'

'Well, if you want to take it like that, there's nothing I can do about it,' Ralph Porter said casually.

'I'm glad you realise that,' Amy replied sweetly.

'There is one thing I can do, though. I can stipulate that I do not want that man on my premises again. Either you send another driver or you can consider the contract cancelled.'

She gazed at him open-mouthed, but before any words would come he lowered his voice. 'And remember what I say. Don't trust him, Amy! Especially try not to be on your own with him.'

He turned then, so abruptly that he almost overturned the small three-legged oil heater that provided the only heat in the office; he banged out and a moment later Amy heard the distinctive Morgan engine roar into life.

She remained staring into the yard long after the Morgan had disappeared from view, trembling all over.

How dare he come here and tell her how to run her business! It was just like him, of course, and she supposed he had every right to veto a driver she might send to his premises, ridiculous though it seemed. But as for telling her who she should and should not employ – well, it was brass-necked nerve. Though there had been something rather different in the way he had finished his warning about Ollie. He had not really sounded arrogant – more concerned. And for the first time he had called her Amy, not Mrs Roberts.

Amy felt the sharp, treacherous corkscrew twist deep within her and strengthened her resolve. He had no right to come here and tell her what to do. Who did he think he was? But she would love to know which version of the parting of the ways was the correct one.

Did he jump or was he pushed? she wondered wryly.

Well, whichever, she would have to eat humble pie and ask Herbie to do the timber run tomorrow. She could not afford to lose Ralph Porter's contract over something so trivial. And she didn't actually like Ollie Griffin, anyway. He might well be dishonest, 'ready to do his eye good' as Mam would put it, and she had no doubt he was more likely to be out for himself than to be loyal. But that did not give Ralph Porter the right to come barging in here with ultimatums.

He was an arrogant, conceited, bossy man and Amy was very glad she had let him know exactly what she thought of him.

*

Another week passed and Christmas was now uppermost in everyone's mind. Money was still scarce, but then it had never been exactly plentiful in Hillsbridge except for the lucky few, and families made poor by the long, hard struggle and the continuing shortage of work were determined to forget their troubles and celebrate.

Fattened fowls were killed, drawn and plucked. Plum puddings – which ought to have been made in the autumn, but had been neglected because of the strike – were hastily stirred, wrapped and boiled in the washhouse coppers, and the boys who had so recently been picking illicit coal off the batches were now sent out to hunt for holly and mistletoe.

'When can we put up the decorations, Mummy?' Barbara asked eagerly and Amy dragged out the step-ladder and sent Huw into the attic for the big cardboard box that contained the baubles, tinsel and lanterns.

'They're squashed!' Barbara complained, pulling out a handful of crumpled paper-chains.

'Well, you can always make some more. I'll get you some new strips and glue tomorrow,' Amy promised. The sight of the decorations was opening up the well of misery inside her again. Each and every one of the decorations was stirring a special memory – poignant reminders of happier times now gone for ever.

'Can we have a tree?' Barbara squealed, unearthing the Christmas angel who always sat on the topmost branch while Maureen, diving into the box beside her, pulled out one of the little candle-holders with the opaque sides that lit the tree with red, blue and green light.

'Look – look! Pretty!'

'Be careful. Those break easily!' Amy warned, snatching it from her, but too late to prevent her from pushing in one of the red glass sides.

259

'But can we have a tree!' Barbara clamoured. '*Can* we?'

'Oh, I don't know! Daddy always got the tree!' Amy snapped.

The girls subsided, looking at her with glum faces and Amy felt ashamed of herself for yelling. But as she had said, getting the tree was something Llew had always done. She had no idea when she would find the time to organise it – and anyway the very thought made her so utterly miserable.

'Look, here's Father Christmas!' she said, trying to make amends by pulling out a shiny red ornament with cotton-wool-trimmed cap; the girls fell on it, their disappointment about the tree momentarily forgotten.

Huw was standing to one side, however, kicking at the chair and looking glum and a little left out.

I'm not the only one with memories of other Christmases, Amy reminded herself.

'What do you like to do best at Christmas, Huw?' she asked.

The faraway look extended to his eyes. 'Sing carols,' he said.

Sing carols! Of course. The Welsh in him would make him love to sing, but Amy could not remember hearing him utter one note since he had come into her home. She forced herself to draw a mental picture of what it had been like for him.

'Did you have a piano?' she asked.

He shook his head.

'You sang with your Mam and Dad?'

'No!' His voice was scornful. 'With my mates.'

'Oh, I see.' Carol singing with his mates, door to door.

> Christmas is coming, the geese are getting fat.
> Please to put a penny in the old man's hat.
> If you haven't got a penny, a ha'penny will do,
> If you haven't got a ha'penny, God bless you!

Well, he couldn't do that here. He had made a few friends, it was true, boys of his own age whom he'd met at school, scrapped with and then formed an alliance, but carol singing door to door was something Charlotte had always frowned on and Amy was inclined to agree with her. It was just another form of begging, after all, and the Hall and Roberts families did not go out begging – at least, not if the womenfolk knew anything about it.

But carol singing around the piano in the front room could be fun. I must remind Mam, Amy thought, and make sure we have a session some time this Christmas. The thought of a sing-song evoked other memories of Christmases much longer ago, when Amy had been no older than the children were now, and she felt a little better.

With only a few days to go now to the great day, the schools had broken up. As always, Amy took Barbara and Maureen up to Mam in Greenslade Terrace before going to the yard, but Huw was more of a problem. She did not like to leave him running around at home – although he had never attempted to run away again, it was still a constant worry nagging away at the back of her mind – and had long ago promised Mam not to worry her with him. If Dolly had not been so heavily pregnant, Huw could have spent some time with her boys, Amy thought, but Dolly's due date was fast approaching and her own two boys sometimes seemed to be too much for her, without adding Huw as a third. As for Jim and Sara's Alex, he was rather too old to want Huw around. So most days Amy took the boy to the yard with her. He could watch the trains from there, or go up to the mill and watch the sacks of grain go up and down in the hoist – and once the lorries were back, she could get Herbie to find odd jobs to occupy him.

Considering Huw's rebellious nature, she was surprised how good he was when at the yard, as if going through the gates took him into a different world and the cares of his young life dropped away.

The day before Christmas Eve was cold, dank and unseasonal, but at least it was not actually raining. While she settled herself to doing the last of the book-keeping before the break, Amy suggested to Huw that he might go out to look for holly and mistletoe to complete the decorations at home.

'The bits with the best berries have probably already gone,' she said. 'But you should be able to find some if you go along the lanes.'

'Can I see if Conrad Tucker wants to come with me?' Huw asked.

Amy pulled a face. Conrad Tucker lived in the next rank up from Batch Row and was not exactly the friend she would have chosen for Huw, but that applied to all the boys he had selected as chums, and if they were the ones he felt at home with, Amy didn't feel she could isolate him by laying down the law about it. Better to ease him away from them gently as he got older.

'All right – so long as you don't get up to any mischief,' she warned. 'Keep off the railway line – and for heaven's sake don't go on private property!'

When he had gone she sat day-dreaming for a few minutes about the present she had bought for him – an extra-special penknife with all the latest attachments. He could have done with it to cut the holly instead of his old rather blunt blade, she thought, and enjoyed picturing his face when he unwrapped the gift on Christmas morning. Then, with an effort, she dragged her mind back to the business. Get today over and then she could really concentrate on Christmas.

Lunchtime came and went, announced by works hooters, and Huw did not return. Amy was surprised but not worried. There was a packet of sandwiches and an apple waiting here for him, but she could imagine him preferring to share a doorstep of bread and dripping with Conrad. When they got together boys had no idea of time – unless their tummies acted as clocks.

By mid-afternoon, though, with dusk closing in mistily, she was beginning to grow anxious, unable to concentrate on her work as she constantly scanned the gathering gloom for a glimpse of the still-skinny figure.

He had not returned when the first of the lorries rolled back into the yard – Ollie Griffin and Arty, back from the gravel run. Since Ralph Porter's visit she had been forced to change them around but it was a constant thorn in her side. The gravel lorry was invariably back first and when Herbie had been doing it, he had then had time to take care of any odd jobs about the yard before it got dark. Ollie didn't do that. Oh, he did anything she asked him to, it was true, but she was never convinced he had not found a quick way around it and he failed to see and deal with things himself as Herbie did. No, a week or so of Ollie's work and she was beginning to see what Ralph Porter had meant about him being shifty and lazy.

But perhaps I'm being unfair, she told herself. He may still be working his way in . . .

She glanced up and watched as he and Arty parked the lorry and came across to the office. The wage packets were made up and ready, each with their little extra Christmas bonus tucked inside, and when the men had reported on their day's work she handed them the envelopes.

'Happy Christmas!'

Arty took his and pocketed it.

'Happy Christmas to you, Mrs Roberts. I'm off now, then – I want to catch the shops to buy something nice for my Mum.'

'That's all right, you get off then, Arty,' she said.

But Ollie Griffin made no move to follow him. Instead, he hung around the office, picking up some of the cards which had been sent to the business and glancing at them, and when the door had closed after Arty he turned to Amy with a broad smirk.

'All ready for the off then, love?'

'I've hardly had time to think about it yet,' Amy said tartly.

'Bet the kids have, though. Christmas is a time for nippers.'

His words reminded her of Huw. 'You haven't seen Huw about anywhere I suppose, have you?' she asked. 'He went out looking for mistletoe and he's not back yet.'

'Naw.' Ollie shook his head. He was looking at her with an expression that seemed almost speculative; it made her uncomfortable, as Ralph Porter's look sometimes did, but without any of the pleasure. Then he winked, a slow, slimy closing of one eye, 'Mistletoe, eh?'

'We usually have mistletoe at Christmas.'

'I'll bet you do!' His voice was heavy with innuendo.

'Don't you want to be getting home too, Ollie?' she asked, anxious to be rid of him.

'No hurry,' he grinned.

'Well, I have work to do. If there's nothing else...'

'Just my Christmas bonus,' he said smoothly.

Something in his tone disconcerted Amy and she felt her breath come a little faster.

'Your Christmas bonus is in your envelope.'

He laughed, coming round the desk towards her.

'Oh, I wasn't talking about that sort of bonus. More like a Christmas kiss, maybe...'

'How dare you!' she tried to say, but as he grabbed her the words were lost in a squeak. He was a big man, solid and strong, and he pulled her effortlessly towards him. As her face brushed the shoulder of his overalls she breathed in the dirty, sweaty smell of unwashed material, then his hand was in her hair, dragging her head back and covering her mouth with wet, rubbery lips. His free hand settled on her bottom, pulling her in close so that for a moment she was helpless in his bear-hug embrace. Then, as he lifted his head to grin down at her, she pushed at him with all her might and brought up her hand to connect a stinging blow to his cheek.

Hurt surprise suffused the blubbery features.

'Hey – what d'you want to do that for?'

'How *dare* you!' The words were clear and concise this time, though her voice shook like the rest of her.

He took a step back, rubbing at his stinging cheek. 'Don't be like that, love! You know you enjoy it.'

'How dare you!' Had every other word been erased from her vocabulary? She was repeating the phrase now like a parrot. 'Get out of here, you oaf!'

'Now, wait a minute! Who are you calling an oaf?'

'You! Do you make a habit of this sort of thing?'

Ollie grinned unpleasantly. 'Just give me half a chance.'

'That, Ollie Griffin, is something you will certainly not get from me. What makes you think you can come in here and take liberties with me – Christmas or not?'

'Aw, come on – a pretty woman like you – all this time without a man... Let Ollie remind you what a good time can be...' He was coming towards her again, wheedling, but the menace beneath the insulting sentiments was clear to Amy and she felt a moment's panic.

They were alone in the yard – there was no one within shouting distance – and Herbie would not be back for another hour or so. Fleetingly Amy thought of Ralph Porter's warning that she had ignored so blithely.

'Come on now, love, don't be scared...'

Amy moved swiftly, putting the desk between them again. 'Get out of here, Ollie Griffin!'

'Well, put up a bit of a fight if you like, love. I don't mind. Adds spice...'

'I'm *not* playing games!'

'No?' he sneered, following her round the desk.

She was trapped and she knew it. Glancing round in panic, her eye fell on a heavy glass paperweight on the desk-top and she grabbed it and held it up threateningly.

'One step closer and you'll get this between the eyes!' she warned him.

264

He stopped, his expression changing from half-playful desire to slow anger.

'All right, missus. If it's like that...'

'It is!'

'All right. But if the goods aren't for sale, you shouldn't put them in the window.'

'You ignorant pig! Get out!'

'I'm going – I'm going...'

As he turned to lumber towards the door, she snatched up the wage packet from the desk and flung it after him. It hit him on the shoulder and fell to the floor, the coins jangling.

'And don't come back. You're fired!'

He didn't answer but simply bent to pick up the wage packet, looking at her with so much dislike in his eyes that it turned her cold.

The door was open; a blast of icy air whipped in, banging it to and fro, and then he was gone. She stood trembling. The oaf! The lecherous, filthy-minded oaf! Ralph Porter had warned her about him, of course. But all the same ... *did* people think she was easy game? A woman alone in a man's world? Was that what the town thought of her?

As she crossed to close the door, her knees felt weak. Well, *he* wouldn't be bothering her again. But would there be others? And what was she going to do about the other lorry now that she had sacked Ollie? Oh, why had this happened now, just when things had seemed to be working out so well...?

The sound of a lorry engine again made her stop, holding the door open to look across the yard into the gathering dusk. Herbie. Thank goodness he hadn't come back in time to witness the little scene that had just been played out. If he had, she would have died of shame! The lorry stopped, Herbie climbed down and after him, Huw. She ran out towards them.

'Huw! Where have you been?'

'Picking mistletoe, like you said. I've got a lovely lot...'

'I found him up the lane. The mistletoe's in the back of the lorry,' Herbie put in. 'And that's not all we've got, is it, young Huw?'

Huw shook his head. Even in the half-light Amy could see the excitement in his face and could not bring herself to shout at him any more.

265

'What *have* you got?'

'In the back of the lorry – come and see!'

She followed him and there, in the empty bed of the lorry, she saw a fine tall Christmas tree.

'Where did you get this?' she asked.

'Ralph Porter sent it for you,' Herbie supplied. 'Said he thought you might not have one this year. Did you want me to take it up home for you?'

'Oh yes, please, Herbie!'

'Kind thought, wasn't it? There's a lot of people go on about him, but I reckon he's a fair bloke,' Herbie said.

'Yes.' Amy turned to Huw. 'Do you want to ride home in the lorry with Herbie and show him where to put the tree?'

Huw nodded. His face was aglow, as if a Christmas tree was something that had been beyond his wildest dreams.

When they had gone Amy went back into the office, packing things together with hands that still shook slightly. What an afternoon! And she wished now that she had not been so rude to Ralph Porter when he had come to the yard warning her about Ollie Griffin.

Her face burned a little as she remembered the way she had turned on him. Well, too bad. He had such a high-handed manner that it was all too easy to get annoyed. But she was glad, all the same, that he need never know just how accurate his warning had turned out to be. If she could find another driver fairly quickly, perhaps he need not know until long after the event that she had had to fire Ollie.

I have the whole of the Christmas break to find someone else, she thought. When Herbie comes back, I'll ask if he knows of anyone.

And in the meantime, I'm going to put it all behind me and we'll try to have a really good Christmas!

Chapter Fifteen

In spite of James's failing health, Charlotte had insisted that
No. 11 Greenslade Terrace should be the hub of the family's
Christmas Day, as it always had been.

'It wouldn't be right, not to have Christmas at home,' she
said, and none of her children with the exception of Jack
would have dared – or wanted – to argue with her.

Jack and Stella were going north to stay with Stella's
parents – big Hal O'Halloran, who had been general
manager of the Hillsbridge group of pits until his retirement
– and this decision had caused such a stir that the others had
all known that to refuse their invitation to Greenslade
Terrace would completely spoil Mam's Christmas.

It was true that Sarah insisted on cooking Christmas
dinner in her own home – 'We'd be just too many to all sit
down round one table,' she pointed out – but it had been
planned that she, Jim and the children should come across as
soon as the washing-up was done to join Dolly, Amy and
their families, and Ted, who had arrived on Christmas Eve
with a caseful of presents and enough yarns to keep them all
up to the small hours laughing and exclaiming over his
exploits. Only one thing marred Charlotte's enjoyment in
his homecoming – virtually the first thing he did was to
invite Rosa from next door to join them, and the sight of her
sitting across the kitchen was a thorn in Charlotte's side, try
as she might to put it out of her mind.

Christmas morning dawned bright and clear. In spite of
their late bedtime the night before Charlotte was awake
early, her mind buzzing with all she had to do, and she was
allowing herself a short lie-in while planning her timetable
to dinner when a loud knocking at the back door brought her
sitting bolt upright.

'What on earth...?'

She got out of bed, pulled on her flannel dressing-gown that had been a present from the boys on another, long-ago Christmas morning and padded down the stairs.

Before she had the stairs door open, the knocking came again. Even James, usually bleary this early, was sitting up in bed and calling, 'What be going on?'

'I don't know. I'm just going to find out.'

Charlotte hurried through the scullery and opened the door to see Victor standing there with Bob and Fred, their faces rosy from the early morning cold.

'Victor! What's wrong?' she asked.

'It's Dolly, she's started,' Victor said, his loud voice adding drama to the statement.

'Oh, my Lord!' Charlotte stood aside for them to come in, noticing as she did so that both Bob and Fred were carrying their Christmas stockings, still bulging and tied tightly round the tops. 'When did she start?'

'In the night. I got the midwife to her about an hour ago,' Victor explained, ushering the boys into the scullery. 'We left it as long as we could, but you know how it is and Dolly thought that if you could have the boys...'

'Yes, of course I can. She doesn't want me, does she?' Charlotte felt completely flummoxed. She had managed to be in attendance for both of Dolly's previous deliveries.

'No, it's all right. The midwife's there now. But I'll get back if you don't mind. You know how poorly she's been.'

'Of course, Victor. What about some breakfast before you go? No? Well, this is a tidy kettle of fish, I must say! Fancy choosing Christmas Day!'

She ushered the boys in, repeating, 'Christmas Day! Well, well!'

'It could have been worse,' James said philosophically. 'At least Victor hasn't got to lose a day's work today.'

'I know that, but now it's going to upset everything! Have you had anything to eat, boys? No? Well, I'll get you some breakfast.'

'They want to open their stockings,' James said and Charlotte brightened. It was a long time since she had had children opening stockings.

'Come on then, boys, let's see what you've got! And just think of it – before the day's out you'll have a new brother or sister too! Well, well!'

Bob and Fred dived eagerly into their stockings, pulling out oranges, apples, nuts and some small toys. Their excited shouts filled the house, waking Harry who came downstairs to see what was going on, and Ted who elected to stay in bed for a lie-in.

They were still squealing and laughing when Amy arrived with Huw, Barbara and Maureen, and there was further hubbub while they showed off their presents – rag dolls for the girls and a penknife and shiny new football which Huw was clutching proudly.

'Want me to give you a game, Huw?' Harry asked and the little boy's face was a picture.

'Oh yes, please!'

'He's thrilled to bits, isn't he, Amy?' Charlotte said when they had gone outside.

'I don't think he's ever had a real family Christmas before,' Amy replied. She was looking wan, Charlotte thought, but putting a brave face on it all the same, and her heart went out to her daughter, struggling through her first Christmas without her husband.

But the fact that Dolly was in labour was overriding all else, making it difficult to concentrate on anything, and Charlotte was glad to have Amy's help with the dinner.

'Perhaps we ought to send some up for Victor,' she suggested anxiously as they peeled potatoes. 'Harry could take it – or Ted.'

'But it would be cold long before they got there,' Amy pointed out. 'Anyway, if the baby arrives soon, maybe Victor will be here after all.'

'If he is, one of us ought to go up to be with Dolly,' Charlotte said. 'Oh dear, it's such an upset, Amy!'

But dinner-time came and went with no sign of Victor and no news. Although they observed all the usual traditions, down to the ceremonial entry of the pudding, flaming in a drop of brandy with a sprig of holly sticking out of the top, they were all preoccupied and it was the children whose voices were raised the loudest in the chorus of 'We Wish You a Merry Christmas'.

Washing up, Charlotte voiced what they were all thinking; 'Oh, I shall be glad to know it's all over! Our Dolly's been worrying me, being so poorly.'

Dinner over, Ted announced that he was going next door to see Rosa, while Harry took the opportunity to ask if it was all right for him to pop up and take Margaret her Christmas present.

'I suppose so – as long as you're both here when Jim and Sarah come,' Charlotte said. 'Remember you haven't seen your brother for a long time now, Ted.'

'I'll be back, don't worry,' Ted said, but by the time Harry was ready to go Jim and his family had arrived and Charlotte was nagging him: 'I don't think you ought to go out yet, Harry. It looks as if nobody's bothered with them. And our Alex does like to see you; you're the only one near his age.'

The afternoon wore on and Ted came back, bringing Rosa with him. She looked as lovely as ever, slim as a wand in a bright red dress that Charlotte privately thought was much too short, and made both Amy and Sarah feel positively plump by comparison. Her oval face was flushed and her dark eyes sparkled, but there was an air about her that Charlotte could not quite fathom – a kind of fervent determination, as if her diamond brightness covered some serious purpose. But Charlotte was too worried about Dolly to let Rosa occupy her thoughts for long.

'Harry, I wish you'd run up and find out what's going on,' she said as teatime approached.

He pulled a face; he knew Margaret would be wondering why he had not put in an appearance, but he also knew that anxiety was spoiling Charlotte's Christmas and it seemed selfish to put his own interests first at such a time.

'All right,' he agreed.

'And take some ham up. Poor Victor can't be having much of a time of it either,' Charlotte suggested, getting out the big traditional ham she'd scrimped and saved for, cutting thick slices and wrapping them in greaseproof paper.

'Be you staying for tea, Rosa?' James asked.

'Of course she is!' Ted replied for her, and Charlotte could have crowned them both. She wanted only the family around at Christmas and at a time like this, worried as she was, the feeling was intensified a thousandfold.

It seemed to Charlotte that Harry was never going to come back, and when he did his anxious face did nothing to allay her fears.

'What's the news?' she demanded.

'None. The baby still hasn't come. The doctor's there now. I think they're concerned about her, Mam.'

270

'Oh, I feel so helpless!' Charlotte exclaimed. 'I think I'm going up there myself.'

'It's too far for you to walk, Mam,' Amy said. 'You've been on the go all day.' Lately she had been concerned that Charlotte was overdoing things with James permanently invalided – and guilty, too, that she had laid more at her mother's door by landing the girls on her every day. 'You know how done up you get with the hills at the best of times.'

'Don't talk so soft! There's nothing wrong with me!'

They all looked at one another. 'Maybe we should get Cliff Button to run her up in his taxi?'

Harry was despatched again to seek Cliff Button's services, but he came back with the news that Cliff was away for the holiday.

'Who do we know with a car?' Ted asked.

'I can't think ...'

'Oh, do stop worrying, all of you! I can walk!'

'No, you can't, Mam. You'll be making yourself bad. There must be *somebody* with a car ...'

Amy sat quietly, chewing on a nail. She could think of somebody with a car – Ralph Porter. But did she dare bother him, on Christmas Day of all days?

'I'm going and none of you are going to stop me!' Charlotte had her coat on, brushing aside all protests and Amy made up her mind. She would swallow her pride and ask Ralph Porter. He might refuse – probably would – but after all Mam did for her, Amy owed it to her to try at least.

'If anybody's got change for the phone, I'll go and ring Ralph Porter,' she said.

They all looked at her in amazement.

'Ralph Porter? The timber man? How do you know him?'

'I do business with him.'

'Oh Amy, I don't think you should bother him ...'

'What about Eddie Roberts – your brother-in-law? He's got a car.'

'Yes, but he's not on the phone and I wouldn't ask him if he was,' Amy said. 'I'm afraid I'm not on very good terms with Eddie.'

They searched their pockets to come up with the change and Amy set out along the Rank for the nearest phone box. She didn't know Ralph Porter's number, she realised, but that hardly mattered. Mrs Coombs, the operator, in whose

271

cottage front room the Hillsbridge exchange was situated, would be able to tell her for certain.

At the thought Amy pulled a face. Knowing Mrs Coombs' reputation she would probably listen in to the conversation. Well, it couldn't be helped; this was an emergency.

As she waited for Mrs Coombs to connect her, Amy's nerve almost failed her. Then the bell was ringing and she heard Ralph Porter's voice on the line, deep and unmistakable.

'Hello?'

'It's Amy Roberts,' she began. 'You'll probably think this is the most terrible cheek, but I wondered if you could possibly do something for me. My sister is having a baby, she's been in labour all day and my mother is so worried she's insisting on going to see what's happening. But Dolly lives right up South Hill Gardens. It's too far for my mother to walk there and back in the cold night air and I was wondering if you... well, if it would be too much of an imposition to ask if you could run her up there in your car...'

Ralph Porter laughed out loud. 'Is that all? What a relief! I thought you were going to ask me to act as midwife!'

'It's no joke,' Amy said a little shortly.

'No, I'm sure it's not. Where does your mother live?'

'Greenslade Terrace. Off Conygre Hill. *Would* you...?'

'Now – or after dinner?'

Amy started. Dinner? They had had dinner hours ago. Then she realised – in Ralph Porter's world dinner was at 7 or 7.30 pm, not midday. How peculiar! she thought. Fancy having your Christmas dinner in the evening! It's enough to cause raging indigestion.

'Now, if you could. I promise we won't keep you from your dinner.'

'All right. Give me ten minutes.'

Amy half-ran back along the Rank. She found Mam struggling to ease her feet into her stoutest shoes with the help of the shoe-horn and still arguing.

'I don't know why you're all kicking up such a fuss about it. I've walked it hundreds of times...'

'It's all right, he's coming,' Amy said breathlessly.

They looked at her in awe, but only Ted voiced what they were all thinking. 'Is he sweet on you, Amy?'

'Of course not!' Amy snapped, but she was glad all the

272

same that she had the excuse of running to explain why her cheeks were suddenly pink.

Hardly had Amy got back when they heard the sound of a motor car engine approaching along the Rank.

'He's here,' Amy said unnecessarily.

'Oh my Lord – Amy, I wish you hadn't!' Charlotte was still protesting as Amy bundled her towards the door.

'Come on, Mam, we can't keep him waiting.'

As she opened the door, other doors opened along the Rank and curtains moved. Everyone wanted to see who was driving along Greenslade Terrace in a motor car on Christmas evening. The realisation flustered Charlotte still more and embarrassed Amy, who thought Ralph Porter would be disgusted by the nosiness of their neighbours. But he seemed totally unaware of the stir he was causing, sitting there in the flying-helmet and leather jacket that made him look a little as if he intended taking off at any second.

'Ready, then?' he asked casually.

'Oh, this is kind! Amy shouldn't have bothered you...' Charlotte gabbled. 'But how do I get in?'

In the light spilling out of the house from the wide-open door, Amy saw his wry smile and felt the small treacherous imp dart within her.

'You'll have to climb in, I'm afraid. Wait – let me help you.'

He swung one plus-four-clad leg easily over the low-slung side of the car and went round to the passenger side where Charlotte was surveying the contraption doubtfully.

'It isn't very big, is it? Oh dear, there won't be room for Amy to come too. You won't be able to get in, Amy. There's hardly room for me.'

'Of course not. It's a two-seater, Mam,' Amy said hastily, hoping Ralph wouldn't think for a moment that she had expected to ride too.

'Oh dear, oh!' Charlotte, who had never ridden any closer to the engine than the back seat of Cliff Button's stately taxi, groaned with dread at the idea of being squashed unceremoniously into this strange red capsule, but mis-understanding her, Ralph Porter turned to Amy.

'Did you want to go too?'

'I knew there wouldn't be room,' Amy reaffirmed.

'I'll come back for you if you like.'

'Oh no...'

'Your mother would feel happier if you were there. It's no trouble.' He turned his attention to helping Charlotte. 'Look – you'll have to get straight over like this – mind you don't burn your leg on the exhaust pipe – that's it...'

With a certain amount of heaving and pushing from behind, Charlotte was eventually manoeuvred over the Morgan exhaust which ran, motor-cycle style, along the side of the car, and squeezed down into the seat.

'Are you all right?' Ralph Porter enquired.

'It's a good job I'm not any fatter,' Charlotte puffed. 'I wouldn't like to go too fast like this. You will drive careful, won't you, Mr Porter?'

Amy thought he might either laugh or snort out a sharp retort, but he did neither. Instead he replied with perfect courtesy, 'Don't worry – I'll get you there in one piece, Mrs Hall.'

'And you won't go too fast?'

'I promise.'

'Oh, well then, here goes!' Charlotte said with the expression of an adventurer taking off into the unknown. Ralph Porter started the engine and it roared into life, making Greenslade Terrace echo for a few moments with the sound that reverberated round race-tracks across the world. As they started off, Amy had a sudden thought and ran after them shouting, 'Mam – your hat!' But too late. The wind caught the brim of Charlotte's best felt and though she made a grab for it, the hat flew out of her grasp and began bowling back along the Rank towards the family, gathered to see her off.

'Quick, Huw, get it!' Amy shouted. Huw, who, remembering the disaster of his last encounter with Ralph Porter, had been watching proceedings from the safety of the doorway, dived out nimbly, retrieved the hat and brought it to Amy. By the time she had dusted it down the car had turned the corner of the Rank and all the family began talking at once.

'Well, I never! Mam in a motor car! Ralph Porter's motor car!'

'How's she going to get out again, I'd like to know?'

'Did he say he was coming back for you, Amy?'

'Come on inside, all of you! You're letting in all the cold air.' That was Sarah, practical as ever, and in the general

274

milling about as they all went back into the house, Amy had a chance to think.

He had said he was coming back for her. Would he? Perhaps she ought to get ready in case. Her breath was coming a little too fast, her pulses hammering a tattoo of something like bottled-up excitement. Because of Dolly, she told herself. But no – they were *worried* about Dolly, not excited...

She took Barbara and Maureen to one side.

'Listen, if Mr Porter comes back for me I'm going to see how Auntie Dolly is. You two must stay here until I get back.'

'When? When will you be back?' Barbara asked tearfully. All the excitement of the day had overtired her and seeing Gran disappear in a strange-looking motor car had been the last straw.

'I don't know, Babs. It depends on Auntie Dolly.'

'Don't go!' Barbara wailed and Maureen, without understanding, joined in.

'Come on, Babs. Come and show Grampy your picture book,' James invited, referring to one of the Christmas presents Charlotte had produced for her grandchildren from her magical 'corner' – the secret, out-of-bounds-place between her wardrobe and dressing-table where surprises had traditionally been kept since Jim, Ted and the others had been small.

But Barbara refused to be sidetracked. 'I want to go with Mammy.'

'Go Mammy!' Maureen echoed, adding to the chant.

'For goodness' sake, quieten then down, Amy!' Sarah warned. 'You know your Dad can't stand a noise.'

But to the surprise of all of them, it was Huw who came to the rescue.

'You don't want to go in that noisy old car, Babs.'

'Do! Do!'

'No, you don't. I went in it once and I don't want to go in it again.'

'You're not going?' Barbara asked.

'Nope.'

'You're going to stay here with me and Maureen?'

'Yes.'

'Oh, all right then.' Satisfied, Barbara curled her arms

275

around Huw's neck; if her hero was staying, that was all that mattered. But instead of relief that the problem had been resolved, Amy felt a twinge of disquiet. She wished Barbara was not quite so obviously taken with Huw. She wanted the children to get on well together, of course, but this was total blind hero-worship. Where Huw led, Barbara would follow. This time, of course, it was working to her advantage, but Huw was unpredictable and still basically wild. Amy had the uncomfortable feeling that the only real reason for his not getting into more mischief in the last couple of months was that he was still feeling his feet – in a strange place and still a little stunned by the events that had changed his life. But give him time and she could see storms ahead. There was a wilfulness alongside the wildness, a determination to have his own way that, coupled with a sense of mischief and perhaps frustration, might give rise to all sorts of problems. Bad enough if she had to sort him out when the time came, but if Barbara was there, tagging along, involved with and supporting Huw at every turn, it would be ten times more difficult. And – be truthful, Amy, she told herself – she didn't really want Barbara idolising and perhaps copying a boy whose mother had been a loose-moralled good-time girl, no matter who his father was.

Amy put on her coat and went to the door to see if there was any sign of Ralph Porter returning. As she opened it she almost collided with Ted and Rosa, who were standing just outside.

'Sounds like a car coming,' Ted informed her.

'Oh! Is it...?'

It was. The bright red Morgan turned along the Rank and Amy could imagine all the curtains twitching again as it passed. She ran back into the living-room.

'He's here. I'm going now. Be good now, won't you, children? Do as you're told till I get back. I don't expect I shall be long...'

Once again they all trooped out, with the exception of Huw who watched by peeping through the curtains.

'Is there any news?' Sarah asked.

'I couldn't say. I dropped your mother and came straight back.'

'I suppose I get into the car the same way Mam did,' Amy said.

''Fraid so. Look out for the exhaust!'

Ralph Porter came round to help her as he had helped Mam, and as his hand cupped her elbow she was swept up suddenly on a wave of awareness. There was nothing intimate about the gesture, but the gentle pressure of his fingers and the very nearness of him lit fires within her. Flustered, she hoisted herself over the side of the car and dropped down into the bucket seat, waving and calling 'Bye-bye' to the children to hide the turmoil inside.

This time he had not turned off the engine – the car vibrated with pent-up power and with the front and side close around her like a metal skin, Amy was aware of another stab of excitement. Like Mam, she had never ridden in a car such as this before, but instead of making her nervous, the thrill of being so close to that powerful engine – combined with the overwhelming awareness that Ralph Porter seemed able to arouse in her – mixed and effervesced into a heady cocktail. As the car pulled away she forgot her embarrassment, forgot the children she was leaving behind, forgot Dolly, labouring all Christmas Day. She was exhilarated suddenly, as if the car were a time capsule freeing her from all her worries, all responsibilities. The wind was in her hair, streaming it away from her face, and she lifted her chin, letting it blow the breath back into her throat.

Lovely – lovely! Too lovely for words! She was weightless, fluid, a part of the whipping wind and the throbbing engine, part of the black night through which they were roaring. She wanted it to go on for ever and when she felt him easing off the speed and coasting to a stop outside Dolly's house, she longed to shout, 'No – don't stop! Let's go further – anywhere! Just drive, please!'

He killed the engine and turned to look at her as she sat with hair tumbled, eyes streaming tears down her flushed cheeks, mouth parted with almost sensuous pleasure.

'You enjoyed that, didn't you?' he asked.

'Oh yes!' She sounded breathless, but for the moment the wind had blown away all traces of awkwardness. 'I wanted it to go on for ever!'

'Well, you're not really dressed for open-car motoring in the middle of winter. Much further and you'd probably be freezing. But if you like, I'll take you for a ride some other time.'

'Oh, I'd love that!'

'Make it a Sunday afternoon – or tomorrow, if it comes to

that. You won't be working on Boxing Day and neither shall I.'

'But the children...'

'Isn't there someone who could have them for an hour?'

'Well, yes, I suppose so...' It was so tempting – she wanted so badly to repeat the experience. 'Yes, I'm sure I could arrange something.'

'Good.' He smiled at her, his mouth twisting sideways. 'Better make it about half-past two. It gets dark so early at this time of year.'

'Yes.' She would sound ungrateful, she thought, to say she wanted it to be in the dark, just as it had been tonight. 'Now I suppose I'd better go and see what's happening to Dolly,' she added regretfully, not wanting to leave this wonderful escapist world and come bumping back to reality.

'Shall I wait?'

'Oh no – we'll be all right to get back. The one way's not so bad and I haven't any idea how long we shall be.'

'Sure?'

'Yes, quite. You've done enough already. I don't know how to thank you, Mr Porter.'

'I was happy to help. There's one thing you can do though and that's stop calling me "Mr Porter". My name's Ralph. All right?'

'Yes, all right.' She tried to say it and couldn't bring herself to. 'And thank you again.'

Before she could hoist herself up out of the car seat the front door of Dolly's house opened and Victor was framed against the light.

'Amy! Is that you?' he called in his loud voice.

'Yes. Is there any news?' she called back.

'She had the baby ten minutes ago. Another little boy.'

Another little boy. Amy went weak with relief, then joy surged up in her and she turned to Ralph laughing and grabbing his arm unself-consciously.

'Did you hear that? A boy! Oh, that's wonderful, isn't it!'

'Yes. I'm glad.' He freed his arm, slid it along the back of the seat to circle her shoulders and pulled her towards him. 'Merry Christmas, Amy.'

His lips touched her forehead and it was like the prince's kiss to Sleeping Beauty, but with the effect in reverse. Her laughter died, though her lips remained parted, her joyful animation froze, even her breath seemed suspended. She sat motionless as his lips skimmed her nose and found her mouth. The pressure was cool but firm and lasted only a moment. There was no time to feel panic or desire, no time to think or react. But when he released her she felt a quick, sharp sense of loss.

She sat for a moment, stunned. He came round the car to help her out and she trembled at his hand on hers and the rock hardness of his body as she stumbled against him. But he made no attempt to kiss her again, simply steadied her and held her away.

'I'll see you tomorrow then?'

'Yes, tomorrow.' Amazingly her voice sounded normal. Then he was back in the car and driving off, nonchalantly waving as he went.

Amy stood in the gateway, steadying herself against the wooden post for a moment. Thank heavens Victor had gone back into the house; she needed this moment alone to compose herself. Like the blood running back into a cramped limb, she was aware suddenly that she was coming back to life ... muscles, veins, nerve endings all tingling. She raised a hand to outline her mouth, remembering the feel of his lips.

All these years since I met Llew I never kissed another man, she thought. Now, in less than a week, I've been kissed twice. But how different they had been – the one slimy, presumptuous; the other undemanding, casual almost, but very pleasant – an experience she would not be averse to repeating.

The front door opened: it was Victor again.

'Amy! Whatever are you doing? You'll catch your death hanging about out there. Come on in and see Dolly and the baby.'

There was a spring in her step as she went up the path. The world was full of surprises. And tomorrow she was going to see Ralph again ...

Ralph. I called him Ralph, not Mr Porter, even if it was only to myself, she thought, and pleasure ran through her veins like warm sherry.

Amy could not go up right away because the doctor and the midwife were still in attendance, so she and Mam made a pot of tea and washed up some of the cups that were stacked in the kitchen – half-emptied cups which had sustained them through that long day.

'Thank the Lord it's all over and our Dolly's all right,' Charlotte kept saying.

'Another boy though! I think Victor would have liked a girl.'

Amy kept up the surface chatter, but underneath she was wondering: Should I tell Mam about Ralph – ask her to have the children tomorrow? But no, she couldn't bring herself to do it. Perhaps they could go next door for an hour and then Mam need never know; Amy had the feeling she would most definitely not approve.

After a while they heard the doctor come clattering down the stairs, exchange a few words with Victor in the hall and slam out to go back to his interrupted Christmas celebrations. Then the midwife came down; not Peggy Yelling in this part of town, of course, but a thin, nervy-looking woman who rejoiced in the name of Nurse Bird and was naturally enough nicknamed 'Nurse Stork'.

'Can we go up now?' Charlotte asked eagerly.

'Nurse Stork' nodded and Amy ran ahead of her mother up the stairs. Dolly was lying back against the pillows, her face as pale as the snowy covers. Her hair was tangled, not curly but in lank wisps, as if the nurse had attempted to comb it and given up because Dolly was too tired and weak to be bothered. As Amy entered the room she forced up heavy eyelids to reveal lack-lustre blue eyes.

'Hello, Amy. What are you doing here?' Her voice was slurred.

'Come to see you, of course. How are you feeling?'

'Glad it's over. What a day! And they say the first is the worst! Still, he'll be worth it. He's over there, have a look at him.'

Amy crossed the room to the crib and peeped inside. The baby lay there, a small damp scrap in a tight white binder, and her stomach contracted. Then, as she looked at him, a strange feeling of unease crept over her. She couldn't put her finger on it, except that it had to do with the look of him and as she gazed a kind of cold dread grew on her. Was there something wrong with him? Oh, surely not...!

Charlotte was beside Amy now, peering into the crib.

'Oh, isn't he beautiful!' she exclaimed, her voice full of emotion. Amy pushed her own terrible doubts to one side. She was mistaken, she had to be.

'He's a real Christmas baby, Dolly,' she said.

'Yes. I think we ought to call him Noël,' Dolly said drowsily.

'Noël! That's a nice name! Dolly...'

But Dolly's eyelids had drooped and she was asleep.

Charlotte and Amy tiptoed downstairs again. In the scullery the midwife was washing her hands at the sink.

'Which of you two is staying the night then?' she enquired.

They looked at one another and at her.

'Someone has to,' the nurse said briskly. 'She can't be left; she didn't have an easy time, you know, and she needs her rest.'

'Well, I can't,' Charlotte said. 'I would, and willingly, but I've got Dolly's other two children at home and my husband is an invalid. Surely Victor arranged for someone to come in?'

'Well, there's nobody here, is there? And I want to be getting home. I've been here long enough already.' Nurse Bird looked meaningfully at Amy.

'*Me?*' Amy said, horrified.

'It looks as if you'll have to,' Charlotte said. 'The nurse is right; Dolly can't be left and there are some things Victor can't do. She needs a woman here, Amy.'

'But what about the children?'

'I'll make up beds for them. They'll have a lovely time all together with Bob and Fred.'

'Oh, I don't know,' Amy protested. 'I didn't come prepared.'

'I'm sure our Dolly can lend you what you need.'

'But I'm no nurse, Mam. I'm just not made that way.'

'Amy, don't you want to help your sister out? You've been glad enough of a bit of help yourself over the last year, I don't mind telling you. It's a bad job if you can't repay some of it...'

'Yes, all right, I'll stay.' Amy knew when she was beaten, but that did not prevent her from worrying about her own commitments. 'Where's Victor anyway?' she asked.

The scullery door opened as if on cue and Victor appeared. 'Did I hear somebody mention my name?'

'Yes. Where have you been, Victor?'

'Down the Rank to let Annie Toogood know what's happening.'

'There was no need to go down, was there? You could have made her hear from here,' Amy said spitefully.

Charlotte shot her a look. 'Amy's offered to stay with Dolly tonight,' she said.

'Oh, there's no need for that.'

'But Victor, there *is*. Dolly mustn't put her feet to the ground on any account. And the baby will need attention, too.'

'That's all right,' Victor stated placidly. 'Annie Toogood will be here in a minute.'

'Annie... oh, that's why you've been down to see her!'

'I fixed up weeks ago for her to come in when it was Dolly's time. But seeing it's Christmas and we had a houseful with the doctor and the midwife, I thought there was no need for her to come up until it was all over.'

'I see. Well, that's a good job, Victor,' Charlotte said and Amy felt almost guilty as relief overwhelmed her. Charlotte was right and she should have been only too pleased to help her sister. But she already had so much on her plate that she sometimes felt it would drive her crazy, and besides...

If I'd had to stay with Dolly, I would never have managed to go out with Ralph tomorrow, Amy thought. And realised again just how much she was looking forward to it.

'Well, Victor, if you've got everything fixed up, I suppose we might as well be getting on home,' Charlotte said. 'It'll take us a while to walk it. I'm glad I've seen the baby, and I'm glad everything has gone off all right. But what a funny Christmas it's been! All upside down!'

Amy said nothing, but as they set out for home she silently echoed her mother's sentiments. It certainly had been a peculiar Christmas. But at least there had been no time for grieving, no time for settling into sad memories of Christmases past. Instead there had been new life, new experiences, new hope. And for that she was grateful.

*

In the darkest corner between the washhouse and the bake-oven, Rosa Clements and Ted Hall stood close together in each other's arms.

It was not the most private place in the world – if they turned their heads they could see quite clearly the lighted windows up and down the Rank – and sounds of laughter, merry-making and the occasional swell of voices raised in singing carols as families clustered round their front-room pianos drifted to them on the cold night air. But with their own families gathered in their small terraced houses, it was the best they could do.

'I'm glad you came home for Christmas, Ted,' Rosa whispered.

And Ted, his senses swimming from the intoxicating nearness of her, murmured his agreement. 'I'm glad I did, too.'

The way she affected him when they were together was a constant source of amazement to him – there was an attraction so primitive that the air between them almost hummed with the strength of it and it drove all else from his mind. It had not always been that way, for as a boy he had been irritated by the skinny raven-haired urchin who had followed him everywhere. And as a young man he had been too besotted with his beloved Becky to notice her. But when his grief had begun to dull a little and he had discovered that life still had to be lived, there was Rosa – grown to a woman almost without him noticing – her eyes sloe-dark in her olive face, her body lissom, her voice soft as the wind in the trees and her spirit as free as that of the travelling fair-man who had fathered her. Ted had found himself wanting her . . . and not only physically. There was something about the wildness of her that called to him as like calls to like and at times he thought that if he settled down one day, it would be with Rosa.

The trouble was that he seemed quite unable to settle down. Since leaving the army at the end of the war he had become a wanderer. The life he led would not have suited most people, who seemed to strive for the very things which made him claustrophobic – one steady job to keep them going week after week until they retired exhausted, or died. But he loved the freedom and the variety, loved the feeling of being answerable to no one but himself.

Sometimes, as he swung in his window-cleaner's cage high above London or wriggled his toes in the sand on Weymouth beach, he thought of Rosa. Maybe one day I will marry her, he told himself. Maybe one day when I'm about forty and I've had my fill of freedom. But not yet . . . Not yet.

It was only when he was with her and the attraction between them flared strong and bright that he thought: I want her now! I can't wait that long!

And that Christmas night in 1926 was one of those occasions.

With the soft reflected light making her face glow and the scent of her hair teasing his nostrils, Ted felt the desire strong and urgent within him. He had been aware of it even in the house with all the rest of the family there; every time their eyes met he had wanted to touch her. Now he *was* touching her and still it was not enough.

He moved his hand from her waist to the swell of her breast and she did not move away. Instead she squeezed her hips closer, her mouth seeking his with urgency and fire. He had never met anyone else who could kiss the way she did. There had been many other girls in other places, but none of them had stirred his senses as Rosa could.

Beneath his fingers her breast was firm and full and her legs, masked only by the wispy fabric of her skirt, moved enticingly against him.

'Hey, you're driving me crazy!' he said softly, wanting to crush her, kiss her, take those voluptuous breasts into his mouth and enter her body with his.

'Am I?' Her voice was breathless but there was a note of caution too, something that almost might have been fear. It sobered him for a moment and he held her away slightly.

'What's wrong?'

'Nothing.' But her tone was guarded.

'Don't lie, Rosa. Tell me what it is. What are you thinking about?'

For answer she tried to kiss him again, but he evaded her lips.

'Don't think you can get out of it like that. I want to know!'

She said nothing and he persisted, 'What is it? You're not usually like this. Is it something I've done?'

After a moment she laughed softly. 'That's ironic.'

'What do you mean?'

'Not something you've done, Ted. More something you *haven't*.'

'Like what?'

'Like telling me you love me.'

'Oh, Rosa . . .' He was beginning to wish he had not started this conversation.

His impatience was a knife in her heart and she cried out, 'You really don't want to talk about it, do you? I believe it's still Becky Church with you, even after all these years. Do you still use me as a stop-gap, Ted? Do you? Do you still close your eyes and pretend I'm Becky?'

'Rosa!' he protested, shocked. His desire had gone now and gooseflesh raised on his arms. What was she talking about? He had never pretended she was Becky. But to hear her say so was almost like sacrilege.

'I suppose you thought I didn't know,' Rosa went on. 'But it's true, all the same, isn't it? She was the only one for you. I've tried, oh how I've tried to make you forget her, but it's no use. Oh, I'm sorry, I didn't mean to say it like this. I was going to be sensible and just ask you . . . just try to find out . . . if there was any hope for us. But it hasn't worked out that way.'

He was still stunned by the suddenness of her outburst. 'I don't know what to say . . .'

She laughed – a small, bitter sound.

'No, I don't suppose you do, Ted. I've waited so long for you to find out what to say, but I don't suppose you ever will. Nothing has really changed in all these years, has it? Perhaps we should call it a day . . .'

Ted experienced something almost like panic. This whole thing was beyond him – what had started as an encounter like all the others had turned somehow into something quite different. Then, as Rosa pulled away from him, he found his voice.

'Don't go!'

She hesitated, fluttering uncertainly like a bird caught in a snare, and he went on urgently, 'I don't know what brought this on but you're wrong, Rosa. You're not a substitute for Becky, you never have been. It's true that I did . . . think a lot of her.' He could not bring himself to use the word 'love'; it didn't figure very largely in his vocabulary, though he *had* loved Becky with all his being. 'But that's a long time ago now. And you and me – we've got something special, haven't we?'

'Have we?' She sounded eager, yet still half-afraid.

'You know we have. I've always thought we would finish up together.'

Her breath came out on a sigh. 'You never said so before.'

'No. Well, perhaps I've been afraid to. I'm such a bad lot, Rosa. You know me, I can't seem to settle anywhere. And I've got nothing to offer.'

'That's not true,' she said. 'I think you've got a great deal.'

'I can't think of a thing. I haven't any money, I haven't got a proper job and I'm not even sure I'd be able to stick one for long. We'd be like a couple of tramps!'

'I wouldn't care,' she said recklessly. 'But I can't go on like this, Ted. I have to know one way or the other whether there's any future for us.'

They stood in silence for a moment while from one of the houses the strains of 'While Shepherds Watched' wafted out on the crisp air. Above the stars were shining, very cold, very bright.

'Well, supposing I asked you to give me six months to get myself sorted out? Would that be any help?'

'You mean you want me to go on waiting?'

'Yes, I suppose that's what I mean. I'm not really sure... And it is a lot to ask... Only one thing I do know... I don't want to lose you. I couldn't marry you at the moment, it wouldn't be fair. But maybe something will turn up...'

It was vague, but her heart soared. He didn't want to lose her; he wanted her to wait. Knowing that was enough. So long as he wanted her to, she would wait for him for ever.

'All right, Ted,' she said.

And as he took her in his arms again the electric attraction between them sparked and flared once more, blotting out doubts and uncertainties, dissolving fears for the future. For together, the present was all that mattered.

Chapter Sixteen

The next day Amy was ready and waiting for Ralph Porter by 2 o'clock.

'You're going next door for a couple of hours,' she told the girls. 'Mammy's going out.'

'Huw! What about Huw?' Barbara clamoured.

'Huw is a big boy and he is going to stay here.'

'On his own?'

'Of course on my own,' said Huw.

'Me stay too!' Barbara begged.

'No, Barbara is going next door with Maureen,' Amy insisted.

She was not altogether happy about leaving Huw alone, but there was no alternative. He was much too big to be foisted onto Ruby Clark next door, and she didn't think he would do anything silly while she was out.

'It won't be for long, anyway,' she told them all.

Huw eyed her suspiciously. 'Where are you going?'

'For a ride in a car.'

'Whose car?'

'Mr Porter's.' Say it lightly, she told herself. But she didn't fool Huw and his face tightened to a scowl.

'Why are you going for a ride in *his* car?'

She drew a comb through her curls. 'You ask too many questions.'

'He's horrible!' Huw stated.

'He is not horrible. Just because he was angry with you for sleeping in his coal-house...'

'He *is* horrible!'

'Well, I haven't got time to argue,' Amy said. 'Come on, girls, what toys do you want to take next door with you?'

They sorted some things into their Christmas stockings

happily enough and Amy saw them next door. She was still not completely convinced that Ralph Porter would actually turn up – last night now seemed to be a little like a dream. But to her surprise when she peeped out of the window just before 2.30 pm there was his car drawn up at the kerb. And before she had time to put on her coat he was up the path and knocking at the door.

'Ready, then?'

'Almost. I didn't know if you really meant it.'

'Well, of course I meant it! Lucky it's fine though. Have you got a scarf?'

'Yes.'

'We may as well go, then.'

'Right. Bye, Huw! Be good now.'

But she was unhappy about the look in his eyes. It haunted her as she climbed into the Morgan, very aware in the daylight of the amount of leg it was unavoidable to show.

Ralph Porter was a gentleman, however. He was not looking.

'Your sister and the baby are well, are they?' he asked.

'Yes.' Amy had now put behind her the twinge of doubt she had experienced when looking at little Noel. 'It was very nice of you to help us out as you did.'

'I was pleased to. I had been wondering for a long while how I could get into your good books.'

She looked at him quickly. He was concentrating on the road, not looking at her, but there was a slight twist to his mouth. She blushed scarlet and was glad of the wind whipping roses into her cheeks to disguise it.

'Where are we gong?'

'Up onto the Mendips, I thought. Does that suit you?'

'Yes, of course. Fine...'

They had to drive right by Dolly's house and Ralph slowed down.

'Do you want to go in and see your sister?'

'No, not today. Not now.' The wind took her words and blew them back at her. Would he think her heartless, not wanting to see Dolly and her new nephew? But this was her treat and she wanted to leave the real world behind for a while.

Through the outskirts of Hillsbridge and neighbouring High Compton they drove, then they were out in the open country. The trees, bare for winter, stretched gnarled brown arms to the sky; hedges and low dry-stone walls divided up a rolling vista of fields. The road ran arrow-straight and Ralph Porter built up speed so that they rocketed along it. Amy had no inclination for talking now – and no breath either. She clutched her hands together in her lap, eyes shining above flushed cheeks, curls whipping from beneath her scarf.

When at last he began to slow down, she was laughing with the tears streaming down her cheeks.

'How was that?' He was motoring more sedately, looking sideways at her.

'Lovely! Lovely! Oh, it's such fun...'

'You should laugh more often, Amy!' The strange note in his voice sobered her and she looked at him quickly, seeing the hard line of his profile etched against the blur of hedges skimming behind it.

'There isn't always a lot to laugh about,' she said.

He eased the car into the verge and stopped the engine.

'You're a very unusual woman,' he observed.

'Me? Why?'

'I wonder how many would be able to do what you have done? Not many would even try and I expect you encountered a lot of opposition.'

'Yes, I did,' she admitted.

'A woman is expected to stay in the home and raise a family, to be looked after by her man.'

'That's all very well if she's got a man to look after her.'

He smiled wryly. 'That's your excuse, but frankly I don't think you're the stay-at-home type. Anyway, you have everything well in hand with that business and it seems to be working.'

'Partly thanks to you,' she said. 'I value your contract. And by the way, you were right about Ollie Griffin. I've had to tell him to go.'

Ralph's eyebrow went up, but he didn't ask for any details and she was glad. Instead, to her surprise he asked, 'And what about the boy?'

'What do you mean?'

'The lad you have living with you. Why did you take him in?'

For all the talk it had caused in Hillsbridge, not many people had asked her the question straight out and his directness disconcerted her.

'I felt sorry for him. He had nowhere to go.'

'But why should you have offered him a home? Surely you had more than enough on your plate already?'

'He came from the same valley as Llew. His mother was an old friend...' The story concocted, told and retold, had never sounded less convincing.

'So you took him in?'

'Yes. I couldn't stand to see him sent to a home. He might have been a young Llew...'

'Yes,' Ralph's eyes were watchful, 'he might have been.'

She shivered suddenly, convinced he could see through her.

'Cold?' he asked.

'No.'

'Perhaps we ought to be getting back anyway. It will be dusk soon.'

I don't mind, she wanted to say. These are lovely, stolen hours and I want them to go on for ever.

But she knew she could not do that. Huw was back at the house alone and the girls would be waiting for her to collect them.

'I suppose you're right,' she said regretfully.

He drove back by a slightly different route. Birds were winging in dark skeins across the leaden sky now and the wind numbed her cheeks and lips. Hillsbridge town was almost deserted and she was glad. Imagine the talk if many people had seen her – 'Amy Hall out car-riding! Whatever will she do next? Where were her children, I'd like to know? And that boy she took in – funny thing to do, if you ask me...'

But instead of striking a sour note, the thought of the gossip made her giggle. Oh, how they would love to know the truth, all of those women with nothing better to do than speculate! But what was funny about that? She must be intoxicated by the ride – and perhaps a little intoxicated by Ralph Porter too...

He stopped the car, putting his arm along the back of the seat as he had done the previous night, but not touching her.

'Now that the ice is broken and you don't think me quite such a monster, perhaps you wouldn't turn me down if I were to ask you again to have dinner me with one night?'

She laughed, a little self-consciously.

'Well, will you?'

'Yes. All right.'

'So I have redeemed myself a little,' he said with a twinkle.

'Yes, but have I? Remember what I did to your car...'

'That,' he said, 'is best forgotten.'

He helped her out of the car and she was still laughing as she went up the path. It was true what he had said, she did not laugh enough. But there had been little enough to laugh about in the past months. Now...

She opened the door and went in. It was dim inside.

'Huw!' she called.

No answer. In the kitchen she lit the gas and it flared brightly.

'Huw, where are you?'

Still no answer.

Surely he hasn't run away again, has he? she wondered anxiously. But his boots were in the corner and his new knife was on the table. He hadn't gone without his boots before and she didn't think he would go without them now, or without the new knife.

She went along the hall calling his name and pushed open the door to the front room. Then she gasped with horror.

The Christmas tree had fallen down! Tall as it was, it reached right across the room so that she was almost stepping on its topmost branches. At its base the bucket in which it had stood was overturned, spilling earth out on to the carpet, while along its entire length lay a horrifying debris of shattered baubles, crushed candle-holders and sadly trailing tinsel.

How on earth had it come to fall? It had been safe – she had taken great care to make sure of that. She took a cautious step into the room, grasping hold of the tree and levering it up. As she lifted it, more baubles came off and fell to the ground, smashing into smithereens of coloured glass. She managed to get the tree upright and held it there, afraid to let it go in case it fell again. But no, it seemed as stable as ever and as she moved her hand away it stood there, sadly bedraggled but perfectly safe. Puzzled, she surveyed it. What could have made it fall over? It was a mystery.

But right now the most important thing was to clear up the mess before the children saw it. They would break their hearts at the devastation – she could have cried herself to see all the ornaments which had given so much pleasure and become part of the Christmas tradition lying there shattered on the floor.

She went into the hall on the way to get a dustpan and brush, and saw a movement in the shadows at the top of the stairs.

'Huw, is that you?' she called.

No answer.

'Huw! What are you doing up there in the dark?'

He came down a step.

'The Christmas tree has fallen over. Did you know?'

He froze. And looking up the stairs at the small figure shrinking there in the gloom, she knew the truth.

'Huw, come down here at once!' she ordered.

Slowly but obediently he came, dragging his feet, trying to avoid her eyes.

'You did it, didn't you?'

Silence.

'Come on, Huw, you might as well admit the truth. You pushed the Christmas tree over!'

Silence still.

'If you don't tell me the truth right this minute, you will go to bed with no tea and no supper. *Did you push over the tree?*'

A small sound emerged that might have been 'Yes.'

'Come on, Huw, I can't hear you.'

'Yes.'

She resisted the urge to take hold of him and shake him until his teeth rattled. 'But why? Why should you do such a thing?'

A shrug.

'Come on, Huw, why? You've made a terrible mess and caused a lot of damage and I want to know why.'

He kicked one foot into the other, saying nothing.

'*Huw!*' she threatened.

He looked up at her, looked away again. 'You went out with him.' His voice was soft, resentful. 'Why did you have to go out with him?'

'Him? You mean Mr Porter?'

'Yes.'

'Why shouldn't I go out with him?'

'Because...'

'Because what?'

'You just shouldn't. I don't want you to.'

'But Huw, I'm entitled to have friends. Because I have friends does not give you the right to behave this way.'

Another shrug.

I'm getting nowhere! she thought. He was angry with me, so he did this. I'd like to give him the biggest hiding of his life, but what good would that do? Perhaps I'm as much to blame for leaving him alone. After all, who could know what goes on in his mind?

'Well, Huw, whatever your reasons you can now help me clear up the mess you've made before the girls come in and see it. They're going to be very upset, I hope you realise. There's no way I can replace the baubles you've broken. And your punishment will be seeing their faces and knowing it's all your fault.'

His lip was jutting and she thought she saw it tremble. But she ignored it resolutely. He was not going to get away with this. She fetched the dustpan and brush and handed it to him without a word. Then she tried to arrange the baubles that were left undamaged so as to conceal the tell-tale gaps in the tree's trimmings while Huw swept.

'Finished?' she asked at last.

He nodded.

'Right. Go and tip the bits in the dustbin. I'm going to fetch Barbara and Maureen.'

For all her efforts to conceal it, there were howls and a good many tears when Barbara discovered the damage. Amy did not tell them how it had happened, but Huw kept well out of the way in any case, sitting in a corner flicking his penknife and not answering when he was spoken to.

By the time the girls were in bed, Amy had had enough of him. 'I think you can go to bed, too, Huw.'

He got up and made for the door without a word, though the hunch of his shoulders spoke volumes.

'I'll be up in a minute to tuck you in,' she told him.

When she went up the stairs minutes later there was only a hump under the bedclothes to show he was there. She crossed to the window, drawing the curtains to shut out the light, and with her back to the bed heard a peculiar choking sound.

Huw crying? Almost unheard of!

She waited a moment, then crossed to the bed.

'Goodnight, Huw.'

A pause. Then a strangled, 'Goodnight.'

She was half-way out of the door when she heard a snuffly voice call her name and she stopped, looking around. There was still virtually nothing to be seen of Huw, just the top of his head. He didn't want her to see him, she guessed.

'Yes, what is it?' she asked, slightly impatient.

'I – I'm sorry.' The tone told her what an effort the apology had cost him. She hesitated. Instinct made her want to take him in her arms, but Amy knew Huw would not like that. So she contented herself with bending over the bed and rumpling the bit of hair she could see.

'It's all right, Huw. But for heaven's sake don't ever do such a thing again, will you?'

'No.'

'It did no good, did it? It didn't even make *you* happy.'

'No.'

'So why did you?'

'I wanted to show you.'

'A very silly thing to do. And I still have a right to a life of my own, you know.'

He didn't answer and she rumpled his hair again.

'Goodnight, then, Huw. Don't lose sleep over it, will you?'

So that was that, she thought, as she closed the door and went back downstairs. There was no telling what he would do if upset about something, but at least he was sorry now – and he had had the courage to say so.

It was a beginning.

*

While Amy was out riding in Ralph Porter's motor car on Boxing Day afternoon, in the front room of the house at Tower View Harry was trying to explain to Margaret why he had not visited her as he had promised on Christmas Day.

'I just couldn't get away. You know what families are . . .'

'Yes.' But it was said in a small voice.

'And as if it wasn't enough with all of them there and Mam getting uppity in case they thought I was neglecting them, our Dolly had to go and have her baby.'

'Oh.'

He looked at her, surprised by her lack of interest.

'Don't you want to know all about it? I thought women were supposed to be barmy about babies!'

'Mm. I suppose so.'

'It's a boy and they're calling him Noël. Bit of a stupid name, if you ask me.'

'I think it's nice.'

'What's the matter with you?' he asked.

'Nothing.'

'I did want to come. I just couldn't. I've got a present for you too. I wanted to give you that.' He pulled out a package, wrapped in bright paper and tied with red twine. 'Here!'

'Oh, Harry!' Eyes shining, she tore at the wrapping and opened the package to find a black moiré band nestling in a bed of tissue paper. 'Oh – it's beautiful! I've always wanted one, how did you know?'

'I'm glad you like it.'

'I do! Can I put it on?' She fastened it round her wrist with fingers that trembled with excitement and stood for a moment looking at it in delight. Then:

'I almost forgot! I've got a present for you. When you didn't come yesterday I made up my mind not to give it to you, but now . . .'

'What is it, then?'

'Wait and see!'

She disappeared and came back with a small box, gift-wrapped.

'Happy Christmas, a little late!'

He unwrapped it. Inside the box was a fountain pen.

'Oh, a pen!' He was surprised – he didn't do much writing.

'Do you like it? I thought . . . well, you're so keen on getting involved in politics and things and Dad's always having to write letters . . .'

He brightened. They were taking him seriously!

'I suppose you'll be wanting to address envelopes and things . . .'

'I should think so.'

'Thanks, Margaret.' He pulled her towards him and kissed her. Her lips were sweet, soft and pursed like a child's and she wound her arms around him, pressing her slender body close.

'Oh, Harry, I was so miserable when you didn't come yesterday.'

'Were you?' He kissed her again. The feel of her body close to him was setting him on fire, starting desire in the pit of his stomach and making him forget Christmas presents, his ambitions for the future, the Labour Party, everything. But at the same time a small, separate part of his brain was reminding him that he was in George Young's house and Margaret's parents were in the room next door and likely to come in at any time. With an effort he prised himself free, crossing the room to pick up one of the cards displayed on the sideboard – anything to give him something else to think about.

'This is nice – oh, it's from Owen Wynn-Davies! Your father's still in touch with him, then?'

'Yes.' But the joy had gone from her voice again and he sensed she had retreated into herself. Vaguely he was aware he had said the wrong thing, though unsure how he had offended.

There was a silence, then she said in a small voice, 'Why do you come to see me, Harry?'

'Ugh?'

'Is it really to see me – or is it because of my father? Sometimes I can't help wondering. Would you still come if my father wasn't who he is?'

Irrationally he was irritated. He had bought her a present, had kissed her and wanted her and then she asked a silly question like that. What did she want him to say?

'Of course I come to see *you*!'

'That's all right, then,' she said. But her voice was still flat.

He moved impatiently. There was no work to do today and with Margaret in this mood he could think of nothing to say.

'Perhaps I ought not to stay too long.'

'But you've only just come! We could have a game of shove ha'penny if you like. Someone gave us a board they'd made...'

'All right.' Playing shove ha'penny meant going into the other room so as to have a table to put the board on... and that meant George and Gussie would be there and he would not be alone with Margaret and the disturbing emotions which he knew he must control. 'Perhaps your Mum and Dad would like to play too?'

'Yes,' she said, 'perhaps they would.'

There were tears glistening unshed in her eyes, but he was too busy trying to pass her in the doorway without touching her to register them. It was only later when he was at home again that he thought of it – and then he was only puzzled.

Tears? Why should Margaret be crying? Either he had imagined it, or else...

Women, I shall never understand them, thought Harry. Pigeons are far, far simpler.

But all the same, the way she had made him feel was very pleasant. Perhaps next time they would be really alone and he could pursue it. Remembering the feel of her lips and her body, Harry certainly hoped so.

Chapter Seventeen

With Christmas over it was time to return to the problems of the business, but the break had refreshed Amy and she could hardly wait to set the wheels of the lorries rolling again. The one problem which had nagged away at the back of her mind during the break was the need to find a driver to replace Ollie Griffin, but when she met Herbie at the yard to discuss plans he had a suggestion to make.

'There's always my brother Cliff,' he said. 'Since the strike, money's so short that nobody seems to want a taxi, and what business he does get is usually in the evenings. I reckon he'd be only too glad of the job.'

'Do you think so?' Amy asked, relieved.

'I did mention it to him over the holiday,' Herbie informed her. 'I couldn't say anything definite until I'd spoken to you, of course, but I can see him tonight if you like and I reckon I can vouch for him being here in the morning.'

'Oh, that would be marvellous, Herbie!' Amy said.

Sure enough, next morning Cliff Button put in an appearance at the yard, sauntering into the office with the air of a man who knew he was dispensing a favour.

'Our Herbie says you need a bit of assistance.'

'I want to take on a temporary driver, yes,' Amy said, determined to start off on the right footing. 'My regular man is likely to be off for a couple of months at least. After that I'm not certain what will be happening, but there's always the possibility that if things go well I shall be wanting to increase my staff anyway.'

'I'm your man, then.' Cliff winked and Amy felt a momentary qualm. Self-employed for as long as she had known him, he had had the initiative to start up the first taxi service in Hillsbridge if not the business acumen to make a success of it. She couldn't help wondering how he would take to working for someone else – particularly a woman. But she was too relieved at having a second reliable driver to worry about that overmuch just now.

'Right, Cliff, we'll just run over the terms of employment and then you can make a start right away,' she suggested.

*

It was two days later that Amy heard the sound of a motor car in the yard and looked up from her books to see Ralph Porter drawing up outside.

At once her pulses quickened and her hand flew to tidy hair through which she had been running her fingers as she worked. But at the same time she was aware of feeling something like dismay. She had hoped he might stay away from her for a while; his presence was altogether too disconcerting, occupying her mind and senses when she needed every bit of strength and wit for coping with the endless problems of day-to-day life.

Over the past few days she had thought about Ralph Porter more than once and was no nearer understanding his sudden change of stance. Why had a man she had always considered arrogant, rude and overbearing – typical of the ruling classes who ground ordinary families underfoot – become not only a man she felt able to turn to in a time of emergency but also someone whose company she actually enjoyed? Almost as puzzling was her own attitude towards him. Dislike and awe had given way to something uncomfortably like attraction and Amy had to admit that, like Ralph Porter or hate him, he was certainly a man it was impossible to ignore.

Away from him, and worrying over the mish-mash of emotions he had aroused in her, Amy was sure of nothing – not sure, even, if she completely trusted him. Was there some ulterior motive behind his apparent change of heart? Did the leopard ever change his spots? But if there was a reason, she was unable to fathom it – and unable too to prevent the quick

298

flash of pleasure she felt when she saw his car in the yard outside.

She half-rose from her chair, but before she could reach the door he had come in, stopping for only a quick, perfunctory knock.

'Good morning.'

'Hello,' she said a trifle breathlessly. 'What brings you here? Is everything all right with the lorry?'

His eyes twinkled darkly.

'Now why should you assume this had to be a business visit? I've come to make sure you keep your side of the private bargain we made. You're going to have dinner with me – remember?'

Her pulses gave another involuntary leap. 'Oh – I don't know about that...'

'Well, I do! It was definitely part of the arrangement and I was going to suggest New Year's Eve. Then we could see in the New Year together.'

'Oh no, I couldn't possibly stay out that late. The children...'

'Get someone to stay with them.'

'Oh no, not that late. Besides, I'd never be fit for work next day – and I don't think you would either!'

His mouth twisted humorously. 'Let me worry about that.'

'No – I really couldn't. Not on New Year's Eve.'

'I hope this doesn't mean that you're going back on your part of the bargain?'

There was something about the way he was looking at her that sapped her will; she felt it draining from her like blood from an open wound and reacted as she always did to weakness – by using the quick weapon of her tongue.

'I wish you wouldn't hustle me this way! Just because I had to ask you to help us out...'

He laughed outright. 'If I didn't "hustle", as you put it, I wouldn't be where I am today. Anyway, it's not such a bad idea, is it? I thought you enjoyed our ride.'

She didn't answer.

'All right, then,' he said. 'If you can't make New Year's Eve, you can't... but there has to be another evening. You can't make excuses for every night of the year.'

'Why not?'

'Because I should be very offended and you wouldn't want to offend a client, would you?'

'That's blackmail!'

'No, it's not, it's a fact. So give in gracefully, Amy, and have dinner with me?' As she hesitated he went on, 'Pheasant's in season and my housekeeper cooks it to a turn. I'll pick you up and take you home too – perhaps that will sway the balance seeing it's my car you're interested in, not me!'

His eyes were twinkling, his mouth trying not to laugh and she felt the wicked imp of desire twist within her.

'Well . . .'

'Does that mean yes?'

'I suppose it does.'

'When shall it be, then? The day after New Year's Day?'

'I suppose so.'

'You sounded almost enthusiastic then! Shall we say seven?'

She nodded. 'Seven.'

'Good.' He glanced at his watch. 'I have to be going, but I shall be looking forward to our next meeting.'

When he had gone Amy found herself totally incapable of continuing with her work. Over and over again she kept hearing his voice, seeing his face with its half-mocking smile.

What is the matter with me? she asked herself. Why can't I put him out of my mind? And why do I go so weak inside when he looks at me the way he does? Is it because there is some truth in what Ollie Griffin said . . . that I have been too long without a man, so that when one who is attractive and masterful comes along, I can't resist?

The thought shot a streak of shame through her.

Oh, Llew – am I betraying you by feeling this way? I love you still . . . is it wrong to want the company of another man? But I don't even know if I *do* want his company. I'm not sure of anything any more . . .

There was also the worry of what to do about the children for the evening. Ruby Clark would sit with them, she was sure, but would Huw prove difficult? She would have to have a word with him – and with Ruby, asking her to keep a special eye on him.

As she had hoped, Ruby agreed to come in during the evening and on New Year's Day she broke the news to Huw.

'I'm going out tomorrow night, Huw. Ruby will be here to

look after the girls and I want you to be especially good and help her all you can.'

'Why?' Huw asked.

'What do you mean – why? Because Ruby's a friend and I don't want you to cause her any worry.'

'No – why is she coming at all?'

'Because I can't leave you and the girls alone.'

'Why not? I always stayed on my own when Mam went out.'

'That's as maybe, but it's not something that I do.'

His face told Amy what he thought of it, but he didn't say any more. Little by little she was gleaning glimpses of his past – and a pretty unsatisfactory past it had been in her opinion. Small wonder he was wild – the miracle was that he was not far, far worse. What kind of mother would go out and leave small children alone? she wondered. Not the kind Llew would have wanted for his son.

Any doubts she might once have had about Huw's parentage had disappeared now; she had put them out of her mind. Had she not thought Llew was Huw's father, she could never have coped. It was as simple as that.

The following evening she planned to get everything ready for Ruby in good time, but last-minute hitches made her late. Maureen's clean nightdress had mysteriously gone astray, the milk for Barbara's good-night drink had boiled over and Huw was obstinately late coming in from playing around the block. In the event she had precious few minutes left to get herself ready and was still trying to finish her make-up and brush her curls into some semblance of order when she heard the sound of a car and, looking out of her bedroom window, saw the Morgan outside.

Grabbing her bag, she rushed in to kiss the girls and issued a few last-minute instructions to Ruby and Huw on her way out.

'The girls should settle down now – I won't be late. And Huw – you will behave yourself, won't you?'

Then she dashed down the path.

'Sorry, I meant to be ready, but you know how it is...'

'No, I don't.'

No, of course he wouldn't. Everything in his house would run on well-oiled wheels, she thought.

There was a slight awkwardness between them when they reached Valley View, made worse by Amy's memories of the last time she had visited his house. Ralph took her coat and showed her into the drawing-room.

'Sherry?'

'Thank you.'

The glasses and decanter were heavy crystal in which the sherry glowed rich amber. Sipping it, she felt the beginning of lightheadedness. Careful, she thought; she was not used to alcohol and had not eaten all day.

'Dinner's all ready, Mr Porter.' The voice from the doorway was slightly reproving and Amy turned to see the voluminous figure of Mrs Milsom, the housekeeper, hovering there.

'Thank you, Mrs Milsom. We shall be in directly,' Ralph said, cool as ever, but when the housekeeper had wobbled out he gave Amy a wry smile.

'I think perhaps we should drink up and not be long about it! Mrs Milsom is an excellent cook, and she gets very upset if her meals are kept waiting in the kitchen.'

'Oh dear, that's my fault,' Amy said. 'I'm sorry.'

'Not to worry. Are you ready?'

He led the way along the dim hall. The dining-room door was standing ajar and he pushed it open and stood back for her to go in. Amy registered a large, pleasant room, sparsely furnished as was the drawing-room with furniture of plain, dark oak, but no trouble had been spared to make the table attractive. Here, heavy silver cutlery and crystal goblets had been set out on snowy white damask, candles glowed red in a silver candelabra and Christmas roses had been arranged in a low bowl. But only two places had been set, she noticed.

'Isn't your sister eating with us?' she asked, surprised.

'She's away.' Ralph drew out a chair for Amy to sit down. 'We had a quiet Christmas, but now she's gone to spend New Year with cousins of ours in Gloucester.'

'Oh, I see.' Amy was half-relieved, half-disappointed. She was curious to meet the reclusive invalid who was a mystery to half the town, but perhaps having to make polite conversation would have been an effort. Would Ralph have invited her had his sister been at home, she wondered?

As if reading her mind, he laughed.

'It's all right – you'll be perfectly safe with me,' he said in an amused tone.

Hardly were they seated than the first course was served – creamy home-made soup – followed by the brace of peasants

Ralph had promised. There was no doubt about it; Mrs Milsom was a superb cook and with Ralph constantly refilling her glass with a fine wine the like of which she had never tasted before, Amy felt her lightheadedness returning.

It was not an unpleasant sensation though, she thought. At least the awkwardness had gone now and words seemed to trip off her tongue with enjoyable ease. She found herself recounting stories which had never seemed funny before and laughing at them; Ralph too was entertaining – or so it seemed to Amy. Even when the talk turned to business, there were amusing moments as Ralph described the 'steamers' he had bought for his business some years earlier.

'Not one of my best ideas,' he admitted, 'though they seemed the way forward at the time.'

'I suppose they made all your drivers seasick!' Amy giggled. 'What could you do with a steamer in Hillsbridge? The river's hardly big enough for a rowing-boat!'

'Not steamer *ships*, steamer *lorries*,' he told her mock-sternly. 'Big Fodens. Superb things to look at, of course, but much too heavy. The unladen weight was 6-7 tons, so by the time you added on the fuel and the water to make the steam, it was almost up to maximum.'

'Maximum?' A bubble of wine went up Amy's nose.

'Maximum weight. You do know, I suppose, that you can only go up to 12 tons.'

Amy giggled again. 'Of course I know. Why do you think all my drivers are so amazingly thin? I pick them that way on purpose. And my lorries never, ever get pulled in to a weigh-bridge by the police. Don't you think that's something?'

'I certainly do. I also find it most surprising. If I were a policeman, I'd pull your lorries in whenever I could in the hope that I'd find an offence – and an excuse to call upon the very attractive lady owner.'

'Mr Porter! I think that is scandalous!'

'Mrs Roberts! I thought we had agreed you were going to call me Ralph.'

'When you blithely talk of arresting me? Not likely! Anyway, go on – I want to hear all about your steamers. How did they work?'

'Just like any other engine – with a fire and a funnel.'

'And you had to light the fire every morning?'

'Well, yes. It could be kept in overnight if you wanted an early start, but that left a lot of clinker. No, the best way was to clear out the fire box and start again.'

'Oh, I shouldn't want to be bothered with that!' Amy declared. 'It's bad enough having to do my kitchen grate every morning, without having to do a lorry as well!'

'They had their advantages and at least they didn't have to keep going to Bristol for overhaul, the way the petrol lorries do.'

'That,' Amy said, feigning a haughty attitude, 'is not my problem! '

'But think of the time saved!'

She shrugged. 'Well, if they were so marvellous I am just amazed you no longer have them. What did you do with them?'

'Sold them for scrap.'

'Oh, that's a crying shame!'

'Would you have wanted them?'

'No.'

'Well, there you are. You can't expect anyone else to want them either.'

'Oh, I don't know. It seems such a terrible waste! "Waste not, want not," Mam always said. Though you don't seem to be wanting for anything, do you?'

Her face had gone serious suddenly, the laughter dying. He leaned across the table, his fingers covering hers.

'Amy, you are getting maudlin.'

'Maudlin? What's maudlin?'

'What happens sometimes when you drink too much wine!'

'I haven't!' But her head was singing and his face in the candlelight was a little blurred. She blinked, focusing, and as her eyes met his she became suddenly, startlingly aware of his fingers on hers. There was a tingling in her skin like the sharp but feather-light prickles of a small electric shock and the warmth where his fingers lay seemed to be spreading a glow that suffused her body.

For a moment she sat motionless, her eyes magnetised by his while everything in her seemed to be stilled to a breathless, waiting hush. Even her heart and pulses seemed suspended; she was nothing but eyes that held his and a hand that lay, trembling with awareness, beneath his touch.

He rose from his chair then, somehow managing to relinquish neither eyes nor hand as he came round the table. As she looked up at him – so tall and ruggedly good-looking, towering above her – her pulses began to beat again, hammering fast and unevenly at her wrists and throat. Then he was bending over her and his face was going out of focus.

Ralph . . . no! she wanted to say, but no words would come. She could not have spoken them – no, not to save her life. She wanted him too much, wanted to feel his mouth on hers and the eager leaping response of every nerve, both on her skin and deep within the yearning heart of her.

His breath touched her first, a warm whisper, and then his lips . . . vibrant, drawing all that longing to one focal point. One moment she was taut and aching, the next he was urging her slowly to her feet and her knees felt weak, too weak to support her. She swayed, but he held her and as the length of his body pressed against hers she was alive and aware again, soft and fluid, while sensations of exquisite needle-sharp desire ran shivering through her.

For timeless moments it seemed she hung there, suspended just beyond reality, while the world around them ceased to exist. One of her arms was around him, feeling the long, taut muscles of his back beneath the well-cut jacket, the other hand on the nape of his neck where his hair grew down to meet his collar.

And his fingers were in her hair, too, holding her lips against his while his free hand supported her.

When he lifted his mouth from hers she wanted it again, wanted to melt into him, but as he held her away the world slowly righted itself once more so that she seemed to see them as two characters in a drama, standing there locked in each other's arms. Panic began then, rushing in to take the place of desire, and with it a fearful tumult of uncertainty. *What am I doing? What am I feeling?*

He began to draw her close once more, but she pulled away.

'Ralph – please . . . no!'

'Why not?' His voice was low, urgent.

'Because . . . because I don't want you to!'

'That's not true,' he said softly. 'You *do* want me to!'

'I don't! I don't know what I want . . .'

He let her go and she sank back into her chair, knees trembling.

'Amy.' He crouched down beside her, his face level with hers. 'I once told you that you didn't laugh enough. You've laughed a lot tonight!'

'Because I've had too much to drink. You said so yourself!'

'No. Well, yes, maybe, but not just that. You've laughed because you're alive. You've found that out tonight. You're alive. You didn't die on your husband's funeral pyre like some Greek heroine.' She caught her breath and he took her hand, holding it in his. 'You owe it to yourself and to him to go on living. Don't try to fight that.'

'I can't... I don't know...' She was close to tears.

'All right.' He released her hand, stood up and returned to his chair. 'I won't press you. But think about it, will you?'

She could not look at him but stared down at her plate, seeing it through a mist. Then, as suddenly, she seemed to get a grip on herself and lifted her chin with a jerk, her voice falsely bright.

'I'm sorry – I'm sorry. I'm being stupid, it's a lovely dinner...'

'And it's not over yet, far from over.'

'Oh, but I don't think I could eat another thing...'

'I hope you can! Mrs Milsom will be mortally offended if you don't try her excellent apple pie.'

'All right, then. Just a little...'

The forced normality lasted throughout the meal. Mrs Milsom appeared with what was indeed the most delectable apple pie Amy had ever seen let alone tasted, and somehow she managed to eat a little of it. Then there was coffee and a liqueur which Ralph said was called Drambuie. It burned her throat but left a warm trail wherever it touched, and she began to feel better again.

'Do you know I've scarcely had a drink in my life before tonight!' she said with a small, dry laugh.

'Well, I hope I'm not going to turn you into an alcoholic!'

'I shouldn't think so. I couldn't afford to drink, even if I wanted to.'

'You do smoke sometimes, though?'

'Sometimes,' she admitted.

He took out his cigarette case and passed it to her. The lighter flared and as she drew in the smoke it seemed to find the same place inside her head as the sherry.

'I think when I've finished this cigarette I ought to be going home,' she said.

Ralph did not argue and she thought: I've probably upset him. He saw this evening as a cosy party for two and now I've spoiled it all. Well, I can't help that.

She ground out her cigarette into the crystal ash-tray.

'It was a lovely meal. Can I see Mrs Milsom, to thank her?'

'I'll call her; she'll be pleased to know you enjoyed it.'

Mrs Milsom responded promptly to his summons and flushed with pleasure at Amy's praise.

'It's nice to cook for somebody as appreciates it,' she said, with a meaningful glance at Ralph.

Driving home in the open Morgan, the wind whipped coldly against Amy's flushed face and added a twist of exhilaration to her mood. There were no lights showing at the windows of her house and she sighed with relief. It probably meant that the children were all tucked up in bed, Ruby was in the sitting-room at the back of the house and all was well.

She tried to get up and out of the car. 'Wait – I'll help you.' Ralph came round to the passenger side and she began scrambling out, but being still slightly unsteady she caught her foot on the edge. His steadying hand was on her elbow, but as she jerked forward she collided with him and he caught and held her.

'Careful now!'

The contact of their bodies brought the blood rushing to her cheeks again and for a moment she thought he was going to kiss her again. Breath caught in her throat and the same heady mix of desire and panic flooded through her. But though he held her for long seconds, his face just inches away from hers, he made no attempt to do so.

'I'll be in touch.' His voice was both tender and decisive, his breath caressing her lips.

Amy felt her knees tremble again. 'Ralph...'

He released her. 'Come on, I'll see you to your door.'

His arm was around her waist and somehow her legs moved. Then something made her glance once more at the upper windows of the house and she saw the small white blur of a face between the screening curtains of the little house. Huw. Huw... watching for her... Huw seeing her in Ralph's arms. A tiny voice of alarm spoke within her, but was overwhelmed by the tumult of her emotions.

Ralph waited while she fumbled in her bag for the key and unlocked the door. She climbed the step and they stood briefly looking at one another, their eyes now directly level. Then he smiled, turned and was gone, striding down the path with the easy gait that characterised him – a man who knew what he wanted, a man who almost always got his way.

Amy closed the door. The house was quiet, there was not a sound to be heard except the buzzing of the blood in her ears. With trembling hands she hung up her coat and tidied her hair with her fingers.

'Is that you, Amy?'

'Yes, Ruby, it's me. Is everything all right?'

'Fine! I sang the girls to sleep – they were no trouble.'

'They like that.' Once, in another lifetime it seemed, Amy had sung the girls to sleep. Now there was rarely any time for such special moments.

'But Huw's a strange one, isn't he?' Ruby commented.

'Why do you say that?'

'I don't really know – it's just the way he is. I think I'd be worried about him if I were you, Amy.'

'He's still settling in,' Amy said, wishing she could convince herself. 'He had the most terrible time, but he'll be all right.'

'If you say so. Well, now that you're home I'll be going, Amy.'

'Yes. Thanks, Ruby. I'm really grateful.'

'That's all right. It's a pleasure to see you able to get out once in a while.'

When Ruby had gone, Amy set about her usual jobs that made up her bedtime routine – clearing up generally and setting the breakfast things ready for the morning – but it all seemed to take a great deal longer than usual. Upstairs at last she looked in on the girls, who were both sleeping soundly, then opened Huw's door a crack.

'Good night, Huw.'

There was no reply and she opened the door a little wider. The lump under the clothes told her he was in bed now, but she felt he could not possibly be asleep.

'Good night, Huw,' she said again.

But still there was no reply and Amy withdrew. There was no way she could make him speak to her if he didn't want to. And perhaps I was mistaken anyway, she thought. Perhaps I just imagined his face at the window and he was tucked up in bed and asleep all the time.

For all the torrent of emotions she had been experiencing, the wine acted as a drug and Amy fell asleep the moment her head touched the pillow. But it was still dark when she found herself suddenly and completely awake once more.

For a moment she lay trembling, a little from the suddenness of her awakening, wondering just what had disturbed her. Then from somewhere in the house she heard a thud, and froze. Someone was downstairs! She sat up, straining her ears for another indication, but there was none. A cold bright moon shining in between her curtains illuminated the clock beside her bed - 5 o'clock. Carefully, as if she herself might make a sound to alert whoever was downstairs, Amy pushed aside the cover and got out of bed. Beneath her feet the linoleum was like ice; it sent a shiver up her warm legs as she reached for her dressing-gown and pulled it on over her flannelette nightdress. Her door creaked as she opened it and she turned back into the room for a moment, wondering what she could use to protect herself from any intruder. There was nothing there, but she remembered her umbrella in the stand at the foot of the stairs. She must creep down and get that . . . then investigate.

Softly, her breath coming in shallow gasps, she went down the stairs. Once the umbrella was in her hand, she felt bolder. Where had the sound come from? The front room? No, she didn't think so. The kitchen, more likely. She went along the hall and threw open the door to the living-room.

'All right! Who's there?'

No answer . . . but the door to the kitchen banged, making her jump, and a blast of cold air whistled round her. Cold air? What . . .

She went into the living-room and then stopped, gasping in dismay. Her eyes had grown accustomed to the dark now and what she saw was a scene of complete devastation.

The table which she had set for breakfast before going to bed was now completely bare - the check cloth which had covered it and all the crockery and cutlery were on the floor. As Amy took a step into the room she trod on something hard - the sugar bowl. Then as she backed away, her toes went deep into the gritty spilled sugar.

What a mess! But this was not the work of a burglar. Her nervousness disappeared and in its place anger came rushing in.

'Huw!' she called furiously. 'Huw - where are you?'

For answer the door banged again. She crossed the living-room, picking her way over the debris. As she had thought, the back door was wide open but of Huw there was no sign. She ran to look out, but the cold moonlight showed no one on the path along the side of the house and the first thrust of panic shot through her anger. He must have gone again... made his gesture and gone. Oblivious of her bare feet, she ran out on to the path as far as the pavement, from where she had a clear view up and down the road. Empty! No movement, no sign of life anywhere. She pressed her hands against her mouth.

Oh God, what now?

And then she remembered her sudden awakening. Something must have brought her sharply to consciousness. Had it been the noise when he had pulled the cloth and everything on it from the table? If so, that was not many minutes ago, so he could not have gone far.

As she turned back towards the house, the sight of the coal-house door gave her inspiration. He had hidden in a coal-house once before; might he have done so again?

The door was unlatched and she pulled it open. The dark here was complete and she could see nothing, but she could hear breathing... rasping breathing that was almost a sob.

'You might as well come out, Huw. I know you're there,' she said in a stern voice.

After a moment's hesitation she saw a shape detach itself from the shadows. As he came towards her she planted herself squarely in the doorway.

'And you needn't think you're going to get away with this, either,' she said.

He went to slip past her and she caught his shoulder so roughly that he squealed in pain.

'In!' She propelled him into the kitchen, slamming the door after them and latching it. Then she lit the gas-lamp and turned to look at him – cowering, yet defiant still, in the corner by the sink.

'Huw, I'm ashamed of you!' she yelled. 'What can you be thinking of to do this? Look at the mess you've made – just *look!*'

He didn't answer, just stood there, his lower lip jutting, hands clenched. He was fully dressed, she noticed.

'Were you going to run away again?' she demanded.

He shrugged.

'I expect you were. You couldn't face me after this, could you? I've done my best for you, Huw; I've really tried to make you feel at home and this is how you repay me. *Oh!*' She was beside herself now and it was all she could do not to take him and shake him like a rag doll, or hit out at him with the umbrella she still held. 'I should have taken Mr Porter's advice and let him give you a darned good hiding the first time you ran away. Then perhaps you'd be behaving better now!'

A small strangled sound escaped him and she realised he was crying.

'*Why*, Huw?' she demanded.

'I told you. I don't want you to go out with *him*.' The words were barely audible, muffled by his hands as he rubbed at his face and running nose. 'He's hateful – and I saw you . . . you and him . . .'

'You were spying on us, weren't you?'

'No, I . . .'

'You *were*! I saw you at the window.'

'I heard the car and looked out.' He snuffled. 'And I hate him! *I hate him!*'

He looked so pathetic standing there, black dust from the coal smeared in dirty streaks across his wet face, and her anger died.

'Why do you hate him so?' she asked softly.

'Because . . .'

'Because he was angry with you when he found you in his shed?'

He shook his head, not answering.

'Then why?'

'Because . . .' A long pause, and he covered his eyes with his forearm. 'Because I don't want him to take you away.'

'Take me away . . .?' she repeated, not understanding at first, then slowly his meaning seeped through. Huw was jealous. No . . . more. He was afraid. She was his haven now, the one thing to cling to in an alien world, and he saw Ralph Porter as a threat to all that.

'Oh, Huw,' she said softly, melting inside with a blend of love and pity and pride. She had thought his behaviour was evidence of her failure, but it wasn't. Just the opposite, it was because she had succeeded – succeeded far more than she had dared hope. He needed her. But he was so insecure, so terribly *lost*, that he could not bear to share her even for an hour.

'Huw, come here,' she said gently.

He looked at her, half-afraid, from behind the crook of his arm.

'Come here,' she said again and held out her arms to him.

311

Still he hesitated – then, slowly, sheepishly, he came towards her. She took him into her embrace, holding his thin body close, oblivious of the coal-dust that rubbed off onto her dressing-gown, and felt him shake with sobs.

'Silly boy. You silly, silly boy.' But she spoke with sadness now and not reproof. 'There's nothing for you to be afraid of, honestly.'

'I thought you would send me away...' His words were staccato hiccoughs.

'Of course I wouldn't send you away!'

'*He* would.'

'He couldn't, Huw. You're part of my family now.'

'Not... like the girls are.'

Above his head she raised her eyes heavenward. 'Just like the girls!'

But she could sense that nothing she could say would convince him. He had been hurt too much, his world overturned too forcibly. Had he ever seen his mother with other men, she wondered? Was there some link in his child's mind between that and losing her? His mother had died, of course. She had not deserted him, but perhaps he had somehow made the connection and seen it as some kind of inevitable punishment. But whether or not that was the case, Ralph Porter presented a threat to him that he could not bear. And at such times he hit out in the only way he knew, creating havoc and causing damage, desperately screaming for attention although until he was completely broken he did not know how to plead.

'It's very early still,' she said softly. 'I think you should go back to bed for a little while.'

He clung to her, shivering... a ghost of the surly, defiant boy he could sometimes be. She pushed him gently up the stairs and into his room, where she helped him out of his dirty clothes and into bed. That would be more dirty sheets to launder, but no matter. This was not the time to insist on washing, she knew.

'Try to get some sleep now.' She smoothed back his hair gently and dropped a kiss on his forehead.

'Stay with me... please...'

She dropped down to crouch beside the bed, his hand held in hers; he lay still, snuffling occasionally, but less and less frequently as the minutes ticked by. She was cold, now, and cramped, but dared not move away until at last his breathing became deeper and more even. Then she disentangled his fingers from hers and pulled the sheet up to cover him.

Amy rose awkwardly. Her eyes felt heavy and her head thick, but there would be no more sleep for her tonight. Soon dawn would be breaking, another cold January day, but before that she had much to do clearing up the mess downstairs in the living-room.

In the doorway she paused to look back at him and a mist of warmth and pity suffused her. He was in her keeping, this child. Whatever needed to be done to repair the damage to his young life, she must do it.

With a sigh, Amy closed the door after her and went downstairs to begin another day.

Chapter Eighteen

Over the next few days Amy found herself thinking constantly of the problem of making Huw feel more secure, but only one of the ideas which occurred to her seemed to present any real and lasting solution.

The Adoption Act had become law in the New Year – perhaps if she could legally adopt him he might feel, in his own words, as much one of the family as the girls. What that would entail and how to set about it she was not sure, so at the first opportunity she made an appointment to see Arthur Clarence, the solicitor.

It was a cold, bright January day, but little sun seemed to find its way into the frowsty office and Amy thought that working here, day after day, year in year out, it was small wonder that Arthur Clarence seemed as dry, dusty and dull as the leather-bound books that lined the walls or the piles of deeds tied up with pale pink tapes which were stacked against the desk and in every corner.

'Well, Mrs Roberts, you are interested in the new Adoption Act, is that it?' Arthur Clarence's voice too was dry, scratchy as an old twig. 'It's a good piece of legislation, so far as I can tell, and should regularise matters in a good many homes. But I'm not at all sure that it will be of any help to you.'

'Why not?' Amy asked. 'I have the care of Huw Griffiths and I simply want to "regularise" it, as you put it.'

'But it's not that simple, Mrs Roberts,' stated the solicitor.

Amy shifted impatiently. Of course nothing ever *was* simple to Arthur Clarence; it was from complicating things that he had made his money.

'I want legal custody of Huw,' she explained. 'I don't want him to think I can turn him out if I feel like it, or that anyone else can take him away. He's very insecure and I believe adoption would give him a feeling of permanence. And in case you think I haven't thought this over very carefully, I have. I'm quite prepared to be solely responsible for him until he grows up.'

'Very commendable.' But he said it looking down his nose, all the same, as if his approval was lip-service only. 'Nevertheless, from my understanding of it, I do not believe the new legislation allows you to be considered in this way.'

'Why not?' Amy asked huffily.

Arthur Clarence shuffled papers in front of him, searching for the relevant details.

'In order to put yourself up to the court as a prospective adoptive parent, you have to satisfy a number of conditions. How old are you, Mrs Roberts?'

'How old?' Amy bristled again, then thought better of it. 'I'm twenty-four.'

'As I thought. An adoption order may not be made where the applicant is under the age of twenty-five years. And there is more. The boy is eight, you say? That means there is an age difference of only sixteen years between you. The restrictions are such that even if you were twenty-five years old – which I admit you will be next year ...' he paused to smile dryly at his own joke, ' ... you would not be permitted to adopt a child less than twenty-one years younger than yourself.'

'But that's stupid! I shall never be more than sixteen years older than Huw!'

'Exactly.' Arthur Clarence pursed his lips together and pushed his spectacles up on his nose. 'There is an exception. If the applicant – yourself – and the child – Huw – were within the permitted degrees of consanguinity.'

'Con-sang-*what*?'

'Consanguinity.' He rolled the term off his tongue with obvious pleasure. 'The relationships as set out in the Book of Common Prayer which preclude marriage between members of a family.'

'You mean if Huw and I were related?'

'Precisely. But you are not.'

Amy swallowed. She remembered how as a child she had once come upon – and read with fascination – a table in a prayer book that listed all the people a man or a woman may not marry, but the details now eluded her. Could it be that Llew's relationship with Huw would make it possible for her to adopt him? She didn't know. Oh, it would be awful to have to sit here and admit it to this pompous old stuffed shirt, but if that was the only way...

'Supposing he was my husband's son,' she said haltingly, 'does that come under – what did you call it – consanguinity?'

'Yes, I believe it does. But surely you are not suggesting...?'

She pinched her lips together and looked at him squarely. 'Yes, Mr Clarence.'

Behind his spectacles his eyes went beady and for a moment he appeared to be uncharacteristically lost for words.

'Would that mean I could adopt Huw?' she persisted.

'Well, yes, but...' Arthur Clarence was beginning to recover himself. 'Are you certain of this, Mrs Roberts?'

'I'm satisfied it's true, yes.'

'But proof... do you have any proof?'

Her heart sank. 'Not really. I think Llew's family all know it's true, and I know Llew paid money towards his upkeep after the man Huw called his father died.'

'But your husband was not named as Huw's father on his birth certificate?'

'No.' She had obtained that when his old home in Wales was broken up and knew that Huw's father was registered as Idris James.

'Well, then, I foresee difficulties,' Arthur Clarence said with satisfaction. 'To prove your consanguinity might be difficult – nay, impossible. The court would have to be convinced that such a claim was true and not just a fabrication invented by you in order to press the matter through. I think it very unlikely you would succeed.'

'But surely it would be worth trying?' she persisted.

'Would it? I'm not sure. It would not be a very pleasant experience, having accusations against your late husband bandied about in this way and his – uh – behaviour analysed and discussed. You would have to bring what witnesses you could, would you not, and they would have to testify as to what they knew of the matter... it could cause a public scandal and as I'm sure you know, Hillsbridge is rather short of topics of conversation at present.'

Amy felt her heart sink. He was right, frowsty old campaigner that he was. If the details of the hearing became public property, they would spread like wildfire. Mam would be dreadfully upset, Llew's mother and Eddie would never forgive her and there might be repercussions on the business. Most important of all, Huw himself would become the centre of attention. There would be no way she could keep the truth from him. And who knew what additional strain it would place on him to learn suddenly and shockingly that the man he had always called 'Dad' was not in fact his real father at all? It might prove the last, disastrous straw.

'I do urge you to consider this most carefully,' Arthur Clarence continued. 'Don't leap into doing something you may live to regret. Far be it from me to decide for you, of course, but is it so very bad to continue as you are? The boy has been placed in your care – why not leave it at that? Why stir up a hornets' nest when there is no need?'

Amy nodded, seeing the sense in what he was saying. She only wanted to do what was best for Huw and if all the details of his past life and parentage came out into the open, it could make matters worse rather than better.

'I'll leave you to think it over,' Arthur Clarence said, bringing the interview to a skilful close.

As she rose, Amy heard herself say, 'You won't tell anyone what I've told you, will you?'

'I shall treat it as a professional confidence, of course.'

But the solicitor was smiling slightly. Amy's words had confirmed to him that her mind was already made up and she did not want the truth made public. She would be taking no further action in the matter of adoption and the knowledge was a relief to him.

As he had said, something like this was certain to cause a scandal. Mr Edwin Roberts would be far from pleased to have his brother's name dragged through the mire – and Mr

Edwin Roberts was a very good client of Arthur's.

*

As Amy entered the yard gates she saw a Morris motor car drawn up to the office steps and a figure pacing about outside, glancing pointedly at the watch which hung just below the third button of his waistcoat.

Sam Gain from the Quarry Company.

He saw Amy coming and strode across the yard to meet her. 'Morning, Mrs Roberts. You're here, then.'

'Yes. I'm sorry – have you been waiting long?' Amy had sensed annoyance in Sam Gain's manner and was anxious to smooth the ruffled feathers. The quarry company was her longest standing contract.

'Long enough. I was surprised to find the place unattended.' He fixed her squarely. 'It would explain a thing or two though, I suppose.'

'What do you mean?'

Sam glanced at his watch again, dropped it and thrust his hands into his pockets.

'I suppose I might as well come straight out with it. I shall be late for my next appointment if I take time to beat about the bush – and lateness is one thing I can't abide. That's the reason I'm here.'

'Lateness...?' The penny dropped and she said sharply, 'Are you trying to tell me we have not been on time with your loads, Mr Gain?'

'That's right; it's taking too long these days. When Herbie Button used to do my work you could depend on him being there when he should be. Now...'

'The lorry is late? Picking up loads or getting them delivered?' Amy asked.

'Both. And I'm sorry, but it just won't do. If you can't provide me with a driver who is reliable and punctual, I shall have to look elsewhere.'

'Oh no, please don't do that!' Amy exclaimed in alarm. 'I'm glad you've told me about the trouble you're experiencing. I had no idea. Why Cliff Button should be taking too long, I don't know, but I assure you that I shall find out and make certain it doesn't occur again.'

'Fair enough!' Sam Gain started to go, then turned back. 'I think I can tell you the why, by the way – or at least the

317

where. There's a transport café up on Mendip with a waitress who seems to have quite a name among the men, and your lorry has been seen outside there a time or two.'

'Really?' Amy said, annoyed. 'Well, thank you for telling me. I shall certainly speak to my drivers. You'll have no further cause for complaint.'

'I hope not.'

'You won't. That's my word, Mr Gain.'

When he had gone Amy stamped into her office. How dare Cliff Button dilly-dally in a transport café and get the firm a bad name! Perhaps he thought he could get away with that sort of thing because he was only employed as a temporary driver or, more likely, because his boss was a woman – if so, he was very much mistaken! Besides, it was an attitude which could spread all too easily to the younger men, and that she would not tolerate.

All day she simmered and by the time both lorries were back in the yard, she was absolutely determined on one thing – no one was ever going to have cause to complain about the punctuality of Roberts Haulage again.

She went out into the yard. Herbie had the bonnet of the lorry up, checking it over while Cliff was leaning against the cab, arms folded, chatting as he watched his brother work. The two mates were sorting chains into piles and stopping occasionally to kick a stone to one another.

Amy crossed to them. 'Could you all step into my office for a minute, please?'

They looked up at her, surprised by the authority in her voice.

'Can I just finish doing this, missus?' Herbie asked.

She hesitated momentarily. It was not Herbie she was gunning for; he was a good worker, one of the best. But she didn't want to leave anyone out of this pep-talk. Company policy was company policy . . . and she had to impress herself on them as the boss, too. If Cliff felt his brother Herbie was above her authority, he might take advantage of it.

'No, come now, please Herbie, if you would,' she said crisply. 'What I have to say won't take long.'

They followed her across the yard, looking at one another and wiping their hands on the bundles of rags they carried in their pockets.

In the office she stood behind her desk, waiting until they were all assembled, then she raised her eyes and looked from one to the other of them in turn. Beneath her gaze they shuffled uneasily, but none of then said anything.

'I expect you're wondering why I wanted to see you all,' she said at last. 'Well, I'll tell you. I've had a complaint today from a customer of ours – Gain's Sand and Gravel. Mr Gain is not satisfied with the timetable we're keeping – in fact, he is so dissatisfied that he came here to see me about it and threatened to take his custom elsewhere.'

Varying degrees of guilt coloured three of the four faces and Amy homed in on Cliff.

'Why has your lorry been late picking up and delivering, Cliff?'

His eyes moved shiftily and he shrugged his shoulders in a gesture which purported to be puzzled by the criticism whilst dissociating himself totally from the inanimate guilt of his lorry.

'It's my belief that you've been spending too long in a certain transport café,' Amy went on tartly and saw a dark flush colour Cliff's face and neck.

'Surely we'm entitled to a cup of tea, missus?' he protested.

'A cup of tea, yes – but not at the expense of the schedule,' Amy snapped back. 'It takes perhaps five minutes to drink a cup of tea. And Mr Gain would not have been here complaining if you had been only five minutes late.'

'It's not my fault if they take a long time to serve us,' Cliff grumbled.

'Very true,' Amy agreed, 'but your problem all the same, I'm afraid. If you can't drink your tea and be on the road in time to keep to the schedules, I'm afraid you will just have to go without the tea until the job is done.' She ran a hand through her hair, tossed her head to loosen it again and met the men's eyes levelly. 'This is a small business and the service we can offer is limited – in some ways we cannot hope to compete with larger concerns. But one thing we can do is ensure that we are both prompt and reliable. Promptness and reliability are going to be the hallmark of Roberts Transport from now on – and *your* watchwords! That's what I called you together to say. We are a small team, but we're going to be a good one – and there is no room in it for slackers. In future I shall be watching the schedules very carefully and I won't stand for any slip-ups. Is that understood?'

She looked from one to the other again. The two mates

319

were exchanging uncomfortable glances, while Cliff looked red and resentful. Only Herbie's face was totally unreadable.

'That's all, then. You may as well get on with your work,' she finished. 'But I hope you will remember what I have said. I want this to be the finest transport company for miles around and if we all pull together, we can do it. But I can't – and won't – carry passengers. There's no room for them in Roberts Haulage.'

Realising they had been dismissed, the men filed out of the office and Amy stood for a moment breathing deeply on the nervous euphoria of having exerted her authority for the first time.

The euphoria lasted exactly an hour. Amy was still in the office, working on new and tighter schedules, when there was a tap on the door. She looked up, impatient at the interruption. Cliff and the two young mates had gone home, she knew – she had seen them leave the yard half an hour earlier – so she guessed it must be Herbie who, still pottering about, had come on some problem.

'Come in!' she called.

Herbie opened the door and entered. There was a hesitancy in his manner, yet at the same time a kind of purpose, tight-coiled, which she had never noticed in him before.

'Is there something wrong?' she asked.

'Yes, missus. There is.' He paused, looking at her with a set face.

'Well, what is it?'

'I don't think I can work for you any more.'

Amy went cold. 'What on earth do you mean?'

'What you said just now, missus... well, if that's your attitude, I don't think I can work for you.'

'But Herbie, for goodness' sake! I wasn't getting at you!'

'I worked for Mr Roberts from the time he started up this business,' Herbie went on as if he had not heard her. 'He never had any complaints. I've done my best to carry on the same way and help out all I can, but a man's got his pride. I mean to say, it's bad enough working for a woman, but to have to stand and be told the way you told us, well...'

'Herbie, listen to me!' Amy was trembling; she felt as if the bottom had dropped out of her world. 'I had to say something – you must see that! If the company gets a bad reputation, we won't get any new work and we shall probably lose what we have. I thought a pep-talk was called for and that it was best to speak to all of you together. But I promise you that none of what I said was aimed at you. You're above reproach. It was Cliff...'

'I know that,' Herbie said implacably.

'Well then, why...?'

'He's my brother, isn't he? And it's because of me that he's here. I feel responsible, like.'

'But you're not his keeper, Herbie! He's been wasting time because of some waitress in a transport café, if what I hear is true, and he has to be told about it. I don't pay him wages to sit around drinking tea and chatting up some fancy piece, even if he is your brother. But I certainly don't hold *you* responsible.'

'That's as maybe, but I've thought it over, missus, and I reckon it's best if I give in me notice.'

'But Herbie!'

'That's all, missus.' He turned and left the office, stubborn decision written into every line of his tall, stooping frame. For a moment Amy sat staring after him in absolute horror. Herbie wouldn't leave Roberts Haulage – he *couldn't*! She would never manage without him! He was responsible for so many things which she didn't have a clue about – and even leaving all that aside, she had come to rely so much on his calm, dependable presence. Oh, how could she have been so foolish as to upset him – and all because of that brother of his and his eye for a woman! Yet even as the panic and sense of desolation mounted, Amy knew she had done the right thing.

She must not let the staff get away with slacking. They must have a standard to work to, or the whole thing would fall apart.

But she couldn't let Herbie go either – she couldn't! There must be a way to keep him...

It came to her in a flash: promote him! Give him some responsibility for looking after the yard instead of just using his expertise – and perhaps put him over Cliff and the others as well. She would have to offer him a raise in pay, and heaven only knew where that would come from, but that would not be the main incentive. It would be the assurance that he was appreciated, needed, which would enable Herbie to swallow his pride and continue working for a woman – if anything could do it, that is.

321

Shaking with anxiety, Amy left the office and went into the yard to look for Herbie, but he had already gone and she realised it would be tomorrow before she could put her suggestion to him. If then. Supposing he expected his notice to take effect immediately? What would she do about that – and about tomorrow's deliveries?

Amy spent a sleepless night worrying about it and next morning she was at the yard early, before any of the men arrived. Sick to her stomach she watched the gates, wondering how she would ever cope if Herbie failed to turn up. But long before dawn she saw the lights of his bicycle turn into the yard and she went out to meet him.

'Herbie, could you come in a minute, please? There's something I want to say to you.'

He came, standing awkwardly in the doorway, turning his cap round and around between his hands.

'Herbie – if I upset you yesterday, I'm very sorry. Though I do truly feel that I only said what had to be said. No . . . just a minute!' she said hastily as his set expression became more mulish. 'As I told you, it wasn't you I was getting at for one moment, but I can see that you were hurt at being lectured with the others when in fact you are my right-hand man. Well, I should like to ensure that can never happen again. If only I can persuade you to stay on, Herbie – and I hope and pray I can! – I would like to make you up to foreman. There would be a bit extra in your pay packet and quite a lot of extra responsibility. Well, in fact, I suppose it wouldn't mean you doing much more than you do at present, but it would give you more authority – and make it official.'

She paused, biting her lip. His expression had changed not one iota, but was still totally blank. Her heart was thudding. Was it too late to make amends? Was he still going to insist on leaving?

'Oh please, Herbie!' she said desperately. 'I do need you! Without you, I don't think Roberts Haulage can survive!'

'Well, missus . . .' Herbie's voice was slow, giving nothing away. 'Well, I'm very touched that you should want to put me in charge, but . . .'

Her heart sank. She had lost him! Then above the hammering of the blood in her ears she heard him say, 'I were coming in to see you this morning, anyway. I spoke in haste last night and I were a bit upset, I admit it. But . . . I couldn't walk out and leave you. No, I couldn't 'ave done that.'

'Oh Herbie, thank goodness!' she cried.

And in that moment she could have thrown her arms around his stooping frame and hugged him, oily overalls and all.

*

Two evenings later Amy was busy ironing when there came a knock at the front door. She popped the flats back on to the gas-ring and went to answer it.

'Ralph!'

'Hello, Amy.'

Her pulses had begun the erratic pounding which the mere sight of him seemed to engender. 'What are you doing here?'

'I said I would be seeing you. Aren't you going to ask me in?'

She experienced a momentary stab of panic. Huw was in the living-room, playing some records on the gramophone and sorting through a box of old postcards she had found to amuse him. What behaviour would it provoke if she were to walk in with Ralph? But she could hardly leave him standing on the doorstep.

'Come in. We'll go in the front room.'

'The kitchen would be fine by me.'

'No!' The kitchen would be within earshot of Huw and he would be able to overhear everything they said.

She led the way into the front room, where she lit the lights and the gas fire. The atmosphere in the room was icy - it had not been used since Christmas - and she shivered.

'It will warm up in a moment - excuse me while I just take my irons off, will you? And oh ... do sit down ...'

On her way through to the kitchen she spoke anxiously to Huw. 'All right, Huw? Having fun with the postcards?'

'Yes. They're good ...' But he was too engrossed to look up and she thanked her stars for the gramophone blaring 'Valencia'. When she returned to the front room Ralph had not taken a seat but was standing in front of the gas fire warming himself. As she came in, he moved away to allow her to share the warmth.

'This is a surprise! I haven't anything to offer you, I'm afraid, except a cup of tea ...' She felt she was blabbering like an idiot, but the words came tumbling out all the same.

'It's all right, I don't want anything – I've just had dinner.' How did he manage to remain so calm, so self-possessed? It was not fair that some people should be like that while she . . . 'I came to ask when I'm going to see you again,' he continued.

Her heart lurched and suddenly she felt as if she had gone hollow inside. From the moment she saw him on the doorstep she had known why he was here, of course – and known too what she must say to him. She had been over and over it since Arthur Clarence had told her it would be impossible for her to adopt Huw legally – the one thing which she had thought would give him stability and free her to live her own life without worrying about the effect this might have on him. But knowing what you had to do and actually doing it were two entirely different things. Believing you were right did not make it any easier.

'Well?' Ralph was looking at her quizzically. 'How about dinner again one evening? Or would you rather go out somewhere? I know how you love riding in the car.'

She took a deep breath. 'No, Ralph, I can't.'

His eyes narrowed – the only betrayal of any emotion. 'Well! You said that as though you meant it.'

'I do mean it. I can't go out with you again – not for a while, anyway. I did enjoy myself the other evening, but it would be better not to do it again.'

'May I ask why?'

She glanced towards the door and lowered her voice. 'Because of Huw.'

'The boy?'

'Yes. I had terrible problems with him after last time.' She went on to outline what had happened and Ralph's face grew grim.

'I could have told you that you would have trouble with that one. Why did you take him on?'

Her lips tightened. 'I think that's my business.'

'Ouch!' He smiled ruefully but it did not reach his eyes. 'All right, I concede it's your business as to why you took him on. But surely you don't propose to let him rule your life? He needs taking in hand.'

'He needs love and security and I should be failing if I didn't give him that. Right now he sees you as a threat. Oh, don't you see, Ralph, he's had a terrible time! He lost his mother, his home, his friends. Now he's afraid of losing me.'

'That's ridiculous!'

'You know that and so do I. But Huw doesn't and it will take time and patience to make him understand.'

'And in the meantime you intend to deny yourself any life of your own?'

'I have a life!' she said hotly. 'I have a very full life.'

'So you've decided to turn me down and tell me you're not going to see me any more!'

'I can't, Ralph. I can't!'

'Because of a child!'

The hardness in his voice frightened her. It was always there just beneath the surface – that cold, biting edge that made him totally different from Llew. Llew had been enthusiastic and emotional, quarrelsome sometimes, yet sentimental enough to be swayed by her and she had always felt she could get him to see her point of view. Ralph... Ralph was a man who would hate to be beaten, he would make a fierce enemy and a poor loser. She wanted him – yes, even now, although he frightened her a little, something basic and primeval about him called to her in a way she scarcely understood. But most of all she wanted Llew – his tenderness and understanding. She had hurt him, hurt him so much by her taunts during those last days before he died and now she would never be able to make it up to him, tell him she had not meant what she said. Would she have been able to hurt Ralph in that way? She doubted it. And to give in to him now, to give into her own compelling desire for him, would be one last betrayal of Llew.

'It's not just because of Huw,' she said softly, 'it's because of me as well. It's too soon, Ralph.'

'You're afraid of what people might say?'

'No!' She hesitated, then admitted, 'Well, perhaps that too. They might see it as a slur on Llew and I wouldn't want that. Oh, I know it would be me they'd be talking about and calling names, but that's not what I would mind. It would be the reflection on Llew – the suggestion that I couldn't have cared much for him. They would pity him, don't you see? I don't want that; I want them to remember him as a man worthy of his wife mourning for him. And me... well, I couldn't feel right about it, not on any account. So that's why I can't see you any more.'

'I see.' He moved abruptly. 'It seems you have made up your mind.'

'I'm afraid so.'

'Don't be afraid.' That hard edge was there again. 'Being *afraid* doesn't suit you. You're at your best with all guns blazing, Amy.'

She was unsure quite how to take that and as she stood looking at him quizzically, he moved away towards the door.

'Well, that's it then, isn't it?'

She nodded. Her throat was full suddenly and she couldn't speak.

'Don't go!' she wanted to say, but knew she must not. As she watched him walk away down the path the tears welled into her eyes, but she brushed them away impatiently.

Don't be such a fool! It's the best thing. Everything you said to him was no more than the truth. It *is* bad for Huw and it *is* too soon to be seen with another man.

Then why, oh why, do I feel as if the bottom has fallen out of my world all over again?

She closed the door, blinked hard and blew her nose. In the living-room Huw glanced up from his postcards.

'Who was that?'

'Oh, just someone to see me,' she said casually, mastering the threatening tremble in her voice. But Huw was already engrossed in his postcards once more. It was all right – the danger had passed – he didn't know who it was.

Amy went back into the kitchen and got on with her ironing.

*

Although it was a relief that the strike was at last over, with Christmas and the New Year behind him Harry was aware of a sense of anti-climax.

At least so long as the strike had lasted there had been something to work for, a sense of purpose overriding everything he did. Now he was back in his job underground – one of the lucky ones – but he was no longer satisfied with that. Carting coal was back-breaking work, but like the rest of the family he was fit enough to cope without too much trouble and though he emerged from the pit each night physically tired, he had enough energy left to feel frustration and something like anger.

The return to work had been on surrender terms – the men were worse off now than they had been when they first went out on strike eight long months ago – and the despair in their eyes made Harry fearful for the future. He had been so determined to do something – anything – to further the cause, but like the others he had achieved nothing and sometimes he wondered if he ever would.

Perhaps Mam had been right to try to steer him away from the pits, he thought. Perhaps he could leave and make a life elsewhere. But somehow, deep down, he knew that was not the answer.

He still wanted to help men like his father and how could he ever do that if he left the pits? But by the same token, what could he do if he remained where he was? He was such a small cog in the great wheels, a nonentity – who would ever take notice of him and what he said?

The answer came to him one day when a new deputy – or 'examiner', as they were known locally – came to work at Middle Pit. Frank Horler was a Purldown lad who had spent all his working life out in the Duchy mines, but Harry knew him slightly through the pigeon fanciers' circles and had never thought of him as being particularly bright. Solid, yes. A good worker, yes. But hardly brainy. And he was not that much older than Harry either – at least twenty-one, of course, otherwise he could not have taken his ticket – but a young man compared with most of the examiners Harry had known during his time underground.

As Harry listened to his drawling voice and watched the slow, deliberate way he went about his tasks, he found himself itching with impatience. Later, as Frank Horler aired his less-than-scintillating views on the politics of Ramsay MacDonald and the Labour Party, Harry thought: Good grief, I'm brighter than he is! If he can be an examiner, why can't I?

He turned over the idea as he dragged his putt of coal along the narrow roadways, his knees scraping over the shining black-sprinkled ground, ducking his head to avoid an overhang here and there.

An examiner! If he was an examiner, it would be the first step towards respect and recognition. And it would be reflected in his paypacket, too. But how to set about it? Harry disliked the idea of talking it over with Frank or any of his workmates. It would seem presumptuous, he thought, and he could almost hear the comments his enquiry would arouse:

'Oh – thinks 'e's too good for us, s'know.'

'You – an examiner, Harry? You bain't hardly out o' your napkins!'

No, Harry decided there was only one person to talk to, and that was Adam Barker, the manager. He might put him down, too, but at least his mates would not be there to see it.

It took all of Harry's courage to knock on the manager's door the following afternoon. An interview had been requested and granted. Now when he found himself face to face with the the small, compact man with the leathery lined face, dressed as was his wont in the highly unsuitable garb of tweed jacket and plus-fours, Harry found his nerve almost failing him.

'Right, lad, what was it you wanted to see me about?' Adam Barker was known not to suffer fools gladly and Harry pulled himself together.

'I want to study for my Examiner's Ticket and I need your advice on how to go about it.'

'That's putting the cart before the horse, isn't it?' Adam barked.

'What do you mean?' He had already succeeded in taking the wind out of Harry's sails.

'Surely the question you should have come here to ask me is whether or not I think you're up to *taking* your Examiner's Ticket?'

'I'm sure I could do the job,' Harry said stoutly. 'I have no intention of staying a carting boy all my life.'

'That's unlikely, anyway. Carting will be done away with when the Guss Committee reports, I shouldn't be surprised. Never mind that hardly any of those shouting about it have the first idea what they're on about. It's a matter where heart, not head, rules. What do you think about it, Hall?'

Inwardly Harry winced. He had taken the device too much for granted to resent it greatly, and he knew well enough the arguments in its favour. Seams here in Somerset were thin, roadways too small for tubs. If other, more expensive methods of getting the coal away were forced upon the owners and the pits therefore became uneconomic, jobs would be lost. But the Miners' Association had taken up the emotive contraption as their *cause célèbre*, the symbol of their oppression. Harry was in a cleft stick and he knew it.

'The guss and crook will go eventually – it's bound to,' he said now. 'What we have to do is hope it's not outlawed until something has been found to replace it – something that will work as well here as in other coalfields.'

Adam Barker raised an eyebrow. 'And what do you think that might be?'

Harry considered. 'Some kind of low contraption on wheels, maybe. Though I'm not sure how well wheels would run on the uneven ground. A band conveyor would be better, if there was room for it.'

'Hmm.' Adam Barker was looking at him with new interest. He was not used to carting boys coming into his office and talking with such intelligence and foresight. 'So you want to take a step up in the world, do you?' he said, bringing the conversation back to Harry's own future.

'Yes, I do. But I don't know how to set about it.'

'How old are you?'

'Sixteen. Going on seventeen.'

'Too young to sit the exam for another four years or so,' the manager commented. 'When you're eighteen or nineteen, you could start Examiners' classes up at the Higher Elementary School. You know about those classes, do you?'

'Not really,' Harry admitted.

'They're run a couple of times a week and you learn all you need to know. But as I say, there is no point in starting them for another year or so. What's your general education like?'

'I went to the Board School,' Harry said defensively.

'And left as soon as you could, no doubt? Well, if you want my advice as to how to get on, I'll give it to you. Go back to school!'

'Leave the pit, you mean?' Harry asked, aghast.

'No – go to night school – Evening Continuation Classes. You can take instruction in general subjects – arithmetic, English, drawing, geography – and get a certificate at the end of it. Anything you learn will stand you in good stead for when you're old enough to go to mining classes.'

'You think so?' This was not quite what Harry had had in mind.

'That's my advice, for what it's worth. And if you have the time, you could go to first-aid classes too. The St John Ambulance Brigade run them and a certificate in first aid is always an asset to anyone going underground. I tell you this: if I'm appointing an examiner and one of the candidates can do first aid, he's always my choice.'

'Has Frank Horler got first aid?' Harry asked.

'He has indeed and he did a fine job when a man was injured by a roof fall at his last pit.' He looked sharply at Harry. 'Your eyesight and hearing are good, I take it?'

'Yes – of course...' Harry looked puzzled.

'There's a stringent test for eyesight and hearing,' the manager explained. 'You have to be able to see well enough to read percentages of fire-damp, and hear well enough to be aware of any roof movements... timber cracking and the like. But I don't envisage any problems for you there. You're young and healthy – and you're a likely lad; I'm only surprised that you haven't come to my attention before this.'

'Well, thank you...' Harry was flushing with pleasure.

'A likely lad,' Adam Barker said again. 'Work hard, Hall, and I see no reason why you should not set your sights higher than examiner. Think of working towards your Second-Class Certificate of Competency.'

'You mean... an under-manager's ticket?' Harry could hardly believe his ears.

'Yes – and your First-Class-Manager's. In fact, for a lad of your ability it might be worth your while to miss out the Second Class and go straight for the First. In that case, if you can fit it in with all the other studies, it might be an idea to learn something about surveying. That's something you can always practise.'

'Yes, sir. And thank you.'

The manager was on his feet, the interview clearly at an end. Slightly dazed, Harry made his way out of the office. A pale sun was warming the rough-hewn lias stone of the row of cottages, the saw-pit shed and the frame house on the opposite side of the yard, and glancing dully off the grey slate roofs. Harry walked into the sunshine, his mind spinning.

He had asked for advice and had certainly got it – far more than he had bargained for. Under-Manager... Manager... it was beyond his wildest dreams, but when Adam had talked about it so matter-of-factly it all seemed possible. Anything seemed possible at this moment.

Harry ran a hand through his hair, letting his breath come out on a soft whistle.

It would mean a great deal of hard work, very little free time and the shelving, for the time being at any rate, of any political ambitions. But if at the end of it he could be manager of a colliery – well, wouldn't that be worth any sacrifice? People would have to stand still and listen to him then. He could do things his way.

He stopped for a moment, turning to look at the head-gear that towered majestically above the squat, dust-blackened colliery buildings, feeling the first stirrings of excitement. A colliery manager – responsible for the lives and livelihood of men like his father and his brother. Power undreamed of!

Yes, thought Harry. That's what I'm going to do and the rest will follow.

He stuck his hands into the pockets of his trousers and, still deep in thought, crossed the yard which might one day, he thought, be his domain.

Chapter Nineteen

Winter lingered and sometimes it seemed as if spring would never come. The wonderful summer was long forgotten now and the greyness had settled back around Hillsbridge... spreading, absorbing, tainting all it touched.

The sky was grey, heavy and laden, and the smoke from the pit chimneys rising into it was not black but merely another, darker, shade of grey. The batches, muddied by the persistent damp, had no shine of jet; the grass and bushes merged against them – a greenish grey, yes, but still predominantly grey; the ash and sycamore and beech trees raised bare arms as if to attract some attention to bring hope to their grey lives; the tall forked elms provided safe cover for the greyish nests of the rooks which cawed and grumbled as they swooped down to sit on the grey-painted railings that fringed the river. And the town itself was and always had been grey, every stone and slate – the church, the chapel, the shops, the pubs, even the magnificent Victoria Hall, home of dances and the billiard rooms, scene of the human lottery in 1918 when names had been drawn from a hat to send them to the hell that was France, which now looked out at the grey Cenotaph inscribed with the names of some of the men who had stood on the steps and heard their names called that day.

Grey, grey, all of it grey – and none of it greyer than the flatness Amy experienced each night when the end of the day meant the end of the panacea ... work. From morning to night there was little time to think of anything else – unless it was how to keep home life for the children as normal as possible. But once they were in bed and an exhausted Amy turned out the lights, there was restlessness and regret. And sometimes, in the sharp, lonely wakefulness, the disturbing memory of the way Ralph Porter had made her feel during the short time they had been together.

She never saw him now – had not done so for months – and at first she had dreaded the imagined embarrassment of coming face to face with him again. But when he did not come to the office to settle the account – telephoning to suggest a more businesslike arrangement of payment by cheque through the post – she felt ridiculously cheated; and when one afternoon towards the end of February, his car had turned into the yard, all the emotions she had thought firmly under control surfaced once more.

'Ralph – hello,' she said, composing herself with difficulty.

'Hello, Amy.' His cool voice and frosty expression gave her an almost physical shock. 'Can you spare me a few minutes?'

'Yes, of course.'

'It's purely business,' he said, as if she needed reassurance. 'I've come to tell you that I'm leaving Hillsbridge for a while.'

'Oh, are you?' Ridiculously her heart had fallen away into a pit deep inside her.

'Yes, I'm going to Gloucester. You remember that my sister was there at the New Year? When I went up to collect her, I realised the possibilities the place offered and I intend to set up a depot with a view to expanding my foreign contacts, import and export.'

'Oh – I never thought of Gloucester as a port,' she said.

'It's on the mouth of the Severn and I've had the opportunity of taking a lease on a property right on the docks. It should make an excellent timber yard.'

'I see.' But she did not; she could think of nothing but: 'Ralph is going away!' Though she had no intention of letting him know that.

'I'm putting in a manager to run the business here for the time being,' Ralph went on, 'so you need not have any worries on that score. In fact, I should like to arrange a long-term contract for your lorry to continue working for us. A year, I thought, if that's agreeable to you?'

'Yes, of course . . .'

'I have the papers here; I thought it would be a good idea for us to get things on an official basis before I go. I don't know how available I shall be afterwards.'

'You'd like to tie it up now?'

'That's the general idea. Now, if I tell you a little about the arrangements I've made for my absence . . .'

As they talked business, Amy fought to keep her mind on the subject in hand. But she was still uncomfortably aware of him, uncomfortably conscious of knowing how it felt to be in his arms. It was no basis for a professional relationship. Perhaps it was just as well he was going away.

The discussion over and the relevant papers signed, he rose with an air of finality.

'Right. It seems there's nothing left then but for me to thank you for the way your firm has been handling my loads and hope that everything continues to run smoothly.'

'I see no reason why it should not,' she replied.

'No, neither do I. By the time I come back, Amy, it wouldn't surprise me if you have a fleet of half-a-dozen lorries and so much business that my account is very small fry indeed. Your husband would be proud of you.'

There was something in his tone she did not understand, but she had no time to ponder it.

'Goodbye, Amy.'

'Goodbye, Ralph. Good luck with your new venture – though I'm sure you won't need it!'

He smiled briefly; the twist of his mouth wrenched at her heart.

'One always needs a little luck. A lot of enterprise, a lot of imagination, a lot of determination and nerve. But a little luck too. Without that, the rest can all be undermined. Now . . . I'll be going. I have a great deal to do and I'm sure you have too . . .'

She nodded. 'Always.'

In the doorway he turned back suddenly. 'Oh, just one more thing before I go – I thought you might like to have this.'

He took a small box from his pocket and handed it to her. Mystified, she opened it, then caught her breath.

Her engagement ring – the ring she had sold to the jeweller in order to pay off her debt to him!

'My ring!' Startled, confused, she looked up at him, but his face was expressionless, giving nothing away.

'It came into my possession and I thought you would like it back.'

'Oh!' A dozen questions were occurring to her – how had he known it was hers, to begin with? But the way in which he had given it to her forbade her asking and she said inadequately, 'Thank you.'

'That's all right. As long as you're pleased.' He did not add that he had hoped to return it to her under happier circumstances, yet instinctively she knew this was the case – and knew, too, that by choosing this moment when intimacy was at its lowest, he was in effect terminating the relationship that might have existed between them.

Sadness at the finality of it obliterated the joy she would otherwise have felt at having her precious ring returned, and as she watched him walk away across the yard the emptiness was yawning in her again – that inescapable sense of loss which had nothing to do with logical thought.

'Oh Ralph! Oh Llew!' she whispered and the tears gathered thickly at the back of her throat.

*

At the end of February Ivor Burge came to see Amy to tell her he was now fit to resume work, and she was left with no alternative but to tell Cliff Button she no longer needed him.

On the one hand she was sorry to have to do it – since her pep-talk Cliff had really put his nose to the grindstone and given her no further cause for complaint. But she never felt totally at ease when telling him what to do. Cliff had been his own boss for too long to be happy talking orders and she also suspected he might try to take advantage of his brother's newly elevated position the moment her back was turned.

'Don't let it worry you, missus,' Cliff said when she broke the news to him. 'I was glad to help you out when you needed me, but I've been thinking of setting up on my own account again for some time now. I reckon that if I was to take my car to Bath, get it properly licensed and all, I could do a roaring trade. There's more call for taxis in towns.'

'I'm sure you're right,' Amy said and thought: What is it I do to my drivers? Cliff would be the second to leave the district after departing from her employ, for Ollie Griffin, she had heard, had gone off to London – 'looking to see if the streets are paved with gold', Herbie had said and Amy had been relieved to hear it. She was still embarrassed by what had happened at Christmas – outraged, yes, but embarrassed too – and had had the unpleasant feeling that he would tell everyone he met about how he had tried to compromise Mrs Roberts, probably adding a few embellishments of his own to the tale into the bargain.

But now he was gone and Amy hoped he never came back. The city could swallow him whole and she would only heave a sigh of relief. But Cliff was a different kettle of fish.

'If ever you want to come back, just let Herbie know,' she told him now. 'I know I'm not in a position to keep you on at the moment, but who knows what the future will bring?'

'Right you are, Mrs Roberts. And I'll say just one thing – it hasn't been half as bad working for a woman as I expected,' Cliff said.

Amy knew that from him this was praise indeed.

*

Winter crept towards spring on muddy, leaden feet. The wind was still biting, the sky grey and cold and last year's dead leaves blew about in forlorn drifts beneath trees that bore the first brave spears of palest green. But in the front gardens of the houses along Greenslade Terrace snowdrops clustered, purest white against the brown, and the crocuses made cushions of gay purple and yellow.

Spring should be a season of hope, Charlotte thought, but somehow this year was not and the lowering sky and bone-chilling cold seemed to reflect her mood of depression and anxiety.

I'm getting older, Charlotte told herself. I feel the cold more. And because I'm uncomfortable, I look on the black side of things and worry more.

But that was not the whole story and she knew it. The worries were real enough – and there were too many of them to brush aside lightly.

With the exception of Jack, each one of her children was

causing her moments of anxiety at least, and some of the problems were enough to constitute a nagging ache in her heart.

Naturally, of course, she was concerned about Amy. Charlotte had never agreed with what she was doing, either with the business or about the boy Huw – 'she's made a rod for her own back there' she said to James more than once.

'She had to do what she thought was right,' James replied, 'and she'll make a fine lad of him yet. She's a winner, our Amy.'

But it was more than he could say when Charlotte's worrying turned to Harry. Placid as he was, even James had his reservations about the wisdom of what Harry was doing. Studying already for his Deputy's Certificate and him still dragging putts of coal – 'It don't seem natural,' his father said. 'It's all very well wanting to get on, but why can't he do it quiet-like, the same as our Jim's a-doin' of?'

Charlotte said nothing to that. In her opinion 'getting on quiet-like' would take Jim precisely nowhere. She was pleased and proud of Harry's ambition and what worried her more was his involvement with the Labour Party. She had never trusted politics or politicians ... with the exception, of course, of Mr Lloyd George whom she idolised – and she was unable to escape from the nagging certainty that somehow, sometime, the Labour Pary would use Harry and then cast him aside, or even get him involved in something crooked or deceitful and leave him to carry home the can. No, Charlotte didn't like it, nor did she like the way he seemed able to think of nothing else. All very well to be ambitious at rising seventeen, but Harry was obsessed and no good would come of it, she thought gloomily.

The progression of thought led her on to Jim, whom James had held up as an example of the way Harry ought to be shaping his life.

Heaven forbid! thought Charlotte. She knew he and Sarah lived in fear of his losing his job at the pit – with all the unemployment, he would never get another – and recently Charlotte had noticed he was developing a cough. Surely he was too young yet to be succumbing to the lung disease? It was just a winter cough, for sure. But it niggled away at the back of her mind anyway, a harbinger of winters yet to come.

All these minor anxieties paled into insignificance, however, beside the one great worry which was so enormous and horrifying that she could bring herself to mention it to no one.

For some time now, Charlotte had been worried about Noël, Dolly's baby, who in her opinion was not developing as he should. The suspicion woke her, sweating, in the middle of the night and started a sickness in the pit of her stomach whenever she peered into his cot.

At first she told herself she must be mistaken. It was probably merely impatience which was making her think that Noël should be responding more – grasping a finger, focusing his eyes and managing a bright, gummy smile. Memory always played false with these things and her other grandchildren had probably been just the same as babies. But all the while a small voice deep inside kept saying she was *not* mistaken – there *was* something different about that flaccid stare and the droop of the mouth issuing its constant stream of dribble. Even the shape of him struck her as vaguely wrong somehow – his head seemed to be growing at a faster rate than the rest of him.

Charlotte watched him with gnawing anxiety as winter eventually gave way to spring and spring to summer. In June, when he was six months old and still showing no signs of doing any of the things she felt sure he should be doing, Charlotte decided she could bury her head in the sand no longer.

'I'm worried about our Noël,' she said bluntly to Dolly one day when she and the boys came to visit. It was a perfect June afternoon – the sky a soft deep blue, the warm air heavy with the smell of the tar-spraying machine in the road outside and, closer by, the delicate perfume of the lavender bushes where bees hovered and buzzed. 'Aren't you worried about him, Dolly?'

Dolly's blue eyes became guarded. 'Why should I be? He's ever such a good baby.'

'That's just it,' Charlotte said. 'He's *too* good. And he doesn't seem to take any interest in anything. Now I'm sure that by his age our Bob and Fred . . .'

'You can't compare them!' Dolly cut in sharply. 'It does no good to try. They're all different, you should know that.'

'Of course I know it,' Charlotte agreed, 'but he should be taking more notice than he does.'

Dolly picked Noël out of his pram and settled him on her ample lap. His head lolled forward and a stream of dribble ran onto his knitted matinee jacket.

'Well, you're the only one to ever suggest such a thing, Mam,' Dolly said, sounding hurt. 'If you haven't got anything nice to say about Noël, you'd do better to say nothing at all.'

Charlotte sniffed. If Dolly was closing her eyes to all the signs at the moment, there was nothing she could do about it.

'We'll just have to hope I'm wrong, Dolly, that's all. But if I'm not . . . well, the sooner you get the doctor to have a look at him the better, in my opinion. And remember, I'm always here if you need me.'

'Thanks, Mam.' Dolly's lip wobbled suddenly and Charlotte thought: She has her doubts, just like I have. She's only trying to pretend otherwise.

The confirmation made her go cold inside, turning the nightmare dread into reality. What would they do? How could they cope? How survive the shame? A grandchild of hers and something wrong with him! For a panicky moment the future swam before her eyes, like a churning sea seen from a boat-deck in a storm. Then cold common sense threw her a lifeline.

It's our Noel, she told herself. He's still our Noel, no matter what. And anyway we might both be wrong.

The figure of a girl turned the corner of the Rank, walking along towards them and momentarily all thoughts of Noel and his possible disability were driven from Charlotte's mind.

Rosa Clements. What was she doing home? She came sauntering up the Rank, the summer breeze blowing her short pleated skirt against her legs and moving her fashionably bobbed cap of raven hair.

'Hello, Mrs Hall. Hello, Dolly. I'm glad I've seen you. I was going to knock at the door anyway.' Her tone was light, conversational, denying the antagonism which had always existed between them, but there was a note of something Charlotte could not quite understand. Jubilation?

'Why's that then, Rosa?' Charlotte asked coolly.

'I had a letter from Ted at the weekend.'

'Really?' Ted was in Ramsgate for the summer, working as a bathing-chair attendant. 'Well, you're highly honoured, Rosa, I must say.'

Rosa ignored the jibe. 'He wants me to go down and see him.'

'Oh, does he indeed?'

'Yes, and I'm going down next week. Just thought I'd tell you, in case you want me to take anything for him.'

'We'll let you know. Thanks, Rosa.'

When she had gone Dolly and Charlotte exchanged looks.

'Do you think anything's going to come of that in the end?' Dolly asked.

And Charlotte remembered that Ted was yet another of her children she worried about – footloose, seemingly the eternal rolling stone, drifting from one job to another, one place to another.

'There's nothing I would like better than to see our Ted settle down,' she said thoughtfully, 'but I might as well tell the truth, Dolly – I hope it won't be with Rosa.'

*

Rosa was looking forward to the weekend. Since Christmas, when she and Ted had reached an understanding of sorts, their relationship had changed subtly. To the outside world their lives were continuing much as always – Rosa still living and working in the Post Office Stores at Withydown, Ted in Ramsgate for the summer – but they were in regular contact and whenever she could Rosa travelled down to spend time with him. Slowly, oh so slowly, they had become more committed, looking towards a future together, though at present they had no definite plans.

Ted's precarious occupations would not support a wife, that much was certain, but Rosa had begun to feel that one day something would turn up and to be less fearful that he might find someone else.

The day after she visited Greenslade Terrace, her spirits were high. As she worked she pictured him working too on the busy beach, his skin tanned golden brown from constant exposure to sun and salt, his hair bleached even fairer than usual. Her heart turned over with love for him. She imagined the room in his lodgings where they would be together – small, cramped, with a worked sampler over the bed, rag rugs on the floor and faded cretonne curtains at the window that overlooked a row of identical houses in a narrow back street. But the impersonal dinginess of the room meant nothing to her. It was made beautiful because it was where his arms would be around her again, glorified by the aura of romance that surrounded every moment they spent together.

I love him, Rosa thought. I love him and I truly believe now that he loves me. He is a rover, but in his way he really cares. The thought warmed her, lightening the mundane everyday tasks, speeding and yet slowing the moments before she would be with him again until time seemed a stupid, topsy-turvy thing.

She was serving a customer when the cold suddenly hit her and for a moment she stood stock-still, her heart almost stopping as the sharp shaft of unexplained dread ran through her like an electric shock and the chill it left wherever it touched made her tremble.

Ted, she thought. Something's wrong with Ted!

The customer was looking at her curiously and she tried to push the weight of the premonition away from her, but it was useless. Useless too to pretend she was being foolish and over-imaginative. Over the years Rosa had come to know and trust her own intuition; never had it let her down. She remembered now that other time, years ago, when she had known Ted was in danger. He had been in France then and with men falling all around, it had not been so strange to feel suddenly that something was desperately wrong with him. Nevertheless, she had been right; she had realised afterwards that the fear she had experienced then had coincided more or less exactly with the moment when he had fallen. Now this same certainty shook her, dispelling every scrap of happiness and replacing it with foreboding.

But what could she do? It was years now since Rosa had made any attempt to use 'the power' she had once felt was within her. Now, as she sought frantically for some way out of the slough of terror that enveloped her, she remembered it. Had she ever really possessed any power? She didn't know, but in her helplessness she knew she had to try at least.

As the customer left the shop she crossed to the door on urgent, shaking legs and turned the sign to 'closed'. Then she ran up the stairs to her own flat. She had nothing to aid her but her own intuition now; there was no time to go to the woods or the open country as she had once done. With trembling fingers she pulled from the drawer the one thing which made her feel close to Ted – a photograph he had sent her, showing him standing beside a beach hut clad only in a pair of rolled-up trousers. A further rummage produced the nearest thing to her old closeness with nature – a necklace she had once made for herself from empty acorn shells and dried berries. Then she sank to her knees with the photograph on the ground in front of her, the necklace clasped between her hands. When she closed her eyes the strength of her emotion seemed to close in around her, a suffocating blanket which cut off breath, and she summoned within herself every ounce of will... concentrating, concentrating, while the room retreated from her and she became an island, a small powerhouse of indescribable force.

Let Ted be all right. The words came from deep within her, a silent shout that echoed within every vein and pervaded her whole being. *Let Ted be all right.* The world shrank with it, reverberated to it. Nothing else mattered. Nothing else existed.

For long, timeless moments she remained there, no longer even wondering what was wrong, thinking of nothing but the need to find a way of helping, even at this distance; some way of mustering the fates to avert disaster.

How long she remained there, motionless, she never afterwards knew. Only at last, exhausted by the effort, she opened her eyes. The acorns on the necklace had cut deep into her hands, leaving sharp scarlet imprints; she felt numb and weak; her head throbbed and her eyes were heavy.

Had she done any good? She had no idea. The fear was still there, and her own helplessness depressed her.

If the power had ever been there, it had deserted her now. Weak and shaking, Rosa pulled herself to her feet. The shop downstairs had to be attended – she couldn't stay up here. Somehow she had to carry on.

Mustering the last dregs of her will-power, Rosa left the privacy of her room and went back down the stairs.

*

It had been a routine morning for Ted – as routine as life as a bathing-chair attendant ever could be.

The weather was good, warm and clear in spite of a strong breeze coming off the sea, and the beach was packed with holidaymakers – men snoozing in bathing chairs, their heads covered by knotted handkerchiefs; women holding up their skirts around their legs to reveal glimpses of pink bloomer legs, paddling in the breakers at the water's edge; children digging in the sand and filling moats with toy tin buckets of greyish sea water. But there were few swimmers. The red warning flags were out, fluttering at either end of the beach, and the few bathers there were kept cautiously to the shallows. The currents were dangerous here and from time to time there was a fatality, but for the most part holidaymakers respected the sea and its moods.

Towards lunchtime, during a lull, Ted wandered along to the refreshment stall for a cup of tea. Tom Bargett, who shared lodgings with him, worked on the stall and they chatted idly as Ted drank his tea and bit into a warm but tasty pork pie.

'I told you Rosa's coming next weekend?'

'Yes. Nice girl. You're lucky there, Ted.'

'I know. Some day I'm going to marry her.'

'Marry? You? You're mad. Stick with your freedom, lad, and have the best of both worlds.'

'That's all very well, but I can't keep her hanging on for ever.'

'I wouldn't be in too much of a hurry if I were you.' Like Ted, Tom was a free spirit. All the lads who worked on the beach were the same. 'Have some fun first!'

'I've done that, Tom. I've had my fun and sometimes I think it's time I settled down. But it's not that easy. What have I got to get married on?'

'Who wants anything?'

They remained in companionable silence, Ted leaning against the refreshment stall and surveying the beach casually. All these people enjoying themselves. All these people, their hopes and dreams shelved temporarily while they took a holiday, or even just a day away from reality.

Suddenly he stiffened, seeing that a small crowd had collected at the water's edge, looking out to sea. A child's scream carried on the stiff breeze above the crying of the gulls. The atmosphere, relaxed and normal a moment ago, had changed dramatically now and there was a chill in the warm sun. Something was happening – something was very wrong . . .

'Swimmer in trouble!' The shout was relayed up the beach, passed like an eddying ripple, charged with the high tension generated by the realisation of imminent tragedy.

The two men at the refreshment stall strained their eyes out to sea.

'Bloody fool! Surely he must have seen the flags flying!'

'Yes – there's always one though that thinks he knows better.'

'Look – there goes Seb!'

Seb Murphy, the lifeguard, was another friend of Ted's and during the long summer evenings they often shared a pint in a sea-front bar. Big, brawny, a fine swimmer, he attracted a great deal of attention on the beach, drawing the girls like wasps to a jam-jar. Now he ran on pumping, athletic legs, darted through the watching crowd and splashed into the breakers. As Ted and Tom watched, the water swallowed him so that they could see nothing but his head and his arms, executing a perfect crawl stroke as he made for the distant and wildly-waving figure of the bather in trouble.

'Seb'll get him,' Tom said. 'Stupid idiot – wonder who it is? Some holidaymaker, I suppose.'

The scene was set like a tableau: the sea, deceptively calm, hiding its dangerous swirls and eddies but strong enough to pull the best of swimmers out and down; the two heads bobbing; the widening fringe of watchers at the water's edge. Seb was nearer now and Ted thought: Tom's right. Seb will get him this time. But still he did not relax. His own muscles were taut and flooded with adrenalin, part of his mind alert and waiting, his eyes strained out to sea. The currents were so treacherous, so unreadable. Until Seb had the swimmer safely on the beach, nothing was certain.

A few more yards and suddenly they saw the even stoke falter.

'He's in trouble!' Tom shouted.

It was as if the lifeguard had suddenly stopped swimming. His arms still moved, but he was no longer making ground towards the flailing figure.

'Christ, Tom, he needs help!' As Ted spoke he was peeling off his shirt and Tom too sprang into action, vaulting the tea-stall and yanking at the buttons of his own shirt.

'Come on!'

There was no time to worry about the dangers, no time to be afraid of the deadly, treacherous currents. It never occurred to Ted that he too might be swallowed up by the dark water – his own safety was as unimportant a part of his reckoning as it had been when he had crawled on to the battlefield in France in a vain attempt to rescue a young fallen soldier. If he had thought at all he would probably have retained faith in his own immortality – others die, I go on for ever. But there was no time for thinking beyond the certain knowledge that two men were in peril in the foaming water and he himself was a strong and confident swimmer. Learned first in the river at home as a boy, the art had been practised and perfected through the years of working at coastal resorts, and as he and Tom reached the water's edge neck and neck and the breakers splashed cold as ice on his sunwarmed legs, he did not flinch.

A few steps and the water was waist-deep. Ted dived into a wave and began swimming strongly. At first it was easy – the ebb tide carried him away from the shore and as he breasted each wave, he could see the bobbing heads nearer than before. Seb was now close to the swimmer in trouble and, thinking he might yet reach him, almost turned back. But some perverse instinct kept him going and as he rode the next wave he was astonished to see Seb further away again – flailing, struggling.

The edge of the current, Ted thought; there must be an undertow there. Useless to try making straight for the drowning boy; he would only hit the undertow as both the others had done. He changed direction, swimming parallel with the shore. Then as he turned out to sea once more a large wave caught him, buffeting him backwards and filling his mouth and nose with stinging salt water. Coughing and gasping, he fought to right himself and trod water for a moment. A second wave caught him still breathless, but he managed to avoid another mouthful and his next view of the other swimmers showed him Seb farther than ever from the now clearly panicking boy.

He's going to drown, Ted thought. Unless I can get to him quickly, it will be too late. He struck out seawards again, his thoughts now all channelled, tunnel-like, to his single objective. *Get to the boy.* Sure enough his strategy seemed to be working and the tide and his own strong strokes took him closer, almost within reach. The boy had seen him and Ted had a view of his face for the first time – young, thirteen or fourteen perhaps, drenched, terrified, exhausted. Another stroke and Ted too felt the undertow. With all his might he battled against it. Two strokes, three . . . almost within reach.

He opened his mouth to yell to the boy to hold on and the sea-water filled it, making him choke again. His eyes were stinging now as well as his throat, but it was almost as if he was detached from his own body. The channelled mind could think of nothing but the boy. Another stroke, another – he couldn't get closer, for the waves were negating all his efforts. But the boy was trying to reach him now; he struck out with wild kicks and suddenly lunged for Ted, grabbing his shoulders with vice-like hands, struggling in terror and dragging him down. Realisation of the new danger burst on Ted like an exploding shell the moment before the water closed over his head:

Drowning men drown their rescuers.

The clinging arms were everywhere, octopus-like, the boy's strength suddenly enormous. Ted struggled to free himself, aware with that small thinking part of his brain that now he had to fight not only the sea but also the boy. After seemingly endless moments his head broke the surface again and he gasped life-giving air into his bursting lungs; then the boy's grip tightened once more and they were under again. Down, down, then back to the surface, water swallowed with air and coughed out again, hands pushing, grabbing, fighting – and all the while the sea pulling at his legs.

Ted's swimming experience had never included life-saving. Seb would have known how to deal with the boy had he been the one to reach him first. Ted did not. But instinct was strong. It's him or me, Ted thought, and as they both broke surface coughing and spluttering, somehow he managed to free his right arm. Then hastily, before the boy could grab him again, he brought his fist crashing into the lad's screaming, gasping face. Life-saving experience Ted might lack, but in his time he had done plenty of fighting. Briefly, before the sea closed over him again, he saw the boy's expression turn to one of surprise, then he went limp and his deadly grasp around Ted's neck and body relaxed. Ted pushed him away, surfacing and fighting to regain breath. The boy was sinking, washed over by the relentless waves, and all Ted could see was his hair, like brown floating seaweed. As his own panic receded, so determination returned and he grabbed for the boy's hair. Technique was unimportant now; swimming – and holding onto that tuft of stringy wet hair – was all that mattered.

From somewhere Ted found a reserve of strength he had not known he possessed. On to his side he went, grasping the boy's hair with one hand and swimming with the other, kicking strongly with legs kept going only by that miraculous fount of inner strength. The battle now was enormous, the waves seemed intent on taking him further out to sea. But somehow he kept going – kick, pull, hold on, swim. He could see the beach, horrifyingly far away, with the mass of helpless figures at the water's edge. Would it never come closer? Kick, pull, swim! Behind him half-covered by water, the boy was unconscious now. Swim, for Christ's sake, swim – or you'll take in a corpse! Is the coast nearer? How can it be so far away? I shall never make it! Yes, you will. Keep going, Ted. Keep going!

The one thing which never occurred to Ted was to let go of the boy and save himself. It was unthinkable that all this should be for nothing. Exhausted, arms and legs aching with weakness, he fought on. The waves buffeted, lifted and dropped him, and salt in his eyes meant that now he could hardly see and the beach was not only distant but blurred too. The sea seemed to be in him as well as all around him. He was a part of it, yet somehow separate, a small insignificant entity. For the first time he felt awe for the enormity of the ocean, its power and invincibility. But it was a fleeting impression only. His whole being was concentrated on reaching that distant shore and on keeping those aching, shaking limbs pumping.

Slowly, painfully slowly, he pressed forward. For what seemed like a lifetime, he appeared to be making no progress at all. Then, almost unexpectedly, he realised he was closer and new determination lent him fresh strength. The tide was still running strongly, but gradually he was beating it. He forced himself on, trying not to notice that the gap, though narrower, was still daunting. *All that effort and I'm still so far out!* No, don't think of that. Just keep going!

And then, suddenly, his legs dipped and he felt shingle beneath his feet. Strangely, instead of refreshing him, the contact seemed to drain him momentarily. He gasped, taking in another mouthful of sea-water which almost choked him.

There was a mist in front of his eyes now, blotting out the beach, and the sea seemed to be thundering in his ears. Oh God, all this and I'm going to drown! he thought. But there was no more panic, only peace. And in the thundering of the waves he seemed to hear a voice, a woman's voice – crooning, gentle, speaking wordlessly to him, urging him on..With his last remaining strength he responded to it, his limbs moving automatically, his senses dazed by exhaustion. A little further – a little further...

And then, just as he felt he could keep going no longer, there were people in the water around him, hands reaching for him. Briefly he felt the urge to fight them as he had fought with the drowning boy, but he had no energy left. Dimly he was aware that he was still holding on to that handful of hair; hands were prising his fingers loose. There were voices, but he could not make out the words; they were indistinct, coming from a long way off. His feet were on the shingle now, the grit shifting beneath his toes as he stood up. He saw someone lift the boy bodily; he lay limp in the rescuing arms, his head lolling, that life-saving hair flopping wetly across the broad, sunburned forearm.

Somehow Ted kept walking until the water reached only his thighs, then his knees. An unexpected wave hit him from behind, covering his back once more and the resulting undertow shifted the sand from beneath his feet. Suddenly his knees were buckling, the water was rushing up to meet him. His chin went under, grazing the ground, and the sea covered his head. And as the roaring grew loud in his ears once more, Ted lost consciousness.

*

Afterwards, looking back on the scene on the beach which followed the rescue, Ted always saw it as fragmented scenes of a nightmare – some parts standing out in vivid relief, some unreal, as if it had not happened to him at all.

There had been a crowd around him when he regained consciousness, but a silent crowd gaping in awe and half-enjoyed horror. The beach had been gritty and warm beneath his skin, the sun beating down on his body. Yet he had felt cold, chilled to the marrow, teeth chattering when he tried to speak. He remembered thinking how funny it was to feel the heat of the sun and yet not be warmed by it, remembered wondering if his trousers had been ruined by the salt water and, most stupid of all, whether there was a queue for bathing-chairs because he was not there to deal with it. But these were the acceptable reactions busying his mind, keeping it from thoughts too horrific to contemplate.

He was lucky to be alive. Ted knew it the moment he opened his eyes and saw the sky blue above him, and briefly savoured the full thrill of living. He was lucky to be alive – something, or someone had been looking after him.

But others had not been so lucky.

Tom, who ran to the sea with him, as anxious to help as Ted had been, was dead – lost in those same treacherous currents. So too was a holidaymaker, a man whose name Ted never even knew. Seb, the lifeguard, struggled exhausted back to the beach and was to spend the rest of his life beneath a burden of unjustifiable shame because in the event he had been unable to carry out the job for which he had been trained and was paid.

But the boy, a local lad who should have known better than to swim when the red flags were flying, was alive. After a spell in the local hospital he was released, none the worse for his brush with death. Because of his bravado and foolishness, two men were dead and two other lives changed for ever.

For in the aftermath of gratitude and anger, pride and humility, Ted was sure of only one thing: his days of drifting were over. By some miracle his life had been spared and it was time he did something with it.

And the one thing he wanted to do was marry Rosa.

Chapter Twenty

As she so often did, Charlotte heard the news from Peggy, who came bursting in waving the morning's edition of the *Daily Mirror*.

'Lotty – have you seen this? It's your Ted!'

'Our Ted? Whatever are you talking about?'

'Here – look – on the front of this paper!'

'Oh, Peg, it can't be!' Charlotte exclaimed. But she took the paper from Peggy all the same and gasped as she saw the photograph, identical to the one Ted had given Rosa. 'Oh my Lord, it is! Whatever has he been up to?'

'Read it, Lotty!' Peggy was bursting with excitement. 'He's only saved a boy – that's what he's done! And two other men got drowned trying! Oh, I couldn't believe it when I saw it first! I had to get our Colwyn to read it as well, to prove I wasn't dreaming. But your Ted – well, he always was a one to leap in where angels fear to tread, wasn't he?'

'Hush up, Peggy!' said Charlotte. 'I'm trying to read what it says.'

'What be going on out there?' James called from the kitchen.

'It's your Ted! He's a hero, that's what!' Peggy went running in, intent on being the one to spread the news, while Charlotte pored over the *Mirror*.

Like Peggy, she could hardly believe it, even though the photograph was unmistakably Ted, and the report was there in black and white before her eyes, under the banner headline:

SEAFRONT BATHING DRAMA – GALLANT RESCUE BY FORMER COLLIER

'Our Ted!' she whispered. 'Oh, my Lord!' She was shaking all over.

'Are you all right, Lotty?' Peggy asked, coming back into the scullery. 'You've gone as white as a sheet. Come on, let's put the kettle on and have a cup of tea.'

'I shall be fine in a minute, Peg. It's just such a shock! I can't take it in. And two men drowned! That could have been our Ted! Whatever will he do next?'

'But he wasn't drowned, Lotty, so there's no point in thinking about it,' Peggy said sensibly. 'Sit down and I'll put the kettle on.'

Charlotte did as she was told, but she was quite unable to stay still for two minutes. 'Silly boy! Fancy going into the sea with the flags flying! You'd think he'd have had more sense...'

The kettle boiled and Charlotte burned her mouth as she sipped her tea when it was much too hot. But still she couldn't stop shaking.

'What are we going to do about it?' she asked.

'We can't do anything. We shall just have to wait for our Ted to get in touch,' James told her.

'Oh, I wish our Harry was here! He could go up and tell Dolly. And our Amy too!'

'Calm down now, or you'll make yourself bad,' James advised. 'They'll see it in the paper. And if they don't, somebody will tell them soon enough. One thing's for very sure – this is going to cause quite a stir in Hillsbridge!'

'He's right, Lotty,' Peggy agreed.

'If there's one person who ought to know, it's Rosa Clements,' James went on. 'Didn't you say she was going down to see Ted next weekend? She ought to know.'

'Oh, Rosa!' Charlotte snapped. 'Never mind about his brothers and sisters as long as *Rosa* knows!'

James said nothing, withdrawing into himself as he always did if an argument was in the offing.

Charlotte was very blinkered when it came to Rosa, in his opinion, but he had no intention of telling her so. She wouldn't listen to him, so he might just as well save his breath. And as he had said, this news was big enough to travel without any effort on their part. Rosa would get to hear soon enough – if she didn't know already. Sometimes James thought that she knew more than any of them.

Rosa, of course, had seen the report for herself the moment the papers arrived at the Post Office Stores. But the shock she experienced had been quite different from that felt by Charlotte. For though to see Ted's face looking up at her from the front of the *Daily Mirror* had stopped her in her tracks, the surprise was made all the sharper by the realisation that the drama had happened yesterday at just the same time that she had experienced such a chill of fear.

While she had been on her knees praying in the only way she knew for his safety, Ted had been fighting for his life. And her prayer had been answered!

Ted was a hero, of course. He had risked his own life for that of some unknown boy. But it never occurred to Rosa to doubt that she had been instrumental in helping him – she was as certain of it as she had been when other results had followed her childish 'spells' of long ago.

I may not be a witch, but there *is* a power in my veins along with my gypsy blood, thought Rosa. I must never misuse it, or it will desert me. But so long as I treat it with respect, I know it is a force to be reckoned with.

Even living with it as long as she had, this was an awesome thought.

*

If Hillsbridge was buzzing with the news that one of its sons was a hero, it was nothing to the stir that the drama had created in Ramsgate.

There was anger towards the foolish local lad who had been the cause of the whole ghastly business; there was sadness for the two brave men whose lives had been lost; and there was adulation for Ted, who had managed by sheer guts and determination to bring the boy to safety. His name was on every lip and wherever he went, someone wanted to shake him by the hand or slap him on the back. Reporters by the dozen turned up to interview him; photographers posed him again and again in front of the beach huts and beside the bathing chairs; total strangers offered him congratulations and gifts of cigarettes.

To his shame, Ted found that once he had recovered from the first shock of his ordeal and the loss of his mate, he was secretly enjoying all the attention. He had never been shy – how could the leading light of the Hillsbridge Concert Party be shy – but neither was he conceited and the people of Ramsgate warmed to the unassuming, easygoing Somerset man who seemed to them to embody everything a hero should be.

From the day of the rescue onwards, Ted never had to buy himself a pint in a pub; his landlady, though in floods of tears over Tom's tragic death, ensured that only the very best of everything found its way onto his plate; and the Ramsgate Corporation, for whom he worked, made it clear that they appreciated having a man like him in their employ.

Ted found himself recommended for an award from the Carnegie Hero Fund Trust and was glad to hear that the two men who had died were not to be forgotten either. The Carnegie Certificate, impressively framed, would not do them much good, he thought, but the grant of £25 each towards providing headstones for their graves was only right, and when he heard that his own grant would be less than half that sun, he did not feel in the least aggrieved. After all, they had lost their lives. He had lost nothing – unless of course he counted his salt-stained trousers!

But the repercussions of his act of heroism did not end with the adulation and the £10 award, welcome though that was...

It was the day of the inquest, held to establish the cause of death of Tom and the unknown holidaymaker. Ted had dreaded it – there was nothing to be enjoyed in reliving the tragic side of what had happened and the formal recognition of the deaths of two fine men, and for Ted the sombre Coroner's Court evoked too many memories of his own brush with the law at the Assize Court in Bristol.

As he emerged into the bright June sunlight he was feeling sobered, despite the words of praise from the coroner which still rang in his ears; at first when the stranger approached him he hardly noticed, then made to brush him aside.

'I'm sorry – I've got to get back to work.'

'I'll walk along with you then.' The stranger fell into step beside Ted, walking with a noticeable limp. He was a tall, well-made man, his lined face brown as a nut, his bushy-white eyebrows perfectly matching a thatch of snowy hair. His voice was deep, with an unfamiliar accent that struck chords in Ted though he did not recognise it. He had heard that voice before – and recently – though he could not place it.

A moment later the stranger jogged his memory. 'I was there when you brought in the boy. I don't suppose you noticed me?'

'Yes, I did.' That voice had been there on the edge of his consciousness when he had come round to find himself lying on the beach.

'You did a fine job. I would have been in there myself if I were twenty years younger. Not now though... not with my leg.' His tone said that he regretted not taking part in the rescue, but was totally without either bravado or self-pity – simply a statement of fact.

'You are wondering why I wanted to talk to you, I expect?' he went on. 'Well, the fact is that I have a proposition to put to you. From what I gather, you have been a miner, but now you're working here as a chair attendant on a casual basis only.'

'For the summer, yes.'

'Why did you leave mining?'

Ted glanced at him, surprised by the question. 'There

352

didn't seem any future in it; I was a carting boy, and likely to be for the next ten years.'

'A carting boy?'

'Dragging putts of coal from where it's hewed to where it can be taken to the surface. A human donkey in harness, my mother used to call it. Anyway, the war came and I joined the army and never went back. I wouldn't be able to now; there are too many men after too few jobs and the bosses have got it all worked out.'

'So what will you be doing at the end of the season?'

Ted shrugged. 'I don't know. Joining the ranks of the unemployed, I should think.'

'As I anticipated.' The stranger was not looking at Ted, but staring ahead with narrowed gaze, a habit gained from searching wider horizons, more open landscapes. 'Ever thought of going to Australia?'

'*Australia?*' Ted was almost speechless. 'No – why?'

'It's a great country. Mind you, I'm prejudiced – it's my home.'

'You're Australian.' So that was the reason for the unfamiliar accent.

'The name's Stuart Wells. I'm in copper. Have been for most of my life, and I've built up quite a nice little business, if I do say so myself. Anyway, the point is that when I saw how you handled yourself the other day I thought: Stuart, that's just the kind of lad you could use – plenty of guts and determination. Then when I heard you were likely to be out of a job soon, I made up my mind to have a word with you. I didn't know how to get in touch, but I guessed you would be at the inquest. So . . . here I am!'

'You came especially to see me?' Ted asked.

'That's about the size of it. The fact is that I'm offering you a job, if you're interested.'

'What sort of a job?'

'A position at the mine. You would start at the bottom, naturally, but once we see how you shape up, who knows? One thing about Australia is that there are plenty of opportunities for a man to get on if he wants to. Not like it is here. It's a young country, growing, not pulling in its horns for a depression. And copper's big business. I reckon I can guarantee you a good living and maybe more. It's up to you.'

'I don't know what to say.'

'Don't say anything for the moment. Think about it – only don't take too long! I'm only here for a few more days, then I'm in London for a week and after that I sail.' He pulled a card out of his pocket and scribbled on the back of it. 'Here – this is the address where you can reach me. As I say, Australia is a land of opportunity and if you're the man I think you are, you'll be ready to grab it.'

Ted's mind was whirling. Australia! The other side of the world! But he liked the sound of it – the idea of travelling to an unknown country for an unspecified job appealed to his sense of adventure. And he liked the stranger too; there was a directness about him that inspired confidence. Besides, on the whole Ted was a trusting soul; his attitude towards people had always been to think well of them until they did something to make him change his mind, and generally he was not disappointed. It came to him that this was the kind of opportunity which presented itself only rarely – the door that slammed shut if you failed to walk swiftly through it. And hadn't he been wondering what the hell the future held for him and Rosa?

'Supposing I was to take up your offer – would I be able to bring a wife?' he asked.

The stranger looked at him sharply. 'You're married?'

'No, but I want to be. There's a girl I've kept waiting too long.'

'I see. I was expecting you to be able to travel light. Women get homesick and they can be a burden.' He spoke with the air of a man who has long since discarded any such fetters.

'Rosa's no burden,' he said. 'She would go wherever I went.'

'It may be rough to begin with,' warned the Australian. 'Housing, for instance, is very primitive.'

'I don't think she would mind that. She's been raised the hard way, like me.'

'Well, that's up to you. As I say, think it over. Talk about it with your girl – Rosa, you call her? And then let me know.'

'Right,' Ted said. 'I will.'

After they had parted company he looked at the card. The printed side gave the name: 'Stuart Wells. Queensland Copper Inc.', with an address in Brisbane. On the reverse, the man had written the name of a Ramsgate hotel.

What's he doing here anyway? Ted wondered, but it was a fleeting thought only. His mind was too busy turning over

354

the possibilities the suggestion offered. A new life in a new country, thrown at him just like that. It was incredible, and yet...

It could be the answer, Ted thought, excitement beginning deep in the pit of his stomach. He had always liked a challenge – and this was a greater challenge than he had ever faced before, greater even than his battle with the sea. Then he had leapt in without thinking to save the boy. This situation gave him time to consider and the conclusion he reached could alter the whole course of his life – and Rosa's too.

Deep in thought, Ted made his way back to his lodgings. But already he was fairly certain what his decision would be.

*

Two days later Rosa arrived in Ramsgate. She had booked into a sea-front boarding house and Ted, taking time off from his work with the bathing chairs, met her at the station.

'Ted!' She dropped her cases and flew into his arms. 'Ted – oh, it's so good to see you! I've been so worried about you!'

'There's no need, I'm all right.'

'Yes, thank goodness! But you might not have been. Oh, when I think about it...'

'Don't! Listen, I've got so much to tell you.'

'Yes, I want to hear all about it.'

'Not about the drowning. Something else. But not here...' He took her case.

'What, then?'

'About us.'

'What *about* us?'

'Don't be so impatient; it doesn't suit you.'

'How can you say don't be impatient? Tell me, Ted, please!'

'All right. How do you fancy going to Australia?'

'*Australia!* You're joking!'

'No, I'm not. I've had the offer of a job in Australia. We could go if you like.'

'Australia!' She felt as if someone had knocked all the wind out of her. 'It's crazy! How would you get the offer of a job in Australia?'

'It's a long story. I told you it ought to wait until we were somewhere quiet.'

'But you must go on now! You can't tell me this much and then just stop!'

'All right. We'll get a cup of tea.'

They turned into a café Ted knew and when they were sitting either side of a corner table, he lit a Woodbine.

'This is the gist of it, then. I met a bloke – an Australian himself. He waylaid me after the inquest they held on Tom and the other chap who got drowned; it seems he was there when I brought in the boy. Well, the upshot is that he offered me a job.'

'In Australia?'

'He's in copper, in quite a big way by the sound of it. They mine it out there like we mine coal here, I suppose.'

'And what would you be doing?'

'He didn't really make that clear, but he did say I would be able to work my way up.'

'In his company? In Australia?'

'Yes.'

'Ted,' Rosa looked at him narrowly, 'has it occurred to you this may all be some kind of nasty joke?'

Ted drew smoke, his face suddenly hurt.

'Oh, I don't think so. Who would do a thing like that?'

'Plenty of people.' Suddenly she felt years older than him; how could he be so naive? 'Some folk delight in doing wicked things.'

'Oh, not him,' Ted said confidently. 'He was genuine, I'd bet my life on it.'

'Well, it sounds pretty funny to me.'

He drew on his cigarette, crestfallen. But after a moment, his optimism began to return.

'Well, so what? What if it is all a joke? Australia's real enough. And it's true what he said – I've heard it before. It's a young country with opportunities for anyone willing to work hard and not afraid of taking a risk. And now I come to think of it, I'm pretty sure I read somewhere that they arrange assisted passages for immigrants – pay for us to go, you know? So even if this job does turn out to be a dud, what's to stop us emigrating anyway?'

'Ted!'

'No, listen, Rosa, I'm serious. I don't know why I never thought of it before. There are no jobs here. I doubt if I could get back down the pit even, and I don't want to do that in any case. So how the heck can I ever expect to be able to make

356

enough to keep a wife and family? But Australia... well, we could give it a try, couldn't we? Things couldn't be worse than they are here and might be a lot better!'

Rosa sipped her tea in silence. Another girl might have pointed out that at least here, in England, they had the family to fall back on if things became really rough, whereas in a strange country they could be penniless and homeless, amongst strangers. But Rosa had never been one to regard her family as a haven. Her mother had been too pathetic to lean on, her 'father' – resenting her despite trying not to do so – had been no steady rock in time of trouble. Like Ted, Rosa was a free spirit. But she was also more cautious. She at least had a good job, with a room of her own, the like of which as a scruffy child she would never have imagined could be hers in her wildest dreams. It was a lot to lose. And yet...

This is what I've wanted and waited for, Rosa thought. Ted... offering me a future. So why am I hesitating for even one moment?

She looked up at him over the rim of her cup. 'If we went to Australia, would we be married?' she asked directly.

A surprised expression crossed Ted's face. 'Well, of course!'

'You didn't say so.'

'I took it as read.'

Happiness bubbled in her, but suddenly she couldn't resist the urge to tease him. 'Suppose I didn't want to get married?'

'You mean...' He looked bewildered and alarmed. 'But I thought...'

Rosa laughed. She couldn't keep it up – it was no good. 'Idiot! You know very well I want to get married.'

'Oh, that's all right, then.' His face cleared. 'I don't know how we would manage about these assisted passages if we weren't married.'

'But don't you think you should ask me properly?' she pressed him.

'Here?'

'Why not?'

'Somebody might hear.'

'I don't care if the whole world hears.'

'All right. Are you going to marry me, Rosa?'

'Is that it? The best you can do?'

'If you think I'm going down on bended knees here in the Stuffed Canary, you've got another think coming!'

She giggled. 'It's never called that, is it?'

'Stuffed Canary – Singing Canary – Canary Café – what's the difference?'

'Oh well,' she returned to the proposal, 'if "Are you going to marry me, Rosa?" is your final offer, I suppose I shall have to settle for that.'

Across the table her eyes, sloe-dark and sparkling, were laughing into his and it seemed to him suddenly that they held all that was beautiful in life – the river dancing over the stones, the warmth of summer's sun, the crisp cold of a starlit sky above white hoar-frost, the bright darting splendour of a dragonfly, the strength, grace and patience of a hovering hawk. And not only that, his past was there too – and his future. All he had ever been . . . all he would ever be. And he remembered the still, calm voice which had spoken to him over the roar of the waves when he had come close to drowning along with the others in the treacherous currents – it had been Rosa's voice!

He leaned towards her, love melting him, making him forget any embarrassment.

'Will you be my wife, Rosa?' he asked in a low voice.

Her throat thickened and her eyes turned misty.

'Yes, Ted. There's nothing I should like better,' she replied huskily.

Across the table-top their fingers met and touched, then twined. And the moment of shared happiness obliterated past hurts and built a shining bridge towards an unknown but promising future.

*

Rosa had been wrong to doubt the integrity of Mr Stuart Wells. The decision made, Ted contacted him at the address he had given and was not disappointed. After a long talk details were finalised, and Ted left bearing a letter formally offering him employment with the Queensland Copper Company, together with a sheaf of printed advice on how to apply for an assisted passage for himself and Rosa, plus the papers which would authorise their emigration to Australia.

When she heard the news, Charlotte was shocked beyond belief.

'Australia!' she repeated over and over again. 'And I

thought our Jack was far enough away, down in Minehead.
But Australia!'

'P'raps they won't go. There's time enough for them to
change their minds,' James said.

But once the wheels had been set in motion, it seemed
nothing would stop them. The passage came through,
arranged for the end of August, and before she knew it
Charlotte found herself having to help organise the
wedding.

'I don't know why they had to leave it until the last
minute,' she grumbled, but all the same she was flattered that
her house and not that of the Clements had been chosen as
the base for keeping up the celebrations.

'I know things are better next door since Walter married
Molly, but she's not had our practice with "putting on a
do",' she confided to Peggy, who had helped her with
organising everything from christenings and funerals to big
street parties in celebration of coronations and jubilees.

'Don't you worry, Lotty, we'll put on a spread that will be
remembered for a long time,' Peggy assured her. 'How many
did you say are coming?'

'Getting on for forty, all told,' Charlotte said. 'How shall I
ever manage to get them all in?'

'Well, at least it's summer. Pray for a fine day and then
they can all spill outside. Unless you were to hire the Miners'
Welfare Hall of course.'

'I'd rather have them at home,' Charlotte declared.
However, thinking about it afterwards, she decided it might
be best to enquire about hiring the hall. If it was a wet day
things would be very cramped indeed in the small house.

Eventually the hall was decided upon. 'I do want to give
them a proper send-off,' Charlotte said. 'If we had the hall,
perhaps we could have a band and a bit of a dance round
afterwards.'

The arrangements had all been made when Ted dropped
his bombshell.

He had come home for the presentation of his Carnegie
Hero Fund Trust certificate and the £10 cheque. There had
been a grand 'do' in the Victoria Hall attended by the press,
and so many Hillsbridge people that they could not all get
inside but had to spill out on to the landing and down the
stairs, and Charlotte had been riding high on a wave of pride.

But at home once more, her delight was soon forgotten when Ted told her his news – the sailing date had been brought forward and he and Rosa would have to leave almost immediately after they were married, on their wedding day in fact.

'Oh my Lord, whatever shall we do?' Charlotte asked in panic.

'We shall all be there to see them off, that's one thing,' James consoled.

'I know that, but I don't like it!' Charlotte was close to tears. 'Just imagine – they're going all that way and we shall have to say goodbye to them in front of everybody else!'

She didn't add what was on her mind – that it might be the last time they ever saw Ted. But knowing her as he did, James read her thoughts.

'Don't look at it like that, Lotty,' he said gently. 'He went off once before, didn't he, to France? And he came back then.'

Charlotte turned away, busying herself with packing the breakfast dishes together. *We were younger then,* she wanted to say. *We had our health and strength. Now, at our time of life, you can never be sure. Ted might come back, but it could be too late for us.* But she didn't say it. There was no point in dwelling on it. And of the present there was so much to do that she was able to forget herself in preparations.

The wedding day dawned grey and overcast, with a slight drizzle falling.

'I just hope it clears,' Charlotte said. 'I don't know what Ted will do if it's raining when it's time for him to go. We can't have him and Harry turning up looking like drowned rats!'

Though cars had been ordered for the rest of the family, Ted had insisted that to save money he and Harry – who was to be his best man – could walk down the hill to chapel.

'You know what they say – rain before seven, shine by eleven,' James protested calmly.

'You'd better be right or we shall have to get Cliff Button to come up for him after all!' Charlotte said.

But there was no need for that. By 10 o'clock the sky had begun to clear and by the time Ted and Harry had to leave there was 'enough blue to make a pair of sailor's trousers' as Charlotte put it.

She gave them both 'the once over', approving their smart suits and the carnations tucked neatly into their buttonholes, trying not to think about the suitcases packed ready for departure and stacked in the bedroom upstairs. But as she watched the boys walk away along the Rank, her throat thickened.

Ted was not at home a great deal, but in the past she had always known he would be back again, cheering any occasion with his banter and his nonsense. Now she found herself wondering whether she would ever stand at the door and watch him walk along the Rank again, and briefly she seemed to see all the milestones of his life condensed into one moving kaleidoscope: Ted, four years old and going to school for the first time, looking smart in spite of the hand-me-down trousers and the no-nonsense boots; Ted coming in from play, socks falling down, shirt hanging out, covered more often than not in mud and dust; Ted, leaving for his first day's work at the pit, proudly carrying his bait in a spotted handkerchief and later, when he went underground, the tallow candle to put in his helmet too. She pictured him more grown-up, leaving to take part in a concert party, looking dashing in his Sunday suit and later, in his soldier's uniform, going off to France. All leave takings, all steps further and further away from her and the home where he had been born and raised – culminating in today, his wedding day when she felt he was finally cutting all ties. She stood for a moment with her heart in her mouth, then from the house she heard James call to her and she thrust the memories aside and went to help him get ready, worrying a little as to how he was going to cope with the physical strain of getting to chapel and on to the Miners' Welfare Hall and back again.

It would be the first time since her husband's illness that he had left the house and although they had the car booked, she knew the effort was sure to 'do him up'. But James had insisted that he could not miss his own son's wedding and she had known that to say too much about her own misgivings would be both pointless and cruel.

In the event, when the car arrived she and Cliff between them were able to get James outside and into the back seat without too much trouble. James had really nerved himself up for the occasion, it seemed, and though she could hear his chest rattling noisily as he sank back against the dark red leather, and his eyes looked a little far away, he was managing to smile. As the car drew away Charlotte looked back at the Clements' house. The door was open and there were obviously a host of comings and goings, but of Rosa there was no sign.

And that was as it should be, thought Charlotte. It was not right for the bridegroom or his family to see the bride before the wedding.

Outside the chapel quite a crowd had congregated, jockeying for vantage positions along the pavement. Charlotte recognised most of those waiting and wondered briefly what they were thinking. As yet, she had not completely reconciled herself to the match. Then, as she and Cliff helped James slowly into chapel, she was amazed to see how full it was. Ted had always been popular, of course, and his recent act of heroism had brought him to fresh prominence. Charlotte saw a great many people whom she would not have expected sitting in the back pews, and exchanged nods and smiles with them.

At the front Ted was sitting with Harry; he turned and grinned at his mother and father. Not in the least self-conscious, Charlotte thought, contrasting him with the nervous bridegrooms both Jim and Jack had made. Behind him the rest of the family were gathered, all dressed in their best – Jim, Sarah and the children; Victor attempting to keep the boys quiet and making far more noise than both of them put together, and Dolly nursing the baby who, as usual, was not making a sound. Behind them sat Jack and Stella, effortlessly smart, and Amy with Huw and the girls. Looking at them, Charlotte felt a thrill of pride. There were so few girls in the family, but Barbara and Maureen more than made up for that. Amy had them both dressed alike in pretty powder blue, and not for the first time Charlotte thought what a pity it was that they couldn't have been bridesmaids. But it was not to be that kind of wedding; there had been neither the time nor the money for frills and furbelows and Rosa, setting aside her childhood dreams of white silk and orange blossom, had decided the most sensible thing was to be married in a costume in which she could also travel.

Knowing her, though, she would look good whatever she wore, Charlotte thought with another slight touch of rancour. And a few minutes later she was proved right as the organ began the strains of 'Here Comes the Bride' and every head turned to see Rosa come through the doors on her father's arm. A costume she might be wearing, but she looked stunning none the less, the tailored suit of steel-grey serge set off by a softly flounced blouse in fuschia pink. Her shoes, too, were pink, and she carried a small spray of matching roses. Charlotte glanced from her to Ted and when she saw the look on his face as he watched Rosa coming towards him, any doubts she might have had about the wisdom of the match melted away.

I believe he has got over Becky Church at last, Charlotte thought, relieved. That look was for Rosa alone – a look of love, admiration and something which might almost have been humility. Rosa might not have been Charlotte's choice for her son, but if she could make him happy . . . well, that was really the only thing that mattered.

The service seemed to pass in a flash, the crowded chapel swelling the singing for the hymns yet maintaining a hush for the making of the time-honoured vows. Then almost before she knew it, Ted and Rosa had made their way back down the aisle and she was left – with the help of Jim and Jack – to get James outside and into a car that would take them on to the Miners' Welfare Hall.

'Nice service, wasn't it, Lotty?' he wheezed as they drove through Hillsbridge, but she was a little disconcerted to realise he was taking little or no interest in his surroundings. After not having been out of the house for so long, she had thought he would be eager to look at everything and everyone, but he did not seem at all interested.

The Miners' Welfare Hall had been organised for a sit-down spread, long trestle tables covered with snowy-white cloths and set with plates of ham salad and dishes of pickles. Peggy was there to make certain everything was in order and Charlotte felt satisfaction as she saw the guests tucking in. But she had difficulty in eating a thing herself; food seemed to stick in her throat, even though she had had little breakfast. She was full of nerves and emotion, she thought. James too ate sparingly, but then he always did. The meal finished, there were the usual speeches with anecdotes to make everyone laugh, but Charlotte was sickeningly aware that the moment of departure was approaching rapidly.

'They'll be going soon,' she murmured to James. 'Everything was ready for them at home, wasn't it?'

'Stop worrying, Lotty,' James replied. He was beginning to look tired and Charlotte wondered if it might be a good idea for him to go in the same car as Ted and Rosa. It had been arranged that Cliff should take them home to collect their cases and then go on to the railway station, and some of the younger guests had already set out to walk down to give them a send-off. But it was too far back into the centre of Hillsbridge for the majority of the guests to do so and Charlotte had decided she would have to stay at the reception and act as hostess. James could go home, as far as it went, but it didn't seem right for him to depart in the same car as the bride and groom and when Charlotte put it to him, he insisted that he was all right where he was for the time being.

'Car's here!' The murmur went round the hall and Charlotte felt her throat close with nerves. This was it, then. They were going! Rosa and Ted had been making a round of the hall, having a word with every one of the guests and saying their good-byes... now they turned and came towards Charlotte and James.

'I suppose it's so long then, Mam,' Ted said.

'Yes, I suppose it is, Ted.' Her voice gave away nothing of the turmoil within her. 'Now you will let us know how you are, won't you, as soon as you can?'

'We will, Mrs Hall,' Rosa said.

'And take care, both of you.'

'You too. Mam, Dad, thanks for everything...' There was an awkward pause with everything and yet nothing to say.

Charlotte stood up shakily. 'I just wish you weren't going so far away...' She checked herself. 'Oh, come here, both of you!'

She moved towards them and they were all in each other's arms, hugging and clinging.

I can't let him go! Charlotte thought in panic. I'm going to hang on to him and make a fool of myself and he will never forgive me...

Gathering herself together, she gave them a little push.

'Get on with you now! You don't want to miss your train...'

'No, we'd better go.' They bent over to hug James too and kiss him on his smooth pink forehead. 'We'll come back to see you as soon as we can save the fare. Or maybe you can come out to see us!'

'Oh! That's very likely, I must say!' Charlotte laughed shakily, tears very close. 'Go on, I'm coming to see you off, but your Dad will have to stay here.'

They kissed him again and the faraway look in James'

blue eyes was very intense. Ted's eyes, too, were suspiciously bright, but Rosa's only sparkled. She was excited, happy to be Ted's wife at last and looking forward to her great adventure. She was leaving behind nothing that she cared about, she was taking it all with her.

As they went towards the door, all the remaining guests clustered after them. Charlotte stayed very close to them, moving in a dream. Outside the car was waiting, Cliff Button standing ready to open the door.

'Goodbye – good luck – write, won't you?'

'Ted? Write? He doesn't know how!'

'Good luck, both of you. Make your fortune and come back filthy rich!'

'Give our love to the kangaroos...'

'Goodbye!'

More hugs, more kisses, then they were in the car. The engine purred into life and through the open window Ted caught his mother's hand.

'Take care, Mam. Look after Dad.'

'Haven't I always?' She was choking on the words now. Oh, to be able to pull him out of the car, to hold him in her arms and never let him go! Ted, Ted, what will I do without your nonsense to worry about? What will I do, knowing you're too far away to come if I need you? I still have the others, but it doesn't make up for you going. Nothing could make up for that...

The car had begun to move and his fingers slipped over her hand. She stood immobile, her hand still outstretched but holding only air. Through the mist of tears she saw them waving out of the back window, but their faces were indistinct. And then the car had swept away around the corner and they were gone.

Around her she heard the buzz of excitement and emotion, but she seemed separate from it, isolated suddenly in a lonely world of her own. The emptiness inside her was a physical pain. They had gone! She had known for weeks now that they were going, yet somehow she had not believed it. Now it was a reality, inescapable, no longer an unwelcome phantom which she could push to the back of her mind. They had gone and she might never see them again. Australia was on the other side of the world.

'Mam!' She was aware of an arm around her waist and turned to see Jack. 'Mam – I'm taking a car load down to the station to see them off. Do you want to come?'

She thought for a moment. He hadn't left Hillsbridge yet ... she could still see him again ...

'What about it, Mam? Dad will be all right here, won't he?'

'No,' Charlotte said, making up her mind. She had said goodbye and she couldn't face them again. Watching the car go had been bad enough – seeing them off on the train would be unbearable. She took a handkerchief out of her bag – one of James's big white ones – and blew her nose. 'No – you go, Jack, and take Amy and Dolly. I'm going back to sit down with your Dad.'

'Sure, Mam?'

'Sure.'

'Come on, then.' His arm was still around her, urging her back inside. James was sitting where she had left him, still looking far away.

'That's it then, Mother.'

'Yes, that's it,' she said, amazed to hear her own matter-of-fact tone.

'Who would have thought it?' James mused. 'Our Ted – going to Australia?'

And she thought: Yes, who would have thought it? When we began, just the two of us, I never guessed what life would hold. It's nothing but a series of farewells.

The band had begun to play, guests were dancing. And the emptiness inside her was echoed by the jaunty yet haunting tune which somehow seemed to sum up everything about Ted:

> Heart of my heart, I love that melody.
> Heart of my heart brings back a memory,
> When we were kids on the corner of the street.
> We were rough and ready guys,
> But oh, how we could harmonise.
> Heart of my heart meant friends were dearer then.
> Too bad we had to part.
> I know a tear would glisten if once more I could listen
> To that gang that sang Heart of my Heart.

Chapter Twenty-One

It was October and Hillsbridge was buzzing with the news. Old Dr Vezey had retired, leaving a vacancy in the practice which Oliver Scott was returning to the town to fill. As a young doctor he had been extremely popular and had married Grace O'Halloran, daughter of 'Big Hal', general manager of the Hillsbridge Collieries, and sister of Jack's wife, Stella. Now, it seemed, they were anxious to return to the area.

'I heard they've been edging for the chance for some time,' Peggy told Charlotte.

Charlotte had good cause to remember Oliver Scott with gratitude. He had been marvellous when Amy had had her terrible accident and fallen into the tub of scalding water; at first she had had her doubts as to whether he was old enough and experienced enough to cope, but when she had seen the way he gave Amy the will to survive she had formed a deep-founded respect for him. 'If it hadn't been for him, I don't know if our Amy would have pulled through,' she had often said, and there was more than a little truth in it. Quite apart from the treatment any doctor would have meted out, Oliver Scott had somehow given Amy the will to survive and for that Charlotte never ceased to be thankful.

She told Amy the news when she came to collect the girls, adding all the embellishments which Peggy had imparted.

'They're buying one of the big houses up by Captain Fish's,' she said, 'I wondered wherever they got the money from – they say doctors don't earn that much, though of course it's a darned sight more than you or I will ever have in our pockets. But I suppose Hal must have left them all right.'

Big Hal had died the previous year, just six months after his wife, and Hillsbridge had commented on how sad it was

367

that they had enjoyed so few years of retirement – but then, how many people did enjoy many?

'I shall be very glad to see him back anyway, Charlotte said now. 'If anybody can get to the bottom of what's wrong with our Noël, Dr Scott can.'

She was still very worried about Noël, who seemed to be so far behind other babies of his age.

But Amy had something other than the return of Dr Scott on her mind, welcome though that would be.

'I've been thinking, Mam, about our Barbara and Maureen,' she said, setting down her empty teacup. 'I've been worrying for some time that they're getting too much for you and I thought perhaps I ought to try to make other arrangements.'

'What do you mean – other arrangements?' Charlotte asked sharply.

'Someone to look after them – well, someone to look after Maureen, anyway. Babs will be starting school after Christmas.'

'Yes, and if she comes here to the Board School she can come down after and have her tea with Maureen while she's waiting for you to collect her, just the same as she does now,' Charlotte pointed out.

'I'd rather like her to go to the school just up the road from our house,' Amy said. 'And I think I could afford now to pay someone to mind Maureen. Things have been looking up just lately.'

It was true – Roberts Haulage was at last beginning to acquire a reputation as a fast, reliable operation and both lorries were now fully occupied most of the time. On occasions there was more work than Amy could handle. Only the previous week the quarry company had asked if it would be possible to take on extra deliveries and Amy had been very grieved to have to refuse. She had spent a sleepless night wondering if she could afford the payments on another lorry, pored for hours over schedules and considered sounding out Herbie with regard to the possibility of taking Cliff back on the payroll permanently. But from Herbie's progress reports it sounded as though Cliff was doing quite nicely with his taxi service in Bath, and in any case to take on another driver just now would be like putting the cart before the horse. It was best at the moment to squeeze the best possible use out of what she had, one way or another.

But the more complicated the rotas became, the longer the hours Amy had to work in the office. Feeling it would be well worth the expense, she had a telephone installed and that saved her quite a lot of time, but nevertheless her concern that she was taking her mother's help for granted had grown day by day. Enquiries had revealed that Ruby Clarke would be willing to look after the girls for a reasonable consideration and the scheme had the added attraction that, after a hard day's work, Amy would be able to return straight home instead of making the long walk to Greenslade Terrace and back again. She had thought Charlotte would be pleased at the prospect of having her days to herself again, but now, seeing the hurt expression on her mother's face, Amy realised she had been wrong.

'Leave them with someone else?' Charlotte said, sounding shocked. 'I don't like the idea of that; they're settled into their routine here.'

'I know that, Mam, but I also know what a handful they can be,' Amy argued. 'You and Dad aren't getting any younger and I don't want you making yourself ill on my account.'

'We're all right, we enjoy having them,' Charlotte said stoutly. 'It's the children you've got to think about, and they're better off with their own family.'

Amy sighed. Charlotte was not making this easy for her.

'I know, Mam, and I'm really grateful for all you've done. But I don't want to go on putting on you. Ruby's very good with them, anyway, and she's quite happy to have them through the week.'

'You've already asked her then?' Charlotte said, affronted.

'Well, yes, I have. And she can take them starting on Monday.'

'In that case there's no more to be said.' But Charlotte's look warned Amy that a great deal more *would* be said, both now and in the future. Charlotte was not one to let things go so easily – but then neither was Amy. When it came to making up their mind and sticking to it, mother and daughter were as stubborn as one another.

The following week Amy set the new routine in motion and at once discovered it was even more of a boon than she had anticipated. Not only did she have a longer working day, but she felt more businesslike somehow. The inevitable chats with Charlotte when she delivered and collected the children had broken any train of thought she might be pursuing about the business; now her enthusiasm continued in an uninterrupted stream from the time she woke in the morning until she fell asleep at night. She attended to the needs of the children when they were with her, of course, but somehow she was able to keep it all on two levels, without the intrusion of adult conversation and arguments and the insidious serpent, gossip. In fact, there were days when Amy was so engrossed that she wished she could leave the children with Ruby until bedtime – and once or twice she did send home to ask if it was all right to do just that. But she knew Ruby was not keen on having Huw, who had always regarded her with a certain amount of suspicion, and was afterwards overwhelmed with guilt despite the fact that the girls seemed none the worse for their extended stay in Ruby's cheerful and untidy home.

'The thing is that there really is so much to do these days!' Amy confided to Ruby when she collected the girls and Huw after one of her long sessions, but in fact that was only half the truth. It was not only the daily routine which kept her office light burning late – it was all the thinking and planning which was occupying her and taking up every waking second.

Gradually, during the months since she had been in charge, Amy had come to realise that it wasn't enough to fight for survival; she also had to expand. The two things were synonymous really – stand still and you were lost. From the time when she had accepted her first contract this had begun to seep home to her – a lesson constantly held up before her in the shape of Ralph Porter.

As far as Hillsbridge was concerned, he was already more than successful – he was rich and powerful too. But he was not satisfied with what he had achieved and had moved out into deeper water, extending his empire.

And I must do the same, thought Amy.

Sitting in her office, wearing her coat because the guttering oil stove did little to keep out the creeping chill of winter, she drew up a list of ways to expand Roberts Haulage.

A new lorry was the first priority – the only way to take on more work and increase turnover – but that and the two extra men she would need to run it were only the tip of the iceberg. There were other things she needed not only to make the business efficient but also to give the right impression to those likely to hire the service she could offer.

Even with the telephone she had put in, the facilities at the yard were very basic. A rest room was needed to accommodate the men, with toilet facilities and a kettle so that they could brew themselves a cup of tea without invading her office. That would become even more important as the number of employees increased. Extra storage space would be virtually a necessity – the present ramshackle store was already overflowing with spare parts, ropes, chains and all the other paraphernalia of haulage. And a petrol pump and tank on the premises would mean a good deal of time saved each day and simpler accounting too – one bill to pay, one log to keep and it would all be up together.

And there is something else I could do with, thought Amy. Transport of my own. A car!

As always, the idea shocked as well as thrilled her. It seemed in some ways a terrible self-indulgence. Yet at the same time, common sense told her it was becoming almost as inevitable as the installation of the telephone had been. She had to be mobile, she could not spare the time for walking to see far-flung contracts. Now that she no longer had to make the long daily trek to and from Greenslade Terrace she found herself begrudging even the time it took to walk from home to the yard and back again. A car would save her that...

And more... It would be exactly the advertisement she needed to tell the world that Roberts Haulage was alive and thriving. There were still so few cars in Hillsbridge that they were the ultimate status symbol even for a man – and she was a woman! Amy couldn't think of a single woman she knew who owned a motor car.

Hunching her coat more snugly around her, she stared into space and pictured it. It need not be a big car like Cliff Button's – it would only have to carry her and the children. It need not be a spectacular one like Ralph Porter's – a nice little Model T Ford or an Austin would more than fill the bill. At the thought, Amy tingled with anticipation. She had always wanted to be able to drive and the episode when she had taken out the lorry had done nothing to deter her. Oh, the fun of being able to control a fast-moving vehicle – the heady freedom of sailing past cyclists and pedestrians with a cheery wave! And seeing their faces pea-green with envy, too!

But where was the money coming from for all these

ventures? Even based on her own rough calculations a good deal would be needed – far more than she had seen come back in profits over the last year.

Well, there was only one thing for it. If she didn't have sufficient money then she would have to borrow it. This was another thought to bring her heart lurching into her mouth, for Amy had always been brought up to live within her means. In a family like hers, if there was not enough ready money to stump up for something, then you went without. Mam had never been one to buy from the tally-man or have groceries 'on the slate'. 'Pay your way' had been her byword and, drilled into Amy as the maxim had been, it had become her way of life too. Now the prospect of owing more money than Dad would have earned in a whole year during his working life made her feel physically sick, yet at the same time she was intoxicated by her own daring.

It's the only way, Amy thought. If I am ever to make anything of this business I must start to think big – and have confidence in what I'm trying to do.

Her mind made up, she reached for the telephone. Not only did she need confidence in herself – she needed to impress others with the viability of Roberts Haulage – and the first person to convince was the bank manager.

Amy had met him only once – a big, bluff man with a face coloured purplish by too much business concluded over lunchtime tipples – and she stood as much in awe of him as she did of the rest of the professional hierarchy of Hillsbridge. But she had not the slightest intention of letting him know that.

I used to be nervous of Arthur Clarence, Amy told herself. But he's only a man and so is the bank manager. Just remember that!

A few minutes later, with an appointment fixed for the following afternoon, Amy continued to remind herself of the fact, but when next day she marched in through the impressive bank door, it took all her willpower to buoy herself up for the interview ahead.

In the event she need not have worried. The bank manager greeted her genially, listened to what she had to say and spent what seemed like a lifetime examining the accounts she had brought with her. Then he sat back, looking at her through his rimless glasses with an expression of apparent approval.

'Well, Mrs Roberts, you will be pleased to know that I

believe I can accede to your request.'

Amy tried to hide the rush of surprise and relief she was experiencing. 'You mean you'll lend me the money?'

'The *bank* will lend you the money,' he corrected primly. 'I believe that what you are proposing is very viable. There are men, and plenty of them, who would feel it unwise to finance a venture by a woman. But I am not one of them. In my experience, women have just as good a head for accounts as men – and why not? After all, in most households it is the woman who holds the purse-strings. And you have already proved yourself more than capable of running the firm. I must confess that I did have some initial misgivings on that score, but to keep the business together as you have done is testimony enough. As for the nature of your undertaking, transport is a thing of the future. Before we can look around the horse will be disappearing altogether and there will be lorries everywhere – a great pity, some would say, but that's progress for you. We can no more hold back the clock in that sphere than we could cling on to the spinning jenny.'

'That's more or less what Llew used to say,' Amy said. 'He even said he could foresee the day when road transport would take some of the business away from the railways. Lorries can go where trains cannot, after all.'

'He may well have been right,' the bank manager agreed. 'Now, to details...'

An hour later Amy was back in her office flushed and excited by success. The money she needed was available – and it had all been easier than she had dared hope. But that was only the first step towards the expansion of the business. Now it was up to her to capitalise on it.

Suppose I can't do it! she thought, a moment's fearful doubt assailing her. Suppose I can't keep up the payments on the loan...

This was a thought on which she could not afford to dwell for long. There was so much to be done ... so many decisions to take, so much to organise and plan.

One day Roberts Haulage will be as well-known a name in transport as Ralph Porter's is in timber, she told herself.

It was a goal worth aiming for.

*

During the next few months Amy worked as she had never

worked before. Christmas and New Year came and went – the first white Christmas in the district for twenty-one years, the old folk said – and though she wrapped presents and filled stockings as she always had, it was receipt records, delivery tickets and schedules that occupied her mind, together with the problems of frozen engines and snow-blocked roads! By spring Roberts Haulage was beginning to look like a flourishing concern. Two more men had been taken on – one already an experienced driver, the other a young man keen to learn while working as a mate – a petrol pump had been installed in the yard and work had begun on a new stone store. With a rest room for her men in mind, Amy had acquired an old railway carriage at a very fair price and that was now installed alongside her own office.

Then, when the weather turned for the better, with clear blue skies taking the place of heavy gunmetal grey, and the buds began to burst on the trees around the perimeter of the yard, Amy took delivery of her new motor car – a neat Model T Ford which sparkled like a black diamond in the bright April sunshine.

'I want you to give me some lessons, Herbie,' she told her foreman with all the authority that was now second nature to her. 'Just one or two – enough for me to know what I'm doing.' And not have a repeat of the fiasco when first I drove the lorry, she added silently to herself.

'I should think that would be a very good idea,' Herbie said in his slow way. 'If you hadn't asked, I was going to suggest it myself. When do you want to start?'

'Now?' Amy said. She felt like a child at Christmas who could not wait to begin playing with a new toy.

'The lorry's due back any time now for the stone job.'

'So what?' Amy said gaily. 'Surely Ivor can see himself in this once?'

Herbie nodded. 'If you say so. You'm the boss, Mrs Roberts.'

'I do say so! You can start the engine for me this time, Herbie – I know I shall have to get used to doing it myself, but I'm so shaky with excitement I don't think I could turn the handle.'

'Do 'ee really think 'ee ought to drive in a state like that?' Herbie asked doubtfully.

'Oh fiddle, why not? As soon as I start concentrating, my nerves will settle down. You'll see.'

'Well, I hope so. I don't want too many shocks, mind,' Herbie warned her, but there was a philosophical twist to his mouth. If Mrs Roberts wanted to start driving here and now, Mrs Roberts would do it – and it had better be with him rather than without him.

To Herbie's amazement, however, Amy seemed to take to driving the Model T like a duck to water. She started off with a skip and a jump, it was true – 'kangaroo juice', Herbie murmured – and she had a problem or two at the steep hill junction, but her steering though a little wild was acceptable, and in spite of the fact that she approached bends with a speed that made his hair stand on end, Herbie was grudgingly forced to admit that Amy was a very promising pupil.

'I would never have thought a woman could do it,' he commented later to Cliff. 'But there you are, life's full of surprises!'

Amy, had she heard him, would have retorted that it was no surprise at all. There was no real physical effort involved apart from swinging the starting handle, a knack that still eluded her, and she could see no reason why it should be considered a man's prerogative to drive a motor car.

And she did enjoy it so! The same feeling of freedom and excitement which had buoyed her up when riding as a passenger in Ralph Porter's car lifted her again as she settled herself behind the steering wheel, the fact that the Ford was not quite in the same class as the Morgan being more than made up for by the fact that it was *hers*. After a few lessons she airily dismissed Herbie as tutor.

'There's no need for you to waste your valuable time, Herbie,' she told him. 'With so much to be done at the yard, I really can't ask you to come joy-riding with me.'

But the truth was that she wanted to be alone in the car. Herbie's spare, overalled figure seemed to clutter up the passenger seat and she was terrified too that he might leave oily marks on the floor or upholstery. And she felt so very *grand* driving alone, sitting bolt upright so as to reach the pedals, curls blowing in the breeze. When she drove through town, passing people she knew, she longed to wave gaily but was afraid to let go of the steering wheel and lose concentration. There was not much traffic on the roads, but she had no intention of colliding with any of it. Once was more than enough for her and the little bump she had shared with Ralph Porter was nothing compared with what might happen if she frightened one of the big dray-horses that pulled the baize-covered station delivery wagon, or startled the baker's rather frisky pony.

One afternoon when she had been driving for two or three weeks, Amy took her Model T – or Trixie, as she had christened it – into town to do some shopping.

It was a risky move, she knew – she could hardly leave the engine running whilst she was in several different shops – but she had to get used to starting the engine by herself sometime and thought it might as well be now. She drove around the triangle in the centre of Hillsbridge trying to choose the best place to park, and eventually after two full circuits she decided upon one corner of the station yard. She drew up and parked alongside the picket fence where hoardings advertised the merits of Newbery's Furniture and Carpets. Then she climbed out and walked briskly around to the shops she needed to visit – Fords, the drapers in South Hill for some darning wool and elastic; the chemist's for another bottle of cough mixture in an effort to get rid of the cough which had plagued Barbara since the winter; and Reads, the hardware shop, for some screws and plugs which Herbie had asked for so that he could continue improving the new drivers' rest room at the yard.

Amy did not particularly like the hardware shop. It was small and poky, with uninteresting items like washers, nails and tacks all crammed together in heavy wooden drawers. High-stacked, unidentifiable boxes full of equally unidentifiable miscellany lined the walls, and a narrow staircase led up to a store-room which, judging by the regularity with which the assistants disappeared there, contained just as much stock as the shop. How anyone ever found anything was a marvel, Amy decided, buying the screws and leaving as quickly as possible.

One port of call remained – the Co-op Grocery Store. Amy had most of her staple needs delivered, orders being made up from lists on specially printed forms and taken out on a round once a week. Her groceries always arrived on a Monday afternoon and were left in a large cardboard box just inside the coal-house, 'so the cats can't get at it', the Co-op man always said.

But this was Thursday and already the cheese had gone, demolished by a hungry Huw. Amy wanted to replace it and also get some biscuits for the men at the yard to have with their tea. It was coddling them, she supposed, but she firmly believed in the benefits of a contented work force.

In direct contrast to the hardware store, the Co-op Grocery was an impressive shop, double-fronted, with large vaulted windows and doors that opened majestically from the top of a flight of steps. Inside, a wooden counter ran the length of the shop on one side, carrying displays of tinned biscuits and hiding the less attractive commodities – sacks of flour and sugar which were weighed up into blue paper bags, also rice and dried fruit. On the other side another counter, equally long, was topped with a marble slab and sectioned into two – the cheese counter and the bacon counter. From each serving point, overhead cash railways whisked away both money and a little paper 'check' bearing the shopper's membership number so that the purchase could be totted up towards the prized 'divi' which was paid out at the end of each quarter. The cash railway was similar to the one Charlotte had loved – and seen wrecked – when she had worked in the County Stores during the Great War, but with one modification. This railway not only received wooden cups that zinged along the wires on the ground floor; it also had an added refinement in that it could cater, by means of something like a minuscule dumb waiter, for cash spent upstairs in the furniture shop, which also had a small hardware department. 'Perhaps I could have got the screws I wanted there instead of going to Reads,' thought Amy.

She bought the cheese and the biscuits she wanted and paused just inside the doorway beside a display of high-stacked cereal boxes, wanting to check the contents of her purse. The shop was busy with customers coming and going, and a buzz of conversation ran constantly beneath the tinging and clatter of the cash railway. As she sorted her change, sixpences and shillings from threepenny-bits and copper, Amy suddenly became aware of two voices which she could hear above the rest.

'Who does she think she is, I'd like to know?'

'Just what I say! Only went to the Board School like the rest of us, but to see her riding around in that car you'd think she was Lady Muck!'

The speakers were hidden from Amy by the boxes of Quaker Oats and the voices, though local, were unidentifiable. But Amy was suddenly, chillingly aware that *she* was the subject of their conversation.

'Of course, she always did think herself better than anybody else. Dancing along with ribbons in her hair when she was a kid. Remember?'

'And you may depend one or other of that family is always in the news. Her brother thought he was somebody, too, going in for teaching. And after he married Hal's daughter – well, that was it, wasn't it? A sight too big for their boots, all of 'em!'

Amy was trembling now, indignant but shocked. One part of her wanted to march round the stack of Quaker Oats and confront the gossips; another longed only to sneak away unseen. What could she say to them? There was no point in making a scene. They were not spreading lies, just passing opinions. But who were they? She was not even sure she wanted to know. For a moment she stood undecided, wishing the ground would open and swallow her.

'Well, I must get on.'

'Yes – look, you'll miss your turn . . .'

The speakers moved away and without stopping to think, Amy dived out of the shop. Her face was burning. How awful! she thought in confusion. How awful to think that people could say such things about her . . . and about the rest of the family too! Did others think – and say – the same? It was jealousy, of course, sheer jealousy, but . . .

Oh, I could die! Amy sobbed silently. Thank goodness they didn't know I was there! Suppose they saw me afterwards . . . ?

She cast a quick look over her shoulder while still half-running across the gravelled forecourt of the Co-operative Stores. Nobody looking, nobody staring . . . Then some sixth sense screamed a warning at her and she jerked back her head to look where she was going. Three broad steps ran the length of the forecourt down to road level, deep at the valley side, shallower as the hill rose to meet the forecourt. She knew they were there, of course, she just wasn't thinking. Now she attempted desperately to alter her stride, but it was too late. Her speeding feet were running away with her and she teetered on the edge of the top step before lurching forward. The second step she cleared completely, but as she hit the ground her ankle turned and she went sprawling across the pavement, bumping her forehead as she fell on the wheel of a cart drawn up at the kerb.

For just a second she lay there, stunned. Then, into the shocked vacuum – What have I done? What's happened? – came rushing the embarrassment and shame. Oh, they'd see her now, those women who had been talking about her! They'd see her lying here in the gutter! She tried to rise, but as she did so the giddiness began, swirling around her.

'Hey, missus, why don't 'ee look where you be going?' The voice of the haulier whose cart she had collided with was irate, but there were other voices, kindly and concerned, with anxious faces to match.

'Are you all right? Goodness me, what a tumble!'

'I'm all right,' Amy tried to say, but the words were going away from her and the faces were blurred and distorted like reflections in the Hall of Mirrors on the pier at Weston-Super-Mare.

'She's not all right. She's going to faint...'

She heard what they said, but it seemed to have nothing to do with her. Desperately she tried to focus, to pull herself back from the brink of blackness, but it was useless. She was in a limbo world, full of panic and acute embarrassment. Vaguely she was aware of arms lifting her, supporting her, but she was no longer able to make out what the voices were saying or even to understand what was happening. The numbness in her head was beginning to turn to pain, a pain that spread like thick cold treacle over the whole of her face and sharpened into a central point as if a steel bolt was being driven into her temple. They were carrying her and the jolting increased the pain and swirled the mists of dizziness.

'Don't... don't...' Amy mumbled, but nobody seemed to be taking the slightest notice of her.

Timeless moments. She was indoors now – there was no longer sunshine hurting her eyes and the voices were flatter and closer. And then another voice, different yet oddly familiar, a voice that might have been part of a dream.

'Fine. You can leave her with me now.'

The dizziness lifted a little and Amy realised her head was between her knees, pressed down by fingers on the nape of her neck. She drew a deep breath and another, concentrating on fighting her way back to full consciousness, then as the pressure relaxed she lifted her head and found herself looking up into the face of Dr Oliver Scott.

Briefly the shock almost overcame her. She had known he

was back in Hillsbridge of course, but this was the first time she had seen him – the first time she had seen him in fifteen years, if it came to that, apart from the brief encounter when Jack had married Grace's sister, Stella – and in that first startled second Amy became a child again. Instead of being here in his surgery next door to the Co-op, where anxious passers-by had carried her, it seemed she was back in Greenslade Terrace as a nine-year-old, racked by the pain of so serious a scalding that he had referred to her as 'parboiled', and looking with adoring eyes at the young doctor who provided the only bright spot in days which stretched end-to-end, boredom interspersed with agony.

'Dr Scott!' Her voice was faint.

He looked down at her, mild brown eyes crossing the passage of years.

'Amy. It's Amy Hall, isn't it?'

'Yes.' Amy Hall. How strange to be called that now! Yet people here about did still think of her as Amy Hall, just as she still called girls she had known all her life by their maiden names.

'It's all right, Amy, don't try to move for a minute.'

The pain sharpened and jabbed at her temple and she winced.

'My head...'

'You've banged it.' He lifted her chin, parted her lids with his fingers and looked into her eyes. 'You took quite a spill, didn't you? You shouldn't have been in such a hurry.'

'I wasn't. I...'

'Don't try to talk just now.' He bent over her and a lick of hair flopped across his forehead. He doesn't look a bit different! she thought, surprised. Not even any older...

'Well, Amy, you've nothing broken.' As he straightened up, leaning back against his desk, she had a full-length view of him – stocky frame filled out with the years and made stockier by the cut of his good tweed suit; square, fair-skinned face; capable freckled hands, thrust now into his trouser pockets; feet, also looking square, in heavy brown brogues. The very look of him inspired confidence in her now just as it had done all those years ago.

'A stupid thing to do, wasn't it?' she said shakily.

'It was rather.'

'It was my own fault, I wasn't looking where I was going. Oh dear, I do feel peculiar...'

'I expect you do. The best thing you can do is get home and rest. Where do you live now?'

'Hope Terrace. But I can't go home. I must go back to the yard. There are things I have to do . . .'

'Not today. They will just have to manage without you.'

'I'll be fine!' She tried to get up, but the dizziness returned immediately and she sat back again quickly. 'Oh, maybe you're right.'

'I certainly am. It would be very silly to work any more today. Now, how are you going to get home?'

'My car is parked by the station.'

'Well, you're certainly not up to driving it. You would be a danger to yourself and anyone else on the road.'

'I suppose so. Perhaps I ought to telephone for Herbie . . .'

Oliver Scott glanced at his watch. 'I'm leaving here now; I have a few calls to make. I could drop you at home on the way.'

'Oh, I couldn't trouble you!'

'No trouble, it's practically on my way.'

'Well, if you're sure . . . But could I telephone Herbie anyway, to tell him what's happened?'

'I'll ask my nurse to do that. Come on, my car's outside.'

Leaving the surgery, Amy felt conspicuous and embarrassed.

'That's my Ford,' she said as they passed the station yard. She disliked leaving it there, but could see she had no choice.

'It's a nice car.' He sounded surprised. 'You've done well.'

'I've tried. In the beginning it was just that I wanted to carry on with what Llew started, but somewhere along the line it became more than that. I think I'm doing it for me now.'

This was no more than the truth, but it was the first time she had admitted it, even to herself.

'It's astonishing. But then, you always did have determination.' They were nearing Hope Terrace now. 'Tell me where to stop,' he said.

Outside the gate he put on the handbrake and turned to her.

'Now, is there someone who can pop in and keep an eye on you for the next twenty-four hours or so?'

'Whatever for?' Amy asked.

'Just to make sure you don't suffer any ill-effects. If you were to get sleepy, or sick, something of that kind, I should want to know about it. Is there someone?'

'Not really,' Amy said. 'You know I'm widowed?' As she said it she felt the bleakness of the phrase, but the sharp edge of pain was missing.

'Yes, I was very sorry to hear about it.' He paused for a moment, thinking. 'What about a neighbour? There's no necessity for her to stay all the time so long as she keeps an eye on you.'

'I suppose there's Ruby,' Amy said, thinking this was all rather unnecessary. 'But surely you don't think...'

'I'm sure there is nothing to worry about, but it's better to be safe than sorry and you wouldn't want to go into hospital, would you?'

'Hospital! Certainly not!' Amy said, horrified. 'Really, I'm fine now, you know. There's no need...' But his stern face convinced her. 'All right, I'll ask Ruby,' she agreed.

'And you will call me if you're at all concerned?'

'Yes.'

He waited until he saw her turn the corner before driving off, but when Amy heard him go she hastened across to her own door without knocking on Ruby's. She didn't want to cause a fuss. She was all right now – a bit shaky, maybe, with a throbbing headache, but otherwise fine. There was no need to bother anyone else.

But it was nice of Dr Scott to be so concerned. He was still the same caring doctor who had found it in himself to buy a teddy bear and a pound of butterscotch for his frustrated young patient all those years ago, even if he was now a married man with two daughters, the elder of whom must now be older than Amy had been at the time of her accident.

The knowledge was strangely comforting. For the first time for years, Amy felt inexplicably as if there was a safety net spread out beneath her, arms ready to catch her if she fell, capable hands willing to pick up the pieces.

It was a good feeling.

Chapter Twenty-Two

On the following Sunday morning, Dr Scott's car drew up once more outside Amy's gate.

'I just thought I would look in to see how you were,' he said.

Amy, in the middle of cooking a joint of pork for Sunday dinner, was flushed from the heat of the kitchen and a little disconcerted at being caught in the homely floral wrap-around apron which Ruby Clarke had given her at Christmas and which, though not at all her 'style', at least kept her dress clean of grease splashes.

'I'm fine,' she said.

'No ill-effects?'

'Not really. I had a headache for a couple of days, but I suppose that was only to be expected.'

'And it's gone now?'

'Well...' She hesitated. 'I did have a kind of sharp pain in my temple earlier on this morning. It lasted for half an hour or so and I must admit it made me feel quite odd.'

'In what way?'

'Oh, shaky.' That was an understatement. The pain had been intense and had made her feel not only shaky but sick too and her skin had gone clammy and cold. But she didn't want to make too much of it.

'And it's gone now?'

'Yes, I feel fine.' She brushed her hand across her face with a quick, dismissive gesture. 'See, the bump didn't come out as badly as I expected. I thought I might have two lovely black eyes – or one, at least. But it was just a lump and a graze, and my hair covered that.'

'That saved your vanity then,' he teased.

'Thank heavens! I could hardly do business looking a

fright.' Out of the window she caught sight of Barbara and Maureen, setting out their dolls for a pretend tea-party on the small square of lawn, and she called to them. 'Come in a minute! There's someone I want you to meet.'

They came, chattering and giggling, Barbara holding Maureen by the hand. When they were introduced, Amy was hoping desperately that they would make a good impression. As a child herself she had idolised the doctor so, and now she wanted her own children to do the same. Oliver Scott shook hands solemnly with Barbara and rumpled Maureen's hair. 'This one's very like you were when I first knew you,' he said, winking at Barbara, who promptly tossed her curls and pranced around precociously.

'Huw – where's Huw?' Barbara asked.

'I think he's gone out to look for his friends,' Amy said. Oliver Scott's glance lifted from Barbara.

'Huw – the boy you took in?' he said questioningly.

'That's right.' Amy held his eyes defiantly, daring him to ask more. 'Dr Scott, you will have to excuse me or else dinner will never be ready.'

He smiled, the friendly yet slightly earnest smile which creased his face so that his eyes almost disappeared.

'Oh dear! I know how impatient hungry youngsters can be. I won't hold you up any longer. But I might look in again, if that's all right?'

'Yes, of course!' She felt edgy suddenly. Because of her re-membered anxiety to see him when she was a child, perhaps?

After he had gone she regaled the girls with the story of her scalding and how Dr Scott had got her well again. They listened, eyes round with wonder. They had heard it all before, but it was a story that never failed to impress – especially now they had seen the other main participant in the drama.

'He said he would come again – will he?' Barbara demanded.

'We shall have to wait and see,' Amy said. She rather thought that, having satisfied himself of her recovery from the fall, he would not come again – unless, of course, it was to present his bill. He had not charged her yet . . . and she hoped he wasn't going to tot up a home visit!

A day or so later however and she was beginning to hope he would call, charge or no charge. The pain in her temple had returned several times and on each occasion it had stopped her in her tracks so that she had to sit down, sweating and trembling, until the spasm passed. At first she thought no further than the sharp pain, but when it hit her for the third time in less than twenty-four hours, Amy found herself beginning to be frightened.

I didn't know I could feel so ill! she thought as the white-hot knife-thrust dulled to an echoing throb and the sickness in her throat sank to nausea. Suppose I did some damage to myself when I fell – something really serious? Could it be that the blow went inwards and the blood has formed a clot?

Things 'going in' had always been one of Mam's bogey-men – anything from damp to measles had been warned against – and Amy herself could think of several people who had dropped dead from strokes and haemorrhages.

If something like that happened to me, whatever would become of the children? she wondered, the fear so intense that it almost started the pain again.

If Dr Scott did not come back, she would go to see him, Amy decided. But in between whiles, when the pain lifted completely, it seemed no more than a bad dream, something far too trivial to be bothering the doctor with; then she would think: Perhaps it's going to be all right. Perhaps it won't come again. And what time have I got for waiting in queues in the doctor's surgery?

But the pain did come again – and so did Oliver Scott, calling in one evening on his way home from his rounds.

'Feeling fit now?' he asked.

'I'm not sure,' Amy said and went on to describe the 'turns' she had been experiencing.

'Hmm.' His serious expression disconcerted her a little. 'Perhaps I ought to take a good look at you.'

She submitted to his examination, but when he had finished he could be only vaguely reassuring.

'There doesn't appear to be anything obviously wrong. But I shall keep an eye on you just the same.'

'You don't think ...' She could hardly bring herself to say it. 'You don't think I'm going to die, do you?'

Not a muscle in his face moved. 'I don't think so.'

'I'm just being silly, then.'

'I wouldn't call it silly,' he assured her.

'I would. But I can't help worrying about what would become of the children if I – well, if anything happened to me. Mam would look after the girls, I suppose. They would be better off with someone younger, but I can't imagine her letting them go, even though it would be a terrible struggle for her and not much fun for them. I don't know whatever would happen to Huw. Mam wouldn't have him, that much is for certain; she didn't approve of *me* having him! And who else would take him in? It really would be an institution for him this time, and the poor kid's had so much upheaval already...'

She broke off, running a distraught hand through her curls.

'Oh Amy, Amy!' Oliver Scott touched her elbow. 'Stop worrying! It isn't going to happen.'

'How can you be so sure?'

'Because I'm a doctor and I say so. You've bumped your head, that's all. In a few months from now, you will have forgotten it ever happened. That's my prediction.'

Amy's face cleared. She wanted nothing more than to be reassured and even in the midst of anxiety she was impatient with herself for being a worrier.

'I'm sorry to have been such a nuisance,' she said briskly.

'A nuisance - you, Amy? Never!'

'Yes. I can be where the children are concerned. My excuse is that I'm solely responsible for them. I don't mind that - well, I haven't much choice, have I? But when it comes to imagining that I might die and leave them ... to be honest, that's just like a nightmare. It's no use - however good others might be, they wouldn't really do the same as I do. Kids need their mother - girls especially. And Huw, of course, is a special case...'

He noticed how her face softened when she spoke of Huw. What had possessed her to take in the boy on top of all her other responsibilities, he wondered. Well, whatever the motive, she was clearly very fond of him now, treating him as if he was as much her own as the girls and worrying about him too.

He pressed her elbow again. 'You can take it from me that they will all have their mother around for a good deal longer. Someone like you is not so easily killed off, Amy!'

'Good.' There was a lift of determination in her voice, as if she was dismissing the fear, and it struck Oliver yet again what a formidable woman she had become. Attractive, yes - with her looks that was obvious - and intelligent and vital. But formidable too, with a strength partly inherited and partly nurtured in those dark days when she had lain on the sofa in her childhood home, her back raw, and later gathered the courage to learn to walk again. Life had not treated her easily, golden girl though she had once seemed to be. Yet she had come through it all with spirit and determination, allowing nothing to get her down for very long. How different from the way in which some people reacted to the problems – often much smaller – in their lives. Mountains produced mountaineers, he supposed, while molehills produced only moles...

The thought made him smile briefly.

'You mustn't overdo things, though,' he said. 'I suppose it's a waste of my breath telling you that, but if you have any sense you will listen to what I say. A blow like you had can affect you in all sorts of ways...'

'I thought you said I was all right!' she interposed sharply.

'I said you're not going to die. But it does sound to me as if your body is crying out for rest. Take my advice and give it what it needs.'

Amy tossed her head. 'Oh, I can't rest! I've far too much to do. There are new contracts to quote for, for one thing, Then I have a new young man starting next week and workmen coming in to put up a new store. I can't possibly take a holiday.'

'I wish you would stop putting words into my mouth, Amy! Did you hear me mention a holiday? It would do you good, of course, but I know better than to even suggest that. No, what I said was *take things easy*. For everyone's sake – not least the children.'

'All right, I promise to try,' she said. But he knew she would not.

During the next few weeks Amy continued to experience the pains in her head. Sharp and debilitating as ever, they came sometimes two or three times a day, each one lasting for anything up to half an hour, accompanied by the cold sweats and nausea and subsiding to leave her weak and trembling. But she tried not to be so frightened by them and when Oliver Scott called – something he was beginning to make a habit of – she made light of them, though his visits evoked in her a mixed response. It was comforting to feel he was 'Keeping an eye on her' but also disconcerting, for she couldn't help wondering if he was more concerned about her than he was prepared to admit.

Then gradually she became aware that the pains were coming less often, lasting a shorter time and having less drastic effect on her, and when she told him so he smiled his slow, cheek-creasing smile.

'There you are, what did I tell you? You're on the mend.'

But still he continued to drop in whenever he was passing, sharing a cup of tea in the comfortable clutter of her kitchen, talking to Barbara in the same serious grown-up way he had once talked to her, and discussing boys' topics with Huw, whose first suspicion of him seemed to have deepened into something close to respect.

Spring became summer. Amy almost forgot she had ever had the pains, so seldom did they now come, and life continued in the same busy pattern as before. But still Oliver Scott's car regularly drew up outside the house in Hope Terrace, and one afternoon during the school summer holidays when she went to collect both the girls from next door, Amy was shocked when Ruby Clarke made mention of it.

'I see the doctor was at your place again last night; his car was there when we came home from the whist drive. Nellie Newth was quite concerned when she saw it – wondered if there was something wrong – but I told her that we've got quite used to it, and he just pays a social visit now and then.'

'That's right.' Amy managed to remain aloof. She had always thought there was more gossip exchanged than cards played at the weekly whist drives and was annoyed now to think that she had been the subject of some of it. The memory of the two women in the Co-op discussing her still rankled, too; though she thought Ruby was unlikely to talk about her in that way, she seemed to hear the voice of others who would:

'Who does she think she is, eh? The doctor calls on her, you know. Oh no, nobody bad in the house, but he calls all the same. Makes you wonder, doesn't it?'

Amy drew herself up now. 'We are very old friends, Ruby,' she snapped. 'I have known Dr Scott since I was eight years old and if anybody wishes to make something out of that, you can be sure they will get a flea in their ear if *I* hear about it!'

'Oh, I'm sure no one would, Amy,' Ruby replied hastily.

The conversation left an unpleasant taste in Amy's mouth for a few days, but she was too busy to worry about it for long.

Although she did feel a pang of misplaced guilt the next time Oliver Scott arrived unannounced at her door, she made sure to invite him inside in a voice loud enough to carry across the alleyway to Ruby, should she be listening.

As always, Oliver settled himself on the high-backed kitchen chair, swinging it up onto its two back legs in a manner Amy would have swiftly reprimanded Huw for copying. But there was something slightly withdrawn in his manner, as if beneath his easygoing professional front he was hiding a secret sadness. It was not the first time during his visits that Amy had noticed this, just as she had also observed that a cup of tea and a chat always seemed to lighten his mood so that the jocularity became natural instead of forced, but she had always refrained from mentioning it.

Today, however, was different and as she placed a cup of tea on the scrubbed wood table beside him, Amy said, 'You're very quiet.'

'Am I?' He looked almost startled. 'Well, maybe I am. Maybe I have things on my mind.'

'What kind of things?'

'Oh, nothing worth talking about.' But there was a shadow in his eyes as he said it and she felt instinctively that something was making him unhappy. Then, almost instantly, she dismissed the thought as fanciful. Oliver had a lovely wife and two beautiful children; he was successful and sought after in his chosen calling, and had even managed to buy himself into a practice in the very place where he wanted to be. Why on earth should he be hiding some mysterious secret sadness?

'How are Grace and the children?' she asked, as she always did.

'Fine,' he murmured, but the veil did not lift.

'I saw them the other day,' Amy went on.

Oliver's head came up with a jerk. 'Oh?'

'Just across the street. They were walking along the pavement outside the rectory and I was parking in the station yard.'

'Oh yes, your famous car. You've caused quite a stir in Hillsbridge with that!'

'I don't know how I should manage without it now,' she said. 'I'm surprised Grace hasn't asked you if she can have one.'

Again the troubled look seemed to close his face. 'Grace

did learn to drive, but she hasn't done so for some time now. She had a slight accident and it unnerved her.'

'Oh dear – nothing serious, I hope?'

'She had a confrontation with a motor-cyclist. The lad came off worst, of course, and broke a leg, and the whole thing was pretty unpleasant. Now I'm afraid Grace is nervous even riding with me.'

Remembering the horrible experience of running into Ralph Porter's car, Amy said, 'Well, I can understand her, I suppose.'

But this did not tie in with ner image of Grace, all the same. The woman she remembered had been so full of self-confidence that it would have been more in character for her to berate the unfortunate motor-cyclist, Amy thought.

Abruptly she changed the subject. 'Have you seen Dolly's Noël lately?'

Oliver Scott shifted his chair on to all four legs. 'She brought him to the surgery last week. He's a fine boy.'

'Yes.' Amy bit her lip. Physically Noël *was* a fine boy – sturdy, with rosy cheeks and the mass of fair curls which were a family heritage. But all their early fears had turned out to be justified – mentally Noël was still a baby, his eyes round and vacant, mouth lolling to emit a constant fine stream of dribble down his chin and on to the front of the little blouses that Dolly changed two or three times a day.

When the first tide of distress had spent itself, Dolly had taken the blow stoically, being blessed with her father's gift of calm acceptance. But Charlotte was still 'in a way' about it and Amy, to her shame, found herself unable to take to the little boy. He disconcerted her, making her see a side of life which she preferred not to think about. Now, however – since he was a patient of Oliver's – she was relieved to be able to talk about him and steer the conversation away from the obviously vexed subject of Grace.

'Whatever will become of Noël?' Amy asked, pouring tea.

'Immediately, or in the long term?'

'Both, really. I suppose he's happy enough at the moment; he doesn't know anything different. But when he grows up a bit, won't he realise he's not like other children?'

'Unlikely.' Oliver took the cup from her and spooned sugar into it. 'Boys and girls like him are quite often very happy people.'

'But surely he'll get teased?'

'I should imagine his two older brothers will be very protective of him. They may squabble amongst themselves, but just let an outsider say a word out of place and I can picture how the fur would fly!'

The back door opened then, cutting him short as Huw came in, black as a pot from head to toe.

'Huw!' she exclaimed. 'What *have* you been doing?'

He shrugged, looking not at her but at the doctor, his expression glowering. Oh, surely he's not going to turn against Oliver the way he did against Ralph! Amy thought... and wondered why the thought of Ralph could trigger off a little twist of excitement although she had not seen him to speak to for more than a year.

'Where have you been?' she asked again.

'On the batch.'

'I can see that!' He looked at her as much as to say: Well then, why did you ask? and she went on, 'You know I don't like you going on the batch. It's a filthy place – and dangerous too. All that loose dust and rubble – you tell him, Dr Scott!'

Oliver smiled ruefully. 'You'll never stop boys going on the batch, Amy. Just be glad the other two are girls.'

'That's one thing Dolly won't have to put up with so far as Noël's concerned,' Amy fumed. 'At least she can keep an eye on him – except of course when he goes to school. *If* he's able to go, that is.'

Huw, kicking off his boots in the corner, muttered something.

'What did you say?' Amy asked sharply, still annoyed with him.

'Nothing.'

'You did, I heard you. What did you say?'

'I said "the funny school". I suppose he'll be going to the funny school,' Huw mumbled.

'What do you mean – the funny school?'

'The one for kids who aren't all there. *You* know.'

'I do not know...' Amy began, but Oliver Scott cut in:

'He means the Special School. It's run by a very good woman. There are eight or ten pupils from all around the district and she does wonders with them, though of course they have shorter hours than the ordinary school – something like half-past nine until two o'clock.'

'I never heard of that,' Amy said, thinking: How long have

391

I lived in this place? I thought I knew everything and everyone!

'Yes, I'm sure Noël will be able to go there when he's a bit older,' Oliver went on and as the conversation drew her attention away, Amy forgot to wonder how Huw had known what she did not – of the existence of the special school.

Later, when Doctor Scott had gone and Huw, scrubbed clean in spite of his continuing aversion to soap and water, was sitting curled up in the fireside chair with his cigarette card collection, she asked him about it.

'How did you know about the school?'

Huw did not even bother to look up. 'Everybody knows about the funny school.'

'*I* didn't.'

'Haven't you ever seen the funnies going there?'

Amy winced. 'Don't call them that, Huw. It's horrible. They're children just like you.'

'No, they're not. I've seen them going round the street, great big boys holding on to their mother's hand – I'd never hold anyone's hand!'

'When have you seen them?' Amy asked, astonished.

'Oh, some mornings . . .'

'But you're at school yourself!'

'In the holidays,' Huw muttered and though his head was bent over his cigarette cards, Amy had the distinct impression he had gone red.

'But surely when you're on holiday the special school must be on holiday too!' she challenged.

'Oh, I don't know – stop getting on to me!' Huw complained and Amy sighed, her annoyance at Huw's attitude to the children forgotten as this new problem reared its head. She had thought Huw had settled in well . . . almost too well. And now this!

Huw's school was a good mile out of Hillsbridge, so if he had been in town when the children were being taken to or from the special school, then he had no business to be. Had he been playing truant? This was something she had not thought of before, despite his attempts to run away; certainly she had had no complaints from the headmistress who, if not exactly ruling with a rod of iron, certainly used tempered steel. But there was no other explanation and Amy made up her mind; she would have to ask for an appointment to see the headmistress to find out if Huw had been skipping school. For the moment there was not much point in pursuing the matter, though; it would only fuel the build-up of resentment.

'Right, Huw, it's your bedtime,' she said sternly. 'But just one more word before you go upstairs. If I ever hear you refer to the Special School as the "funny school" again, or call names at the children who go there, you will be in serious trouble. Do you understand?'

He said nothing, but his face remained set in the mulish expression and Amy went on, 'Just think yourself lucky, Huw, that you were born whole and well. Children like Aunty Dolly's Noël will never be able to do all the things you can do, and you would do well to remember that.'

His head still bent, he muttered something unintelligible.

'What was that?' Amy asked crossly, suspecting something rude.

'I said that at least they've got mums and dads, most of them,' Huw repeated.

Amy went cold inside. So despite all her efforts he was still grieving, he still felt alone in the world. Guilt swamped her. Perhaps she had not done enough? True she had given him a home, probably better than he had had before, but she could never replace his mother. And she was so seldom there. Could she have made him more secure if she had been less tied up with the business? But whatever the ifs and buts, he still carried his burdens and counted himself less well off than children like Noel who, for all their disabilities, were part of a secure, loving family.

'Oh Huw!' she said softly, searching for words and knowing that anything she said would be inadequate. 'Huw, I know it's not like having your own mother, but you have got us. And we do love you.'

He did not answer and looking at the scrubbed face above the untidy shirt collar, the scowling expression, the grimy-nailed hands clutching possessively at the cigarette cards, she thought: It's true, I do love him. I took him in because I felt responsible, but somewhere along the line I have grown to love him. With all his trying ways, I've come to love this little boy.

'Come here,' she said.

When he didn't move she went to him, pulling his face

against her breast and folding her arms around his skinny shoulders. For a moment she hugged him tight, then held him away.

'Maybe I don't take the place of your mother, but to me you're the son I never had. Remember that, eh?'

He nodded slowly.

'Bed, then. And remember too that for you there is always tomorrow. Lots of tomorrows!'

Another nod. But after he had gone upstairs Amy sat for a long while thinking. Would he ever recover from his experiences? She didn't know. But she determined to make an even bigger effort to fill the empty corners of his heart. Yet even as she reached the decision, she doubted her own ability to carry it through.

*

At the front-room window of the house in Tower View, Margaret Young stood twitching the curtain nets in order to get a better view of the road. Occasionally people appeared, walking up the pavement – a couple strolling hand in hand, a girl pushing a bicycle, a man walking a small mongrel dog. But the one she was looking for had not come into sight. Harry had arranged to collect her and take her to the pictures and he was already almost fifteen minutes late.

Margaret strained forward so as to see an extra few feet of road, chewing on her lip. Unless he came soon they wouldn't get a good seat, but would be forced right to the front of the cheap seats where the screen towered above and the huge flashing images made your head ache. Worse still, they might miss the beginning of the film altogether and she did so want to see it. *The Jazz Singer* with Al Jolson, the 'Singing Fool', in the leading role, was the first so-called 'talkie'. It had caused a sensation when it was released the previous year and now, after a long wait, it was actually being shown here in Hillsbridge.

Margaret had been delighted when Harry offered to take her to see the film. She saw so little of him these days. His ambition had switched abruptly from local politics to studying at evening classes with a view to getting promotion at work, and he had spent very little time with her for months now. Even his precious pigeons had been pushed into the background. Now that his ambitions had taken off, flying faster and higher than the best homing bird, he had lost interest in the breeding process and was selling off his stock to the youngest Brixey boy. But Margaret was puzzled as well as dismayed and irritated by the shift in his priorities.

'I can't see why you need to be studying every evening when you won't be old enough to take your exams for ages yet,' she had objected. 'Even I don't study all the time and I've got to take my matric long before you can sit for your examiner's certificate.'

'It's not just studying school subjects,' Harry had tried to explain. 'The more I can learn about the pits, the better chance I shall have. I'm going to be the youngest manager in Somerset one of these days, just watch me!'

'I thought you wanted to get into politics,' Margaret said.

'I did. Perhaps I shall still do that. But nobody will take any notice of me unless I make something of myself first. And this is the way to do it.'

'But you must have some fun; you can't work all the time,' Margaret argued. 'I never see you these days, Harry.'

'Come with me when I go out to practise surveying, then,' he suggested.

To begin with she had done as he said, trotting along behind him carrying coloured pencils, paper and all the paraphernalia he was acquiring. But it was depressing to be alone with him in lovely deserted meadows where the summer-sweet hedges made shady secret places, when he took far more interest in his calculations than he did of her; frustrating to see his enthusiasm reserved for the unexpected evidence provided by a knoll or ridge, instead of the touch of her hand; hurtful to know he was exulting in a correct assumption rather than a stolen kiss. She could not converse with him, for she knew nothing of the language of surveying, and these days he seemed uninterested in the anecdotes and the bright, happy chatter which had once delighted him, so she relapsed into silence while the feeling of rejection rose to suffocate her.

I don't think he wants me for myself at all, she thought. I doubt if he ever did. When his interest was in politics, he picked up with me because it was a way of getting in with my father. Now his ambitions have changed, he doesn't want me any more.

It was not in Margaret's nature to be morose or self-pitying, but as the joy went out of her relationship with

Harry she found herself sinking deeper and deeper into depression.

I love him, she thought, desperate with all the passion of first love. I know he's my first boy-friend, but I don't want anybody else, ever. And if he really doesn't want me, I shall be an old maid. The tragedy of it brought tears to her eyes and sometimes – after another evening when she had failed to communicate with him and he had left her with no more than a quick, perfunctory kiss – she cried herself to sleep.

Sometimes Margaret tried a new line foreign to her nature, endeavouring to persuade him into some outing or other, and sometimes she succeeded. When she did, they seemed to return to that early easy communication they had shared and her soaring heart would whisper that anything was possible. But more often than not her suggestions were met with an excuse and for this reason, if for no other, she was delighted when he had agreed to take her to see *The Jazz Singer*.

'I must admit, I'd like to see it myself,' he said and Margaret, hopes soaring, had thought: Perhaps this could be the turning point. If he really enjoys it, it might make him realise there is more to life than studying and surveying.

That afternoon she raced through her allotted homework as soon as she got home from school, grateful there were no lengthy essays to write or vocabularies of Latin or French words to learn. Then she went up to her room to get ready.

I wish I could have a bath, thought Margaret as she pulled off her print dress which was slightly damp beneath the arms from hurrying home, it would be lovely to have a scented bath like a lady in a novelette, with soft swirls of foam to tickle my chin and talc to match the soap and leave a perfume on my skin that would drive Harry wild with love for me.

But a bath, scented or otherwise, was out of the question. The house did have a bathroom – Gussie had had the small spare bedroom 'done over' – but there was no supply of hot running water. Instead there was a massive copper, heated by a popping, spluttering gas jet; the water had to be ladled out into the bath with a metal dipper, while simultaneously filling large saucepans to help with the transfer at the tap at the base of the boiler.

The whole thing constituted what Gussie called 'a performance' and meant that baths were restricted to once a week – 'Friday Bath Night' had been the order of the day when Margaret was a child, though now she was older it had become a movable occasion.

But whatever else, baths were not something to be embarked upon lightly as a quick freshener before going out, so Margaret did what she always did – took hot water in a jug and poured it into the shallow porcelain basin with its decorative trim of pink roses that stood on the wash-stand in her room.

Her toilet completed, she took her newest dress from the wardrobe and held it up to admire it. The dress was white, with an extravagantly pleated skirt and a big sailor collar trimmed with navy blue braid and a small capstan motif. Dare I wear it? she wondered. The seats in the picture palace were never as clean as they might be and white would show every mark. But oh, she did so want to look nice for Harry . . .

Recklessly she put on the dress and then turned her attention to her face. A touch of lipstick was the most she usually wore by way of make-up, but today she had confided to one of her more daring classmates that she was going to the pictures and consequently had been offered a pot of rouge, a pencil liner and a pair of tweezers to attend to her feathery brows. For half an hour she experimented, turning herself into a fair imitation of the fashionable flapper girls.

Gussie's face was a picture when she saw her daughter, but with admirable control she managed to restrain herself from saying anything. She knew how much Harry meant to Margaret and had also seen the heartache he had caused her recently. In her own way she had even shared in her pain. Now she felt that if dressing-up for the occasion would make Margaret happier, that was all that mattered. Arms folded around herself, hands tucked into the pockets of her wrap-around floral apron, Gussie surveyed her daughter.

'All I can say is that if Harry doesn't take any notice of you looking like that, then he never will,' she observed.

Margaret giggled, but it was a pleased giggle.

'It's all right then?'

'It's lovely. What time is he picking you up?'

'Half-past six. I've got ten minutes to spare, so I think I'll sit down and do a bit more of my English literature reading.'

But it was no use, she could not concentrate, so she packed away her book and went to look out of the window, watching for him eagerly at first and then with mounting impatience. The mantel clock struck the half-hour, then the quarter, its pretty musical chime hanging in the air. At five to seven, Gussie looked in.

'Harry's not here yet, then?'

'No.' Margaret tried not to sound anxious. 'If he doesn't come soon, we shall miss the start of the picture.'

'Something's happened to hold him up, I suppose,' Gussie said, but inwardly she was as anxious as Margaret. She liked Harry, considering him a steady boy with more ambition than most, but disapproved of the way he treated her daughter. 'I'll be in the kitchen if you want me,' she offered.

Margaret nodded and when her mother had gone she peered out of the window again, wondering if she should go down the road to meet him and so save precious minutes. But she didn't really want to look that eager. Imagine he's just leaving his road now, she told herself. He's coming round the corner, walking up the hill past the cottages, hurrying on the steep bit and he should be coming into view by the time I count to ten... well, maybe twenty. She counted slowly, almost stopping on eighteen-nineteen-twenty. But there was still no Harry.

The clock struck again – a quarter past seven – and Margaret's heart was a lump of lead pressing down in her chest. He wasn't coming. This was not the first time he had let her down, but it was the worst. She had been looking forward to it so much. Tears pricked behind her eyes, squeezed out and rolled in two large drops down her cheeks.

As the unrelenting minutes ticked by, she began to wonder if something had happened to Harry... an accident at work, perhaps. He could be dead and I'm standing here blaming him, she thought in panic. I can't wait any longer – I must go down to his house and find out!

But when she went to the kitchen to tell Gussie of her intention she met with opposition.

'I don't think you should do any such thing, Margaret.'

'But if something has happened, I wouldn't know...'

'I don't think for one moment that anything has happened. At least, not the kind of thing you mean.' Gussie wiped her hands on a teacloth, deciding the time had come for some plain speaking. 'The truth of the matter is that Harry is not as interested as you are and you might as well face it, love. He's got other things on his mind.'

'Oh, I know he's busy – he's so keen to study and get on, but...'

'He doesn't treat you right. If he really cared, he'd be here now. Oh, lovey...' She broke off as she saw the tears well up

398

again. 'It's hard, I know, but sometimes it's as well to face up to the truth. The way you're going on, you will just be hurt time and time again.'

'But he does care – he does!' Margaret grasped at the memory of shared moments, tender touches – the moire band on her wrist.

'Then where is he?' Gussie demanded. 'Look at you ... all dressed up and ready to go – and he should be here, but he isn't. You let him run rings around you, lovey. It's not the way.'

'I don't care!' Margaret exploded. 'I'd rather have him sometimes than not at all. Don't look at me like that! I *would*!'

'Then you will just have to put up with it, won't you?' Gussie said.

Left alone again, Margaret's tears flowed freely, running rivulets of eye-pencil down her cheeks. All hope had gone now and she was not even watching for him when she heard his knock at the door. She jumped up, dashing at her face with her hands and suddenly trembling all over. He was here. Something *had* detained him ... She had known it ...

She ran into the hall to meet him. 'Harry – what happened? I've been so worried ...'

'Sorry I'm late.' But he sounded only marginally concerned. 'I got talking to the under-manager about what I'm doing and I didn't notice the time.'

And suddenly she was not worried or upset any more, just hurt and very angry.

'But we were going to the pictures!'

'I know. I'm sorry. We'll have to make it another night now.'

'But I was all ready!'

'I said I'm sorry ...'

'No, you're not!' she shouted. 'You're not sorry at all. Sometimes, Harry Hall, I hate you!'

A look of utter bewilderment crossed his face. 'But there's always another time.'

'No, there isn't!'

'There is. *The Jazz Singer* is on all the week.'

'Maybe. But we won't be going, not together anyway.'

'Why not?'

He really doesn't seem to know, she thought, sadness almost overcoming the anger.

'Because I can't go on like this; there isn't any point. I'm sorry, but I just can't bear it.'

'But Marg...'

'Don't "but Marg" me! I really like you, Harry, ever such a lot. But I'm just a stop-gap to you. I come second to everything else.'

'I've got to work, Marg, if I'm ever to make anything of myself – you know that. I like you too, but this is my life we're talking about.'

'And I'm talking about *my* life! I don't expect to be the only thing that matters to you. I know you want to get on and I respect you for it. But I won't be made a fool of.'

'I've never done that,' he protested.

'No? What about tonight, then? Look at me – all dressed up and nowhere to go...' She broke off, fighting the threatening tears. 'No, I'm sorry, Harry, but that's it, I'm afraid... Unless you can promise you won't let me down again.'

He shrugged. There was a mulish look on his face now.

'All this fuss – just because we can't go to the pictures tonight.'

'No, not just because of that. Because of all the other occasions when I've been left for a fool too. There was a time when I thought you liked me, but now I can see that even that wasn't what I thought; you just wanted to get in with my father. Now you don't want that any more, so you don't want me either.'

Harry moved to the door. 'I don't have to stay here and listen to this.'

'You'd better go then, hadn't you?' said Margaret.

The moment he had gone she began to cry again, bitter, unhappy tears. But after a while when her sobs had spent themselves, she was aware of a feeling almost of relief. Maybe there would not be any more shared moments, but there wouldn't be any more nights like this one either, waiting in vain for him to come. There would not be the laughter, but neither would there be the pain of rejection.

Perhaps one day when Harry has achieved his ambition, there may be another chance for us, thought Margaret, but for the moment I must put him out of my mind. And avoiding her mother, who was tactfully hiding in the kitchen, Margaret went upstairs to wash her face and change out of the dress that would never now be soiled by the grubby seats in the picture palace.

Chapter Twenty-Three

Autumn came in wet and windy and the inclement weather caused Amy problems and to spare. The high winds ripped the tarpaulin roof of her office, damaged lorry sheets covering loads that were waiting to go out and brought down a tree in the corner of the yard, necessitating extra work for Herbie and the other in men clearing it up.

One evening towards the end of September, Amy was working late. It had been raining all day and the river was running high along the boundary of the yard. Before leaving at five-fifteen Herbie had moved the lorries to the highest points and with the help of the other men secured new tarpaulins over the waiting loads, but Amy was still anxious.

They hadn't had the floods up here since she had been in charge of the business, but there was always a first time. She knew the river was liable to flood and if it did, not only were the things in the yard in danger, but moving the lorries out in the morning would also be a problem. The lane was so low and flat just outside that it was always the first road in Hillsbridge to become impassable, with the bridge connecting the yard to the lane the most vulnerable of all. If the rain kept up, it could be two feet under water by morning and Amy had a full schedule booked for the next day.

As she worked on her books, the rain beat a constant tattoo against the windows of her office and a steady drip-drip came from the corner where the tarpaulin had been inadequately repaired. At last, unable to stand it a moment longer, Amy reached for the telephone to call the builder. Probably he would not be too pleased at being disturbed during the evening, but that could not be helped. At least she was likely to catch him now and with any luck he could put her on his list of calls for tomorrow.

To her dismay, however, she discovered the telephone line

was dead; that must mean an overhead cable down somewhere. She uttered a reasonably ladylike but heartfelt oath. No telephone meant extra work and perhaps lost business. How she had managed before she had one, she could hardly imagine and she hoped fervently that it would not be too long before the fault was discovered and rectified.

For another half-hour Amy worked on. Then a knock at the door almost made her jump out of her skin. With the drumming of the rain she had not heard anyone coming and now for a second she could not think what the noise was. Then she got up to open the door and as the wind took it, blowing it back on its hinges, she gasped her surprise.

'Ralph!'

'Hello, Amy.' His tone was as cool and self-assured as ever.

By contrast Amy was anything but cool. Her heart had given an uneven lurch and as the blood began racing through her veins her skin tingled hotly.

'Can I come in?' he asked. 'It's very wet out here!'

'Yes, of course. Come in.'

He followed her into the office, shaking the raindrops from his flying-jacket with the same careless ease she remembered so well. But there was a constraint between them now and thrilled as she was to see him, she was aware of it. It was almost as if they had gone back to the beginning – to the day when she had run into his car with the lorry. His arrogance was as daunting now as it had been then. Except that then she had disliked him and now...

Now she could not put a name to the emotions that leaped and reared as she faced him for the first time in more than a year. While he had been away, she had put him out of her mind because she had no time for regrets. She had refused to remember the way his touch had excited her, refused to acknowledge the longing for him of which she had been so ashamed. But now, meeting him again so unexpectedly, she was unable to erect a single defence against the power of the attraction he had for her.

'You're quite a stranger.' Tension introduced an edge into her voice which sounded almost hostile. Her knees felt weak and carefully she manoeuvred around the desk and sat down. Ralph casually leaned back against the filing cabinet, but she thought the attitude of relaxation was skin-deep only – beneath the careless pose he was as taut and alert as an animal ready to attack.

'I've been based very firmly in Gloucester,' he replied.

'And how has that worked out?'

'Very well. I now have a depot right on the docks and I've established trade with overseas timber companies, principally in Scandanavia. As a matter of fact, I was over there for an extended stay this summer to strengthen the links.'

'That explains why we haven't seen you in Hillsbridge.'

'Oh, I have been back, but usually at weekends and then mostly I'm only too happy to stay at home and make the most of the comforts I've been missing – not least Mrs Milsom's cooking.'

There was a gleam of amusement in his eyes and the colour came up in Amy's cheeks as she wondered if he was alluding to the dinner they had shared.

'I don't know how you manage it,' she said hastily. 'It must be difficult running businesses in two different places.'

'They're not really two businesses – they're one and the same. And as regards the Hillsbridge end of the enterprise, I've been lucky; I have a good depot manager and good staff. There comes a time when you have to delegate, as you'll discover, Amy.'

She didn't answer. Delegating was something she could not imagine herself ever being able to do. It was one thing to leave Herbie to look after the maintenance of the lorries and the practical problems of the yard – she knew so little about that side of things that it was really only sensible. But the more she learned the more she realised that even that aspect of the business came back to her as the person ultimately responsible; sometimes she would wake at night, arousingly aware that this lorry was due for a service tomorrow or that one needed attention to its horn or tail-light. How could she possibly hand all that over to someone else? Yet it was strange to think that three short years ago it would never have entered her head that she could do any of it.

'Your business seems to be thriving, Amy. I knew it would,' Ralph commented.

Another small shiver ran through her. How was it that the tone of his voice could affect her like that? More sharply than she had intended, she said, 'I hope we've given you satisfaction.'

'Indeed. When the contracts run out, I am sure we shall wish to renew them. And there may be other work. In fact that's the reason I'm here now – to ask how you would feel about taking on longer hauls.'

Ridiculously her spirits fell a little. Fool that she was, she had still been nursing a vain hope that he might have called to see *her*. She should have known better. With Ralph, business was behind most things.

'What sort of longer hauls did you have in mind?' she asked.

He pulled across a chair and straddled it.

'I have a couple of lorries myself at Gloucester, of course, but when the import business is going at full stretch I shall have more customers than I can handle. One answer would be to invest in more lorries but, for reasons I won't go into, I don't want to do that just at the moment. Another alternative would be to use Gloucester haulage firms – there are plenty of them – but I prefer to stay with the tried and tested. And I have enough customers in this area to make it worthwhile to use a Hillsbridge-based company. Generally speaking, the scope of my operation can be fitted into a triangle like this . . .'

Without asking permission, he reached for Amy's pen and began to draw on the back of an envelope which was lying on the desk.

'Are you sure you wouldn't like a clean sheet of paper?' Amy asked, mock-sarcastically.

'Well, yes – if you can spare it.'

'Help yourself.'

For a few minutes they talked over the details of Ralph's proposals and then, almost abruptly, he rose.

'Good! You'll do sums and quote me, will you? I shall be here until tomorrow, but after that you can reach me in Gloucester.'

'You're not going to be here for long, then?' she said. 'I thought perhaps your sister would persuade you to stay for a few days. She must find it rather lonely, with you away so much.'

He smiled briefly.

'Flora's handicap has made her quite a recluse. Mrs Milsom provides all the company she wants and they're very good at making up dummy hands for games of whist – though I suspect they cheat rather a lot! But they don't miss me. I'm no card player and unless there is money at stake, I find it very hard to work up any enthusiasm. Business is much more interesting – especially building up a new branch. You could do worse than open another depot yourself, Amy – in Gloucester perhaps.'

'Oh, I've quite enough on my plate with this one at present!' she retorted, then immediately regretted the ill-considered response. She had no wish to appear narrow and inward looking – Ralph seemed to have such a high opinion of her enterprise, which flattered her – neither did she want him to know how heavily she had mortgaged the business in order to build it up as she had. Some things were better kept to oneself, especially where other business people were involved; moreover Ralph, for all that had been between them, was as shrewd a man as any when it came to making a quick profit. 'As you can see, I was very busy when you arrived,' she went on hastily. 'And to be honest, I shall be here until midnight if I don't get on with things.'

He raised an eyebrow. 'In that case, I won't hold you up any longer.' He moved to the door and opened it. Again the wind almost whipped it from his grasp and threw a flurry of rain into his face. The roar of the river was very loud and he turned back momentarily. 'I wouldn't stay here any longer than you can help, though. It's a wild night and there could be floods.'

'I hope not! I have three full loads to get out of here in the morning.'

'Never mind the morning. How would you get out tonight?'

'I have my car,' she reminded him.

'Once the river breaks its banks, the bridge will be impassable.'

'I shall be all right. Don't worry about me.'

'If you say so. But I'd keep an eye on it, all the same.'

His tone aroused resentment. It was her yard, for goodness' sake – she had sat out two winters here. Yet still he treated her like an idiot . . . or, perhaps, a woman!

'I haven't got time to sit and watch the river rise,' she snapped. 'It hasn't flooded now for two years and I don't suppose it will in the next hour.'

Ralph smiled, one corner of his mouth lifting. 'Good night, Amy.'

After he had gone she returned to her work, but now it was more difficult to concentrate than ever. Ralph had unsettled her, tempted her thoughts away from the comfortable haven of day-to-day events and relationships and reopened old reservoirs of desire. One day I shall really think about the way he makes me feel, Amy promised herself. But not now; I have too much else to do and besides, he was quite right – that damned river does seem to be rising...

For the next hour Amy worked steadily and after finishing what she had intended to do, took an extra half-hour to prepare the backbone of a quotation for Ralph. Then she sat back, thinking once more of his suggestion that she should open another depot, possibly in Gloucester. It would be nice to imagine that perhaps he wanted to work more closely with her, but that could be no more than wishful thinking.

Anything that might have been between you and Ralph Porter ended when you told him you were not interested in a relationship with him, she reminded herself – he's not the one to go chasing after lost causes. But the warning did no good; he was back, she had seen him again and all her old feelings had been resurrected.

At last Amy packed her papers together, turned out the fire and lights and put on her mackintosh. As she opened the door she was met by total darkness, for the wind had put out the gas-lamp which usually lit the stretch of road outside the yard. Turning up her collar, she went down the wood-plank steps of her office and straight into what seemed to be a deep puddle. Her feet, encased in her Russian boots, did not feel it but there was enough to splash cold water up her legs.

'Ugh!' Amy stopped short. She had known the yard was in need of repair, but had not realised it was bad enough to cause puddles like this right outside her office door. After she had taken a tentative step or two forward, the truth hit her. This was not just a puddle, it was the river, encroaching slowly but surely into the yard.

Her heart sank. This was it, then. The rain was still falling steadily and if it kept up all night, by morning the yard and the road outside would be under water. Thank heavens Herbie had moved everything to the higher ground. Thank heavens that her car was on higher ground too!

She waded a few more steps and was then out of the ankle-deep swirls. As she half ran across to her car, she reflected that at least she would get that safely home before the yard flooded. She only wished she could take the lorries and everything else, lock, stock and barrel.

A few turns of the handle and the engine spluttered into life. Amy jumped in, got into gear and then, as her lights illuminated the lower part of the yard, she saw just how high the water already was ... a creeping, rising tide.

The wheels splashed through the puddles as she drove towards the gates and out; then, too late, she remembered Ralph's warning about the river bridge. The front of the car hit the deeper water with a smack, forging a path for a moment, and fatally Amy let her foot up on the accelerator. Afterwards she tried to explain that she had just been trying to slow down; in fact it was an instinctive but totally wrong reaction. When she tried to move forward again the car pushed ineffectively against the water, chugged and stopped. Frantically Amy tried to coax it back to life, but her efforts were useless. The engine coughed and spluttered like a sick old lady and then, with a gurgle, died.

'Oh, my God!' Amy said aloud as she forced open the door and saw the water swirling around the wheels. Even her boots could not protect her now – the icy wetness seeped and oozed between her toes as she waded into it. The starting handle was almost under water and though she grasped it determinedly, she knew her efforts would be in vain.

What can I do? she wondered wildly as she put all her weight behind it. I can't leave the car here!

A sudden rush of longing for Llew filled her. He would have known what to do. But Llew could not help her now.

When first she heard the sound of a motor car engine, Amy thought it must be up in the main road. Then, as beams of light sheared through the darkness, she realised it was coming her way. Splashing, her feet dragging in the water like hooves in quicksand, she ran towards the road waving wildly. The car was coming quite fast and in the total darkness only the headlamps were visible, like great devil's eyes. Then, as it drew level with her, it slowed and she recognised the unmistakable lines of Ralph's Morgan.

Relief surged through her, muted with embarrassment. He had warned her about this and now he was going to see her stuck here just as he had predicted. For an unbearable moment she thought he was going to laugh, but he did not.

'Amy!' he said, his face very straight. 'What are you doing out in all this rain?'

Relief gave way to annoyance. 'What do you *think* I'm doing? My car's stuck in the water! The river's up – the bridge is flooded.'

'Oh dear!' he said solemnly.

'Well, I wasn't to know, was I?' she flared. 'I didn't see it until it was too late and I was in it by then. Oh Ralph, whatever am I going to do?'

'There's not a great deal you can do tonight,' he replied.

'What do you mean? I can't leave it there!'

'Where is it, then?'

'Right on the bridge. Over there!'

'Wait a minute.' He pulled his own car to the side of the road and got out, turning up his collar and walking towards the bridge. Amy followed him.

'It stopped and I couldn't get it to go again. Do you think you could ... ?'

'Not a chance.' He had a flashlight in his hand. Its powerful beam picked up the Model T sitting squarely on the bridge that was beginning to look like an extension of the river itself. 'It will take a tractor to get that out.'

'But where could I get a tractor at this time of night?'

He was paddling around, weighing up the situation.

'The only thing would be to push it back into the yard. How strong are you feeling?'

'Oh ... oh, I don't know ...'

'It's on the flat,' he said.

'But push it back – couldn't we push it *out*?'

'No point. The engine will be thoroughly wet by now and it will have to dry out before you can start it again – even if you had a hill to run down, which you don't. And the road's already partially flooded along by the mill, anyway.'

'But you think we could push it back?'

'We might be able to. Come on, we'll try.'

Back into the swirling water again and Amy grimaced as it squelched into her boots, but said nothing, aware that Ralph would only greet her grumbles with scorn.

'Hmm. You are well and truly afloat, aren't you?' he said drily. 'Let the hand-brake off and put it out of gear.'

'I know!' she retorted.

In the darkness they heaved together. Water sloshed into the top of Amy's boots, but now she was no longer alone it did not seem so bad. Eventually they had the car off the bridge and with Amy leaning through the driver's door to steer, they got it back into the yard and then pushed it as far as they were able towards the higher ground.

'That's about as far as we can go,' Ralph said.

'Will the water reach it there?' Amy asked breathlessly.

'I don't know; depends how much the river rises. But we can't get it any higher. And I think the rain's easing off now.'

It did seem that it was not pouring down quite so hard.

'Come on, I'll take you home,' Ralph offered.

'Oh no, I couldn't bother you...'

'No bother, you're wet through.'

'I shall be all right.'

'I've heard that before. Do as you're told for once!'

Warmth spread through her, dispelling the cold. She went with him and when they reached the deep water on the bridge he turned to her. 'Come on, I'll carry you through.'

Before she could protest that a little more water in her boots would hardly make any difference, he had swung her up as if she were a child. One arm was beneath her knees, the other hard and strong around her back, and beneath her cheek the leather of his jacket was wet, cold and shiny. She relaxed against him, revelling in the contact and in the feeling of being completely within his power, yet at the same time cared for, cherished.

Beyond the water he paused for a moment, still holding her. He had left on her car lights and they illuminated a section of his face – the strong lines, the deep shadows, the mouth hard yet oddly sensual. Something twisted deep within her, turning her stomach to water, and she longed suddenly to have those lips on hers. In that instant, memory reminded her exactly how they would feel... as hard as his arms, yet also tender, drawing her soul out of her body. A small sigh escaped her and she half closed her eyes, waiting for that imagined kiss. Instead, she felt him relaxing his hold on her and setting her down. Disappointment screamed in her, and a sense of loss, but almost instantly she was equally aware of her defences going up. If he should realise what she had been thinking... she'd die! She moved away from him abruptly with a little laugh which came out closer to a snort.

'Thanks, Sir Walter! It's just as well I haven't had the time to put on too much weight!'

'I expect I could still manage you,' he said. 'Now come on, you'd better get home and change out of those wet things.' But there was a sharp edge to his voice and she cringed inwardly again, wondering if he *had* known what she was thinking.

As he drove her home she hunched in her seat, shivering from time to time. He was right – the cold and wet were beginning to get to her. Outside her house he leaned across and opened the door for her but not even his nearness, still intoxicating as it was, could keep her teeth from chattering.

'Go and have a hot drink or else you will be a candidate for pneumonia.'

'Oh, I haven't the time to be ill!' she returned tartly. 'Thanks for the lift, Ralph – and for your help.'

'Glad to be of assistance.' But again the irony of his tone left her wondering if half the pleasure had come from being proved right. He had not actually said, 'I told you so', but still . . .

'Good night. And thanks again.'

'Good night. I'll be seeing you.'

Ruby had brought the children round from next door and put them to bed. She was a gem, Amy thought, worth every penny she was paid. Now she was sitting in the kitchen with Huw, who was pointedly ignoring her while chewing his way through a doorstep of bread and cheese she had found for him.

'Ruby, I'm sorry I'm so late!' Amy went on to explain the reason for her delay, but at the mention of Ralph's name Huw stuffed the last of the bread and cheese into his mouth and slammed out of the room. Amy sighed. Apparently Huw couldn't stand him and Ralph's absence had done nothing to ease that deep but unfounded dislike.

'I'd better go and change,' she said to Ruby. 'I wish I could have a hot bath, but I don't think I can be bothered to wait while the water hots up. I'm going to try to have an early night.'

When Ruby had gone, Amy found she hardly knew what to think of first. There were all the worries about the floods and the yard, her waterlogged car and the out-of-order telephone. But somehow all of this was subordinate to thoughts of Ralph. And when all her jobs were out of the way and she crawled gratefully into bed with the luxury of her stone hot-water-bottle – in use for the first time that autumn – it was the things he had said which kept popping into her mind.

So many of his comments could be imbued with hidden

410

meaning if you scratched the surface – the suggestion of starting a Gloucester depot, the faintly ironic 'Glad to be of assistance', even his parting comment: 'I'll be seeing you'. But then again it might mean nothing. That was the trouble with Ralph, you never could tell.

It's only wishful thinking on my part, that's all, she told herself. But nevertheless the tiny flame of excitement was sparking deep within her and when she fell asleep, her body curled around the stone curve of the bottle, it was as if she was feeling his arms around her once more, strong and infinitely tender... and as she fell asleep, her lips parted on the pillow in a long, imagined kiss.

*

Next morning Amy sang as she sorted clean clothes for the children and prepared their breakfast.

I must be crazy, she thought. I have to face a day with all sorts of problems and yet I'm happy. And she knew it was because of Ralph, her hopes for what might yet be resurrected between them and perhaps the half-remembered dreams of the night, too.

With Huw and Barbara despatched to school and Maureen safely installed with Ruby, she set out to walk to the yard. The rain had stopped at last, though the sky still looked heavy and the winds had brought down many of the leaves prematurely from the trees so that they lay in sad, sodden drifts on the saturated ground.

As she reached the top of Porter's Hill she slowed her step, wondering if she should walk down past Ralph's house. Driving, she never went that way – his scathing comments so long ago about it being a private road still rankled. But walking... it was so much quicker, and besides...

Admit it – that's just an excuse! she told herself. You're hoping you might see him!

Her breath came a little unevenly as she walked down the hill, looking at the house while trying not to make this obvious. But there were no signs of life and, a little disappointed, she turned her back on it and continued walking along the lane towards the yard.

As it came in sight, she strained her eyes to see what sort of state things were in. The road above the yard certainly wasn't flooded – though she could remember times when it had been under water – and as the yard itself came fully into view she heaved a sigh of relief. Once the rain had stopped the river must have started going down, and though streams still gushed down out of the sloping fields above, running broad rivulets across the road, there were only puddles and patches of thick sludge to show for the muddy water which had risen the previous night.

Her car and one lorry were well above what had been the tide-line; the other lorries were not to be seen – clearly the river bridge was now passable and they had already left for their day's work.

As she unlocked her office, Herbie emerged from the new spares shed.

'Good morning, Herbie.' There was a lift in her voice. 'Come in and we'll have a cup of tea.'

He followed her, wiping his hands on the piece of rag which usually hung out of the back pocket of his overalls.

'What a night! We were lucky not to get flooded out. Looks as if the water came into the yard,' he remarked.

'It did.' She put on the kettle before unbuttoning her coat and sitting down. 'You noticed I had to leave my car here last night? The bridge was flooded and I very nearly got stuck . . .'

She went on to relate what had happened and Herbie listened, shaking his head sorrowfully.

'I'm sorry, missus. If I had known what was going to happen, I'd have stayed on. But I didn't think you would be late like that.'

'It was my own fault, Herbie. And anyway, Ralph Porter helped me.'

'Hmm.' Herbie's look said if anyone had to help her, it ought to have been him. 'So he's home again, then?'

'Only until today.'

She was about to tell him about the possible new contracts when he went on, 'I thought I saw him yesterday, driving up the hill. Came to take his young lady to meet his sister, I shouldn't wonder.'

A nerve jarred warningly through her. 'His young lady?'

'Well, he had someone in the car with him. Very posh she was, too – just the type you'd expect him to go for. Wearing one of them new-fangled hats – you know, a bit like a turban, I always think.' (Herbie had once served with the army in India.) 'But on her I must say it looked good, though she had too much paint and muck on her face.'

'His young lady! You shouldn't jump to conclusions, Herbie. He could have been just giving someone a lift. After all, *I* was in his car last night . . .' Amy said brightly, though a hollow was beginning to open up inside her and she knew she was grasping at straws.

Herbie, quite oblivious of the effect his words were having, shook his head.

'I wouldn't have thought you'd see the likes of her in Hillsbridge if weren't for somebody like him. And my missus was only telling me t'other day that she'd heard he might be getting married soon. That housekeeper of his had told her sister. Now that would be a turn-up for the books, wouldn't it? What with him seeming like a confirmed bachelor.'

Amy said nothing. The joy was seeping out of her with every word he spoke. It was only gossip of course, gleaned third-hand, plus a glimpse of a glamorous woman in Ralph's car, but still . . .

Why should I imagine he has been leading a celibate life in Gloucester? Amy thought miserably. He's a very eligible man and he can't occupy all his time with business.

'Now, missus, the lorry for Harfords got off all right . . .' Herbie turned the talk to the subject he was most comfortable discussing and with an effort, Amy followed him. But when all the day's business had been ironed out and Herbie had gone back to his work, she found herself still thinking of Ralph with a sinking heart.

Yesterday, seen through rose-coloured spectacles, the encounter had seemed laden with promise. Now it was the negative aspects which loomed large – the coolness between them when he had first arrived, the alacrity with which he had put her down after he had carried her through the water, the businesslike way he had discussed the possible new contracts . . .

Amy closed her eyes, biting hard on her knuckles.

I don't want to do it, she thought. If I quote for those runs to Gloucester and get the work, it will mean seeing more of him, talking to him on the telephone . . . and I don't want to. When there had been the chance of resurrecting their relationship she had welcomed the prospect, but if Ralph had a sweetheart – or even wife! – the contact would be torture.

But it's business and you have to do it! she told herself. And answered as much with her head as with her heart: But if

413

every time you have to speak to him it upsets you this much, it's just not worth it. You'll be snappy with other customers, careless about details and the rest of the contracts will suffer.

Without stopping to think about it any more, she reached for the telephone and asked for Ralph's local number. Mrs Milsom answered, telling her that he had already left for Gloucester. But when she rang there she was informed he had not yet arrived. Taking time off to be with his lady friend, perhaps? Firmly Amy pushed that thought aside. At least she did not have to speak to him; she was put through to a clerk and left a message for Mr Porter to say that at present she felt unable to offer a quotation for the long-haul journey. However, she hoped the local contract would continue as before. Then, with a feeling of resignation, she returned to her day's work, but the problems she had hummed over earlier closed in on her now – silly, niggling irritations which combined to produce a nerve-jarring whole. The last straw came when her newest driver returned to confess that he had been pulled in by the police and reprimanded for not having his load properly secured. Amy flew at him, blaming him roundly and dismissing his excuse that when he had left it had been cold and wet and his fingers had been too numb to fix the ropes securely.

'I won't have it!' she snapped. 'Don't you realise you could have caused a serious accident if you had shed your load! You might have killed somebody!'

'I'm sorry, Mrs Roberts,' the boy said miserably.

'And so you should be. This is a responsible firm and we have a reputation to maintain. Did you know that a new transport firm has started up out at Stack Norton? They haven't taken any business from us yet, but if we were to get a bad name, then they might. Next time – if there is a next time – you'll be fired.'

The boy left, red-faced and disgruntled, but Amy could not find it in her to feel sorry for him. She was too sorry for herself.

There are times when I wish I had never started this, she thought. I could be a housewife and mother, putting all my energies into bringing up my family, doing all the things I never have time for now. Instead, here I am trying to do a man's job and letting life pass me by. I'm becoming a harridan, and then I wonder why Ralph goes off and finds a woman who has the time to spend making herself *look* like a woman...

Although the river appeared to have gone down considerably the sky was still leaden and Amy made sure that Herbie had placed the lorries well above the flood-line before she packed up, much earlier than the previous night. She didn't feel like working late again; all she wanted was to get home, spend some time with the girls and Huw and then be alone to wallow in her misery.

But even at home the petty irritations continued. When she cooked supper she discovered she had run out of Bisto and Huw - sent up to the general store on the corner to get some - delayed to play fivestones with some of his pals, so that she had to wait, fuming, and eventually go out to look for him. When she returned, the potatoes had boiled dry; then Barbara came hanging round her skirts sniffing and complaining of a sore throat.

'I suppose she sat in school in wet socks yesterday - and that cloakroom runs with water,' Amy thought irritably. 'Now if she's starting a cold it will go through the house - that's all I need!'

'Can I go down to Rex Parker's?' Huw asked when they had finished eating.

'Yes, as long as you're back by half-past eight,' Amy told him, thinking it would be sure to be nine o'clock. But Rex was one of Huw's more acceptable friends and she liked to encourage him to keep the sort of company least likely to lead him into trouble.

The girls tucked up in bed, she sat down for a few minutes and lit one of her cigarettes. The days when she had had to smoke out of the front-room window were over - now she smoked when she liked and the habit was growing. But tonight not even that brought her any comfort and when the doorbell rang, she wondered for a wild, wonderful moment if it might be Ralph.

Opening the door, however, she found Oliver Scott on the step. Amy was surprised. He had not called quite so often lately and now he reminded her faintly of a wandering puppy, standing there with a lopsided and slightly guilty smile, rumpling his sandy hair with a big hand.

'I was just passing, so I thought I would look in and see how you were getting on...'

'Come in.'

In the kitchen the clothes the girls had discarded were piled in the easy chair, waiting to be taken upstairs. Amy picked them up and plonked them on the table.

'Sorry about the muddles.'

'Don't worry about it. Muddles can be nice – they make a room homely.'

'Do they?' Personally Amy hated muddles, but since they always seemed to materialise round her she had learned to live with them.

'We never have muddles.' He sounded oddly regretful.

'Lucky for you!'

It was just as if he had not heard her, as he continued, 'Grace won't have it. She can be very strict. If I or the girls leave anything lying about, woe betide us!'

Amy was unsure what to say. Though the sentiments were ordinary enough, his tone made them deeply personal. Oliver rarely talked about his wife, she realised suddenly, but when he did there was always this feeling of . . . what? Unhappiness, almost. It was understandable for him to speak of her sometimes with that edge of irony – nobody could be happy all the time. After a row or even a pettifogging but persistent disagreement, she might have used the same tone to talk about Llew. But Oliver *always* sounded the same when Grace's name was mentioned.

'If she's so fanatical about tidiness, I think I would be tempted to leave a few things about on purpose to annoy,' she said wickedly, watching him out of the corner of her eye.

'I couldn't do that.' He sounded so definite that she turned to look at him fully and caught an expression more clear-cut than mere unhappiness. He looked worried, she thought, out-and-out curiosity getting the better of her.

'Why not?'

His grey eyes, totally devoid of laughter now, flicked up to hers hastily as if to assess her reason for asking.

'Why not?' she pressed him again.

'In Grace's state of health, that wouldn't be wise.'

'What do you mean? Is she ill?' Amy asked, unable to contain herself. 'I didn't know, Oliver. Is it serious?'

A slight pink flush coloured his cheeks. 'She's not physically ill, Amy. But her mental stability is balanced on such a fine knife-edge that we don't do anything to upset her if we can help it. This tidiness thing is just one of her foibles.

416

She has always been fanatical about it and now, well, a muddle can wind her up as quickly as anything.'

'Oh, you mean it gets her in a temper.' Amy had never had any experience of emotional or so-called 'nervous' troubles.

Oliver ran his fingers through his hair, leaving it standing up like the prickles of a rather curly hedgehog.

'Not exactly. Snappy, yes. But mostly very, *very* strung-up.'

'So why don't you just tell her to calm down?'

'It isn't that simple.' He sat down in the chair where the offending clothes had been, staring into the fire that was sending showers of wood-sparks up the chimney. 'I said just now that she's not physically ill, but when the other problems are really bad they *make* her physically ill. Worse, she refuses to go out when she's like that – won't speak to anyone, even.'

'*Grace* won't?' Amy, who could remember Grace as the leading light in Ted's old concert party, was flabbergasted. 'But she was always such a one for...' she broke off. She could hardly say 'showing off', although the expression had been on the tip of her tongue. 'She was always such a good mixer,' she ended lamely.

'That has nothing to do with it, actually,' Oliver explained, as if to a patient. 'Quite often it is those with the seemingly brightest personalities who suffer most in this way.' His voice trailed away and he spread his hands helplessly on his knees. 'It's not easy for any of us, Amy. In fact, there are times when I wonder where it will all end.'

'I had no idea,' Amy said formally, but his dejection – so contrasting with his normal easygoing manner – was eating into her, evoking sharp sympathy which had nothing to do with understanding.

So this was the cause of those sudden moments of unhappiness – the 'secret sadness' she had detected and dismissed because it seemed just too ridiculous. Grace was no longer the girl he had married – she had become a pale shadow of that vibrant, vivacious creature who had been called more than once 'the belle of Hillsbridge'.

'Is it because of her illness that she won't drive, either, Oliver?' Amy asked, remembering the conversation about the car.

'It's all connected. She won't drive, she won't communicate, even the smallest decision is beyond her – really little

417

things, I mean, such as what we should have for dinner or whether or not she should buy a new dress. And it seems that nothing I can do or say really helps her. I'm a doctor; I spend my life helping people to cope with their ailments, real and imagined, but I can't do a thing for my own wife...'

'Oliver, I don't know what to say...'

He got up. 'You don't need to say anything. I shouldn't be burdening you with my troubles, anyway.'

'Don't be silly. What are friends for?'

His eyes narrowed until they were almost lost in the folds of his cheeks. Then suddenly he reached out to grasp her arms, holding them gently.

'Oh, Amy, Amy – if only she could be more like you!'

Unexpected tears filled Amy's eyes because she felt so sorry for him. He was a good man, a kind man who dispensed caring and compassion along with the old-fashioned potions and the modern drugs. He deserved a happy family to go home to at the end of a long day. Instead he returned to more problems, all the more enormous because they were personal, and the emptiness of a marriage in which he had become not husband but custodian. She ducked her head, twisting away so that he should not see the tears.

'Oliver, I must get on. I have so much to do...'

'I know; I'm going now. This was just a flying visit, since I was passing.' His tone was absolutely normal except for the slightest wobble on the final syllables. The intimacies of the past few minutes might never have been. 'How's your head now, by the way? Not troubling you any longer, I hope?'

'Sometimes,' she admitted, 'but *only* sometimes.'

'Let me see, how long is it now since the accident...?' It was just like a professional visit now, Amy thought wryly.

'I think I shall survive, doctor,' she joked and for just a moment his mask slipped again.

'I'm sure you will, Amy. You *are* a survivor,' he said.

Chapter Twenty-Four

During the next two weeks Oliver Scott did not call on Amy even once. He's embarrassed because now I know a great deal about personal matters which he would have preferred to keep to himself, she thought.

After the torrential rains the weather had turned fine. There were clear days when the sun was warm once the early nip had melted from the air, and the leaves – those not brought down prematurely by the high winds – made splashes of red and gold against the heavy azure sky. It was Indian summer at its best, and in more ways than one it was the lull before the storm.

Half-term for the schools was kept at the beginning of October, and this year Jack had offered to have Huw for the week's holiday.

'It's a bit cold for the beach, but I'm sure we can still find plenty for him to do,' Jack wrote and Amy had accepted the invitation eagerly on Huw's behalf. It would be good for him to have a change of scene and, knowing her brother, Amy felt sure he would give Huw a holiday to remember. Why, he might even take him up in one of those new-fangled engineless aeroplanes, or 'gliders' as they were called. Gliding was the very newest sport and Jack, with his love of flying, had been one of the first to take it up.

'Crazy, I call it,' Charlotte had said irritably. 'After his experiences in the war, I should have thought he would have been only too glad to keep his feet on terra firma!'

But she accepted that Jack, a grown man if he was still her son, would do exactly as he pleased.

'I should put your foot down and say that Huw can't go up, if I were you, Amy,' she advised, but Amy just smiled. If Jack were to take Huw up it would probably make his holiday, she thought.

Jack and Stella arrived in Hillsbridge on the Friday evening and stayed the night with Mam in Greenslade Terrace.

'We were invited to stay with Grace and Oliver, but quite honestly I don't think Grace is up to it,' Stella confided to Amy when they called to collect Huw on the Saturday morning.

'I'm sorry to hear that,' Amy said, wondering whether Stella would think it odd if she failed to ask what was wrong with Grace, or whether the very fact of asking would give the game away that she knew the truth.

'It's her nerves,' Stella went on confidentially. 'She's never been properly right since Frances was born. I saw it happen to others when I was nursing, but I never expected it to happen to Grace. She was always such a bright, outgoing sort and it must be dreadful for her.'

'And for Oliver,' Amy said.

'Well, yes. The trouble is that it's always the relatives who get the sympathy when someone's suffering with their nerves,' Stella maintained. 'Always a case of "poor so-and-so has such a picnic with his wife", while nobody spares a thought for how ill she may be feeling. It's a popular assumption that the victim could pull herself together if she chose, but it's not as simple as that, believe me.'

'I expect you're right,' Amy said, but privately acknowledged that she came within that category herself. She could hardly find it in her to spare sympathy for Grace, who had everything and yet was seemingly unable to appreciate how lucky she was.

Jack and Stella left with Huw fairly early on Saturday morning so that they would be back in time to make the most of his first day, while Amy took Barbara and Maureen for her weekly visit to the market. Unless it was pouring with rain she never took the car on Saturday mornings – the walk had become almost a ritual.

At the top of Porter's Hill she glanced to her right automatically. The house was out of sight from here, but even passing right by it, Amy had not seen Ralph since the night of the floods and assumed he was still in Gloucester. But she looked all the same, because she was still irresistibly drawn to any contact with Ralph.

Sometimes during the intervening weeks she had thought about her decision not to quote for the long-haul journeys and regretted it. Herbie might have been mistaken in what he had said, yet she could have severed all contact with Ralph because of it. Besides which, she would have liked the challenge and comfort of the extra work. Several times lately she had heard the name of the new Stack Norton transport firm mentioned and, though she had not noticed any falling-off in business because of it, she was aware that at some time or other competition might have to be faced – if not from them, then from anyone else who might decide to buy a lorry and set up a company.

She was almost into Hillsbridge when Barbara squealed, 'There's a car coming, Mammy! A car!'

She had been bending over to adjust Maureen's bonnet as she walked, but now she glanced up and went weak inside. There was no mistaking that car – big and classy, bright red at a time when most cars still came in a choice of two colours – black or black! It was Ralph's Morgan.

Flustered, she found herself wondering frantically whether or not to wave and then, as the car drew closer, she froze. There was a woman in the passenger seat and as it passed Amy got a clear view of a fine-boned face beneath an emerald green cloche hat, framed by the collar of an emerald jacket. Beside her, Ralph raised a hand to Amy in mock-salute. Then they were gone and Amy was left feeling as if the bottom had dropped out of her world all over again.

It was true then, what Herbie had said, and not just idle gossip. And if Ralph was here in Hillsbridge with her again, then the affair must be on a serious basis.

Perhaps he *is* going to marry her! thought Amy wretchedly. And then, as defiance rushed in to anaesthetise the pain a little: Well, good luck to him. If that's the kind of woman he wants, let him get on with it – and much good may it do him. She'll spend all his money for him and make his life a misery with her demands. Still, it's his funeral!

It never occurred to Amy to wonder if she might be judging unfairly. She was opinionated enough to believe one quick glance was sufficient for her to sum up the character accurately – and too hurt to want to credit Ralph's lady friend with even the smallest asset.

'Mammy, you're hurting my hand!' Maureen complained and Amy loosened tension-tight fingers.

'Sorry, my love.'

'What's wrong, Mammy?' Babs chirped in.

'Nothing,' Amy said and told herself the same: There is nothing wrong – nothing at all. Well, there is nothing *different* anyway from what it was yesterday. You may be just a bit wiser – and that can't be bad. So forget it – forget Ralph and forget the hoity-looking woman in emerald green.

But she could not forget. It hovered at the edges of her mind, casting long shadows and colouring everything she did and thought...

With Huw away the house was surprisingly quiet.

I didn't realise how noisy he was! Amy mused and then came to the conclusion that probably it wasn't *just* Huw who roared about the place, but the fact that when he was there he encouraged the girls to join in with noisy games. Left alone, they were playing quietly apart from the occasional inevitable squabble. Bedtime too was completed at the girls' earlier time, and Amy found herself almost at a loose end.

As always, of course, there was plenty to do if she cared to look for it, but she didn't feel like doing anything. She tuned into the wireless, but listening to music could not prevent the thoughts of that morning's encounter from whirling chaotically around in her head. I must admit they do make a good pair, she thought grudgingly. No doubt she had the same kind of background as Ralph and like it or not, she would be an asset – superb when it came to entertaining, knowing who should sit where and what cutlery to lay. I'd be totally dependent on Mrs Milsom if ever I found myself in that position – and if she did anything wrong, I wouldn't know!

But the emptiness inside her was complete. It was all very well to try to be philosophical about it – that didn't ease the ache of broken dreams or lift the heavy weight around her heart.

She decided to get in some more coal. It was chilly in the evenings now and she thought she could do with the comfort of a fire.

While she was in the coal-house she heard a car stop outside and peeped out to see who it was. The vehicle was out of sight, hidden behind the hedge, but someone was walking up the path – someone whose bowed head made him look almost like an old man.

'Oliver! Is that you?' she called.

'Yes.' His voice sounded strained too.

'Wait a minute – I'm in the coal-house...' She emerged

with her bucket and he followed her round to the back door. As the pool of light from the kitchen caught his face, she drew in a shocked breath for he looked ten years older than when she had last seen him – haggard, middle-aged, his round face falling into pouches of distress. Her first thought was for Jack, Stella and Huw driving back to Minehead. Had something happened to them? Was Oliver bearing terrible news? She began to tremble right down to the tips of her fingers.

'What's the matter?' she asked sharply.

'You haven't heard, then,' he said heavily and her blood seemed to turn to ice. So there was something she didn't know! She closed the door, leaning heavily against it.

'Heard what?'

'About Grace.'

'Grace?'

'My wife.'

'No. What about her?'

'She tried . . . oh God, Amy, I don't know how to put this into words . . . she tried to do away with herself.'

Amy stared in disbelief, straightening away from the door. It was Oliver who was sagging now and she pulled a chair forward for him.

'You mean commit suicide?'

He nodded.

'But how?'

'Like so many people do, she went down to the Mill and jumped in the river.'

'Oh, my God!' Amy pressed her hands over her mouth and closed her eyes tightly for a moment. Then, 'Is she all right? She didn't succeed, did she, Oliver?'

'No, she didn't succeed, thank God! Someone saw her acting strangely and followed. Then, when they heard the splash and the scream . . .'

'She screamed?'

'The cold water brought her to her senses and she panicked – tried to get to the bank. But the river is deep and overgrown just there and Grace can't swim. She would have drowned without a doubt, but the man who had followed her alerted the manager at the Mill, who was working late, and between them they managed to get her out.'

'Oh Oliver, it's terrible!' Amy said, distressed. 'Where is she now?'

Oliver sat forward in the chair, head bowed, big hands rumpling through gingery hair.

'In hospital.'

'Suffering from shock, I suppose? Where is she – at the Cottage Hospital?'

The crown of gingery hair moved slowly from side to side. 'No – no...'

'Not the Cottage Hospital? Then where...?' Amy's voice tailed away as the truth dawned. 'Oh, Oliver, you mean she's...'

'In Wells. The asylum. I've fought it, Amy, as long as I could, but there comes a time when you have to give in and face up to the facts. There's nothing I can do for Grace, but somebody's got to do something to help her, for Christ's sake! She can't go on like this. It's terrible for her and for us, and I never know what she's going to do next. How could I leave her in charge of the children? She might do anything, I just can't trust her.'

'So you've had her put away?'

'For the time being. Oh, Amy, don't say it like that! It sounds so cold and hard. Not that there *is* a nice way of putting something like that. Believe me, over the years I've tried to couch that kind of thing in gentle phrases for my patients – the brutal truth is that there's no way to soften it, not when it's your own wife.'

'She's in the best place, Oliver,' Amy said inadequately.

'Yes, I know. I've said *that* to patients a good many times, too,' he replied. 'That doesn't help either. And there's more... she might face criminal proceedings. Christ, what a mess!'

Amy looked at him sadly. This was her childhood hero, the man whose golden image had lightened a thousand dark hours for her. Now he was as much in need of help as she had ever been.

'Would you like a drink?' she asked. 'I can't offer you a choice, I'm afraid, but I do have half a bottle of brandy in the cupboard, strictly for emergencies.'

He didn't answer and she went into the front room for the brandy, pouring out two glasses. When she pushed one into his hand he gulped it back and she came over to give him another.

'Go on, I can spare it. The bottle hasn't been touched since Babs had a bilious attack last Christmas...'

There was a long awkward silence. Oliver drained his glass for a second time and again Amy tipped golden liquid into it. He looked as if he could drink the bottle dry and still it would not do him any good, she thought.

'Whatever made her do it?' she asked after a moment, speaking more to herself than to him. 'I know she hasn't been well for a long while, but she must have got worse all of a sudden.'

'Something triggered her off, obviously.' Oliver rolled the glass between his hands. 'If you ask me, it might have been seeing Stella this morning that did it.'

'Seeing *Stella*?' said Amy incredulously.

'Between you and me, Grace is very jealous of Stella.'

'But why should she be? That's just silly!'

'There's not necessarily too much reason behind these things,' he pointed out. 'But Grace was the one who always seemed to have everything.'

He laughed in a self-deprecatory manner. 'Grace obviously wouldn't agree with you.'

'Then's she's mad!' Instantly she could have bitten out her tongue. 'I'm sorry, I didn't mean that . . .'

'I told you, when she's ill Grace sees things in a different perspective from when she's well. And I've been a disappointment to her, no doubt. I believe Grace liked the idea of marrying a doctor, but she didn't expect me to bury myself in a country practice, especially not back here in Hillsbridge. It would have suited her very well if I had gone in for a consultancy, in Harley Street, say. For all that she was born and bred here, Grace is a city bird. I have thought for some time that maybe it was a mistake to come back. I even wondered about moving again. But for my own selfish reasons, I fought against it.'

'You mean because you're happier in the country?'

'That – and other things.' He looked up at her, his face haunted, and as their eyes met she knew with startling suddenness what those other things were. It was there, etched in those expressive brown eyes, a longing that he would never – *could* never – put into words.

In that moment of confused certainty, Amy found herself piecing together the clues which had been there all the time had she only had the insight to recognise them. The times when he had come just to sit in her kitchen. The tension which grew when she mentioned his wife and family. His words just the other day: 'If only she could be more like you, Amy!'

Somewhere along the line Oliver had stopped seeing her as the little girl he had once eased away from death's door. At some stage he had looked at her and seen a woman – a woman he wanted. He had hidden it well and Amy had never suspected for a moment. But now, after a day that must have been a living hell for him, he had turned to her as the one person in Hillsbridge in whom he felt able to confide, the one person he wanted to be with.

The knowledge overwhelmed her. Her idol had feet of clay. Yet somehow he was the more attractive for being human. Once, a long time ago, he had sustained her in time of need; now she had her chance to do the same for him.

As the tenderness welled up in her, she dropped to her knees beside him, tentatively touching his hands. His eyes came up to meet hers again and the look in them was as nakedly obvious as ever. Beneath her touch, he turned his hands so that his fingers grasped hers and she did not move away.

Pity was stirring warmth in her and his touch was evoking sharp, sweet memories of other touches. But most potent of all was the heady cocktail stirred in her by the knowledge that she was needed. Oh, it was so long since she had been needed! More than two long years. Ralph didn't need her, he never had. Ralph needed nobody – but if he ever did, she was not the one who would fill his need. The woman in the emerald toque would do that.

The pain twisted in her again, too hurtful to bear and her breath came out on a small sob.

Oh Ralph, why isn't it you here, holding my hands? Why – why? What sorry creatures we are – I'm crying inside for Ralph and Oliver's crying for ... for what? For Grace, his wife, mother of his children, who tried to take her life today – or for me, because he thinks I'm all the things she isn't: brave, happy, strong ... But I'm not, Oliver, I'm not! I'm a human being too and I'm afraid of the future without Llew or Ralph ... afraid ... afraid ...

'Amy.' His voice was low, husky with desire, and he pulled her gently towards him so that she was held between his knees. Brown eyes held blue and she felt the strength draining out of her.

I don't love him ... But he's here; he's real, living,

breathing flesh and he needs me. We need each other. It's been so long, dear God, so long...

Her skin was tingling now, each pore crying out for his touch. Breathless it seemed she hung there, suspended over the abyss of desire which could blot out thought, drain away conscience. Right or wrong – what did they matter? What did anything matter? He was here and she was here, two souls drowning in a sea of misery.

His hands left hers, sliding up her arms to her elbows and then to her shoulders. They paused there, gripping, and as the pressure increased so her chin lifted until the tendons in her neck were taut. She could see his face above her, too close to be distinct, and the smell of his shaving soap was in her nostrils.

When his mouth covered hers she gasped deep in her throat. His kiss was so hungry that it seemed to squeeze the breath from her and gave no leeway to draw another. In panic she twisted her head from side to side but he refused to let her go, his fingers biting into her shoulders, his mouth devouring her. Just when she felt her lungs would burst he released her lips and as she drew breath she was aware that every one of her senses had been heightened. She pressed closer, winding her arms around the solid barrel of his chest and when his hands slipped from her shoulders to the back fastening of her dress, she only moved towards him.

The fastening gave and as he eased the dress down over her shoulders her skin seemed to yearn up to his touch. His fingers traced the lines of her back and as they moved around to caress her full breast, she felt herself coming alive inch by inch. Her head was pressed against his chest; she could hear his heart hammering beneath her ear and she wriggled in close so that their bodies were pressed close together, and eased her fingers between the buttons of his shirt, stretching out to fan over his chest with its covering of crisp reddish hair.

Then his mouth was on hers again and he was pressing her back, back... lowering her until she was lying full length on the rug, his mouth still covering hers. The weight of his body was driving her crazy and she tried to part her sensitised thighs to have him still closer, but she could not move. Fully clothed apart from her bared breasts, she was tinglingly aware of his nearness; just as her need rose almost to screaming pitch he shifted slightly to reach down and pull up her skirt.

'Oliver...' She arched, aching, tingling, her whole being concentrated in that one throbbing centre of her body. He moved away briefly and as he did so the knock came at the door.

How is it that passion can be running so high in one moment and stone cold the next? The knock made Amy freeze and she knew from Oliver's absolute immobility that he too had reacted in exactly the same way.

My God, there's somebody at the door! The kitchen door! Just a few feet away! For a brief second they clung together, then into that silence when even breath was suspended the knock came again, loud and insistent.

Panic flared and Amy tried to move.

'Quick – quick – get up...' Her voice, though a whisper, was harsh with urgency and Oliver clamped a hand over her mouth.

'Ssh! Keep quiet and they might go away!'

'No!' she whispered through his fingers. 'Whoever it is will know we're here; they have seen the light. I'll have to answer it!'

Oliver swore softly, but he let her move and she scrambled to her feet, pulling down her skirt and hoisting up the bodice to cover her breasts and shoulders.

'Quick – do me up!' she hissed.

His fingers fumbled against hers as they struggled with the fastenings. She ran her fingers hastily through her hair as she hurried to the door, glanced over her shoulder to see Oliver straightening his clothing and opened it.

Ruby Clarke stood there with a brown paper parcel in her arms.

'Amy, this came for you while you were out...' She broke off, looking past Amy and seeing Oliver. 'Oh, I'm sorry, I didn't know you had company...'

Later, Amy was to think: Liar! You must have known – must have seen the car outside. You came especially!

But in that awkward moment she could only wonder: Will she know? Is it obvious what she interrupted?

Her cheeks were flushed, she could feel them burning and was painfully aware of her tumbled hair and imperfectly fastened dress. Should she invite Ruby to come in? Would it look stranger still to leave her standing on the doorstep? She glanced round at Oliver again – he too was flushed, the pink blush that is so disfiguring on people with red hair was staining his face and extending down his neck. She decided against asking Ruby in and took the parcel from her hastily.

'Thanks, Ruby. I don't know what this can be – I wasn't expecting anything...' She knew she was gabbling, her voice conveying the fluster she was feeling. 'I won't stop if you don't mind. Oliver is here and we were talking...'

'Yes, I can see that,' Ruby said. She sounded almost triumphant, as if she had confirmed exactly what she had come to find out. 'Don't worry, I can't stay myself, Amy. I'll see you tomorrow.'

When she had gone Amy closed the door and leaned against it, shaking.

'Oh, why did she have to come? I don't believe it! How awful!'

Oliver, clearly shaken, was still straightening his clothing, patting pockets and now that it was too late, neatening his tie.

'Who is she?'

'My neighbour. She's very good with the children, but such a gossip... Oh Oliver, do you think she noticed... do you think she knew?'

'God, I hope not!'

'But she must have! How could she *not* know? It must be written all over us... oh, I could die! And what about you? It could be serious, couldn't it?'

'Yes. But she couldn't *know*.' Oliver was trying to compose himself. 'There was nothing to see.'

'Only us. We look – well, we hardly look as if we've just been chatting, I'm sure! Oh my goodness, it's awful – it couldn't be worse. Ruby, of all people...'

'I ought to go.' Trying to move decisively, Oliver kicked into the chair, his guilt and embarrassment obvious. 'Amy, I'm sorry; I've put you in a terrible position.'

'It wasn't your fault alone. It was mine too. Well, it just happened, didn't it?'

'But I should have known it would. And with Grace in hospital... Christ, if she gets to hear about this...'

He was fumbling in his pockets. 'My keys. Where are my damned keys?'

She saw something gleaming in the middle of the carpet. 'Here. They're here.'

He took them. 'I must not come again. It's a bit late to say that I suppose, but...'

'Oh, don't say that! Maybe she didn't realise...'

'We can't afford to take the chance. I'm going, Amy; I should never have come.'

'No, I know. Oh, Oliver, I hope it will be all right...'

In the doorway he paused. 'I'm really sorry, Amy.'

There was no secret desire in his eyes now, only haunted anxiety, and Amy realised she had never been anything for him but an escape from reality. He had wanted her, yes, but only because she represented all the things in which at this moment Grace was lacking. But that was not to say he had stopped caring for his wife. With the possibility of scandal rocking Hillsbridge, with his very career in jeopardy, his first thought had been to worry what Grace would say or do if she came to hear of it.

'Don't worry, Oliver, if anyone asks me I shall deny everything,' she assured him.

He nodded. 'Yes. Well, thanks for that anyway, Amy.'

When he had gone she sank into a chair, covering her face with her hands as all the possible horrors of discovery raced before her closed eyes. If Ruby suspected, if she talked... oh, how will I ever hold up my head again? Amy wondered.

Then her natural optimism began to take over.

Perhaps Ruby had not noticed. Perhaps she wouldn't talk. For the moment, at any rate, this was all she had to hold on to.

*

It was, of course, a vain hope, as Amy knew next day when she met Ruby hanging out the washing – the suspicion and the secret delight of having been the one to walk in on the intimate scene was written all over her. And within a couple of days Amy was sure that Ruby had shared her knowledge. She saw people looking at her and whispering... hoped it was imagination fired by a guilty conscience and knew it was not.

Then, on the third evening, she had a visitor when Eddie Roberts came knocking on the door, his face like thunder.

'Amy, what the devil are you thinking of?'

'What do you mean?' she demanded, though she was shaking inside.

'There's talk everywhere about you and Dr Scott. Do you mean to tell me there's nothing in it?'

'Talk? What talk?' Sick to the core, Amy took refuge in sharp attack.

'Don't play the innocent with me, Amy. You must know about Grace?' When she did not answer, he went on impatiently, 'She tried to drown herself down by the Mill – and they're saying she did it because her husband was carrying on with you.'

Amy gazed at him aghast. 'You can't be serious!'

'I am, perfectly serious. His car's been seen outside here a good many times since they came back to Hillsbridge. People notice these things – you should know that. In a place like this it spreads like wildfire.'

'Then they have wicked minds, that's all I can say!' Amy flared.

'You don't deny he's been visiting you, then?'

'Why should I deny it? I have nothing to be ashamed of. He comes to check up on me – I had terrible headaches after my fall.'

'That's all right, then,' Eddie said pompously, then had second thoughts.

'What about last Saturday night? The night Grace – well, did what she did. He wouldn't have been making a professional visit then. But he was here, wasn't he?'

Amy shrugged angrily. 'If you say so.'

'I'm not the one who says so, it's Ruby Clarke. She's been saying so all over Hillsbridge – and a good deal more besides. She says . . .'

'Yes?' Amy demanded defiantly.

He faltered, then continued, 'She says she caught the two of you at it,' he stated. His voice was loud and accusing and the words hung in the air and echoed in her ears.

Her first reaction was cold, debilitating fear. They had been found out, Ruby had talked! Then her anger returned with a rush, heightened by the edge of underlying guilt.

'How dare you?' she demanded. 'How dare you come here accusing me and judging me? Who the hell do you think you are?'

Eddie took a half-step backwards.

'Your brother-in-law. That's who I am.'

'Huh!'

'I know you don't like me, Amy, and we've never got on. But Llew was my brother and I won't see him made a fool of. He had a good name in Hillsbridge; people respected him.'

'And why shouldn't they respect him now? It's a sorry state of affairs if I can't have friends call to see me without people making up all these wicked lies...' But there was an uncertain note in her voice now and her cheeks flushed. Sensing that he had found her most vulnerable spot, Eddie drove on to the attack once more.

'Is it lies, Amy?' he demanded.

Her flush deepened. 'Yes. Yes – of course it's lies! Ruby certainly did not "catch us at it" as you put it. She burst in on a private conversation. Oliver was upset – confiding in me. I was the first person he had felt able to talk to all day. Haven't you one ounce of common sympathy in your body? His wife had tried to drown herself and he had to have her taken down to Wells. Think how you would feel! You'd be only too glad to be able to talk it over with someone, wouldn't you? Well, so was Oliver. But there aren't many people he *can* talk to. He's a doctor and people take their troubles to him, not the other way around.'

'Oh yes, and what makes *you* so special?' Eddie asked, heavily sarcastic.

'Don't ask me. He treated me when I was a little girl and nearly died. He was like a father to me. This is the first chance I've had to repay him – and you have the nerve to come here saying...'

'I wasn't the one who said it,' Eddie argued hastily. 'I'm only telling you what others are saying. And to be truthful, you can't blame them. A young, attractive woman like you, widowed and on your own – when a man comes calling on you, people are bound to talk.'

'Let them!' He stared at her, shocked. 'Let them, I don't care!' she repeated.

Eddie drew in a deep breath so that he swelled with his own self-importance. 'You don't give a fig for propriety, do you?'

'What do you mean by that?'

'The way you carry on. I might as well tell you now I'm here, Amy – the whole family has been shocked by some of the things you do.'

'Oh? Like what, may I ask?'

'Running a business isn't very ladylike, for a start.'

'But better than letting you get your hands on it!'

'Smoking – driving a car – bringing that boy here...'

She was shaking with fury now. 'That boy, as you call

432

him, is your brother's son, don't forget!'

Eddie went white. It was as if he had forgotten this, or at any rate pushed the knowledge to the back of his mind.

'You would have swept him under the carpet, I suppose!' Amy raged on. 'Pretended he didn't exist? You would have let Llew's son go to an orphanage or an institution!'

'Keep your voice down!' Eddie implored, looking anxiously around at the still-open kitchen window.

'Why should I? If people are determined to talk about me, then I'll give them something to talk about!'

'Amy, for the love of Mike! I've got a reputation to keep up, even if you haven't!'

'Yes, that's it, isn't it?' Amy accused. 'That's why you're so concerned about my moral welfare – because you're worried what people may say about *you*. I've heard how you're hoping to get on the council when they have the next election, Eddie Roberts. I suppose you want to look whiter than white so that everybody will vote for you? Well, I'll tell you one who won't! I've seen you in your true colours. Brother-in-law? I'd be better off without one. And if you're not careful, that's what I shall tell the whole of Hillsbridge. Now – get out of here – and don't come back!'

'But Amy!'

'Get out!' She opened the door and in the end he went hastily, anxious the neighbours should not hear more of the quarrel than was inevitable.

For a few minutes Amy stood with her hands bunched to fists, shaking with temper. What right did he have to come here and tell her how to live her life – him with his fancy ways and an eye on making a name for himself. And she was disappointed in Ruby, too. Some friend she had turned out to be!

Well, there was only one way to stop her spreading more stories – and that was to counter-attack. Amy went to the bottom of the stairs, listened to make sure there was no sound from the children and then went round and banged on Ruby's door.

'Amy! What a surprise!' Ruby gushed but her guilt was written all over her.

'What do you mean by spreading stories about me?' Amy demanded.

Ruby took a step backwards. 'I don't know what you mean.'

'Then I'll tell you! You called on me on Saturday night when Dr Scott was visiting me. Now it has got back to me that you've been telling people you caught us behaving improperly. I should like to know what you mean by it, Ruby.'

'Well, I . . .' Confronted by the fruits of her willing gossip, Ruby was at a loss for words. 'It's not true, I didn't say that!' she blurted.

'"Caught us at it". Those were the words used to me.'

'Oh, I didn't! I *never*!'

'You must have said something, you're the only one who would.'

'His car was outside. Anybody could draw conclusions.'

'Not anybody. *You*, Ruby.'

'But I didn't say *that*. You know how people twist things, they put words in your mouth and . . .'

'I've got just one thing to say to you, Ruby. If you don't go back to the people you've talked to and tell them you blew the whole matter up out of all proportion, I shall have you up for scandal. And don't think I wouldn't, just because we're neighbours. Not that this is a very neighbourly thing to do, anyway.'

'Well!' Ruby gasped. 'I've certainly tried to be neighbourly – and this is all the thanks I get for it! I take it you won't want me to have the littl'uns any more, seeing what you think of me!'

Amy hesitated, cold reality driving a knife into her anger. It was so convenient, Ruby having the children . . .

'Look, Ruby, I've had my say. I'm upset, I won't deny it – wouldn't you be upset with such rumours flying round Hillsbridge about you? Not only that, have you thought how serious this could be for Dr Scott if anyone believes what you've said? He's a good man and an excellent doctor, but if people thought – well, his career could be ruined.'

'Well, all I can say is that he should have had more sense than to act the way he has,' Ruby said nastily.

'Promise me you'll stop spreading the rumours and we'll forget the whole thing.'

'Not likely! You've just said things to me you had no business saying. It's not my fault if you and Dr Scott want to mess about!'

'For the last time . . .'

'I won't say it outside any more because I've got no proof.' Ruby was red in the face now. 'But you know and I know exactly what was going on when I came knocking at your door. So don't come the injured innocent with me, Amy Roberts. And I'll tell you something else – I'm fed up with seeing you act like Lady Muck. I've been pleased to help you out, but if you think that gives you the right to come round here telling me a thing or two, you've got another think coming. All right?'

'All right!' Amy was shaking again. 'If that's the way you want it. But I meant what I said, Ruby – any more talk and you'll find yourself in court!'

'And you'll find yourself bankrupt! Nobody's going to do business with a husband-stealer!' She slammed the door and Amy was left trembling with hurt and anger.

She simply could not believe that Ruby had said such terrible things to her. 'Bankrupt!' 'Nobody would do business with a husband-stealer'. And 'Lady Muck'! Was that what Ruby thought of her? It was horrible – everyone seemed only too ready to turn against her, to think the worst.

All along the Rank the back doors were firmly shut now for the evening and Amy suddenly found herself thinking of the doors in the Rank at Greenslade Terrace. In memory it seemed that when she had been a child they were always ajar, the sun in summer evenings slanting in to make diametric patterns on faded linoleum, the warmth from the constantly burning coal fires creeping out in winter to greet you and envelop you in an aura of welcome. Even when the doors had been closed, as these now were, Amy had not felt excluded by them. She had known that the moment she knocked and peeped inside someone would greet her: 'Amy! What are you doing here? Come on in, my love!'

But no longer. Standing there in the deserted yard, feeling totally alone as if antagonism, not warmth, now lurked behind the closed doors, she realised for the first time that not all the fruits of success are sweet.

I've done well for myself, Amy thought. And other people don't like it. Oh, they might be nice enough to my face, but what do they say about me behind my back? The things that Ruby, my *friend* Ruby, said to me just now? That's the only time I hear them said out loud – when I've upset somebody enough to get them really rattled. Otherwise I go on in blissful ignorance.

But oh, how pleased they must be to have something to say about me! How they must enjoy making the digs!

The thought was a frightening one, because suddenly Amy could see with what delight the story about herself and Oliver must have been passed from lip to lip. But as she thought about it, her emotions went full circle and her anger began again, searing yet healing.

It was pathetic, people like Ruby stoking up jealousy for sheer spite. They could do as well as she had if they put half the energy they expended on scandal-mongering into making something of themselves. And they certainly were not going to mar her success now.

With a characteristic lift of her chin, Amy turned and crossed the yard to her own house.

Chapter Twenty-Five

The last few months of 1928 were a difficult time for Amy – a time when problems mounted and she felt as if she were running constantly in thick, sticky treacle.

The confrontations with Eddie Roberts and Ruby Clarke had upset her more than she cared to admit, bringing home to her the gulf which was there ready and waiting to open between her and her own people, creating practical difficulties which had to be resolved by more confrontation.

Approached about having Maureen again until alternative arrangements could be made, Charlotte was understandably cool, though triumphant.

'You see, Amy? You can never trust outsiders. And to think those children were in her care!'

'I'm sure she never said or did anything to harm them,' Amy said.

'You can't be sure of that. A woman who could make up such dreadful lies...'

'It's nice to know you trust me at least,' Amy said drily.

'Anyone who knows Oliver Scott would know there couldn't be any truth in it!' Charlotte declared. 'He's a gentleman. But you should have had more sense than to have him there, Amy. People will talk – you ought to have known that. And look at the trouble it's caused!'

Amy said nothing. Whilst asking a favour, she was in no position to utter the kind of sharp retort which came to her lips all too easily these days. And there was no doubt that she had stirred up a hornets' nest.

Grace was still in Wells, undergoing 'treatment', while the town buzzed with speculation as to what that might mean. A suicide always caused a stir, giving the rest of the population an opportunity to enjoy a shiver of horror as they wallowed in the gruesome details; although Grace's attempt had been unsuccessful, the fact that she was both Hal's daughter and the doctor's wife more than made up for it.

'Good thing somebody were on hand to fish her out, or those two little girls would be without a mother!' Walter Clements commented to the rest of his cronies gathered round the corner table in the Miners' Arms, and Stanley Bristow added, 'Good thing she didn't jump under the Pines. Couldn't have changed her mind then, could she?'

There was a murmur of agreement and Reuben Tapper, one-time railway porter, nodded vigorously. Jumping beneath the wheels of the Pines Express which thundered through Hillsbridge twice daily was one of the most popular and spectacular methods selected by Hillsbridge suicides – and certainly, as Reuben could testify, one of the messiest.

In the Miners' Arms, as on street corners and doorsteps all over Hillsbridge, talk of the suicide attempt progressed naturally to the reasons behind it and in every case blame was heaped on Amy.

Oliver Scott was popular and highly respected; no one could imagine the doctor doing anything improper. But Amy had been the subject of gossip more than once and as a result she was condemned universally with scarcely a word spoken in her defence.

'She always were a bit flighty,' Stanley Bristow said and Tommy Brixey, who had once fancied his chances with her before being put firmly in his place, added, 'Hoity, too. Though much good it did her, marrying a foreigner.'

Again there was a murmur of agreement. Although Llew, had he lived, would now have resided in Hillsbridge for six years, he was still regarded as a foreigner – and by the same token, so was Eddie. Unless he could get himself adopted as an official Labour Party candidate, he would have an uphill struggle to get himself elected to the council here, which he was so anxious to achieve.

'D'ust think 't will go any further?' Walter Clements asked. As a former neighbour of Amy's, he felt a little awkward being a party to discussing her morals and preferred to steer the conversation onto a less personal level. 'They do say as how a doctor can get right in the muck over this sort o' thing.'

Heads nodded sagely, but it was left to Stanley Bristow to say what they were all thinking.

'It's no more than talk at the moment and they'd have their work cut out to get him for nothing but talk – unless Grace or Amy have their say, of course. And what good would that do either on 'em? It's a damn shame! I can mind when Grace were just a girl, and she used to sing with our concert party. She could charm the birds off the trees, honest she could, and when I think she's come to this, well, I could break my heart. But if the doctor do get into trouble, I reckon we all ought to stand by 'un. He's a good bloke, one in a million, and a lot of us have got cause to be grateful to 'un. What d'you say?'

One by one they nodded:

'We could do a lot worse than Dr Scott.'

'Ah, we could – he were very good to my missus when she had thick bronchitis – and he didn't send his bill in all that quick, neither.'

'He's all right. Amy Hall's a fast piece – bound to be. T'ain't right, a woman doing what she does.'

'And there's summat funny about that boy she's got living there too, if you ask me. Do 'ee think she 'ad 'un afore she were married?'

So the talk went on, stopping only when Jim Hall and Dolly's husband Victor dropped in for a pint. And it was not confined to the Miners' Arms, either. It spread through the town like the first trickle of floodwater, becoming murkier and deeper as it passed from mouth to mouth in the queue at the Co-op bacon counter, hummed along the row of men who squatted collier fashion against the wall on County Bridge, and, most daring of all, spiced up the slow minutes for those waiting their turn at the doctor's surgery.

Almost universally the story was the same. The doctor could not be held to blame; if there was anything in the story, then without a doubt it had come about because of Amy

438

Hall. She was 'a one' and always had been; she wore her skirts far too short for a woman her age, even if it was the fashion; she was on her own all day down at that yard of hers with just men for company. It wasn't right – no wonder she'd run into trouble now; the only surprising thing was that it hadn't happened long ago.

At first, Amy was unaware of the proportions the talk was reaching. She had other things on her mind. Business was slackening off and since nothing had changed in the running of Roberts Haulage, she could not understand why.

One morning when she went into the office, Herbie was waiting with yet another piece of unwelcome news.

'Leech Gravel don't want us this week,' he told her bluntly. 'They've just telephoned to say they've made other arrangements.'

Amy's face dropped. Leech Gravel was a small but regular hiring. 'Why should they cancel?' she asked.

Herbie shook his heads. 'They didn't say.'

'Well, why didn't you ask?'

Again Herbie answered with a small shake of his head. Amy wondered briefly if he was keeping something back, but Herbie was a man of few words who was happiest simply getting on with his jobs in the yard. It was just like him to take the message and ask no questions.

When the second firm – a small timber merchant from Withydown – telephoned to say they would not require the Roberts lorry this week, Amy was unable to conceal her dismay. Joe Bray, the owner, was a friendly little man who usually did his business by coming into the office and chatting over a cup of coffee and a cigarette.

'Forgive me asking, but why won't you need us this week, Joe?' Amy enquired. 'Business is all right, is it?'

'Yes, business is fine,' he murmured uncomfortably.

'Then why... ?'

There was a long pause and Amy began to think they had been cut off. Then Joe said, half-defiantly, 'We thought it was only fair to give that new transport firm over at Stack Norton a try.'

Amy felt the skin prick on the back of her neck.

'Oh, haven't we been giving you satisfaction, then?'

'It's not that. But it seems only right to let them have a week's work sometimes, seeing they're trying to get started.'

'I see,' Amy said – but she did not. The other firm had been in operation for some months now and Joe had not felt the need to give them a week's work before. Why now?

But deep down a small unwelcome voice was suggesting a reason. Perhaps it was all to do with the gossip. She had been tarred as 'no better than she should be' – a woman who got the respectable doctor into trouble and drove his wife to suicide – and people were not anxious to be involved with her. Was it Joe's wife, concerned about the business chats over coffee and cigarettes, who had laid down the law? Or was it Joe himself, a good chapel-going man with a highly developed set of morals, who had decided to transfer his business, temporarily at least? Whichever, it meant another job lost – the second in a week – and Amy was seriously worried. The business had been ticking over nicely, but she had not been so inundated with work that she could afford to lose regular customers in this way.

As Joe hung up Amy heard another click on the line, closer to home and quite distinctive. Damnation! she thought. It's that woman at the telephone exchange, listening in again!

That was the trouble with the telephone. Sitting in her own front room, the woman who operated the Hillsbridge exchange could plug in to whatever conversations she chose – and she was never slow in broadcasting what she heard. In no time it would be all over town that Roberts Hauláge was in trouble, and even if that was still an exaggeration at the moment, it might not be for long . . .

Amy's heart sank. She hated the idea of people saying the business was failing even more than she hated being branded a scarlet woman, for the business was her pride and joy. But there was no doubt about it, and as the weeks went by she was forced to admit that things were not going well. Apart from the two lost contracts, there was a shortage of casual hirings, with only one new booking coming in over a month. Too much of the time the lorries were idle. But the bills still had to be paid and the bank loan still ate up the fast diminishing profits.

How long would it take to ride out the storm? Amy wondered. How long before the talk died down and people began coming to Roberts Haulage again – if indeed that was the reason? Or would that never happen? If her former clients were satisfied with the new haulage firm, then they might very well stick to it. Well situated for both quarries and woodlands, Amy could not think why it hadn't taken off at her expense the moment it opened up.

In an attempt to drum up business, she spent a whole day drawing up a list of likely clients and telephoning round to them, but this too was a frustrating affair. In the bigger and more prosperous firms she found herself being fobbed off by a lady clerk without ever reaching the principal or even the transport manager; and though she was given a polite enough reception by the small one-man businesses, her persuasive powers got her precisely nowhere.

Could it be that she had been wrong to attribute the falling-off in business solely to the rumours about her reputation? Amy wondered. Was it rather the cautious expansion of the last few years was grinding to a halt and firms were pulling in their horns? For a little while it had seemed that the golden years might be just around the corner not only for the men who had survived the Great War, but also for those too young to have known anything about it. When the Kellogg Pact had been signed by every nation of the world, ensuring that conflict would never again be used as a solution to problems and promoting lasting peace, it had spread an umbrella of hope over the nation, even here in the depressed Somerset coalfield. But now, as she made her telephone calls, Amy sensed a change of mood which had nothing to do with her escapade with Oliver Scott – and hardly knew whether to be glad or sorry that that might not be the sole cause of her problems.

If only I had someone to talk it over with, it would not be quite so bad, Amy thought wretchedly. But there was no one. Mam wouldn't understand – she never had. Her watchword had always been caution, and any advice she had to give now would probably centre around disposing of the assets and making sure Amy had a credit balance in a piggy bank rather than owing money to 'the proper bank'; the latter being one of the few buildings in Hillsbridge which, along with the billiards hall and the mortuary, were beyond Charlotte's pale – places in which she would never be persuaded to set foot.

In any case, Mam was far too preoccupied these days to talk about anything but the King's health, Amy thought. In the middle of November a lung infection had laid him low and the daily bulletins on his condition were not encouraging. Always an ardent royalist, Charlotte followed the downhill progress as the cold turned to congestion of the lung, tutting knowingly when an increase in fever was reported and shuddering when pleurisy was mentioned.

'Poor soul – with all those doctors, you'd think they'd be able to do something for him, wouldn't you?' she commented regularly and on the day when Amy was worried sick about the balancing of her accounts, all Charlotte could talk about was that the Prince of Wales was racing home to London from 'somewhere between Lake Tanganyika and Dar-es-Salaam'.

'He's a wonderful man, but I hope and pray he won't become King just yet,' Charlotte said. 'Now, Amy, what were you saying about the lorry?'

'Nothing,' Amy said wearily. 'At least, nothing that would interest you half so much as the next bulletin on the King's health.'

'You're getting very cheeky, Amy. I don't like it,' Charlotte scolded her.

By the beginning of December the condition of His Majesty was improving a little, though the strain on his heart was giving cause for concern, but Amy's problems had done nothing to diminish. She still had the long-term contracts, of course, but they would not produce sufficient work to keep the lorries fully occupied and she found herself wishing she had not been so hasty in rejecting Ralph's request to quote for the long-haul journeys. Perhaps there was still a chance for her in that direction, she thought. Going back and crawling to him would not be easy – but it might produce more work.

She tossed it over in her mind for a few days, anxiety fighting with pride, but eventually – faced with the prospect of laying off one of her drivers, and with a bleak Christmas looming – Amy decided it was no use being squeamish any longer. If there was any possibility of getting the extra work she needed, then she must go all out for it.

She reached for the telephone and placed a trunk call to Gloucester, but when at last she got through she was told that Mr Porter was in Hillsbridge.

'I can give you the number where he can be contacted,' the impersonal voice told her over the roarings and cracklings on the line.

'I have the number, thank you,' Amy replied.

She disconnected, then sat for a moment with the receiver held between her hands, getting used to the idea that he might be just up the road. Then she called his home number.

Amy had expected the housekeeper to answer it, but in fact it was Ralph himself whose voice came down the line.

'Ralph, it's Amy.' She made an effort to sound cool and businesslike. 'I telephoned your Gloucester office, but they told me you were at home.'

'That's right. My sister has been poorly and I've come home to pester the doctor who's treating her.'

Amy went cold. Had Ralph heard the rumours? She did not imagine Oliver was his doctor, since the Porters would almost certainly be private patients and on the list of one of the more senior doctors in Hillsbridge. All the same, at the rate the gossip had travelled, nothing was impossible.

'I'm sorry to hear she's ill,' she said lamely.

'She's improving now, though in her state of health that's probably the most we can hope for,' Ralph said. 'What can I do for you, Amy?'

She drew a deep breath. 'It's about the long-haul journeys. If they're still on the cards, I'd like to quote for them.'

'I see.' He paused. 'I'm sorry, Amy, but when I thought you weren't interested I made alternative arrangements.'

'So I'm too late,' she said in a small voice.

'I'm afraid so.' Another pause. 'You haven't given any further thought to opening another depot, I suppose?'

She half laughed – it was almost funny that he should be talking about opening another depot when she had scarcely enough business to keep one going – but the laugh came out closer to a sob.

'I don't really think...'

'Amy, is something wrong?'

Wrong? Only that I'm in one hell of a mess. Unable to pay my debts. Liable to lose everything... That was what she wanted to say.

'No. No. I'm fine.'

'You don't sound it.'

'I've got a bit of a cold, that's all.'

A pause. Then Ralph asked, 'Are you at the yard?'

'Yes.'

'And will you be there for the next half-hour?'

'Yes. Why?'

'I'm coming down to see you.'

No! she thought wildly. I don't want to see you! It won't do any good, you'll just confuse things again. And I won't be able to hide the fact that I'm close to my wits' end . . .

But she heard herself saying, 'Oh, right. I'll be here . . .'

During the five minutes or so before his car drew into the yard, Amy did her best to compose herself, though her mind spun with conjecture as to why he was coming. But when she saw him walking towards her office, collar turned up to shield his face from the icy wind, shoulders hunched, cigar gripped tightly between his lips while the smoke blew away in curls and puffs, her heart seemed to swell within her so that breath was almost cut off.

Fool! she told herself. Why do you let him do this to you? He was never right for you and he found someone else. This is a business visit only . . .

She opened the door of the office and he came in, the cigar smoke instantly perfuming the small, cramped room.

'That's better. Telephones are fine for convenience, but there's nothing like conversing face to face.'

'No,' she said. 'Do you want a cup of tea?'

A corner of his mouth lifted. 'There you are, demonstrating the point, you see. A telephone never offered me a cup of tea! Yes, if the kettle's on, I could drink a reservoir.'

She busied herself with the familiar motions. He was perched on the corner of the desk and she could feel his eyes following her. When she put down the mug beside him he spooned sugar into it, then, still stirring, looked up to meet her eyes.

'Is the business in trouble, Amy?'

It was so direct, so unexpected that she was taken completely off guard. So he had heard the rumours, she thought in panic. But his questioning eyes were still holding hers and there was no time to think of an evasive answer. She drew a hesitant breath.

'There are a few difficulties . . .'

'What kind of difficulties?'

'We haven't been so busy. We've lost a couple of regular hirings, through no fault of our own, and the extra business just hasn't come in. It's not a catastrophe yet, but we're not big enough to absorb that kind of loss of business.'

He nodded, his eyes narrowed, his lips a tight line around the half-smoked cigar.

'What do you mean when you say it's no fault of your own?'

'We've done the work quite satisfactorily. Neither firm has

ever had any cause for complaint.'

'So why have you lost them?'

She bit her lip. 'A new firm of contractors started up over towards Stack Norton a while back. I think they're getting our business,' she hedged.

'Why?'

She shrugged. It was making her uncomfortable, the way he was sitting there firing questions at her. And she did not want to tell him about Oliver Scott.

'*Why* are they getting your business?' he repeated.

'Perhaps because they're closer to the quarries and the woods that are being cut.'

'No. No, that won't do. It's a good six months since they started up. If your clients were going to change for that reason alone, they would have done so before now. Besides, it makes no difference to them, does it? An extra four or five miles on your journey is neither here nor there. Choosing the nearest haulier might influence new trade, I grant you, but the others would stick with the tried and trusted when there's so little in it. There must be more to it than that.'

'Well, I'm sure I don't know.'

'Then you should find out!' He drummed his fingers impatiently on the table top. 'The answer must lie in the way the two firms are being run. Word travels fast in this kind of business...'

'What do you mean?' she demanded, stung by his criticism.

'I mean that you've done wonders, Amy, but you're not really business-wise yet. There's something you're missing.'

That was the one key which could unlock what Amy believed to be the truth – the accusation of incompetence.

'I'm missing nothing,' she retorted. 'It's not my business that's at fault; it's the wicked gossip that's been spread about me.'

'Gossip? What gossip?'

So he hadn't heard!

'Dr Scott, an old friend of mine, called to see me a few times and people are only too ready to put the wrong interpretation on it.'

'Oh, I see.' But there was a slight hardening of his expression.

'It's hardly my fault if his wife has suicidal tendencies,' Amy flared. 'The silly woman has everything she could wish for, yet she tried to drown herself and somehow or other I found myself getting the blame, though it had nothing to do with me. People can be so unfair!'

'Yes, they can.' He looked at her narrowly through his cigar smoke and for a moment she thought that in this probing mood he was about to ask her whether she was sure there was nothing in it. Then he drew the last smoke and ground out the cigar butt in the ashtray on her desk. 'I still don't believe it can be anything but coincidence. It must be to do with the way the two businesses are run.'

'I don't agree,' she argued. 'All my troubles started along with this stupid, malicious gossip. You don't know what people round here can be like.'

'Oh, but believe me, I do!' he said drily. 'I've been the subject of gossip and speculation for as long as I can recall. But I can't see it interfering with your type of business. It might be different if you were running a little shop with a lot of old pussies for customers, but a businessman isn't likely to be influenced by such a thing. He has more important things to think about.'

'Perhaps. But his *wife* might think about it,' said Amy bitterly.

'Possibly. But how many wives have a say in details such as who gets the transport contract in a business? Most wouldn't even know their husbands were dealing with you. Would you have known who Llew's contacts were when Roberts Haulage was his concern and his only? I doubt it. The only people a wife gets to know are those her husband brings home to wine and dine. No, it's far more likely that there's a simple rational explanation for all this. Have you checked how your charges measure up, for instance?'

'No, but...'

'Well, you should. You've gone for the typical woman's explanation – the emotional one – without getting down to the basic practicalities. This new firm is probably under-cutting you – maybe even running some journeys at an unprofitable level in order to get the business away from you. Then when they've bankrupted you and have the field to themselves, they can charge whatever they damned well please. What you have to do is beat them at their own game. Get on the telephone and ring everyone you can think of...'

'I've tried that. I couldn't even get past the desk clerks...'

'Another disadvantage of being a woman – they don't take

you seriously. Well, you must try again. Persistence and sweet talk is what you need. And something special to offer... You must tell them you're cutting your profit margins to the bone in order to give them the best possible deal...'

Listening to him, Amy thought of the unpaid bills, the books that refused to balance, the overdue payment on the bank loan.

'But I couldn't afford to cut profit margins...' she protested.

'You must! It's the only way. Listen, Amy, you have to get that business back whatever the cost. If you lose it now, you may lose it for ever.'

'I know.' It was a vicious circle, closing in around her. Ralph was right, she was sure; it was on such bold decisions that he had built up his own successful enterprises. But suppose it didn't work? She would be the one left with the pieces to pick up - though probably they wouldn't fit together any more. 'I don't think I can do it,' she said despairingly. 'No, don't look at me like that - I just can't! It's all very well for *you*, you're a man and you're respected. But me...'

She broke off, shaking her head and he leaned forward.

'Don't talk like that, Amy, it doesn't suit you. You're a fighter...'

Sudden tears welled in her eyes and she felt very, very tired. A fighter? Perhaps. Sometimes it seemed that she had been fighting all her life. But that wasn't true, of course. Except for the battle for her life when she was a child, she had had things easy until Llew had died. There had always been someone to look after her, to cosset her. But in the last few years all that had changed. So many problems she had faced - and all the time alone. There had been no one to back her over the fostering of Huw, no one to turn to on decisions concerning the business, the children, the running of the house. She had coped with it all, but somehow she didn't feel 'fighter' was the right way to describe herself - 'plodder' maybe would be more to the point.

I'm a plodder, she thought, wallowing in a rare bout of self-pity. I do my best to take the obstacles as they come, but that's not enough. Now I have to face up to doing new costings, new estimates, wheedling, cajoling, trying to sound confident although my chin is on the floor, hoping and praying it will work out, worrying about the consequences if it doesn't and knowing that if this set of problems is resolved there will be a fresh lot around the next corner, and the next . . .

She felt heavy suddenly – eyes, cheek muscles, arms, legs – as if the responsibility was a physical weight pulling her down. The office was claustrophobic, just a part of the trap that held her, and she twisted restlessly.

'Well, Amy?' Ralph asked.

She dropped her head into her hands and her fingers made thick, dark patterns across her blurring eyes.

'I don't know if I can go on with it. I've had enough.'

She felt his eyes on her as he reached into his pocket for another cigar. Then he said lightly, 'If you feel like that, you could always marry me.'

For a brief, glorious second she thought he meant it and her heart leaped so that it made her feel sick. Then cold common sense knocked her sharply back to earth. How typical of him to make fun of her!

'Well!' she laughed shortly. 'I don't think I'm quite that desperate.'

He lit his cigar and the fragrant smoke curled around her again.

'Good! There's fight in you yet.'

'There certainly is. I might be down, but I'm not out. You're right, I can't let this stupid tin-pot firm get the better of me.'

'That's the spirit. Don't underestimate them, though.' He swung off the desk. 'I'll be going then. But remember – if things get rough you know where I am. OK?'

When he had gone she sat for a while still breathing in the smoke of his cigar and thinking. Marry him indeed! What a thing to joke about! But oh, if only it had not been a joke . . . how good it would be not to have to worry any more. To be able to leave the decisions and negotiations to someone as strong and capable as he was. To forget the business and be just a wife again . . . *his* wife . . . It was a dream, of course. But what a lovely dream . . .

Amy shook herself back to the present, deciding she would make an early start in the morning. And she would do as Ralph had suggested. First she would work on her costings; cut them to the bone. Then she would get in touch with everyone she could think of and make them offers they couldn't refuse. Christmas was coming – perhaps she should invest in some bottles of Scotch and ply them around amongst likely customers. It was bribery, of course, but she would call it goodwill.

Next morning, fired with new determination, Amy set out half an hour earlier than usual. And it was while she was parking her car in the yard that she heard a lorry coming along the lane from the direction of Ralph Porter's timber yard. She looked up with a mixture of curiosity and professional interest. It was a smart lorry, bigger than hers and new-looking – laden with timber. She got out of the car to watch it pass, then caught her breath at the sight of the legend inscribed on the cab:

D. FRICKER, STACK NORTON.

The new firm – the one which had been stealing her business – *and* coming from Ralph's timber yard fully laden! Frowning, she watched it rumble away up the lane, but before it was out of sight there was another on its tail, identically new and also laden with timber! Almost unable to believe her eyes, Amy watched as the second lorry followed the first past the mill and up the hill, disappearing out of sight behind the winter-brown hedges. Then she slammed shut the door of her car and half-ran across the yard to the store.

'Herbie! Are you there, Herbie?'

'Oh, good morning, missus.' Herbie was coiling ropes. 'You'm in early this morning.'

She ignored the comment. 'Herbie – do you know what I've just seen? Two lorries belonging to that new firm from Stack Norton! And it looked as if they were coming from Ralph Porter's yard!'

She had expected him to be as staggered as she was. Instead, he said in his slow way, 'Oh, ah. Very likely.'

'What do you mean – very likely?' she demanded.

'They've been doing that pretty reg'lar these last few weeks. This is about their time.'

'You mean to tell me you knew?'

'Well, yes, missus, to tell the truth I have seen 'em.'

'You didn't tell me.'

'No.'

'Why not?'

'There didn't seem no point upsetting of 'ee . . .'

'No point!' She was almost speechless. 'But you know that *we* do work for Mr Porter!'

'Ah. It do seem a bit off,' Herbie agreed. 'I s'pose it's all on account of Mr Porter being in with the girl.'

'What are you talking about, Herbie?'

'The Fricker girl. Daughter of the owner. You remember I told you he had a lady-friend? Well, that's who it is.'

'Oh!' Her head was spinning. The young woman she had seen in his car – the one in the emerald green toque – could she be the daughter of the owner of the rival firm?

'But I didn't think it was anyone local,' she blurted. 'She looked so... sophisticated!'

Herbie expressed no surprise that Amy had seen the girl. 'She's been away, from what I hear. There's money there – they sent her off to Switzerland or somewhere. Not that I'd call Stack Norton local, anyway. You wouldn't know folk from over there. *I* wouldn't...'

'Well, no, but...'

'I'm not surprised at Mr Porter picking up with her though,' Herbie went on. 'Just his sort, after all that education. And not only that – he's always been as sharp as needles when it came to the business side.'

'What do you mean?'

'Can't be bad, can it? Inside contact like that with a transport firm. And she's the only child. It'll all be hers one day – and his, I s'pose, if he does go and marry her.'

Amy said nothing; she couldn't. Too many thoughts were rushing at her. Ralph – romancing her when first she took over Llew's business – trying to get in with *her* maybe, with an eye on Roberts Haulage? And then later, when he had first put up the suggestion that she should tender for his long-haul jobs: 'I don't want to buy any more lorries myself at the moment for various reasons,' he had said. Could it be by that time he had seen the chance of getting into haulage himself, through the girl he had met?

'I'll tell 'ee summat else, now we'm on the subject,' Herbie continued. ''Twouldn't surprise me if Ralph Porter weren't behind Frickers pinching our business. They picked up very sudden, didn't they? I don't know, of course. But it makes you wonder, don't it?'

'Yes,' Amy said. 'It makes you wonder.'

She was still stunned, her mind whirling, but anger was beginning to prickle in her, an unquestionable feeling that she had been played with... made a fool of.

'If you want me, I shall be in my office, Herbie,' she said.

The first hour was too busy to allow Amy time to think very deeply, though the puzzlement and anger continued prickling at the back of her mind. Then the telephone rang.

'Hello. Roberts Haulage.'

'Mrs Roberts? This is Don Fricker. I thought it was time you and I had a chat. Are you available sometime today?'

'Mr Fricker.' She hesitated, giving herself time to think. Refuse – you have nothing to talk to him about. But curiosity was too strong. And besides – perhaps it was time to get cards on the table? 'Yes. I'm available. What time do you suggest?'

'No time like the present, I always say.' His tone was forceful, not slow-drawn in spite of the Somerset accent. 'I can be with you in half an hour.'

Stall. Just a little. Don't let him think you've got nothing better to do than sit here and wait for him.

'Make it an hour. I'm rather busy just now.'

'Really? All right – in an hour.'

She replaced the receiver and sat biting her lip. Why had he said, 'Really?' like that, as if he had not expected her to be busy? And why was he coming? Was it coincidence, or something more?

Well, in an hour I shall know, thought Amy.

With difficulty she concentrated on some more booking and then, five minutes before he was due, she heard a car come into the yard. She straightened her desk, patted her hair into place and ran a lipstick over her mouth; funny how these small feminine habits could bolster confidence. How did a man achieve the same end – with a cigar, perhaps? Or did a man not need his confidence bolstered? There was a knock at the door. 'Come in,' she called.

Don Fricker was a big man, heavy-jowled, with an expression of false bonhomie that Amy felt instinctively might conceal a bullying nature. Try as she might, she could detect no resemblance to the girl she had seen in Ralph's car. She held out her hand and he took it, pumping vigorously.

'Pleased to meet you at last, Mrs Roberts.'

'Do sit down, Mr Fricker. To what do we owe this visit?'

He sat, unbuttoning his jacket and leaning forward.

'A woman after my own heart. You don't waste words! All right – I'll come straight to the point. Like I said on the phone, I thought it was time you and I got together for a chat.'

'What about?'

'Business, what else?' He chuckled at his own joke. 'We're in the same line, aren't we? You have heard of me, I expect?'

'Heard, yes.' Play it cool; give nothing away.

'I expect you have.' He chuckled again. 'As a matter of fact, I think I've taken some of your trade.'

She said nothing, staring at him stonily.

'That's true, isn't it?' he persisted.

'I really couldn't say.'

'Come now, Mrs Roberts. You know it and I know it. No point beating about the bush. You've done well for a woman, but I reckon that now you've got real competition, you're struggling.'

'Mr Fricker, I don't know that I care to discuss my business with you. Please say what you've come to say.'

'Now, there's no call to get on your high horse. I have a proposition to put to you.'

Her mind worked overtime. Was he going to suggest some sharing arrangement? 'What kind of proposition?'

'I want to buy you out.'

The directness of it made her catch her breath.

'Look, Mrs Roberts, I warned you I'm a straight man, and I'm putting it to you straight. I'll take your yard, your lorries and your assets. Staff I can't guarantee; I like to choose my own. But I think you'll find my offer reasonable. I've been doing some sums and...'

'Just a moment, Mr Fricker. What makes you think I'm interested in being taken over?'

'The state of your business,' he said calmly.

'And what do you know about the state of my business?'

A slightly shifty look distorted the bluff features.

'Stands to reason. You've expanded and now you're having to pull your horns in. You're in trouble, Mrs Roberts, and I'm offering you a way out. I'm prepared to take you over, lock, stock and barrel. Now...'

Take her over, lock, stock and barrel! Take over Roberts Haulage – absorb it into Frickers – her business... Llew's... and after all the effort she had put into it! It was unthinkable! She could hear his voice going on, quoting figures and consolidating his offer, but the words had become a blur and the anger was beginning again.

Why had he chosen today to come with a take-over offer? Was there some connection with Ralph's visit yesterday? Oh yes, now that she came to think about it, there had to be!

'Mr Fricker, please listen to me,' she interrupted. 'I don't know what has prompted you to come and make me this offer, but I really feel I should tell you that you're wasting your time. Roberts Haulage is not for sale.'

The bluff features hardened a little. 'Come now, Mrs Roberts, listen to what I have to say.'

'I have listened. Perhaps now *you* should do the listening. This is my business and that's the way it's staying.'

'You would do well to consider...'

'I don't need to consider. I'm sorry you have had a wasted journey. Good day, Mr Fricker.'

'Now just a minute...'

'Good day, Mr Fricker.' She had risen and he did the same.

'This isn't wise, Mrs Roberts.'

'I'll be the judge of that.'

'And not a very good judge, I'd say. Well, you've had your chance. I've offered you good money when all I needed to do was bide my time. You haven't heard the last of me, I promise you. But next time, there won't be money on the table.'

'That makes no difference, since there's nothing to buy.'

'There won't be by the time I've finished, certainly. You'll regret turning me down. I made the offer out of the goodness of my heart, because I felt sorry for you...'

Sorry, my foot! Amy thought furiously. When did you or anyone else make an offer because you felt *sorry*? No, you want my business and you thought this was a good time to get it. And the whole thing *stinks*!

'I don't think there's any more to say.' Amy moved to the door.

'All right.' The mask was down now. 'I'll pick up your few assets much cheaper when they're sold off to pay your debts. It will save me a bob or two, Mrs Roberts.'

'We shall see about that,' Amy retorted.

After his car had pulled out of the yard she stood shaking with anger.

Oh yes, it was all adding up now, wasn't it? The reason Ralph had been to see her yesterday... everything. She had wondered what his real purpose was, when there had been nothing to say which could not have been said on the telephone. He had come to pump her about the business and when she had been fool enough to pour out her heart to him he had let her, with never a mention of the fact that he was connected with the Frickers. Then presumably he'd gone straight home and telephoned Don Fricker to confirm what they had suspected; no doubt advised that this was a good time to press for a take-over. A take-over which would net Roberts Haulage not only for the opposition but, eventually, for himself as Don Browning's son-in-law.

Oh, she had always known it was business first and last with Ralph, but she had never realised just how far he would be prepared to go for his own ends – or how low he would sink. How could he have done it – sat here and talked the way he had when all the time...

And what about that joky marriage proposal? she thought. Had he been joking? Or had he, even then, been hedging his bets? The latent anger fanned to fury and Amy reached for the telephone.

He answered it immediately; had he been expecting a call from Don Fricker to report on the success of his proposals? Amy wondered.

'This is Amy Roberts,' she said formally, her tone barely concealing her fury. 'I just wanted to tell you what I think of someone who could do what you've done.'

'Oh? What have I done?'

'As if you didn't know!' she flared. 'You must think me a perfect fool, Ralph.'

'I certainly do not! I have every respect...'

'Respect! You wouldn't know the meaning of the word! How could you do it? Sit here and pump me about the business, pretend sympathy, when all the time you wanted Roberts Haulage for yourself! I've had Don Fricker here this morning making an offer, and very well primed about my problems. You were very prompt in reporting to him, I must say. When did you do it? When you arranged the day's schedule, I suppose. Oh, when I think what a fool I've been...'

'Amy...'

'Don't "Amy" me! Yes, I have been a fool, I admit it. Fool enough to trust someone whose only motive is to further his own interests. You said yesterday that I had a lot to learn about the ways of business. Well, let me tell you – I have learned a great deal very fast. I've learned things today I never expected or wanted to learn. But I promise you this ... I shall never be so naive again. And you won't find Roberts

Haulage going down so easily. I'll make a success of it if it's the last thing I do!'

'For heaven's sake, Amy...'

'That's all I have to say. Goodbye, Ralph.'

She slammed down the telephone and when it rang a moment later she stonily refused to answer it. Let it ring. If it was Ralph trying to get back to her in order to try to mend bridges, she didn't want to know.

What he had done was despicable. But she'd show him that Amy Roberts was not beaten so easily. As she told him, she'd get the business back on its feet again if it was the last thing she did. And from now on she would do it with no holds barred. Oh yes, she had learned a thing or two today, most importantly that to be successful you had to be unscrupulous. She didn't like it, but there it was. One way or another, Roberts Haulage was going to survive – more than survive. And whatever she had to do in the effort she would do it.

*

With a cold ruthlessness she had not known she possessed, Amy set about pulling back Roberts Haulage from the brink of disaster. Her first act was almost suicidal. Taking her courage in both hands, she cancelled all contracts with Porter Timber. This meant a loss of business which might have proved disastrous, but Amy looked on it as cutting away diseased growth – taking the bad apples out of the barrel. Better to lose the trade than to have the contact constantly festering at the back of her mind, she reasoned; better to get rid of it cleanly and leave herself free to work and expand without the feeling of being indebted to someone she could not trust.

Then, with the same singlemindedness, she set about drumming up new business to fill the vacuum. If Frickers, with Ralph Porter behind them, had been able to take business from her, then it must be possible to take it back again. She worked tirelessly, throwing caution to the winds along with scruples, snatching at every opportunity, cajoling, wheeler-dealing, planning, often late into the night. She threw herself into it so wholeheartedly that there was no energy left over for regrets, no time for nursing an aching heart, and before long her efforts began to pay off.

Roberts Haulage was becoming known once again for its competitiveness and reliability; dealing with the go-ahead Mrs Roberts began to be the fashionable thing to do.

The day Joe Bray telephoned to ask if she would take on once more the work that Frickers had been doing, she knew she was winning.

'They're all right, I suppose – but it's not like dealing with you,' he told her, friendly but faintly apologetic, and triumph ran through her veins like wine. But she was too intent on winning the next contract, and the next, to throw her hat into the air.

For all her success, however, there were still times when one of the lorries was standing idle and Amy knew she could not afford to have it so. One night she racked her brains over endless cups of tea and cigarettes and next morning she had a suggestion to put to Herbie in the form of a ready-made decision – the way she always did things nowadays.

'Herbie, I'm going to start using the old lorry to haul coal.'

Herbie looked at her without surprise. He had become used to what he privately called 'Mrs Roberts' brainstorms'.

'Haul coal? Where to?'

'To customers, of course. There's a ready market in towns like Bath and Bristol. We could collect the coal from the pits, get it bagged up here and establish a round. I see no reason why it shouldn't work quite well alongside the haulage business, and it will be something regular we can fall back on. If we mean to stay solvent we have to expand and this would be far more manageable than going into long-distance haulage, for the moment at any rate.'

'If you say so, Mrs Roberts.'

'I do.'

And so the coal haulage business began and soon it was taking off so well that Amy was forced to acquire another lorry and employ a clerk for the specific job of dealing with the bookwork entailed.

Another year and she had another idea – charabanc outings were becoming highly popular, so why not add a further sideline to the business and run outings in summer? Cliff Button, who had given up his attempt to be a town taxi-driver, was now back in Hillsbridge but according to Herbie was not doing too well – he would be ideal for the job of charabanc driver, for he was good with people and knew the area well. A small garage at Purldown which had tried somewhat half-heartedly to corner the market in day trips, was now in difficulties; Amy, with good returns from the other branches of the business, made an offer and took over their charabanc.

The diversifying of the business could have produced weak links, but Amy's driving determination ensured this did not happen. As the months passed, success piled on success. In the world outside, however, the depression was gathering in intensity, bringing empires crashing and causing widespread hardship to rich and poor alike. Millionaires committed suicide rather than face ruin, a terrifying run on the Bank of England almost bankrupted the country, the Government itself fell. But in Hillsbridge, one woman refused to be deterred from her planned expansion. Closing her eyes to the panic that was sweeping not only England but most of the Western hemisphere, seeing only a small firm with the potential to expand in a world where motor transport was becoming ever more necessary, she worked and planned accordingly.

Soon Amy was no longer able to handle every aspect of the business herself. She took extra staff onto the pay-roll, had an accountant to advise her on financial details and became a valued client who was greeted cordially when she visited the bank manager or her solicitor, Arthur Clarence. To the name of Roberts Haulage was added Roberts Transport, separate yet allied, and Amy found that a finger in extra pies meant a wider circle of contacts and reverberations of success which spread ever further like the ripples from a stone dropped in a pond.

As her business interests grew, so her personal concerns became less and less important to her. She still ensured that she had time to spend with the children, but her life was compartmentalised. Maureen joined Barbara at school and Amy employed a girl to come in every day to clean, cook, wash and look after them both after school and during the holidays – a girl old enough to be reliable, yet young enough to do as she was told. Rita Carter was neat, earnest and respectable, glad to have work when her father and brother, both former miners, were unemployed. Amy knew she would have none of the problems with her which she had experienced with Ruby Clarke.

That breach had healed to some extent – the two neighbours were on speaking terms once more – but there was a restraint between them which had not been there before the Oliver Scott episode, and Amy was never quite able to forget how ready Ruby had been to gossip about her. In fact, for a while she had worried that Ruby might exact her revenge by writing to the authorities to report Oliver for betraying the Hippocratic oath, but mercifully the whole thing had blown over, with Grace eventually making a partial recovery and the family leaving the district. From the night when their friendship had so nearly overstepped the boundaries, Amy had never seen Oliver alone again, and that too had been a tremendous relief. She felt she could not have looked him in the face without blushing. She knew she had courted disaster in encouraging his friendship and that she had been blind and stupid not to realise where it was leading. Had *he* realised? Amy sometimes wondered. That he loved Grace was in no doubt; just what had he been thinking of to play with fire the way he had done?

But it was safely over now and Amy was determined to ensure there would be no recurrence. All in all, relationships with men were a good deal too dangerous to dabble in, she decided. It was best to keep them on a strictly business level. That way neither hearts were broken nor fingers burned – and all energies could be concentrated on something far more profitable.

Sometimes, just sometimes, an element of loneliness crept in and Amy found herself longing in the night for a shoulder to lean on, someone to talk to, the warm contact of another human body. But with the coming of morning she always pushed such longings aside. Better to be self-reliant – the one person you could trust in this world was yourself! Better to be in a position to make your own decisions about your own future. Better to have no one but yourself to blame if things went wrong – and not have to look over your shoulder and wonder what someone else would think of the choice you had made.

Would I ever have found myself if Llew had not been killed? Amy wondered. And again: would Llew have proved a sufficiently good businessman to weather the storms as she had done? She pushed it away as a disloyal thought. Of course he would!

But nothing could deter her from the sense of purpose which permeated her days. And nothing could detract from the pride she felt in what she was achieving single-handed.

Chapter Twenty-Six

Minehead beach was deserted, a band of sand and greyish shingle which followed the curve of the bay. Above the town the mound of North Hill – that in summer would blaze with heather and gorse – rose darkly majestic and seagulls mewed and cried as they rode the gusting March wind. On a fine day it was possible to look across the water to Barry and the Welsh coast which bounded the Bristol Channel on the opposite side; today it was obscured by mist and the muddy sea, whipped into off-white horses, merged into the leaden sky.

On the bleak beach one lone figure was walking, head bent so that her chin was buried in the upturned collar of her fur coat, hands thrust deep into the warm cavities of her pockets. Amy Roberts' Russian boots scrunched and turned on the shingle, but she scarcely noticed; she was too deep in thought.

Decisions, decisions... sometimes during the last few years it had seemed life consisted of nothing else. Even now, while taking a short, well-deserved holiday staying with Jack and Stella, she could not leave them behind. But the decision she was making now was one of the most pleasant she had had to reach.

It was March 1932 and Amy was making up her mind to buy a plot of land on which to build a house.

I can't pass it up, she thought. It's too perfect in every way!

The moment it had come on to the market she had felt the tiny, satisfying thrill she was coming to recognise when she was confronted with something good: a piece of land within easy reach of the yard, sufficiently high up the hill to be beyond reach of the flooding river, with a pleasant outlook, surrounded on three sides by allotments, bounded by mature

459

trees and fronted by the lane which led to the Mill. An ideal site for a house, secluded yet accessible and already in her mind's eye she could see the way it would be – red brick, perhaps, with bay windows each side of the front door, a gravelled drive and a garage for her Model T Ford. She had made enquiries from Eddie Roberts straight away, for he had now moved from insurance into the business of buying and selling houses, and was working for the firm of auctioneers and estate agents who had that piece of land on their books.

There was a high reserve price on the plot, Eddie had told her – because the vendor was in financial difficulties, Amy suspected – and she had held off from making a decision to bid for it there and then. What was more, the auction was to be held at the George during the week she was on holiday.

'That decides it then, I suppose,' she had said a little glumly. 'I can't let everyone down – this holiday has been planned for so long!'

Eddie, giving his impression of 'Honest Joe', had leaned on the polished counter of his office so that his face came in line with hers.

'Tell you what I'll do for you, Amy. If you decide to go for it, give me a ring and I'll put in the bid for you – I can't say fairer than that, can I?'

'All right,' she'd agreed. 'I'll think it over, Eddie.'

Now, with the auction arranged for the following day, she knew that the time for thinking was over. If she wanted the plot, she had to phone Eddie Roberts with her offer tonight.

Do I want it enough to perhaps pay over the odds for it? she asked herself. And almost immediately the answer was there, clear and unquestionable: Yes, I do want it. Almost without realising it I have set my heart on it. And it would be a fitting crown to my success, the right kind of house for the proprietor of Roberts Haulage.

As she lifted her chin from the sheltering collar of fur, the wind whipped her hair across her cheek and blew breath back into her throat, fanning her excitement. Oh yes, it would be such fun to plan a new home, so satisfying to be amongst the elite who lived not in ranks and terraces but in a detached house, and to know that she had achieved it out of her own efforts, her own enterprise. Once before she had contemplated moving, but that had been a step down into the poor area of Batch Row. How different this would be!

I've not done badly, Amy thought with justifiable pride

and knew this was an understatement. When she had begun, she had nursed only one ambition – to keep going the business which Llew had started. But from that small seed Roberts Haulage had grown into a profitable and highly successful concern. And now she was going to build her final edifice to Llew's memory and she must call it after him – after the Welsh village where he had been born, perhaps. That would be nice and very fitting.

Her mind made up, Amy turned, looking for a moment out to sea, and as she watched a gull detached itself from the rolling grey water, spiralling up into the mist above. So the white specks tossing on the waves were not all sea-horses. There were seagulls too, seagulls who rode out the storm and then rose, wheeling and crying, to soar on the wind.

And that's a little how I feel, Amy thought. I rode out the storms and now I'm up there, soaring, experiencing the exhilaration and the tiny twinge of fear. I know what it's like to be high, high, high!

So I shall go back to Jack's and phone Eddie. What will he think, I wonder, when he knows that I've made up my mind to go for the land? I suspect he won't like it much.

That thought too gave her pleasure and she turned again, walking back along the beach, now anxious only to set her latest plan in motion.

*

Charlotte heard the news as she so often did, from Peggy.

'So your Amy's after that plot of land down by the Mill, then! It'll be lovely for her, won't it? So near to her yard. Oh, she has got on well, Lotty.'

Charlotte's eyes narrowed; this was the first she had heard of it! But she had no intention of letting Peggy know that. It was so humiliating, your own daughter doing things and you not knowing a thing about it.

'How did you get to hear?' Charlotte asked.

'They were talking about it in the Co-op. I expect it came from Edna Denning at the call office. She doesn't miss much, that I do know, and I saw her coming out as I went in.'

'Hmm!' Charlotte snorted. 'Something ought to be done about her. It's not right that she should listen in to people's conversations.'

'No, it isn't really.' Peggy didn't sound very concerned,

though. She had never used a telephone in her life, so the thought of Edna Denning listening in to conversations had no personal relevance. And besides... 'I'm not sure I wouldn't do the same,' Peggy admitted with a chuckle. 'All that news going right through your own front room! It must be very tempting!'

'But not *right* at all!' Charlotte insisted. 'Telephone conversations are private – or ought to be. You have to pay enough for them!'

'But what about your Amy? You must be proud of her, Lotty. Come to think of it, I should think you must be proud of all of them. What with Jack teaching and Ted doing well in Australia and Harry – well, he'll be manager soon, from what I can hear of it.'

'Not for a couple of years yet. He can't take a manager's post until he's twenty-five,' Charlotte said, but it was true – she *did* feel a thrill of pride when she thought how well her children were doing. When at first Harry had started studying, she had thought he might be over-reaching himself, but last year he'd taken his Second Class Certificate of Competency and passed with flying colours; the manager had wanted him to miss it out and go straight for his First Class, and Charlotte thought privately that if he had done that, he would have passed it just as easily. But Harry had been cautious, explaining that with a Second Class he would be able to start shot-firing right away and keep an eye open for under-managers' posts to apply for, whereas if he failed the First Class he would still be stuck on the starting line and handicapped by the knowledge of failure as well. But he had done well, without a doubt, and the fact that one day he would probably be running a pit, and responsible for the lives and welfare of men like his own father and brother, gave her a glow of pride whenever she thought about it.

Ted was doing well by all accounts, too. He didn't write as regularly as Charlotte would have liked, but then he had never been much of a pen-pusher and his letters when they did come, though hopelessly out of date, seemed to radiate a spirit of optimism. Ted and Rosa were happy in Australia. The work was hard and they missed England, but the money which was there to be earned more than made up for that. Already they had their own house and though his description of it had made Charlotte wrinkle her nose and think: 'It doesn't sound much like *my* idea of a house!' she supposed that in a different country one must expect things to be different, and if Ted and Rosa were happy with it that was really all that mattered. And it certainly seemed they were happy – and now their first baby was on the way. When the letter bearing the news had arrived, Charlotte had shed a private tear. It seemed so long since she had waved good-bye to Ted on his wedding day – and now there was going to be a new baby, her grandchild, and she might never even see it. It was all very well for Ted to write that they would be coming home for a visit as soon as they had saved the fare; Charlotte was under no illusions – that was a promise he might never be able to keep. Australia was such a very long way away!

But if he was still in England, he would probably be out of a job, Charlotte consoled herself. Far too many men were out of work and though Jim fortunately had managed to keep his employment at the pit, Dolly's Victor had been on the dole for a while after Captain Fish had died suddenly the previous year. The new owner of his house had not required the services of a gardener/handyman and Dolly and Victor had been in what Charlotte termed 'a hole' until Victor was fortunate enough to get himself taken on by the council. Now he was sweeping the roads, and though this was not exactly Charlotte's idea of an ideal occupation, at least it meant that Dolly had a wage packet coming in to feed and clothe the family.

Yes, all in all, the children had all done very well and if it was true that Amy was going to buy a plot of land and build herself a house, that was good news too – though Charlotte could not help wishing that her youngest daughter would settle down and marry. It wasn't right really, her doing a man's work, and there were plenty of 'good catches' about whom Amy could have for a husband if she wanted them, Charlotte was sure. But there it was, whenever she said as much to Amy she had ended up getting her nose bitten off, so it was prudent to keep her opinions to herself. Amy had always done as she pleased and Charlotte could not see her changing now.

'You know, from the time your Amy was a little girl I always knew she was going to do well for herself,' Peggy said now. 'You could see it in her then, couldn't you? Yes, when I heard she was after that plot, I said to myself: Well, I always knew it. I always knew Amy was going to be a somebody. And I was right, wasn't I? And to think *I* brought her into the world!'

Charlotte said nothing.

'Let's just hope she sees you and her father all right now she's so well-off,' Peggy commented.

Charlotte drew herself upright. 'She doesn't owe me anything, Peggy.'

Peggy looked surprised. 'But you're her mother. It's only right...'

'She didn't ask to be born,' Charlotte said sharply. 'None of them did. I've done my best for them because they're my children, but I shan't look for anything in return. So long as they come to see me from time to time, that's all that matters to me.'

It was a forward-looking view, out of step with the Victorian view of the family still mainly adhered to, and even as she said it Charlotte was not sure she believed her own words. But with children as independent as hers, what other way was there of looking at things?

I suppose she'll tell me all about it when she comes home again, Charlotte comforted herself. And at least Peg doesn't know it was news to me. That's one thing to be grateful for!

*

Amy came home from Minehead at the end of the week.

'It hasn't really been holiday weather, has it, missus?' Herbie said when she put in an appearance at the yard, and she was forced to agree. But then, who could expect to be able to go to the seaside in March and paddle or sit in a deck-chair on the beach?

'The children enjoyed it – Jack's so good at thinking of things for them to do and Stella feeds us up like Christmas turkeys,' she said. 'As for me – well, it gave me a chance to do a lot of thinking I never have time for at home.'

'I bet you'm glad to be back, for all that,' said Herbie, who had never spent a night away from his own bed in his life and never wanted to.

Amy smiled. 'I must say I'm not sorry,' she agreed.

It had been good to take a break, but now she was eager to be back in harness and keener than ever to set her plans in motion for her new house.

She intended to get in touch with Eddie Roberts immediately she reached the office that first morning, to see how the auction had gone – just how much her plot had cost her, and what the next step would be. Indeed, as she passed the plot on her way to work she stopped for just a moment to look at it proprietorially, planning just where the house would stand, where the drive would best lead in from the road and whether there would be room to have apple and plum trees in the back garden – something she had always dreamed of. But once at the yard there were so many jobs to catch up on that there was no time for contacting Eddie until late afternoon, and when eventually she did find the time to put through a call to him, it was only to be told he was out of the office.

'Can I take a message?' the young lady clerk asked.

'You can tell him I rang, yes,' Amy said, leaving her name and noticing the hesitation in the girl's voice when she discovered to whom she was speaking.

Is that because I'm his sister-in-law, or do I merit respect in my own right? Amy wondered, faintly amused and deciding on balance that it was probably the girl's awe of Eddie which lay behind her deferential manner. After all, Eddie was quite an important person these days – not only in charge of the estate agency but also a public figure. He had put up for the council at the last elections and been one of the 'Labour Six' who had been elected *en bloc*.

'He'll want to be in touch with me about the land at Mill Lane,' Amy explained now.

'Yes, I see. Well, I wouldn't know anything about that,' the girl said awkwardly. 'You'll have to speak to Mr Roberts himself.'

'Ask him to call me, will you?' Amy instructed and put the phone down, thinking: Eddie, you're slipping. You should have somebody in the office who can fly the flag better than that when you're not there!

By the time she was ready to go home Eddie had not called back and she made a mental note to contact him again first thing in the morning. The sooner all this was signed and settled, the better she would be pleased.

Since her success Amy had had a telephone installed at home as well – one of the few houses in Hillsbridge to be so privileged – but it seldom rang except on matters of business and when it did the children usually scrambled to be first to answer it.

When it rang that evening soon after she had put the girls to bed, she heard the squeak of bedsprings and the patter of feet on the lino and had to call up to them to go back to bed.

'I'll answer it! You two should be asleep!'

The two guilty faces peeped between the banisters for a minute longer then disappeared as she shouted again: 'Barbara! Maureen! Do as you're told!'

Then she reached for the shrilling telephone, thinking that at least Huw never rushed to answer it.

Huw had a healthy mistrust of the instrument and in any case he was in the kitchen working albeit with bad grace on some homework his teacher had given him. He could be a clever student if he tried and the teacher had realised it. The trouble was that he had no interest in studying; all he really wanted was freedom.

Amy sighed and gave her head a little shake.

'Hello. Amy Roberts speaking.'

'Amy – it's Eddie.' How could anyone inject so much bluster into three simple words, she wondered?

'Eddie! I was trying to get hold of you this afternoon. I wanted to find out how the auction went – and how much you had to go to in order to get the land for me?'

There was a slight hesitation. Then he said, 'There was a lot of interest in it, Amy. Far more than I ever expected.'

'You mean it's cost me?'

'Not exactly.'

'What do you mean, not exactly? Did you have to pay over the odds to get it for me or not?'

'I didn't get it. You were outbid.'

She felt sick. '*What?* But I gave you plenty of leeway. Far above the valuation.'

'I'm sorry, Amy, but there it is. The land sold for £100 more than you authorised me to bid. I didn't feel I could go any higher.'

'Oh!' Disappointment yawned in her. 'Oh, Eddie, couldn't you have contacted me when you saw the way things were going?'

'You were on holiday and I could never haved reached you in time. They don't hang about at these auctions, you know. Anyway, it's no use crying over spilled milk now. The land's

466

been sold and that's all there is to it!'

His jaunty tone annoyed her. Eddie hadn't wanted her to have the land, she was sure. No doubt he was jealous of her success and disliked the idea of his sister-in-law having a better house than himself. When he had been forced to drop out of the auction, he'd been delighted more than likely.

'I don't believe you really tried for me, Eddie,' she fumed. 'Surely you could have done something if you really wanted to? After all, we're family, though I know that's never made much difference to you. I wouldn't expect you to cross the road to help *me*, but the children – your own nieces and nephew – Babs and Maureen and Huw too, though I know you don't like to admit it. Your own brother's children! I should have thought you would take them into consideration.'

'I'm sorry you feel like that,' Eddie said stiffly. 'But really this conversation is getting us nowhere, Amy.'

She swallowed at the knot of anger. 'I daresay you're right. Who outbid me, anyway?'

A pause. 'I'm not sure I'm at liberty to tell you that.'

'Oh, stuff and nonsense! It was a public auction, wasn't it? How can there be anything secret about it?'

Another pause. Then Eddie said, 'The land was sold to Ralph Porter.'

She nearly dropped the telephone. 'What? What does he want with it?'

'I really couldn't say. Now, if there's nothing more, I'll wish you good night, Amy – and leave you to cool down.'

She slammed down the telephone and stood with her nails biting crescents into her palms. Ralph Porter! Over the last couple of years she had scarcely heard his name, nor had she wanted to. But the feeling of rivalry and betrayal had never quite left her. She had trusted him – *wanted* to trust him – and he had gone behind her back to the opposition.

Things had not worked out as he planned, though – or on the other hand, perhaps they had! Ralph was so devious one could never be quite certain. But whatever the reason, the expected marriage between Ralph and Erica Fricker had never materialised. Instead, there had been a big society wedding the previous year, when Erica had married a Swedish timber merchant – one of Ralph's contacts, Amy supposed. When she had seen the photograph and the five-column report in the *Mercury*, Amy had felt a sharp, twisting

467

triumph. So Ralph had lost her! He must have introduced her to the Swede and she had preferred him. Oh Ralph, how funny – all your scheming and then you lost the girl and her father's business! It was only afterwards she had thought it unlike Ralph to lose anything he wanted, and had wondered whether perhaps things had worked out in such a way that he had changed his mind. That theory had been borne out when she had noticed that the lorries passing by on their way to the timber yard no longer bore the name of Fricker emblazoned on their cabs. Instead they were Ralph Porter's own – specialist timber lorries which carried far more wood than any general purpose haulage lorry could transport.

No, on reflection, whatever had happened had probably been to Ralph Porter's advantage – he would have made sure of that. As to how Frickers Transport had been affected, Amy didn't know. They were still in business, for she saw them about from time to time, but their paths never crossed and she was unconcerned. Perhaps nowadays they drew their business from firms closer to home.

However, none of this affected the surge of anger she felt as she considered the fact that Ralph had outbid her for the plot of land she wanted so badly.

Why? she asked herself now. He couldn't want it to build a house – not for himself, at any rate. His own house was more than adequate for his needs and he spent little enough time in it. Amy could only think his motive was spite... and a little bit of paramountcy. Yet spite was not a vice she would have attributed to Ralph and his importance hardly seemed to need proving. Ruthless as he might be, such petty failings somehow seemed beneath him.

A thud close at hand brought Amy's attention back to the hall where she still stood by the telephone. She spun round, thinking for a moment that the girls had disobeyed her and crept downstairs. Then she noticed that the door leading to the cupboard under the stairs was ajar. She waited, brow wrinkling, but silence prevailed. A mouse? They did run about the house from time to time and she had to set traps for them. But no mouse would have made such a loud thud, especially this early in the evening, with all the lights still blazing.

She went along the hall, threw open the door and saw a figure standing in the cupboard looking out at her.

'Huw! What are you doing here?'

'I wanted some string. I . . .'

'Then why didn't you ask me for it?'

'You were on the phone . . .' There was a strange, mulish set to his face, and his eyes were defiant. He's been standing there listening! she thought and her temper flared again.

'How dare you creep about! If you knew I was on the phone, you should have waited!'

He stared back at her with the same defiant look, masking something else . . . puzzlement? Confusion? She didn't know, and wondered with a sudden shock how long he had been there and how much he had heard. Snatches of the conversation played themselves over in her mind and she thought: Oh Lord, did he hear what I said about him being Llew's son? Desperately she tried to recall her exact words, but they were elusive now. All she knew was that she had made mention of it to Eddie and Huw could have been within earshot.

During recent years she had wondered sometimes if she should tell Huw the truth about why she had taken him in, but had always decided against it. What good would the truth do him? Surely it would only unsettle him more. Better to let him keep his identity intact. But it niggled at her all the same, the fear that at some time he might find out and in a way not of her choosing. Now she was suddenly afraid that moment might have come and cold panic added to her anger.

'I won't have it, Huw, do you hear? When I'm on the phone, it's private. I don't want big ears listening to everything I say. So remember that in future, please!'

The way he was staring at her was disconcerting. Where did he get that look from? Certainly not from Llew, despite those clear blue eyes which for her had been the first confirmation of the truth. She found herself thinking of the woman who had been his mother. Was it from her that look came? Though Amy could recall every word of the conversation they had had on that dreadful day, though she could still picture the weary figure dragging up the hill in front of her, the features had been quite lost. No matter how she tried, she could never summon them up. Yet now it seemed to her that it was the woman who stared at her accusingly through Huw's eyes . . . Llew's eyes . . .

'Have you finished your homework?' she asked abruptly. A nod. 'Can I go out?'

She hesitated. It was dark outside now, and cold. But she

wanted to be on her own, to think. She couldn't face the
thought of him sitting there, watching her.

'Where are you going?'

'Oh, I don't know. Just out.'

Where did he ever go? she wondered. The same places as
the other boys, she imagined – the river, the woods, the
railway line, the batch. Hours and hours wasted doing
nothing. But she could remember her own brothers being
just the same, with the exception of Jack.

'All right, then. But don't be late.'

He didn't answer, just knelt down to retie the lace of his
boot, winding it tighter around his ankle and finishing with
a double knot which would take ages to wriggle free at
bedtime. But when he had gone, she felt a moment's sharp
regret. She shouldn't have taken it out on him; it was not his
fault that Ralph Porter and Eddie Roberts were such perfect
pigs. When he came home she would make it up with a cup
of cocoa and a plate of his favourite chocolate biscuits.

She went back into the sitting-room, eased her feet out of
her shoes and into slippers and subsided onto one of the
dining chairs.

It was the first day after her holiday, and she felt like a dish-
rag already. Was it ever worth going? Being away for a week
meant things slipping through your fingers, work piling up,
decisions not made. Dimly she remembered what Ralph
Porter had said to her once about delegating, but she
thought: No, this business is my life. It's not only a source of
income, it's taken the place of my husband. And one day,
perhaps, it will have to take the place of my children as well.

She stretched wearily, but though she was upset by what
had happened, there was no feeling of defeat now. The last
few years had taught her one thing at least, that she could
touch the bottom and come up fighting. Whatever life chose
to throw at her, she could weather it. Even in the midst of
setbacks it was a comforting thought, and Amy smiled to
herself.

Tonight she would sleep on it. Tomorrow she would
decide what to do.

Chapter Twenty-Seven

Huw went slowly down the hill, kicking any stone that lay on the path and imagining he was scoring a marvellous goal for Hillsbridge. It was his favourite dream, one that never failed to cheer him up, and after a few minutes he felt his spirits lifting.

He had no idea why Amy had flown at him so – it didn't seem to him that he had done anything very terrible by being in the cupboard under the stairs when she was on the telephone – but he was used to her by now, used to her volatile moments and the warm remorse that followed. And life wasn't really so bad. He had enjoyed the week's holiday at Minehead, even though the weather had not been good enough for Jack to take him up gliding as he sometimes did, and he was beginning to take for granted the advantages which had come his way with Amy's success – enough money in his pocket to stand buying gob-stoppers and sticky buns for his less-affluent pals, a brand-new bicycle and the car, which he could not wait to be allowed to drive. The only real thorn in his flesh was having to go to school. Huw looked back nostalgically to the balmy days in Wales when he had played truant. Mam never seemed to mind too much, while Amy became really furious if she thought he had missed so much as an hour. He hated lessons; he thought they were a complete waste of time. But next year he would be fourteen and able to leave. What he was going to do concerned him not one jot. He'd be free – and that was all that mattered.

Further down the hill he saw two figures he recognised standing under a gas-lamp and sharing a crafty Woodbine – Stuart Seymour and Gordon Tamlyn. He had called at Gordon's house earlier and his mother had said he was out;

now Huw was glad to see the lads.

''Lo, Stu. 'Lo, Gordon. How be on?'

Stuart coughed over the Woodbine and offered it to Huw. 'Want a drag, Huw?' Huw accepted and passed it on to Gordon. 'Anything doing tonight?'

'Naw. It's getting too foggy to do anything much.'

Huw glanced up. The gas-lamp was making a splurge of light in the gathering mist. Another half-hour and the fog would come right down, closing in, clammy cold.

'We could go down the hut,' Gordon suggested.

They looked at one another.

'We could play five-stones or have a game of cards in there.'

There was no need to identify 'the hut' further, for the other boys knew exactly where Gordon meant – a wooden structure in Ralph Porter's timber yard. It was a favourite place with them, though not one they used too often because of the risk of getting caught. But when they did use it, the danger added spice.

'Well?' Gordon prompted.

'Yeah.' Stuart hesitated, but Huw jumped in quickly. He had overheard Amy mention Ralph's name on the telephone; clearly he was one of the reasons for her being upset. Breaking into the hut and spending an illicit hour there seemed a fitting revenge.

'Good idea, Gordy. We haven't been in the hut lately.'

The shared cigarette was ground out and they started off down Porter's Hill, walking shoulder to shoulder until they came within sight of the windows. Then they kept to the side of the road, creeping in Indian file in the shadow of the hedge. The lane was usually the most dangerous part, as it was lit by the occasional lamp and within view of the house, but tonight the mist obscured them enough to make it reasonably safe. Through the barbed wire fence they went and across the yard between the high piles of timber to the large shed which stood in the far corner.

Made of wood-planks, its door tight-fitting and pad-locked, the shed was to all intents and purposes secure. But the boys knew otherwise. On one side there was a gap between the planks, too narrow for a man to climb through but allowing just enough space for a boy.

They lined up beside the gap, Huw keeping look-out while the other two crawled through, then following himself, lying prone and wriggling, wriggling, until first his body was in and then, by inching back to the widest space, his head. Inside he rolled over and got up, the familiar feeling of triumph exciting him. Just to know you had breached a Porter stronghold was exhilarating enough, the fact that it gave cover for a game of five-stones or cards was an added bonus.

Inside the shed was divided into three by means of wooden partitions – one 'room' taking up a full half of the hut, while the other half was bisected by another partition. The large 'room' was bare and more or less empty except for a few cans and containers and a tangled heap of chains and ropes, but the inner sections were piled high with boxes and bundles of papers and records which had been turned out from the main filing system but not thrown away. The boys had investigated them once, but found them deadly dull – a mass of unintelligible figures and references – and now they ignored them completely, going straight through into the large room. There they arranged a pile of ropes in a corner and squatted down on the scratchy hemp 'cushion', Stuart producing a pack of cards from his pocket. It was just possible to see the cards by the light of the nearest gas-lamp as it shone through the square, high-up window and they played pontoon for a while, using odd bits of sticks as tokens. Huw, acting as banker, did well and before long the other two boys had no tokens left.

'This isn't much fun. You always win,' Gordon complained.

'Trouble is, it's so bloomin' cold!' Stuart added.

On that they were all agreed. Sitting in one place, they had grown cold without noticing it. Now they shivered, pulling their jackets around them and hunching their shoulders to retain what little warmth they still had.

'P'raps we'd best go home.'

'But it's early yet.'

'Tell you what, we could light a fire!' Gordon suggested. The others regarded him suspiciously.

'See – we could built it on that concrete,' he continued. 'It looks as if it's for a fire anyway.'

Certainly the square slab of concrete set against one of the walls of the hut looked as if it might have been intended as the base for a coke stove. Whether there was once a stove which had been dismantled later, or whether it had never been installed at all, the boys didn't know, but there was no sign of a stove or stove-pipe now – just the blackened concrete base.

'What could we light a fire with?' Stuart asked. 'We ain't got nothing to burn.'

'There's plenty of wood out there!' Gordon jeered. 'And I've got some matches for me fags, haven't I?'

It was good enough for them. Huw and Stuart wriggled out between the boards again, collecting sticks and the driest pieces of wood they could find and passing them back to Gordon. Then they climbed inside again and gathered expectantly around the bonfire which Gordon had built on the concrete slab.

'Come on, then, light it! What are we waiting for?'

Gordon produced the matches and struck one, but the wood was damp and unwilling to catch. Huw fetched a few of the sheets of yellowed paper from the back room, screwed them up and placed them beneath the stick; by blowing hard on this they managed to produce a flicker of flame which ran up one twig in an uncertain path before dying again.

'It's going! It's going to go!' Stuart encouraged. 'Try again!'

Huw fetched more paper and the three bent determinedly over the smouldering pile, alternately fanning and sheltering it. But the damp sticks still proved stubborn.

'Good job we ain't got to cook our supper like this,' Stuart commented. 'We'd starve, wouldn't us?'

'It's never going to go,' Huw said. 'Come on, let's go in the other room and have a game of five-stones. It'll be more comfortable on the boxes than it is sitting on this rope.'

He and Stuart went off into the inner sanctum, but Gordon hung back, reluctant to give up on his idea.

'Oh, let him stay and mess about with it if he wants to,' Huw said. 'We'll have a game, shall we?'

He and Stuart settled down on the damp boxes as well as they could, dealing the cards between them and ignoring the sounds from the outer room where Gordon was still fiddling with his fire. Then a sudden whoosh! made them jump almost out of their skins.

'Crikey! What was that?'

They rushed to the doorway to see a visibly shaken Gordon backing away from the now blazing fire. In his hand he was holding one of the cans.

'What was that? What did you do?' Huw asked, while across him Gordon was explaining loudly, 'I think it's petrol. I put some on the fire to make it go...'

'It's going now all right!' Stuart cackled.

Huw was aware of a stab of alarm. Certainly the fire was going – flames were licking around some chunks of wood which Gordon had stacked on it. But showers of sparks were spiralling up towards the tarpaulin roof and a couple of sticks thrown out by the force of the explosion were burning on the wood-plank floor of the hut.

He ran to them, trying to kick them back, but instead one landed on a small patch of spilled petrol and within moments an area of the floor was burning.

'We've got to put this out!' Huw instructed.

'What with?' For the first time Stuart sounded frightened.

They looked around them. There was nothing to hand but the pile of hemp ropes.

'Try them!' They dragged out the ropes, trying to bundle them together into a cushion to stifle the flames, but as they threw it haphazardly they succeeded only in scattering the fire and several other small patches where Gordon had dripped petrol began to burn.

'Come on, let's get out of here!' Stuart yelled in panic.

'No, you idiots, we've got to put it out!' Huw was stamping on the burning wood with his booted feet and when the other boys did not reply, he turned to see them threshing their way out of the gap in the planking.

'Come back! Help me!' he yelled, but they took no notice.

Frightened, he turned back to see that the fire was worse than ever. He almost followed his friends through the plank-gap to safety, but a vision of Amy's fury if she got to find out about this stopped him. He tried again to blanket the flames with the ropes, but in vain; then, as a last desperate resort he tore off his jacket and beat at the fire. One section succumbed, dying to a pile of glowing embers, but on the other side of the concrete slab he suddenly noticed a trail of fire snaking across the floor.

Why should it do that? he wondered, momentarily puzzled. Then, as he realised it was heading straight for the petrol can which Gordon had set down under the window, he knew. More spilled fuel, short fuse to a fireball!

The fear he felt then was so sharp it was white-hot, exploding through his veins. He beat the licking fire to the petrol can, picked it up and hurled it at the window. The glass smashed as it went through, but the cap – loosened by Gordon – came off and more petrol spilled out, splashing onto Huw's hand and the floor and filling the air with heavy fumes. Then, as the fire reached the saturated patch, the floor and the wooden wall beneath the window went up in a mass of flames.

In that moment Huw knew there was nothing more he could do to contain the fire. In utter panic he rushed across to the gap in the planks, dropping to his knees and trying to wriggle himself through. But getting in and out as a lark was one thing; trying to force himself through with a raging fire behind him and panic in his heart was quite another. His head stuck, his shoulders stuck and when he attempted to push through a leg, the thick heel of his boot caught on the plank. The smoke was in his nostrils now and in his mouth, thick and acrid, choking him; showers of sparks flew upwards and with a faint roar the roof caught.

The panic shot through him again, fierce and licking as the flames. I'm not going to get out! he thought. I'm trapped! But in the midst of the terror there was a tiny area of calm which seemed to visualise the scene as clearly as if he was somewhere above, looking down on it all.

He saw beneath him the blazing hut, the petrol cans outside the window exploding with the heat, himself trapped as the fire gained strength around him. It was the most peculiar sensation he had ever experienced.

Then he was coughing again, his eyes streaming as he threw himself once more at the wretchedly small gap which was his only way out... And felt in his heart the terrible certainty that it was hopeless.

*

Amy was still sitting in the kitchen deep in thought when she heard the hammering on the door.

'All right – all right – I'm coming!'

She opened it to see two small dishevelled boys.

'Mrs Roberts! Quick – quick!'

'There's a fire! Huw...!'

They were so out of breath that it was a moment before she could make out what they were saying.

'Calm down, lads! What is it?'

'A fire down at the timber yard! Huw's trapped!'

'Huw?' Still she could not comprehend. They weren't making sense.

'Huw! He's still in the shed! It's all afire! Quick!'

Their panic got through to her in spite of their incoherence and she looked from one to the other, cold fear beginning in the pit of her stomach. Stuart and Gordon. Huw's friends. But no Huw...

'Quick missus! Come quick!'

She stopped for nothing more. Something was terribly wrong. She reached inside the door for her old mackintosh, pulling it on as she followed them. Half-way up the path she realised she was still wearing her slippers, but that scarcely mattered. As the boys began to run, Amy ran too, screaming at them and trying to get them to explain.

'What is it? What's happened? Stuart – where is Huw?'

As they reached the open ground behind the Rank she saw the flames, searing orange through the mist.

'Oh, my God!' She stopped, appalled. 'Fire!'

'Yes – yes!' They were chattering, gibbering. 'Quick!'

'Has anybody rung for the fire brigade?' she asked, thinking of her phone, trying to be calm. 'The hooter hasn't gone, has it?'

Almost as she spoke it began, a shrill siren echoing through the darkness and the mist. Somehow it added to the nightmare atmosphere and she began to run towards the fire again. The boys ran with her but then at the bottom of the hill they hung back, fascinated yet afraid and guilty, knowing they were responsible for the holocaust that met their eyes. The hut was well ablaze, but now the fire had spread and whole piles of timber were blazing, sending showers of sparks into the air while smoke hung in a heavy pall over everything. It blew into Amy's face, stinging her eyes and throat; she coughed, turning and twisting. The boys were at her heels again and she grabbed hold of Stuart's arm.

'Where is Huw?'

'In the hut. We were in the hut...'

'Oh, my God,' she said again.

The gate to the yard was wide open now and she ran through it, her feet turning on the uneven ground. The hut was a ball of fire, blazing fiercely. In the light of the flames she saw a tall figure she recognised.

Ralph! He must have been at home, seen the flames and

come down. She ran towards him, all differences forgotten as hysteria rose in a choking tide.

'Ralph! Ralph...'

He turned and saw her. 'Get out of here, Amy! Get away – go on!'

'No! Ralph...' she grabbed his arm. 'Huw's in there! The boys said...'

'Huw? Where?'

'In the hut! They said...' She turned, but the boys had gone. 'They said he's in the hut!' she screamed.

'How can he be? It was locked.'

'I don't know. But they said... they said...'

'All right. All right, Amy.' He was searching in his pockets and she heard the jangle of keys. 'Stay here!' he instructed and then began to run.

She couldn't do as he told her but began to run after him, dodging between the showering sparks and the blazing timber.

The door of the hut was still standing, though through the window the flames danced and leaped. Ralph was fumbling with the padlock and as the door swung open the fire came roaring out.

'Huw!' she rushed forward. The hut was an inferno, the heat seared her face and she screamed in panic – jumping back, then rallying. 'Huw! I must get to him...!'

As she darted forward he caught her, taking her arms in an iron grip. She half swung round, fighting him. 'Let me go! Let me go! Huw...!'

'You can't! Amy...'

'I've got to! Let me!' She was sobbing now as well as screaming. 'He's in there... he's in there... oh, God... Ralph...'

But his grip did not relax and he dragged her away. As her feet scrabbled on the ground one slipper came off and she kicked out of it, still fighting and crying, 'Huw! Huw!'

'You can't go in there! No one can.'

Above the roar and crackle and the sound of her own cries she heard the jangling bell of the fire-engine coming closer, rattling down the lane and screaming into the yard. Even before it had stopped the firemen were leaping down, strange alien figures in hastily-buttoned jackets and helmets. Then the hose snaked down and through blurred and streaming eyes she saw them rush with it towards the river. There were shouted instructions now adding to the general chaos, and after what seemed a lifetime the water came gushing through the hose, a steady jet playing on the blaze.

Ralph still held her and, unable to look any more, she turned her face into him, sobbing helplessly.

How long it took for the fire to be brought under control, Amy never knew, but it seemed an eternity. Never in her life had she known such complete, debilitating fear. It paralysed her, taking the use from her legs, leaving her unable even to control the sobs which still racked her. But eventually the last flame flickered and died and there was nothing but blackness and the stench of sodden and charred wood. As some of the firemen turned their attention to the piles of timber that still burned, others went in and out of the hut – dim moving figures against the backdrop of darkness and rising smoke, damping down the embers. The fire chief, a portly man whose full-time occupation was running his own firm of building contractors in the town, approached Ralph.

The moment she realised he was there, Amy grabbed at him frantically.

'Huw! Did you find Huw?'

In the glare of the fire-engine lights, his face was smoke-blackened and sombre.

'There's nobody alive in there, Mrs Roberts.'

Her blood seemed to turn to ice. Nobody alive!

'Oh, there must be! There must . . .' Again she made to start towards the hut, again Ralph restrained her.

'For God's sake, man, what took you so long?'

'Trouble with the hooter. It was locked up and we couldn't get to it to blow it. The men all had to be contacted one by one. They did well, considering . . .'

Amy felt hysteria rising again. What were they talking about? A fire hooter locked up – men who had done well – when Huw . . . She shivered convulsively, a moan coming out on her trembling breath.

'Let me go! I must look . . .'

'No! It's not safe in there. As soon as they can, my men will make a search and if there's a body, they'll find it.'

A body. *Huw*. And then she was screaming again, though the sound was thin and almost drowned by the noise of the water pump and the shouts of the men as they damped down the hut and extinguished the remaining pockets of fire.

'Mr Porter – there you are.' It was Sergeant Eyles, bustling and businesslike, but he stopped short as he became aware of Amy standing there. 'What's going on here, then?'

'It's Huw! He's dead...' Amy began incoherently and Ralph put an arm round her shoulders.

'It's all right, Amy. Hush, now. Well, Sergeant, this is about the size of it...' He went on to explain, relaying the facts as he had gleaned them from Amy's hysterical account.

When he had finished, the policeman's face was as sombre as the fire chief's had been.

'Boys – boys!' He shook his head. 'But you're not absolutely sure he's in there, by the sound of it?'

'If he isn't, then where *is* he?' Amy cried. 'They said he was there; they left him...'

'Well, if he is, the firemen will find him,' Sergeant Eyles said, his matter-of-fact tone chilling Amy yet again. 'Now, the best thing you can do is to get home. Unless Mr Porter will take you into his house for a cup of tea, of course? You could do with one by the look of you, and it's as well you're not here if...' He nodded meaningfully.

'You can come to my place if you like, Amy,' Ralph said. 'But I expect you'd rather be at home.'

'Home,' Amy said in a dazed tone, wondering what it was about the word which was striking chords somewhere in her. Then she remembered and her hands flew to her mouth.

'The children – they're on their own! I didn't even lock the door! I never thought...'

Ralph and Sergeant Eyles exchanged glances.

'Come on, I'll take you, Amy,' Ralph said and to the policeman: 'I'll be back, though there's not a great deal more I can do here tonight.'

Though still dazed she tried to run but her legs were unsteady and she was shaking so much she almost fell. Ralph's arm went around her, supporting her. They did not speak on the lane; words seemed superfluous, and in the car she was possessed by a sense of nightmare urgency, a longing to get back to the girls and make certain that they at least were safe.

The house was in darkness except for the patch of light from the kitchen window. It looked just as she had left it, so normal it had no place in this nightmare, but she had a sudden precognition of the long hours of the night stretching before her, hours when she would be unable to sleep, waiting for the knock on the door, hours when she would be alone . . . so alone. How did I ever believe I could be self-sufficient? she wondered. Such a short time ago she had been so sure she had faced the worst that could happen to her, the darkest moments of her life. Now she was aware once again of her painful vulnerability, the way in which fate could suddenly turn and deal a body blow – and her sense of aloneness when it did. If something terrible has happened to Huw – if he is dead – I shall never get over it, she thought.

'Amy, if you need anything . . .'

Ralph's face in the glow of the street lights was all strength and shadows and it tore at some deep part of her. He would not utter platitudes. That was not his way.

She turned quickly and ran down the path to the house. The door was on the latch as she had left it and she pushed it open and went into the kitchen with its bright, enveloping light.

Everything was just as usual. Not a world where terrible things happened but a safe, pleasant, warm world. Somehow it only intensified the feeling of nightmare as she stumbled through the kitchen and into the living-room. And then she saw him!

Crumpled up in the big wing-chair, chin resting on chest, at first she thought she was imagining things, then she thought he was dead. She grasped at the table edge for support, a soft scream rising in her throat, but the sound did nothing to wake him. He remained motionless – small, bedraggled-looking, his face and bare arms blackened with soot, jagged scratches trickling rivers of dried blood between the dirt on his legs. Though still supported by his securely-tied boot, one foot lolled out of the chair to give the appearance of a rag doll, and in spite of the chill in the room now that the fire had died to nothing more than embers, he wore no jacket.

As the first shock passed, relief and exultation flooded in and suddenly Amy was laughing and crying at the same time, hardly able to believe that after all the agony and her worst fears he was here, alive and safe, curled up in her favourite chair.

'Huw!' she ran towards him, unable to contain herself and he stirred, rubbing at his grimy face with blackened fists. Then as he saw her he came wide awake, guilt shadowing his eyes.

'Oh, thank God, you're here!' She was gabbling, the words tumbling out one on top of the other. 'I thought – oh, you don't know what I thought! The boys said that you . . . where *were* you?'

For a moment he did not answer, but the guilt was there, written all over him. Suddenly she was angry, her fear and shock transmuting all the terrible emotion of the last hour and exploding to fury.

'Where were you, Huw? You were in there, weren't you – in the hut? You started that fire!'

His eyes, red-rimmed, were full of fear. 'We didn't mean to . . .'

'You didn't. . . . !' She broke off. 'I've been worried sick about you! I thought you were dead! The place is burned out, you know that, do you? And the timber yard – it's been the most terrible fire! You were responsible, weren't you? *Weren't* you?'

She had him by the shoulders, shaking him.

'You did it! You and those . . . those *stupid* friends of yours. I should never have let you go out tonight. Well, you won't again. Not with them anyway. I shall see to that. Oh, Huw, how could you be so stupid? How *could* you?'

'We didn't know . . . we didn't think . . . I tried to put it out . . .' His teeth were chattering as she shook him, repeating his words.

'You didn't know. You didn't think. I'll teach you to think!' She was beside herself now out of control, the words pouring out in a hysterical stream, until a sound from the doorway made her stop and swing round.

Barbara stood there, eyes round with bewilderment and fear. In her nightgown she looked like a small, crumpled cherub. Then as Amy hesitated, still gripping Huw's arms, she ran across the room to grab wildly at her mother's sleeves and skirt.

'Mummy, don't – don't! You're hurting him!'

The temper went out of Amy in a rush, leaving her weak and trembling. Her arms dropped to her sides but Huw still stood there, paralysed by the ferocity of her attack.

'Oh, what's the use . . .' The note of hysteria was still there in her voice. 'What's done is done. Huw, you're black. I'll put the water on so that you can have a bath. And Barbara, go back to bed.'

'No, Mummy! Mummy, what's happening? Tell me,

Mummy...' Barbara was sobbing now, but still clinging to Huw.

'Nothing, Babs. It's all right.' She drew breath as another thought struck her – the firemen still searching the ruins of the shed for Huw's charred body. 'Huw, you go and fill the boiler. Babs – come on, I'll put you back to bed. Then I have to make a telephone call.'

She took hold of Barbara firmly and bundled her up the stairs. The child went unwillingly, but Amy was in no mood to either pacify her or explain; her frayed nerves simply would not allow it. She put Barbara into her bed and drew up the covers.

'Go back to sleep now. And not another sound. If you wake Maureen, I shall be very cross.'

The child's eyes peeped at her over the coverlet, wide and frightened, and she bent to kiss her, forcing her voice to come out steady.

'It's all right, Babs. Nothing for you to worry about, I promise. Huw has been naughty, that's all.'

If only that *were* all, she thought, going back downstairs on legs which still felt like soggy cotton wool. Who should she telephone to say that Huw was all right? Ralph's house? The police station? She wasn't looking forward to doing it, but it had to be done. She settled on the police and the phone was answered by Sergeant Eyles' wife, an officious little woman who, totally dominated by her husband, did her own dominating whenever and wherever she could.

'Sergeant's not home at present. He's out dealing with a fire.'

'Yes, I know.' Swallowing her embarrassment Amy explained the situation, enduring the woman's ill-disguised snorts of disgust.

'All right, I'll let him know as soon as I can. And he'll be coming to see you, no doubt – and the boy.'

Oh, Lord, Amy thought, the full implication of what Huw had done coming home to her. Huw and the other boys had been responsible for a serious fire, so there was bound to be a police investigation.

When she finished on the telephone she went to talk to Huw, who was struggling to fill the boiler.

'We better have a chat while the water's boiling,' she said wearily. 'And you had better tell me exactly what happened.'

She took him back into the living-room, where she sat him

down and crouched beside him.

'From the beginning,' she instructed.

She was calmer now and her calm communicated itself to him. Haltingly, his eyes avoiding hers, he related what had happened in the shed. When he had finished, she sat back on her heels.

'Oh Huw, Huw, why did you do it? Why did you go in there? Surely you knew you shouldn't? And playing with matches...'

'I did try to put it out.' His eyes were frightened and suddenly, without warning, she was remembering a long-ago Sunday when Ted, her brother, had been accused of letting out a neighbour's pig to root among the parsnips. Only a small girl herself, she had been terrified by the consequences she envisaged – at worst, the police coming for Ted; at best, a winter without root vegetables to fill their hungry bellies because they would be forced to replace those spoiled by the pig. The dread had been similar to what she was experiencing now. But how long ago it seemed – and how harmless compared with this mess!

She shivered, hiding it from Huw.

'All right, go and have your bath now. The water will be hot enough. I'll come and help you get it ready. Then I'll make you a milky drink.'

In the bathroom the walls were dripping with condensation. As she dipped water, the steam rose into her face and she was unsure whether the droplets on her cheeks were perspiration or tears.

'Get undressed.'

Obediently he took off his shirt, then stood in his vest and shorts waiting for her to go. He was too big a boy now to let her remain while he bathed, but she looked at him for a moment all the same, at the once-thin limbs which now had filled out and grown sturdy; the shoulders, broad and brown above his white vest, even though it was winter; the thick brown hair falling over his smoke-streaked cheeks; and in spite of her anger and anxiety, she was overwhelmed with tenderness.

She had come so near to losing him. This strong young body could so easily have been reduced to charred flesh and bone. But it hadn't happened. The shed might be a burned-out shell, the timber yard devastated, but Huw was alive and almost unharmed. The rest were material things and replaceable – if she had to foot the bill for the damage, well, so be it. It was only Huw who was irreplaceable and he was here, safe beneath his own roof. Amy whispered a prayer of thankfulness, then went out, closing the door behind her and leaving Huw to his bath.

Chapter Twenty-Eight

Through the long hours of the night Amy slept little, weary though she was. She was too tense still and each time she closed her eyes, she found herself reliving the nightmares of the evening. The smell of the smoke was still in her nostrils, the sounds of the fire still in her ears and the terrible scenes – some real, some imagined – there in vivid splashes of colour before her eyes. It was a cold night but Amy lay sweating and then, when she pushed the covers aside, the night air crept in chill rivers down her neck and back so that she was soon shivering violently.

Even when she did manage to banish the ugly images for a little while, sleep would not come. For into the void moved the haunting worry as to what the sequel might be to the disastrous events of the evening.

Whether or not he had intended it, Huw had been responsible with the other boys for the fire, and there were certain to be repercussions. Sergeant Eyles' wife had said the police would want to interview him. Might that in turn mean criminal proceedings? Though she had now drawn the covers around her shoulders once more, Amy shivered. Huw must have committed several offences, now she came to think of it, though just what they might be she was unsure. Trespass, certainly. Was that an offence? She didn't know. And starting the fire – arson? Or criminal damage? He was too young to be brought up before the Magistrates' Court, of that she was fairly certain, but there was a Juvenile Court;

this was where she would have had to apply if she had gone ahead with her attempts to adopt Huw legally, she supposed. The people who sat on the bench were pillars of the community, known for the severity of their outlook, dedicated to turning what had been known as a lawless area not so long ago, into something approaching respectability.

As she pictured Huw facing them, her heart seemed to fail within her. He would have to admit he was guilty and throw himself on their mercy. But what would they do with him? Suppose they decided to teach him a lesson and sent him away to a Reformatory School? That would not be unheard of, and it was the very place from which she had been so determined to save him. Or supposing...

As the terrible new thought struck her, she went cold again, lying very still. Supposing they decided she was unable to control him – would it be in their power to take him away from her? It might be – she didn't know. But the vulnerability of her position was frightening, since she had no legal claim over Huw at all. For a long while now she had not even thought of it; now she found herself wishing with all her heart that it had been possible to do more than simply take him in. She had given him her love along with a home, looked on him now as her own son, but officially he was not. To the outside world he was an orphan and if the magistrates, those all-powerful guardians of the peace, decided he would be better off somewhere other than with her, she was most dreadfully afraid there would be nothing she could do about it.

*

First thing in the morning, Amy telephoned Arthur Clarence. There was no delay now, for she was a valued client and instead of being questioned as to her business or requested to make an appointment, she was connected with the solicitor himself immediately.

'Good morning, Mrs Roberts. And what can I do for you?' Arthur Clarence's tone was formal but cordial.

'I need your help. Something rather dreadful has happened.' She went on to explain and the solicitor listened in silence, only tutting occasionally to let her know he was still there on the other end of the line.

'What's the position, Mr Clarence?' she asked when she had finished. 'Is Huw likely to find himself in court? Is there a possibility I might lose him?'

'Dear me, what an unfortunate state of affairs!' She could imagine Arthur Clarence drumming with his finger-tips on the desk top, mentally flicking through his dust-dry legal books. 'Let us take this step by step, shall we? First the matter of trespass. That's a civil matter and the police would not be interested in it. But breaking and entering, maybe. That is a criminal offence and the police might very well ask themselves what the lads were doing in the shed – whether perhaps their intention in breaking in was to help themselves to something which did not belong to them.'

'Oh no, Huw didn't want to steal anything!' Amy said hastily. 'There was nothing there to steal anyway, from what I can make out. The place was just used as a store for old records.'

'Hmm. Well, a charge of arson wouldn't stand up – there was no malicious intent, was there? But nevertheless the boys were responsible for causing a great deal of damage.' He paused, considering while Amy waited. It was not in Arthur Clarence's nature to reach any decision lightly. 'It is my opinion that the police would be unlikely to take any action unless a complaint is made,' he said at last.

'A complaint?'

'If Mr Porter should decide to press charges, then they may be forced to do something. Your best course of action, as I see it, is to have a word with him – throw yourself on his mercy, so to speak. If you can persuade him to let the matter drop, then I think it may all blow over. Otherwise...'

'I see. Thank you, Mr Clarence.'

'Not at all. Let me know what happens, won't you? If the worst comes to the worst, I shall do my best for you, of course. But let us hope it won't come to that.'

She replaced the receiver and stood with her hands pressed to her head. It was beginning to ache with the dull heaviness that came from a sleepless night, spreading until she felt as if she were wearing a too-tight cap. So there was a chance that the police would not prosecute. But it would depend on Ralph and she could not guess what his reaction would be. Last night he had been very good, it was true, but by morning light he might be feeling differently. Memories of past encounters rushed into Amy's mind. A man who could double-deal as he had done over the Frickers Transport contracts, or who could buy a plot of land he didn't really want just to prevent her from getting it, could do anything. Where business was concerned he was unpredictable – no, he wasn't. He was predictable in that, should gain be involved, he would put scruples and personal loyalties firmly aside. And the fire last night had involved him in considerable loss. If claiming on his insurance meant establishing the guilt of the culprits, then Amy felt horribly sure he would do it.

Unless, as Arthur Clarence had suggested, she could persuade him to do otherwise.

The prospect sickened her. Throw yourself on his mercy, the solicitor had said and the very words grated on her taut nerves. She had always hated crawling to anyone and now, after the years of antagonism, to have to crawl to Ralph would be degrading. Strange, she thought, how easy it had been to accept his comforting strength last night. But last night had been different and she had not stopped to think about the niceties of the situation then; she had been too frightened and worried. Today, in the cold grey light of morning, it was a different thing entirely. But still, if that was the only way, she would have to swallow her pride. If it would save Huw, it was worth it.

She reached for the telephone again, then hesitated. Perhaps this would be better done face to face. The girls were already at school, but she had let Huw sleep in. Now she went upstairs to his room.

He was sleeping soundly, his face pink and innocent above the snowy sheets.

'Time to wake up, Huw.' She shook him. He opened one eye, then as he came awake and remembered the events of the previous night, his face became troubled. 'Get up, Huw, and get dressed. We're going to see Mr Porter. You are going to apologise for all the trouble you have caused, and I am going to do my best to see the matter ends there.'

A flash of fear shone in the blue eyes. He lay motionless and she jerked the covers off him.

'Come on, now. There's no point in putting it off. I'll make you some breakfast and I want you downstairs and ready to eat it in five minutes. Right?'

His usually healthy appetite was diminished this morning and he picked at his bacon, pushing it around on his fork.

'Eat it up,' she ordered, deliberately hard. She saw him swallow it with an effort, watching him in the mirror as she applied lipstick. Then she bundled the dishes into the sink; Rita could wash them when she came. Another quick phone call to the yard to tell her clerk she would be late and then she was ready, waiting while Huw forced his feet into his best boots. Then she inspected him minutely. Clean shirt, clean shorts, clean jersey – at least she had taught him something. When first he had come, he would have climbed back into the clothes he had taken off last night, filthy as they were.

In the car he sat silent, staring out of the windscreen. Her hands trembled on the wheel.

'Now all you have to do, Huw, is say you're sorry and tell Mr Porter that you didn't mean to start a fire. And then I shall tell him how you tried to put it out. That is the truth, isn't it?'

He nodded, not answering.

'You'll find your voice when we get there, I hope,' she said.

In the valley, the smell of smoke still hung heavily in the misty air. Amy was glad she could not see the shed or the timber yard; she never wanted to see it again. When she got out of the car, Huw hung back and she waited for him, taking firm hold of his arm.

'Come on, my lad.'

She led him to the front door and rang the bell. After a few moments it was opened by Mrs Milsom. She showed no pleasure at seeing Amy; it was as if the dinner she had prepared for her on that long-ago night had never been. Now, her chins seemed to wobble with indignation.

'Yes?'

'Can we see Mr Porter, please?'

'He's not here.'

'Oh . . .' This was the one thing Amy hadn't thought of. 'Is he at the yard?'

Mrs Milsom's lips tightened, the only firm line in the whole of her jelly-like body.

'I couldn't say. Though in view of what happened last night, I should imagine it's quite possible.'

'Thank you. We will look for him there. Come on, Huw.'

They had reached the car when she heard a call and turned to see Mrs Milsom waving. 'Hang on a minute!'

She stood waiting and the housekeeper puffed over to her. 'Miss Porter wants to see you.'

Amy was unable to contain her surprise. *'Miss* Porter?'

'That's right. If you'll come this way...'

Amy gave Huw a little push. 'You go and sit in the car and wait for me,' she instructed him.

Then, puzzling to herself, she followed the housekeeper back up the path. All these years and she had never so much as set eyes on Ralph's sister. Now, at this time of the morning, just when she would have expected an invalid to be resting, she had been summoned to the presence. Why?

The hall of the house was exactly as she remembered it. It smelled of polish, as if someone had already been hard at work, but the faint aroma of cigar smoke still lingered, clinging to the heavy curtains at the door. On one side of the hall a door stood ajar – the housekeeper pushed it open wide and stood aside for Amy to enter.

Her first impression was of the lightness of the room compared with the rest of the house. Cream flower-sprigged curtains were opened wide to let in what light there was on this murky morning, and on a centrepiece in the ceiling three bulbs within tinted glass shades cast an additional golden glow.

The room was dominated by a bed, the brass swirls and balls on the ornate head and foot catching the golden light and fragmenting it into small sparkling myriads. A fire burned in the wide and gracious grate and brass fire-irons treated the reflected light in the same way as the bedstead. A cane card-table in front of the window was covered by an embroidered cloth, a tapestry-topped commode occupied a discreet corner, delicate china ornaments and spring flowers brightened every corner. Two high-backed wing chairs were drawn up, one on each side of the fire. The chair facing the door was empty but for piled velvet cushions, but above the back of the other Amy glimpsed the top of a head, dark but peppered with streaks of iron grey.

She crossed the room, her feet making no sound on the rich Indian carpet.

'My dear Mrs Roberts.' There was warmth in the educated voice. 'I'm so glad to meet you at last.'

Miss Porter hardly looked the frail invalid Amy had expected. Were she standing, Amy guessed she would be almost as tall as Ralph and her face, though pale and gaunt, was also strong-featured. Her hair, plaited into two thick braids, fell from a centre parting almost to waist-level, her hands lay calmly in the lap of her rich blue dressing-gown. Only her eyes, dark-rimmed, showed the signs of her suffering.

'You must excuse me for not being dressed yet.' There was a generous curve to the well-shaped mouth when she smiled. 'I'm afraid it takes me a while to organise myself for the day.'

A week ago – yesterday, even – Amy might have added her own sharp silent aside that Ralph's sister had nothing to organise herself for anyway! But today, face to face with a woman she knew instinctively to be remarkable, the thought never so much as crossed her mind. Miss Porter might see no one, but that did not mean she would not make the effort to live life to her own routine within the confines of her room, and one of her tenets would certainly be that she must be dressed before lunch – probably before 'elevenses'; but never, ever, before breakfast.

'Do sit down,' she said now, indicating the chair opposite her own, and when Amy did as she was bid she was treated to a half-curve of Miss Porter's open smile. 'That's better. Now I can see you properly. And I have so wanted to meet you. I've heard so much about you and I know how highly Ralph thinks of you.'

Amy scrutinised the strong face, looking for signs of insincerity, but there were none. As far as she could tell, Ralph's sister meant what she said.

'What have you heard of me, I wonder? I think I'm looked upon as something of a mystery in Hillsbridge, am I not?' Again that twinkle, as if she might be enjoying her notoriety.

'Oh, I wouldn't say that exactly ...'

'Well, I would. At best I expect I am referred to as a recluse – at worst, a witch. The simple truth of the matter is that my health is not good, though I think even the stories of that are exaggerated in the town. I had two bad doses of rheumatic fever as a child and a third when I was in my teens. That left me with a severe heart problem which restricts me considerably. But still I am fortunate in that I have all I need here. I love to read, I write a little poetry – Ralph may have told you. And for the past year or so I have been researching the life of Edith Cavell, with the idea of perhaps writing a biography. I suppose you think it strange that someone as limited as I am should take a woman of such strength and courage as my subject.'

'Not at all,' Amy interposed.

'I admire her tremendously. Had I been able, I suppose I would have liked to do what she did. As it is ... well, I think myself fortunate to have the time to study the things that interest me – and Mrs Milsom to play a rubber of bridge or whist for relaxation. I'm also very lucky to have a brother like Ralph.'

Amy said nothing. Miss Porter's hands moved slightly in her lap and she noticed that the skin was almost transparent over the blue ridges of her veins.

'Now we have the introductions out of the way, let us talk. You came to see Ralph this morning.' There was no inflection in her voice, but Amy knew it was a question.

'Yes.'

'Because of what happened last night?'

'Yes. My son ...' (How easily those words slipped off her tongue!) 'My son was one of those responsible and I wanted him to apologise.'

'I'm sure Ralph will accept his apology.'

'Yes, but ...' Amy hesitated. Unaccountably she was beginning to feel this woman might be an ally. 'I was hoping to talk to him as well. You see, I am extremely worried as to what the outcome of all this is likely to be. I might as well put my cards on the table, Miss Porter ...'

'Flora,' Ralph's sister interposed. 'We can use first names, can't we? I really feel I know you as Amy.'

'Yes, of course.' Amy paused for a moment and then went on, 'The fact of the matter is, I am afraid that if this comes to court Huw might be taken away from me.'

Seeing the other woman's look of surprise, she realised that however much Flora Porter might think she knew about Amy, this was one area about which she was definitely in the dark.

'I said just now that Huw is my son,' she said quietly. 'That is not strictly true. In fact he's an orphan I took in five years ago now. Adoption was not possible, so I have no legal rights at all where he's concerned. Which is why I'm particularly worried that the magistrates might decide I am not capable of bringing him up ...' She sat forward, her hands knotting in her lap. 'Huw's not a bad boy; he shouldn't have been in the shed, I know, but he didn't mean any harm. It was just an adventure to him. And he did stay behind to try to put out the fire ... and it very nearly cost him his life.'

A corner of Flora Porter's mouth lifted and the gesture reminded Amy of Ralph.

'Boys will be boys, you mean?'

'I suppose so. Oh, I don't want to make excuses for him. I realise the seriousness of what he did. I just want to say how sorry I am and try to persuade Ralph to let the matter rest there.'

'I shall certainly tell him what you have told me, if you would like me to,' Flora Porter said. 'I can't answer for him, of course – Ralph is a law unto himself . . .'

'I'm sure he is.'

'. . . but I should be very surprised if he did anything to hurt you.'

Amy's mouth twisted into a wry smile and she stood up, about to thank Flora Porter for her time. But the other woman's eyes were holding hers and the shadows in them were tantalisingly deep, full of hidden meaning.

Amy caught her breath, waiting.

'Yes, Ralph is ten years younger than me, so I have had plenty of opportunity to get to know him pretty well. He is a man who disguises his feelings, but as far as you are concerned . . .' She let her voice trail away, then stretched out a blue-veined hand towards Amy. 'I mustn't detain you any longer. You have a great deal to do, I'm sure, and it would be selfish of me to keep you talking. But I promise you I will speak to Ralph about your anxieties. And I hope that perhaps you will come to see me again when you feel you can spare the time.'

'Yes, of course. And thank you.'

Mrs Milsom appeared in the doorway, so perfectly on cue that Amy wondered if perhaps she had been listening. A strange companion for a woman like Flora Porter, she thought, unless of course she had other attributes besides cooking skills and a liking for a game of cards hidden beneath her flabby exterior.

As Amy followed her back along the hall, she found herself wondering just why Flora Porter had wanted to see her and what, if anything, she had been trying to tell her. That Ralph cared more for her than he ever admitted? If so, he had a strange way of showing it. And though she acknowledged she liked Flora, it occurred to Amy that a woman of her intelligence who was alone so much would almost certainly look for ways of amusing herself. Perhaps the little scene in which she had just taken part had been just that – an entertainment for a bored and lonely woman.

The morning air still smelled of smoke. It hung in the mist that was refusing to lift and Amy thought that never again would she smell it without experiencing a chill of fear, the echo of the terror she had lived through the night before.

She walked back along the drive her head bent slightly. Then suddenly she was upright, eyes crinkled into a frown, lips parting with surprise.

Her car had gone!

For a moment she stood, uncomprehending. It couldn't have gone! But the drive was empty and, when she half-ran out of the gate, so was the lane beyond.

'Huw!' she said loudly, accusing the open air. 'Oh Huw, what now?'

But she knew. She did not have to be a genius to work it out. Afraid of having to confront Ralph Porter, he had run again – and this time he had taken her car with him.

But he can't drive, she thought in panic. He doesn't know how! Oh, she had seen him watching when he sat beside her and often he had begged to be allowed to try out the gears and pull on the hand brake in readiness for the day when he would be old enough to take the wheel. But that was not driving.

Anxiously Amy looked up and down the lane. No sign of him. Well, it was unlikely he would have gone *up*. Negotiating the sharp turn out of the drive in that direction would have been beyond him. So he had probably gone *down*.

Slipping the handle of her bag over her arm, Amy began to run. Urgency was pointless really – she knew she would never catch him – but the need for action drove her on. Then, as she rounded the bend and the T-junction of the hill with the lower lane came into view, she stopped short again, her hand flying to her mouth.

There was her car, at a crazy angle across the road. And the front wing was crumpled into the bonnet of Ralph Porter's Morgan.

In that first moment, Amy experienced an uncanny sensation of *déjà-vu*. The accident had happened not more than a few hundred yards from where she had run into the Morgan with the lorry years ago. History had repeated itself . . . almost. But this time the inexperienced driver was Huw –

and of him, or Ralph, there was no sign.

Oh heavens, this is all I need! Amy thought in a master-piece of understatement.

The crackle of twigs on the other side of the hedge attracted her attention and she swung round to see Ralph climbing through the iron V-gate into the lane. The collar of his flying-jacket was awry, his trousers stuck with dead leaves and his face dark with anger. Instinctively she slipped her bag off her arm, clutching it to her as if it were a shield.

'So there you are!' Ralph was breathing heavily, but this did nothing to detract from the cold anger of his tone. 'Why can't you keep that boy of yours under control?'

'What happened?' Amy asked foolishly.

'What *happened*? I should think you could see what happened! He was driving your damned car and he ran into me.'

'Where is he? Is he all right?'

'How should I know? He was sufficiently all right to take to his heels and make a run for it. I couldn't catch him; if I had, I would have given him a taste of what he sorely needs – a damned good hiding. Just how the hell do you think you're bringing him up? As if it were not enough to cause all the trouble he did last night, now he's smashed up my car. Something will have to be done about him. And if you won't do it, *I* shall!'

Amy swallowed. Her instinctive reaction to criticism of the way she was raising Huw – indignation – was on this occasion tempered by her own anger towards the boy. If she could get her hands on him now, she'd like to do exactly as Ralph suggested – give him a hiding he would not forget in a hurry.

'Come on, we'd better take a look at the damage, I suppose.' Ralph's fury was barely under control and as he strode down the hill towards the cars, Amy had to run to keep up with him.

'Is there much damage? Exactly what happened?'

'He came swinging round the corner, straight into me. Look, dammit, the head lamp's gone . . .'

Amy hung back, almost afraid to look. She did not want to see the damage to her own precious car, much less to Ralph's Morgan.

'I'm sorry,' she said inadequately.

'I should think you damned well are! What was he doing with the car, anyway?'

'We came to see you...' she began, but he wasn't listening and she realised he had not expected an answer.

'Well, we can't leave them here. Let's see if we can push yours back far enough for you to get the starting handle in it. Then if you leave the road clear for me, I can limp home.'

Miraculously they were able to get both cars started, though as she moved off Amy could hear the grating of protesting metal and rubber.

'You'll be hearing from me!' Ralph shouted above the racket and she felt sick with apprehension. She had taken Huw to see Ralph in an effort to put things right. Now matters were a thousand times worse. If there had been any possibility that he might forgive Huw for starting the fire it was quite certain he would never forgive him for damaging his car.

It was afternoon before Amy had time to think about Huw again and wonder where he had gone when he fled from Ralph's wrath. Her own car had been taken away for repair – she didn't want to be without it any longer than could possibly be helped – and all the details which had arisen from the accident and the fire had had to be attended to on top of the day's normal work. Well, wherever he was he would come home when he was hungry, she supposed. He had wasted enough of her time already with his nonsense for today and she had no intention of allowing him to waste more by worrying about him.

When she reached home, she opened the door to the comfortable rattle of teacups. In the living-room Rita was giving the girls their tea – crumpets freshly toasted and oozing butter, stewed apple spiced with cloves and 'plain' cake on which she was allowing them to spread some of Charlotte's home-made gooseberry jam. She looked up smilingly as Amy came in, seemingly unaware of the traumas the day had brought, and Barbara and Maureen set up a clamouring.

'Mammy, you're home! Have you got anything nice for us?'

'Mammy, did you see the fire? Is it out now?'

'Mammy – Mammy...'

Amy kissed them, her eyes moving swiftly around the room. 'Where is Huw?'

'Don't know, Mammy. Mammy, listen, at school today ...'

'Has he been here, Rita?'

'I haven't seen him, Mrs Roberts.' Rita lifted the tea-cosy, peeping inside to check the contents. 'There's a cup of tea in the pot if you'd like one.'

'No, thank you, Rita,' she said absently. 'Haven't you seen him at all today?'

'No. But then he would have been at school, wouldn't he? Perhaps he went home with a friend afterwards.'

'Perhaps he did,' Amy said, not wanting to go into long explanations that Huw had certainly not been to school.

She went upstairs to change out of the costume she now wore to the office and into a pair of neat casual slacks. Mam hated them – 'Women were not made for wearing trousers,' she always said, and Amy had to agree she was not really tall enough to carry them off. But they were so comfortable.

Night was falling, the darkness closing in with the swiftness of early spring, and with it the mist was thickening once more. A nasty night – not at all the sort of night to be out as Huw must be in the thin jacket he had been wearing this morning.

He's skulking somewhere, afraid to come home, thought Amy. Well, let him skulk! But by the time it was completely dark, she was becoming really worried. Huw was always unpredictable; in his present mood, heaven only knew where he would go or what he would do.

She put on her coat and boots. 'Rita, would you stay a little longer? I'm going out to look for Huw.'

The girl – who had already promised the girls a game of 'Sevens' before their bedtime – readily agreed, and leaving the three of them sitting up around the table with their heads bent over the cards, Amy walked down the road to the Seymour house. The door was opened by Stuart's mother – and she was none too pleased to see Amy.

'No, I haven't seen your Huw and I don't know that I want to!' she snapped in response to Amy's enquiry. 'He's a bad boy – leading our Stuart into trouble like he did. I've had the police here today, I suppose you know that? I've never had such a thing before!'

'I don't think you can blame Huw entirely for that,' Amy said hotly. 'They were all in it together.'

'That's as maybe, but our Stuart would never have done such a thing if he hadn't been led. Disgraceful, I call it!'

'Well, would you at least ask Stuart if he's seen Huw?'

With bad grace she did as Amy asked, but returned with a negative answer.

'No, our Stuart hasn't seen him all day. And won't either, if I have anything to do with it!'

Amy left, feeling annoyed as well as anxious and wondering whether a call on Gordon Tamlyn would produce the same result. As she walked along the road she saw a group of boys coming towards her, taking up most of the pavement, and recognised several of Huw's cronies amongst them.

When she reached them they split to let her pass and she repeated her question about Huw. Some of the lads shook their heads and went to walk on but one, an undersized lad with a shock of hair in a pudding-basin cut, spoke out.

'I saw him at teatime, missus. We went out to Withywood to pick up some stick and he was wandering about out there.'

Withywood was half a mile out into the country, one of the old mines in and around Hillsbridge which had not been worked for a generation. Surrounded now by the woods which had given it its name, it was a favourite summer haunt with some of the local lads; however, Amy had always told Huw to keep away from it, as she had heard that the company which had owned it had gone bankrupt rather suddenly and closed the place down without even covering the shafts properly.

'What was he doing out there?' she asked now.

The boy shrugged. 'Dunno. All I know is I saw him...'

'Thank you.'

The boys walked away, leaving Amy wondering what to do next. Surely Huw was not still out at Withywood, alone in the dark? Should she go home and wait for him to decide to do the same? Or should she go and look for him? The knot of anxiety inside her was growing, fuelled by the sharp memory of last night's horror, and she decided on the latter course.

Her mind made up, Amy went home, told Rita what she intended to do and collected her strongest torch. Then she set out again, along the lonely lane that led to Withywood. With the mist closing in around her, her footsteps echoed eerily and several times she stopped, looking around with the uncomfortable feeling that she was being followed. But she saw no one. Once a loud noise close by made her jump and scream, but it was only a lone cow sticking its nose over the hedge and Amy gathered herself together and walked on.

There were two cottages at the corner of Withywood Lane; their lighted windows made small warm patches in the mist, but when Amy had passed them the darkness closed in around her once more. Somewhere, far away, she heard the whistle of a railway engine, a mournful wail in the night; then there was nothing but the deep shrouded silence.

At the end of the lane she paused. Ahead of her the dense woodland formed a thick girdle which she knew stretched to the top of the railway embankment; to her right was the site of the old workings, overgrown now as the woodland had encroached onto them. As she shone her torch, a slight break in the mist showed her the tumbled piles of brick and stone, tumbledown remains of the derelict buildings which had once housed winding engine and screens, and the gaunt finger of the pit chimney, still pointing drunkenly towards the sky.

At one time someone had made an attempt to fence in the old workings; now the barbed wire had been broken down in many places. Shining her torch, Amy found a gap and climbed through. Underfoot the ground was rough – stony in places, and soggy with drifts of dead leaves in others. Brambles snared at her slacks and she was glad her legs were covered, though she wished she had stopped to change her shoes for stouter boots before coming out. For a few moments she picked her way tentatively, then stopped and called Huw's name. But the mist tossed her voice back at her and there was no answering sound.

Still calling, Amy stumbled on deeper into the old workings. Beside the ruined engine-house she stopped, shining her torch through a gap in the tumbledown walls, but the light only glanced eerily around the uneven hunks of stone.

She went on across the old yard, cracked now, and heaving. Then quite suddenly her feet encountered something different and she stopped dead, shining the torch at her feet. Wood planks . . . and rotten by the feel of them. Was this the old shaft? The skin prickled at the nape of her neck and she backed off hastily, terrified by the thought of the sheer nothingness which might be beneath her feet, then kicking tentatively at the rotting timber with her heel. She felt it splinter and in one place her heel sank right in, almost throwing her off balance.

It wasn't safe . . . it shouldn't be allowed. Suppose she had stepped onto it? She could have gone through, fallen to her death like the out-of-work miner who had thrown himself down another uncovered pit-shaft somewhere out beyond Purldown just a few weeks ago. And not only would the main shaft be hidden somewhere here beneath brambles and wild grasses, but probably ventilation shafts too – smaller, but just as deep. The nape of her neck prickled again; she had no idea where any of those shafts might be.

And what about Huw – suppose he was here in the dark? Would he be as careful as she was being, or would he blunder along blindly? She opened her mouth to call his name again, then closed it. If he was frightened of the consequences of being found, he might run, heedless of the hidden dangers in the undergrowth. Perhaps he had done so already. She closed her eyes, pressing her hands against her mouth as she imagined the ground giving way beneath his feet, seeming to hear his scream echoing as he plunged into the depths of the earth. Then, with a conscious effort she pushed the image from her mind. No such thing had happened. It couldn't have. If Huw had been meant to die, surely he would have died last night in the fire? But she couldn't shake off the cold premonition of impending doom.

Shining her torch on the ground in front of her, she moved on, skirting the workings. Strange to think men had once earned their living here, mining the black mineral from beneath the earth, bringing it to the surface, sorting it, grading it. Once the now silent air would have echoed with the clang and thud of machinery, the feet of men and horses would have trodden where she now stumbled, carts would have queued for some of the good coal while the rest went down the incline to the railway sidings, while the waste would have been taken away in tubs for dumping on the batch – the man-made mountain of black dust built up behind the workings.

With the torchlight illuminating the ground at her feet, Amy failed to see the barbed-wire fence until she collided with it. She jumped back, crying out, pressing her scagged hand to her mouth and tasting blood. She had not realised how close she was to the steep railway embankment, but now the beam of her torch showed the ground falling away beneath her on the other side of the barbed wire, black and loose with spilled coal-dust between the odd scrubby sapling that somehow had taken root. Across the valley an owl hooted – another living thing here in the night – but the mournful sound only accentuated the loneliness, and sick despair came rushing in to fill the empty place inside her.

It was useless. Huw wasn't here – and if he was, she could never have found him.

I will try just once more, Amy thought, and cupping her gashed hand to her mouth she called, 'Huw! Huw – are you here?'

The mist seemed to absorb the sound of her voice and she was about to turn away when she heard it – a small, thin cry, seeming to come from below her. Hope flared, then died. An animal, perhaps? A mouse squealing in the talons of that marauding owl? But no, a mouse could not make a sound as loud as that had been, not even in the extremities of terror. She froze, listening. And the cry came again, not animal but distinctly human. A small, frightened cry for help.

Again Amy cupped her hands to her mouth. 'Huw! Is that you? Where are you?'

'Here! Down here!'

'Down here?' Down the embankment? Surely not! With the mist playing tricks, it was almost impossible to tell.

'Down where?'

'Here – here! I fell! My leg...'

Following his thin, echoing voice she felt her way along the fence. The light of her torch picked up more piles of stone and ruined walls as she edged her way around a waist-high buttress and stopped, appalled to find herself teetering on the edge of nothingness.

'Auntie Amy!' His voice seemed to be coming almost from beneath her feet. 'Here! I'm here!'

She inched forward, crouching down. 'What are you doing down there?'

'I fell. I was running... I didn't see it...'

'Can't you climb up?'

'No! I hurt my leg. I think it's broke...'

Amy shone the torch and its beam picked up his small white face.

'Auntie Amy, I'm ever so cold too...'

She shifted the beam of the torch so as to take a look at the

501

trap into which Huw had fallen. What the ruined walls had once housed, Amy did not know. A sump of some kind, perhaps? An inspection chamber? It hardly mattered. The drop into it was ten feet at least and sheer.

She leaned over looking for footholds, handholds, anything, but could see none. But even if she could climb down, there was no way she could lift Huw to get him up – or take him home, if his leg was injured. She would have to leave him and go for help, and she didn't like that idea at all. It was unlikely that she would find either telephone or car in the cottages at the end of the lane, and it would take at least another half an hour to get home, then perhaps as long again to contact someone who could drive back to Withywood. An hour in all ... and it would seem a lifetime to a boy who was frightened, cold and in pain. If only there was someone with her – if only her car wasn't laid up for repair – if only ...

But wishful thinking was wasted time and energy. She was on her own.

'Now listen, Huw, I'm going to find someone to get you out of there,' she said.

'Oh, Auntie Amy, don't go ...'

'I have to, Huw. We can't stay here all night.'

'But I'm so cold ...' She could hear his teeth chattering and she took off her coat and held it down to him. 'Here you are. Put this on. I'm going now, but I'll come back as quickly as I can.'

'But Auntie Amy ...'

'Be sensible, Huw!' she snapped.

She straightened up, still unwilling to leave him though there seemed to be no alternative, and stood for a moment shivering herself in the cold, clammy night air. Perhaps if she gave him the torch it would be some comfort for him? But in that case she would never find her way back out of the workings. And the lane was so dark ...

She turned, looking into the blackness ... It was complete, enveloping. And then suddenly she was aware of a path of brightness spreading yellow in the mist, and heard the sound of a motor engine.

A car – out here? She could hardly believe it. Who would drive out here at night? A courting couple, perhaps? But few men young enough to be courting in the woods would own a car. Someone who had missed their way, then? Would they turn round and go away when they realised they were in a cul-de-sac? On no, they mustn't go, whoever it was...

Almost heedless of the hidden dangers which had worried her just now, she began to run. Her foot caught in a tree root and she tripped and fell, sprawling for a moment in the undergrowth, then picked herself up again and hurried on towards the lights, calling as she went even though she knew she would never be heard.

'Wait – wait – don't go...'

The lights were still there, thank God! Her breath came fast and uneven. Then suddenly she was aware of another sound – someone coming towards her through the undergrowth? She checked, then ran on... and cannoned into a body. Hands caught at her arms, steadying her, and she smelled the unmistakable aroma of leather.

'Amy! Steady on!'

'Ralph?' She couldn't believe it.

'Yes. What's going on?'

'It's Huw. He's fallen and he's in some kind of pit. I can't get him out and I was going for help...'

He steadied her, still holding her by the arms. 'Where is he?'

'Over here. I didn't know what to do. I think he's broken his leg and the hole's so deep. Thank goodness you're here! But... why *are* you here?'

'I went to your house. Rita told me where you'd gone and why, so I thought I'd better come to look for you. And a good thing I did! Amy – you're shivering. Where's your coat?'

'I gave it to Huw. He was so cold...'

'Here, you'd better have mine.' He took off the leather jacket and gratefully she let him put it round her shoulders.

'Come on, now. Show me where he is.'

She led the way back through the undergrowth. At the wall she stopped.

'He's down there – see? Huw – I'm here. Ralph is too. We shall soon have you out of there.'

How Ralph was going to achieve this when she could not, she did not stop to think. She only knew that somehow he would.

'All right, let's have a look. Lend me your torch a minute, Amy.' Ralph was skirting the pit. A moment later he called, 'It's not so deep on this side. Hang on, Huw, I'm coming down.'

She stood, nestling into the sheepskin collar of his jacket.

'Round here, Amy. Careful, now. Can you hold the torch for me?'

'Yes...' She shone the beam for him and watched him climb over the edge and drop into the pit. As he picked Huw up she heard the boy's cry of pain and winced.

'Take hold of him, can you?'

She did as he said, crouching down and sobbing softly at Huw's moans, then closing her arms around him and holding him fast.

'Oh Huw, Huw, you silly boy! What will you do next?'

Ralph was climbing up now, pulling by his arms and rolling over on to the damp but firm, ground. Then he took Huw from her, lifting him easily. The boy moaned again, then was quiet.

'Come on. I left the car on the road.'

'Be careful! There are shafts...'

'Shine the torch, then.'

She preceded them, picking out a path with the beam of the torch. The car, pulled in close to the perimeter of the old workings, was a large shape against the darkness. Not the Morgan – another vehicle.

'My car is being repaired, so I've hired this one,' Ralph explained.

He opened the rear door and lifted Huw in carefully. Amy slipped in beside him, cradling the boy against her.

'Mr Porter...' he muttered fearfully.

'It's all right,' Amy said. It was useless to be angry with him now. More to the point, she ought to be angry with herself for not reassuring him more effectively. She was convinced now that when he behaved stupidly, it was just his way of reacting to what he saw as a threat. This was a sorry end to a couple of disastrous days.

From the driver's seat, Ralph said, 'We'd better take him to the hospital.'

'Will there be anyone there to see him?' It was a cottage hospital, staffed only by family practitioners.

'They'll have to get someone then, won't they? My doctor will come if they call him.' His tone said: He'd better! and Amy thought: Thank God for Ralph! It was almost incredible the way he seemed to be there, just when she needed him most. This was beginning to be almost a habit.

Thankfully she settled herself back against the seat, pulling Huw's head onto her shoulder.

'You see, silly? There was no need to run, was there? Everything is going to be all right, you'll see. And from now on, my lad, you're going to stop worrying me to death!'

Chapter Twenty-Nine

'Ralph, I don't know how to thank you.'

The warmth of her kitchen encompassed her and she stretched out her hands to the fire. Ralph sat on one of the upright dining chairs, legs splayed, his hands cupped around a mug of tea that Rita had brewed on their return.

Now she had gone and Ralph and Amy were alone, the cottage hospital having elected to keep Huw in overnight.

'I'm just so glad you knew where to find us,' Amy said. 'If I hadn't told Rita where I was going, and if you hadn't come to look for me, I don't know what I should have done.'

'You shouldn't have gone out there at night on your own. Frankly, Amy, I think you need taking in hand.'

He looked at her over the rim of his mug, as if expecting her usual quick retort. But for once, Amy was subdued.

'It's Huw, isn't it?' he said after a moment. 'He's causing you all sorts of problems.'

'Oh, I know it seems that way, but he isn't a bad boy really,' she said hastily. 'He's just terribly insecure. He's been very stupid, I know, but in the circumstances it's quite understandable.'

'But he's had a good home with you for some years now.'

'I know, but it goes so deep with him and I think he's still afraid – afraid of authority and afraid I might send him away. And I've been afraid too – that I might lose him. If the powers-that-be were to decide...'

'Yes, Flora told me.' He set down his cup. 'Why did you take him in, Amy?'

She turned to look at the fire. The flames danced and leaped up the chimney, mesmerising her, and suddenly she wished she could tell him. After all these years of lies and half-truths, how marvellous it would be to stand up and admit, unashamed, the reason why she had taken Huw into her family, fought for him, kept him and loved him.

But the habit of silence was too strong and Ralph was an outsider. You didn't tell outsiders your business.

'It's all right,' he said behind her. 'You don't have to tell me; it doesn't make any difference.'

'Difference? To what?'

'To the fact that I still want to marry you.'

She spun round. The flames into which she had been staring seemed to have etched themselves onto her pupils, so that she could see them still – gold and orange with dark centres, leaping against the hard-hewn angles of his face.

Happy surprise leaped in her like the flames, lighting every corner and bathing her in warmth. Then, as she looked at him sitting there with elbows resting on the table, so casual, so totally unlike the picture of a man proposing marriage, her ready defences flew up.

'Is this a joke? Because if so...'

He held up his hands in mock-surrender.

'No joke. And don't look so surprised. It's not the first time I've asked you, after all. You turned me down before, of course.'

'Don't be ridiculous!'

'Surely you can't have forgotten so soon! Oh, it seems a long time ago now, I grant you. You were in difficulties with the business, I seem to remember...'

'And you were double-dealing with Frickers!'

'So you do remember! I wasn't *double*-dealing with Frickers, though.'

'How can you deny it? I saw the lorries leaving your yard with my own eyes.'

'Doing runs you had already declined to tender for!'

'And as for asking me to marry you, since you were supposed to be going to marry Miss Fricker you can hardly be surprised that I didn't take your proposal very seriously.'

'Amy, there is something very wrong here. I never had the slimmest of designs on Erica Fricker.'

'I saw her in your car and I heard...'

'Gossip, I expect. You of all people should know what gossip is like in this place.'

She felt herself colour slightly and decided the subject

might be best left alone. She had no wish to know the details of any affair he might or might not have had with Miss Erica Fricker.

'Anyway, I might as well tell you that I don't intend to let you turn me down a second time,' Ralph went on smoothly. 'You might have been able to build up a successful business, you might be a very determined lady. But you're not safe to be left alone!'

She opened her mouth to protest but the happiness was there, spilling in again through every pore, and she was remembering so many of the moments of their tempestuous relationship, shaken together so that they danced and spun in a bright kaleidoscope. There had never been – or so it seemed to her – a time when he had not stirred her in some way. To hear his name or catch a glimpse of him had always started a restlessness inside her which could be stilled only by resolution and the imposition of work, work and more work. To be with him was a sweet storm, sending waves of conflicting emotion to drown all reason. To feel his touch... she shivered now, delicious pinpricks electrifying her skin at the very thought of it. Yet there had been resentment too, and mistrust and fear. Fear of getting too close to him, fear of the strength of her own emotions. And always, always there had been sparks between them, it seemed – rivalry flared so easily. Why, even now there was the little matter of the piece of land she had wanted...

'Wait a moment, Ralph,' she heard herself say. 'You say you want to marry me. But what reason on earth can you give me for some of the things you've done? Only a couple of weeks ago, you outbid me for a piece of land I wanted so that I could build myself a house. You couldn't have wanted it yourself, so why did you deprive me of it?'

'Would you believe it was because I thought that if you had a brand-new house of your own, you would be less likely ever to consider coming to live in mine?'

'But that's silly...'

'You'd better believe it, because it happens to be the truth. How did you find out that I was the one who'd bought it, anyway?'

'As you yourself said, it's impossible to keep secrets in this place!'

His mouth twisted wryly and he got up, perching against the table edge. 'I suppose I asked for that. Anyway, you haven't given me an answer yet, Amy. I've waited a long time for you – I don't think I can be patient much longer.'

'I suppose if I were to say "this is so unexpected" it would sound like a cliché. But it's true – it *is*. I can't believe you're serious enough to warrant a serious answer.'

He reached across, taking hold of her by the wrist and pulling her towards him. Taken unawares, she was unable to resist and stumbled against him; then before she could move away his arms were around her, holding her tight, and his mouth was on hers, hard and inescapable. Beneath its pressure she felt her own lips soften, then move in irresistible response. A surge of longing made her weak and pliant, her head spun, her body became fluid and moulded to his; her legs, hardly strong enough to support her, were trembling. For timeless moments the whole of her being was drawn up into the exciting vortex of his kisses. Then he pulled away slightly, looking down at her, his eyes dark pools reflecting fragments of light from the glass shades on the gas-lamp.

'Now do you believe I'm serious?' he asked.

She tried to break away. His nearness was so disconcerting, upsetting all preconceptions, making her want nothing more in the world than to say, 'Yes, Ralph, yes. I believe you.'

'Well?'

'I don't know...'

'Come on, my love, think of the advantages.' There was a rough edge to his voice now which she recognised as barely-controlled desire. 'You wouldn't have to worry about them taking Huw away from you any more, for one thing. Keeping him seems to matter a great deal to you. If we were married, I could adopt him.'

Again she tried to pull away. 'Oh Ralph, don't play with me like that. It's not fair! And besides...'

'Besides what?'

'How do you know he wouldn't run away again if he thought he was going to have to live with you?'

He laughed outright. 'You make me out to be quite an ogre, don't you? But seriously, I don't think he would. You said yourself he's not a bad boy. He just needs stability and a firm hand.'

'But I couldn't marry you just for that; it wouldn't be right.'

'Not just for that!' He pulled her close again. 'I'm in love with you, Amy, and I think you're in love with me. The difficult part is getting you to admit it!'

The weakness was beginning again, turning her knees to jelly and speading in warm rivers up her thighs. The smell of his leather flying-jacket and the aroma of his cigars was in her nostrils, dizzying her, the longing was an ache which began deep in the heart of her and spread and trickled through every vein.

Oh yes, it was true, she was in love with him. She had loved him for so long – so long! Even in the days when Llew's death had been too fresh to allow her to admit it, she had known where her heart lay. And nothing had happened to alter that. Not their many differences, not the long months and years when she had put him out of her mind. The potency of the attraction between them had still been there, an ember waiting only to be fanned once more to a fierce flame.

And now Ralph had said he loved her too. Said it casually almost, as if it was something he had come to take so much for granted it hardly needed to be said at all. How like a man – especially a man like Ralph! Deal with the practicalities and let passion speak for itself. And the words became for him an irrelevance.

But not for me, Amy thought. He has said he loves me and he wouldn't say that unless he meant it, never in a million years. And the happiness leaped in her again, along with the new confidence and the certainty.

'Admit it!' His face was close to hers, she could feel his breath on her mouth and beneath its touch her lips moved.

'Yes, Ralph.'

'Yes, you love me?'

She nodded wordlessly.

'And yes, you'll marry me?'

Another nod.

'Good.' It was soft yet jubilant, almost a sigh. 'When?'

'I don't know...' A moment's panic. 'Ralph, it won't be easy. I'm used to doing things my own way...'

'I know that! But I'm as bad. A confirmed bachelor, that's what Flora calls me.'

She laughed, a small, intoxicated giggle. 'I thought that's what you were!'

He smiled, his eyes crinkling. 'So I was – until I met you.

Do you know, Amy, I think I knew the day you ran into me with that damned lorry that you were going to be the one who was different.'

'Oh, Ralph!'

The yearning was beginning again, creeping and shooting through her veins. 'I knew too.'

'You did?'

He lifted a hand, tracing the outline of her face beneath the curly cap of hair and spreading out to cup her chin between his outstretched fingers and thumb. Then, holding her face square to his, he kissed her again, his lips touching first her forehead, then her nose and lastly her mouth.

At the fusion of their lips the fires sparked again, pure, sweet and explosive as he crushed her in his arms. Her hands slid beneath his flying-jacket and explored the sinewy length of his back beneath the tailored fabric of his shirt. How beautiful he was! Strong and lean, totally male. Delight shivered through her and she moved beneath his touch, now wanting nothing more than to abandon herself to him. But unexpectedly he pulled back, holding her away, and her turbulent emotion was shot through with a sense of rejection.

She looked up at him quickly, wondering in that second if even now he was about to destroy her again. But his eyes, meeting hers, were serious.

'I haven't waited for you this long to take you here, in a kitchen.'

She understood and understanding was like a light going on in her heart. He was right. This moment of commitment was special for them both – too special to be snatched at and sullied by the impression of sordid and illicit lust.

She held out her hand to him. This might not be the place, but it was certainly the time. Tiredness and fear had receded now, and she wanted to drive them out for ever.

Without speaking he took her hand, following her along the hall. At the foot of the stairs they paused to kiss again and then, arms about each other, climbed unsteadily to the landing. At the door of the girls' room Amy listened intently for a moment, but there was no sound except their even breathing.

As she pushed open the door of her room, the first qualm hit her. Llew's room. Llew's bed. It was six years now since he had died, but it made no difference. Her faithfulness to him all that time had left untouched the memory of him here in this room.

Sensing her hesitation, Ralph moved his hand up to squeeze her shoulder and she curled in on herself, wanting him yet unable now to bring herself to cross the Rubicon.

'Ralph – I'm sorry – I don't think I can...'

There was a moment's silence when she felt his fingers tighten on her shoulder, then relax. Glancing up, she saw his face had a shut-in look.

'That's all right,' he said lightly, but she saw the hurt in his eyes and knew guilt. Perhaps she was wrong to hold back now. He would not try to persuade her, would not seduce or take advantage of her. Press her to marry him, yes, but not this. He had too much respect for her. She caught her lip between her teeth, fighting against the barrier in her own mind. She had been a widow for six years. She had loved Llew and remained faithful to his memory all that while – no one would expect her to remain celibate for ever. And she didn't want to hurt Ralph – hadn't they hurt one another enough?

She drew a steadying breath, taking a step into the room – and as she did so the qualms fell away. This was her room now, it had been so for six years. The bed might be the same piece of furniture, but the coverlet and the sheets were different – champagne silk to which she had treated herself when a good contract came through, instead of the crisp white cotton of her marriage bed. The dressing-table and washstand might occupy the same positions, but now they looked like the furniture of a woman's room, the dressing-table top covered with pots and potions; small decorative china ornaments and lace-edged mats remitted the starkly functional appearance of the pink-rimmed jug and basin. Even the curtains were different, pretty sprigged flounces instead of the plain cerise which had hung at the windows when Llew was alive.

This was her room – it had seen her triumphs and her tears. And if Llew's ghost lurked somewhere here, surely he would understand what she was doing and give her his blessing?

'Amy, if you don't want to...' Ralph said.

'It's all right.' She turned to look at him, her eyes holding his.

'Are you sure?'

'Yes.'

They were in each other's arms again, kissing with tender restraint – the calm before the storm. Then Ralph began to undress and another qualm caught her, sobering her and filling her with shyness.

Her scars – the evidence of her scalding as a child – were still there, as they always would be, across her lower back and buttocks. Ralph knew nothing of them and she forgot them herself most of the time, for they were as much a part of her as the shape of her chin or the colour of her hair. But now, as he began to loosen the buttons of her blouse, she held taut, terrified he might be revolted by the mutilation.

'Ralph – wait . . .'

'What now?' His tone was rough; he had wanted her for too long.

'My back – I was scalded when I was a child – it's not very nice . . .'

His breath came out low and husky and with gentle firmness he moved his hands to the waistband of her trousers.

'Show me.'

'Ralph . . .'

'Show me!'

He undid the button and slid his hands inside her slacks; although she froze inwardly, she was unable to resist.

Then she felt his fingers moving over her back, tracing the imperfections, and shyness made her cringe. But when she looked up at him fearfully, there was nothing but love in his eyes.

'Poor Amy,' he said softly. 'It must have been a terrible scalding.'

'It was, but it doesn't matter now. All that matters is that I want to be beautiful for you and I'm not . . .'

'Oh Amy, that's nonsense! You *are* beautiful!'

Her slacks slipped to the ground; as she moved her feet slightly to step out of them, she caught sight of the reflection in the dressing-table mirror and held her breath to see the two bodies reflected there. They were total opposites – the one hard, lean and muscular, the other softly rounded; curves and hollows, both bathed in golden light. And his hands still rested gently on the scars.

A mixture of emotions welled up in her again – gratitude, humility, love – and guilt that she should have done him the injustice of thinking even for a moment that he might be repelled by something so essentially superficial. But still she could not help wishing that the whole of her body was smooth and white for him; still could not overcome her shyness and her reluctance for him to see her imperfection.

'Please don't look, Ralph,' she said. 'I don't want you to look.'

His face softened. He had thought he could exorcise her embarrassment with frankness. Now he realised that even more important was the illusion she wanted to preserve.

He kissed her, biting at her lips with tender passion, then slid his hand away from her scars and down the backs of her thighs to her knees, lifting her with effortless ease and carrying her to the bed. As her skin encountered the silk sheets she clung to him, arms winding tightly around his neck while he bent over her, covering her with kisses. The warm tide of desire rose once more to drown the shyness and the doubts and she pulled him down to her, hungry for the feel of his body next to hers.

Oh, the electric excitement when bare flesh touches bare flesh, when every tiny movement of every nerve and muscle awakens an answering response! She lay in a state of aroused ecstasy, wanting him closer, within her even, yet at the same time wishing to prolong the glorious anticipation of those singing moments.

His lips followed the line of her throat and shoulder, sucked softly at the smooth creamy skin where the swell of her breasts began, moved down the valley between and traced moist, warm circles on the curve of her belly. Then as she thrust up her hips towards his face, he knew she was ready.

With a movement that was urgent yet at the same time almost lazily graceful, he moved onto her. She gasped softly beneath his weight, wanting nothing now but to accommodate his seeking body and be one with him.

And Ralph, drowning in her, knew that the wait had been worthwhile and that now, in the end, mastering her had been the only way to win her. But oh, the softness beneath that hard-boiled and assured front! Oh, the capacity for loving which had been denied so long! As their bodies merged and joined, as they moved in unison towards the crescendo that seemed to bring the stars and moon down to earth, his love was as great as his desire; together it was a combination more powerful than anything he had known before. And instinctively he knew it was the same for Amy.

Her head moved against the pillow, soft moans escaped her. But happiness and passion were synonymous now, uniting to obliterate tiredness and fear, driving out loneliness and doubt, filling her with the confidence that there was nothing in the world which could not be overcome by the strength of their union.

At the last he cried her name and her own spent passion was suffused with warmth. She curled her legs around his, unwilling to let his body leave hers, until gradually they dropped from the pinnacle to the plateau below and from the plateau into the smooth green valley of contentment.

Lying langorous, her head in the crook of his shoulder, she thought again of Huw and of the question Ralph had asked her. She had wanted to answer before and been unable to speak. Now, softened by the intimacy of shared love, she knew she must remove this last barrier.

'Ralph, you asked me why I took in Huw.'

'It doesn't matter, my love. I'm sure you had your reasons and if they are good enough for you, they are good enough for me.'

'If we're to be married, I think you should know the truth.'

She felt him stiffen slightly. 'All right. If you feel you want to tell me. But only if you want to.'

'I do. I told you once before that it was because he came from the same valley as Llew. That's true – but there's more to it than that.' She paused, then said simply, 'He's Llew's son.'

She felt the tension go out of Ralph's body and knew what he had feared she was about to say – that Huw was her son, born out of wedlock, cared for by God-knows-who until the opportunity presented itself for her to have him with her . . . after Llew's death perhaps?

'I didn't know of his existence until after Llew died,' she said and went on to tell him the whole story of how Huw's mother had come to see her and then died in the lodging house.

'I couldn't let him go into an institution,' she ended. 'Not Llew's son. So I took him in.'

Ralph raised himself on one elbow, looking down at her. 'Does Huw know?'

'Oh, no! No, of course not. He believes he's the son of a miner who died in a roof fall underground. It isn't that I didn't want to tell him the truth – I thought it would be better for him not to have his world turned upside down. He had been through enough. And yes,' she added in a small voice, 'I suppose there *was* an element of just not wanting to tell him about Llew. I suppose I wasn't very anxious for anybody to know that my husband...' she broke off, then put in hastily, 'Though it did happen before I knew him, of course.'

'Of course.' Ralph's eyes smiled down into hers. 'You're a remarkable woman, did you know that, Amy? Even more remarkable than I thought. Don't worry about Huw, we'll sort him out.'

Her lips curved in a small, contented smile. How wonderful to hear him say 'we'. It was more comforting than she would have believed possible to feel she did not have to struggle on alone any more, that Ralph with all his cool strength would be there beside her.

Why had it taken them so long to overcome their differences and surrender to the inevitable, she wondered. But in one way she was glad it had happened that way. The intervening years had taught her so much, about life and about herself. She had taken on the business and built it up alone – her achievement owed nothing to anyone but herself and of course Llew who had started it. Had she taken Ralph's offer of marriage seriously when first he had spoken, he would have been the one to drag Roberts Haulage out of the slough – or at least, she would always have felt it was his success. Now she was prosperous. Now the whole world could see she was marrying Ralph because she wanted to and for no other reason. As for him...

Ralph would never have married her with any other motive in mind, suddenly she was sure of that. Had he wanted control of her businesses, he would have found some other way of getting it. A marriage of convenience would never be his style. And the way he had made love to her just now was further proof, if she needed it.

From the bedroom along the landing a child's cough brought her sharply out of her dream world and back to reality. Barbara – that recurrent winter chest was troubling her again. Reluctantly Amy moved.

'I'll have to go to her.'

Ralph's hand circled her neck, pulling her back for one last kiss.

'Don't worry about it. There will be plenty more times,' he said softly.

And Amy, replete with satisfied love, knew that he was speaking the truth.

Chapter Thirty

Within a few days Hillsbridge was buzzing with the news that Amy Roberts was to marry Ralph Porter. The wanton business lady and the confirmed bachelor! A merger of power with power.

Before they could hear it from anyone else, Amy told the children. Babs and Maureen were thrilled and excited, their main concern being whether they would be allowed to be bridesmaids. Yes, Amy assured them, they most certainly would be, and their faces glowed like small pink suns as they contemplated it.

Huw, freshly home from hospital with his leg in plaster, was less sure. He glowered a little and sulked, but Amy explained to him with firmness and love that she had to be free to make her own decisions about her own life.

'At the moment I'm lucky, Huw – I have you and Babs and Maureen,' she told him. 'But one day you will all be gone. You will have your own lives to lead – exciting things to do and places to see. But I should be left here all alone.'

'We wouldn't leave you alone,' Huw said stoutly and Amy felt a glow of satisfaction at the sign – rare enough – that he had accepted the love she had given him.

'You say that now, but when you're a bit older you will see it differently,' she assured him. 'Of course you must feel free to live your own life – that's the way things should be. You don't want to feel you must worry about a middle-aged lady like me!'

'You're not middle-aged. You're young!'

She smiled again. 'Maybe now. But give me time!'

Charlotte was the next obstacle and as Amy had expected, she was less than ecstatic about the match.

'Oh Amy, are you sure it's the right thing?' she asked when Amy broke the news to her. 'He's - well, he's so different from you. And never having been married, he's bound to be set in his ways.'

'No more than I am,' Amy said stubbornly. 'Yes, Mam, I quite expect the fur and feathers will fly sometimes. But then, it wouldn't be like me if if didn't, would it?'

Charlotte snorted and said nothing. It was true that Amy was the most volatile of her children - sometimes she wondered where the fire had come from when the others were so placid, never realising it was her own spark which was rekindled in her youngest daughter.

'Well, they bain't going to be seeing that much of one another, be 'em?' James commented. 'Unless our Amy's going to give up everything and go off to Gloucester, of course.'

'No, I'm certainly not going to do that!' Amy said hotly, aware that one of the bones of contention niggling at her mother was the fact that Ralph had had to leave for Gloucester the day after his proposal and so been unable to be formally introduced to Charlotte and James as their future son-in-law. 'We'll work something out, don't worry.'

'Oh, I bain't worrying,' James said mildly. 'Just wondering, that's all.'

'And when is the wedding to be?' Charlotte asked. 'We shall want a bit of notice, you know.'

'We haven't set a date yet, but I can't imagine it will be long. There's no point in waiting, is there? And you need not worry yourself about arranging anything. We'll do it all.'

'Oh, I see. I suppose an *ordinary* wedding wouldn't be good enough for Mr Porter.'

'Mam, don't be like that,' Amy pleaded. 'It certainly won't be like a first-time-round wedding, of course. We're not two youngsters. I won't be wearing white this time and he won't be having a "knees-up" in the Miners' Welfare Hall. I should imagine it will be a quiet wedding, just relations and close friends, with a reception at a hotel - the George, perhaps. But really we haven't had time to discuss it yet.'

Charlotte sniffed, still looking put out, and Amy put an arm around her shoulders.

'Do try to be happy for me, please, Mam. I love Ralph and

he loves me. Don't you think it's time I settled down again?'

Beneath her embrace, Charlotte moved a trifle impatiently.

'I suppose so. Well, yes, it's true – you ought to have a husband. But Mr Porter...'

'Just so long as he's good to her, Lotty,' James put in. 'That's all that really matters, isn't it?'

'And he will be,' Amy said confidently. 'Oh, I know he's got a reputation as a hard man, but he can be very kind. Don't you remember how he took us up to Dolly's the night Noël was born? And he bought back my ring from the jewellers...'

'He did *what*?' Charlotte said sharply and Amy realised she had said too much. Mam did not know she had once had to sell Llew's engagement ring.

'Oh, nothing. It was a long time ago,' she said hastily. 'Now, I promise you I'm going to be happy. So will you please stop objecting and spoiling everything?'

Charlotte gave a quick impatient nod and Amy was surprised to see tears glistening in her mother's eyes.

'Well, he wouldn't be my choice, but as your Dad says... as long as he's good to you...'

A week later Ralph was back from Gloucester and the arrangements for their future were some of the first subjects he raised when he and Amy were alone.

'You realise there will have to be separations for a while at least, don't you? I can't turn over the Gloucester end of the business to anyone just at the moment. But what I intend to do is to set things up so that I can eventually supervise everything from here. It will mean a certain amount of travelling, but at least we shall be able to make this our home base.'

Amy smiled. 'I was hoping you would say that.'

'Well, I know you'll want to retain control of your businesses and it is important that the children should be unsettled as little as possible. Now – come here. I have something for you.'

'For me?' She was as excited as a child and her pleasure thrilled him as he drew a small box from his pocket.

'No prizes for guessing what it is.'

'Well, it's certainly not an elephant!'

'I said no prizes. Hold out your hand.'

'Which one?' she teased.

'You know damned well which one!' He took her left hand and spread it out on his knee. 'Just one small problem, Amy. You're still wearing someone else's ring.'

Her face went sombre. Llew's wedding ring, which she had worn since the day he had placed it on her finger; somehow it had never occurred to her to take it off. Now she knew it was for her to do this – it was not something she could expect Ralph to do for her.

Without lifting her eyes she took hold of the ring and slipped it off. Momentarily sadness flooded her, but it was bitter-sweet and haunting, not sharply painful. Her finger looked unnaturally bare as she took the ring into her left hand and with some difficulty eased it on to the third finger of her right hand.

'You don't mind if I wear it there?' she asked.

'Of course not.'

He opened the small box and she saw the engagement ring he had bought her, a sapphire set in the centre of a cluster of diamonds.

'Oh, Ralph!'

'You like it?' He lifted her hand and put the ring on her finger.

'It's beautiful! And it fits! How did you know...?'

'I checked your ring size a long time ago,' he said and she coloured slightly, remembering again her first engagement ring. Had Ralph decided so long ago that he wanted to marry her? How incredible it seemed now.

The ring sparkled and winked blue fire at her.

'Sapphires – to match your eyes,' he said. 'For a wedding present I shall buy you earrings to match, if you would like them. And a necklace for your birthday.'

'Oh Ralph, you're spoiling me!'

'Only because I want to. And because I think you deserve a little spoiling.'

Amy couldn't speak. She was too happy.

'Now, we must make our plans,' he said.

The wedding was arranged for Easter Monday, less than a month away, and it was to take place in the parish church. Charlotte sniffed about this, too, when she heard; like most mining families, the Halls were chapel folk and always had been, and Charlotte felt that already Ralph was enticing Amy away from her roots. But Amy, too happy to snap at her mother, pointed out that since Charlotte was a less-than-

519

regular worshipper, it was hypocritical of her to protest. Because of the shortage of time, it was decided a special licence would be safer than relying on the reading of banns, and so this was applied for.

The following Sunday, Ralph took Amy and the children out to lunch at a hotel in Wells – 'to give them a chance to get to know me,' he said, and Amy was delighted by the instant rapport that was established between them. Maureen was coy and, after being persuaded to drink two glasses of 'fizzy-pop' between courses, very giggly; Barbara flirted shamelessly, sitting on Ralph's knee at every opportunity; and even Huw responded to the way Ralph treated him as an equal, allowing him to order for himself from the betassled menu and holding a long and solemn discussion with him about the Morgan motor car.

Afterwards, driving home in Amy's Model T – which they had been forced to use since the Morgan would never have accommodated all of them – Ralph raised the subject again.

'I suppose I shall have to get something bigger, since I'm acquiring a ready-made family,' he said with a wry smile.

'Oh, you couldn't get rid of your Morgan!' Amy protested.

'Certainly not! I meant in addition to that. We shall have a car each and a family car. How would that suit you?'

'Beautifully,' Amy said, relieved. For her, Ralph and the Morgan were synonymous.

Amy had prepared a Sunday afternoon tea – fruit and cream, currant bread spread thickly with farmhouse butter, small iced cakes and an enormous shiny-topped cherry cake. Although she and Ralph were still too full of lunch to be able to eat much, the children managed to tuck in again. Afterwards, while she was washing up, Ralph played ludo for a while with the children, then came into the kitchen where she was stacking away the last of the clean dishes.

'OK, then?'

'Ralph, you're marvellous with them! They've taken to you so well; I would never have believed it.'

He grinned. 'I'm a man of many talents. I hope you realise your good luck?'

'Oh, I do! I do!'

'Good! Can you bear to talk business for a minute?'

She cast a quick glance towards the living-room and he intercepted it.

'Don't worry, they're fine. They're setting up the

tiddlywinks now and I should think we shall be in for an all-night session!'

She closed the cupboard door and turned to face him, wiping her hands on the teacloth.

'Are you sure it's business you want to talk about?' she teased.

'Quite sure! There will be plenty of time for other things later. It's about Frickers Transport.'

Instantly he had her attention, just as he had known he would. Her eyes narrowed and it occurred to him once more that Amy could be a dangerous enemy. She never forgot an old score.

'What about Frickers Transport?'

'They're in trouble.'

'How do you know?' But she could guess. All such snippets of information were hashed and rehashed in the private room at the George – and Ralph had been there with his usual drinking cronies last night. 'How bad is it?' she asked.

'Very bad, by the sound of it. They owe money all over the place. I suspected as much. Their name has been in the paper too often lately over petty offences – hardly a week goes by but one of their drivers is brought before the court for something or other.'

'But paying their fines wouldn't be enough to ruin them, surely?'

'Of course not. They're just the visible symptoms of an internal disorder – think about it. Last week they were summoned at Bridgwater for having a lad driving one of their lorries, when they know as well as we do that the new traffic laws don't allow anyone under the age of twenty-one to drive a heavy motor. Why did they do it? Because a lad comes cheaper than a trained man and they thought it was worth the risk. The week before, it was a lorry with defective tyres – three of them right down to the canvas, according to the policeman who stopped them. They got away with that – heaven knows how – but the fact remains that the tyres should have been replaced long ago. And it's not so long since one of their little two-tonners ran away and into a herd of heifers – remember? One animal was killed outright, one had to be destroyed and the drover was put in hospital. More evidence, if you work it out, that the lorries are not being properly maintained.'

Amy nodded. 'You're right, of course. I hadn't really thought about it. The less I have to think about charming Mr Fricker, the better it is for my health.'

Ralph laughed. He knew of Amy's hearty dislike for Don Fricker and in fact shared her view that he was a thoroughly disagreeable man, though he did have an extremely attractive daughter. Once upon a time, when Ralph had despaired of ever making headway with Amy, he had considered whether or not he should make some overtures to Erica. But she had had eyes for no one but the son of his Swedish contact, and Ralph had been sufficiently in love with Amy to be glad he had not been tempted to settle for second-best. Now he leaned back against the kitchen table, watching Amy's face as she contemplated the problems facing her bitterest rival.

'You think he's on the slippery slope, then?'

'I do.' He picked up a stray cherry which Amy had failed to notice on the table top and popped it into his mouth. 'I think that you could finish him off any time you cared to.'

She considered. Finish him off. Undercut him, promise a better service, gobble up his remaining business. It wouldn't be difficult. Rats always desert a sinking ship, she thought. And it would be poetic justice. Wasn't it exactly what he had tried to do to her once, when he had known she was down? But there was another away, a little costlier perhaps but cleaner and more satisfying.

'I'd rather take him over,' she said.

Ralph half smiled. It was incredible what the years of fighting had done for her – though perhaps that hard edge of determination had always been there and was only now honed to a fine cutting edge.

'Careful, Amy!'

'Why?'

'You don't want to burn your fingers. This is a bad time and things are likely to get worse before they get better. There's a depression, you know.'

'I know that.'

'Not only that, transport is getting more competitive and cut-throat. For instance, the railways are intensifying their operation, and intend to replace a lot of their horse-drawn wagons with motor vehicles so that they can run a complete source-to-destination service. It will be quick and convenient for a good many firms to use them.'

'I can compete.'

'Well, that has to be your decision. Think about it, though.'

'I have thought,' she stated.

He grinned. 'You have become one hell of a business-woman, Amy. All right, you want to take over Frickers. How do you want to go about it? Shall I put out some feelers for you?'

She thought for a moment, the memory of Don Fricker's visit to her that day when she had been scraping rock-bottom still fresh and clear in her mind. At the time she had blamed Ralph for putting him up to it – now she knew better. Without doubt Fricker had carefully planned the demise of Roberts Haulage and gleaned information as to how well his undercutting and wheeler-dealing was working through the usual channels of tittle-tattle – conversation between the drivers, for instance. As for the timing of his visit to her, Amy was now sure that it was pure coincidence that it had occurred the day after she had talked to Ralph. Knowing that the attempt to put her out of business had been all Fricker's own work meant that all her smouldering resentment was directed at him alone, and the memory of his readiness to destroy her decided her now.

'Find out what you can for me, yes. But leave the negotiating to me,' she said.

'He'll never sell out to you, Amy.'

'We shall see about that.'

The rest of the evening she was withdrawn, thinking and planning. Next morning she made telephone calls to her accountant, bank manager and Arthur Clarence. Then, with the facts and figures at her finger-tips, she telephoned Fricker Transport.

'Mr Fricker, it's Amy Roberts. Can I come out to see you?'

'Mrs Roberts!' His tone was bluff as ever, but she detected a note of anxiety. 'To what do I owe the honour?'

'I think I can tell you that better face to face. Shall we say an hour?'

A hesitation. 'Make it an hour and a half, Mrs Roberts. I'm rather tied up just now.'

She smiled, remembering the way she had hedged with him. The boot was certainly on the other foot now.

'All right. An hour and a half.'

As she drove out to Stack Norton, Amy felt elated with

excited anticipation. Don Fricker's yard was just off the main road and as she turned into it, she noticed two lorries parked up. They looked less than cared for, the bright paint mud-spattered and fading, traces of rust on the beds. Not the best of stock to take over, but with a little money spent on them they could be assets once more instead of liabilities. And she liked the positioning of the yard, too. Out here, close to the quarries, it could make a useful depot.

Don Fricker came to the door of his office to greet her, but his hearty manner – like his voice on the telephone – revealed telltale signs of anxiety. She followed him into the office – bare, functional, with pin-up calendars dwarfing the charts on the walls. Amy made a mental note that these would have to go!

He pulled out a chair for her and then settled himself in his own large, worn swivel-chair without waiting for her to sit. She studied his face. It had fallen into heavy pouches and the veins which criss-crossed red and purple on his cheeks and nose made her wonder if he was drinking too much. Cause or effect? she wondered. Had the business run into trouble because Don Fricker was drinking the profits, or had he turned to the bottle to drown his sorrows?

'Well, Mr Fricker, I know you haven't any more time for beating about the bush than I have,' she said. 'So I shall come straight to the point. I have a proposition to put to you. I know you're having cash problems and I'm prepared to bail you out.'

The heavy jowl dropped. 'You..?'

'That's right. I'll put in my accountant to go through your books and my garage manager to put the lorries in good order. It looks as if some money needs to be spent on the depot too – a few hundred at least, though that's just a rough estimate based on what I saw on my way in. All in all, I think this could be a profitable base if it was properly run.'

As she spoke, his emotions seemed to run the full gamut. Surprise verging on disbelief, indignation verging on anger. When she paused to look at him directly, he struggled to find his voice.

'What's behind this, Mrs Roberts? You're not offering this out of the goodness of your heart.'

'Of course not.' She half smiled. 'My price is a controlling interest, Mr Fricker: the business registered, shares properly floated. And I should want at least sixty per cent of them.'

His mouth dropped open again. 'You're crazy!'

'I don't think so. I'm not offering to buy you out outright as you did with me, because I'm convinced you would refuse, just as I did. What I am doing is offering you the chance to keep your company intact – so long as I have the controlling interest.'

Silence hung between them for a moment, then Don Fricker asked heavily, 'Why?'

'Why don't I just wait for you to fold up, you mean? Oh, I think that would be a pity. I don't want you here as competition, it's true. But as another shoot from the main stem of my company, it would suit me admirably.'

'And if I refuse?'

'I don't think you will. I don't think you can afford to. But if you do, then I shall just bide my time. I might even help you on the downward slope. Let's face it, Mr Fricker; I can take your remaining business any time I like. But I would prefer to take over a going concern. So you see – it's advantageous to both of us.'

He was silent and she sensed that she had taken the wind right out of his already slackening sails. Don Fricker, of all people, hated to be bettered by a mere woman.

He rose now. 'I'll think it over, Mrs Roberts.'

'Don't think too long, otherwise there may be nothing left for me to take over. Remember that this way the firm has a chance of survival and you still have a job.' She paused in the doorway. 'Just one thing – I should expect you to cut down on your drinking, Mr Fricker.'

Without waiting for his reply, she left. The adrenalin was pumping through her veins and she thought: Oh, I enjoyed that! It may cost me and I may live to regret it. But it was worth it, just to see his face!

Two days later she received the call she was expecting; Don Fricker was ready to accept her offer. And as she put the details into the hands of her accountant and solicitor, Amy experienced one of her purest and most unadulterated moments of triumph.

Chapter Thirty-One

Easter – and the day of Amy's wedding – approached with
lightning speed. With all the arrangements in hand, she took
time off to go to Bath and choose a dress to wear. The weather
was still poor, wet and cold, so with Dolly's help she settled
on a dress of fine sky-blue wool, with a brown hat and shoes.
The children were also a problem; having promised Barbara
and Maureen that they could be bridesmaids, she was obliged
to dress them accordingly, but she was anxious to avoid them
catching cold. She and Ralph were going away for a few
days' honeymoon and as Mam would be looking after the
girls she wanted them fit and well – not taking a shower of
germs into the house where, in the hot unventilated
atmosphere, they could all too easily thrive and be passed on
to Dad, with his bad chest. Eventually she settled on long-
sleeved dresses of ivory piqué, with bonnets and muffs in a
colour to tone with her own dress. They looked sweet – so
sweet that the swell of pride brought a lump to her throat.

The week before the wedding was a busy one – not only
was she finalising the takeover of Fricker Transport, but also
supervising the removal of their personal effects to Valley
View House so that they could move in directly she and
Ralph returned from their honeymoon.

'I expect there will be a lot of things you will want to do
with the house,' Ralph said amiably.

'I wouldn't want to tread on Flora's toes,' she assured him.

'You won't! Her room is her castle, but beyond that she's
never taken any interest – understandably. And I've never
had the time or the inclination. It's been kept clean and that's
about the most that can be said. You can have a field day,
Amy.'

'Yes,' she said, pleased. 'I think I will.'

The rooms were all so fine and big that already she could visualise what she would like to do with this one and that, though the first priority would be to make the children's bedrooms into refuges where they could feel comfortable and at home as soon as possible.

'No regrets about the house you planned to build?' Ralph asked.

'None – well, maybe just a few,' she qualified.

He reached into an inside pocket. 'Well here, my dear Mrs-Roberts-soon-to-be-Mrs-Porter, is your other wedding present. I promised you a necklace, didn't I, but here's something on account.'

Puzzled, she opened the envelope he handed her. Inside was a legal document.

'The deeds to my piece of land!' she exclaimed. 'Is that what it is, Ralph?'

He nodded. 'Right first time. Just in case you should change your mind and decide you can't bear to live in Valley View House!'

'Oh, Ralph!' She was touched.

His face softened. 'I just want you to be happy, Amy, and I can hardly believe my luck that your happiness seems to coincide with mine.'

'I know. We *are* lucky, aren't we, Ralph?'

'Very!'

'Except perhaps with this wretched weather.'

'Perhaps we shall even be lucky with that.'

As the weekend approached, however, that seemed unlikely.

'I don't know what it's coming to,' Charlotte complained as a dismal Easter Sunday followed a Good Friday and Easter Saturday which must have been amongst the coldest and wettest on record. 'In my young day, we were always able to go out picking primroses at Easter. You couldn't now, though. You'd get "shrammed".'

'I don't expect it's so different really. Some years are nice, some years not. It's just the way you remember it,' Harry said, but Charlotte snorted her disagreement. Harry was an under-manager now, but still living at home, and she was determined he should not try to impose his opinion at home as he was able to do at work.

She was proud of him, of course, as she was proud of all

her children – and glad too that his future now seemed assured.

Harry was a good boss, from what she could hear, and always interested in the welfare of the men. Just lately there had been a succession of representatives of the Federation calling at the house, and she knew they were consulting with him about future prospects. The last working agreement guaranteeing the men a seven-and-a-half-hour day was due to expire in the summer, when the bosses would be likely to seek a reduction in wages. From the titbits of talk she had overheard, Harry was siding with the Federation and doing what he could to ensure the men's hours and wages would not suffer. She was pleased he was being true to his class, but a little worried too; she didn't want him to harm his own career and in this life you had to look after 'Number One'.

'I was wondering, Mam, if our Amy would mind if I invited someone along to the wedding,' Harry said now.

'Oh, who?'

'Margaret Young. I ran into her yesterday. You know she's away at college training to be a teacher? Well, it's the holidays now and she's home for Easter.'

'I shouldn't think our Amy would mind at all, just so long as you let her know there will be one more to sit down,' Charlotte said.

*

'Margaret, there's someone to see you,' said Gussie.

Margaret, who had been reading one of her interminable study books, looked up in surprise.

'Someone to see me? Who?'

'Harry Hall!'

'Harry!' She put down her book too quickly and stood up, straightening her skirt. 'What a surprise!'

But somehow it was not. Though she had hardly seen him over the last few years, when they had bumped into one another in the street the previous day she had known from the quickening of her pulses that she was still as drawn to him as when she was a giddy, very-much-in-love schoolgirl – and the look on his face told her that he felt much the same.

Now she went to the door with a ready smile on her face. Harry was standing there, smartly casual with a raincoat loosely thrown on over his Oxford bags and fashionable Fair Isle pullover.

'Harry – how nice to see you! Are you going to come in?'

'I'm a bit wet,' he apologised.

'Don't worry about that. Take off your coat.'

When he did so, she looked at him and saw that he had filled out; saw too the sense of purpose about his stocky frame.

'You're a very important man now, Harry,' she said as they settled down facing one another in the front room, where once they had sorted clothes to be handed out to needy families during the General Strike.

He laughed. 'I wouldn't say that.'

'I would! Under-manager at your age! That's quite some achievement!'

'I haven't achieved what I set out to do yet. I made up my mind a long time ago that I was going to do my best to get a better deal for men like my father. But I haven't managed it and sometimes I think I might have got sidetracked.'

'Maybe. But still...'

'That's the trouble with life, isn't it? So many byways to choose from. I thought if I could make something of myself, people might listen to me. Now I'm not so sure. Be you ever so mighty, there's always someone mightier!'

'Once upon a time you had political ambitions.'

'And they haven't been completely swamped – just set aside for a little while. But one day...'

'Is that why you're here?' she asked.

'No,' he confessed, 'I came just to see you. Amy is getting married tomorrow and I wondered if I could persuade you to come to the wedding with me.'

'Oh – I don't know! Isn't it a bit late for that?'

'I don't think so. One more or less will hardly make any difference.'

'I don't know if I have anything suitable to wear.'

He laughed. 'The perennial woman's excuse! Please come, Margaret.'

She hesitated, remembering all the good times they had shared. He had caused her heartache once, but she had been so young then – too young. It wouldn't have worked, she had realised that a long time ago. His ambition had been clear-cut – or at least, overriding – and she would have been in danger of sacrificing everything to it. Though painful, the break had given her the chance to pursue some ambitions of her own. She had been able to pass her exams, decide on her future, gain her place at teacher training college and ... yes, do a little growing up. Perhaps this time things would be different.

'All right – if you're sure your family won't object.'

'They won't,' he promised.

'And provided I can find something to wear!'

He appraised her, noticing how trim she looked in her sweater and skirt and the way her brown hair fell prettily into the long bob around her face. Then his eye fell on her wrist and she held it out, laughing a little.

'Yes, you see I still wear your moiré band.'

'And I still use your pen. It saw me through my exams.'

It was still there, that bond, strengthened rather than diminished by the years of separation.

'It looks as if the most important thing I shall need tomorrow will be an umbrella!' said Margaret.

And as they laughed together it seemed for a moment as if the sun might be coming out from behind those heavy grey clouds for at least two of the wedding guests.

*

It was still raining on Easter Monday morning and by lunchtime the weather had worsened to hail, with the occasional rumble of thunder.

'It cleared up for Ted's wedding,' Charlotte said. 'Let's hope it clears up for Amy's.'

She was to be disappointed, but thankfully it mattered less. This time there was a fleet of cars laid on to take the guests to the church, and ushers with umbrellas to protect them from the downpour as they walked along the churchyard path to the porch.

Amy would have liked James to give her away, as he had when she married Llew, but he was really no longer fit to do it and, as he said philosophically, 'I gave 'ee away once, Amy. I can't very well do it twice!'

So Jim, as her eldest brother, had been commandeered to do the honours. He arrived in good time, squashed into a stiff collar and his best suit, his hair (beginning to recede) well slicked-down, and ready to supervise the departure of the excited children.

'Now behave yourselves in church, won't you?' Amy said as she saw them off.

'Don't worry about them. This is your day, Amy,' Jim told her. 'You're all ready, are you?'

'Yes. Let me pop upstairs just once more,' Amy said.

'Don't be long, then.'

'It's my prerogative to keep them waiting a little while!'

Leaving him downstairs keeping an anxious eye on the mantel clock, Amy went up to her room. She had no reason for going back – she was completely ready – but she had wanted to spend just a few quiet moments with her thoughts.

It was the last time she would be alone in this room. Already it was beginning to look bare and most of her things had already been taken to Valley View. But it was still her room – where she and Llew had spent the nights of their married life – and she wanted just a moment to say goodbye to it.

Standing beside the bed, she let her eye roam around every corner. There was the crack under the window that once she had worried about.

'Suppose the house is subsiding?' she had said to Llew. 'With all the mine workings hereabouts, you never know.'

'Don't worry about it, Amy. The house will be here long after you and I have gone,' Llew had said.

Well, he had been right there.

Then there was the coffee-stain on the carpet, a bedtime drink she had spilled one night when Llew had grabbed her unexpectedly for a kiss.

Sharp nostalgia twisted in her then, a potent mixture of sadness mingled with her happy anticipation of the future.

Oh Llew, you do understand, don't you? she asked silently. I have to go on living. And I've done my very best, truly I have. I've built up the business that meant so much to you. I've brought up your son. And whatever happens to me in the future, I shall never forget you, I promise. But I can't spend the rest of my life alone. So please, please understand...

The silence in the room was complete. As she breathed it in, still looking around, suddenly it seemed to her that Llew was there beside her, unseen yet all around... in the crack on the wall and the coffee-stain on the carpet, in the very air she was breathing. She stood motionless and as the feeling of his presence seeped into her, the doubts and sadness seemed to melt away.

Llew knew and Llew understood. He was giving her his blessing. She felt it at the very core of her being, without any doubts, and from the calm still place deep inside she knew nothing but gratitude. Her fingers closed on the stem of her shower bouquet and she held it out.

'This is for you, Llew,' she said softly. 'After the wedding, I shall put it on your grave. But there will be other people about then, so I'm telling you quietly now.'

For a moment longer the gentle silence lasted and Amy felt completely at peace. Then from the foot of the stairs Jim called, 'Amy – are you ready? The car's here!' and she returned swiftly to reality.

'It's all right – I'm coming!' she called back.

Then, with one last look around the room, she went downstairs.

*

As Jim had said, the car was waiting. When Amy went out to it, several neighbours waved and called their good wishes and she waved back, beginning to feel a little as if she was living a dream. In spite of the rain there were more people waiting outside the church, sheltering under umbrellas and watching for the bride. She took Jim's arm, composing herself, and walked along the path between the ages-old gravestones, passing beneath the ancient sundial on the church wall with the inscription which meant so much to all who read it.

> When as a child I laughed and wept
> Time crept
> When as a youth I thought and talked
> Time walked
> When I became a full-grown man
> Time ran
> When older still I daily grew
> Time flew
> Soon I shall find in passing on
> Time gone.

The church was almost full in spite of the small guest list. Amy was aware of a sea of faces turned to watch her come in on Jim's arm, and of the heavy scent of the spring flowers which decorated every nook and cranny in the window sills and the old stone pillars. She smiled automatically, checked that the girls were lined up side by side ready to follow her and nodded to Jim.

'All right,' she whispered breathlessly.

Then they were moving down the aisle between the pews and the rows of smiling, backward-looking faces. She saw Jack and Stella, Dolly holding onto Noël whose red, shiny face was beaming happily at her, and on the other side of the aisle the dark hair shot with grey that belonged to Flora Porter. She had time to register a moment's regret that Ted and Rosa could not be here, sharing her wedding day with the rest of the family, and then she had eyes for no one but the tall figure waiting at the end of the nave, immaculate in his morning suit. As she neared him he turned to look at her and their eyes met in a long, shared smile. And then the rector began the words of the time-honoured ceremony which would make them man and wife:

'Dearly beloved, we are gathered together . . .'

*

As the Morgan climbed the long rise out of Hillsbridge, Amy caught at Ralph's arm.

'Can we stop, just for a minute?'

'Stop? Don't tell me you're walking out on me already! We've only been married three hours!'

'No, I'm not walking out. I just want to take a last look at Hillsbridge.'

'We shall only be gone for a fortnight.'

'I know. But just one look. Please!'

He pulled into the side and she got out, crossing the pavement to lean both elbows on the wall. Beneath her the field dropped away, humpy green, to the tangle of soot-blackened buildings, the railway lines, the yard and tall brick chimney of Middle Pit. Beyond the church tower rose square and grey; still further and encircling the town, the banks rose again, shades of emerald in the evening sun which had eventually broken through the storm clouds.

'Funny old place, isn't it?' Ralph said.

She didn't answer. Funny old place, maybe. Some might even say ugly – a scar on the softly rolling country. But all the important things in her life had happened here – the joys and sorrows, the triumphs and disasters. The hills that encircled Hillsbridge had contained her life and all its milestones. Somehow she had a feeling they always would.

'The Emerald Valley,' she said softly.

'Mm?' Ralph questioned, but she only shook her head. It sounded too romantic and foolish even for a wedding day.

'Ready then?' Ralph touched her waist lightly and she turned so that all she could see was the road, winding up ahead of them.

'Ready,' she said.